THE
BURNING
LAND

VICTORIA STRAUSS

An Imprint of HarperCollins*Publishers*

This is a work of fiction. Names, characters, places, and incidents are products of the author's imagination or are used fictitiously and are not to be construed as real. Any resemblance to actual events, locales, organizations, or persons, living or dead, is entirely coincidental.

EOS
An Imprint of HarperCollins*Publishers*
10 East 53rd Street
New York, New York 10022-5299

First Eos paperback printing: December 2004
First Eos hardcover printing: February 2004

Printed in the U. S. A.

10 9 8 7 6 5 4 3 2 1

Enthusiastic acclaim for
VICTORIA STRAUSS'
THE BURNING LAND

"A most impressive accomplishment—large in scope, unusual in subject matter, literate in style, intelligent and thought-provoking. Ms. Strauss' eye for detail is outstanding . . .The world she creates possesses a complexity and convincing solidity I've rarely seen equaled."

Paula Volsky

"Strauss has created a highly original and complex world . . . Her plotting is devious and unpredictable and yet never forced, because the characters always act in believable ways, true to themselves. And boy, when she depicts evil, it makes your flesh crawl!"

Dave Duncan

"Powerful, frightening . . . compelling . . . thought-provoking . . . strong characterization and fine story-telling."

Cincinnati Enquirer

"Skillfully crafted, with a soundly stated central argument: that humankind corrupts the very beliefs it conceives itself to be honoring."

Andre Norton

"A complex and ultimately compelling fantasy that will engage thoughtful readers and leave them eager for the next installment."

Jacqueline Carey

Books by Victoria Strauss

THE BURNING LAND
THE GARDEN OF THE STONE
THE ARM OF THE STONE

Arsacian Pronunciation

"**X**" is pronounced "sh"—as in Axane (Ah-SHANE); Caryax (Car-YASH); Darxasa (Dar-sha-SA).

The stress in proper names is generally placed on the last syllable—as in Santaxma (San-tash-MA); Baushpar (Baush-PAR); Sundit (Sun-DIT)—except . . .

. . . A circumflex (^) indicates a long "a" sound (as in "father") where stress is placed on that syllable—as in Ârata (AH-ra-ta); Râvar (RAH-var); Habrâmna (Ha-BRAHM-na); Vâsparis (VAHS-par-is).

The Doctrine of Baushpar

We the Brethren, incarnate Sons and Daughters of the First Messenger of Ârata, leaders of the Âratist faith and guardians of the Way of Ârata, do promulgate these seven principles, which we hold and assert to be the true wisdom of the church:

1. That the capacity for shaping is the gift of Ârata, a reflection of his own power of creation, and therefore divine and precious.
2. That the use of shaping is governed by human will in service to human desire, and therefore fallible and dangerous.
3. That because it is divine and precious, shaping must be honored; that because it is fallible and dangerous, shaping must be guarded.
4. That men and women who have vowed the Way of Ârata, having sworn their lives to Ârata's service and renounced in his name the failings of doubt, ignorance, greed, complacency, pride, and fear, are of all human beings best suited to

     accomplish both these tasks; and that all shaping, therefore, shall be gathered within the church.

5. That of all uses of shaping, the most proper is the glory and remembrance of Ârata through ceremony and observance.

6. That no practitioner of shaping shall employ it otherwise, lest any come to follow the dark ambition that has lately brought such a plague of death and misery upon Galea.

7. That no practitioner of shaping shall own more power than any other, that there may not come to be rivalry and contention between them, and that this equality shall be accomplished through use of the drug manita.

Thus the god's gift will be employed fittingly and by those fit to its employment, and the conflicts lately ended will never come again.

To this promise we the Brethren set our hands, in the holy city of Baushpar, in the land of Arsace, on the continent of Galea, in this ninety-second year of the second century Post Emergence.

GALEA

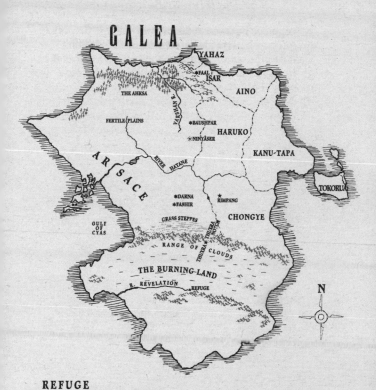

YAHAZ
*FAAL I.
ISAR
AINO
THE AHKSA
FERTILE PLAINS
Vinshan R.
*BAUSHPAR
HARUKO
*NINYÁSER
KANU-TAPA
ARSACE
RIVER HATANE
*DARNA
*FASHIR
*RIMPANG
CHONGYE
GRASS STEPPES
GULF OF CYAS
RANGE OF CLOUDS
THE BURNING-LAND
R. REVELATION
REFUGE
N

REFUGE

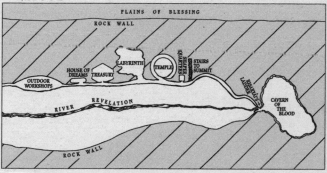

PLAINS OF BLESSING
ROCK WALL
OUTDOOR WORKSHOPS
HOUSE OF DREAMS
TREASURY
LABYRINTH
TEMPLE
SHELTER QUARTERS
STAIRS TO SUMMIT
RIVER REVELATION
SHADOW LOWER
CAVERN OF THE BLOOD
ROCK WALL

THE
BURNING
LAND

Prologue:
The Messengers' Tale

*(The first story told by Brethren foster parents
to their spirit-wards)*

This is the story of the Messengers—of the beginning of our faith and of its end. It is also our story, the story of the Brethren, whose task it is to guard the Way of Ârata. You know it already, little one, for some of it you have lived, and all of it you have learned before, in other incarnations. But the reborn soul does not recognize itself at once, and so we tell this tale each time you open your eyes anew upon the world, that you may remember who you are.

In the time before time, All That Was and All That Was Not came together in union, and a million gods were born. Each god went out to create a world. The god Ârata made our world—Ârata, as tall as the sky, with skin colored like the heart of flame and eyes and hair like new gold. To men and women, whom he made last and loved best, he gave the gift of his own power of creation, so that we could shape anything we chose. Only the shaping of life did he withhold from us. For if we human creatures could shape life, we would be gods ourselves.

Eons came and went: the primal age, when everything in existence was perfect, and Ârata ruled in unbroken com-

munion with all living things. Now, Ârata was a bright god,
for his nature derived from All That Was; but other gods had
more of All That Was Not in them, and these gods made
cold, barren worlds. One of them, the dark god Ârdaxcasa,
became jealous of his brother's beautiful creation, and decided to take it for himself.

Ârata and Ârdaxcasa fought. One by one the lands were
stripped of life and sank below the waves. At last only our
own great land of Galea remained. There Ârata defeated his
Enemy, in a burst of light so powerful that Ârdaxcasa's flesh
was turned instantly to ash. Only his bones were left. Ârata
buried them, each in a different place, so that the Enemy
should never again be whole.

Then Ârata lay down upon the wasteland the battle had
made, to sleep and heal. He was grievously wounded, and
his golden blood poured out around him, alight with his divinity—if you had been there to look at him, little one, it
would have seemed to you he lay amid a lake of fire. Slowly,
slowly, the ground closed over him, and the earth took on the
flame color of his skin. That is why, ever since, we have
called his resting place the Burning Land.

As Ârata fell into unconsciousness, the communion between his great mind and the small minds he had created was
severed. Our world was abandoned to the emptiness of the
cosmos. Time began its cruel flow, and death came into being. It is for this reason that we speak of the time of Ârata's
slumber as a time of exile.

But there was even more than this to burden humankind.
The burst of light that destroyed Ârdaxcasa's flesh spread
the ash of his being over all Galea. Every living creature
breathed it in. A piece of the Enemy's cold dark nature took
root in us, beside the warm bright nature Ârata had given us.
Thus evil was born into the world. From that moment, all
people were at war—each man within himself, every man
with every other. Even the earth did battle. Ârata dreamed,
and because his nature is creation his dreams took form.
Good things came of that—soft breezes, new plants and
creatures, the Aspects that to the ignorant seem separate

gods but in truth are only Ârata's memories of his waking self. But dark things came as well, from Ârata's dreams of pain—storms and quakes, plagues and demons, floods and drought. These, too, Ârata dreamed into being, in a world that had never known such things.

The ages passed. Ârata slept on. The world sank deep into corruption and godlessness. Ah, it was a monstrous time, little one—almost as if the Enemy, and not Ârata, had won the victory. At last the chaos became so terrible that Ârata could no longer rest. Rising a little way toward wakefulness, he shaped a summoning dream, and sent it out in search of a righteous man.

The man it found was Marduspida, a jeweler of the city of Ninyâser in the kingdom of Arsace. Marduspida had a fine home and a handsome wife and thirty strong sons and five graceful daughters. He did not wish to leave all he owned and loved and journey into the Burning Land, as Ârata's dream commanded. Six times, out of the flaws that are most deeply rooted in the human soul, he rejected Ârata's summons—once from doubt, once from ignorance, once from greed, once from complacency, once from pride, and one last time from simple fear. But Ârata's dream had chosen true. In the end Marduspida could not deny its call. He bid his wife good-bye, said farewell to his children, and set off into the Burning Land.

Marduspida walked without ceasing. The food of the gods nourished him, and the nectar of paradise slaked his thirst. Still the blazing sun beat upon his head and the hard ground burned his feet and the hot winds seared his body, and by the time he reached the place where Ârata lay he was scorched and wounded, worn thin as a shadow. He sank down upon the sands and fell into a sleep as deep as death.

Ârata came to him then in dreams. For seven days and seven nights Ârata came, in the form of a man with skin as red as fire, and hair and eyes of golden flame, and terrible wounds on all his limbs. Ârata gave Marduspida the wisdom of the universe. He told Marduspida of the path that men and women must follow during the time of his slumber, to overcome the dark nature of the Enemy inside them—the path of faith and action we call the Way of Ârata. He told Marduspida of the glorious promise of his awakening—of the time of cleansing that will follow, when all living things will rise to be burned in Ârata's holy fires, seared clean of both the ash that is our birthright and the darkness we have added to that burden; of the return of the primal age, when Ârata will rule as he did before, and all creatures will exist again in pure and perfect bliss.

At last, when the dreaming was finished, Ârata ordered Marduspida to return to the world, and write down all he had heard in a book to be called *Darxasa*, which in the tongue of the gods means *Book of Waiting*. Then from one of his thousand wounds he took a drop of his fiery Blood, which the passing ages had rendered as hard as crystal, and set it on the sands as a sign. And he said to Marduspida:

You are only the first. Watch always for the next. He will be born out of a dark time. He will come among you ravaged from the burning lands, bearing my Blood with him. One act of destruction will follow on his coming, and one of generation. Thus shall you know him. He will bring news of me, and he will open the way, so that my children may be brought out of exile.

Marduspida woke, and found the shining crystal of the Blood beside him. He took it up and returned to Arsace, and wrote down all the words that are in the *Darxasa*. When he was done he read them to his sons and daughters, who became his first disciples. Together, Marduspida and his children spread word of Ârata throughout the kingdoms of Galea, that all men and women might understand and follow the Way of Ârata. Marduspida became known as the First Messenger, and his sons and daughters . . . can you guess, little one? His sons and daughters became known as the Brethren.

On his deathbed, our father Marduspida bequeathed to us the golden necklace he had made with his own hands to hold the crystal of Ârata's Blood, and bid us guard the Way of Ârata for all our lives. Beside his grave, we thirty-five swore a solemn covenant: We *would* guard for all our lives. We would not allow our souls to fall asleep with the passing of our mortal flesh, as the souls of ordinary men and women do, but suffer them to remain perpetually wakeful, born always into new vessels, so that the world might never lack the guidance of the first faithful.

So it has been ever since. For twelve centuries our souls have been awake, traveling without cease from one body to the next—a journey that will continue until Ârata rises, and the primal age blooms again. But every bargain has two sides, little one. For this long, long life there is a price. When the age of exile ends, we will end with it. Of all the souls on earth, only the souls of the Brethren will not rise into the perfection of the new primal age.

It is not a thing to fear. Does a laborer not grow tired at the close of day? Is it not sweet, when a task is completed, to lie down and rest? So it will be for us, when the time comes.

This then is your inheritance. Ârata slumbers still. Humankind waits on. And we Brethren work, and guide, and guard, and wait—for the coming of the Next Messenger, for the opening of the way. For the time when we, like Ârata, may sleep.

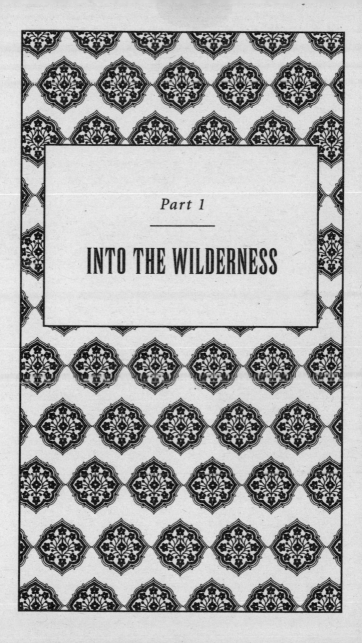

Part 1

INTO THE WILDERNESS

—1—

The rush of water caught Gyalo full in the chest. It felt completely real; he gasped and leaped aside before he could stop himself, brushing at his face and clothes. Even as he did, he understood the trick, and straightened up again, angry at himself for being taken in.

He thought he could see the one who had done it: a skinny postulant with the yellow headband of a trainee Shaper, leaning over the back of a passing parade cart and grinning in Gyalo's direction. Packed in around him, other trainees tossed blessings to the crowd: a shower of spangles, streamers of transparent gauze, a burst of rainbow brilliance. These were not true shapings, which changed and shifted matter and properly could be performed only in the context of Âratist ceremony, but illusions, substanceless manipulations of light and air: a symbolic reminder of the sacred power bestowed by the god on humankind before time began. They vanished even as the spectators laughed and snatched at them.

The water had not been entirely illusory, though. Gyalo could feel dampness on his cheeks, and the fine golden silk of his Shaper stole was spotted with wet. Under other circumstances he might have seen the humor in it—the people nearby clearly did, though in deference to his Shaperhood they hid their smiles behind their hands—but he had spent time and care dressing himself, and so he was not amused.

"Here, Brother." One of the bystanders, a young Arsacian woman, offered him her stole. "For your face."

She spoke shyly, but laughter twitched the corners of her mouth. Well, Gyalo thought, it *was* funny. Ruefully, he smiled at her and took the stole.

"Thanks for your charity, lady," he said, giving it back into her hands. "Hopefully I can manage to keep dry the rest of the way."

She giggled. "Great is Ârata," she said, making the god's sign. "Great is his Way."

"Go in light."

Gyalo moved on. To his left the spectators were a mass of packed bodies and laughing faces; to his right the procession trundled along, an exuberant juggernaut of color, noise, and smell: ox-drawn parade carts festooned with ribbons dyed in the god's colors; groups of Forceless monks on foot, beating drums and blowing kanshas, great trumpets that curved over the shoulder and made a sound like a mythic beast dying in agony; drays bearing huge wood-and-gilt statues of Ârata in his four guises of World Creator, Primal Warrior, Eon Sleeper, and Risen Judge; litters with smaller images of some of Ârata's more powerful Aspects—Dâdarshi, Patron of luck, Skambys, Patron of war and weather, Hatâspa, Patron of fire and weaponry, Tane, Patron of crops and the moon—carried by hymn-singing devotee-priests. Between these groups walked postulants with rods of burning incense, and more monks shouting out rhythmically: "Wake, O Ârata, wake. Wake and deliver your children from exile."

Like the blessings, the cacophony was symbolic: No one imagined that all this noise could actually rouse the god. It was meant for the human spectators, to remind them of the waiting that was their lot, that had been the lot of every living creature since Ârata first lay down to sleep. It echoed deafeningly back from the high blood granite walls that enclosed the avenue; Gyalo's ears rang from it, and his eyes burned from incense smoke. Another day he might have ducked through one of the archways that gave access to the tangled side streets, in search of a less crowded way to go. But though he had long known Baushpar's plan by heart, he had never actually set foot in the holy city until six months earlier, and the map in his head did not always guide him properly. He could not risk, today of all days, getting lost.

Which reminded him, with unwelcome sharpness, that he was nervous.

The avenue terminated upon a vast walled square paved in russet ironstone, at whose center rose the monumental bulk of the First Temple of Ârata. The Temple's original core had been erected more than eleven centuries before, but it had been expanded many times since then, in a score or more of different styles and motifs lent harmony by the yellow honey granite of which the whole was made. Images and carvings covered every inch of the huge façade, worn to varying degrees of featurelessness by time and weather, but here and there, where the construction was newer or there was protection from the elements, showing sharper and more perfect. Above it all a dozen domes reached toward the sky, like fat lotus buds about to open. Recently regilded, they reflected light even on this overcast day; when the sun shone, they were blinding.

Gyalo had been raised on tales of the First Temple's magnificence, and it justified the stories in every respect, even marred by decades of neglect and the more substantial depredations of the Caryaxists, who had helped themselves to floor tiles and wall inlays and anything made of metal, and scraped all the gold leaf off the image of Ârata Eon Sleeper that reclined at the Temple's circular core. Still, the Temple was too huge, and—even for the Caryaxists—too sacred to be razed or ruined, as other temples and shrines and monasteries all over Arsace had been. It rested on the ironstone paving, a golden island atop a russet sea, as colossal and serene as the dreaming god himself.

Gyalo and the procession parted company—the procession moving left, preparing to round the Temple, Gyalo

turning right, toward the square's western side. The spectators made way for him, dipping their heads respectfully and
making the sign of Ârata as he passed. Elsewhere the square
was thickly populated by food vendors and offerings-sellers,
but there were none here. The western wall marked the
boundary of the Evening City, a labyrinth of courts and offices and suites that, from the first days of the church, had
been the seat of the Âratist leadership. For the past eighty
years it had stood empty, for the Caryaxist rebellion had
sent the Brethren into exile. But the Caryaxists were gone
now, and the Sons and Daughters had taken back their
home.

The red gate at the wall's midpoint was unlocked—meant
not to bar entry but to remind those who passed through it of
the separateness of the men and women who lived on its
other side. It gave onto a long courtyard paved in the same
ironstone as the square. At the court's far end, a pavilion with
a yellow-tiled roof marked the entrance to the Evening City.

Four guards stood duty inside, clad in the white stoles of
the Forceless and displaying on their arms and cheeks the
sinuous tattoos of ordinates from the kingdom of Kanu-Tapa,
where Skambys, Patron of war, was the most important of the
Aspects, and martial arts were part of Âratist training. Behind them rose two great sets of vermilion-painted doors.
Those on the left, which gave access to the offices where administrative work was done, were open. Those on the right
were closed. Beyond them lay the living quarters of the
Brethren, where no one went without permission.

Gyalo approached the guards' leader. He came here daily,
in his capacity as aide to the Son Utamnos; the guards all
knew him, a fact they acknowledged now by ignoring him
completely. This time, though, his purpose was different.

"I have a summons." By custom, he spoke Arsacian, the
common language of the church. "From the Bearer."

The leader's bored, superior expression did not change.
He took the message cylinder Gyalo offered and scanned the
paper inside. Turning, he nodded to one of his subordinates,
who disappeared through the right-hand doors. The leader

handed the summons back to Gyalo and withdrew his attention again, as thoroughly as if Gyalo had ceased to exist.

Under other circumstances Gyalo might have been annoyed at this display of Tapati arrogance, but today he was too distracted. His apprehension flowed through him like water. It was unexpected, this anxiety—not the feeling itself, for given the identity of his summoner some degree of nervousness was to be expected, but its acuteness. Had not Utamnos, warning him to expect the summons, told him that its purpose would honor him? Yet Utamnos either could not or would not reveal what the purpose was, giving him instead a list of documents to read in preparation: accounts of the Caryaxist occupation, descriptions of Thuxra City, the small body of writings on the Burning Land. Over the past four days the mystery had become more and more oppressive. Now, waiting in the pavilion with only the disdainful guards for company, Gyalo felt nearly ill with accumulated stress.

The guard returned, another Forceless monk behind him. The monk scrutinized Gyalo's summons and tucked it into a pocket of his gown.

"Come," he said.

He led the way through the doors on the right, into rooms and corridors familiar to Gyalo from his visits to Utamnos's private suite, and then into regions Gyalo did not know. Everywhere was magnificence, both intact—astonishing floor mosaics, intricately carved columns and door frames, gorgeously stenciled ceilings, majestic galleries flanked by graveled courts—and marred—defaced murals, derelict gardens, ruined atriums, shattered carvings. The Caryaxists had been great graffitists, and the returning Âratist leadership had found much of the Evening City decorated with revolutionary slogans and lewd cartoons. Despite the priority given to the removal of these, a few still remained, ugly scrawlings in red paint like blood, yellow paint like bile: Ârata's colors, used to mock him.

Gyalo's guide delivered him at last into a large chamber with a coffered ceiling and a floor of red tile. "Wait here," he directed, and departed.

Gyalo paced the length of the room, halting before the windows. They faced onto a small garden—not overgrown, like many of those he had just passed, but exquisitely restored, with clipped shrubs and carefully raked gravel paths. The warm air smelled of roses. He closed his eyes and breathed deeply, seeking calm. He was aware of the beating of his heart, the ebb and flow of his apprehension.

There were footsteps behind him. He turned. A man in white-and-crimson clothes was passing through the doorway, followed by two Tapati guards and a teenage boy. The man towered above all three of his companions; he moved with the swift forceful stride of someone who assumed without considering it that he would be made way for. Gyalo had seen this man many times—had heard him speak many times, too, in rich tones that made all words beautiful—but always from a distance, always surrounded by scores, even hundreds, of others. He had never, at this point in his career, thought to stand solitary before the Blood Bearer, incarnate Son of Ârata's First Messenger and elected leader of the Âratist church.

He came forward and sank to his knees on the cool tiles. He bowed his head, crossing his hands before his face, and said, in a voice that shook only a little:

"Great is Ârata. Great is his Way."

"Go in light," the Bearer replied. "Get up."

Gyalo obeyed. The Bearer was about forty years of age, with broad handsome features and heavy-lidded eyes. An intricate image of the sun, Ârata's symbol, was tattooed in red upon his forehead. He had the tawny skin and heavy bone structure common in the kingdom of Haruko, where he had been born in this incarnation; the great weight of muscle he carried was apparent in his corded neck and wide shoulders and the round hard sinews of his right arm, left bare by the traditional draping of his white stole. Like all vowed Âratists he kept his chin and skull clean-shaven, and wore the monk's uniform of loose trousers and knee-length sleeveless gown—though his were made of lustrous red silk, rather than Gyalo's plain linen or the coarse cotton worn by the Forceless.

On the Bearer's chest rested the badge of his office, a thick gold chain with a pendant cage of gold wire, inside which gleamed a honey-colored jewel as large as a man's clenched fist: the Blood of Ârata. The Blood was round in shape and naturally faceted; a core of living flame seemed to dance at its heart. All vowed Âratists wore a smaller simulacrum of this necklace, hidden beneath their clothing, but the most cleverly crafted of these could only suggest the splendor of the original. If Gyalo had not known what the jewel was, he would still have sensed its sacredness, in that shuddering brilliance that was unlike anything else in the world—so much more beautiful, and so much stranger, than was apparent from a distance.

"Your master told you to expect this summons, yes?"

With difficulty, Gyalo wrenched his attention away from the jewel. "Yes, Old One."

"Your master holds you in high esteem." The Bearer's eyes moved across Gyalo's face, as if measuring him against that assessment. "He tells me that he relies on you beyond any of his other aides."

Gyalo bowed his head. "His confidence honors me, Old One."

"Come." The Bearer turned and strode toward the chair his guards had brought forward and placed at the center of the room. Gyalo followed, halting a little distance away and arranging himself in a posture of respect, his eyes cast down and his hands clasped before him. He was conscious of the guards at the Bearer's back, and of the boy, kneeling quietly on the floor at the Bearer's feet. The boy was also Haruko-born, paler of skin than the Bearer, but with the same strong bones and heavy-lidded almond eyes. His black hair hung loose, and he wore the plain white tunic and trousers of a postulant. But the sun tattoo on his forehead, and of course his presence, marked him for what he truly was: another incarnate Son, too young yet to take up the burdens of leadership but old enough to observe his elders in the performance of their duties. Infant Sons and Daughters were given to the adult Brethren to raise as their own: This boy, Vimâta, was both the Bearer's spirit-brother and his foster child.

"Tell me about yourself," the Bearer said. "Where were you born?"

"In Rimpang, Old One." Rimpang, capital of the kingdom of Chonggye, was home to the largest Âratist center in Galea after Baushpar; the Brethren had taken refuge there upon their flight from the Caryaxist rebellion. "My mother was a cook in one of the convents. She died when I was seven. The nuns gave me to the monks to raise."

"Had you no other family?"

"My father. But he was a soldier, and stationed elsewhere. There were only the monks to take me in."

The Bearer shifted in his chair, crossing one leg over the other. His broad face was attentive, as if he were hearing these things for the first time. Gyalo had no doubt, however, that the Bearer already knew everything that was to be known about him. This recital was, in some way, a test.

"Did your father ever return?"

"Yes, Old One, about a year after my mother died. He wanted me to have a military career, not a religious one. He demanded that I be taken from the monastery and given to him. The monks told me I could choose, and that if I wanted to stay, they would honor my wishes. I decided to stay. My father was angry—he tried to get the courts to intervene, he even petitioned the overlord of Rimpang province. But then he was called away. He never came back. I heard later that he died in the Jingya epidemics."

"Why did you decide to stay? You didn't yet know you were a Shaper. And you were very young—too young, surely, to know what you desired for the rest of your life."

"From the time I can remember, Old One, Ârata has called me. One of the earliest memories I have is of the Rimpang temple core—the image of Ârata Creator, the incense and the candles, the offerings and the silence. I loved the silence—I thought I could feel the god within it. I think I always wanted to vow the Way, though I never truly understood that until my father tried to make me a soldier."

"You would have come to the Way in any case, being what you are, whether your father wished it or not."

"Yes, Old One. But most Shapers never choose their service—they are chosen, by their ability. But I *did* choose, before ever I knew what I was. I feel blessed to have been granted that chance."

The Bearer studied Gyalo; at his feet, Vimâta gravely echoed his spirit-brother's attention. The Bearer's heavy-lidded gaze was extraordinarily direct, and also extraordinarily opaque. Gyalo could feel the force of the powerful personality behind it; he could see the ancient intelligence that lived in those eyes. But he could not begin to guess what the Bearer might be thinking.

"Go on," the Bearer said. "You became a postulant, then."

"Yes, Old One. I completed my training, and swore the Sixfold Vow. I was assigned to work in Rimpang library while I studied for my Shaper ordination. After I was ordained, I took the administrative examinations. The Son Utamnos selected me from the position lists. I served him for five years in Rimpang, and for the past six months here in Baushpar."

"You give a very brief account of yourself. I understand your exam scores were extraordinary."

"I was told so, Old One."

"Come now, no false modesty." The Bearer smiled a little. "My Brother Utamnos informs me that you have an acute grasp of your own abilities."

Gyalo felt himself flush. "I do know my strengths, Old One. I try to know my weaknesses also."

"Ah." The Bearer picked up the jewel on his chest, his blunt fingers caressing the wire of its cage in an absent, habitual gesture. "It is quite a skill, to understand one's weaknesses. Most people have some notion of their talents, but few know their failings half so well. And often it is an ignorance deliberately cultivated."

Gyalo could not take his eyes off the Bearer's fingers, probing gently at the golden lattice. What was it like to touch the Blood of Ârata? Did it radiate warmth like the blood it had been, or chill like the crystal it had become? Did the god's divinity resonate in it, as his immanence did in the silence of his temples? Or had its nearness grown so familiar that the Bearer no longer noticed such things? There was an offhand quality to his gesture that suggested this.

The Bearer's brows were raised again. Gyalo struggled to rein in his thoughts.

"I agree, Old One," he said. "I strive to avoid self-deception."

"According to Utamnos, you are unusually diligent in that regard. He says you turn toward the truth even when it is painful for you to do so." The Bearer paused. "He also tells me that your manita dose is unusually high."

This time Gyalo felt his face go scarlet. "Then he must have told you, Old One," he said carefully, "that my dose is stable, and has been for some time now."

"Indeed. And that, prior to its stabilization, you never attempted to abuse your shaping, unlike some who require frequent dosage adjustment. That you yourself approached him, in fact, when you sensed your tether had become inadequate."

"Yes, Old One. As any Shaper should."

"And yet other Shapers have fallen into apostasy that way. Those with naturally strong abilities especially find it difficult to accept the limitation of the drug. Haven't you been tempted?"

The room seemed to have grown very still. The Bearer's eyes gleamed, unblinking as a hawk's; the jewel, with which he no longer toyed, shone on his broad chest like a tiny sun. Beside him, his spirit-brother was an attentive shadow. Gyalo understood, with sure instinct, that this was not just another question; a turning point of some sort had been reached.

"When I started my Shaper training, Old One," he began, "I did resent manita's grip upon my shaping. Because of that, and also out of curiosity, I did things I shouldn't have done, experimented with my ability in ways I knew were forbidden. I won't excuse myself by saying I was only a boy, or that I hadn't yet taken the Shaper vow, or that most trainee Shapers do the same. I knew the Doctrine of Baushpar, I knew the words of my teachers, and so I knew it was wrong. That should have been enough."

He drew a breath. Images of that time stirred uncomfortably in memory: If he tried, he could still recapture the ghost of the desire that had driven him, the breathless mix of shame and guilt and excitement his secret explorations had produced. It was not easy to talk of this. His preceptor in Rimpang had known, and he had confessed to Utamnos early in their association. But to no one else.

"As I grew older, and my understanding of the Way of Ârata deepened, it *did* become enough. But I cannot lie—I was still curious, and it wasn't always faith that kept me pure, but only will. Then I was put to work in Rimpang library. I have an interest in the past, in the history of the church. I came upon the firsthand accounts of the Shaper War. I'd never seen such documents—all I knew of the War was the texts that are given in the postulant classes. I read them all, every account I could find. And I came to understand—not just to accept through my training or to hold through my vows, but to truly *understand*—the need for limitation. Shaping freed to human will, to human desire, is a terrible anarchy. Those who follow it in that way don't care for what it is, but only for what it can do. They may begin by acknowledging its sacredness, but always they grow corrupt, and end by pursuing greed and gain. And down that road lies catastrophe.

"So my answer to your question, Old One, is this: The cure for desire is knowledge. I see that road too clearly now ever to set my feet upon it. Since that time, I have not been tempted."

The Bearer's eyes held his. For a moment there was silence. Then the Bearer smiled—fully this time, though his eyes remained hooded. Beside him the boy Vimâta smiled also, a graceful mirror.

"Your master promised you would impress me," he said. "He was correct."

Gyalo bowed his head. He felt as if he had stood in the path of a whirlwind, and been passed over. "You honor me, Old One."

"To business, then." The Bearer shifted again in his chair, a restlessness that did not suggest impatience so much as the driving demand of an energy too great to be held still. "Obviously, I haven't called you here just to question you. I understand your master has set you to reading the accounts of that abomination, Thuxra City?"

"Yes, Old One."

Thuxra City was a prison, built by the Caryaxist government ten years after the uprising that brought it to power, as part of its transition from egalitarian revolution to authoritarian state. Over the years, as hardening ideology and popular unrest bred escalating repression, Thuxra grew to enormous proportions. In addition to political prisoners and ordinary people accused of a wide variety of anticommunal offenses, many vowed Âratists were confined there, monks and nuns who defied secularization orders, or were found to have taken vows in secret, or were discovered in more active forms of resistance, such as smuggling dissidents to safety across Arsace's borders.

Thuxra stood on the far side of the massive range of mountains known as the Range of Clouds, at the edge of the Burning Land. There were many practical reasons to build a prison in such a hostile and isolated place, where escape meant death, and only the prisoners and those who guarded them knew exactly what went on inside. But it was ideology that had caused the Caryaxists to situate Thuxra in Ârata's sacred land—a deliberate defilement of holy ground, a powerful demonstration of their contempt for the Âratist traditions that for centuries had kept the Burning Land inviolate, disturbed only by pilgrims and holy men. One of the Brethren's most urgent priorities was Thuxra's dismantlement.

"Before Thuxra," the Bearer said, "Caryaxist officials used Arsace's existing prisons to hold vowed Âratists whom they did not choose to execute or secularize. Sometimes, though, to save space and also because it was considered . . . appropriate, vowed Âratists were banished directly into the Burning Land."

Gyalo drew in his breath. "I'd thought that was only a rumor, Old One."

"Unfortunately very little of what we heard about the Caryaxists during our exile in Rimpang has turned out to be rumor. The faithful were marched over the mountains, stripped naked, and chased out into the Land. Any who attempted to return were killed." The Bearer smiled, this time with singular grimness. "It's all documented. They were dedicated record-keepers, the Caryaxists.

"The practice ceased once Thuxra was built, for the Caryaxists discovered the Land could be mined, and it was more profitable to keep all their prisoners alive for labor. It was assumed, of course, that the banished Âratists had perished. It's a deadly environment even for a man at full strength, which those poor souls most certainly were not. However . . ." The Bearer paused. "For some decades now, our Dreamers have been dreaming of something odd, deep inside the Land. They are vague, these Dreams—the Dreamers can't even say, really, what it is they sense. It's there, though, where nothing ever was before, some sort of . . . disturbance, far out in the wastes. Until recently, not knowing a great deal about what was going on inside Arsace, we had no reason to assume it was anything but natural—volcanic eruption, or something of the sort. But now, with the records available to us, we think it might be human—or more precisely, the exercise of a human power."

"Do you mean . . ." Gyalo was incredulous. "Do you mean to say there are survivors?"

"We think it's possible."

"But how? The Land is waterless. There's nothing to eat, nothing to live on."

"In the *Book of the Messenger* it's written that the Messenger was nourished on the food of the gods and the nectar of paradise when he followed Ârata's dream into the wastes. It seems those things may not have been entirely miraculous. There is sustenance in the Land, and water, for those who know how to find them—the Caryaxists discovered this during their time at Thuxra, as they pushed outward in search of gems and copper and gold. On the other hand . . ." Again the Bearer paused. "The records show that only Dreamers and Forceless were banished in this way. Whatever else you may say about the Caryaxists, they weren't fools—they understood the risk of unbound shaping, which is why they were so relentless in their pursuit of Shapers. But suppose a Shaper, or perhaps more than one, decided to pass himself off as Forceless to save his life, and was taken along with the others?"

"And without manita—"

"Exactly."

Gyalo was silent, considering this possibility—that Shapers released from the tether of manita and forced into the Burning Land had used their ability to save themselves, and that their descendants had survived. There had been many Shaper apostasies over the course of Âratist history, particularly during the centuries just after the Shaper War and the formulation of the Doctrine of Baushpar, as the church took steps to gather all shaping to itself; but they had been quickly discovered and dealt with. Even the most vigorous had lasted no more than a decade. This desert community, on the other hand, would have existed for seventy or more years—two, possibly three, generations without manita. It was a staggering idea.

"So you believe that shaping is causing the disturbances the Dreamers have dreamed, Old One?"

The Bearer shook his head. "Truly, at this point, all is speculation. We know nothing for certain, not even that there were Shapers to begin with. But whatever the truth may be, we must discover it. We cannot tolerate the possibility that human beings may languish in such dreadful exile—nor can we countenance such a disturbance of Ârata's sacred resting place. If there are survivors, they must be found and brought back to Arsace."

Gyalo felt as if the floor had just shifted, very slightly, beneath his feet. The events of the past days—the summons, the reading, Utamnos's evasiveness—fell abruptly into place inside his mind. "A rescue expedition," he said.

"Yes. King Santaxma in his generosity has agreed to equip it, and also to provide a military staff. We must be grateful for His Majesty's eagerness to aid the church in this urgent matter."

One would not guess, from the formality of the Bearer's manner, that he and Santaxma were fast friends, and had been so since childhood. Santaxma was the scion of the only branch of the Arsacian royal family to survive the massacre that brought the Caryaxists to power; he and the Bearer had grown up side by side in Rimpang, dreaming a shared dream of Arsacian freedom. They came to power together also, Santaxma crowned King-in-Exile only a few months after the Bearer's election. Together, they embarked upon the fulfillment of their vision, Santaxma raising men, the Bearer raising money. Now Santaxma reigned again in Arsace, and the Brethren ruled once more in Baushpar—a dual restoration, but a single triumph.

"Know," the Bearer said, "that this decision has not been lightly made. We detest the necessity of intruding upon the god's rest. But Ârata has already been disturbed, over and over, by the death and suffering the Caryaxists brought into his sacred land—and by these survivors, if indeed that is what they are. We will add only briefly to his disquiet, and when we are finished his peace will be entirely restored. The god who created us, who made us out of his own bright nature, would not expect us to set tradition above service, when so great a wrong may need to be put right."

"I understand, Old One."

"I suspect you also understand that you are to be part of the expedition."

It was true. Even so, to hear it spoken stole Gyalo's breath. "I will do my best to serve, Old One."

The Bearer raised his brows. "You sound uncertain."

"I confess, Old One . . . I do not understand why I have been chosen."

"How so?"

"I'm a Chonggye ordinate, Old One. I've lived almost all my life in Rimpang. My knowledge is of history and administration. I have no martial training, and barely any familiarity with travel. I wonder that you would not want someone . . . more experienced."

"You are physically strong. That's clear to look at you. You're a competitive runner, I believe?"

"I was, Old One. It's been some time since I competed."

"The point is that you are fit, and accustomed to endurance. Martial matters needn't concern you—that is what the soldiers are for. As for experience . . . no one has experience of the sort of journey you will be undertaking. In that, you are at no greater disadvantage than the others." He watched Gyalo a moment, shrewdly. "Your doubt is natural. But know that a great deal of care has gone into planning this expedition. You will be leaving from Thuxra City, as the lost Âratists did. You will have a man from Thuxra to show you the ways of survival in the Burning Land. The soldiers will cope with the practical aspects of travel . . . and other areas in which their skills may be needed. There will be Dreamers to serve as guides. There will be Forceless to help you prepare those you may find for return to Arsace. And there will be you, a Shaper, to maintain the requirements of ritual, to supervise the other Âratists, to record the journey—and, if necessary, to provide a historical perspective on Shaper apostasy, from your close knowledge of the Shaper War. So as you can see, it's not for your knowledge of a sword or your travel skills that you've been chosen."

Gyalo bowed his head. "I understand, Old One. Thank you."

"The soldiers will arrive within the fortnight, so if you've any outstanding business, take care of it now. My Sister Sundit is overseeing the travel plans. She'll summon you for briefing in the next day or so."

"Yes, Old One."

"In the meantime, don't speak of this to anyone other than the Brethren—not even to your fellow aides. The purpose of this expedition is not generally known. We do not wish to stir more speculation than we must."

"I understand, Old One."

"Come." The Bearer stretched out his right arm, his powerful muscles flexing. "I will give you my blessing."

Gyalo approached and sank to his knees, bowing his face so that all he could see was the gleaming silk of the Bearer's trousers and the upturned toes of his embroidered indoor shoes. The Bearer's hand descended upon his head, the palm wide and warm against his shaven scalp, the fingers easily encircling his skull. It was a gentle grip, but he could feel the leashed power of it, the weight of flesh and bone in the arm above.

"Go in light, child of Ârata, vowed servant of the god. May your bright nature lead you forward, and your ash-nature follow after you. May the light of Ârata overflow your soul, and the darkness of the Enemy never trouble you. May your faith guide you, and your obedience keep you, and your compassion lend you strength. These are all the tools you need. In the name of Ârata, in the name of his First Messenger, in the name of his church, by the power of his sacred Blood, I give you blessing. Go in light, child of Ârata, vowed servant of the god."

The Bearer's fingers tightened briefly, then withdrew. But it seemed to Gyalo that he could still feel the burden of that great hand—a metaphorical burden now, of expectation and purpose. The sinews of his neck ached with tension. He rocked back onto the balls of his feet, and stood.

"Thank you, Old One."

"Journey well, Brother Gyalo." The Bearer's hand had descended to lie lightly upon Vimâta's sleek black head. "Go in light."

Gyalo bowed. "Great is Ârata. Great is his Way."

One of the Tapati guards led him back through Evening City, turning aside when the doors to the entrance pavilion came in sight. He walked homeward in the twilight. The people of Baushpar had gone indoors to their suppers, and the streets were all but deserted. He picked his way through the litter of the procession—heaps of ox dung and shreds of ribbon and clots of straw, and here and there a little piece of shining matter, the remains of blessings that an inexperienced trainee Shaper had invested with too much substance. But he scarcely saw these things. The Bearer's necklace hung before his inner eye: the gleam of golden lattice, the quiver of flame at the heart of the crystal of the Blood. Soon, very soon, he would walk the red sands from which that crystal had come. He had to breathe deeply and set his feet hard upon the ground to convince himself he was not dreaming.

— 2 —

Full night had fallen by the time Gyalo reached the monastery to which he was assigned. Properly, he should have had rooms in the Evening City; but Shapers were in short supply, and the Brethren's aides, who normally performed only temple service, had been temporarily parceled out among the monasteries and nunneries to fill the gap. Above the entrance, the Five Foundations of the Way of Ârata were written out, so that no one should enter here but with thought of the god: Faith, Affirmation, Increase, Consciousness, and Compassion. Gyalo touched his thumb and smallest finger to his eyelids in the sign of Ârata as he passed beneath.

Until recently, this monastery had been empty. The Caryaxists had blockaded Baushpar soon after they took control of Arsace, making it almost impossible for tradesmen or travelers to get into the city. Departure was permitted, though, and within a decade the secular population had vanished, seeking better conditions elsewhere. The vowed Âratists, left behind, cared for the city as best they could; but since vowing the Way was now forbidden, there were no new postulants to take the place of the monks and nuns who died. The Brethren, returning in triumph, found a place of ghosts, its buildings derelict, its streets littered with debris. Yet beneath the deterioration, Baushpar was whole. The city was an ancient and powerful symbol, gifted to the faith by King Fârat, an early convert of the First Messenger, who had made the Way of Ârata the state religion of Arsace. It was from Baushpar that Marduspida sent his followers out to preach the word of the god in foreign lands. It was to Baushpar that Marduspida retired when he could no longer travel; it was in Baushpar that he died. Even the Caryaxists, apparently, had been unwilling to challenge such a weight of history—or perhaps, more pragmatically, they had simply feared that to destroy the holy city would tip the people of Arsace over the line into revolt.

Over the year and a half since Santaxma had regained the throne, vowed Âratists from every kingdom of Galea had poured into the city, eager to assist in the task of restoring Baushpar to its former glory. The secular population returned also, reclaiming abandoned villas, opening shops and reestablishing businesses. In some areas the work was only begun: the Evening City, for instance, where the wealth of ornament and artwork must be painstakingly re-created from imported materials. In others it went more quickly. The refurbishment of this monastery had already been complete six months ago, when Gyalo arrived.

The evening meal was in progress in the ground-floor dining hall. The food smelled enticing; but Gyalo turned away, and climbed the wide staircase to the third floor, where the Shapers lodged. In Rimpang he had had a suite to himself, but here he had only a single chamber. It was comfortably furnished, with ochre-tinted plaster walls, two round windows covered by hinged wooden screens, and a cabinet bed with carved doors. Everything had been beautifully restored; there was no obvious sign that the chamber had stood abandoned for decades. But he had lived there long enough to mark the spots where different graining spoke of replaced floorboards, to count the cracks in the worktable's mother-of-pearl inlay, and to learn by heart the shape of the mildew stains on the shelves of the storage cupboard—a subtle legacy of damage, persisting beneath the bright façade of renewal.

Sitting down in the room's only chair, he drew his simulacrum from beneath his gown, took it off, and laid it before him on the table. His taste for luxury was modest; this necklace, purchased from a renowned Rimpang jeweler, was one of the few extravagances of his life. Its chain and wire cage were neither brass nor silver gilt but pure gold; the jewel inside, somewhat smaller than the Bearer's, was glass—but cut, not molded, its facets sharp enough to wound, as the real Blood's were. Inside the jewel glittered a representation of the flame at the Blood's heart. Gyalo had asked the jeweler how it had been incorporated into the glass; the man refused to say, but swore that his was the most faithful reproduction available anywhere. Having seen the real Blood close, Gyalo knew the jeweler had not lied. The flame was static and did not shed light, but in all other ways it was a remarkably accurate representation.

Never before had it failed to give him pleasure. Yet in this moment, the memory of the true Blood fresh in mind, it seemed cheap—a bauble, a gimcrack. He had thought it an act of reverence four years ago to spend nearly a year's allowance on it; now it seemed merely vanity. Better, almost, to have kept the knot of molded glass he had worn before— a thing that represented, as all simulacrams must, but did not dissemble, as this one did.

He put it on again. It settled heavily against his chest, cool at first, warming with his body heat. At least, he told himself with halfhearted irony, it would not tarnish with his sweat and turn his skin green, as he traveled in the Burning Land. A small value, for the fortune it had cost.

The Burning Land.

He had spent much time wondering, before this afternoon, what might lie behind the Bearer's summons. But even his wildest speculations had not approached the truth: that deep within the desert exiled Âratists might survive, either by the miracle of some unknown oasis or the practice of the basest apostasy; and that he, Gyalo Amdo Samchen, was to be part of the expedition sent to find them. In the time it had taken him to cross Baushpar, the idea had lost none of its strangeness. Even now it made him feel unsteady, as if the floor beneath him were not quite solid.

Intellectually, he understood why he had been chosen. Yet it was precisely true, what he had told the Bearer—he was a man of thought, of learning, who had passed the whole of his life within the sheltering confines of Rimpang's great Âratist complex, and, until King Santaxma's restoration to the throne, had never thought to leave it. Though he had read widely, he possessed little direct experience of the world, little firsthand knowledge of its hardships. The greatest hunger he had ever felt was the pang of a missed meal. The greatest injury he had ever suffered was an arm broken in childhood. The deepest exhaustion he had ever known was the fatigue of a footrace, a tiredness that carried with it a trained athlete's assumption of quick recovery.

According to the accounts he had read over the past days, the Burning Land was a place of unmatched brutality—an endless expanse of rock and sand and scrub, where the sun beat like a hammer on the helpless earth, and rain fell only rarely. Few who went in came out. Those who did reported no inland rivers, no hidden pockets of abundance to succor the wanderer. Even if, as the Bearer said, there were men who knew how to survive in such a place, travel would be grueling. How would he withstand those trials? Would he endure with honor? Would his weakness shame him?

Would he return?

That was the real question, of course. It had hovered, unspoken, behind the Bearer's instructions; it rose like a wall now inside Gyalo's mind. It was not quite the first time he had faced the possibility of dying. In the decade and a half of chaos and civil war that followed on the death of the Voice of Caryax, many regions of Arsace had fallen entirely to lawlessness; journeying to Baushpar, he had traveled roads roamed by bandits and renegade Caryaxists, who were said to kill vowed Âratists on sight. But his party, which included Utamnos, had been guarded by a full company of Exile cavalry, providing not just a promise of protection but a deterrent to attack. In the desert, the enemy was not physical. It could not be fought off with bows and swords. A display of force would not discourage it.

Consciousness, he thought, invoking the Fourth Foundation of the Way. *I am conscious now: of my fear of dying, of my fear that I may prove myself less strong than I would wish. I know my capabilities, but only within the limits of my life till now. How will I fare when I am tested?*

Yet even as he stood before his fear and named it, he was aware that fear was only part of what he felt. Something else, brighter and more urgent, had been planted in him today. To walk in the footsteps of the First Messenger. To set his feet upon sacred ground—not in the random wandering of a pilgrim, not in the defilement of the Caryaxists, but in the dedicated service of Ârata. To see, perhaps, the ancient signs of the gods' titanic struggle—parched channels where rivers had run, the shadows of leaves etched into rock, the ghostly traces of a land that once had been as verdant as Arsace. He, Gyalo Amdo Samchen, would experience those things. What might he discover in the Burning Land? What might he learn?

He caught his breath. Since he could remember, he had sought knowledge. Yet even as he acquired it, he recognized the limits of his learning, bounded as it was by his worldly inexperience and his confinement in Rimpang. These limits had been transcended by the Brethren's return to Baushpar, which allowed him to cross a land and explore a city he had known only in tales, almost as a myth. In the past months, however, as wonder faded into familiarity, he had realized, with an understanding that was not quite acceptance, that he had simply come to another place he would never leave.

Now, though, he *would* leave—on a journey that might take his life, but would also teach him more than he had ever imagined he might know. And not from books, but firsthand, through his own direct experience. This was what he wanted.

Through his fear, he knew it—this journey. This chance. This change. No matter what lay at the end of it.

For a little longer he sat at the table, dreaming. At last he got to his feet and crossed to the meditation alcove set into the space between the end of the cabinet-bed and the outside wall. He lit a cone of incense and settled himself on the cushioned meditation bench, back straight, hands loose upon his thighs. Closing his eyes, he began the breathing exercises that would aid his descent into contemplation.

Ârata could not be prayed to: sleeping, he did not listen. Even among vowed Âratists, there were many who preferred to approach the god in a less distant guise, through one or another of his Aspects—facets of his personality dreamed into being over the course of his eonic slumber, directly active in the world and therefore capable of hearing the prayers of those who followed them. But Gyalo had never been drawn to these bits and pieces of the larger whole. It was the totality that called him—Ârata himself, utterly inaccessible to human consciousness and yet profoundly immanent within the world. For those who worshiped in this way, the only path was meditation, undertaken in the knowledge that the barrier of Ârata's oblivion could not be pierced, but only mirrored a little within the limits of the human soul.

Usually Gyalo descended into the darkness within himself, riding the ebb and flow of breath. Today, though, an image possessed his mind. He seemed to fly above an ocean of scarlet sand, an undulating eternity of aureate light and burning dunes. Deeper he went, and deeper. The world of grass and water fell away. Far off, at the red horizon, the hills seemed to hold the contours of a sleeping face, too vast to be properly apprehended: the face of Ârata, waiting for him in the wilderness.

Two days later Gyalo was summoned by the Daughter Sundit. He was generally familiar with all the Brethren, from his duties for Utamnos and the council meetings he had attended; but he had actually come face-to-face only with a few, for the Brethren associated mainly with one another,

avoiding contact with ordinary mortals beyond the members
of their own private staffs. Sundit, a close friend to Utamnos,
was one of the few. Characteristically, she did not make him
stand while she spoke to him, as other Sons or Daughters
might have, but bid him be seated and served him refresh-
ments. Her briefing was thorough. By the time he was dismissed, he knew the route the expedition would take to
Thuxra City inn by inn and monastery by monastery, and had
learned how it would be equipped down to the last tent pole.

"We may not know what you'll find in the Burning Land,"
she told him in her matter-of-fact way. "But we can at least
be absolutely certain of how you reach it."

The military escort arrived within the week: a cavalry
company of twenty commanded by a captain named Teispas
dar Ispindi. As the leader of the expedition's religious contingent, Gyalo was called again to Sundit's chambers to be
introduced. Teispas was a compact man in his midthirties,
with hawkish features and black hair; he was smoothly po-
lite, with the proper degree of respect for Gyalo's Shaperhood, but behind his courtesy Gyalo sensed a deep reserve.
Pure-blood Arsacians regarded themselves as Galea's original inhabitants and looked down on the peoples of the other
kingdoms, who were of a different racial stock; but it
seemed to Gyalo that something other than snobbery lay behind Teispas's remoteness.

Gyalo spent the afternoon before his departure in his
small office in the Evening City, taking care of final matters
and setting in order the many books and scrolls that littered
his desk, so that those who came later to fetch them could
more easily return them to their places. Over the past days,
driven by the sense that thorough intellectual preparation
might offset his lack of practical skills, he had requested
from the Brethren's library every document he could think
of that might be relevant to the journey: reports by the liberators of Thuxra City, a history of the Shaper War, several
accounts of Shaper apostasy through the ages, a book describing Arsace's sacred sites—from which he had taken
notes, for he intended to visit as many as lay within easy dis-

tance of the travel route. Yet the more he read, the more the vistas of his ignorance opened out before him. Now, gathering up the mass of material, he could hardly have felt less prepared.

Finished, he blew out his lamps and went into the workroom, where the cadre of clerks and copyists under his supervision labored at assessing, compiling, and reproducing documents on the refurbishment and restaffing of Arsacian monasteries and temples. Many had worked for him previously in Rimpang; they did not know the truth of where he was going, but they knew he would be gone for at least a year, and they lined up to say good-bye, offering blessings and good wishes, amulets for luck, and trinkets to leave along the way at the shrines of Jo-mea, the Aspect who watched over travelers. In his unsettled frame of mind, the warmth of their farewells moved him almost to tears. They let him go at last, and he returned to the monastery to join the other Shapers in the ceremony of Banishing conducted nightly in the monastery's small chapel. Then he exchanged his linen stole for one of silk, and set out for his evening appointment: a meal with Utamnos.

Utamnos's valet, a Forceless monk almost as aged as Utamnos himself, met Gyalo at the Evening City's entrance and conducted him to Utamnos's suite. Utamnos was waiting, sitting on a cushion before a low Chonggyean-style table. Gyalo knelt, crossing his arms before his face.

"Great is Ârata. Great is his Way."

"Go in light, Gyalo. Get up. Seat yourself. Are you hungry? I hope so. I've planned a rather special meal."

Gyalo settled himself opposite his master. The residences of the Brethren had been among the first spaces in Baushpar to be restored; this room was so pristine that it looked not centuries old but nearly new. The plaster walls, tinted a deep shade of coral, were muraled to half their height with a stylized design of birds and reeds. Warmth came from several large braziers set on either side of the room, and light from candles in paper cages, resting on their own reflections in the gleaming floorboards. There were no rugs, and little furniture beyond the table at which Gyalo and Utamnos sat. On a pedestal in one corner a slender ash-fired vase held a sheaf of poppies.

According to Âratist belief, the world had been created by Ârata out of his own bright nature, and so was good. The pleasures of the world, therefore, were also good, and it was proper to embrace them. Though vowed Âratists swore an oath of celibacy, they lived without restraint in other ways—especially the Brethren, each of whom possessed a vast personal treasury amassed over the long period of their rebirths. But while some set great store by outward show, others were far more moderate. Utamnos denied himself nothing he desired, yet the whole of his residence reflected the exquisite restraint that defined this room.

Utamnos's valet brought in the meal, which was as fine as Utamnos had promised. They talked of inconsequential things: the coolness of the summer, the progress of Baushpar's refurbishment, the disagreements between the city's secular administration, which believed the church should contribute to the rehabilitation of businesses and private residences, and the Brethren, who wanted the secular population to donate labor for the repair of public works. A candle enclosed in a paper globe sat on the table between them, glowing like a tiny moon.

At last Gyalo pushed away his bowl. "I can't remember when I've had a better meal. Thank you, Old One."

Utamnos smiled. The honorific fit him, for he was ancient indeed, his face deeply creased, his eyebrows white. In this incarnation he was Arsacian, small in stature and slender as most Arsacians were, so dark of skin that his faded sun tattoo barely showed. He wore the cream-colored stole of the Forceless, as did all the Brethren, for the First Messenger and his offspring had not possessed shaping or dreaming ability. Among the Sons and Daughters, only he owned memories of Baushpar in his own body; he had been just four years old when the Caryaxists came. He had wept, on his return, to see Baushpar's defilement. With his own hands he had worked to scrub graffiti from the walls and sweep debris from the neglected courtyards.

"It was my pleasure. I wanted to make a good memory for you while you are traveling."

"It will be, Old One."

"You've explained everything to Tenzen?"

"I spent all the morning with him." Tenzen was another of Utamnos's aides, and would handle Gyalo's duties in his absence. "Everything's arranged, Old One. You'll barely notice I'm gone."

"Oh, I will notice. You are my Third Hand. You know that."

"Yes." Gyalo dropped his eyes, fixing them on the little candle-moon. "I know that."

"I was the one who recommended you for this expedition. Did the Bearer tell you that?"

"No, Old One. But I guessed it. There must be other capable Shapers with administrative experience and knowledge of the repatriation effort, and even some of the learning I possess, who also have experience of the world, of travel and so on. The only reason I can imagine I was chosen was because you spoke for me."

"Very true. And do you know why I spoke for you?"

"I assume you believe me capable of the duties I've been given, Old One."

"You're one of the finest aides I have ever had, Gyalo. Accomplished, intelligent, completely trustworthy. But those qualities, excellent as they are, are not what I value most in you. There is something else, something I've not encountered often in my lives. You have a clean faith. There is no shadow in it, no stain of doubt or ambition or hypocrisy. You see Ârata as he is, in all his power and all his distance. You do not need to deceive yourself in order to believe—you don't need to force the god into a smaller shape, a selfish shape, as those who worship the Aspects do."

"No, Old One. I've never needed that."

"That purity, that . . . honesty, makes you strong." Utam-nos's eyes, amber brown and webbed in wrinkles, were intent on Gyalo's face. "Strong in your soul. Strong in a way that the power of the body, the breadth of experience you believe you lack, cannot match. *That* is the strength you'll need, in the Burning Land. When you find these people, there will certainly be Shapers among them."

"You say 'when,' Old One. I was told it wasn't certain there would be survivors."

"Oh, there are survivors. I've never believed that what the Dreamers have been sensing all these years is natural; why then would they not be able to see it clearly? No. There's some agency at work. Perhaps whoever is there does not wish to be found."

Gyalo shook his head, disturbed. "But who could hide from Dreamers?"

"Perhaps you'll be the one to learn. As for the Shapers—by logic it must be so."

"I'd thought of that, Old One. We learned from the Caryaxists that there is sustenance in the Land, but the banished Âratists didn't know that. If they did survive, they could only have done so by use of shaping."

"Precisely. Now, not all my Brothers and Sisters wish to follow this logic. Even those who concede the probability of Shapers assume they will be weak, for it has been well established that the ability fades if training is not precise. But these exiles were vowed Âratists. Isn't it at least as likely that they remembered their training and passed it on intact? To me it seems entirely possible that what you will find in the Burning Land is not just a community that includes unbound Shapers, but unbound Shapers *at full strength*. It will not be easy for you to experience that, Shaper that you are—or to witness what will have to be done."

"I've known from the start it was a possibility." The release of shaping from the tether of manita created a consuming addiction to the ability, almost a kind of madness, from which sprang all manner of corruption: greed, cruelty, a lust for more and ever more power. Shapers who tasted this addiction could never again be trusted. Captured apostates were rendered powerless by means of massive doses of manita given under supervision—in effect, a lifetime sentence of arrest. Discovered apostates usually fought savagely to escape that fate. This was the true purpose of the expedition's military contingent—to provide the force that would be necessary, should there be Shapers in the Burning Land. "I'm prepared."

"No." Utamnos shook his head. "You cannot be prepared, Gyalo. Oh, in one sense you'll be ready enough—my Brothers and Sisters are wise enough to equip for all eventualities, whether they believe in them or not. But in other ways . . . If I am right, you will encounter apostasy of a kind that has not been seen since just after the Shaper War. You've studied the accounts, you know all about the corruptions and the abuses . . . but you cannot possibly know what it will be like to confront such things until you come face-to-face with them. It will be all the harder for you because of your own strong ability, and the possibility of temptation that holds for you. And yet it is precisely for this reason that I trust you above any Shaper I know. It's because you see the danger in yourself, and know so clearly the ways in which you might fall, that you grasp so acutely the danger falling poses. It's because you've explored beyond the boundaries that you know so well why the boundaries are there. The Bearer found this difficult to accept, at first. But I was able to persuade him that a strong, committed, *experienced* Shaper was a better choice than a weaker one with a less subtle understanding of the ability."

Gyalo thought of the questions the Bearer had asked him. Shapers were Âratism's priests, its elite. More educated than other vowed Âratists, more accomplished, they held most positions of authority within the church, and provided much of its administration, from the running of monasteries and nunneries and hospitals and orphanages to the recording of Âratist history and the service of the Brethren. Gyalo had never greatly cared for these trappings of status—it was shaping itself he loved, not just the manipulation of form and matter he performed in ceremony, but the way the world appeared to him when he called forth his ability. Shaping lay in his soul like Ârata's images within the cores of his temples—walled round with training and the restraints of manita, a mighty sleeping thing at the foundation of all he was and all he did, whose dreams, in the form of the rituals he conducted, touched and transformed the very fabric of reality. To shape was to see as Ârata had seen, when he called the world to being. It was to exercise, in miniature, Ârata's own creative power. It was, briefly, to return the god to active life within the world. Of all men and women on earth, only a Shaper could do these things.

Gyalo was aware that his ability was dangerous—not because of his childish experimentation, which was not so very different from others', but because it was so strong. It had come upon him early, and with unusual violence—a sudden access of visions and hallucinations that swallowed him whole for days, while the manita masters struggled to find the dosage that would properly tether him. It was a delicate balance, requiring that shaping be bound into latency yet remain accessible to the trained will. Most Shapers needed frequent adjustment at first; Gyalo had needed more than most, and from the start his tether had been larger. By the time he turned fifteen his dosage had leveled out, but small increases had still been necessary well past the time of his Shaper ordination, at the age of twenty-five.

And yet he understood that what Utamnos had said was true. The difficulty of his shaping talent, the struggle he had had to wage to master it and himself, made him stronger than those who had not needed to fight so hard. In spite of himself, he still dreaded the physical perils he would go out the next day to confront. But spiritual danger he did not fear.

"He asked me about that, Old One," he said. "About apostasy. Whether I'd ever been tempted."

"And of course you answered honestly."

"I told him what I told you, when I first began to work for you."

"He liked you, you know." Utamnos smiled, his dark face creasing. "He told me so."

"I'm honored, Old One."

"You are also lucky. He can be capricious in his judgments. If he'd taken a dislike to you, nothing I could have said would have persuaded him to send you."

There was an edge to Utamnos's voice. He did not often allow himself to be so unguarded; but Gyalo knew, as few beyond the Brethren's immediate circle did, that there was conflict between Utamnos and the Bearer. Though the souls of the Brethren were infallibly reborn, their characters in any given incarnation were much affected by their physical forms, and they often found themselves at odds, like members of a large family whose loyalty is beyond question but whose personalities rub one another raw. In his present body, the Bearer was much concerned with politics; it was part of his dream of post-Caryaxist reconstruction that the Brethren take a place in the Lords' Assembly, gaining the church, for the first time in Arsacian history, a political as well as a religious voice. Many of the Brethren supported this—but some, Utamnos among them, believed that the church had no business with affairs of state. Utamnos was the eldest of the Brethren, not just in his present body but in the original order of the First Messenger's children, and when he objected to a course of action, the Bearer was obliged to listen, and, often, to obey. But in this Utamnos had not been able to sway his spirit-sibling.

"I have a gift for you." Utamnos reached beneath the cushion on which he sat and brought out a package folded into patterned paper. "To keep you company on your long journey."

Gyalo unwrapped the little bundle. It was a book, bound between covers of yellow horn: *Dream Songs,* by the eighth-century devotional poet Tsantse Jo Dokha. The stanzas were written out on fine creamy paper in the original Chonggyean. Gyalo ran his fingers lightly along the lines of brush-stroked characters, so different from the flowing cursive of

Arsacian script. They had been his first learning, and were still his favorite to read.

"It's an exquisite gift, Old One. Thank you."

"I'll think of you, Gyalo." Utamnos's expression softened. "Under the sun, upon the sands. See that you take care. See that you come back to me."

Gyalo felt his throat tighten. He lowered his head and occupied himself with slipping the book into his pocket.

There was the sound of an opening door. A small dark-haired boy came trotting toward them.

"Look who is here!" said Utamnos, turning. "What are you doing out of bed, my bright boy?"

"I had a dream," the child whimpered.

"Oh, a dream! Come, let me make it better."

Utamnos held out his arms. The boy ran to him. Gyalo saw the involuntary grimace as Utamnos caught him up, and thought, as he often did these days, that his master was growing very frail.

"There, there, my sun-child, my treasure," Utamnos murmured, stroking the boy's curly black hair. "What did you dream that was so terrible you couldn't stay in bed?"

The boy shook his head, burrowing into Utamnos's embrace. All the Brethren were precious, but this little boy was especially so, for he was Arsacian. For the past eighty years, Sons and Daughters born into Arsace had gone unfound; by the end of the Caryaxist tyranny, the number of recognized Brethren had dwindled from thirty-five to twenty-two. Most of the lost Brethren could not be recovered until their next rebirth—it was possible for them to recognize what they were, and to access the store of their reborn wisdom, only if training began when they were very young. But two Sons had died within the past six years and had not been replaced, and it had been hoped their reincarnations might still be found within Arsace. This child was the first: Ivaxri, eighteenth of the Messenger's thirty sons.

"It is late," said Utamnos. "I should get him back to bed. Let me give you my blessing."

Gyalo rose and went to kneel at his master's side. Utamnos's hand came to rest gently on his head—not a weight, as the Bearer's had been, but a caress. Gyalo felt emotion rise in him again—love for this old man, who had recognized and indulged his hunger for learning, who had freely forgiven his youthful sins, who had treated him not as a servant but almost as a son. Would Utamnos still be here, in this form, when Gyalo returned? It was pointless to feel sorrow at a Son's or Daughter's physical passing; yet so much of Gyalo's love for his master was bound up with the ancient shape Utamnos now wore. It would be impossible not to grieve.

"Go in light, child of Ârata, vowed servant of the god," Utamnos said softly. "May hardship overlook you. May pain forget you. May you endure gladly, and return safely. Go in light, my helper, my friend, my Third Hand."

His grip withdrew. Gyalo looked up, into his master's face—and into the face of Ivaxri, who had lifted his head from Utamnos's chest. The boy's expression was grave, his eyes intent; it was not the gaze of a child at all, but the detached, fathomless regard of a soul so old there was nothing it had not seen, peering out from behind a mask of childish flesh. Gyalo felt a coldness run along his spine. He did not often confront such a stare, for the older Brethren sought to spare those who served them, and the younger soon learned to do so. But now he saw, fully present in Ivaxri's wide unblinking eyes, the whole cold *otherness* of the Âratist leaders, their incomprehensible unlikeness to ordinary beings.

Ivaxri reached out one small hand, and set the tip of his index finger on Gyalo's forehead. "Go in light," he said, with his baby tongue that could not yet properly form the words. Then he burrowed into Utamnos's stole again.

Gyalo got to his feet. "Go in light, Old One."

"Great is Ârata. Great is his Way." Utamnos smiled. In his eyes there was only warmth. "Travel well, Gyalo."

Gyalo woke at dawn, as he always did, even now that there were no bells to mark the time.

The room in which he lay was a wreck. The plaster ceiling was gone; only the lath remained, tacked precariously to the beams that supported the floor above. The walls had fared a little better, though their original white was faded to the color of spoiled milk. One window screen was intact, a lovely filigree of twining vines, its long-unoiled wood desiccated and brittle; the others had broken or fallen out. Debris covered the floor—chunks of plaster, bits of wood, scraps of fabric, and, everywhere, the litter of birds: guano, feathers, animal bones.

The monastery of which this room was part stood on the desert side of Thuxra Notch, the pass that gave access through the Range of Clouds to the Burning Land. Like other small monasteries in remote locations, it had survived the Caryaxist takeover without dispersal of its religious population and, for ten years after the fall of the old government, carried on more or less as always, maintaining the track through the pass and providing lodging for the pilgrims who came to see the sacred desert for themselves—not many, in those anti-Âratist times. It might have been left alone indefinitely, to die slowly by attrition, had it not been for the construction of Thuxra City, which brought it to the Caryaxists' attention. It was targeted for closure, Caryaxist-style. Soldiers came to execute the monks; their bodies were left unburied on the ground outside, and the monastery's salvageable goods were hauled away.

The monks' bones had been collected by the Exile Army, soon after the liberation of Thuxra City, and brought to Baushpar for interment. The Caryaxists had burned the monastery's papers, and the monks' names would never have been known had the soldiers not found, inscribed in still-legible red paint on the wall of a third-floor chamber, a message: *Remember us,* followed by sixty names. Gyalo had searched it out the previous evening and stood before it for some time.

The Dreamers, repelled by the aura of death that hung around the building, had argued against camping there. Kai-do Seiki had been especially vehement. In the end she had given in, but her complaints and exhortations annoyed and tired everyone—especially Gyalo, from whom, as usual, she demanded support.

Thinking of Seiki, Gyalo sighed and rose.

Shivering, for it was early autumn, and the mountain nights were cold, he took his meditation square from his travel pack. Settling himself cross-legged, he meditated for the space of two thousand breaths. Then, rising to his knees, he crossed his arms before his face and spoke the Affirmations with which every Âratist, vowed and secular, greeted the day:

"Ârata is the one god, now and forever. Ârata is the bright god, and darkness does not touch him. Ârata sleeps, but one day will wake. I affirm my faith in Ârata, deny my ash-nature in his name, and rejoice in the promise of his rising. Great is Ârata. Great is his Way."

Returning to his travel pack, he dug out a large leather

pouch and a flat silver box. The pouch, lined with several layers of waxed silk, held two years' supply of manita—far more than would be required for this journey, but he liked to err on the side of caution. Inside the box, each cradled in its own felt-lined compartment, was a tiny silver scoop, a silver tube slightly flared at one end, and a disc of beaten silver about as big as his palm.

He removed the items and arranged them before him on the meditation square. Opening the pouch, he spooned eight measures of fine brownish powder onto the disc, then bent and used the tube to inhale them—four in one nostril, four in the other. The drug struck him immediately, a burning at the back of his throat, a flare of light before his eyes, a buzzing in his brain. It passed almost at once, leaving his mind and vision clear. So accustomed was he to these sensations that he scarcely noticed them.

He put the manita equipment away, wadded all his spare clothing and undergarments into a bundle, took his razor, and descended to the ground floor, where the rest of the party slept. The soldiers, who had laid out their pallets with military precision in what had been the monastery's dining room, were already stirring. Avoiding them—not out of any particular aversion but because he had had enough of human interaction after the disputes of last night, and wanted to bathe, as he had wanted to sleep, in peace—Gyalo slipped out the back.

The arid hills that made up this portion of Thuxra Notch spread out before him, bracketed to the east and west by towering snowcapped peaks, glowing pale apricot in the light of the rising sun. The dry earth was broken everywhere by rock, like skin worn down to the bone; it supported only short tufted grasses and the occasional scrubby bush. Nevertheless, the monks had made gardens, enclosing areas and building them up with manure from their goats and chickens. In addition to the food crops, they had grown a small supply of manita—the shade posts still stood, though the gauze that had covered them was long since rotted away.

Only a handful of Shapers could ever have been needed here, for ritual and supervision, but there was not a monastery anywhere with a patch of ground and a reasonable climate that did not grow manita plants and maintain a preparation specialist to dry and process the leaves. There was still some manita here, in fact, in a zinc-lined box in the storage cellar, alongside heaps of desiccated root vegetables and dried-up crocks of salt meat. Out of curiosity, Gyalo had tested it: Even after all this time, it had the burn and flash of a fully effective drug.

At the stream that ran in a rocky channel a little distance from the derelict gardens, Gyalo stripped and squatted on the bank to wash his clothes. He was careful to measure his movements; the Notch was lower than the peaks around it, but still well above the tree line, and he had discovered how easy it was to lose his breath even in the most ordinary activities. The water was snowmelt, rushing down from higher elevations, and his hands quickly grew numb. He spread the garments to dry and, gathering his resolve, waded into the shallow flow and knelt there, splashing water on himself until he could no longer endure it. He returned to the bank and waited for his shivering to diminish, then shaved his face and scalp by touch, a trick he had mastered long ago.

He was warm by the time he was done, for the sun had risen high enough to flood the floor of the Notch, and there was no wind today to chill the air. He set the razor aside and closed his eyes, raising his face to the light. A sense of well-being possessed him, composed of many small awarenesses: the sun on his flesh, the pleasure of being clean, the morning hunger in his belly.

Travel suited him. The daily promise of new sights and experiences, the novelty of passing each night in a different place: He loved these things, and beside them the monotony of travel rations and unbroken days of riding and even the tiresome demands of the Dreamers seemed inconsequential.

He had walked the crowded streets of Ninyâser, Arsace's capital, with its brick-paved streets and graceful multistoried dwellings, so different from the low buildings of earthquake-prone Chonggye or the massive granite structures that dominated Baushpar. He had sat in meditation in the shadowed core of Ninyâser's temple, where a newly gilded image of Ârata Creator gleamed like the sun glimpsed across a void of night. Just outside the town of Darna, he had laid offerings before the colossal image of Ârata Warrior rock-cut into a cliff, and paid his respects at the adjacent religious complex, whose administrator, with whom he had corresponded about issues of staffing and refurbishment, received him with great cordiality. He had made several detours to visit the holy sites that lay near the expedition's route: the forest clearing where King Fârat first embraced the Way of Ârata; the Cave of the Steadfast, where a group of early Âratists was walled in alive for proclaiming that Vahu, then worshiped as a separate deity, was only an Aspect of a greater god; the hill above the River Hatane, where the First Messenger had stood so long and proclaimed the Way so passionately that his feet had left imprints in the stone. Here Gyalo was disappointed, for the shrine built around the imprints was being restored, and wooden scaffolding had been placed over them for protection.

Of course, he had also seen things much less inspiring. Santaxma was less than two years restored to the throne; in many ways it was astonishing what had been accomplished in that time. Yet the shadow of eight Caryaxist decades still lay long across Arsace. For every shrine or temple or monastery restored and repopulated, two more lay vandalized and empty. For every Âratist hospital or orphanage put back in operation, half a dozen stood vacant. Even now Caryaxist slogan banners could be seen, and many people still wore the dull peasant garb the Caryaxist government had imposed as part of its campaign to abolish the distinctions of rank. In the south, where there had been civil war upon the Voice's death, whole villages lay in ruins; in Arsace's fertile center fields lay fallow, grown up in weeds. There was little land that had not been at least preliminarily reclaimed by its pre-Caryaxist owners, but putting it back into use was a complicated and contentious task. The

Caryaxists had done away with most forms of ownership, freeing serfs and combining farms and peasant holdings and private estates into vast agricultural plantations; now boundaries must be resurveyed and conflicting claims sorted out one by one. There was also the question of what to do about the plantation workers, who believed they, too, had a claim upon the land.

Yet even these sober sights did not diminish the pleasure Gyalo took in the process of the journey. He was aware that his enjoyment was unlikely to survive the Burning Land, which would bring at last the trials he had wondered about, and feared, in Baushpar. Still, he was no longer haunted by dread. There was a timelessness to the constant motion that soothed his soul. He felt, if not precisely severed from his ordinary life, suspended somewhere beyond it, weightless and serene.

The sound of voices roused him. He got up and began to pull on his still-damp garments.

"Playing washerwoman, Brother?"

It was one of the cavalrymen, Haxar, with his companion Sauras and several others. Santaxma's Exile Army had included men from all the kingdoms of Galea, but expatriate Arsacians were its core; Haxar and the rest were pure-blood Arsacian, born and raised in the refugee communities of Haruko. Their military pedigree was more distinguished than most, for they had been among those who rode with Santaxma through the streets of Ninyâser after it fell, and followed him on his famous pilgrimage through the Hundred-Domed Palace, as he reclaimed his heritage room by room.

"I thought I'd take the chance while there's still running water," Gyalo replied.

"Why bother, Brother?" Sauras inquired with a grin, dumping an armload of waterskins on the stream bank. "It won't be long before we're desert-bound. You'll be caked so stiff with sand and sweat, you won't even remember being clean."

"Well, I'll be clean today at least," Gyalo retorted. "You might profit from my example. I can smell you from here."

"He hasn't let a drop of water touch him for two weeks, Brother." Haxar pulled the stopper from one of the skins and plunged it into the stream. "Ârata's thousand wounds, that's cold! How'd you stand to get in it? . . . He thinks if he lets the dirt pile on thick enough, he won't be burned in the desert sun."

"If he doesn't die before, from the bloody stench," said one of the other soldiers, amid guffaws from his fellows.

"You'll be laughing out of the other side of your faces soon enough," Sauras said. "Meantime, I'm taking bets. Care to wager, Brother?"

"I'm not a gambler, Sauras. But if I were, I think I'd bet against you." Gyalo finished gathering up his clothes. "Are the Dreamers awake yet?"

"Awake and making trouble."

Gyalo sighed. "I'd better go, then."

"Rather you than me, Brother!"

Their laughter followed him as he made his way back.

The moment he entered he was confronted by Rikoyu, the Forceless monk who provided dream interpretation for the two Dreamers. Gyalo did not particularly like Rikoyu, a stolid, humorless man whose literal-mindedness completely belied his delicate and subtle profession; but it was impossible not to feel sympathy for him, for the Dreamers treated him dreadfully, and he bore the brunt of their many petty dissatisfactions and angers.

"She wants to see you." Rikoyu's face and voice, as always, were impassive; only his use of the pronoun betrayed his agitation. "Can you come?"

"Yes. Of course."

Gyalo set his laundry aside and followed Rikoyu to the room the Dreamers, after some argument the night before, had chosen. Inside, the litter of the floor had been swept into one corner, and the Dreamers' portable beds set up: long boxes made of boards held together with removable pegs and strung with rope lattices, into which thick cotton-stuffed mattresses were fitted. Posts were thrust into brackets at each corner, supporting drapes of diaphanous crimson silk. Senri-dai Tak's drapes were still closed—Gyalo could just see him through the translucent fabric, lying on his back with his hands crossed on his chest, as composed as a corpse—but Kai-do Seiki's had been looped aside, and she was sitting up amid a welter of red coverlets.

Unlike shaping, the power of dreaming had not been given by Ârata at creation, but was born into humankind after the god lay down to sleep—a final gift perhaps, a solace for the years of exile. Through special visions of their slumbering minds, which in their vividness and complexity were not at all like ordinary dreams, those with dreaming ability were able to travel out across the world in sleep. With training, Dreamers could learn to set their destinations and control their actions, to call in Dreams at will and send them out with precision. Mystic Dreamers drugged themselves to unconsciousness, striving to touch the edges of Ârata's own slumber. Working Dreamers sold their ability to rulers engaged in espionage, or to merchants who wanted to track the progress of trade caravans. Charlatan Dreamers (and charlatans who were not Dreamers) sold nonexistent services to the gullible, claiming they could dream the future or influence what was to come.

To the First Messenger, Ârata revealed a greater truth. The Dreams of human Dreamers touched the earth, as Ârata's did. Human Dreams might thus be made into a tool to combat the evils and disasters that Ârata's dreams of pain brought into being—to fight these things on their own terms, as the dreams they were. Thus the Path of Dreams was born. Where there were droughts, Âratist Dreamers dreamed of rain. Where there was plague, they dreamed of health. Where crops were blighted, they dreamed of growth; where there was famine, they dreamed of abundance. In this way the chaos of existence was held, if not at bay, at least in equilibrium, so that Ârata's agony could not overwhelm the world as it had in the dark centuries before the First Messenger's coming, when plagues and tempests and monsters had stalked humankind without respite.

Âratist Dreamers avoided contact with the outside world, whose hard, unmalleable reality they found distasteful. They spent their lives cloistered in monasteries and nunneries, sleeping fifteen hours at a time and rarely leaving their beds even when awake, existing in a silent, rarified universe of opulent rooms and dim light and soft foods, where devoted servants waited on them hand and foot, and every whim was instantly gratified. Most were pale, languid creatures with little physical strength and no practical skills, incapable of fending for themselves in even the most basic ways. During the mass secularizations imposed by the Caryaxists they had died in droves, unable to survive without the special care to which they were accustomed.

"I dreamed last night of death," Seiki said. Like most Dreamers, she was fat, with smooth unweathered skin that made her seem much younger than her true age. "Dead monks, dead bones, dead rooms, dead gardens. Dead, all dead."

"I'm sorry, Seiki," Gyalo said. "These weren't summoned Dreams, were they?"

"Of course not. I wouldn't be so stupid as to summon a Dream *here*. Even so, all that death, all around me . . ." She shuddered. "This is your fault. I *told* you this place would trouble me. As a Shaper, you should have supported me."

It was clear to Gyalo that this was more than just peevishness at work: Sleeping in the monastery really had made her suffer. Being who she was, however, she was incapable of simply saying so. Nearly three months of dealing with such situations had drained him of patience, and he was sorely tempted to make a sharp reply. But it was his duty to smooth feathers, not to ruffle them; in any case, he needed to pick his battles, for there were a lot of them. The coming day of travel would be easier for everyone if he allowed Seiki to browbeat him a little.

"I'm sorry," he said again, soothingly. "It must have been very distressing for you. Did Tak have trouble, too?"

Seiki clutched at her red coverlets. "What do I care about *Tak*?" The two Dreamers disliked each other only slightly less than they disliked the other members of the expedition. "It's *me* we're talking about."

"Well, we'll be leaving in an hour or two. The bad influences will be behind you. You'll be able to put it out of your mind."

"Yes, but what if this place has clouded my dreaming?" Effortlessly she switched from accusation to anxiety. "What if I can't call in my Dreams? I *need* to call in my Dreams. Everyone is *depending* on me."

"You won't be clouded," Gyalo said firmly, as if to a child. "You're too powerful a Dreamer, Seiki. You have the skill to dream true, no matter what the circumstances. That's why you were chosen to guide us through the Burning Land. There aren't many who would be capable of that."

"Or of whining so much while they're about it," interjected Tak, with sluggish spite, from behind his crimson draperies. Gyalo ignored him.

"Once we reach the Burning Land, you'll dream just as you always have. Everything will work out for the best— you'll see. We all have faith in you. We are all so very grateful you are with us. I promise to make sure we never stay in a place like this again."

"I could report you for this, you know. Even if you do serve the Brethren."

Gyalo drew a breath. At such times it required real effort to remember that he did not actually detest Seiki, that in her helplessness and arrogance she was pitiable rather than hateful.

"Was there anything else you needed?" he asked quietly.

Seiki's eyes moved around the room, as if searching for some reason to keep him. "I suppose not."

"Then I'll be going. I've a Communion service to prepare."

"Yes, yes." She waved a plump hand. "Go if you must."

He turned away. Her voice followed him out.

"*Well?* What are you *standing* there for? Go see why my attendant hasn't brought me my breakfast yet."

"Yes, Sister," Rikoyu said. There was not a trace of emotion in his voice.

The expedition departed an hour later.

The road they traveled was broad and well graded. Before the building of Thuxra City, it had been a simple horse track; nothing else was needed, for only pilgrims sought out the Burning Land. But with the opening of the prison, a proper road became necessary, and the track had been widened and improved so it could comfortably accommodate large wagons or several prisoners walking abreast.

The party made good speed, riding from just after dawn to just before dusk, camping on the road, strung out in the order of travel: the soldiers first, led by Teispas, with their grooms and spare mounts and packhorses; then the enclosed coaches of the Dreamers, in which their attendants also traveled; then Gyalo and Rikoyu; and finally the two additional Forceless, Sittibaal and Zabdas, who had joined the party in Ninyâser. Gyalo could sometimes hear them as they rode, talking in the language of Yahaz, their native land. They were not Perpetuals, put to Âratist training since childhood, but Second Lifers, who had vowed the Way as adults—former military men, both of them, who kept to themselves. They were cooperative travelers and required little supervision.

It was Teispas's habit to ride the length of the column three or four times a day, to make sure all was as it should be. A little over a week after they left the ruined monastery, he reined in at Gyalo's side.

"How goes it, Brother?"

"Well enough, Captain."

"That's sensible." Teispas nodded at the cloth Gyalo had wrapped around his head to protect his shaven scalp. "The sun's fiercer than you realize. The air's different this side of the Notch, have you noticed?"

"Yes. Drier. Sometimes I think I can smell the desert."

"You should get your first sight of it soon." Teispas wiped

the sweat from his forehead. Each day of the descent had been a little warmer than the last; the captain still wore his scale hauberk, but like the other soldiers he had removed his helmet. "I'm told there are a number of overlooks."

They rode on in silence. Teispas was a formidably competent organizer, and under his direction the journeying had run as smoothly as a sand clock; he was an efficient soldier as well, as Gyalo had learned in the lawless regions south of Ninyâser, where the party had twice come under bandit attack. Over the weeks they had established an amicable relationship; there was respect between them, even a certain liking. Yet Gyalo could not say he knew the captain better now than on the first day they had met. Even at his most cordial, Teispas was separated from others by an impenetrable wall of reserve.

"I've been given orders," Teispas said abruptly. "We're to keep close while we're at Thuxra City. We'll be barracked in the custodians' compound—it's separate and enclosed, and we're not to go out of it. We're not even to go about within it unless we have an escort."

"Ah," Gyalo said, surprised; Sundit had not mentioned this. "Very well. I'll warn the others."

"I hope *she* won't be a problem." Self-disciplined as he was, Teispas could not quite hide his loathing for Seiki, who had driven him to distraction with her demands and whims on the way to Baushpar. His gratitude to Gyalo for relieving him of this duty had made the first bond between them. "It'll be very awkward if she decides she must go sight-seeing."

"Well," Gyalo said wryly, "since she invariably wants the opposite of what she's offered, perhaps I'll tell her that sight-seeing is a requirement of our stay."

"And that not to do it will insult our hosts." Teispas grinned, a wide, wolfish expression. Gyalo had thought him entirely humorless when they first met, but in fact the captain possessed a fierce dark wit, which emerged infrequently, like flashes of light from a well-curtained room. "Then she'll be sure to stay indoors." He sobered. "This is important, Brother. I'm counting on you to manage it."

"I can't imagine why any of us would want to go about. Thuxra City isn't exactly the sort of place one wants to tour." He studied Teispas's hard profile, which as usual revealed nothing. "Why is it so important?"

"Just manage it." Teispas's voice was flat. "Will you do that?"

"Yes. Yes, of course."

"Good." Without further word Teispas pulled his horse aside, and spurred it toward the front of the line. Gyalo was left puzzled, and unaccountably uneasy.

A few days later, the Burning Land came in view. Beyond a steep curve in the road the cliffs dropped away, and the Land was there—a stunning immensity of flat red ground and patchy green-and-yellow scrub, sweeping without variation all the way to the horizon. There was more red in some places, and more green elsewhere, and here and there a scrap or strip of brown or gray or amber; but in essence wherever the eye fell the view was the same, a monotony as astonishing in its way as the gargantuan scale of it. The horizon was lost in a lavender haze of distance; above this, the sky paled, then deepened to the purest blue Gyalo had ever seen—and the most barren, for it was empty of birds, empty of cloud, empty of everything except the harsh brilliance of the sun.

The others checked their pace to look, then rode on. But Gyalo pulled his horse out of line and urged it toward the edge, and sat gazing down until he felt he might spread his arms and soar outward, like the birds that did not fly here. He had formed images of what the Land might be like, based on his reading, but the reality of it banished them utterly. He had not expected it to be beautiful; but beautiful it was, in the burning color of the ground, the green haze of vegetation, the blinding sapphire of the sky—alienly, forbiddingly, breathtakingly beautiful. He thought of the First Messenger, crossing the Notch twelve centuries before: Had he paused on this very precipice, perhaps, looked out over this very vista?

He became aware that someone had drawn up beside him:

Rikoyu. The interpreter stared down at the Land, an odd expression on his usually stolid face.

"It's so flat," he said.

"Not completely." Already, Gyalo's eyes were adjusting to the contours of what lay below; he could see that it was not as unvaried as he had first thought. "I think that's a fold of hills, over there." He pointed. "And there, too, to the west. And perhaps something higher, toward the southern horizon . . . but it's not easy to tell from such a distance."

"So flat," said Rikoyu, as if Gyalo had not spoken. "I can't . . ." He drew an audible breath. "It's hard to believe we'll really travel there."

Gyalo looked at him, stiff in the saddle, hands clenched upon the reins. Rikoyu, he realized, was afraid. Of the trials of crossing such an alien land? Of the presumption of treading on holy ground?

"We're well equipped and well prepared," he said, gently. "We go in Ârata's service. There's nothing to fear."

Rikoyu did not reply. After a moment he turned his horse and rode off after the others. Gyalo remained a little longer, his eyes moving on the wastes, drinking in their immensity. The air against his face was hot; he could taste its dryness. Beneath this land, he thought, Ârata slept—invisible, concealed. Yet in every particle, the soil spoke his presence, for it was the color of his skin: the color of the fiercest flame, the color of the hottest coal.

"Great is Ârata," he whispered. "Great is his Way."

The wind seized the words and bore them up into the endless sky.

They came down at last onto the parched red flatlands where Thuxra City stood. Because of the way the foothills rose and the road curved, the prison had been hidden as they descended, and so Gyalo's first view of it was face-on, from a distance of about half a mile: a great ribbon of black wall, quivering and distorted with heat. A pair of gates was set two-thirds of the way along its length, closest to the right-hand edge. Along the longer, left-hand side, changes in the masonry testified to Thuxra's several expansions, as its ever-growing population outstripped the existing walls' ability to hold them. Gyalo found it extraordinarily ugly—not just in itself but in its harsh man-made presence in this untouched land. He thought he would have seen it so even if this had not been a sacred place, and the walls a terrible defilement.

Atop the walls, guard enclosures curved outward at regular intervals. They were empty, for Thuxra was no longer an active prison: Its captives had been sent back to Arsace soon after its liberation, its mining operations terminated. The only work that went on here now was the reclaiming of equipment for reuse elsewhere, preparatory to Thuxra's complete dismantlement; the only inhabitants were the Exile soldiers in charge of that task, and, for some of the officers, their families.

Someone was watching, though, for as the party neared, the gates began to swing inward. Beyond lay an immense paved courtyard, itself bounded by high walls. Directly ahead, a wide opening gave onto the complex of stables and workshops and warehouses that had once kept Thuxra running. The wall on the right was pierced by a latticed gate—the entrance to the custodians' compound. The wall on the left was set with four wooden doors. Every captive brought here—by cart or on foot, in long trains or in groups of two or three—had passed through one of those doors: first stripped naked, then set to wait as custodians recorded their names and physical characteristics, then herded away according to their crimes: political prisoners through the first door, religious offenders through the second, civilians through the third, violent criminals through the last.

The party halted where the prisoners had stood, while Teispas dismounted and went to greet Thuxra's military administrator, who was approaching with several of his aides. It was breathlessly hot. The thick walls seemed to swallow sound; an odd dead silence filled the courtyard, muffling the voices of the men, even the noise of the horses' hooves and harness. Still, distantly, Gyalo thought he could hear a rhythmic booming, like a battering ram against a metal gate, and, behind it, the babble of voices—Thuxra's workers, engaged in the task of dismantlement.

He looked toward the doors—closed forever, the prison spaces behind them empty. He had prepared himself for this experience, as he prepared himself for most experiences, by reading: studying a plan of Thuxra drawn up by its liberators, scanning many of the liberators' accounts. The scrim of that familiarity lay across this strange place. But it was only a surface familiarity, and his knowledge was only paper knowledge, and as days ago above the Burning Land, he found himself forced to acknowledge its limitations. He had believed himself prepared to enter this place, where so many horrors had been done; but in what he felt now, he understood he was less ready than he had thought.

At last the signal was given to dismount. Grooms came to take the horses. The baggage was unloaded, the Dreamers helped from their coaches and settled into their litters. The administrator and his aides ushered them toward the custodians' compound.

Beyond the gate lay a different world. A graveled thoroughfare ran between graceful pastel-hued villas, each set within its own lush garden. Everywhere was greenery, and astonishing quantities of water—leaping in fountains, running in artificial streams, cascading into gazing pools. The air smelled of grass and wet. Gyalo, staring around him, felt as if he were dreaming. The awful heat was the same, as were the walls of Thuxra, rising dark above the green; beyond that, there was not the smallest sign of prison, or of desert.

The soldiers were led away to barracks, and Teispas and the vowed Âratists were conducted to the administrator's house, which was larger than the rest and enclosed within a bigger garden. Gyalo's room was lavishly appointed, with a high Arsacian-style bed and choice carpets on the floor. Bowls of flowers had been set upon the windowsills. A manservant stowed his travel pack and the boxes of his ceremonial equipment, then conducted him to the bathhouse, where yet more water, piped in and heated by some invisible method, steamed in round wooden tubs.

They gathered for the evening meal on the wide porch at the house's rear. The air was cooler, touched with the scent of flowers from the garden. Both Dreamers had chosen to sleep, but Teispas, Gyalo, and the two Forceless monks were present, as was the administrator and three of his aides, and a woman whom the administrator introduced as Kaluela, his wife. She bowed to Gyalo, then took his arm and drew him to the chair by hers.

"There's plenty here, below the ground," she said, in response to his question about the abundance of water. "More than enough for all Thuxra's needs, even when it was full."

"Yes," said the aide seated opposite. He was Tapati, and wore the full-skirted red surcoat and wide gold sash of Exile dress uniform. Like many non-Arsacian Exile personnel, he affected the aristocratic Arsacian styles that had been current before the coming of the Caryaxists: Gold rings hung in his earlobes, and his hair fell to his shoulders in carefully waxed ringlets. "Say what you will about the Caryaxists, they were clever engineers. The irrigation methods they worked out are quite extraordinary."

"One wouldn't know there was desert here at all," Gyalo said.

Kaluela smiled. She was Tapati also, plump and handsome, with slow-blinking amber eyes, discreetly enhanced by cosmetics, and golden skin that looked as if it had never felt the touch of the desert sun. Like the aide, she was dressed Arsacian-fashion, in a high-waisted gown of green-and-purple silk, her black hair coiled atop her head and the backs of her hands painted with delicate designs. There was a calmness about her, a kind of placid grace; in other circumstances Gyalo might have enjoyed her company. But he was not comfortable in this tiny mock-paradise. Its dishonesty repelled him, its denial of the environment that surrounded it; it disturbed him to see Exile personnel so easily ensconced, as if they had forgotten what Thuxra had been. He was distracted also by the impression that he could hear distant shouting, as in the courtyard this afternoon. He knew it was only the sound of workers, laboring into the night; but in a small, irreducible part of himself it seemed that what he heard must be the crying of Thuxra's victims, as if Thuxra's walls had absorbed their suffering like the desert heat and still breathed it back.

"Water transforms everything, Brother," Kaluela said. "This desert soil is actually very fertile, once you irrigate it. We cultivate much of our own food here, outside the walls, though not on such a scale as the Caryaxists did. And inside there are the gardens." She gestured toward the dim green tangle beyond the lamplit porch. "Of course you have to work to keep it wet—in this heat you can't neglect it even a day."

"That must require a lot of labor."

"Yes. Fortunately we were able to keep the servants who were here originally."

"You employ the Caryaxists' servants?"

"Not servants," the aide said. "Prisoners. The Caryaxists used every resource they had. They took men and women from the prison population and trained them to domestic service. As you can imagine, it was considered a desirable assignment."

"They're free now, of course." Kaluela looked uncomfortable. "And we pay them a wage. But it did seem sensible to keep the people who had been here, since they knew how to run things."

Gyalo found himself unwilling to imagine that anyone who had been imprisoned in this place would choose to stay, wage or no. Unless they had not been given a choice? He glanced at the two middle-aged women who stood a little distance away, waiting to spring to the service of anyone who dropped a napkin or needed more wine. They wore neat, well-made dresses; their quiet faces bore no mark of suffering or reluctance.

"They came to a place where there was nothing, the Caryaxists," the aide said. "And they built an entire self-sustaining community. They used everything that could be used—people, space, materials. Because of the conditions here, they invented things that had not been known, used methods that had never been tried. It's extraordinary, some of the things they did."

"Really, Dorjaro," Kaluela said. "Sometimes I think you actually admire them."

Dorjaro shrugged. "Hating what they did doesn't mean I can't acknowledge their ingenuity."

"I confess I feel pity for them," Kaluela said. "Not the men, of course, but the wives and children. They weren't responsible, surely. They left everything behind when they fled, even their clothing, even the children's toys. The other wives and I packed it all up and shipped it back to Ninyâser, to be given to the poor."

"That was compassionate of you, lady," Gyalo said.

She leaned toward him, enclosing him in her perfume. "I'm so glad you're here, Brother. I've often thought about them, those poor Âratists sent out to die. I'm so glad you'll be setting their bones to rest in Ârata's bosom."

That was what those at Thuxra had been told of the expedition's purpose; only the prison administrator knew the truth. "You have a kind heart, lady."

"I'll pray for you while you're gone, to Jo-mea and Dâ-darshi. For luck, and safe return."

She brushed her fingers across the Âratist charm she wore at her neck, a sun-symbol made of gold. She was devout: Gyalo had seen the Aspect shrines, a dozen or more of them, in a shadowed room at the back of the house.

At the other end of the table, the administrator leaned forward. "We were hoping, Brother, that we might ask a favor of you while you're here. Some of us have been at Thuxra for close to a year, and in all that time we haven't had a chance to take Communion. We'd be grateful if you'd conduct a service for us."

"That's no imposition at all," Gyalo said, sincerely. "I'll be glad to do it."

The administrator smiled. He was stout and handsome like his wife, though considerably older. Alone among his colleagues, he eschewed Arsacian fashion: His ears were unpierced, his hair cropped short in Tapati military style. "I'll make the arrangements. Would midday tomorrow be acceptable?"

"Yes. It would be helpful to know how many might attend."

"Well, that's the imposition, I'm afraid, Brother. As many, perhaps, as four hundred."

"Four *hundred*?" Gyalo could not conceal his astonishment. "I had no idea there were so many people here."

"There is much work to do at Thuxra, even now."

The dinner finished soon afterward. The aides departed, and the guests sought their rooms—all but Teispas, who remained behind to speak with the administrator on some private matter.

The bedchambers led off an open gallery at the back of the house, running the length of the second floor. Gyalo paused by the balustrade, gazing out over the garden and trying to clear his head, which ached fiercely. The night had grown almost chilly. The sky was studded with an astonishing number of stars, and the moon, half-full, seemed brighter than on the other side of the Range of Clouds. The air smelled moistly of grass and flowers, and, intermittently, of something less pleasant, reminding Gyalo of the odor of Baushpar's back alleys, where the sewers were yet to be repaired. The sound that had distracted him at dinner—the noise of shouting, the calling of Thuxra's ghosts—was no longer audible.

"Peaceful, isn't it?"

It was Teispas, coming up silently as he often did, so that it almost seemed he had materialized out of thin air.

"Ârata!" Gyalo pressed a hand to his racing heart. "You just frightened me out of a night's sleep."

"I'm sorry." For an Arsacian, Teispas was tall, but still he had to look up to meet Gyalo's eyes. "It wasn't my intent."

"It's extraordinary. I've never known anyone who could move so quietly."

"Too many years spent surprising sleeping sentries, I suppose."

Gyalo glanced out again at the moonlight. "It *is* peaceful. If I didn't know where I was, I'd never guess."

"That's the point, isn't it?" Teispas grinned his fierce grin. "To inflict pain and misery every day, and turn your back on it every night. The best of all possible worlds—for a torturer, anyway."

"So I have been thinking also, more or less. It disturbs me to see our people so comfortable here, as if they had forgotten the history of this place. Dorjaro . . . the aide who sat across from me at supper . . . seemed to regard it all as little more than a fascinating exercise in engineering."

"Well, it is that, you must admit."

Gyalo shook his head. "Soon enough it will be nothing. I have been reminding myself of that."

Teispas turned toward the garden, resting his forearms on the wide sill of the balustrade. He had removed his sash and draped it around his neck; his surcoat hung unbuttoned, and his hair, released from its normal tightly braided club, fell loose across his shoulders. He was absolutely still. It was one of the first things Gyalo had noticed about him, this capacity for stillness—not a tranquil settling or a watchful readiness, but a halting, a closing, as if he had abandoned his body and gone elsewhere.

"I need to tell you something," he said.

"Yes?"

A pause. Teispas drew a breath. "There are still prisoners in Thuxra."

The first thing that sprang to Gyalo's mind was the two women at dinner. "Prisoners," he repeated.

"Yes." Teispas stared steadily down at the garden. "Not everyone who came here was accused of religious or political offenses. There were real criminals, guilty of real crimes. They can't be set free, obviously, and the Arsacian prisons don't want them. No one knows what to do with them. And we Exiles aren't like the Caryaxists, are we? We don't just kill the people who offend us."

"You're telling me there are people still locked up here?" Gyalo said, disbelieving. "That Thuxra is still *operational*?"

"A portion of it, yes. Until an alternative is found."

"But . . ." For a moment Gyalo lost the words. "But

Thuxra was emptied before the salvaging began. I've seen the reports. I've read the letters."

Teispas did not reply.

"How do you know this?"

"I was briefed before we set out."

"So that's what I heard tonight." *The ghosts of Thuxra,* Gyalo thought, *not ghosts at all, but real.* "I suppose it explains why there are so many people here. They need jailers."

"Partly. As the administrator said, there is yet much work to be done. I understand the prisoners have been useful in that regard."

"Who is responsible for this? Does the King know of it?"

"I can't tell you that."

"Can't, or won't?"

Teispas said nothing.

"How long will it go on, then?"

"Until a disposition of the prisoners is made."

"But until they're disposed of Thuxra cannot be dismantled!"

"Exactly." Teispas smiled a little, wryly. "I wouldn't recommend you hope for a quick resolution."

Gyalo turned back toward the garden. His shock was beginning to yield to anger. Dismantling Thuxra meant not just tearing it down, but completely eradicating it: The materials of which it was made were to be hauled away, so that not a chip of stone, not a crumb of mortar, not an iota of Thuxra's being might remain to defile Ârata's resting place. On this matter church and state had spoken with a single voice—or at least, they had done so just after the Caryaxists' fall.

But obviously at some point secular expedience had taken precedence over faith. The Brethren would never have tolerated such a decision—they would have insisted that Thuxra be emptied even if it meant setting bandits and murderers free to roam Arsace. So the secular authorities had undertaken deliberately to deceive the leaders of the church, even, it seemed, to the production of false reports. The audacity of it took Gyalo's breath. Distant as Thuxra was, its personnel confined as securely as its inmates, there was little risk the deception would be uncovered—unless, as now, by vowed Âratists inconveniently present. Teispas's stern warning, on the way down into the Land, suddenly made better sense.

But that raised another question.

"You obviously weren't meant to reveal this, Captain—"

Teispas made a sound that was not quite a laugh.

"—in fact, that was probably why you were briefed, wasn't it? So you could assist in keeping it from me and the others. Why would you tell me, then? Why would you take such a risk? You could lose your career."

"At the very least." Teispas shook his head. "I don't like the political game that's being played here. I don't see why I should play it, too. I've gotten a sense, these past weeks, of the sort of man you are, Brother—I think you'll use the information wisely. Besides . . ." He paused. "Isn't it what any good Âratist would do?"

There was something very odd in the way he said this. "It's what any Âratist *should* do," Gyalo replied. "I can't think of many Âratists who *would* do it, however. If that's really your reason, you are truly a man of steadfast faith."

Teispas pushed himself away from the balcony and turned to meet Gyalo's gaze. He was not a handsome man: His features were too harsh, his skin too weathered, for that. But his was an arresting face, with its hooked nose and arrogant mouth and perfect arching brows above the blackest eyes Gyalo had ever seen. Normally it was controlled, watchful, remote. Now, though, it was alive with feeling. Teispas's lips parted; for a moment it seemed he would speak. But then he closed his mouth again. His face smoothed, the animation vanishing back into the deep place from which it had briefly emerged.

"Good night, Brother."

He departed as silently as he had come, passing out of the moonlight and into the darkness of the gallery. A few moments later Gyalo heard the soft sound of a closing door.

A servant came the next morning to guide Gyalo to the hall the administrator had chosen for the Communion ceremony.

A crowd was already waiting: Exile personnel, their families, the Dreamers in their litters, Rikoyu. All carried meditation squares and strings of Communion beads. They made way for him, their voices following him: "Great is Ârata. Great is his Way."

Inside the hall Gyalo dismissed the servant and began to set up his equipment at the dais that rose at one end: a small gong to announce the ceremony, a red-and-gold kneeling cushion, a collapsible wooden altar draped with a yellow cloth, a folded square of linen, and five polished brass bowls. Into the first four bowls he placed a ball of copal amber, a pyramid of red onyx, a cube of black granite, and a heap of rock salt. Into the last, set behind the others, he poured a small amount of consecrated oil.

He knelt on the cushion and closed his eyes, preparing to summon his shaping ability. He had not slept well the night before; the shock of Teispas's revelation was still with him. But as he turned his mind to the familiar discipline he felt that care, and others, slip away. It was one of the blessings of ceremony, this transition into timelessness, this journey beyond the mundane.

He could not say—no Shaper could—exactly what he did. The release of a shaping ability was something that could not be described, only grasped. Nevertheless his human mind, enslaved to the concreteness of words and images, struggled for comparisons. It was a loosening, like shedding a constricting garment. A searching, like scanning a crowd for a single face. A shifting deep within himself, drawing every facet of his consciousness into new alignment. A widening, as of an infinitely indrawn breath. And finally, an equilibrium, a weightless point of balance. Training focused a Shaper's skill, and manita bound it: A Shaper functioned on the knife edge of symmetry between these two opposing principles.

Gyalo opened his eyes. His Shaper senses were free, as much as the tether of the drug would allow. The world seemed wider, more dimensional, pulsing with forces and currents invisible to ordinary senses, alive with shadings and textures imperceptible to ordinary vision. To see as a Shaper did was to awaken to the true reality of being: that the apparent solidity of things was in fact a complex illusion of force and light, that below every apparently fixed and permanent entity lay a wholly different truth of flux and change. And yet it was not random, this unending dance of process; there was pattern in it, pattern in each thing that *was*, from the moment of its origination to the moment of its dissolution. The gift of the Shaper was to perceive those patterns. The skill of a Shaper was to manipulate them.

Many Shapers found the altered mode of perception uncomfortable or frightening or even sickening, and spent as little time with it as duty would allow. But from the first, Gyalo had loved it—this brief glimpse of a truer truth, this tiny, metaphorical resurrection of Ârata to active life within him. This was how Ârata himself had looked upon the world in the moment of creation—or at least, as near an equivalent as the human mind could manage. The only indulgence he had ever allowed himself, since the age of eighteen, when he had formally and forever renounced his youthful penchant for transgression, was to summon his shaping earlier than was strictly necessary, before the ceremonies he conducted rather than in their midst.

Picking up the small baton that lay beside the gong, he struck six slow strokes. The crowd flowed into the hall. To Gyalo's Shaper senses, each individual trailed light, auras of shimmering color as varied as their faces. All living things owned such an aura. There was pattern in it, as there was in everything, but it was not a pattern a Shaper could read, for Ârata in his wisdom had not granted human beings the power to shape living things.

When all the communicants had entered, and the doors had closed again, Gyalo began. "Praise Ârata, lord of this world."

"Great is his dominion," the communicants responded.

"Praise Ârata, who made the lands and seas, the plants and creatures, the sun and moon and all other things."

"Great is he who creates, and sets things in their place."

It continued, a series of statements and responses designed to recall to the worshiper the might of the god, the beauty of the world, the origin of all things in perfection and their ultimate return to that state. The Banishing, the other major Âratist ritual, was a reminder of humanity's separation from the god; lamentation accompanied it, a bitter litany of loss and exile. But Communion was a celebration of closeness, of connection. With each statement and response, the communicants told off a bead; absent a Shaper, it was possible for any Âratist to perform this much of the ceremony him or herself.

The responses done, Gyalo spread his hands above the altar.

"In praise and in remembrance, we come together in this place to take upon ourselves the signs of Ârata and of our faith in him. In praise and in remembrance, I, his vowed servant, invoke the power that was his gift to humankind, the power with which the world was first brought to form. Through me, Ârata opens his eyes once more within the world. Through me, he touches it again, in change and in creation. In praise and in remembrance, I call the light of Ârata to being within me, within the substances I transform, within you who offer yourselves to receive them."

Gyalo focused his shaping will on the brass bowls one by one, grasping the patterns of their contents, drawing them delicately into new alignments. The amber became a pool of honey. The onyx became a little hill of russet sand. The granite became a drift of black soot. The salt became clear salt water. In the energy of transformation, bits and pieces of substance flew off and were consumed: Each change was accompanied by a flash of light, a puff of sound like an outblown breath.

"Come forward."

The Dreamers were first. Assisted by Rikoyu, Seiki knelt before the altar. The blue-white of her lifelight was a bare margin around her body, but it was almost too bright to look upon. Her eyes were closed, her habitual scowl smoothed away. Angry as the Dreamers sometimes made him, Gyalo could not doubt the purity of their faith, for he saw it daily in this ceremony.

"Who receives the marks?"

"Kai-do Seiki," she whispered.

Gyalo dipped his right index finger in the honey and marked her left cheek. "The blood of Ârata." He dipped up the sand and marked her right cheek. "The earth under which he sleeps." He touched his left index finger to the water and marked her forehead. "The tears of exile." He touched the ash and marked her chin. "The stain of sin. Remember."

Seiki crossed her arms before her face. "Great is Ârata, the one god, the bright god, the god who sleeps, the god who will wake. I affirm my faith in Ârata, deny my ash-nature in his name, and rejoice in the promise of his rising. May it be soon."

"May it be soon. Go in light, daughter."

Next was Tak, his lifelight bluer than Seiki's and not as strong, but flaring out a great distance around his body. After Tak came the administrator—his light was pale amber, run through with darker currents—then Kaluela with her little daughter Eolani, both mantled in the softest rose. Sittibaal and Zabdan were next, and those soldiers of the expedition who were present, then the rest of the communicants, beginning with the administrator's aides. One by one, Gyalo spoke the words and marked them all. He had to stop, once, to transform more materials.

Last, he administered Communion to himself. Then he dipped his fingers into the consecrated oil to cleanse them of all residue of change and used the linen cloth to wipe the oil away.

"By the grace of Ârata and in remembrance of his creation, I, his vowed servant, have transformed these substances in his name. Now I banish what was changed, so it may be his again."

Again he held his hands over the bowls, unmaking all they held. He unmade the oil as well, and the linen that had cleaned his hands. With vanishment, as with transformation, came a pulse of light and sound.

"Go in light, all you who have gathered in Ârata's name."

"Great is Ârata," they chorused. "Great is his Way."

The communicants rose and left the chapel. For a moment after they were gone Gyalo sat unmoving, watching the world with Shaper senses; then he closed his eyes and let go of the equilibrium he had achieved, allowing manita's tether to pull his shaping back into latency. When he opened his eyes again, the world looked as it always did. As many times as he experienced it, it was a shock, this return to unaltered perception. There was always, for just an instant, a desire to flee back into himself and recapture what he had let go.

He had arranged to divide the communicants into two groups, so they would not have to wait so long and he might have a chance to rest. Toward the end of the second ceremony he recognized Teispas—who, characteristically, had chosen to lose himself among Thuxra's personnel rather than precede them as was the privilege of his rank. The captain's face showed nothing as he received the marks; his dark eyes, as usual, were remote. His lifelight was deepest indigo, shading toward azure at its edges.

At last it was over. With the servant's help, Gyalo packed his equipment and left the hall. He was hoarse from hours of speaking, light-headed with the fatigue that always followed a protracted release of his shaping ability. But he felt cleansed. Within this monument to hatred, he had sown a seed of holiness—a promise, it seemed to him, of Thuxra's final dissolution.

— 4 —

In all, the party was four days at Thuxra, while the prison administrator oversaw final preparations, and the travelers received instruction in riding the camels that would carry them into the Burning Land. It seemed to Gyalo that the grooms and others must surely find it puzzling that such quantities of men, food, and equipment were being mustered for a simple burial expedition; but no one appeared to wonder at it.

The camels, indigenous to the desert's perimeter, had been domesticated by the Caryaxists as an alternative to mules and horses, for they were impervious to the sun, would eat nearly anything, and were able to go almost entirely without drinking as long as there was enough fodder to be had. They were trained to a variety of spoken and physical commands, but they were also lazy and ill-tempered—Gyalo spent much of the first morning of training trying to avoid being bitten by his mount (improbably named Cirsame, after the heroine of the epic poem of the same name), who was able to swing her long neck around with frightening swiftness to snap at his feet and ankles. He was reluctant, as the instructor advised, to beat her with the stick he had been given; but at last he gave in and thrashed her with all his strength, and thereafter they got along much better.

The travelers welcomed the opportunity to rest. Even Seiki was content. For Gyalo, though, it was a trying time. Thuxra had repelled him even before Teispas's revelation; afterward, his revulsion was painful. Under other circumstances he might have been preoccupied by anxiety, in this pause before the journey's true beginning; as it was, he could not wait to be gone.

On the morning of departure he took breakfast with the others, then returned to his room, where he drew out his travel journal and inserted between its leaves the letter he had composed on the night Teispas spoke to him. He placed the journal in one of the red-and-gold pouches the church used for its priority correspondence and sealed it. On the address tag, he wrote Utamnos's name. Given the letter's contents, he did not want to leave the pouch with the administrator, even sealed; so he had decided on what he hoped was a better alternative.

There was nothing more to do: His belongings were packed, and the boxes with his ceremonial equipment had been taken yesterday for loading. He closed his eyes, breathing deeply. Then, with the letter pouch and his travel pack, he left his room.

He and the other vowed Âratists had been instructed to gather on the house's porch and wait for escort. He was early, for he planned to go in search of Kaluela. But as he rounded the turn of the stairs he saw her in the hall below, Eolani at her side.

"Will you give us your blessing, Brother Gyalo?" she asked, as he approached.

"Of course."

He set down what he carried. She knelt with stately elegance, pulling Eolani down beside her, her red silks pooling around them both. He placed a hand on each dark head. He had come to like Kaluela very much, and also to pity her.

Because of her husband's unpredictable profession, she was accustomed to making the best of the circumstances in which she found herself, but her loneliness was clear, and her dislike of Thuxra. She had not said so, of course. No doubt there was a great deal she was forbidden to say.

"Go in light, children of Ârata," he said softly. "May you find peace and all its comforts. May Ârata's brightness illuminate your hearts. May the Enemy's shadow spare you. In Ârata's name I give you blessing. Go in light."

"Thank you, Brother."

Kaluela rose. Eolani pressed herself against her mother's side, gazing up at Gyalo with large brown eyes. Gyalo smiled at her; he had a tenderness for children, and Eolani owned something of her mother's pleasing grace.

"I've a favor to ask you, lady," he said.

"Of course, Brother. Anything."

"I have a dispatch that needs to reach Baushpar." He took the letter pouch from atop his travel pack and held it toward her. "It's for the Son Utamnos. I'd like it to go separately, not with other mail, and as quickly as possible. Can you arrange it for me?"

"Oh!" As he had hoped, she was pleased. She took the pouch reverently in both soft, painted hands. "I'd be honored, Brother. A messenger will start across the Notch this very day."

"I'm grateful. For this, and for the hospitality you've shown us."

"It's been a joy to have you in my house. I'll pray daily for your safe return."

"Thank you."

She made the sign of Ârata. "Great is Ârata. Great is his Way."

"Go in light, lady." He smiled down again at Eolani. "And you too, little lady."

She smiled back, a sudden illumination of her small face. "Will you give me a gift too, Brother?"

"Eolani!" her mother admonished.

"No, no. Perhaps I do have something." He crouched down, so that his eyes were on a level with the child's. "Watch closely, now." He reached a little way into himself, to the outer edges of his ability, until the world stirred around him and odd colors hovered at the corners of his eyes. Because he touched his skill so lightly, the tether of manita was barely perceptible; it was easy as breathing to draw the light and air above his outstretched hands into a delicate pattern of illusion, so that what seemed to be a glittering, transparent scarf took shape upon his palms.

"There." He draped it gently across Eolani's hair. "You look very pretty."

"Ohhh." She put up her hands wonderingly. "Is it real?"

"No, sweetheart. We Shapers are only allowed to shape real things to honor the lord Ârata. But it should last until you go to bed tonight."

"Say thank you, Eolani," Kaluela prompted gently.

"Thank you, Brother!" Eolani smiled, radiant, then looked up at her mother. "May I go show Nurse?"

"Yes, darling."

She scampered up the stairs, clutching the illusion around her head and shoulders.

"Thank you, Brother," Kaluela said. "You've made her happy."

"It was my pleasure."

She seemed to hesitate. "Farewell, then."

She turned and moved softly down the hall, toward the open porch at the house's rear. She passed from shadow into light, her red silks blazing briefly to brilliance, and was gone.

When the vowed Âratists reached the courtyard, they found the party assembling under the supervision of the prison administrator and Teispas. In addition to the original group of twenty-eight, there were ten camel-handlers, a former mining prospector skilled in desert survival, and seventy pack camels loaded with equipment: tools, cooking utensils, candles, ten days' supply of water in metal-lined barrels, and a year's stock of flour, rice, dried beans, dried meat, salt sticks, and pellets of dried apricot paste to prevent mouthrot sickness. These supplies were calculated only for the expedition; it was assumed, if survivors were found, that they would be able to provision themselves for the return journey.

Each traveler had been issued a knife, a pair of flints, a tin bottle for the daily water ration, and a hooded muslin robe—a protection as essential as water, for though it would soon be winter in the Burning Land, the sun was always an enemy. Bedrolls, tents, and personal belongings were strapped to the riders' mounts; for the soldiers, this included their weapons and armor, which were impossible to wear in the desert heat. Only the Dreamers would travel unrobed and unencumbered, in curtained litters borne between pairs of specially harnessed camels.

A little apart from the rest, five more camels bore what appeared to be large rolls of sheepskin. Inside this padding were fifty clay globes of manita powder brought from Baushpar, meticulously prepared according to the recipes King Vantyas's artificers had used during the Shaper War. Shattered with force, the globes would fill the air with the dust-fine drug, instantly incapacitating anyone who breathed it in, for manita burned like acid in the eyes and lungs of those who were not used to it. In the hour or so it took to recover, the drug would have time to work its inhibiting effect on its victims who were Shapers.

There were so many riders, so many beasts, so much shouting and milling about, that for a while it seemed no kind of order could be reached. But at last they rode out, to the cheers of Thuxra's staff, many of whom had gathered to see the party off. It was a long parade—by the time Gyalo emerged, the procession stretched before him like a swaying, dun-colored serpent, its head already coiled around the far corner of Thuxra's walls.

At the prison's back lay its middens, great pits dug over the years to receive Thuxra's massive amounts of waste. Most had been covered over with earth by the Exile reclaimers; the stink that enwreathed them was probably only a ghost of what it had been, but it was still noxious enough to cause Gyalo to wrap a fold of his robe across his mouth and nose. It was this he had smelled the other night, he realized, foul beneath the sweetness of the administrator's garden.

Where the middens ended, the broad highway that provided access to the mining areas began, running straight as a carpenter's rule toward the southern horizon. The party rode between huge pit mines that descended into the earth like giants' stairsteps, past mountainous piles of tailings and regions of trenched areas and open cuts. The cloudless sky was an enamel bowl clamped hard upon the earth; the sun burned down from it like white-hot iron, kindling the red soil to a brilliance that could hardly be looked upon. Flies spiraled around Gyalo's head, lighting on his skin no matter how he waved his hands or drew his robe across his face, and sweat ran into his eyes so relentlessly that after a while he lost the will to wipe it away. The camel saddle grew steadily more uncomfortable. He had been taught how to prop his left foot on Cirsame's neck and hook the right under his knee, but as often as he got himself settled Cirsame would twist her head or shrug her powerful shoulders, knocking him out of position and pitching him painfully against the saddle's wooden pommel.

Worse days of travel were to follow, but this first was the one that remained most vividly etched upon Gyalo's mind. Time dissolved. Each breath, each jolting camel footfall, held a new experience of eternity. Overhead, the sun did not seem to move at all. But then, abruptly, it was evening, the blood orange light of sunset tinting the sands an unearthly pink, and a halt was called at last. When Cirsame knelt for dismounting, Gyalo found he could hardly stand. Sittibaal and Zabdas were as badly off as he, while Rikoyu, whose light skin had burned even through the protection of his muslin robe, needed assistance to dismount. None of them had the strength to unsaddle and hobble their camels or to pitch their tents; the camel-handlers and the soldiers, themselves exhausted, did these things for them, a silent kindness that made Gyalo feel as useless as a child.

With darkness came new suffering. The desert sands held

none of the day's heat, and the nights were as frigid as the days were broiling. Gyalo lay shivering, desperate with exhaustion yet too miserable to fall properly asleep, drifting between strange dreams and a wakefulness just as surreal, in which moonlight washed like silver mist through the gap of his tent flap and the night was filled with the skitterings and rustlings of the desert's nocturnal inhabitants. The rising light of dawn woke him fully, wretched in mind and body. He lay on his back, staring up at the dun-colored canvas of his tent and cataloging his discomforts, which now included not just aches and pains, but the stink of his sweat-rank skin and clothing. He thought of the hours to come, of the heat and the light and the flies and Cirsame's harsh gait, and felt a falling within himself, a kind of clutching dread.

The others were stirring. He forced himself to rise, groaning at the protests of his abused muscles, and dug into his pack for his meditation square. As he did he realized, with shock, that this was the first time in nearly twenty-four hours that he had thought of Ârata, or of the fact that he traveled holy ground. Shame gripped him. His misery had made him selfish; the desert had become for him merely a desert, a place of tribulation, as if he were no better than a Caryaxist.

He turned his mind to meditation and the Affirmations, striving to accomplish these things with a whole heart—and with intent for the future, so he would not forget again. Then, still stiff and weary but with a sense of restored perspective, he hauled himself to his feet and went out to see how the others fared.

It took the party three days to pass beyond the mines. The Burning Land, or at least this portion of it, was fantastically rich in metals and gemstones, as the Caryaxists had discovered. The gemstones had been mined by free Arsacians, to whom the Caryaxist government gave claims in exchange for a percentage of their yield, but the metal mining had been carried out almost exclusively by prisoners. Their barracks stood by the roadside, abandoned to heat and dust, the pressure wells that had supplied them still capable of pro-

ducing water. Equipment remained also—carts, hoists, barrows, buckets, digging implements of every kind. Close to
Thuxra, the reclaimers' efforts were apparent, but the farther
the party traveled, the fewer signs of work they saw. Gyalo,
appreciating for the first time the magnitude of the task to be
accomplished, understood that the delay in Thuxra's dismantling was not entirely a lie.

True to the public purpose of its mission, the party paused
wherever human bones were found. It was not likely that any
of these were banished Âratists; hundreds, perhaps thou-
sands, of Thuxra's captive workers had died in their chains,
and it was certainly they who were buried in the limed pits
near the barracks areas, some so lightly covered that the
bones jutted through, weathered as driftwood. But Gyalo,
speaking the words of the interment ceremony, banishing
twigs and stones into the void of pre-being in lieu of the offerings of a proper funeral, made no distinction, and neither
did the others.

The mines fell behind at last, and the party moved on into
virgin scrubland. They marked the way they had traveled
with cairns of stone, or, where there were no stones, with
one of the red-and-gold marker posts they carried. Each evening, Gyalo noted the day's progress in his spare travel journal and drew maps of the terrain, indicating their route with
a trail of tiny footsteps.

Heat and flies and saddle aches were only the beginning
of the trials of desert travel. The daily water ration, though
adequate for survival, was never quite enough to slake
Gyalo's thirst. Sand got into everything, chafing skin already
sore from sweat and sunburn, and the itchy irritation as his
hair and beard grew out made him scratch his face raw. The
miseries of his body prevented proper sleep; the monotony
of travel rations sapped his appetite. There was a whole cata-
logue of dangers for which he must be constantly alert—sun
poisoning and heat delirium, snakes and scorpions, big
lizards whose bite was powerful enough to amputate a hand
or foot. There were insects whose bites carried fever, and

plants whose stems wept poisons, and thornbushes whose barbs worked themselves so deeply into flesh that they had to be cut out. There were freak storms—sandstorms that blew up out of nowhere, rainstorms that dumped water as if from a giant's bucket, making the dry river courses run again and turning the plains briefly into lakes.

He often thought, during this early period of travel, of the Shapers Utamnos was so certain waited at the journey's end. It had been easy to judge them from the distance of Baushpar—easy to say to himself, *I would not yield.* But now, as he learned to understand the true harshness of the Burning Land, he could not help but wonder whether, thrown naked into the desert's searing embrace, he really would be strong enough not to do as the lost Âratists might have done to survive. He had not forgotten that first day of travel, when all thought of Ârata had been driven from his mind.

Slowly, he acclimated. He had an athlete's training and an athlete's stamina, and also an athlete's grasp of the nature of endurance, which derived as much from mental discipline as from physical strength. These things helped him hang on while his body toughened and his skin hardened and he learned to handle his own gear and ride Cirsame as easily as he once had ridden a horse. A few weeks into the journey his appetite had returned, and though a day of riding left him tired, it no longer utterly exhausted him.

Teispas no doubt suffered as much as anyone, but he never showed it. He was a rigorous commander, with no tolerance for shirking or malingering, often harsh in his dealings with his men. But he never asked anything he did not himself give tenfold; and he was scrupulously fair, never yielding to temper or to prejudice. His men respected him; clearly, they trusted his leadership. Yet in this cruel environment, where the only imperative was survival and most of life's inessentials were stripped away, Gyalo saw something that, earlier, had not been apparent: They did not love him.

The soldiers endured stoically, coping with sunburn and thirst and heat exhaustion as they had elsewhere coped with

cold and starvation and dysentery. They seemed largely indifferent to the fact that they traveled sacred ground, and
their cursing of the Land and its discomforts often verged on
blasphemy; but Gyalo's daily ceremonies were far better attended now than they had been outside the desert. Zabdas
and Sittibaal, ex-soldiers that they were, also adjusted with
reasonable ease, but the Dreamers' attendants, who had
spent most of their lives in the comfort of Aino monasteries,
had a much harder time of it. As for Rikoyu, he could not
have managed at all had Gyalo, Zabdas, and Sittibaal not
regularly assisted him. He accepted their help as stolidly as
he accepted his suffering; later, thinking back, Gyalo realized that he could not remember Rikoyu ever thanking him.

Vâsparis, the mining prospector who served as the expedition's guide, seemed little affected by the harsh conditions. He was a small, wiry man with gray-streaked hair in a
braid down his back; his age was hard to guess, for his years
under the desert sun had seared his face and arms nearly
black and dried his skin to the consistency of leather.
Among other practical talents, he possessed an astounding
knowledge of the Burning Land. The parched wastes held
many secrets, but none so great as this: There was sustenance everywhere in them. Nearly all of it was camouflaged
or hidden—starchy tubers that grew underground, fruits that
clustered not at branch tips but at the base of stems, streams
that ran beneath dry watercourses, so that trenches dug deep
enough would fill up with water. Without Vâsparis, the travelers would have ridden past food and water every day, every
hour, and never known it.

Gyalo, always drawn to new knowledge, was intrigued by
the little miner's skill and took to accompanying Vâsparis on
food- and water-scouting expeditions. This pleased Vâsparis,
who was glad to show off his expertise. The Land was full of
plants and creatures that existed nowhere else; Vâsparis had
named many of them, showing, for an uneducated man, a
surprisingly poetic flair. A thorny tree whose branches were
smothered in bloom after the rare desert rains was cataract-

of-gold. A venomless coral-colored snake that flowed along just under the surface of the sand was a rosy sandswimmer. A woody succulent with sap so acid even the camels would not eat it was fireblood bush. The rare sweet-fleshed melons that grew below the ground were kiss-of-paradise.

He and Gyalo found one of these, early in Gyalo's semi-apprenticeship, when Gyalo caught the frayed hem of his trousers on its thorny, leafless vine. Kneeling, Vâsparis dug down into the soft ground and drew out a smooth, amber-colored globe.

"Wouldn't even've looked for this," he said. "Paradises don't usually ripen till later in the season. Here." Taking his knife from his belt, he cleaved the melon expertly in two and held one of the halves toward Gyalo. "Too much trouble to take it back. What the others don't know won't hurt 'em, eh, Brother?"

Gyalo devoured the fruit, rind and all; it seemed the best thing he had ever eaten. Vâsparis clapped him on the shoulder.

"The desert has accepted you," he said. "She's given you the dearest of all her gifts. She'll tease you now, and test you, but she'll never turn her back on you." He shook his head. "You're favored, Brother. I was more than a year finding my first paradise, when I came out from Arsace to be a miner."

"What made you want to come here?" Gyalo asked, curious.

"To get my fortune, of course." Vâsparis grinned, the leathery skin creasing around his eyes. They were an odd reflective gray, like tarnished silver, startling in contrast to the darkness of his face. "It was near twenty years back, when the government was looking to push the mining out past Thuxra and trying to recruit free men to prospect the Land. It was bad times in Arsace then, and the wage was twice what you'd get anywhere else, with a bounty for every new strike. Still, not many went—and not just because they didn't want to leave their families or were scared of dying.

But I've never been much of a man for religion. I didn't see why Ârata should pay any mind to us little creatures scurrying around the edges of his Land. No offense, Brother."

"None taken, Vâsparis."

"So I packed up my things and came. I loved it, right from the first. All of it—the sand, the sun, even the heat." He made a wide gesture, encompassing the burning vastness of the desert, the pitiless reaches of the sky. "'Twas the money brought me, but it's the Land that's kept me. If I could stay, I would. I surely would."

Gyalo could not fault him. Despite the little miner's profession of unbelief, he displayed greater reverence for the Land than any of the Exiles Gyalo had met at Thuxra. And yet it was a very un-Âratist reverence. To Vâsparis, the desert was not the spoiled shadow of a land laid waste by Ârata's and Ârdaxcasa's cosmic battle, but a place complete and perfect in itself. And in a way, he was right. For the Land was far from the barren waste that legend depicted. Its arid face, its strange terrain, teemed with life—as if Ârata's creative power, flowing from him as continuously as his dreams, had brought a whole new world to being above him, across the eons of his sleep.

Eight weeks into the journey, the scrubland gave way to a region of long parallel sand dunes, where the heavy-loaded camels sank to their ankles, and men and beasts alike suffered greatly from thirst. Beyond this difficult terrain lay a range of rocky hills as red as the earth, springing suddenly from the flat ground. There was ample vegetation for the camels, and quantities of water in standing pools around the hills' base, and they halted for several days to rest. On the final morning, Gyalo woke before dawn and climbed the tallest hill. He performed his morning meditation and spoke the Affirmations, then sat watching as the low clouds turned from gray to gold, and the red edge of the sun slipped above the horizon. He thought of the First Messenger: Might he have passed this way, rested in these very hills?

When it was light enough he took from his pocket Utam-

nos's gift, the little book of Dokha's poetry, and opened it to
the place he had marked:

LONGING

> One day
> I traveled under weeping skies
> and slept in wet garments.
> I dreamed of sun
> but still the rain fell.
> One day
> I waited in a darkened room
> and closed my eyes on silence.
> I dreamed of torches
> but none burned.
> One day
> I will wake
> to light.

He looked up again at the vast country before him, the red-
green-gold vistas running to the edge of the earth. It came to
him, in a kind of quiet revelation, that he had found his balance in the journey. He traveled now as he would wish to
travel in this sacred place: mindfully, in physical and spiritual equilibrium.

The party moved on into a more varied region, where the
scrub mixed with patches of sparse woodland. There was
more animal life—bright-plumaged birds and small herds of
deerlike creatures, which Vâsparis, who had never seen
them before, dubbed lyrehorns—and also many wonders.
They rode one day through a field of sandstone pillars, mysterious as the ruins of a lost empire. They traveled alongside
a chasm that split the ground as cleanly as a knife cut, and
was so deep its bottom could not be seen. They rounded pure
white salt pans—the remains, according to Vâsparis, of ancient lakes—and followed dry river courses where gray-
leaved, white-barked trees leaned out above empty sand.

They picked their way across a plain where chunks of emerald and moonstone and yellow beryl lay scattered like windfall fruit. There, many of the men halted to stuff jewels into their baggage, ignoring Gyalo's warnings about stealing from the god.

"We take his food and water," one of them told him angrily. "We take his sand and his thorns and his bloody poisonous snakes. Why shouldn't we take a stone or two?"

"Taking what you need to survive is one thing. Loading yourself with jewels you hope to sell later on is another."

"Who'll know, Brother? We're all alone in these ash-cursed wastes. Who'll know?"

It was Teispas who put a stop to it, with open anger—a lapse in his usually faultless self-control that surprised the soldiers so much that they replaced the stones with a minimum of grumbling. A few of them, though, contrived to hold on to a portion of their booty, as Gyalo discovered a few days later when Haxar—one of the few who had not taken any stones—brought him several men whom he had persuaded to relinquish their gems as an act of faith. Gyalo promised to return them to the desert with proper reverence, and assured the soldiers that Ârata would remember their repentance when the time of cleansing came.

Haxar lingered after his companions left. "Do you think he's watching us, Brother?" He did not speak Ârata's name; there was a superstition among the men that to do so outside the Communion ceremony was unlucky. "Do you think we're in his dreams?"

"Who can say? Perhaps he dreams us, perhaps he doesn't. There's no way to tell."

"But if he does dream us, how will he know we're not invaders, defilers, blasphemers, like the Caryaxists? How will he know we serve him?"

"He'll know it when he wakes, as he will know everything that has ever passed upon the earth during his time of slumber."

"But we've taken his jewels, and cursed his Land, and spoken blasphemy on the soil that covers him. Surely he's angry with us, Brother. Surely those things won't be forgiven."

"Ârata is compassionate, Haxar. He understands our weakness, and forgives what he can. You've added light to your soul by what you've done today. Strive to travel the Land with reverence, to take no more than you need and give back all you can in the form of faith. If you do that, I promise your time here won't stain you."

Haxar departed, though Gyalo thought he still seemed troubled. For a little while he appeared daily at Communion, but gradually his attendance fell off to its former casual level.

The Dreamers' visions led the party steadily south. Gyalo had worried about how they would stand the journey, but under the favored treatment they were given, they bore up very well. By day they reclined comfortably in their cushioned litters, whose gauze curtains could not exclude the heat, but did shut out the piercing light and the ubiquitous flies. At night their tents were the first to be set up. When standing water was available, they drank before the others; when it was not, they received the largest rations from the water barrels.

Characteristically, they were not appreciative, and spent much time complaining about things that could not be changed. Yet though they might make miseries of themselves during the day, every night Seiki and Tak lay down willingly to dream, and every morning recited their visions to Rikoyu. The rigorous training that made it possible for Dreamers to set the subjects of their Dreams and function at will within those settings rendered their visions highly abstract; the images they brought back were often as cryptic as those of ordinary sleepers. Over the centuries an extensive symbology had been codified, allowing skilled interpreters like Rikoyu to make sense of even the most convoluted Dreams. Rikoyu carried with him four fat symbol books, divided into sections for different settings, objects, beings, colors, sensations, and sounds. There was also a thinner volume cross-referencing these, for the context in which an image appeared was also important.

"The hard part, though, isn't working out what the images mean," he told Gyalo, who was fascinated by the process, which he had never before seen firsthand. Ordinarily taciturn, Rikoyu was more than willing to expound upon his craft—the only thing about which, possibly, he was passionate. "It's working out which ones are meaningless. Dreams contain a lot of extraneous imagery—things that rise from the Dreamer's life, his personality, what he had to eat for dinner that night. It's one reason interpreters work with the same Dreamers—you get to know the padding. For instance, Seiki dreams often about oak trees and the color blue."

"Why?"

"Who knows?" Rikoyu shrugged. "The point is that those images can usually be discounted. Of course, it depends on context. Sometimes, if they're connected in certain ways with certain things, they can be significant. But mostly not."

"How do you tell the difference?"

"You have to know the Dreamer. Each one has his own style, his own way of linking things. If someone gave me fifty Dreams written down, without names"—there was pride in his voice—"I could pick out Seiki's or Tak's just by the way the images fit together."

The Dreamers found the Land's emptiness intimidating, and their sleeping minds were often drawn back to inhabited Galea. They did dream of the Land, though, Dreams that centered always around the same three elements: turbulence, distance, and the direction south. This lack of precise detail had dogged Dreams of the desert from the time the disturbance was first detected; it had been hoped the Dreams would gain focus as the expedition moved deeper into the Land. But time passed, and their vagueness remained unchanged. Still, the direction was clear—south, always south—and that was enough to keep the party moving.

Four months into the journey, they came to the most hostile landscape they had yet encountered: a vast plain of pebbles packed flat and hard as pavement, polished by time and the elements to the reflectiveness of glass. The wind that blew

off it was like the breath of a furnace. Even the most desolate of the dunes had supported some vegetation, but there
was none here, nor any other sign of life. Far away at the
southern horizon, a range of twilight-colored mountains
poked up into the sky, some of them showing the flattened
cone-shape of volcanoes.

The party made camp, and Teispas dispatched a pair of
soldiers to survey the terrain. They returned exhausted and
sunburned, to report that they had ridden for two days and
seen no sign of change. There seemed no choice but to try
and go around.

To the east the plain curved north, so the party turned
west. After a day of travel the plain's margin dipped sharply
south. Now, suddenly, the Dreamers' Dreams acquired defi-
nition, producing an array of symbols that, according to
Rikoyu, meant human life and work—still south, beyond the
pebble plain.

They had, it seemed, found the lost Âratists.

But the plain ran on. Scouts sent ahead reported no end in
sight. After a week of this, Teispas called a meeting. He and
his second-in-command, Aspâthnes, were present, as were
Gyalo, Rikoyu, and Vâsparis. Outside, the sun was slipping
over the edge of the world in a glory of gold and orange
cloud; its fading light filtered through the canvas of Teispas's
tent, enveloping the men in ruddy gloom.

"We're sure now that what we've been sent to find lies on
the other side of that plain," Teispas said. "Probably in those
mountains. But it's been over a week, and still the plain goes
on. And the Dreamers have begun to lose focus again. Isn't
that so, Brother Rikoyu?"

"Yes," said Rikoyu.

"We have supplies for only a year. We've been traveling
more than four months, and it'll take us at least that long to
return—longer, if the lost Âratists are with us. We have no
time to waste. But that is what we are doing—wasting time.
For all we know this ash-cursed plain goes all the way to the
sea." He paused. Like all of them, he had lost flesh; he had
not had much to spare to begin with, and now was gaunt as a

ghost. With his tangled hair and overgrown beard, he looked like a castaway rather than the leader of a military expedition. "We must try to scout a crossing."

For a moment there was silence.

"There's bad places in the Burning Land, but no place crueler than the pebble plains." Vâsparis sat cross-legged, his hands resting on his knees, self-contained and easy as always. "There's a little one west of Thuxra City. My partner and I tried to cross it once, but we had to turn back. The sun pounds down on those stones till you'd swear you were frying on a griddle."

"We can travel at night, and take shelter by day."

"That's fine for men." Vâsparis shrugged. "But what about the camels? Nothing for 'em to eat or drink out there. They can go maybe ten days like that—and only if there's good forage at the end of it."

"We can't carry more than ten days' supply of water in any case," Teispas said. "So their limit and ours is the same. We've seen rain clouds above the mountains—it seems likely there's good land there. The scouts can try at the most southern point, where the Dreamers' Dreams were strongest. If they can break through in eight days, it shouldn't take the main party more than ten."

"And if they can't break through?" asked Aspâthnes, Teispas's second. "Or if they don't return?"

"Then we'll move on and try another route. And if that doesn't work, another." Teispas fixed Aspâthnes with a hard black gaze. "And if *that* one doesn't work, I'll concede defeat, and we can go back to slogging along the edge of this ash-cursed plain, until our supply situation forces us to turn tail and go back to Arsace without completing the mission that right now, *this moment*, is finally within our reach."

"Very well," Aspâthnes said. "If the scouts can cross in eight days, and find good land there, I agree it should be tried."

"And you, Brother." Teispas turned his gaze upon Gyalo. "What do you think?"

The question was only a courtesy—Gyalo was in charge

of the vowed Âratists, but he had no voice in the mission's command. But he did not disagree. Since the Dreamers' Dreams had changed, a blazing excitement had filled him. He was as impatient as Teispas to confront the truth they had sought so long.

"It will be risky," he said. "But every day in the Burning Land is a risk. I agree we should try to find a way across."

"Good." Teispas looked toward Aspâthnes. "Two volunteers. I want them to leave this night. See to it."

"Yes, sir." Aspâthnes rose and left the tent.

The scouts departed. The main party came on at a slower pace, until they found the red-and-gold marker the scouts had planted at the point where they had decided to try a crossing. There was good camping close by—a small oasis where water bubbled up to form a pool, and a grove of ghost oaks cast a whispering shade.

The party waited, using the time to patch tents and clothing and repair frayed harness. On the fifteenth day the scouts emerged, exhausted but triumphant, to report that it had taken them seven nights to reach the far side of the pebble plain, where waited verdant land such as they had not seen in all their months of travel.

They set out the night after the scouts' return. The water barrels were full; inessential items had been unloaded and left behind, and the difference made up with green fodder for the camels. They rode till dawn beneath the cold-starred sky. The waxing moon stared down, a half-closed eye; around them the plain lay flat and featureless, glistening with reflected moonlight like a plaque of beaten silver. There were no variations, no landmarks, nothing at all with which to measure motion—a monotony as difficult to bear, in its way, as any physical hardship.

At dawn they halted. Looking back, Gyalo could see no trace of their starting point, nor any sign of the land ahead other than the hazy mountains. Tent pegs could not be driven among the packed stones, so they spread the canvas of their tents across the camel saddles, and beneath this low shelter passed the broiling day. Gyalo dozed and woke and dozed again, tangled in dreams of fire and suffocation. When evening came, the blankets on which he had lain were soaked with sweat, and the stone of the plain burned his feet through the soles of his boots.

The camels bore up well while the fodder lasted, but on the fifth night they began to slow, raising the possibility that the journey might take longer than the nine nights Teispas had estimated. The water allowance was reduced (except for the Dreamers, for whom nothing was ever rationed); the thirsty men grumbled, but were not ready to listen to Vâsparis when he suggested, seriously, that they drink their own urine—a survival technique, he claimed, that more than once had made the difference between life and death for him.

At sunset on the seventh night, the travelers crawled from their sweaty burrows to begin the labor of saddling and loading. Gyalo was unhobbling Cirsame—not that she really needed hobbling, for she was by now too depleted to wander—when he heard a shout:

"Look! Over there!"

It was one of the camel-handlers. He was pointing southward, toward a peculiar disturbance in the sky. High above the plain the air trembled, shimmering like heat haze. The margins of the area were blurred with iridescence.

"What is it?" Sittibaal, who had spread his canvas nearby, came to stand beside Gyalo. "A storm?"

Gyalo shook his head. What it recalled to him, strangely, was Shaper sight: The air around a substance about to be transformed often looked just so. "I don't know."

Faintly came a long roll of thunder. Storm clouds, dark and turbulent, began to unfold at the disturbance's center. They compounded and enlarged, pulsing with sullen lightning. The thunder was continuous now. A swirling irregularity appeared at the storm's eastern edge; after a moment a column of cloud sank slowly down, like a probing finger. It touched down, lifted, touched again.

"I've never seen a storm like that." Sittibaal's voice was hushed. "Have you?"

Gyalo shook his head.

For a time they watched as the cloud-finger investigated the ground, sweeping slowly back and forth, almost as if some invisible hand were shepherding it. At last they returned to preparations. Gyalo had forced Cirsame to kneel when the thunder suddenly boomed louder. He looked up. The storm had grown, eating up much of the southern sky. It was still expanding—the clouds swelling, the black column engorging, like a bladder pumped with air—

No—not expanding. Approaching. The storm was coming toward them, racing along the pebble plain at unbelievable speed. In the instant Gyalo realized this, the wind struck, pressing his clothes against his body. The light dimmed. Wetness struck his face—rain?

Another clap of thunder split the air. Cirsame bellowed and tried to rise; he pulled her traces, attempting to hold her down. There was a confusion of running men, of shouting—then the storm struck, a screaming madness of wind and rain. Lightning flashed, blinding; the thunder that followed was like the earth cracking in two. The wind tried to pick Gyalo up; he wound his wrists with Cirsame's traces and hung on for his life.

There was another flash, another crack. The wind wrenched him savagely around. Pain burst in his shoulder, like nothing he had ever known. Something struck him, crushing him to the ground. And then there was nothing in the world but agony and the storm.

Gyalo was not certain, afterward, whether he lost consciousness, for he remembered little of what happened once he fell. But at last he became aware that the storm had gone. He lay on his chest, his face turned on the uneven surface of the pebble plain. His left arm was pinned beneath him. The shoulder felt as if hot iron had been thrust into the socket; it was so painful he could barely breathe. A weight lay across his legs and hips. He knew without trying that he would not be able to pull free.

He opened his eyes. Full night had fallen; the moonlit world was still, and very quiet. He could feel the wetness of his clothing, but the plain around him was already nearly dry, the moisture evaporating almost at once from the day-heated stone. Nearby lay a peculiar humped dark shape; his mind, hazed with pain and shock, took a moment to recognize it as a wind-ripped tangle of tent canvas, camel saddles, and what looked like the smashed remains of a water barrel.

Though he could not move his legs and feet, he could feel them: His back was not broken, then. But when he tried to push himself up on his right arm, the pain of his dislocated shoulder nearly caused him to lose consciousness. As he lay, trying to gather strength for another attempt, he heard the sound of voices.

"Over here!" he called hoarsely. "Help! Over here!"

A pause; then footsteps. "It's Brother Gyalo," someone said, and someone else: "Cursed ash of the Enemy, look at all that blood!" And then, before Gyalo had time to feel more than the first edge of panic: "It's not his. Look."

"Oh," said the second voice, which Gyalo now recognized as Haxar's. "I see."

"You three, lift the beast." This, unmistakably, was Teispas. "I'll pull him out. All right. On my count. One—two—three!"

The weight on Gyalo's legs eased. Hands gripped his shoulders. Agony burst inside him, and the world fell away.

He came to, shivering with cold. His rescuers had left him propped against a camel saddle. His arm had been pushed back into its socket and bound to his chest with strips torn from his stole; it was still painful, but bearable. His legs were stiff, but they moved easily enough, and he thought he would probably be able to walk. From hips to ankles, his clothing was black and sodden. *Blood*, he thought. *Cirsame's?* It must have been she who had fallen on him. What had happened to injure her so terribly?

Looking at it made him queasy, so he turned his eyes instead to what lay around him. The moon was near full; its light flooded powerfully down, casting the wreckage of the storm into sharp silver-and-black relief: saddles, blankets, baggage, fallen camels, other things so torn and twisted he could not tell what they were. The devastation spread out along the storm path, a ribbon of debris running across the face of the pebble plain. All was still within this territory of ruin. Even remembering the incredible wind-driven violence of the storm, it was hard to comprehend such utter destruction. It seemed artificial, as if what he saw were not a real catastrophe but some abstract representation of one.

A little distance away, a number of long dark forms lay side by side. From the precise way they were arranged, as much as by their shape, Gyalo knew that they were corpses.

Slowly and with care for his bound arm, he got to his feet. A wave of dizziness seized him; he had to stand, eyes closed, until it passed. Limping, he crossed to the bodies and looked into their faces: five soldiers, a camel-handler—and Sittibaal, the right side of his head reduced to a mess of blood and bone.

Gyalo sank to his knees, his teeth chattering with nausea. Until that moment, despite the havoc all around him and his own pain, everything had seemed oddly distant, as if he were observing as it happened to someone else. But the sight of Sittibaal tore through that false detachment. The weight of understanding fell on him, all at once. The expedition was destroyed. These corpses, this wreckage, the few stunned survivors, were all that remained. Could they surmount such disaster? Or was it the end of everything, come upon them in a fury of wind and rain?

Death had always stood behind this journey, behind all they planned and did. Yet in this moment, with mortality suddenly as close as his hand, it was not of death Gyalo thought, but life—the need to survive, to go forward into the future, to accomplish all he had it in him to accomplish and learn all he had it in him to learn. The force of that desire stole his breath; he felt no fear, but only anger, anger that it might not be possible. *Ârata,* he cried silently into the night, though he knew the futility of such address, *this cannot be what it seems! There has to be a way!*

Sometime later, he was roused by the sound of boots on stone. He lifted his head to see Haxar and one of the other soldiers bearing a corpse. They laid their burden by the others. Haxar glanced toward Gyalo.

"You all right, Brother?"

"Yes," Gyalo said.

They left, moving as if still burdened. Gyalo thought: *If they can work, so can I*. He returned to the bodies, speaking over each the words of final blessing. Then he began to move about, identifying objects and gathering them into piles, whatever he could lift and carry with one hand. It was slow work, and he had to stop now and then to rest, but it occupied his attention, holding away the dread and speculation that might otherwise have consumed him. After a little while he found his travel pack, with everything safe inside it, including his pouch of manita. He felt a relief he did not want to examine too closely. He discarded his bloody trousers for a clean pair; his gown he could not remove because of the binding of his arm, but he compromised by cutting off its blood-stiff skirt. Last of all, clumsily, he wrapped his spare stole around his shoulders.

By dawn, the survivors had fully surveyed what remained. It was a bleak inventory. Out of a party of thirty-nine, there were twelve remaining: Gyalo, Teispas, Vâsparis, seven soldiers, a camel-handler, and Seiki. Teispas and Nariya, one of the soldiers, were unharmed; Haxar, another soldier called Cinxri, and the camel-handler had only superficial injuries. But Gyalo, Vâsparis, and Diasarta, a fourth soldier, were more seriously hurt, and the three remaining soldiers looked likely to die within hours. As for Seiki, she appeared whole, but complained of pain in her side and chest, and seemed to have difficulty breathing.

Of the dead, only fourteen could be located. Tak was among them, his back broken. The rest, including Rikoyu and Zabdas, were gone without a trace, picked up by the winds and carried away. Thirty-one camels were found, twenty-nine of them dead or dying; others might have survived, bolting before the storm, but they were far out on the pebble plain by now. Food was not a problem, for many of the bags of flour and rice and dried meat had been caught beneath half-loaded camels as they fell, if necessary, the camels themselves could be butchered. But most of the water barrels lay smashed to tinder, and of those found intact only seven had anything in them. The rain had soaked the blankets, and left water caught in pots or the hollows of overturned saddles; some of the labor of last night had been devoted to collecting it.

As the red edge of morning sliced the eastern horizon,

the able-bodied survivors gathered to discuss what should be done.

"Saf and Bishti and Gâbrios won't last the day," Teispas said bluntly. He had worked tirelessly through the night; his dark face was strained and haggard, his hands and arms and chest marked with blood that was not his own. "That leaves nine of us. We've five full barrels of water, and two about half-full. If we ration it, it'll last us four, maybe five days. We've more than enough food for that amount of time. We've two camels—with luck, they'll survive a little longer. One can be loaded, and Seiki can ride the other. The rest of us are able to walk. If we start tonight, we have a good chance of reaching the other side. A good chance," he repeated.

"The other side?" Haxar asked hoarsely. His forehead and cheek were bloody from a still-oozing gash in his scalp, and his eyes were swollen with weeping. Sauras was among the dead, one of the last to be found; Haxar had not allowed the others to touch him, but had himself brought his friend to lie beside the other corpses. "Which other side?"

"The southern side, of course." Teispas's tone was sharp. "The northern side is too far away."

"We can't go south." Haxar shook his head.

"Oh? And why not?"

"The god's angry. That's why he sent the storm. He wants us to go back. He wants us to leave his resting place alone."

"Ârata hasn't touched the world deliberately since the time of the Messenger, Haxar," Gyalo said, from where he sat by an unconscious Seiki. "This storm was his dream, sure enough, but only as every storm or whirlwind or catastrophe of the earth and air is his dream. There was no purpose in it."

"No." Again Haxar shook his head. "That was no natural storm. You all saw it—you know I'm right. It was a warning. A message. We have to turn back."

"We can't turn back." Teispas spoke clearly, as if to a child. "We don't have enough water."

"Not for all of us. But what if just five go? That's one barrel each We'll draw splinters. The chosen ones'll go back. The rest . . . well, the rest will die. But at least some will live."

"I will not pick and choose among my men." Teispas's voice was tight. "I won't follow a path that saves only some when there's a way to save us all."

"The captain's right," Vâsparis said. His arm, broken by flying debris, was bound to his chest like Gyalo's; a blood-soaked cloth wrapped a wound in his calf. "Why should only some live when we all can? That's madness. I say go south."

"Then we'll die for sure!" Haxar's voice shook with urgency. "The god'll send another storm, and this time we'll all be killed. Ash of the Enemy! Why won't you see?" He turned to the other soldiers. "Nariya, Cinxri. Diasarta. We've talked about this. Tell them."

The soldiers stirred uneasily. Teispas sighed and passed his hand over his face. "You've said enough, Haxar. Don't make me order you to be silent."

"Captain . . ." It was Nariya, the one uninjured soldier. "Maybe you should listen to him."

"What, you too, Nariya?"

"I'm just saying think about it. I heard what the Brother said." Nariya cast a glance at Gyalo. "But he's only a man. How does he know what the god wants? How's he so sure Haxar's wrong?"

Teispas sighed again. Vâsparis made a gesture of disgust. But Diasarta, his splinted leg stretched awkwardly in front of him, nodded agreement; and though Cinxri and the camel-handler only watched, there was fear in both their faces.

"Haxar *is* wrong," Gyalo said, reaching wearily for the authority of his religious rank. "Ârata is not consciously present in the world. The storm was a dream—a moment of pain, a moment of restlessness. It wasn't sent to punish us, or to warn us, or to bring us a message. It was just . . . chance, bad luck, that we were in its way. I'll grant it's possible that Ârata sees us in his dreams. But we're here to find his own lost faithful, to redress the cruelty of those who denied his divinity. How could such a purpose make him angry?"

Nariya watched Gyalo, brows knotted; but Haxar was shaking his head.

"You're blind, Brother," he said. The febrile intensity had left him; he sounded only tired. "As blind as the rest. Right from the start, there were signs. Every day the sun tried to murder us. Every day the desert tried to cripple us. But did we pause, did we turn back? No. And now here we are, with death whispering in our ears, and still you won't look to the truth."

Teispas had had enough. He rose to his feet in a single surging motion.

"I will hear no more," he said, harshly. "There's only one practical way to save ourselves, and that is to go south. I am still commander of this expedition, such as it is, and those are my orders. That is, unless any of you want to challenge me?" He looked around at the gathered faces, each in turn. Nariya stared at the ground; Haxar tried to match the captain's gaze, but his eyes fluttered and slid away. Teispas let the silence gather a moment, then nodded once, decisively. "Good. Now, we need to rig coverings to get through the day. Cinxri, come with me. The rest of you, stay where you are."

He turned and stalked off. Cinxri scrambled to his feet, not looking at the others, and followed.

Gyalo elected to remain with Seiki, who was drifting in and out of consciousness. He was concerned: She had begun to cough, a deep, painful hacking that produced an ominous froth of pink spittle around her lips. Cinxri and Teispas erected a covering over them, using camel saddles and salvaged tent canvas, and there they lay through the burning day. There was not much Gyalo could do for her, other than give her sips of water from the half barrel Teispas had left with them and blot the sweat from her face, but his presence seemed to comfort her.

He drank a little himself and chewed on some of the dried

meat they had salvaged the night before. His shoulder ached, but he fell asleep anyway, lying on his back and weltering in sweat.

The jerking aside of the canvas covering brought him abruptly awake. There were hands on his ankles and at his shoulders. He gasped in pain; a hard palm came down over his mouth.

"Hush, Brother. I don't want to hurt you. I will, though, if you give me reason."

It was Haxar. He knelt beside Gyalo, half his face a mask of dried blood. He seemed calm, in control; but there was an instability to his gaze, and he blinked rapidly, like a man fighting to hold on to consciousness.

"Do you understand?" Gyalo nodded. Haxar's hand withdrew. "All right. This is what's happened. We've talked it over, Cinxri and Nariya and me, and we've decided to go back. To go north."

"But—"

"*Shut up!*" Haxar hissed; for a moment Gyalo thought the soldier would strike him. "Only five can go. We don't want the captain, obviously, or the Dreamer. Diasarta'd slow us down too much. And you—well, Cinxri thinks we could make you shape water for us, and maybe he's right, but who knows what else you'd do, eh? Or what you'd say about us when we get back?" His unsteady eyes flicked to Gyalo's, then away. "So we're taking Vâsparis, even though he isn't willing, and the camel-handler. They both know the Land. And we're taking the camels and the full water barrels. We'll leave you the half barrels, but we need the rest."

As Haxar spoke, Nariya bound up Gyalo's ankles, and Cinxri looped a leather strap around his good wrist and tethered it to the heavy camel saddle above his head.

"It's just to hold you while we're leaving," Haxar explained. "You'll get free if you work hard enough."

"Don't do this, Haxar," Gyalo said hoarsely. "We can survive, all of us, if we stay together. If you go, you doom us all."

"Shall I tie up the Dreamer?" Cinxri asked.

"No. She's no threat." Haxar braced his hands on his knees and rose to his feet. "I'm sorry, Brother. It's got to be this way."

"Think about the burden of darkness you're taking on your soul. How long do you think it will take for Ârata to burn you back to purity at the end of time? Eons. Eons of pain and fire. Or maybe it won't be possible to cleanse you. Maybe the burning will consume you utterly, so you'll never see the paradise of Ârata's waking. Is that what you want?"

"I've made my choice," Haxar said. For a moment his restless gaze stilled; then he turned away. "Cover them up," he ordered his companions. And then, when they did not move: "Didn't I tell you he'd try to scare us into letting him go? Do it!"

The two soldiers stepped forward. The heavy canvas descended, shutting out the sky, the pitiless sun, the mutineers. Gyalo heard their footsteps, then, for a little while, the sound of bags being loaded, the groaning of unwilling camels, the thuds and curses as the men beat them to their feet. Then silence.

Gyalo hauled himself into a position where he could reach the bonds on his wrist with his teeth. Cinxri had pulled the knot tight, and Gyalo's saliva swelled it even tighter. Still he chewed at it, stubbornly, though he knew that hope was truly gone. *The desert will never turn its back on you,* Vâsparis had told him; if only it could be so, and some miracle rise up off the plain and save them. For the choice was upon him, the lost Âratists' choice, the choice he had prayed he would never have to confront.

The sun was setting by the time the knot gave. It was short work, after that, to get his knife and slice through the bindings on his ankles. He paused to drink a little, and to drip some water between Seiki's lips; then, pushing aside the canvas, he climbed to his feet and limped off in search of Teispas.

The captain lay under a covering with Diasarta and the two other soldiers, his feet roped and his hands trussed behind him. He had made some headway against his bonds, but it probably would have taken him several more hours to get out of them; nevertheless, he did not seem grateful when Gyalo cut him loose. Gyalo freed Diasarta—like Gyalo, he had been tied to a camel saddle with his arms over his head, but it did not seem to have occurred to him to bite at the knots—and checked the others. Only Gâbrios, his head heavily bandaged, was still alive. Then he followed Teispas.

Teispas had pulled Gyalo's travel pack from beneath the canvas that covered Seiki, and turned it out upon the pebble plain. He was kneeling, rummaging through Gyalo's scattered belongings. It was so unexpected that for a moment Gyalo simply stared.

"What are you doing?"

Teispas's moving hands stopped. He held up a leather pouch. "Is this where you keep it?"

"What—" A horrible understanding opened up within Gyalo's mind. "Give that to me."

"I thought so." Teispas sprang to his feet, tearing at the pouch's closures. Gyalo lunged forward, but he was off-balance with his bound arm, and anyway, it was too late. With a wide sweeping motion, Teispas tossed the pouch's contents outward. For an instant a cloud of manita hung upon the air, sharp particles glinting in the last rays of the setting sun; Teispas backtracked rapidly to avoid its spread, his hand clamped across his mouth and nose to protect his breathing. Then the night breeze took it and bore it off across the pebble plain.

Teispas shook the pouch to make sure it was empty, then turned it inside out. He let it fall to the ground, where it lay like a reptile's discarded skin.

"What have you done?" Gyalo whispered. He knelt where he had fallen, supporting himself on his good hand. Teispas knelt also. In the fading light his face was like dark wood—as hard, as still.

"These past hours," he said, "I've been turning things over in my mind. There is no natural way for us to survive. We're at least three days from the end of the plain. They didn't leave enough water for even one of us to get that far." He paused. His black eyes gleamed like polished onyx. "But we have you, Brother. You're a Shaper. You can do as the Shapers we were sent to find did, all those years ago. You can save us."

Gyalo stared at him. He could not speak.

"Don't tell me you hadn't thought of it, for I won't believe you."

"The use of shaping outside of ceremony is forbidden to me." Gyalo's lips were stiff. "My vow forbids it."

"I know. And I can't force you to break your vow. But I've just removed one of the barriers to breaking it. Perhaps you're strong enough to save us even with the tether of the drug—I don't know. But if you're not, you won't have to make the decision now to set the drug aside. I've taken that out of your hands."

"You think that will make a difference? You think I'm not capable of keeping my vow without manita?"

"Oh, I think you are." Teispas spoke with utter calm. "I think you very much are. But I also think you're a man of conscience. Let me ask you something. Do you think Ârata prizes selfishness?"

"What?"

"Do you think he will be pleased with you at the end of time if you allow us all to die on principle, when you have the means to save us?"

"You don't understand." There was a horrible inevitability to the words, as if he had already lived this moment of confrontation. "You don't understand the importance of the Shaper vow."

"There's more at stake here than just a *vow*." Passion roughened Teispas's voice. "There are lives involved besides your own. *There are other people who will die* if you refuse to use your ability. Your life is yours to throw away if you want, but our lives . . . our lives . . . how can you make that choice for us?"

"It's not . . . choice! Choice has nothing to do with it. The doctrines of the church . . . are not situational. My vow is not conditional. I didn't vow for a single place, a single time, a single situation. I vowed for all places, for all times, for all the joys and sorrows and disasters of my life."

"You are just one man, Brother!" Teispas cried. "Will the Âratist church crumble and fall if you break your oath? Will the course of history change?"

Gyalo drew in his breath. "I am not . . . just one man. I am all those who have gone before me. I am all those who will come after me. If I were to do this thing, I wouldn't be breaking just my promise, but all those promises. I wouldn't be betraying just my faith, but the faith of every Shaper who ever kept his vow."

"But who will know? We're alone on this plain—who will ever know what we did here to survive? I'll never speak of it. I'll take your secret to my grave. I swear it."

"*I* would know. *Ârata* would know. And he would not forgive it—no, not even if I saved only you and allowed myself to die. I'd be burned to nothing at the end of time. Not one iota of me would remain. Do you understand? If I break my oath, I will die forever!"

"Your ability was given by the god," Teispas said, softly. "But the oath you follow was made by men. How do you know what Ârata thinks of it?"

Gyalo stared into the captain's implacable face. He was aware he should feel outrage. But there was only horror, opening up within him like the sky overhead, without limit.

"I cannot break my vow," he said into that immensity. "I cannot save you. You've thrown away my manita for nothing."

For a long moment Teispas watched him. "Perhaps I have."

He got to his feet, and began to walk away.

"Do you think you'll pay no price for what you've done tonight?" Gyalo shouted after him. "You'll burn for a long time when Ârata rises again." Teispas paced on as if he did not hear. "I thought you were a man of principle! A man who truly honored the Way of Ârata! How could you tell me the truth at Thuxra and then do this? How could you be so false to your own faith?"

Teispas paused. "Ah," he said, not turning. "But you don't know where the falsehood lies, do you, Brother?"

And he moved on, leaving Gyalo speechless.

For a time Gyalo wandered amid the wreckage of the expedition, looking for manita. He did not really expect to find it; nearly everything had been gathered and sorted the night before, and none of the clay globes meant to subdue apostate Shapers had been found intact. Still, he needed to be sure, needed to know that he had done everything it was possible to do. His heart pounded as he searched; his good hand trembled and his legs were weak.

At last there was nowhere else to look. He returned to Seiki, who was awake and begging weakly for water. He helped her to drink, then, trying not to think about what he was doing, filled a cup and went over to where Diasarta and Gâbrios lay. Gâbrios was still unconscious, though he did swallow the water Gyalo dribbled between his lips. Diasarta was awake. When Gyalo knelt to offer him the cup, he clutched Gyalo's arm instead.

"They left us." His voice held barely contained hysteria. "We're going to die."

Gyalo said nothing.

"I begged them to take me. I said I'd crawl if I had to. But they took the camel-handler instead. They took a *former prisoner* instead of me." His fingers worked convulsively on Gyalo's arm. "Why'd they do it, Brother? Why?"

The moon had set. Gyalo could barely see the scarred face turned toward his own. But his mind's eye showed him clearly the fear that must distort Diasarta's features. Teispas's voice spoke inside his head: *Your life is yours to throw away, but our lives . . . our lives . . . our lives . . .* He could no longer ignore the irony of the water he held. He jerked free of Diasarta's grasp. Water splashed onto the ground.

"Do you want this or don't you?"

For a moment Diasarta stared at him; then he took the cup and gulped greedily, and lay back, silent.

Gyalo took up his Seiki vigil again. Her cough had worsened, and the corners of her mouth were dark with blood. He was certain now that she would die, no matter what he did or did not do. It did not help at all to know that. Teispas's voice droned on inside his head, and nothing would make it stop—*our lives . . . our lives . . . our lives . . .*

Teispas returned at dawn from wherever he had gone, and without a word began to rig up a larger shelter. He did not ask for assistance, nor did Gyalo offer it. By the time the sun was over the horizon—the time when Gyalo would normally have taken his manita dose—the shelter was finished. Teispas picked Gâbrios up and carried him into it. Then he came for Seiki—hauling her on her blanket, for she was too heavy to lift—and then for the water barrels. Gyalo could not imagine where he found the strength.

Diasarta insisted on transporting himself, sitting on the surface of the pebble plain and hitching himself backward with his hands. When Teispas tried to help, he wrenched away.

"Don't touch me!" he cried. "This is your fault! You wouldn't listen to what they said. The god knows you're a good officer in battle, but it's different out here. You can't stand against the enemy, because he's all around us, he's the ground under us and the air against us and the sun on our heads like a bloody branding iron. You've killed us all." Then, half-screaming as Teispas stood staring at him out of a still, dark face: "I'll say what I want! You think I care about rank now, about ash-cursed rules and regulations? What're you going to do, have me court-martialed? We're going to die on this filthy plain! We're all going to die!"

Teispas turned and walked away. Diasarta wept for a time, like a child, not bothering to cover his face. Then, doggedly, he resumed the task of dragging himself into the shelter.

The day rolled by. Gyalo tended Seiki. Diasarta slept. Gâbrios clung stubbornly to life, though he was delirious, muttering words that did not sound like any language Gyalo knew. Teispas sat beside the two water barrels left by the mutineers; he had estimated how much was in them and decided on a rationing system, a postponement of the inevitable that seemed pointless only if one did not know, as Gyalo did, the deeper reason behind it: He was giving Gyalo time to change his mind. His dark eyes never once met Gyalo's, and he did not speak a word. But Gyalo could still hear him—*our lives ... our lives ... our lives ...* Never had Gyalo hated anyone so greatly.

Late that afternoon, he felt the first chills and stomach cramps of manita insufficiency. Manita was habit-forming—an unintended side effect that had served the church well over the centuries, for if will were not enough to prevent vowbreaking, fear of manita withdrawal generally was. Harrowing accounts of withdrawal were part of Shaper training; Gyalo had a very precise idea of how sick the next two or three days would make him. He lay down on his side and pulled his knees to his chest, light-headed with dread. And yet, terribly, the sickness was welcome—for surely, in the wrack of pain and nausea, Teispas's stubborn voice would fall silent.

As the night drew on, an awful restlessness possessed his body, so that he wanted to dig his fingers into his skin and tear it off. The cramping grew worse. When he crawled outside the second time to vomit, Teispas broke the stony silence he had maintained since the previous night.

"What's the matter with you?"

"I'm ill. You threw away my manita." The sun was rising, penetrating the canvas. What Gyalo saw in Teispas's face made him laugh, even miserable as he was. "You didn't know, did you. Manita is addictive. Over the next few days I'm going to get so sick I won't even remember my own name. So much for your plans, eh?"

But the spiteful pleasure of witnessing Teispas's dismay was short-lived. Soon Gyalo was too sick even to crawl outside. He slipped in and out of consciousness, waking to retch, then falling back into tangled dreams. He was aware that someone cared for him—lifting him, cleaning him, giving him sips of water; but he could no longer remember where he was or who was with him.

He dreamed about his life, bright bits and pieces that rose out of the murk of his sickness, then sank again.

He was at his graduation ceremony, putting on the clothing of a vowed Âratist for the first time, bowing his head so his preceptor could fasten a simulacrum around his neck, swearing the Sixfold Vow: to renounce doubt, ignorance, greed, complacency, pride, and fear, the Six Failings that had caused the First Messenger to reject Ârata's summoning dream, and to replace them all with faith, as Marduspida had done when he accepted the burden of the god's call. His breath came short as he spoke the words; he had never felt so unworthy.

. He was a child, waiting behind the nunnery kitchen for his mother to bring him a napkinful of sweet moon cakes, specially baked for the planting festival of the Aspect Tane. His mother stroked his hair, and whispered to him: *Eat them all, they'll make you strong.* The cardamom odor of the cakes mingled with her scent of cinnamon, and he felt a love for her that was almost painful.

He was a postulant, resentment of manita's grip on his budding ability sharp within him, stealing down into the monastery basements to try his shaping skill in ways that were forbidden. He called up patterns he had secretly memorized—more and more, wilder and wilder, intoxicated by the Shaper vision of the world; until he lost control and cracked the flagstone where he knelt, and in terror unmade everything and fled upstairs again, certain his transgression could be read in his face.

He was at his Shaper ordination, his feet dyed red and his hands dyed yellow, chains of flowers around his neck, walking in procession with a dozen others through the courts of Rimpang monastery. The monastery's administrator wrapped each of them in a golden stole, and drew the letters of Ârata's name upon their foreheads in crimson paint, and received their vows, according to the seven tenets of the Doctrine of Baushpar: *I do affirm and believe that shaping is a gift given by Ârata, a reflection of his own creative power, and therefore divine and precious; and to this understanding I submit myself irrevocably and forever. I do affirm and believe that the use of shaping is governed by human will in service of human desire, and therefore fallible and dangerous; and to this understanding I submit myself irrevocably and forever . . .* He wept at the words, beautiful in his mouth. In all his life, he had never known such joy.

He was a child once more, and his father had come to take him off to be a soldier. He crouched terrified in an upstairs chamber, while his father pounded on the monastery door and shouted his name, and the monk assigned to care for him whispered, over and over: *There, there. You're a brave boy. You've made the right choice.* And he put his hands over his ears, for he could not bear the desperation in his father's cries.

He was on the pebble plain, watching as Teispas cast his manita upon the wind—a dozen different times, a dozen different ways. Sometimes he grabbed the pouch before Teispas did, burying his face in it, breathing in the drug as if it were air. Sometimes he missed the pouch, by inches or by yards, and felt again the horror of the loss. Once he did not try to save the drug at all, but simply stood and watched it go, and felt his heart go with it. *Our lives, our lives, our lives,* Teispas chanted as he emptied the pouch. *Our lives . . . our lives . . . our lives . . .*

And then for a time there were no dreams.

He woke, abruptly, to silence. The nausea was gone. He felt empty, as if the whole of him had been scoured out; he seemed to drift, light as paper, upon the quiet that surrounded him. *Am I dead?* he thought dreamily. *Is this the end of time; have I been wakened to be judged?*

He opened his eyes. What he saw shocked him, and he clamped them closed again. But only for a moment. Wonderingly, he looked out upon a world completely changed.

On one level, he saw what anyone would see—the rough canvas an armsreach above his face, the orange glare of sunset bleeding through it. But below, or above, or perhaps inside that ordinary reality lay another. He perceived the essential qualities of the canvas: the pattern of the cotton that composed it, what made it a thing that lasted, what made it a thing that decayed, how it could be pulled apart and scattered into nothingness. He perceived the true nature of the light: its undulant motion, the myriad hues that hid within it. This was the vision of a Shaper—a grasp of pattern, a command of form, an elemental comprehension of being and nonbeing, process and stability—but stronger, wider, deeper than he had ever known it in the grip of ceremony. All his life it had been tethered, even when he called it forth. But now it was free, fully free. He had not had any idea it would be like this.

For a time the wonder of it held him. But his thirst was too great to be ignored. The air under the canvas was noisome, thick with the smell of sickness and sweat and body waste. And the silence was beginning to seem ominous. How long had he been ill? Were the others alive?

His left arm was still bound to his chest. He struggled to raise himself on his right; it was difficult, for he was very weak. Moving brought him a sense of his own filthiness. The others lay around him, in the same positions they had occupied when he first fell sick. To the ordinary observer, they might have seemed dead, so still were they, so ravaged, their eyelids crusted and their lips cracked and swollen. But to Gyalo's Shaper sight, the light of life was visible, flickering green and blue and white and indigo and carmine. Even Gâbrios lived.

The water barrels also lay just as they had. Given the appearance of his companions, it did not seem likely there was any water left. But Gyalo's thirst commanded him. Effortfully he crawled toward Teispas, who did not stir as Gyalo eased the cup from beneath his hand. Gyalo looked into the open top of the first barrel. Nothing. He tried the second. Amazingly, there was a little water at the bottom. He reached in and scooped up as much as he could.

He raised the cup in both hands. The water glinted in the dim light; he saw it, and the pattern of it, and the pattern of the cup that held it. His thirst was awful. Yet something held him back. What if he did drink? He would only grow thirsty again, and soon, very soon, the water would be gone. And what of the others—could he slake his thirst while they lay dying? Or if he denied himself and let them drink, how much longer would they live? A day? Two? He did not think they would thank him for so small a mercy—given that he had the power to save them all.

He set the cup down. Everything had changed, and nothing had: He had slipped into dreams with this question, and found it waiting when he woke. *Choice has nothing to do with it,* he had said to Teispas, but he knew—had known—that his words were false. Everything was choice, even refusing to choose.

"Gyalo."

At first he thought he had imagined it. But when he turned, he saw that Seiki's eyes were open.

"Gyalo," she whispered again.

He picked up the water, and went to her on his knees. The blue-white of her lifelight, once so bright, was the faintest margin around her body. He arranged himself so he could lift her head onto his lap. He held the cup to her lips; she sipped a moment, weakly, then turned her face away.

"Gyalo . . . I must tell you something."

"What is it, Seiki?" He set the cup down. Gently, he smoothed the short, sweat-lank hair back from her face.

"I've been dreaming." She paused for breath. "The way I used to when I was a child, before the training." She gasped again. "Gyalo . . . the Brethren were right. There are people. A city. A city on a river, cut into the stone." She stopped, panting. "And there's a temple . . . a temple to Ârata like any temple in Galea . . . they aren't apostates, Gyalo, they are believers. And something else, something I couldn't see . . . but I thought . . . I thought that Ârata—"

She began to cough, a deep hoarse hacking that shook her from head to foot. The sound of it tore the silence. Diasarta thrashed and muttered, but did not wake; Gâbrios and Teispas never stirred. Blood bubbled from her mouth, and Gyalo turned her head so she could spit it out. At last she lay quiet, her eyes closed, breathing with great effort. Gyalo wiped the blood from her chin and cheeks with his fingers, and cleaned them on his own filthy clothing.

"Gyalo," she whispered.

"Yes."

"When you get back to Baushpar . . . will you make an offering for me . . . in the First Temple?"

Gyalo closed his eyes. "Yes."

"I would like it to be . . . a prayer ribbon . . . gold silk with red stripes. . . ." She paused, wheezing. "And a promise square with my name on it . . . and flowers . . . oh Gyalo, I can't remember . . . you know what's right. Will you do it for me?"

"Yes, Seiki. I'll make a beautiful offering for you."

She opened her eyes, rolling them upward so she could see him. "I did my best." The appeal in her face was like a child's. "I dreamed . . . as well as I could dream. I tried . . . my hardest. Didn't I?"

"You did, Seiki. Oh, you did."

"I don't want to die." Tears leaked out of her eyes, ran down her temples; Gyalo brushed them away. "Will you give me your blessing?"

"Go in light, child of Ârata," he whispered, his hand smoothing her hair. "May you sleep in peace. May you rise in glory. May you sit at Ârata's right hand in paradise. Go in light, child of Ârata."

She was quiet for a time, her breathing a little easier. Then, very faintly: "You were right . . . not to save us."

Four more breaths. Her lifelight shivered, like a wind-blown flame, and went out.

For a long time Gyalo sat with her head on his knees, as night fell and the world grew dark. Around him the others' lifelights glimmered faintly; he could see his own as well, a soft pearlescence illuminating Seiki's still features. Seiki knew, as Teispas could never know, why Gyalo could not break his vow. And yet in this moment, he saw he could not keep it. His shaping was free within him. He could not choose to withhold it, though he knew what that choice meant for him, in this life and after.

He knew something else as well, knew it through the quality of his character that had forced him all his life to turn unflinching toward the truth. He was not strong enough to allow himself to die.

The decision made, a sense of urgency gripped him. Gently he shifted Seiki's head from his knees. He picked up the cup and drained the rest of the water; the relief of drinking brought him strength. He crawled toward the edge of the canvas shelter, pausing briefly to tear at the bindings that held his arm to his chest, for he could no longer bear to be hindered in that way. The shoulder was still painful, but it felt better free.

Outside the shelter, he had to try twice before he could gain his feet. For a moment he stood swaying. The world around him was alive with meaning. All was motion—the eternal exchange of stasis and dissolution, the unceasing dance of becoming, being, ending. He saw the pattern of each piece of wreckage, the pattern of the larger entity they composed; beyond that, he sensed, were greater patterns still . . . as great as the world . . . as great as the universe. . . . It was overwhelming, this unfettered vision. He could barely comprehend it.

He staggered out across the pebble plain. He changed the patterns of the air as he passed through it; a turbulent wake stretched out behind him, a swath of swirling color. It was like dreaming, like drowning, to move this way. At last his legs buckled, and he fell to his knees.

He did not, he realized, know what to do.

Shaper apprentices began their training with the manipulation of light and air. This was easier than working with solid matter, and also safer, because it produced only illusion. Next the apprentices moved to unforming, the banishing of matter into nothingness, for the best way to understand pattern was to unravel it. Last learned was the delicate art of transforming, the skill that lay at the heart of Âratist ceremony. But it was a narrow training, meant only to fit a Shaper's ability to the needs of ritual. Everything Gyalo had ever shaped was small; despite his secret experimentations, he knew only a handful of patterns well enough to re-create them, out of all the millions in the world. The largest and most complex shaping he had ever achieved was a lump of granite that filled his cupped palms.

Water's pattern he knew, from the water in the Communion ceremony. But a palmful of water, two palmfuls, were not enough. He needed a water source—something that would flow, something that would stay. Might it be possible, not to make water, but to free it from the earth? Water flowed underground elsewhere in the Burning Land—why not beneath the pebble plain? Unforming was easier than transforming . . . if he could unform the rock down to where the water lay, surely it would well upward, as it did when trenches were dug at the low point of a dry river course.

He tried to push himself back on his heels, but his arms gave way, and he collapsed onto his side.. Pattern rippled around him. If he waited much longer, he would not have the strength. *Ârata,* he cried dizzily, silently, to the god who did not hear him, *forgive me. I could not make a different choice.*

He breathed deeply, as he did in meditation. He fixed his eyes on the plain before him, opening himself to the configuration of it, feeling for the places where, grasped, it might be pulled apart. He called up all the will he had and reached out.

His Shaper senses met the substance of the plain. It resisted, a thing he had never known before, for he had never before tried to unmake only a part of something, or to unmake so much at once. It was like a blow; he felt his teeth sink into his lower lip. He held on, hooking his will into the pattern of the rock, forcing separation. There was an echoing crack, a blue-white flash. And another. And another and another and another, fusing into a single sound, a single light, sinking as the rock unmade. Gyalo's senses sank with it; he no longer felt his body, his weakness, the plain beneath him. He *was* the light, *was* the sound—pure will, pure power, arrowing downward like a diver. It was joy, and more: It was recognition. For the first time in his life, he knew himself entire.

A final, enormous rending, and all resistance vanished. A titanic force seized him, flinging him upward. For just an instant he saw the stars, spinning toward him; and then his Shaper senses tore loose and he was inside himself again, lying on his face, his arms splayed outward. His heart pounded so he could hardly breathe. The taste of blood was in his mouth. And all around him, there was water.

He lifted his head. The surface of the plain had split. A plume of water fountained upward, raining down again like a summer storm. In the moonlight it was alive with color—violet, green, gold, red. Like light, water held every hue within itself, and his Shaper sight encompassed them all.

I did it, he thought. *I opened the earth and made water flow.*

He rolled onto his back. He opened his mouth and let the water fill it. It seemed the sweetest thing he had ever tasted, and the most bitter. He was truly delivered into the wasteland of his future. What would he do with it? Return in disgrace to Baushpar and live out his years under arrest as an apostate? Exile himself within the Burning Land? Follow Seiki's Dream across the plain, to those who had chosen as he had? Each possibility seemed equally empty, equally meaningless.

A shadow stirred at the edge of his vision. Turning his head, he saw Teispas. The captain knelt, face flung back. His dark skin gleamed with wet. His indigo light flickered around him, not much stronger than Seiki's before she died. His features, in profile, seemed oddly contorted. Gyalo realized he was weeping.

"This is what you wanted," Gyalo said, hoarsely. "Are you satisfied?"

Teispas turned to him. Gyalo had never thought to see such an expression on that hard, closed face, the look of a man who had accepted death and found himself delivered.

"I left it for you," he said, his voice just audible above the pounding water. "The water in the barrel. I hoped you'd wake. I hoped you wouldn't be able to watch us die."

Rage burst within Gyalo. Nothing else could have brought him to his feet; nothing else could have propelled him across the distance that separated him from Teispas. He seized the captain's tattered shirt in both fists. He bent until he was a fingerbreadth from the margin of Teispas's light.

"I have never hated anyone in my life as I hate you," he said, softly. "I could unmake the rock you kneel on. I could let you go and close the earth above your head. Do you believe it?" He shook the captain. "Do you?"

"Yes." Teispas met his gaze, unflinching. "But you could already have killed me, by doing nothing. You won't do it now."

"If I could have chosen not to save you, I would have."

"I know."

"You bear the burden, too. Don't think you'll be forgiven, at the end of time. Don't think you'll escape Ârata's judgment."

"Ârata is dead." All Teispas's guard, all his control, was gone. His face, shining with the colors of water, was utterly naked. "He died of his wounds centuries ago. We are all that's left."

Gyalo was so shocked that for a moment he could not move. Then he released his grip. Teispas tipped forward, just catching himself before he fell. Gyalo walked away, staggering. Pattern reeled around him, overwhelming, incomprehensible.

"Brother," Teispas called after him, then again. "Brother Gyalo!"

"Don't call me that," Gyalo said. "I'm not an Âratist now."

He did not know if Teispas heard him.

Part II

THE DREAMER'S PROMISE

— 6 —

Once, there had been many of them, the hunters in Axane's Dream. They had carried great quantities of baggage and equipment loaded onto scores of hump-backed, long-necked beasts, and they had moved across the Burning Land as if nothing could stop them. But now there were only four. Their animals were gone. Their tattered clothing and their weapons and a few bags and bundles were all they had with them. They had crossed the stone barrens, and reached the Plains of Blessing; they lay among the grasses in a space they had flattened down, sleeping.

Axane had come upon them from the air. She always flew in her Dreams—soaring, swooping, untethered from the earth and from Refuge, the things that bound her when she was awake. Now she wanted to go closer. She was untrained, and could not always make her Dreams obey her; but this time will and Dream were one, and she drifted down like a falling feather.

One of the hunters was long-limbed and harsh; he slept with his eyes tight closed, as if unconsciousness were an effort. Another lay on a makeshift litter, his head wrapped in grimy bandages. The third was scarred across the cheek, his left leg bound to splints; he did not sleep, but kept watch, his back propped against a bundle. The fourth . . . the fourth she recognized, from the first of her visions of these men. He looked like no one she had ever seen in the flesh, though she had often glimpsed such faces in her Dreams—light-skinned, dark-haired, with broad high cheekbones and eyes shaped like melon seeds. He was curled on his side, one arm flung above his head.

What had happened to them? Had they been banished from the main body of the party? Or had some disaster struck, leaving only these survivors?

She hovered above the light-skinned man, gazing down upon his sleeping face. This was not ordinary reality—the air was the air of Dreams, rippling with strange currents and touched with unearthly color, and the world around her was a Dream-world, its perspectives oddly skewed, its edges shading into void. Yet he seemed very close, very solid, as if not just her mind but her body floated there. If she drew near, would he sense her?

As if in answer he stirred, and rolled onto his back. His tunic, torn at the neck, pulled apart, revealing something on his chest, something shining—

Axane recoiled in shock. Her will broke, releasing her violently upward, into the Dream-sky. Abruptly, she was awake.

She lay on her back, eyes wide, heart pounding. Around her bulked the real-world landscape of her night chamber, shadowed in the light of a single oil lamp. It was as ordinary, as familiar as her own body. But in that moment, the final image of her Dream still burning in her mind, it seemed as strange as any place her sleep had ever taken her.

Had she truly seen the Blood of Ârata upon his chest, this stranger who hunted her people?

It had been a brief glimpse, cut short by astonishment. Perhaps she was mistaken. But in her mind's eye the image was vivid and distinct—a gold chain supporting a tangle of gold wires, and inside them a golden, fire-hearted gem. What else took that form, except the Blood? Might it be a Dream-symbol, one of those images that did not literally represent reality but only pointed to some aspect of it? But her untrained dreaming was nothing like the complex, abstract visions of proper Dreamers. Within the framework of her bird persona and the shifted perspectives of her sleeping mind, she dreamed straightforwardly of actual people and things—a fact she had spent careful time confirming, some years back.

What could it mean, then, this stranger arriving from the Burning Land with the Blood of Ârata around his neck?

Her father, or any of the people of Refuge, would not need to ask that question. But Axane did not believe as they did, had not believed that way in years. Unbidden, she heard her father's voice: *Risaryâsi's Promise is fulfilled,* he said inside her head. *The Next Messenger has come, to lead our people out of exile.*

Which would mean, she thought, *that for six years I've been a blasphemer....*

No, she told herself firmly. *It cannot be.* If indeed it was the Blood on the light-skinned man's chest, it had some other meaning. How could it be otherwise? If her people's teachings were wrong, how could Risaryâsi's Promise be fulfilled?

She had first dreamed the hunters four months ago. Soaring above the Burning Land, she glimpsed a light below. She did not will herself to investigate, but all at once, in one of the dizzying shifts her Dreams often imposed on her, she was there, floating like a moth over pitched tents, stacked baggage, the glow of fires.

It was a camp, she realized, like the camps the hunters of Refuge made when they went off in search of game. But what hunters could these be, so deep within the desert? There were men at the Land's northern edge—she had seen them in her Dreams, men in chains who dug into the earth and lived in a vast stone structure at the foot of the Range of

Clouds. But beyond that shallow fringe the Land was empty of humanity, a place so hostile that only Shapers, or those led by Shapers, could survive it—at least, so said the tales of the First Twenty-Three, and in her nighttime journeys she had seen nothing to make her doubt it.

Wondering, she drifted past a tent. A man was in the act of crawling through the opening. He was clad in loose garments that left his sinewy arms bare; his face—slant-eyed, high-cheekboned, entirely unlike the faces of her people— was furred with an uneven growth of beard and haggard as if with illness. He straightened and stood a moment, swaying; it seemed to Axane, for just an instant, that his eyes looked into hers, as if he saw or sensed her Dream-self, though of course that could not be. He rubbed his hands across his cheeks, shook his head, and set off between the tents. At the camp's edge he stopped before a pit dug into the ground, and began to fumble with his clothing. Axane pulled away then, rising into the Dream-sky and soaring on, back to Refuge.

The lack of training that made her Dreams so literal made it impossible for her reliably to instruct herself to dream again of these hunters, or whatever they were. But her curiosity was powerfully stirred, and she was sure it was not just chance that brought her to them five times more, as they made their way across the Burning Land. Usually the camp was the same—banked fires, closed tents, no sign of life apart from a lone sentry and the strange humped beasts tethered around the perimeter. But in her fourth Dream she came upon two men sharing a pipe at the camp's margin. They spoke her own language, with the odd accent her dreaming had taught her to recognize, and their faces were like the faces of her people.

One of them said; "Do you think there's anything to this journey?"

The other shrugged. "What's the difference what I think?"

"I'm curious. D'you really think there can be descendants of vowed Âratists living in the Land?"

The shock of it almost caused Axane to lose her grip upon the Dream.

"Even if there are," said the other, "we'll never find them.

All we know's that they're south. *South!* What's that mean, in a place this size? It's like looking for one tree in a bloody forest."

"That's what I think. We're hunting shadows. We'll go as far as our supplies will let us, then we'll turn tail and crawl back to Arsace, with nothing to show for it but sunburn."

"Can't be soon enough for me. It's a filthy place, the Land. I don't care if it's blasphemy to say so. The sand, the vermin, the ash-cursed heat—every day a new disaster."

"Think about how you'll spend your bounty," the first man said dryly. "That's what I do."

Axane had lain awake that night, her heart racing, her mind on fire with speculation. Why were the hunters seeking Refuge? How did they even know it existed? There were Dreamers in the outside world, she knew; could it be that there were some like herself, not tied to one place—could they have dreamed of Refuge, as she dreamed of the kingdoms of Galea? But the Dreams of Refuge's Dreamers defended it, weaving a veil of illusion to deflect the observation of demons and the malice of the Enemy. Should they not, then, also deflect other Dreamers' Dreams? There was little about her people's faith that Axane had not questioned, but it had never occurred to her to doubt the efficacy of the Dream-veil.

If the hunters really knew so little about Refuge's location, chances were the second man was right: They would pass it by. The Land was vast, and Refuge well concealed. But if luck were with them . . .

There was no one else to see what she had seen. Refuge's Dreamers did not range across the world, as she did; all their strength and skill was used to keep their sleeping minds in place. They would not dream the hunters until they were nearly at the cleft. If the hunters' intent was harmful, that would be much too late.

But if she gave warning, she must reveal herself as a Dreamer. And that was something no one knew.

In the end she decided on a better way. The hunters were still distant—she knew this from the knowledge of the Land she had gained in her Dream-travels. She would give them time to draw closer, then begin to mount the cleft twice a day, morning and evening, to scan the Plains for intruders. From the heights she could see all the way to the stone barrens—a whole day's travel, time enough for Refuge's Shapers to prepare a defense, if defense were needed. Who would know it had not simply been coincidence that brought her to the summit at the proper moment? More than that, if the council saw the intruders for themselves, they would have no choice but to believe they were real.

She had climbed to the summit yesterday evening after supper, and sat there till the sun went down. She had seen nothing. But she had been watching for a large party; if there were only those four left, she might have missed them on the vastness of the Plains.

Their faces returned to her, starved and battered, and she wondered again what had brought them to such a state. When they woke, where would they go? Across the river Revelation to the southern mountains? Along Revelation to the western sea? Or maybe they were close enough to glimpse the light of what lay at the terminus of the cleft—to glimpse it, and follow it to Refuge.

And if they did, and her people saw what the light-skinned man wore around his neck . . . She caught her breath.

The quiet of her room broke upon a great hollow bellowing—the sound of the calling horns, by which the Shapers who kept Refuge's sand clocks daily marked the hours of rising, worship, and sleep. All over Refuge, men and women and children were rising from their beds, spreading their meditation squares, kneeling to speak the morning Affirmation. Axane lay still, listening to the sound of her own breathing. It was her secret act of rebellion against the customs of her people: In the mornings, she did not pray.

At last she threw back the quilt and got out of bed, the dry air of Labyrinth chilly on her skin. From the flame of her little night-light, she kindled the standing lamps set around the

walls. Much of the room's furnishing—the wide bed, the
table and stool, the chest, the brazier and lamps, the clay
pitcher and basin—was standard community equipment, du-
plicated in every chamber in Refuge. But there was also
much she had made or chosen herself, from the wall-
concealing hangings woven of silvery grass gathered on the
Plains of Blessing, to the coiled matting braided and sewn of
the same material, to the quilt on the bed, whose rich night-
shade purple dye she had mixed herself. The twin leaf-
carved household chests had been an intent-gift from her
father, meant as the first furnishing for an apartment of her
own. Things had not worked out that way, though, and so
here they sat.

Discarding her bedgown, she cleaned her body at the
basin and pulled on an ankle-length chemise, made of the
lightest linen that could be woven from Shaper-flax. Over it
went a shorter linen tunic, dyed a deep shade of green and
tied below the breasts with an indigo sash. Most things in
Refuge were utilitarian, as befitted use-objects, but the
plants and minerals of the Plains of Blessing yielded dozens
of glowing dyes, and the clothworkers of Refuge made lavish use of them. She dragged a comb through the curling
thickness of her hair and wound the smoothed tresses atop
her head, fixing them in place with bone pins. Finished, she
examined herself briefly in her small beaten-metal mirror—
a purely practical inspection, for she had long ago resigned
herself to the fact that she was not and never would be pretty.

She laced on her sandals, and from the smaller of the leaf-
carved chests took two packets of infusing herbs, one for
pain and one for appetite. With the packets and a wooden
tray, she slipped past the curtain that closed off her room and
into the passage beyond. To her right, shrouded openings
marked the chambers of her half brothers and half sisters,
her father's second partner, her father's wife, and her father.
Past his room lay the apartment's entrance, and beyond it,
the soaring spaces of Labyrinth, where all of Refuge except
its ordained Shapers lived.

Labyrinth was a great cave, carved by Refuge's original Shapers into the sandstone of the river cleft where Refuge lay concealed. Down either side ran three tiers of galleries, their sheer edges guarded with rope netting. Private apartments led off them, ten to a tier, each with a firepot beside its curtained entrance. Axane's father's apartment occupied the midpoint of the first tier; she emerged directly onto Labyrinth's floor. Its odor greeted her—woodsmoke and cooking, interwoven, as everything in Refuge was, with the dry scent of rock and rock dust. Through the colossal entranceway she could see the red cliff wall on the southern side of the river Revelation, and above it, a slice of morning blue sky.

Preparations were under way at the fire pits that ran down Labyrinth's center. Cooks stirred pots of grain porridge and turned out rounds of flatbread, a staple of every meal, with practiced speed. Trainees cut and arranged a variety of fruits on platters, and set out clay bowls and bone spoons on the plank tables in the eating gallery, a large space hollowed into the back of Labyrinth, with thick pillars left in place to support the ceiling. Axane stocked her tray with dishes and utensils from the store at the gallery's back and carried it over to the fire pits, where she helped herself to food and dipped boiling water to pour over the herb mixtures she had measured into two large cups, all the while making obligatory morning small talk with the cooks. She placed clay lids over the cups to keep their contents hot and returned to her father's apartment.

In the passage she encountered Vivanishâri, Habrâmna's second partner, her brood of children at her heels. Vivanishâri, an unmanifest Shaper of the Mandapâxan bloodline, had been sixteen when Habrâmna declared intent for her, just four years older than Axane. She and Axane had known one another before the declaration, as everyone in Refuge knew everyone else; they had not been friends, but they had not been enemies either. That had changed, with Vivanishâri's pregnancy and subsequent installation in Habrâmna's household, for Vivanishâri was jealous of the favor Habrâmna showed his plain, unmarried, unmanifest daughter. Fearing to displease him by openly displaying her dislike, she satisfied herself with small acts of spite—as now, sweeping past as if Axane were not there, forcing Axane to press against the wall to avoid spilling the contents of the tray. Her children—four boys and twin girls, all of whom had inherited Vivanishâri's lustrous black curls and tendency to stoutness—followed their mother's example.

Swallowing her irritation as she always did, for Vivanishâri's pettiness was not worth the breach of her carefully cultivated façade of calm, Axane resumed her interrupted journey, halting before the curtain of her father's wife, Narstame.

"One is here," she called, the formula for entrance. "It's me, stepmother. I've brought your breakfast."

A rustling of bedcovers, and then a soft: "Enter."

A single lamp burned on a table by the bed, illuminating Narstame's dark face and odd yellow-amber eyes. Under the piled coverlets, her withered body seemed as slight as a child's. The air smelled of prolonged human occupancy, and of sickness.

"Good morning, stepmother."

"Good morning, stepdaughter."

Axane propped extra bolsters at the head of the bed and helped Narstame sit up. Narstame's eyes followed her as she positioned the bed tray and set out breakfast dishes, but the old woman did not speak. She had always been distant, even toward the many sons and daughters she had borne Habrâmna; now, as her body wasted and each day robbed her of strength, she seemed to be turning slowly to stone. Axane pitied her, but that was all. She felt no bond to her stepmother, who had cared for her dutifully after her true mother vanished into the House of Dreams, but without real affection.

"I'll be back in a little while," she said. Narstame, her twiglike fingers wrapped around the cup, nodded.

Axane did not call before ducking past the curtain of her father's room: She knew he would be up and waiting for her. His chamber, originally made for Risaryâsi and occupied by each of Refuge's leaders after her, was larger than the others. There was matting on the floor to soften the chilly rock, but Habrâmna liked the striated multicolored patterning of Labyrinth's sandstone, and the walls—as smooth and rounded as the river-carved contours of the House of Dreams, for Shaper stoneworking could not produce sharp edges—were bare. Apart from the basic furnishing, the room contained only a large round table set about with six high-backed chairs, and a bloodgrain cabinet polished to a soft gloss.

Habrâmna had fewer personal belongings, perhaps, than anyone in Refuge. But this appearance of asceticism was in a way deceptive, for Axane knew her father believed himself the owner of something much larger: Refuge itself. In truth he served at Refuge's sufferance, for he was an elected leader, chosen by community vote from among the eleven members of Refuge's governing council, and could be replaced if he displeased those he led. But in his own mind, he ruled by right. Because he was a good ruler, these opposed viewpoints had never been tested. He had guided Refuge for sixteen years: the longest tenure of any of its leaders, only six years less than Axane's entire life.

He sat at the table in the capacious chair that had been specially made for him. He smiled to see her, and held out his big hands with their swollen knuckles. She set down the tray and bent to receive his kiss.

"How is your stepmother?" he asked, as he always did.

"I left her comfortable." She looked into his face, concerned. "You look tired this morning, Father. Did you sleep?"

"A little." He shifted in his chair, grimacing. Halfway through his fifth decade, he was still a powerful-looking man, with dark, burnished skin and a high-arched nose (both of which, to her misfortune, she had inherited), and eyes as

black and sharp as the obsidian from which the craftsmen of
Refuge made the community's cutting tools. For much of his
life he had been troubled by inflammation of the joints,
which in recent years had become severe enough to handi-
cap him. He could no longer walk without effort, and it was
painful for him to grip and lift heavy objects or to perform
fine actions, such as writing. Because he had always been a
slow-moving, deliberate man, few people besides Axane realized how impaired he truly was. This private morning meal
was a concession to his affliction, for he was in great discomfort just after rising.

"Drink your tea." She set the pain-relieving brew before
him, then went around the room to kindle the lamps. The
chamber sprang to light, its sinuous bands of russet and orange and bone and amber glowing like a desert sunrise. "If
you need it later, I'll make up poultices for you."

"The tea will be enough. You spend too much time caring
for me, daughter." But he smiled, to show it was not a rebuke. "Share the meal with me today. There's much more
here than I need."

She had a dozen things to do, but he often made this request, and she was always prepared for it. "Yes, Father," she
said, and seated herself across from him.

He took the bowl of porridge and pushed the plate of fruit
and bread toward her, waving it away when she offered it
back. She listened as he spoke in his measured manner of
the affairs of Refuge, between slow mouthfuls: the blight af-
fecting the sapona bushes from whose leaves the healers
made a tincture to ease the pain of childbirth; a dispute between two of the senior carpenters; the preparation for refurbishment of the Temple paintings, undertaken every decade
and just about to begin again; his pleasure that Randarid, son
of one of his sons by Narstame, had just manifested as a
Shaper, bringing the total of Refuge's manifest Shapers to
nineteen. Over the years of his growing dependence on Axane, it had become his habit to ruminate aloud like this—not
to gain the benefit of her advice, which she would not have

presumed to offer, but as a way of giving form to his thoughts. She also served as his scribe, writing out orders and schedules and reports at his dictation, sitting by his side at council meetings and taking notes. Still, she suspected it would have shocked the council to know how freely he spoke to her.

At last he set down his spoon, pushed his bowl aside, and folded his knotted hands before him on the table.

"There is a matter I would discuss with you, Axane."

His expression was grave. She felt a stir of apprehension. "Yes, Father?"

"You are a dutiful, obedient, loving daughter. Ârata knows I'd like nothing better than to keep you by my side forever. But I cannot continue to be so indulgent with myself, or with you. I haven't pressed you before now, Axane. But the time has come. You're twenty-two years old. You must fulfill your duty to Refuge. You must have children."

"But I'm barren, Father." Axane's heart had begun to pound. "It's been proved."

. "What, by your time with Ardinixa? Nonsense."

"But Father, he and Biryâsi have a child. I was with him for the entire year, and I never conceived."

"It took him nearly that long to get a child on Biryâsi. And there's been no other, though they've been married two years now. No, daughter." He shook his head. "It's as likely his fault as yours that you never became pregnant by him."

"Father, I'm barren. I'm certain of it. It would be wrong for me to declare intent. To . . . to waste a man's time that way, when he could be getting children on a fertile woman."

"Axane." Habrâmna's face softened. "My dearest child. Don't think I'm not grateful for your care—these past years, with my difficulty, you've been a treasure. A joy. But it is not right for you to sacrifice your happiness in order to tend me. I'm not so selfish—and even if I were, I must think of Refuge. You know the vision, the task, that guides us. You know our purpose here in hiding: to re-create the human race. More than any others before us, we must honor the Third Foundation of the Way and turn our energies to increase. I cannot allow you to exempt yourself, no matter what the reason."

"But Father—"

"No, Axane. My mind is set. Yesterday, I told Râvar that he may declare intent for you."

"*What?*"

"I believe you heard me, daughter."

"You've consented . . . to an intent . . . on my behalf?"

"I have."

"But Father . . ." For a moment she lost the words. "Father, I have the right to choose for myself! You can't . . . you can't just decide for me—"

"I must." His black eyes held hers; there was far too much knowledge in them. "For if I leave the choice to you, you will find a way never to choose."

"Râvar's only eighteen, Father," Axane said, desperate. "I'm four years older. He deserves a wife his own age. A wife who's worthy of him."

"You are my daughter. You are worthy of any man."

"Did he ask you for this? Was this his idea?"

"No, Axane. He did come to me, but only to beg me to speak for him, to try and sway your heart. It was I who decided he would declare."

"Father . . . Father, I'll find another man. I swear I will. I know you're right—I know it's my duty. Just let it not be Râvar. Please. Don't make me keep intent with Râvar."

"Ah, daughter." Habrâmna shook his head. "Can you not see the gift I give you? A man who desires you, a manifest Shaper—the most gifted Shaper, perhaps, in all our history, more powerful even than Mandapâxa himself. And you— you have the blood of Cyras, and the blood of Risaryâsi, to whom Ârata spoke in Dreams. You will breed manifest children, I know it. You must search your heart; you must find gladness in this. And if you cannot . . ." He paused. "If you cannot, you will still do as I bid you, because you are my obedient child. Is that not so, Axane?"

Silence fell, the thick, tactile silence that is only possible inside a great weight of rock. Habrâmna watched her, his black eyes unblinking, his face as stern as the image of Ârata Warrior in the Temple core. It was rare, very rare, that he turned this regard on her. And yet it was always there, behind the smile and the tender looks. She loved her father, and knew he loved her—loved her as he loved no person living. But she also knew that, like Refuge, he considered her his possession, to be used according to his will. Her own desires were irrelevant.

"Yes, Father," she whispered.

A smile broke across his face, so tender, so joyful, that it made her want to weep, or scream: She did not know which. He held out his twisted hands. She got to her feet and knelt by his chair, and let him fold her into his arms. She had imagined, before this moment, that she knew what bitterness was. She had thought she knew what it felt like to be imprisoned. But she had not known.

After a moment he set her away from him. "You're a jewel of a daughter, Axane. No man ever had a better."

Her face felt like stone. She did not trust herself to speak.

He pressed his lips to her forehead and released her. She got to her feet. Turning to the table, she began placing breakfast dishes on the tray.

"Has Râvar said . . . when he will declare?" she asked, not looking at him.

"At the next registration."

"I see." She finished with the tray. "Do you need anything else, Father?"

"Not at the moment. Come to me after the noon meal—I may want you for dictation."

"Yes, Father."

She took the tray and left the room. In the hall she passed Sarispes, oldest of her half siblings by Vivanishâri. His mouth stretched in a grin; he drew breath to make some remark. But she cast him a look of such uncharacteristic fury that the smirk dropped off his face, and he passed her by in silence.

—7—

Like a sleeper, Axane went about her morning tasks. She made the beds, emptied the chamber pots into the latrine crevasse at Labyrinth's rear, filled buckets from the cistern at Labyrinth's entrance to replenish the water pitchers, settled Narstame for the day. At last she returned to her room to begin a second fair copy of next month's task rotation schedule, from her notes of her father's dictation. The creation of records was an obsession for Habrâmna, who believed it his duty to leave a complete account of Refuge for succeeding generations—every document, with the exception of the private journals he kept in the bloodgrain cabinet in his room, must be written out twice, once for use and once for preservation.

But she could not concentrate. The small space of her chamber, ordinarily a sanctuary from the watching eyes and constant work of Refuge, oppressed her. She sat staring miserably at the wall hangings until, abruptly, she remembered she had not yet climbed the cleft to look out across the Plains of Blessing. She had dreamed only the four hunters last night, but that did not mean the others were not out there somewhere. She threw down her pen, jumped to her feet, and quit the apartment.

Outside Labyrinth she turned left, up the wide ledge that ran the length of the cleft's north wall. Below, Revelation leaped violently toward the Plains, its roaring song so familiar she barely heard it. The cleft walls soared above her, the sky trapped between them like a strip of azure cloth; the morning was barely half-gone, but already the air in this deep place was simmeringly hot. She passed the huge rock-carved face of the Temple, then the screened opening of the Shaper quarters, where the ordained Shapers and the older trainees lived. Perhaps fifty steps beyond, where the cleft wall curved inward, a ladderlike stairway was formed into the stone.

She knotted up her skirts and began to climb. She counted as she went, a habit left over from childhood: one hundred, and the sheer wall acquired an easier slope. One hundred sixty-eight brought her to the colony of fingerleaf bushes rooted in a crevice, two hundred nine to a deep fissure that paralleled the steps, exhaling chilly air. At two hundred seventy-three, she emerged upon the summit.

The summit's pebbled sandstone surface was gently rounded, and about a hundred strides across. At Axane's back, the cleft's south wall bulked across the gap made by Revelation, and beyond it a series of time-sculpted cliffs, rising toward mountains that ran east and west as far as the eye could follow. To the north stretched the great panorama of the Plains of Blessing, furred with silvery grass like the flank of a lounging beast. At the Plains' northmost boundary lay the dead expanse of the stone barrens, their wind-polished surface blinding even from this distance with reflected sunlight. To the west, where the cleft sloped down to the Plains, Revelation wound a sinuous path toward the ocean, its banks lined with shadowy stands of timber. East rose more cliffs and, closer, the terminus of the cleft. At night the golden radiance of what was hidden there was clearly visible, massing like mist above the summit, but in the high day the greater brilliance of the sun eclipsed it.

During Refuge's first decade, watchers had been posted here day and night, ceaselessly scanning the Plains for intruders. After that they were not needed, for according to Risaryâsi's revelation the armies of Ârdaxcasa had destroyed themselves, and there were no longer any human enemies to come in search of Refuge. These days, the summit was used only for whitening cloth and drying meat. Desiccating lines and bleaching frames occupied the area to Axane's left, and the two great pulleys by which such things were raised and lowered. Even before she dreamed the strangers, she had often come up here when her time was free, to be alone.

She crossed to the summit's northern edge, unmindful of the dizzy drop to the Plains below. Shading her eyes with her hand, she scanned the horizon as those early watchers had. The sun bore down upon her head and shoulders; a dry breeze blew, carrying with it the spicy scent of the bitterbark trees that grew along the banks of Revelation, molding her gown to her body and plucking tendrils from her carefully coiled hair. As far as she looked, she saw only grass and sky and trees and light. The Plains were empty.

Still she stood, staring west, along Revelation's languorous course. Her Dream hung vivid in her mind. Where were they now, the light-skinned man and his companions?

Duty called; she knew she should go down again. But just then she could not bear the thought of confinement between rock walls. Crossing to the bleaching frames, she ducked into the shade beneath. The linen made a billowing roof above her head, just high enough to allow her to sit upright. She drew her knees up and rested her chin upon them, gazing north.

Briefly, in the climb to the summit, she had forgotten her father's words. But they returned to her now, and her thoughts began again their dreary circling.

She had not grown up fearing union with a man. It was inevitable, after all: a declaration of intent sometime after her sixteenth birthday, a pregnancy, a marriage. Plain and quiet as she was, she was still her father's daughter, and she had had many suitors. In the end she chose Ardinixa, an unmanifest Shaper of her father's bloodline, the Cyran, but sufficiently distanced by marriage to be acceptable.

She did not love Ardinixa; but it was a practical match, and she had thought to be satisfied with it. Nothing could have prepared her for her hatred of the experience. Not the physical aspects—those she liked well enough—but the fact of being tied to him, unable to escape. It was not enough for him that they spent every night together in her room; he wanted also to sit with her at meals, walk with her in the evening, take her with him on hunting trips. Long accustomed to solitude by reason of her secrets, she was burdened both by his intrusion and his assumption of his right to intrude. If she became pregnant, she saw, this was the way it would always be. He would push his way into every moment. She would never be free of him.

Her courses had never been regular, like those of other girls; several times she feared she was indeed with child. But it was never so. That, for him a source of grief and frustration, was for her another step toward deliverance, and she could barely hide her relief each time the blood came. He was angry when they parted, as if her failure to conceive had been deliberate; she knew, though, that the anger masked pain. He was happy now, with Biryâsi and their little boy. He and Axane were cordial when they met, as if the bitterness of their failed union were not common knowledge.

There had been offers since then, but she had refused them all. Her year with Ardinixa had made her certain she never wished to marry; it had also given her good reason not to try again. Refuge's imperative to increase, which required a woman to prove her fertility before she could wed, prohibited her from marrying if she showed herself barren. Yet Ardinixa's difficulty in impregnating Biryâsi, as well as the couple's inability to produce another child, had not escaped Axane, or anyone else in Refuge. She might be assumed to be infertile, but not beyond a doubt.

She set herself to become essential to her increasingly afflicted father, reasoning that if she could make her single status as important to him as it was to her, he would not press her into another intent. It cost her a certain amount of guilt to manipulate him so; yet, she told herself, her care for him was not false, for she would have done the same even if nothing were at stake. Habrâmna relied on her enormously now, in matters both trivial and important. Beyond occasional remarks about passing time, he had never seriously urged her to take another suitor. Even so, she had always known she might receive an order like the one he had given her today. But the removal of her choice—that she would never have expected.

She felt anger rise, trapped and bitter. Her father's great ambition, his desire to beget manifest Shapers for Refuge, blinded him. It was an absurdly unsuitable match. Râvar was as gifted as he was beautiful, a man who should certainly produce as many children as possible over the course of his lifetime; while she was plain, and four years older, and possibly barren. His passionate pursuit of her was considered folly, not just by half the eligible females in Refuge but by their parents, and she knew her resolute resistance was regarded with approval.

How they all will hate me now, she thought.

There must be some escape. The match would certainly be greeted with condemnation; perhaps it would force Habrâmna to change his mind. It was more than a month to the next registration, the quarterly ceremony at which intents were formally pledged and recorded—surely she could think of something before then. And if she could not . . . *Oh Árata*, she thought, though with at least half of herself she did not believe the god could hear her, *let me truly be barren. Let me not conceive. For if he gets a child on me . . .* She felt her breath come short with dread. She would be with him forever then. His sharp Shaper gaze would follow her everywhere, probing at her mask of Forcelessness, prying at her secrets. He sensed she kept them—it was part of what drew him to her.

She closed her eyes, thinking of secrets.

It had begun with her mother, a manifest Dreamer of the Risaryâsan bloodline. As was allowed for men of the Shaper and Dreamer bloodlines, Axane's father had taken her as first partner when it became apparent that none of his children by his wife Narstame would manifest either ability. It was a love match—or so Axane always believed, for her mother was a widow of twenty-six with two half-grown daughters of her own, rather than a ripe virgin as most partners were. And when the union failed to produce children other than Axane, Habrâmna did not set Axane's mother aside, but kept her in his household until she reached the age of thirty-five, and, as all manifest Dreamers must, entered the House of Dreams for good.

Axane was then eight years old. With the obstinacy of childhood, she had convinced herself that her mother would not go—that she would refuse, or that Habrâmna, elected Refuge's leader two years before, would use his authority to keep his first partner by him. Even at the celebration of farewell she had been sure her father was only waiting for the proper moment to announce his decision. When she realized that was not so, she was at first more shocked and angry than bereft. She made scenes; she demanded visits. But by custom, entry into the House cut ties of family and friendship forever. Her father would not break that rule either.

Too furious and distraught to care how she would be punished, she left her room one night very late and crept into the House. It was a strange, frightening place, with its round pink hallways and low pink chambers. And though she knew—as every child of Refuge did—that once Dreamers entered the House they rarely left their beds, she did not know they slept like this—laid out on their backs like dolls, naked under their coverings, their eyes bound closed with strips of linen. She did not know they looked like this— heads shaved, skin pallid, limbs atrophied from lack of use. She did not know they smelled like this—of waste and sweat and sluggish breath, and underneath, something fouler (which, once she gained experience as a healer, she recognized as the odor of bedsores). Even the cleansing herbs strewn across the floors, the little bowls of aromatic ointments smoking above the braziers, could not mask those ugly odors.

She tried to turn back. But in the twining passageways she became lost, and blundered about in growing terror, until suddenly and quite by accident she came upon the chamber where her mother lay. The sight of her, her beautiful hair all gone and her face slack from the medicine Dreamers drank to keep them sleeping fifteen hours at a time, was so shocking that Axane screamed. Once started, she could not stop. Attendants came running. They tried to carry her out, but she clutched her mother's bedframe with both hands and would not let go.

"You're not my mother," she howled at the corpselike woman in the bed. "Where's my mother? What have you done with my mother?"

At last an attendant struck her, stunning her to silence, and they were able to carry her to her father's apartment. A healer was called to dose her with some of the Dreamers' own sleeping mixture. But when she understood what she was being asked to drink she began to scream again, and her father sent the healer away.

"I'll never go to sleep again," she sobbed, clinging to Habrâmna's chest. "I'll never go to sleep again!"

She was not punished. Her father had always been more indulgent toward the child of his first partner than toward his other offspring; or perhaps he realized that the experience had been punishment enough. The image of her mother in that bed was indelibly fixed in Axane's mind. It overwhelmed the memory of her mother's living presence, an ending as final as if she had seen her mother's body wound in gold-dyed burial cloths and set to rest in one of the mortuary caves. For a long time she grieved, as though for someone really dead. When her mother did die, six years later, Axane felt the ghost of that old emotion, but that was all.

The grief passed. The fear did not. From that time it was always with her—the dread that she, too, might manifest dreaming ability, and face a future in that horrible place. The terror when she began to suspect, at the age of twelve, that her fear was fact was like nothing she had ever known. For a time she tried to deny the changes in her sleep. But like other children she had been taught the signs, and the vividness of her nighttime visions, the perfection with which she recalled them, could not be ignored.

At last she gathered her courage and followed a Dream into the waking world. Exactly as she had seen it in her sleep, she found it: a redback ram that had lost his footing on the summit of the cleft and fallen into a fissure, caught by his curving horns in a narrowing of the walls. She had dreamed the ram alive and struggling; now he was still. That was the only difference.

The last of her self-deception fell away as she stood there. She felt the world around her changing, becoming a place in which she, like her mother, was a manifest Dreamer. She thought perhaps she would never move again—that she would remain there until she died of her entrapment, like the ram. At last, because she could do nothing else, she returned to work.

She knew what must come next. She put it off, as if not confessing her ability might change the truth. Days became weeks; weeks stretched into months. One day she woke to the realization that, without ever consciously deciding it, she had set her feet irrevocably upon a path of concealment. She would never speak of it. She would consciously undertake to live a lie.

It was the most terrible of betrayals. The Dream-veil was Refuge's only defense against the tricks and influences Ârdaxcasa sent into the wilderness to tempt its people out of hiding. Maintaining it was the duty of every manifest Dreamer. There would be no forgiveness for Axane if she were discovered—she would be cast out, and even her father would not lift a hand to save her. Yet the possibility of banishment, the guilt of deceiving her father, were not so awful as the prospect of a living death in the House of Dreams. She would do anything—tell any falsehood, commit any treachery—to escape a Dreamer's fate.

Behind her pretense, she continued to dream. At first, like any new manifest, her visions were of objects and places close to home. Gradually, as her untrained ability grew, she began to range outward, to places other Dreamers never saw: south and west toward the ocean, east and north into the Burning Land. And later, still farther north, to the Range of Clouds and beyond—where she seemed to see, in vivid and consistent detail, a world she had been taught did not exist.

At the heart of Risaryâsi's revelation lay this understanding: that Ârdaxcasa and Ârata bestrode the earth again, joined in battle as they had been before history's beginning. In the darkness of that killing time, humanity had destroyed itself, and the kingdoms of Galea lay in ruins. Only the exiles of Refuge survived, in the haven Ârata had made for them: the god's chosen people, the secret future of the human race.

At first, Axane believed that the life and civilization she saw on the other side of the Range of Clouds was the work of demons, or some dark illusion of the Enemy—the very sort of illusion she would have been trained to guard against, had she admitted the truth of her dreaming. This was her punishment for lying, she told herself: to be brought over and over to these alien lands and cities, these demonic human simulacra who did not look or speak like any people she knew. Yet as the Dreams continued, two or three of them a week, she began to realize that they often *did* look and speak like people she knew. And even those she did not understand behaved in ways that were recognizably human. Why should demons seem so much like men at work, children at play, women at domestic tasks? Why should they worship Ârata in temples so much like Refuge's own? How could mere illusions so vividly imitate real life—birth and death and planting and building and art and warfare? Why should they so perfectly reflect the Galean geography she had learned as a child?

In the end, as with the dreaming itself, she could neither fight nor control the change in her. There was no sudden revelation, no moment of truth; she simply looked into herself one day and understood that she no longer believed her Dreams were illusory. She had come to accept them as true visions of a real world. In this true, real world, life went on beyond the Range of Clouds, intact and thriving. There were no demon armies, no ruins, no dark stain of destruction. There was no sign of primal battle, no trace of risen gods. There was no indication at all, in fact, that any of Refuge's teachings were true.

Now, all these years later, she still was not certain where her people's error lay. Had Risaryâsi mistaken the symbols of her Dream-revelation and wrongly interpreted the meaning of Refuge's exile? Was what lay at the terminus of the cleft not a miracle at all—did Ârata sleep elsewhere in the Burning Land? Or perhaps it was exactly what it seemed, and Ârata really had shaken off his slumber. And yet the Cavern had lain empty for all of Refuge's history, and for long before that perhaps. If Ârata had risen, why did he keep himself apart?

She had never been particularly devout—not like her father or Tiyace, her half sister by her mother, who when she was alive had spent much of her free time in the Temple. She hardly remembered, now, what it had felt like to embrace Refuge's faith. Still, sometimes, she missed belief, for it had bound her to the world she lived in. Even when she concealed her Dreams she had been part of it, for it was not the Dreamer's task she rejected, but only her own subjection to it. Now, though, she knew that Refuge's Dreamers dreamed in service to a falsehood. She had become an exile—distanced even in the most intimate exchanges, invisible to those who looked her in the face. A woman without a place, though only she knew it.

Yet she could feel the knowledge in her, shining without being seen, like a lamp in a sealed room. And she knew that if she were offered the chance to extinguish it—to forget, to be part again of Refuge—she would refuse. She would never give up the wondrous things she knew.

The shadows had contracted as she sat thinking. It was close to noon; she really must go down. Still she sat under her canopy of linen, gazing toward the world her people denied. There were times when she was sure she felt it calling her, that wider realm of experience—not the Dream of it, but the reality, in all its inconceivable color and variety. And she remembered the redback ram that had first confirmed the truth of her dreaming—confined beyond escape, yet still, pointlessly, struggling to be free.

She descended at last, casually greeting those she passed, as if it were perfectly normal to descend from the heights at noon, her hair disordered and her dress marked beneath the arms and at the back with sweat. But of course it was not normal, and she knew it would be discussed, as everything even the least bit unusual in orderly Refuge was. Had she been keeping a tryst? Was she shirking a duty? No one would ask her to her face; the pretense of privacy was rigorously maintained, for without it life would have been unlivable. But there was very little a person could do in Refuge that others did not know. Any adult, looking into the eyes of any other, could see his or her whole history reflected back.

She ducked quickly into her room, to smooth her hair and pull a stole across the dampness of her gown, then took her place at her father's table in the eating gallery. Noon was quieter than morning or evening, for a good portion of Refuge's population was absent during the day, hunting or harvesting or tending the fields. Across from her, Vivanishâri chattered to Habrâmna, who sat at the table's head; Axane could tell he was not really listening. At Vivanishâri's side the twins kicked their heels and poked each other with their spoons, and Sarispes, dusty from the carpenters' shop where he was in training, ate as if he were starving. To Axane's left, her older half brother by Narstame conducted a low-voiced argument with his wife, while his seventeen-

year-old first partner, the source of the conflict, sat picking
at her food, wan with pregnancy sickness even in her fifth
month. Axane's second half brother, with his wife and
younger children, occupied the table's far end. By custom,
Habrâmna's six living daughters sat elsewhere, with their
husbands' families.

Axane felt little kinship with these members of her extended clan. Growing up, she had been all but an only child.
Only her half sisters by her mother and Narstame's two
youngest girls were part of her father's household when she
was born; the girls were married and gone by the time she
was three years old, and though her half sisters had remained
for longer, she had never cared for Sitoret, the elder; and
gentle Tiyace, whom she had loved, had died in childbirth
when Axane was thirteen. As for Vivanishâri's children, they
had been taught to dislike Axane, as their mother did.

Habrâmna did not need her after all, so once the meal was
done she left the coolness of Labyrinth and made her way
down the ledge toward the Treasury, where work waited for
her in the herbary. All of Refuge was caves: The sandstone
walls of the river cleft were honeycombed with caverns and
fissures, and Cyras and Mandapâxa, Refuge's two original
Shapers, had taken advantage of this when they made—or
more precisely, unmade—the spaces for the community's
life, work, and worship. Closest to the Plains were the striated curves and hollows of the House of Dreams; next was
the Treasury, where the herbary and indoor workshops and
storehouses were; then came the great spaces of Labyrinth, and after it the vaulting immensity of the Temple, and
finally the abode of the ordained Shapers. Over time there
had been alterations—Labyrinth expanded upward as
Refuge's third generation grew old enough to marry and
breed; the storage areas of the Treasury widened and improved; the Temple steadily embellished with sculpture and
painting. Only the House of Dreams had never changed. It
was just as the First Twenty-Three had found it, seventy-five
years before: a jewel-hued, interlocking complex of passages and chambers so perfectly formed that the Twenty-

Three had at once recognized the hand of Ârata at work, fashioning a home for his beleaguered faithful eons before they ever needed it.

Across the face of the Treasury, the red-orange sandstone had been shaped away to form a series of pillars, each fashioned to a different design. An arched entrance was set at their center; at its apex, presiding over the Treasury's abundance, stood a full-size image of Ârata Creator. He was portrayed as a naked muscular man in the prime of life, his long hair rippling like tongues of flame, his lips curved in an enigmatic smile and his eyes half-closed as if in ecstasy. His arms were bent at the elbows; between his cupped hands he held the sun.

"Axane."

A figure detached itself from the deep shadow between two pillars. Râvar. Axane's heart began to pound. She had not thought to see him until evening. He was not yet ordained, and was supposed to spend the whole of the day in training and Temple service.

He came toward her. He was extraordinarily handsome, his long-limbed body perfectly proportioned, his features pure and symmetrical, his sleek skin amber-gold. Members of the Mandapâxan bloodline often had light eyes; his were cloudy green, the color of Revelation where it flowed beyond the cleft. His black hair hung loose nearly to his waist, crimped by nighttime braiding as was the fashion among Refuge's younger generation; wristlets of wood and bone were also popular, and quantities of them adorned both his arms. His ochre tunic was bound with a sash of sunset red, and looped up to the knee on one side with a red cord, baring one exquisitely muscled golden calf.

"I was hoping you'd come," he said, smiling his curving smile.

At some point, Axane knew, she must confront him. Seeing him now, though, all she wanted to do was turn and run from him. But the entrance to the Treasury was a busy place; and where he had been standing she could see his usual collection of followers: Sonhauka, also a Shaper trainee and his worshipful shadow; his first cousin Kiruvâna, from whom he had been inseparable since childhood; several other friends, carefully dressed in imitation of him. She did not want to give all these people food for gossip.

"I have work to do," she said woodenly.

"Look." He extended a graceful hand. "I've brought you something. It made me think of you."

A feather lay in his palm, green as the emeralds the craftsmen of Refuge tapped out of the rock of certain cliffs, iridescent as the opal chunks scattered across the floors of certain valleys. Axane stood unmoving, her arms at her sides. She did not want the gifts he often tried to give her. She had told him to stop offering them, but it made no difference.

"Ah well." He blinked; there was a pulse of light, a breath of sound, and the feather vanished. "If you won't have it, no one shall."

The Treasury's workers moved past them, going about their tasks. No one watched: In crowded Refuge it was discourteous to pay open attention to others' business. But she could feel the heat of their curiosity; she could imagine what they were thinking, what they would say to one another once they were out of hearing. All at once, breathtakingly, she was enraged—at Râvar, at her father and his blindness, at Refuge itself. The intensity of the feeling frightened her; she drew in her breath and began to walk rapidly down the ledge, not caring where she was going, wanting only to escape.

"Axane!" She heard his footsteps behind her. "What is it? What's wrong?"

She did not answer, hoping he would give up and turn back. But he kept pace, hurrying along beside her. The Treasury fell behind. They passed the House of Dreams, its round pink entrance like an open mouth, and the broad Shaper-made indentation of the cleft wall where tasks the Treasury could not accommodate were carried out: the smelting and smithing of iron, the stretching and treating of hides, the smoking of meat, the threshing of grain. The natural, narrow openings of the mortuary caves lay beyond the workshops; past these, the walls of the cleft began to drop, as the river's westward flow brought it near the Plains of Blessing. There Râvar, tiring of pursuit, grasped Axane's arm and pulled her to a halt.

"What's amiss?" he demanded. "Why do you run away from me?"

She wrenched free. "Because I want to be alone!" She hurled the words at him, surrendering to her anger, hardly caring what she might reveal. "Can't you see I want to be alone? Can't you for once just leave me be?"

He stared at her in what seemed to be genuine astonishment. "Axane, have I done something to displease you?"

She sighed. Her fury was not like his, a towering passion that could darken the very sky; it came upon her quickly and burned out just as fast. She could already feel it ebbing, dropping her back toward the hard, flat despair from which it had briefly lifted her. "My father spoke to me this morning."

"Oh." She saw his comprehension. "Axane, I was going to tell you myself. I was going to explain."

"Were you?"

"Yes! I didn't ask him to order our intent. I wouldn't do such a thing."

"Wouldn't you?"

He opened his mouth to reply, then caught himself and looked around. They were beyond the settlement and its work areas, but not beyond observation: Those who worked the fields regularly passed that way, going to or returning from the Plains. Here as elsewhere, the river had carved caves and fissures into the rock, blind alleyways that offered privacy. Taking her arm again, Râvar led her toward one of these. Entering, they plunged instantly into shadow. The fissure's narrow walls curved and billowed, sinuous as cloth. Perhaps twenty steps along they sprang abruptly outward like a pair of cupped hands. He halted here, and let her go.

"Axane." His face was serious; his river green eyes held her own. "All I wanted was for him to speak for me, to try and persuade you to take me seriously. The rest was his idea."

"Was it?"

"Yes! I swear it. He was the one who decided."

Almost, she believed him. "Well, even if that's true, you gave him the idea, by going to him the way you did."

"What else was I to do?" He threw up his hands, his wristlets sliding. "I'm at my wits' end. You avoid me, you ignore me, you won't even accept my gifts. I just . . . I wanted . . ." He blew out his breath in frustration. "I wanted you to listen. I thought maybe he could make you do that. That's all. How was I to know his greatest ambition was to see you declare intent again? I never would have asked him to give you to me without your consent."

"But you wouldn't refuse me, would you, if I was offered to you without my knowledge," she said bitterly.

"How could I refuse? He's Refuge's leader. He can direct me as he wills."

She turned away, flattening herself against the warm stone of the fissure's wall. What he said was true enough. Still, it was not an honest denial—for this was what he wanted, and Râvar being Râvar, he expected to get what he wanted, an assumption so ingrained that how he got it did not really matter.

She had watched him grow up, though she had never traveled in his orbit, and not just because she was four years older than he. Even as a child he had stood apart—stronger than others, more beautiful, more capable—and he had gathered to him those most like himself. When his shaping manifested, it seemed perfectly natural; of course a boy like Râvar would be a manifest Shaper. The power of his gift, judged to be the greatest born into Refuge since his forbear Mandapâxa, was equally unsurprising—for what other sort of gift would Râvar have? And yet Axane had never fallen under the spell that, as soon as his voice broke, had turned even older girls into simpering idiots in his presence. A little of what she felt was envy—how could she not envy someone so at home within his world, so confident in his endowments? Some of it was caution, for her secret's sake. But much of it was dislike—for his blithe arrogance, his absolute assumption of entitlement, and also for the way that others accepted and excused those things in him.

When first he approached her, just over a year ago at the age of seventeen, she assumed it was some sort of cruel joke and responded accordingly. But he persisted far past the point of jest, and when she saw the disapproval of Refuge's elders and the puzzlement of his friends, she was forced to believe he was sincere. Still she did not take him seriously, for he was just a boy. Whatever bizarre fancy had brought on his infatuation, it could not possibly survive the test of time.

But time passed, and his ardor did not wane. Her steadfast rejection seemed only to increase his determination. The fixity of his interest began to frighten her, not only in itself but in the shadow-purpose she thought she perceived behind it. He could not want her, as some of her other suitors had, for the status she would bring him; it was a foregone conclusion he would be Refuge's principal Shaper one day. But she knew he was ambitious, and she began to wonder whether his eyes might be set on more than Temple service. By tradition, Refuge's leaders were Forceless. Might he see marriage to her as a step toward changing that? Did he think to use her to influence Habrâmna?

She confronted him, speaking to him as an adult, bluntly telling him she did not care for him and enumerating the reasons why a union between them was inappropriate. He listened, his eyes never moving from her face, saying not a word. No one had ever looked at her the way he looked at her, as if he could not tear his gaze away. It made her feel naked, and she hated it.

"This is wrong," she finally said in desperation. "For both of us. You must see that."

"I'll tell you what I see," he replied. "We make a pattern, you and I. We are meant to be together."

"Râvar, this love you think you feel for me is an illusion. I have nothing to offer you. I'm four years older than you. I have no beauty. I have no influence—my father loves me, but I can't make him listen to me, and never have been able to. If you think to reach him through me, you're mistaken."

"You think that's why I want you?" He drew back, affronted. "You can't see yourself, Axane. Not as a Shaper sees you. You are beautiful in your light. Other women are rose, or gold, or azure, but you—you're blue and indigo and shining emerald, all twisted together—so many colors, and all so bright. They're nothing like you, your colors. They aren't calm, they aren't obedient. They're bold and furious, they boil around you like a storm." He drew a breath. "I want to spend the rest of my life looking into them. I want to spend all my days finding what it is inside you that throws off so much light."

That was when she began truly to be afraid—afraid as she had not been since childhood, just after she began to dream. It was no longer simply a question of not wanting him. She knew now that he saw her too clearly, that he sensed the presence of her hidden self. The thought of living with him, of sleeping with him, of spending the hours of her life beneath his eye, terrified her. How long would it take him to pierce her deception? Once he did, he would not protect her. Callow as Râvar was in many ways, the intensity of his faith, the absoluteness of his devotion to Refuge, could not be doubted; he would not hesitate to denounce her. Desperate to discourage him, she dropped some of the pretense behind which she hid, showing him the sharper side of herself, the nature she concealed so that others might take less notice of her. Perhaps if he thought she was a shrew . . . But it only seemed to fascinate him more.

Even so, she had believed she could escape. Eventually he must lose interest, or yield to pressure from his elders, who surely would not allow him to remain single for much longer. All she had to do was continue to resist. But now she was trapped—snared by the conjunction of his frustration and her father's desire.

She pushed herself away from the warm rock and turned again to face him.

"Râvar . . . Râvar, you know how I feel. You know this match is against my will. If we go together to my father and tell him we've decided it's not right, he'll listen. He'll release us. Please—if you really love me, do this for me. Let me go."

"No." Gravely, he shook his head. "This isn't how I would have chosen to win you. But I've got you now. I will not let you go."

"People will be furious when this intent is declared. And your family—you know how your family feels about me. And Gâvarti—"

"If I cared for any of that, I'd have given you up long ago."

"Doesn't it matter to you that this is not my choice? That I'll enter into intent with you only because I've been ordered? That . . . that I cannot *bear* the thought of being bound to you?"

Again he shook his head. "You don't really mean that, Axane. I know you feel something for me. I couldn't love you as I do if there were nothing in you to answer it."

He spoke with utter certainty. She stared at him, silenced by despair.

"Don't be afraid," he said softly. He stepped toward her. His eyes held that look she hated, the look that made her want to fold into herself and hide. "It will be different once we're declared. I'll change your mind, I swear I will. Your desire and mine will be the same."

"Oh?" Anger rose in her again, trapped and futile. "That would be quite a trick. Do think you can maybe change Revelation's flow while you're at it? Or make the day an hour longer?"

He blinked. "That's an ugly thing to say."

"You think that's ugly?" She laughed, a short sharp bitter sound she would not have allowed herself to make before anyone but him. She was often conscious of the irony of it—that it was with him, of whom she most desired to be free, that she was closest to her true self. "Just wait. You think you know me, Râvar, but you don't. You may not be so happy to have me, once you've got me."

His mouth tightened. He turned away, abruptly, leaning against the water-smoothed sandstone and folding his arms. High above his head, the sky was a blue so pure it seemed unnatural; sunlight struck a little way down into the fissure, kindling the rock to the color of living flame. In his red-and-ochre clothes, he looked almost as if he were made from the same material—a man carved, like Ârata above the Treasury entrance, from stone. All at once Axane could not bear it.

"I have work to do," she told him. "I'm going."

"You treat me without respect," he said, his eyes fixed on the ground. "I don't know why I put up with it."

"Good-bye, Râvar."

She turned to go. There was a rush of air, and then his hands, gripping her from behind. He pulled her against him, clamping his arms around her. His wristlets cut into her flesh. His scent enclosed her: the aromatic wood of the chest in which he kept his clothes, the oil he combed into his hair, the tang of sweat.

"I'm not asking for so much." He spoke into her hair. "Just for you to let me love you."

"Let me go." She struggled against the cage of his arms.

"I love you," he whispered. "I want you." She felt his lips on her cheek, her neck. His hands moved to her breasts. She wrenched away, striking out, catching him with her fist. He gasped. She whirled to face him.

"How dare you?" She was shaking. "How *dare* you?"

"We're intended." He held his hand to his side. "I have the right to touch you."

"We're not declared yet. You don't have the right yet."

For a moment he watched her. "Very well. But in five weeks, we *will* be declared. Don't try to push me away then, Axane."

His face was absolutely still. His gaze was as flat as a

snake's. For a long time she had feared the prospect of life
with him. But never before had she feared him, himself.
With an effort of will she turned and walked steadily away.
Any moment she expected to feel his arms again.

On the ledge she paused a moment to collect herself.
Something brushed against her neck—her hair, pulled half
out of its pins. She stopped to coil it up again, with hands
that still shook. The tears she had suppressed all day overwhelmed her; she sobbed aloud, once, twice. Then she
wiped her eyes and, resolutely, turned back toward
Refuge.

The herbary lay on the Treasury's second level, directly
above the entrance, open across the whole of its front to allow the air circulation the drying plant materials needed.
Shelves and cupboards were ranged along its walls; workta-
bles and drying racks and grindstones and pounding slabs
cluttered its floor. It was crowded with healers, and also with
cooks and clothworkers, for the herbary prepared dyes and
seasonings as well as medicinal compounds. The air was
powerful with scent, the aromatic exhalation of all the herbs
and spices, potions and powders, oils and ointments pro-
cessed and stored there.

Axane got a knife from the equipment store and went to
join a group of trainees and junior healers preparing new-
gathered asperil bark for drying. They made room for her,
speaking greeting, never pausing in the rhythm of their cutting. She knew these women, not just as healers but as fellow
members of a closed community—knew their aptitude for
their work, their preferences in dress, their mannerisms of
speech, the private happenings of their lives. Yet though she
was pleasant to all, and companionable with some, none was
a friend. There had been a time just after her dreaming manifested when she had thought her lie must somehow print itself upon her face; in terror of discovery she had drawn into
herself, growing silent and careful. As the habit of deception
deepened the terror waned. But by that time she had acquired
a reputation as someone who kept apart, and it seemed safer

to leave it so. In recent years, as the women of her generation declared intents and began to breed, the gulf had grown wider still. She longed sometimes for the sort of friendship the others shared, for someone to whom she could speak her thoughts, someone from whom she could seek solace. But she had chosen her life, and this was part of it.

Beside her stood Yirime, like her a junior healer. Yirime had given her a sharp glance as she came to the table; now she felt the other woman's eyes again.

"You've a hairpin falling out," Yirime said. "There, at the back."

Axane dropped the knife and put her hands to her hair.

"Better fix your dress too, while you're at it."

Axane looked down, and saw that her gown was rucked up over her sash. She had not even noticed. She tugged it straight, the blood rising in her cheeks.

"Isn't it amazing, the mess a woman can get into, walking down toward the Plains?" Yirime gave her a sly smile. "Never mind. We won't say a word."

The others snickered. Axane's face was flaming. They must all have seen her go down the ledge with Râvar. She did not for a minute believe Yirime's promise of silence; by nightfall, everyone would know she had come back with her hair and clothes disordered.

Yirime's infant, slung on her back in a carrying cradle, began to whimper. "Not again," Yirime said wearily. "He can't be hungry, I just fed him."

"I'll take him for a while, if you like," Axane offered.

Yirime looked at her, surprised. "That would be kind."

Axane reached into the cradle and lifted out the baby, heavy and sour-smelling in his linen wrappings. Turning her back on the other healers, she paced over to the herbary's front.

"There, little one," she whispered, jogging the child gently in her arms. "You won't grow up to be a gossip like your mother, will you? No. Hush, now. Hush."

The baby quieted and slept, his small head in the hollow of her shoulder. The thought of pregnancy had become appalling to her while she was with Ardinixa, and she still most often thought of her probable barrenness in terms of deliverance. But now and then it came to her that she would likely never have a child—that in all her life the only babies she would ever hold were other women's, as she held Yirime's infant now. And she felt the presence of a sorrow whose boundaries she could not properly comprehend, but that would, she suspected, grow very clear as her life drew on.

Distantly came the crash of thunder, rolling long and low beyond the cleft, out on the Plains of Blessing. It crashed again, and then again, the thunderclaps overtaking one another until they twisted into a single rope of sound. And yet the sky, what she could see of it above the south wall of the cleft, was clear. Râvar, she thought—calling up the elements, making storms above the stone barrens as he did when he grew bored or angry. Ordained Shapers were bound by oaths to restrict their power to particular uses, but there were fewer restraints on those in training, and Râvar took full advantage of that, calling winds to amuse himself, opening crevasses, transforming rocks and fallen wood into strange hybrid objects not known in nature. He was careful to go well apart when he did such things, so they would pose no risk to Refuge.

She stood listening, the sleeping baby heavy in her arms. She thought of Râvar's hands on her, and of the way he had looked at her before she left him. She thought of the will that could call up such tearing forces. In the heat that breathed inward from the cleft, she felt cold.

At last, with a final, enormous crash, it was over. She had seen these storms of his before, and knew he did not unmake the tempests he created, but released them, flinging them out across the barrens. At least, she thought, there was no harm they could do there.

She returned to the asperil cutters. She gave the infant back to his mother and worked in silence for the rest of the afternoon.

* * *

That night she lay with her eyes open on the shadowed ceiling of her chamber. She thought of the strangers, and willed herself to dream of them. But she had no Dreams at all.

— 8 —

For four full nights, Axane did not dream. Her sleep was dark and peaceful.

Early on the afternoon of the fifth day she was in the herbary, working with several trainees to make up linen packets for infusions. The girls were bored, and so was she; they traded giggles and whispers and tossed stems and scraps of cloth at each other, but she did not have the heart to reprimand them.

"*Blood of Ârata.*"

The words were hushed. Yet they cut like a knife through the noise of talk and work. Axane turned. One of the cooks, who had gone to nurse her baby by the low balustrade that ran the length of the herbary's open front, stood as if struck to stone, gazing down the flow of Revelation.

"What is it?" someone called.

The cook, riveted by whatever it was she saw, did not reply. Another woman went over to the balustrade, and leaned past the cook; she clapped her hand to her mouth, but everyone heard the sound she made, half gasp, half cry. All across the herbary, healers and cooks and dyers left their work, crowding up to the balustrade. Axane's trainees dropped their sewing and bolted from the table; Axane followed, feeling the sudden breathless pull of premonition. A solid mass of watchers blocked her view. She stood on tiptoe, craning over their shoulders.

And then she saw it.

Down the ledge, a returning hunting party marched toward Refuge. They were ranged in the customary parallel formation. But it was not animal carcasses they carried between them, strung on spears for transport. This time, they had brought back something live: four men. Two carried a litter on which lay a bandaged third; another labored behind on makeshift crutches. Even from a distance, it was apparent that they were not just men—they were strangers. Strangers, in Refuge, where no strangers ever came.

The strangers of Axane's Dream.

She stood transfixed. Along the balustrade, the watchers were as still as the rock itself. There was no sound but Revelation, leaping and shouting in its channel of stone. The procession came steadily on; after it followed a larger procession, Refuge's field workers, trailing behind like children. The light-skinned man walked at the litter's head. The torn breast of his tunic gaped open; his golden necklace was clearly visible. As he passed below the Treasury, the gem inside it caught the sun and threw back living fire.

As one, the watchers gasped.

The procession reached Labyrinth and vanished within. The stasis that had held the women broke. They abandoned the balustrade, rushing for the herbary's exit. Parimene, the senior healer in charge, shouted for order, but no one heeded her. Dizzy with shock, Axane allowed the exodus to carry her out of the Treasury, along the ledge, into the dim spaces of Labyrinth.

A crowd was already gathered—the cooks and their helpers, the younger children and the elders who taught lessons in the afternoon. A clamor of talk rose as those who had been present when the procession arrived described for the newcomers what they had seen: how Habrâmna had been

waiting, with the ordained Shapers and the ten members of
the council (for the hunters had sent a runner on ahead); how
the hunters had been dismissed; how Habrâmna and the others had escorted the strangers to an empty third-tier apartment, and followed them inside.

Axane stood among the herbary workers. Her pulse beat
in her throat; a strange high tension filled her, not quite fear,
not quite excitement, not quite anything she knew. Over the
past days she had continued to climb the cleft, watching for
the light-skinned man and his companions; but the only
signs of life she saw were her own people's, and with each
day it had seemed less likely that the strangers would find
their way to Refuge. She had not been certain if what she
felt was relief or disappointment. Now, suddenly, they were
here, and she still was not sure. She clasped her hands together at her waist, and strove for calm.

"Did you see it, Axane?" It was one of her trainees, beside
her. "Did you see—the one in front—what he had around his
neck?"

"The Blood of Ârata, child," a senior healer answered before Axane could respond. "That's what he had around his
neck. Ârata be praised—the Next Messenger has come."

"You don't know it was the Blood," another woman objected. "We weren't close enough to see."

"I saw," the healer asserted. "I saw as plain as plain. It was
the Blood. There's no doubt in me."

"And he's a stranger," another healer said. "Who could a
stranger be, except the Next Messenger?"

"A demon," whispered a dyeworker near Axane, but so softly only those immediately around her heard.

"Ârata be praised." The senior healer made the sign of
Ârata; there were tears in her eyes. "Our exile is finished.
We can go home."

The crowd continue to grow, as word spread through the
Treasury and the outdoor workshops. It was a strange, subdued gathering. Some, evidently certain of the miracle,
knelt in prayer, telling their Communion beads. Others
talked among themselves, or moved restlessly from group to

group. Most, like Axane, simply waited, gazing up at the apartment where the leaders of Refuge were still closeted with the strangers.

At last Habrâmna and the others emerged. The crowd fell silent at once. Habrâmna led the way down to the first tier; there, still above the gathering but near enough to be easily heard, he came forward to the gallery's edge. The council clustered close behind him; the Shapers stood a little apart. Axane saw that Râvar and Sonhauka, the two eldest trainees, were among them.

"People of Refuge." Habrâmna leaned heavily on his ironwood walking stick, but his powerful voice betrayed no trace of pain or fatigue. Axane could read nothing in his face. "You all know what has happened today—some of you because you saw it, others because you have been told. Know then that we have confirmed these men are strangers, and that one of them bears the Blood of Ârata. This is a moment of great significance for Refuge and its people. But for now, we are still a community. We must still eat and drink, still be clothed and sheltered. I ask you to return to your tasks, to your homes, to your children. For the moment, let life go on as always."

"So it's true?" someone called from the floor. "He is the Next Messenger?"

"He bears the Blood of Ârata," Habrâmna repeated.

"Who are the others?" called someone else.

"They are his companions, who travel with him."

"Where is he?" cried another voice, and another, almost simultaneously: "Why does he not come out to us?"

"He is resting," Habrâmna said. "He and his companions suffered greatly in the Burning Land. They are injured and weary. They need time to sleep and heal."

A chorus of cries broke out. "For how long?"

"Why must we wait?"

"When will he speak to us?"

"When will we know?"

Habrâmna held up a hand. "He will emerge when he is recovered," he said when silence returned. "People of Refuge, be patient. Your questions will be answered, I promise you. We have been waiting decades—a few more days is not such a hardship. Now again I ask: Return to your work. Return to your duties. That is all."

He descended to Labyrinth's floor, the council and the Shapers behind him. Shouted questions followed him, but he shook his head, refusing answer. The crowd made way, then drew in again; the sound of talk rose, louder than before. But people were already beginning, obediently, to disperse.

Parimene rounded up the healers and led them back to the Treasury. Axane moved among them, barely aware of where she put her feet. She had been all but certain that her father must denounce the light-skinned man. For surely the light-skinned man would deny what Refuge named him; surely he would tell Habrâmna and the others who he really was. But Habrâmna had not denounced him—had seemed, in fact, to acknowledge him. Had the light-skinned man accepted Refuge's assumption of his identity? Why would he do such a thing?

In her mind a small voice said, *Because he* is *the Next Messenger.*

No, she told herself. *Galea exists. Refuge's faith is wrong. He* cannot *be the Next Messenger.* And yet she was aware, more acutely than she had been since she first began to Dream, that she had no authority but her own senses for the things she thought she knew. She could not quell the small, superstitious remnant of her childhood training that spoke to her in her father's voice—the part of her that feared to look into the faces of these strangers, and see Risaryâsi's promise looking back.

Who were they, these men? Who were they truly?

Need swelled in her, stronger than fear—to go to them, to find out for herself. What would it be like, to stand before a stranger—someone not of Refuge, someone she did not know, someone who did not know her? What might the light-skinned man tell her, if she spoke to him? What might she learn? Her breath caught; the shimmering tension she had felt as she stood waiting sparked through her again, an emotion so outside the ordinary range of her experience she could not even truly say what it was.

In the herbary, the workers reluctantly took up their abandoned tasks. Their attention was not on their work: Herbs were spilled, utensils dropped, containers misplaced. Axane's trainees were in an ecstasy of excitement, chattering and exclaiming until Axane thought she would go mad. After a little while, unexpectedly, she was delivered: A boy came with a summons from her father.

She went downstairs to the council chamber, where Habrâmna held audience daily to address problems or disputes or anything else that needed attention in the constant, changing flow of Refuge's work and community life. Shades of red and rust and orange dominated here as elsewhere, but the Treasury's sandstone contained more gold than either Labyrinth or the Temple, and a thick yellow band ran below the ceiling like precious inlay. Panniers of oil with floating wicks were fixed to the walls, each flame dimly twinned in the glossy surface of the stone behind it.

Habrâmna sat at a long table made from pale bitterbark wood. With him, locked in intense discussion, was Gâvarti, Refuge's principal Shaper. Râvar stood beside her; he was not only her best pupil but her favorite, and she often brought him with her on Shaper business. Axane waited in the passage until they were done, then went forward, making the sign of Ârata as she passed Gâvarti, keeping her eyes downcast so she would not have to meet Râvar's smoldering gaze.

"Sit down, daughter." Habrâmna gestured to the chair opposite his own. "Were you in the herbary this afternoon?"

"Yes, Father. I saw the strangers arrive."

"Good. Good." He shifted, restlessly, as he did when he was in pain. "You know, then, that two of them are seriously injured, and need a healer's attention. I've sent word to Parimene that she's to provide it. I want you to assist her."

Axane's heart leaped; for a moment she could not speak.

"Surely you are not unwilling, daughter."

"No . . . no, Father. I'm just surprised."

"It isn't only for healing that I want you there, Axane. I need someone to observe these men—their speech, their actions, everything about them. I want you to come to me tonight after supper, and tell me all you've seen and heard. No detail is too small. Do you understand?"

"Yes, Father," Axane said. Then, carefully: "Is anything amiss?"

Habrâmna sighed and passed his hand over his face, the sort of revealing gesture he would not make before anyone but her. "I don't know, Axane. There are questions. It is possible . . . it's possible this man may not be who he seems."

"Not who he seems? But in Labyrinth, you said—"

"I did not think it wise to speak our doubts. Feeling is already running high enough."

"Why do you doubt him, Father?"

"The Blood of Ârata around his neck, his arrival out of the Burning Land—those things would seem to mark him as the Next Messenger. But . . . I don't know if you could see this from the herbary, but he is not like us. His eyes, his skin, his height—he seems to be"—he shook his head—"differently created. And the Blood he wears. The fire at its heart is strange. Not living, but immobile. And it does not shed light."

She had not seen that in her Dream . . . and the jewel had certainly seemed to burn as he passed below the Treasury today. "What does it mean, Father?"

"Who can say? Mandapâxa's histories tell us that there were different races in Galea once. Perhaps Ârata made him like one of those lost peoples, so we might know he's not just any man. Perhaps the Blood he bears, the Blood shed by woken Ârata, is different from the Blood we know, the Blood shed by sleeping Ârata. If that were all . . ." He paused. "But it is not. He denies he is the Next Messenger."

Axane felt her breath catch. "Denies it, Father?"

"When the hunters found him, they saw the Blood around his neck. They fell to their knees to do him honor. They say he became angry, that he called them blasphemers. He did not speak that way to me. But when I greeted him as the Next Messenger, he drew back, as if . . . as if he were affronted and asked why I should say such a thing. When I told him, he turned his back. After that he would not speak at all, no matter what we said to him."

"That's strange indeed, Father."

"It has occurred to me that he is testing us. To see how well we've kept the Way of Ârata here in exile, how faithfully we've followed the precepts of Risaryâsi's revelation. But some of the councilors are uncertain. And Gâvarti fears he's false—sent not by Ârata to deliver us but by Ârdaxcasa to destroy us."

A coldness slipped along Axane's skin. "What do you think, Father?"

"I tell you honestly, child—I do not know. If he is the Next Messenger, how can I insult him by doubting him? But until my doubts are resolved, how can I accept him?" He shifted his body again, grimacing. "Until I know more, I will act as if both are true. I will treat him like the Next Messenger, and I will watch him as if he were a demon. That is why I need your assistance, daughter." He sighed. "I don't like to use you so. Nor would I, if there were any choice. But one employs the tools one has. Ârata laid his hand on me the day I decided you should be a healer."

Fatigue shadowed his proud features. Axane felt guilt turn in her. She knew the truth; she could answer all the questions that troubled him. But how could she speak? Even leaving aside the crime of her long subterfuge, her father was no more capable than any of her people of accepting that men from the outside world could come in search of Refuge. He would not believe her. He would dismiss her Dreams as Enemy-sourced illusions preying on a deception-corrupted mind.

"Father," she said, "you should rest."

He shook his head. "I'm well enough, Axane. Be on your way now. And Axane—not a word of this to anyone. Not even Parimene."

"Yes, father."

"You are my obedient girl."

He reached out his hands. She got up and went to him, and bent to receive his kiss. He held on to her as she straightened.

"Have you and Râvar spoken yet?"

Anger rose painfully, blotting out the guilt. She had not yet forgiven him for the future he had forced on her. "We've spoken, Father."

"Good. Good. Life must go on, Next Messenger or no."

She returned to the herbary, where she found Parimene waiting. The penetrating stare the senior healer turned upon Axane conveyed her annoyance at the delay. Parimene was a stout woman with dexterous hands and small brown eyes like honeyfruit seeds; she treated the sick with inexhaustible kindness but had no tolerance at all for the failings of those who were well and whole. Axane disliked her, something she had never shown by so much as a word or a glance, though she suspected her feelings were fully returned.

Parimene took up a basket of medical supplies and gestured Axane toward a bundle of splints. In silence they set out for Labyrinth. Parimene set a swift pace, light on her feet despite her bulk; her face was calm, as if she had only been called out to treat a knife wound or a broken limb. Inside Labyrinth a few prayer groups remained, but around them the bustle of normal activity had resumed. Cooks and others paused to watch as Axane and Parimene moved past—news spread fast in Refuge, and by now there could hardly be anyone who did not know who had been given the task of caring for the strangers.

The strangers' apartment opened just beyond the head of the stairway. Parimene stepped firmly across the threshold, but Axane paused. Before her stretched the striated stone of the apartment's passageway, gridded with the light and shadow of the lamps that burned in little niches in the walls. It was like every other apartment in Refuge, but not like any of them—it had become the entrance to another world.

She breathed deeply, trying to slow the racing of her heart, and followed Parimene inside.

Three of the men were in the first chamber: the harsh-faced one, the one with the broken leg, and the one with the head wound, stretched out on the bed. Since the apartment was unassigned, the chamber contained only the basic furnishings that equipped all the rooms of Labyrinth—there were no ornaments or amenities, no hangings or matting or extra lamps. A tray lay on the table, stacked with empty dishes; water and clothing had been brought as well, and they had cleaned themselves and replaced their tattered attire with the flowing garments of Refuge. Broken-leg sat on the stool, his crudely splinted limb stretched in front of him. Harsh-face squatted nearby. Their backs were half-turned; they did not see Axane and Parimene in the doorway.

". . . apostates and heretics," Broken-leg was saying. His voice held that odd intonation Axane had heard in her sleep; it made her feel very strange to hear it waking. "I'm not staying a moment longer than I have to."

"You voted with all of us to seek this place." Harsh-face's words were patient, as if he were dealing with a child. "It's shelter. What does the rest of it matter?"

"Bloody prison, more like. We don't even have weapons, thanks to you."

"It was a gesture of good faith to give them up."

"Good faith!" Broken-leg spat the words. "Who asked you to offer up our faith?"

"We need their help, Diasarta."

"Soon as I can walk without this splint I'm leaving. Don't try and tell me different. You don't command me anymore."

"Well, that's true enough," said Harsh-face, this time with open irritation. "No one can command a fool not to be one."

Parimene, who had stood listening, stepped forward, and said in an authoritative tone, "We're the healers sent to help you."

Their heads whipped around in unison. It might have been comical if the situation had been less strange. There was a small, tense pause; then Harsh-face rose smoothly to his feet. He bowed, touching the fingers of both hands to his lips and extending them in a graceful arcing gesture—clearly a sign of courtesy, though his dark face did not relax by so much as a muscle.

"We're grateful," he said. Seen with waking eyes, his features were even harder than in the slightly blurred vision of Axane's Dream. He looked like a bird of prey, with his jutting nose and angled cheekbones and glittering dark eyes— a striking man, if not a handsome one, with a heavy growth of beard and black hair falling in tangled skeins across his shoulders. His face was patched with peeling skin and marked with scabbed cuts and scrapes. "My name is Teispas dar Ispindi." He gestured toward the other man. "That's Diasarta dar Abanish."

"I am Parimene, of the Mandapâxan bloodline," said Parimene, as if she introduced herself to strangers every day. "My helper is Axane, of the Risaryâsan bloodline. Which of you needs treatment most?"

"Gâbrios, over there." Teispas indicated the bed. "He took a blow to the head about three weeks ago. Diasarta's leg is broken, though it seems to be healing well. I'm only bruised and burned."

"And the Next Messenger?"

"Like me." His expression gave nothing away. "Is there anything I can do to help you?"

"I might need you to hold him down." Parimene moved toward the bed. "Axane, the lamp."

Axane set down her bundle of splints and took the small lamp from the table. Her pulse had steadied, but she still felt light-headed and strange. Parimene lowered herself to her knees and began to inspect Gâbrios's bandages. They were neat, marked with faded bloodstains as if they had been washed and reused.

"We didn't expect him to live." It was Teispas, coming up beside Axane so silently that she started a little. "We didn't bring spare linen for bandages."

"There are plenty of bandages here," said Parimene. "Axane. The knife."

"Knife!" Diasarta was half-off the stool.

"She has to cut the bandages off, Diasarta," Teispas said,

quietly. He reached out, and took the lamp from Axane's fingers. "I'll hold that."

But his eyes followed her, and she knew his quietness did not mean he trusted her. And she saw how Diasarta stiffened as she reached into the basket, for all the world as if she might pull out the knife and sink it into Gâbrios's throat. *They're afraid*, she thought. With that, the last of her superstition fell away. These were not demons, or divinities either. They were just men—disarmed and injured and cast among strangers, whom they understood no better than the people of Refuge understood them.

She gave the knife to Parimene, who began to cut through the layers of cloth that bound Gâbrios's head. He looked to be in his early twenties. His limbs were skeletal, and he stank of body waste, though obviously attempts had been made to clean him. His eyelids fluttered as Parimene worked.

"Are there any fits?" she asked. "Does he wake at all?"

"No fits. He wakes from time to time, though I'm not always sure he recognizes us."

Parimene finished cutting and pulled the bandages away, revealing a mass of yellowish vegetable matter.

"These are tilla stems," she said, surprised.

"Is that what you call them? There's a plant in my country that can be used to dress wounds. This . . . tilla . . . looked something like it. I thought it couldn't do any harm."

"Tilla holds away infection. If you've been using it, the wound should be clean."

Beneath the tilla, a long looping gash ran around the side of Gâbrios's head, its edges red and swollen but clear of pus. His hair had been hacked off around it. Parimene touched it here and there, her fingers gentle.

"This is your work, the stitching?"

"Yes."

"It's neat." There was approval in her voice.

"Where there's soldiering, there's stitching." Teispas smiled faintly; there was no humor in it. "I've not lacked the chance to practice, over the years."

"They should have come out some time ago." Praise, for

Parimene, was always qualified. "But you did right to close the wound. I'll remove them now. I don't expect any complications. But . . ." She looked down into Gâbrios's loose, unconscious face. "Head wounds are difficult. I can't say whether he'll recover."

Teispas nodded. "I understand."

"Axane. Go make me a cleansing infusion."

Axane took a healer's bowl of white clay from the basket, dropped into it the proper packet of bark, and descended to Labyrinth's floor. Cooks and helpers crowded around most of the fire pits, but at the sixth, nearly at Labyrinth's back, there was only a little group of trainees making flatbread. Here Axane drew a dipper of water from one of the pots kept always boiling, filling the bowl to the first marked measure. Ignoring the trainees' stares and whispers, she carried the bowl to the benches of the eating gallery and sat down to wait while it steeped.

From there she could see the entrance to the strangers' apartment, glowing softly against the dimness of the third tier. She heard Teispas's voice: *There's a plant in my country that can be used to dress wounds. . . .* From which of the seven kingdoms of Galea had he come? She knew all their names; she had heard them spoken a thousand times in her Dreams and in the history lessons she had memorized as a child. But she had never heard them spoken as Teispas could speak them: in waking time, by a man with living knowledge of the place he named.

And suddenly, with a feeling like a veil dropping or wall tumbling down, she saw that though she had dreamed the outside world, though she had believed in its existence, it was not until now, this moment, that she truly understood it to be real. Real, like the bench she sat on. Real, like the voices of the cooks. Real, like the clatter of utensils, the smell of roasting meat rising from the fire pits. Vertigo seized her. She closed her eyes. For an instant she seemed to hang suspended on nothingness, a space so vast she could not compass it. And yet it had always been there, behind the veil.

"Axane?"

She opened her eyes. A little group of women stood before her.

"Ummm . . . we wanted to know. . . . Have you seen *him* yet?"

She did not need to ask whom they meant. She shook her head. "We're taking care of the others first. They're more injured than he is."

"Oh," said the cook, disappointed.

"Are they very badly hurt?" asked another.

"One has a serious head wound. One has a broken leg."

"Will they recover?"

"Yes. Yes, I think so."

"Can you talk to them?" asked a trainee. The group had begun to swell, more workers drifting over. "Can you understand what they say?"

Axane nodded. "They speak just as we do."

"Are they proper men?" another trainee said breathlessly. She elbowed her companion, who was sniggering. "You know what I mean. Are they like *human* men?"

"As far as I can tell, they're as human as you or I."

"Are they really the Next Messenger's servants?"

The questions came quickly, the cooks speaking over one another and tripping up the ends of Axane's answers.

"Have they done miracles yet?"

"Do they talk of Ârata?"

"Have they blasphemed?" This, darkly, from a woman who stood a little apart from the others; some of them turned to her and exclaimed disapprovingly, but she stood her ground, her mouth thin, her eyes narrow.

At last Axane's infusion reached the proper strength, and she made her escape. At the cistern she added a measure of cold water, filling the bowl to the second marked line, then returned to the apartment, where Parimene was cutting out Gâbrios's stitches. He was awake, moaning and feebly trying to struggle. Teispas had set the lamp down on the bed in order to hold him.

"You may as well tend the leg," Parimene said without looking up, as Axane placed the infusion at her side.

Diasarta did not like Axane touching him. He clutched the edges of the stool as she pushed up the hem of his tunic and ran her hands lightly along his calf. The bone had been set straight, and the break had not torn the skin.

"How did it happen?" she asked him.

"A cook pot hit me," he said, grudging.

"A *cook pot*?"

"There was a storm. The wind threw the pot at me. Like a catapult, it was."

Axane had no idea what a catapult was. "Well, it seems to be healing firm. But it should be resplinted. You'll be more comfortable."

He stared at her. He was a broad-boned man past first youth, with a long mouth like an axe cut. The scar she had dreamed wandered down his left cheek, vanishing into his beard. He was breathing hard—with pain, she had thought at first, though seeing the condition of his injury, she did not think he could be in much pain.

"Let her do it, Diasarta," Teispas said quietly from the bed. Diasarta's eyes flickered, and his tense mouth tightened even more. But he nodded.

"You need to lie flat. I'll help you to one of the other rooms."

"No. Do it here."

With effort, he shifted himself off the stool and lay down on the cold stone floor. She replaced the makeshift splinting with good straight boards and clean padding and linen ties. He relaxed a little as she worked, but his eyes never left her face. When she was done, he tried twice to rise before he allowed her to assist him. He sat swaying on the stool, his eyes closed, as she applied salve to his sunburned arms and cheeks.

Meanwhile, Parimene finished cleaning and bandaging Gâbrios's wound. With Teispas's help, she cut off his filthy clothes and washed his body with the rest of Axane's infusion, and bound him like a baby in linen swaddling cloths. Then she saw to Teispas, which did not take long.

"Where's the Next Messenger?" she asked when she was done.

"At the end of the passage," Teispas said. "I'll show you."

"No need," said Parimene crisply. "The two of you rest now. I'll see more food is brought. We'll return tomorrow morning to tend the boy."

"Thank you." Teispas repeated the graceful gesture of courtesy he had made before. "We're grateful for your care, and for the shelter you've given us."

Parimene nodded. "Come, Axane."

She stepped into the passage. Axane took up the basket and followed. Her heart had begun to race again.

In the last night chamber, no lamps burned except for the small one on the table. The light-skinned man lay on the bed, his back turned. He still wore the ragged garments in which he had arrived. Parimene paused in the entrance, halting so abruptly that Axane ran up against her. She realized, to her amazement, that the senior healer was trembling.

"We are the healers sent to help you." Parimene's normally assertive tone had vanished; the words were almost tentative. The man on the bed did not respond. Parimene took a step into the room. "We've been told you have injuries that need tending."

"I'm not badly hurt." He spoke without moving. His accent was odd, though different from his companions'; his voice was hoarse, as if with disuse. "Leave me some bandages. I'll take care of myself."

"But—"

"Leave it, I said!" And then, quiet again, "I want to sleep."

"Yes. Of course. Axane. The basket. Give it to me, girl!"

Axane obeyed. Parimene stepped to the table, where she set out a selection of items—salves, cloths, rolls of bandages. *Turn*, Axane willed the light-skinned man. *Turn, so I can see your face*. But he did not stir.

Finished, Parimene backed toward the door. "Send for me

if you need me," she said. "Any hour, day or night. My name is Parimene."

"There is one thing. I'd like to shave."

"Yes. Yes, I'll arrange it at once, Next Messenger."

Did he flinch? In the dim light, Axane was not sure, for at that moment the calling horns blew. For an instant the harsh, hollow sound of them filled all the spaces of Refuge, reverberating from the rock, overwhelming the air. The light-skinned man bolted upright, his face stretched with something very much like fright.

"What was that?" he whispered, when silence had returned.

"The calling horns," Parimene told him—hesitant, puzzled he did not know. "It's the hour of worship."

His mouth opened a little, but he said nothing. His gaze had moved beyond her, to Axane, standing just inside the doorway. He stared at her, fixedly, as if he saw something that astonished him. She felt her cheeks begin to burn.

"Come, Axane." Parimene's hands were on her, pushing her backward through the door. "Leave the Next Messenger to sleep."

That was the last she saw of him—a pale face, a pair of wide eyes. The image stayed with her throughout the Temple service, throughout the evening meal, throughout the time she spent with her father. Knowing he would also speak to Parimene, she told the exact truth about what she had seen and heard inside the strangers' apartment, holding back only her own observations—Diasarta's fear, the apparent dislike between him and Teispas, the way the light-skinned man had seemed to flinch when Parimene named him.

Habrâmna was exhausted; he did not keep her long. "I've told Parimene she must take you with her each time she goes," he said as she rose to leave. "Keep watch, Axane."

"Yes, Father."

She dreamed that night, of a city she had dreamed before and knew to be part of the kingdom of Haruko. It was built on stilts above water; canals ran where streets should be, and the walls of its dwellings were painted with strange bright symbols. At its seaward edge, a temple to Ârata thrust gilded domes into the sky.

She woke before the calling horns. Unbearable exhilaration filled her. She wanted to run, to dance, to throw her voice against the indifferent rock of the river cleft, until every echo shouted back what she knew: That the world was vast, and filled with life, and there was more, much more, than merely Refuge.

— 9 —

Suddenly, Axane was popular. Everywhere she went, people stopped her. What did the Next Messenger look like? Had he spoken to her? Was he very ill? Even Vivanishâri allowed curiosity to overcome her usual hostility, waylaying Axane in the passageway and asking for news. Axane was tempted to yield to spite and refuse reply, but she controlled herself, answering her father's partner as she had answered others— vaguely, with many protestations of not knowing or not remembering, as if she had been too awestruck to observe very much.

She and Parimene returned to the strangers' apartment at midmorning to tend to Gâbrios, and again at midafternoon. The first time he did not wake, though his eyelids fluttered, and he swallowed the soft grain porridge Parimene spooned into his mouth, but the second time his eyes opened, fixing wonderingly on Parimene's face.

"Am I dead?" he whispered.

"No," Parimene told him, with the gentleness she offered only to the sick. "You're alive, and we're going to make you well."

He fell asleep again before the food was finished. "You go on," Axane told Parimene. "I'll wait a while, and give him more if he wakes up."

She had feared objection, but the senior healer nodded. "Don't stay too long. You've work to do."

Parimene departed. Axane sat on by Gâbrios's bedside. The silence sang faintly; the lamp flames throbbed a little, as if keeping rhythm with her pulse. At last she rose and went out into the illumination and shadow of the passage. She passed the chambers Diasarta and Teispas had chosen—both were sleeping, Teispas in darkness, Diasarta with all his lamps alight—and continued to the passage's end. The chamber there was just as it had been yesterday: a single lamp flickering on the table, the light-skinned man curled on the bed, his back turned to the entrance.

She halted. She had known since she woke that morning that she would find a way to speak to him alone. Yet now that she was there, she could not think how to begin. The stillness of the room, of the man inside it, was like a wall.

Then his shoulders moved, just a little, and she knew he was not asleep—that he sensed her there, watching. The words came without thought.

"I know you're not the Next Messenger."

Silence, spinning out so long that she thought she had been mistaken, and he was sleeping after all. But then he rolled over, pushing himself upright on the bed. He stared at her—not quite as intensely as yesterday, but still with a fixity that made her skin feel hot and exposed. He had shaved not only his cheeks and chin, she saw with a strange little jolt, but his head, which now was as naked as a stone.

"You do," he said at last.

"Yes."

"Well, then, perhaps you can tell me why so many people here seem to think I am."

"Because you came out of the Burning Land," she told him. "Because you bear the Blood of Ârata."

"Ah." He closed his eyes, as though her words caused him pain. "He said that, too, your leader." His hand rose to grip his necklace, which made a large lump beneath his tunic. "You people honestly believe this thing is the Blood of Ârata?"

"Well . . . yes." Axane paused, remembering what her father had said yesterday. "Why? Is it . . . not?"

"No. It's not. It's a simulacrum. A symbol. A likeness, fashioned from glass and gold."

She could not have imagined such a thing. "But why would you wear a likeness of the Blood?"

"All vowed Âratists do. It's a sign of faith—a remembrance of the Blood Ârata gave Marduspida, the First Messenger." He allowed his hand to fall. "Obviously your people have forgotten that."

"You're vowed to Ârata? As my ancestors were?"

Something seemed to happen in his face, though his features did not change. "I was."

"Were you banished, too?"

For a moment he stared at her. "No," he said. "We were sent."

"Sent? By whom?"

Instead of answering, he asked a question of his own. "Yesterday your leader said something about a Dreamer, a promise. What did he mean?"

Axane hesitated. "It's complicated."

"I want to understand," he said, intensely. "I need to know what has happened to us. Why your people would . . . would mistake me so. Will you tell me?"

"Yes." Axane drew a breath. "If you'll tell me about your people. About your world. Who you are and why you came here."

He smiled, with a bitterness she did not understand. "Why not? In a way, it's what I came to do." He gestured toward the stool. "Shall we begin?"

Axane stepped across the threshold—an ordinary step, onto a floor like a hundred others. Yet for an instant it seemed to her that vast distances flew away beneath her feet, as if she passed not merely beyond the passageway but into some wholly different space. Years of deception had tutored her in self-control; she did not falter, but crossed steadily to the stool and seated herself, folding her hands on her knees.

"I'll tell you the story our children learn," she said, "when they first begin their schooling.

"Years ago, a great evil arose in the world, a terrible persecution of all who followed Ârata. In the kingdoms of Galea, shrines were violated and temples were destroyed, and those who were faithful to the Way of Ârata were murdered and tortured and imprisoned. Some, men and women who had vowed themselves to Ârata's service, were brought over the Range of Clouds and banished into the Burning Land.

"One who was taken for this fate was a Dreamer named Risaryâsi. Most of her companions believed they were being carried to a place where they would be set free. But Risaryâsi knew better. She knew they'd been condemned to die."

The room's single lamp left the light-skinned man half in shadow. He had settled himself cross-legged, his hands braced upon his thighs; beneath level black brows, his eyes were steady on her face. The gaze of a stranger, she thought—not just someone she did not know, but someone who did not know her, to whom she was as much a cipher as he to her. It made her feel self-conscious and strange; but, like the knowledge with which she had woken that morning, she also found it powerfully thrilling.

"Halfway through the journey to the Burning Land, Risaryâsi dreamed a Dream she didn't summon—of Ârata, floating in darkness. With the Dream came three understandings. First, that she was being called to receive Ârata's revelation, as the First Messenger had been."

He drew in his breath at that, but did not interrupt.

"Second, that she must gather together as many vowed Âratists as she could, each with a different skill—planting or weaving or healing, anything a community might need to survive—and prepare them to follow her. And third, that she must find the two Shapers the persecutors believed were Forceless and convince them to join her.

"Risaryâsi rejected her Dream, just as the First Messenger rejected his. But it came to her again and again, and at last she had no choice but to accept it. At night, while the guards slept, she went from vowed Âratist to vowed Âratist, looking for those who would follow her, trying to find the Shapers."

"She must have been an unusual woman, your Risaryâsi."

"Because she dreamed of Ârata?"

He shook his head. "Most Dreamers wouldn't be capable of following such a plan, never mind conceiving it." She looked at him, puzzled. "Never mind. Go on."

"At last Risaryâsi found the Shapers. Their names were Cyras and Mandapâxa, and they'd hidden their shaping in order to survive, for the persecutors had a terrible fear of Shapers, and killed them wherever they were found. Risaryâsi told Cyras and Mandapâxa of her Dream, and what they must help her do. They didn't believe her at first. At last they did—but still they turned away."

"Because of their vows."

"No," she said, puzzled again. "Because they feared to cross the Burning Land."

"They didn't fear to break their Shaper vows?"

"Why should they?"

"Do your people remember," he said, carefully, "that Shapers were required to take special vows? Vows that concerned the use of their ability?"

"Of course. Our Shapers still take those vows."

He blinked. "Your Shapers take vows?"

"Yes."

"What do they swear?"

"To honor shaping as they honor Ârata, whose gift it was. To practice it for need, but never for desire. To turn away from pride, and know themselves as servants. To stand apart from greed and live their lives as guardians."

She could see he was taken aback. Did he assume, because of Refuge's isolation, that its people had entirely abandoned the customs of the world from which they had come?

"These vows," he said. "How do your Shapers fulfill them?"

"They lead us in worship. They preserve the ways of shaping, and teach their skills to newly manifested Shapers.

They bring the rains that water the Plains of Blessing, and shape the Three Essential Elements the Plains don't provide, and make our living and working spaces larger as our numbers grow, and do anything that must be done that human hands can't do."

"Shapers made this place? This . . . Labyrinth?"

"Shapers made all of Refuge, except the House of Dreams."

"I didn't think it could be natural." He gazed around the room, at the glossy rock, the curving angles. "And yet it looks almost water-made, the way the stone is smoothed."

She nodded. "Shaper stoneworking can't make sharp edges."

"Astonishing. I had no idea—" He cut himself off, pressing his lips together. "They must be very strong, your Shapers."

"Yes."

"Yet this seems to be an ordered community. How—" He hesitated, as if searching for the proper words. "Do your Shapers take their vows willingly?"

"Of course."

"Are there never any difficulties? Shapers who resist? Who decide they'd rather serve themselves than Refuge?"

Briefly, she thought of Râvar. "No. Never."

He was silent. His face, in the dim light, was fierce with thought. She did not truly understand his questions—or rather, she had the sense that he was not asking exactly what she thought he asked, as if, though they understood each other's words, they were speaking slightly different languages. She was aware, through her dreaming, that shaping was practiced differently in the outside world—she had never seen the easy daily use of it that was the norm in Refuge. In fact she had never seen any shaping at all, except inside the temples of Ârata, where Shapers in red-and-gold clothing conducted Communion ceremonies that were like and not like those of her people, as well as other ceremonies her people had forgotten or set aside. She had always assumed the difference stemmed at least in part from necessity: Refuge, in its isolation, had greater need of shaping than did the kingdoms of Galea. But in truth she had no idea why things were not the same. She felt it now, the sharp frustration of her haphazard knowledge.

"Go on," he said.

"At last Risaryâsi convinced Cyras and Mandapâxa to go with her. When the persecutors banished them into the Burning Land, they gathered their followers and set off across the desert. Risaryâsi's Dreams guided them, and Cyras and Mandapâxa summoned water from the rock and shaped food from the earth and from the air. Even so, it was a terrible journey. There were fifty when it began, but only twenty-three by the time they crossed the stone barrens and reached the Plains of Blessing.

"The Plains were like a miracle after the Burning Land. The First Twenty-Three were weary—some wanted to stop right there, on the banks of Revelation, and go no farther. But Risaryâsi's Dreams told her they must move on, into the cleft that brought the river down upon the Plains. There, in the cleft's north wall, they found a great round opening, and inside it the rooms and passages of what is now the House of Dreams. In its perfection they recognized Ârata's hand at work, creating a refuge for them, a safe haven. They understood they had come at last to the end of their travels, to the place that was to be their home.

"That night Risaryâsi dreamed again. She saw a great wheel turning. She saw Ârata stirring in troubled sleep. She saw a rain of ash covering all the world. She saw the faithful swallowed up in darkness. She saw twelve black boxes, and in them twelve rods of ivory. She saw a withered branch fill up with sap and sprout leaves the color of midnight. She saw a great eye open, blazing like the sun. She saw a sword of flame sweep across the vastness of the sky. She saw a ruined city rise to wholeness. She saw the wheel once more, turning, turning. And she saw Ârata—Ârata awake, as tall as the mountains, with skin like red coals and eyes and hair like yellow fire.

"Ârata brought his shining face close to hers. Tenderly he greeted her, as a father greets a beloved daughter. She had done well, he told her; soon she could rest. But one task still remained. She must walk the river cleft to its end. She must climb up to the golden light that shone there. At the source of the light a miracle waited; and in the miracle, understanding."

"We saw a light," he said, interested. "At night, rising up above the top of the cleft."

"Then Ârata said to Risaryâsi: *Go, daughter. Walk the road I have prepared for you. You are the first, but many will walk it after you. For time does not run straight, but turns ever around upon itself. And what has been will be, many times, before the circle breaks.*

"Risaryâsi woke and obeyed her Dream. She reached the place where the river pours down into the cleft, and saw the light blazing out from behind it. There, inside the rock, she found the miracle Ârata promised—a great empty Cavern crusted with his Blood, a million million golden drops of it."

"Wait a minute." He held up his hand. "You're telling me that's what makes the light? The Blood of Ârata?"

"Yes."

He shook his head. "That's impossible."

"Why?"

"According to the *Darxasa*—do your people remember the *Darxasa*?"

"Yes. Cyras wrote it down, word for word, just as he remembered it."

"Well, then, you know that the *Darxasa* says that there's no Blood in the world of men, except for the drop Ârata gave Marduspida as a sign. And there won't be again, until the Next Messenger—the *real* Next Messenger—returns to announce Ârata's awakening."

"Yes. But the Blood also flowed from Ârata's wounds, in the place where he lay down to rest."

He was dumbfounded. "Do you mean to say your people believe this cavern is Ârata's actual *resting place*?"

How many times, secretly, had Axane questioned this herself? Yet it was deeply strange to hear another's unbelief—a stranger's unbelief—and it pulled her toward defiance. "Yes. Empty. I told you. Risaryâsi saw him awake."

"But that's—that is—that is completely—" With an effort, he got control of himself. "Ârata rests beneath the ground," he said, carefully, as if to a child. "Not in some cavern in a cliff. Besides, Risaryâsi came upon this place—how long ago? Seventy years? Seventy-five? If Ârata had been awake all that time, the Next Messenger—the real Next Messenger—would have arrived long ago. No. Your Dreamer made a terrible mistake. Your people have been led into false belief."

He was so certain, so absolutely sure. "But what is the Cavern, then, if it's not Ârata's resting place? I've seen the crystals. They're golden, and they have a heart of flame, just as the *Darxasa* says."

"A gemstone of some kind. The Burning Land is full of gems." He shook his head, impatient. "Risaryâsi wouldn't have known what the Blood looked like anyway, to recognize it. Oh, she might have seen it around the neck of the Bearer if she made pilgrimage to Baushpar, but only at a distance. And it's just as likely she never saw it at all, never saw anything but Temple paintings and her own simulacrum. These stones may somehow resemble the Blood, but believe me, they cannot *be* the Blood. Look." Again he gripped his necklace. "My simulacrum proves it. I've been close to the true Blood, as close as I am to you, and I can tell you for a fact that no one who'd really looked on it would mistake what's around my neck for the real thing."

"The council did see the difference. But they thought maybe the Blood of sleeping Ârata might not be the same as the Blood of risen Ârata."

"The Blood of . . ." He drew a long breath. "No. I won't debate this. Go on. You might as well finish the story."

"Risaryâsi sat down to meditate before the Cavern. For a day and a night she meditated. Slowly, she began to understand the symbols of her Dream, and the revelation she had been summoned to receive."

Axane was no longer comfortable with this narrative. She had not thought to consider, as she sat impulsively down to speak it, how he might react; it had not occurred to her that her people's beliefs, which he would recognize as false, might also offend him. Risaryâsi's tale was known to her from a thousand childhood repetitions, so familiar she could speak it word by word without ever thinking about its meaning—but before his stranger's incomprehension, it seemed suddenly foreign, not only in its elements but in the patterns of its phrases, which forced her to speak as if she believed them.

"She saw first that her people's understanding of the world was wrong. Human history was not a straight road to a single end, but a great wheel turning always upon itself. The battle of the gods, the Enemy's incineration, Ârata's long slumber, the rise of the persecutors, her people's flight—those things were meant to happen not once, but many times.

"She saw next how this had come to be. Over the centuries of Ârata's sleep the evils of the world had fed the dark power remaining in the bones of Ârdaxcasa, which Ârata had separated but not destroyed. She saw how the violence that had driven her and her companions into exile became a banquet for that power, rendering it strong enough at last to draw itself back to wholeness. She saw that Ârdaxcasa's return had woken Ârata, and that the gods fought again for mastery of the world, as they had before time began.

"She saw, finally, what must be done. She and her followers were Ârata's chosen people, the seed of a new human dawn. They must build life and faith in this haven Ârata had made for them, preserving the Way of Ârata and the ways of humankind against the day when Ârata vanquished his Enemy and lay down again to sleep. Then they would emerge and rebuild the kingdoms of Galea. And the human race would rule the earth once more, until the cycle turned and the evil rose and the gods woke, and Ârata's chosen were banished once again.

"Risaryâsi returned to the others and told them of her revelation. There was rejoicing, for at last the First Twenty-Three knew their purpose in the Burning Land. In their new home, they rededicated themselves to the service of the god. They vowed to keep the Way during their time of hiding.

They vowed to preserve the knowledge of the world and to pass that knowledge on. And they vowed to give their strength to increase, so that the human race might flourish in concealment.

"And so it is today."

Silence. His eyes had turned from her as she spoke; his face was dark again, absorbed. She waited, surreptitiously studying him. His shaven skull, which had startled her when she first saw it, no longer seemed so strange; she could see, now, how it suited the exotic symmetry of his features, the long eyes and broad cheekbones and wide nose and full mouth. If he had not been so ravaged, she thought, he might be a handsome man.

"So according to Risaryâsi, the history of the world repeats." He spoke without looking up. "Endlessly."

"Not endlessly. One day Ârata will strike the final blow. Then the world will be delivered from the turning wheel of time, and the Age of Exile will be done. The time of cleansing will come, and after it the new primal age."

"But until then the gods rise and battle, rise and battle, again and again."

"Yes."

"And this . . . Next Messenger your people believe me to be. How does he fit into this interminable string of repetition?"

"Ârata said to the First Messenger: *You are only the first. Watch always for the next.* That's Ârata's Promise. Risaryâsi told the First Twenty-Three: *At the end of every cycle there will be a place like Refuge, and at the beginning of every cycle the Next Messenger will arrive to summon its people out of exile.* That's Risaryâsi's Promise."

"*He will be born out of a dark time,*" he quoted softly. "*He will come among you ravaged from the burning lands, bearing my blood with him. One act of destruction will follow on his coming, and one of generation. Thus shall you know him.* But I've done no destruction. Nor any generation either."

"The destruction will be Refuge, when we leave it behind.

The generation . . . no one knows exactly what the generation will be."

"So that's what your people believe I've come to do—lead an exodus back to the kingdoms of Galea?"

"Out of the Burning Land, yes."

"So if I said 'Come, leave all your possessions and follow me,' they would?"

Axane hesitated, uncomfortable with what she seemed to hear in his voice. "I think many would."

"What, not all?" His eyes jumped to hers. "Who would disobey the Next Messenger?"

"Not everyone is sure that's who you are."

"Aha. So there *is* doubt."

"Well, you did deny it. My father told me. And there's your . . . your simulacrum, and the way you look. Your features are not like ours."

"What about this, then? What if I go out onto the balcony outside and shout for everyone to hear that I am *not* the Next Messenger, that the Blood I wear is false, that I have nothing whatever to do with Ârata, that indeed I am as far from him as any man can be? What then?"

"You mustn't do that," Axane said, alarmed.

"Why not? It's the truth."

"You have to understand. My people . . . my people don't believe the world you come from exists. They don't believe there are any human beings left alive anywhere in Galea, except for us. So if you're not the Next Messenger, the creation of Ârata, you can only be a creation of the Enemy, don't you see? A demon, an illusion sent to tempt us out of hiding. I don't know . . . I don't know what will happen to you, if my people start to think that's what you are. There are already some who fear it."

"What am I to do, then?" He struck the mattress in front of him with the flat of his hand, a sudden violence that made Axane jump. "Pretend to be this fulfillment of your people's heresy in order to save myself? What a twisted irony that would be. Or tell the truth and die for it? For myself I don't care, but I think my companions might feel differently. Tell me. What should I do?"

"You must go away from here." Axane met his angry gaze. "As soon as you are able."

"Ah, Ârata." It was agony she heard now, a depth of pain so raw it shocked her. "If only I had cast the ash-cursed thing aside. I knew I should, after I . . . once I . . ." He closed his eyes convulsively, as if shutting out something too terrible to remember. His hand had closed, white-knuckled, on his necklace. "But it was all I had left. Now look at me. It's like some awful joke. I might almost think Haxar was right, and punishment was really possible in this life."

He bowed his head. His body was still, so still she could not see his breathing. She felt again that quality she had sensed as she stood waiting on the threshold, before she spoke the phrase that turned him toward her. It closed him away, like a wall, beyond reach of words. She would not have known what to say in any case, for she did not understand the nature of his suffering. And yet his anguish touched her. She wanted to comfort him, to put out her hands to him, an impulse so strong it frightened her. She did not know this man. She had spent less than an hour with him. Why should she care, even a little, about his pain?

Ah, but you do know him, something in her whispered. *You dreamed him, twice. Long before you ever saw him in the flesh, you knew his face. . . .*

His hand fell. His eyes rose. Softly, he asked: "Who are you, that you know these things your people don't?"

Axane was aware, suddenly, of the silence, of the shadowed spaces of the apartment, empty but for her and him and three sleeping, injured men.

"My name is Axane. I'm a healer. My father is Habrâmna, Refuge's leader."

"The leader?" He raised his brows. "Did your father send you here?"

"No. I came myself. To . . . to tell you about Refuge, to

warn you. And . . . I hoped you'd tell me about your world. About your people."

"But your people don't believe my world exists." His eyes never left hers. "Isn't that what you said?"

"I don't believe as my people do." It made her feel naked to say it, as if she had peeled off not just the protective covering of her long lie, but her very skin. "I haven't for years. Not since I was a child."

"You don't believe that story you just told me?"

She shook her head.

"None of it?"

"I think . . . the beginning must be true. About the persecutors, and my ancestors being driven out of Arsace. And maybe the journey, how the First Twenty-Three got across the Burning Land. But the rest of it . . . no. I don't believe it."

He watched her. "Are you an atheist?"

"An . . . atheist?" She stumbled over the unfamiliar word.

"Do you think Ârata is dead? Or perhaps that he never existed?"

"No," she said, shocked. "No, I don't think that at all. It's just . . . just that I don't believe in Refuge. Over the years, it stopped making sense to me that we were a chosen people, out here in the wilderness. I began to wonder whether Risaryâsi was wrong about her Dream. It began to seem to me that maybe there was no battle, and no Next Messenger would ever come for us." It left out the cause, the catalyst. But she could not confess that, even to a stranger. "You believe as Risaryâsi did before her revelation, don't you?"

"That there's only one history of the world—that the gods battled only once, and Ârata will rise only once, and there will be only two Messengers, Marduspida and the one still to come? Yes. That is the belief of the Âratist church, and always has been. What your people believe, what they practice, is heresy."

Diasarta had also used that word, yesterday. "What is heresy?"

"A deviation from the true way of belief, based on wrong understandings. There are different kinds of heresy. Risaryâsi's, which was her own choice, is not the same as her descendants', since they know no better." He gave her a penetrating look. "And then there's someone like you, who sees the error but doesn't know what to put in place of it. Are there others who think as you do?"

"I don't know. If there are, they've never spoken."

"What of your Dreamers? Do you have Dreamers here?" She nodded. "Do they never dream the kingdoms of Galea? Do they never see the outside world?"

"My people believe the Enemy knows of us, though he doesn't know exactly where we are. He sends his influence into the Burning Land, in the form of false Dreams and illusions and even demons, to find us, to tempt us out of hiding. The Dreamers' task is to spin the Dream-veil, a . . . a kind of obscurity, a distraction, a shield, so Ârdaxcasa's tricks won't locate us. Their minds are trained to remain here, in Refuge. They never dream beyond the Plains of Blessing."

"And in all the years you've been here, not one Dreamer has disobeyed the training?" He sounded disbelieving.

"Perhaps." She looked down at her folded hands. "But none has ever confessed it."

"It might explain something," he said, thoughtful. "For years our Dreamers dreamed your presence in the Burning Land, but never clearly enough to divine what you were. The Dreamers we had with us for guidance dreamed no better, right up until we reached the pebble plain. Your . . . Dream-veil . . . might account for that."

Astonished, she said: "You had Dreamers traveling with you?"

"Yes."

"You let them free? They aren't confined?"

"No." He frowned. "Why do you confine your Dreamers?"

"All manifest Dreamers must enter the House of Dreams, at the age of thirty-five. Once they go in, they never leave it."

He shook his head. "In the kingdoms of Galea, no Dreamer is forced to the Path of Dreams. They may follow it, or not, as they choose."

Axane could not speak, dazzled by the vision of a world

in which a manifest Dreamer might live free. Her own Dreams had never shown her this.

"It must be hard for you," he said quietly. "To recognize your people's error and not be able to admit it. To keep such a secret."

It took her breath away, that he would see this.

"You said you thought the beginning might be true," he said. "The beginning of your story, the persecutors who sent your ancestors into the Burning Land."

"Yes."

"Well, you've got the scale of it wrong. The persecution was only in Arsace—it didn't touch the other kingdoms. But it did happen. The persecutors were called Caryaxists."

Caryaxists. She had heard that word, in her dreaming. "Why did the . . . Caryaxists . . . hate the Way of Ârata?"

"They followed the ideas of a man called Caryax, a scholar who was preoccupied with . . . well, with what he saw as the inequities of Arsacian society. He was also an atheist—he thought that faith was illusion and people's minds were better focused on the world." He frowned. "I don't suppose that makes much sense to you."

"No! I mean, yes!" Here it was at last, the first of the threads that would bind the scattered fragments of her Dream-sourced knowledge into a coherent whole. "Tell me more. Please."

"Well, Caryax was executed for sedition—"

"Sedition?"

"Encouraging others to rebel against authority.. All his books were burned. But he'd gathered followers, and his ideas survived. About twenty-five years later, there was famine in southern Arsace. The nobles hoarded food, and the peasants rose up against them. The son of one of the noble houses was an ardent Caryaxist, and set himself up as leader of the revolt—he called himself the Voice of Caryax. People came from all over the southern provinces to join him. Eventually they marched on Ninyâser. The king surrendered on the promise of safe conduct to Chonggye. Instead he and his family were executed, along with his council and many others."

"Why?"

"Caryax wrote that no advantage of birth or wealth should set one man above another. The Voice thought the best way to accomplish that was simply to get rid of nobles and the wealthy. Dead, they could never rise up and challenge him."

"What about the persecution of the Âratists?"

"Caryax thought that if faith could be deprived of public expression, belief would eventually wither away. So the Voice prohibited Âratist ritual, and seized the church's properties and emptied the monasteries and nunneries. But Âratism didn't wither. It survived, hidden in the minds and hearts of believers, until King Santaxma returned to take his rightful place upon the throne."

"So the Caryaxists no longer rule Arsace."

"No. We're working now to restore what was lost. Your people were part of that. I was a member of an expedition, a . . . a kind of hunting party, sent by the Âratist church to find you and bring you to Arsace."

Axane looked at him, astonished. "You mean you really *were* sent to lead us out of the Burning Land?"

He smiled, without humor. "Yes."

"You said an expedition. But there are only four of you."

His mouth tightened. "There was a storm. We were crossing the pebble plain. It sprang up out of nowhere—a terrible wind, with a finger of cloud that swept the earth. I've never experienced anything like it. It carried off half the expedition, and what it didn't take it tore apart. We are all that's left."

Axane put her hands to her cheeks. The room before her vanished; she saw blackness blooming from an empty sky, heard the howl of distant winds. *Râvar*, she thought. *Of course*. Diasarta had spoken of it yesterday, but she had not put it together until now.

He was watching her. "I take it you've seen such storms before?"

She forced her hands back into her lap. It seemed to her that he should know.

"Our Shapers call storms sometimes," she said. "When it's dry. One of them must . . . must have been practicing. He didn't mean any harm. He had no idea you were even there. There's never been anyone on the stone barrens before."

He stared at her. "One of your Shapers made . . . that?"

"Yes. I'm sorry. I'm so sorry, for you and your companions."

He began to reply, but whatever he would have said was overtaken by the calling horns. Their clamor fell achingly upon the air and died away.

"It's the call to worship. I must go."

"Seiki—one of our Dreamers—said there was a temple here."

"Yes."

"What is your worship like?"

"We assemble in the Temple core. We meditate. We take Communion."

"Communion," he repeated.

She got to her feet. "I'll try to come back tomorrow."

He nodded. But his face was dark again, and she was not sure he had really heard her.

Passing Diasarta's bright-lit chamber, she glanced inside; he still slept, the bolster pulled half across his head. In Teispas's room, a lamp had been kindled. Teispas sat facing the entrance, his hands hanging loose between his knees. His eyes met hers as she went by, but his dark face did not change.

Only as she emerged onto the gallery did she realize that she had never asked the light-skinned man's name.

She descended to the floor of Labyrinth, and went to her room to fetch her Communion beads and meditation square. The familiar sights and smells, the predictable course of the coming hours, pressed in on her like an early twilight. It was this way, sometimes, when she came back from one of her solitary plant-hunting expeditions, moving from an open world into one defined by walls of stone. For a little while, in the small room upstairs, she had been unaware of boundaries.

She left Labyrinth and turned toward the Temple. The joyous clamor of Revelation rose up to greet her. Shadow draped the bottom of the cleft, but sunlight still ignited the summit, reaching a little way down the northern wall, touching the apex of the Temple's sculpted façade.

At its base, the sandstone had been shaped into a colonnade, similar to the one that adorned the Treasury. Above it stood two immense images of Ârata: on the left, the Eon Sleeper, his naked body marked with gaping wounds; on the right, the Risen Judge, the flames of cleansing leaping from his palms. Between the images hung a great wheel, with all the world tangled in its spokes: people, animals, birds, fish, plants, mountains, rivers. The disk of the sun burned at its center, and around its edges danced the moon and stars. Thus was the whole of the Age of Exile represented: from time's beginning in the god's first slumber to time's ending in his stern judgment, and all the spinning cycles in between.

Axane passed beneath the heavy arch of the entrance and into lamplit dimness. According to the lore of Refuge, Cyras and Mandapâxa had shaped Refuge's Temple to match their memory of the temples they had known before their banishment—which by ancient tradition were circular, a central core surrounded by an enclosed gallery that was the only means of access. Along the gallery's inner wall, a continuous chain of painted images told the tale of the world and humankind, worshipers entered at the moment of the earth's creation and followed history around, until, at its finish, they were delivered into the temple core.

Usually Axane hastened past these paintings, which she knew so well she barely needed to look at them. Today, however, she walked more slowly, trying to view them with a stranger's eyes. They had been begun by one of the First Twenty-Three, who had been a temple artist in Arsace, and completed by her children, to whom she taught her skills. Like Cyras and Mandapâxa, she had created them out of her memories of Galea, so perhaps a stranger would find them familiar enough—until, of course, he reached the penultimate panels, depicting Risaryâsi's flight across the Burning Land and the founding of Refuge.

The final image showed the arrival of the Next Messenger. He stood on the air above the cleft, the Blood of Ârata blazing in his hands—a young man, gaunt from his travels, clad only in a breechclout and a wild thatch of hair and beard. Blood trailed down his forearms from the cuts the crystal's razor facets had inflicted on his palms. Yet his expression was serene, innocent of pain. There could hardly be a greater contrast to the troubled face of the man Axane had just left. She thought, with a strange thrill of dread, that even if he never spoke a word about who he was and why he had come, Refuge must see the anguish in him and wonder.

Inside the Temple's core, banks of braziers set around the perimeter cast a smoky amber light that reached only partway up the soaring walls. The ceiling was a vault of shadows. Opposite the entrance a massive image of Ârata Warrior strode out of the stone, a muscled youth in a warrior's kilt, a sword of flame upraised in both his hands. His long hair streamed around him like the corona of the sun, and his lips were stretched in a silent, fierce battle cry.

The congregation was already mostly assembled, kneeling across the core in loose family groups. Axane made her way to the front, where her father sat above the others in a chair. Vivanishâri and her children knelt on his right; behind him were Axane's half brothers and sisters, with their wives and husbands and partners and children. The place to his left was Axane's, and had been ever since she grew old enough to kneel on her own. She spread her meditation square and settled herself, unwinding her Communion beads from around her wrist. She sensed her father's eyes; he smiled at her and turned away again.

The last stragglers took their places. Silence settled on the gathering. Into it, after a few moments, came the Shapers. A trainee led the way, carrying a smoking dish of incense. Behind her walked the eight ordained Shapers, clad in red tunics and stiff golden robes, their copper Communion bowls held before them. Eight more trainees followed, bearing incense vessels, and finally Râvar, the oldest trainee, with the casket that contained the ceremonial substances. He moved with measured grace, his eyes upraised to the face of Ârata, solemn with the gravity of the ceremony. At such times his devotion shone from him like a beacon. But Axane, looking at him, saw bruise purple clouds on a far horizon and shivered.

The procession halted at Ârata's feet. The incense bearers ranged themselves to one side, while the ordained Shapers knelt and set out their Communion bowls. Into these, carefully, Râvar placed the ceremonial substances: yellow beeswax, red sandstone, black obsidian, white salt, and blessed oil. He took up the casket again and retreated, standing ready to replenish as needed.

Gâvarti raised her hands to the congregation. She was among the last of Refuge's firstborn generation, and had known Risaryâsi when she was a child. The braziers behind her lit the stiffened linen of her golden sleeves and made an aureole of her silver curls.

"We gather, as we do each day, to give honor to Ârata, creator and defender of the earth, who in his wisdom chose our forebears to receive his word, and made for them this Refuge to live in safety through the time of the gods' conflict. Let us begin our worship with a meditation upon the beauty of Ârata, which illumines every part of his creation and shines also in each one of us."

Gâvarti bowed her head. Silence descended, broken by muffled coughing, a child's whimper, the rustle of clothing. Axane stared at the floor before her knees, her thoughts drifting as they always did during the meditation.

"Come forward," Gâvarti said, softly.

Axane looked up. Gâvarti was on her feet, her hands extended. Axane turned, following the direction of Gâvarti's gaze; around her, others did the same. There was a sound of indrawn breath, like wind running through leaves. The light-skinned man stood in the core's entrance, framed in the yellow lamplight of the gallery, as still as one of the gallery's painted images.

"Join us," Gâvarti said. "Share our worship."

For a long moment the light-skinned man did not stir. His face was blank, loose, like someone dreaming. Then, slowly, he advanced. The congregants' heads turned to follow him. Beside Axane, Habrâmna pushed himself effortfully to his feet.

"Here is a place for you," he said, as the light-skinned man reached the first rank of worshipers. The light-skinned man shook his head.

"I will kneel." His voice barely seemed to break the quiet.

He matched action to words. For a moment no one moved. Then Gâvarti dropped her arms and lowered herself once more to the floor. Habrâmna braced his hands on the arms of his chair and sat. The congregants turned their faces forward. But Axane still watched the light-skinned man. Her heart beat with dread. What would he do, when Gâvarti asked him to join the ceremony, as she surely would? Gâvarti, Axane remembered, was one of those who doubted him.

"Praise Ârata, lord of this world." Gâvarti began the ceremony.

The communicants responded raggedly, still unsettled by the disruption of their worship. Axane spoke with the others, her Communion beads slipping through her hands. The light-skinned man had raised his eyes to Ârata Warrior, striding eternally out of the rock; his lips did not move.

The responses ended. The ordained Shapers spoke in unison:

"In praise and in celebration, we come together in this place, to take upon ourselves the signs of Ârata and of our love for him. In praise and in celebration, we, his vowed servants, call forth the power that was his gift to humankind, the power with which the world was first brought to form. Here, in our refuge in the Burning Land, we touch the world in change and in creation, as Ârata did when he made it, as he does now to defend it, as he will again when the wheel turns and the cycle is renewed. In praise and in celebration, we call the light of the risen god to being within us, within the substances we transform, within you who offer yourselves to receive them."

As one, they worked the transformations of the ceremony. "Come forward," Gâvarti said. Silence; no one moved. Gâvarti spoke again, beckoning: "Come forward."

Axane saw the change in the light-skinned man's face, as he realized it was he who was meant. He placed his palms on the floor and pushed to his feet. He approached, his body angled a little forward, as if the air were some tactile substance that impeded him, and fell to his knees before Gâvarti's Communion bowls.

"Who receives the marks?" Gâvarti said.

He murmured something inaudible. Gâvarti's brows drew together.

"Who receives the marks?" she repeated, a little louder.

"Gyalo Amdo Samchen." His voice shook on the final syllable, but this time he could be clearly heard.

Gâvarti dipped her right index finger in the first bowl and reached out to mark his left cheek. "The blood of Ârata, past and present and still to come," she said. She dipped into the second bowl, and marked his right cheek. "The sands under which he slept, to which he will return." She dipped her left index finger to the third bowl, and marked his forehead. "The tears of exile, in which each cycle begins." She dipped into the fourth bowl, and marked his chin. "The stain of sin, in which each cycle ends. Remember."

He bowed his head and crossed his arms before his face. His tunic pulled tight across his back; Axane could see how gaunt he was, the points of his shoulder blades like the points of a bird's wings, the bones of his spine marching like stacked pebbles up the nape of his neck.

"Great is Ârata," he said, and paused. The silence that held the core was as dense as the rock around it. Axane's breath halted. At last Gâvarti spoke, finishing the acknowledgment:

"Great is Ârata, the one god, the bright god, the god who sleeps, the god who rises. I affirm my love for Ârata, deny my dark nature in his name, and rejoice in the eternal promise of his awakening, which is now and will be again, in the certain turning of the wheel of time." She began to touch his head in benediction, but then hesitated and withdrew her hand. "Go in light."

He pushed himself to his feet and went back to his place. He closed his eyes; Axane, watching, saw tears spring from beneath his lids and track slowly down his cheeks. A sense of intrusion gripped her. She turned away. But his pain reached toward her, as it had that afternoon, and her throat ached with a grief she did not understand.

The citizens of Refuge came forward to receive the Communion marks, and the sound of voices filled the core. Axane was among the first of the communicants; returning to her place, she saw that the light-skinned man was gone, and looked toward the gallery just in time to see him pass out of sight. Turning to kneel again, her eyes fell on Râvar, standing at Ârata's feet with the casket clutched in his arms. He, too, had marked the light-skinned man's departure. His face was as still as that of the image above him.

The exodus from the Temple was unusually subdued. Many of the congregants seemed too awed to speak of what they had just witnessed. Others talked of the blessing the Next Messenger had brought upon the ceremony. But there were also some who whispered that the Next Messenger had not spoken all the Communion words, that he had wept as he received the marks. What did it mean? Was it a judgment? A test? Something else?

Inside Labyrinth, the evening meal was nearly ready. Axane cleaned the Communion marks from her face and went out to collect Narstame's supper. On her way back, she glanced up at the third tier. One of the cooks was passing into the strangers' apartment, bearing a large tray of food. The image of the light-skinned man—*I know his name now*, she thought, with a strange thrill: *Gyalo Amdo Samchen*— composed itself in the mirror of her mind. She knew exactly how the cook would find him: lying on his bed, his knees drawn up, his back turned to the entrance of his chamber.

—10—

Emerging from her father's apartment the next morning with the breakfast tray, Axane saw that the prayer groups still had not obeyed Habrâmna's request to disperse. They sat in little clusters, reciting prayers or keeping silent vigil, their eyes turned toward the strangers' apartment. They paid no heed to Labyrinth's morning bustle or to the impediment they made to others' progress.

Her morning duties complete, she went to find Parimene, and the two of them returned to care for Gâbrios. Her failure to come back to the herbary yesterday afternoon had not escaped Parimene; the senior healer did not leave her side for an instant, foiling any chance to slip away.

On their way out of Labyrinth they encountered Irdris, one of the junior healers, her Communion beads looped around her wrist and her meditation square folded over her arm.

"Irdris." Parimene halted. "Why aren't you at your duties?"

"I've been saying devotions in the Temple."

"There'll be plenty of time for devotions when work is done. Put your things away and report to the herbary at once."

"I won't." Defiant, Irdris met Parimene's glare. "I'm done with working."

"What do you mean, you foolish girl?"

"Why should we work, now the Next Messenger has come? Refuge will be empty soon. Any day we'll be leaving it behind."

"Oh, really?" Parimene's lips thinned. "And I suppose that in the meantime men won't fall sick, and women won't birth babies? And food will float down from the sky, and we'll all have nothing better to do but loll about and say our prayers?"

"Maybe." Irdris did not back down. "If that's what the Next Messenger decrees."

"Well, that's all very nice. But life goes on, and so must we. That's what I've been told, and that's what I mean to see we do."

"Do as you please, old woman," Irdris retorted. "It makes no difference to me. I'm going to take joy in my last days in Refuge, whether you like it or not!"

She stepped around Parimene and moved swiftly off into the depths of Labyrinth. Parimene stood motionless; her face looked as if it were carved from ironwood. Axane wondered how long it had been since anyone had dared speak to her so.

"The council will hear of this," Parimene said, tightly. "Come, Axane."

Axane spent the rest of the morning in the herbary, helping to remove the fibrous inner layers from the newly dried strips of asperil bark. The women working with her were eager for news; there was little more to tell than there had been yesterday, but they plied her with questions even so, hanging raptly on every detail. When other workers began to drift over to listen, Parimene stepped in to disperse them. "Save your tales for the evening hours," she told Axane, harshly.

They paid their afternoon visit to Gâbrios, and Axane tried to repeat the pretext of yesterday, but Parimene would not allow it. They were shorthanded; five of the junior healers had not returned after the noon meal. "That stupid girl has been talking," the senior healer said, with a grimness that did not bode well for Irdris. Axane felt a frustration so sharp it was close to anger. The face of the light-skinned man, Gyalo Amdo Samchen, commanded her thoughts—marked with Communion substances and tracked with tears, as she had glimpsed it in the Temple; dark with anguish, as she had seen it in the shadows of his chamber. She wanted to know what had drawn him to the ceremony yesterday. She wanted to know why he had wept. She wanted to hear him speak about his world again. She could think only of how she might return.

That night she went to her father's room with salves to soothe his inflamed joints. As she worked, applying the ointment and covering it with linen bandages, he spoke, irritably, about the events of the day. The herbary was not alone in its disruption: In the smithy and the weavery also people had put down their tools and left their work. Women had failed to join the cultivating bands to which they were assigned; men had shirked their hunting tasks.

"I fear it will only become worse." He sat stiffly in his chair, his bedgown pulled up, while she knelt before him, attending to his knees and ankles. "The prayer groups remain, despite my orders—in fact I think there are more now than there were yesterday. Two men beat each other bloody this morning because they could not agree whether the Next Messenger was walking on the ground or above it when he first came into Refuge. At least a dozen people have come to me fearful that the Next Messenger was offended by the Communion service last night, and I can't count the number of times I've been asked when he will emerge again. And there is doubt, much doubt. This afternoon Omida accused me outright of admitting a demon into our midst." Habrâmna sighed. "If only he would speak. If only he would show himself."

"He's ill, Father."

"I know, daughter. But the longer he hides himself away,

the more the rumors will grow. The Shapers are uneasy also. Gâvarti tells me they want to examine him."

Axane's hands stilled. "Examine him, Father? How?"

"Gâvarti did not say, and I did not ask. I'm content to leave Shaper mysteries to the manifest." He sighed again and shifted in his chair, searching for a comfortable position. "I sent to him this morning, asking for an audience, and he refused. Perhaps he is not yet strong enough to put himself on public view, but it seems to me he ought at least to be willing to receive visitors. Did you see him today, Axane?"

"No, Father. Parimene attended to him."

"Well, if he will not let me come in to him, perhaps he will come out to me. Tomorrow I'll offer to conduct him through Refuge. Surely he will want to know how we've lived during our time of exile."

Axane finished with his knees and got to her feet. "Now your arms, Father."

"How I loathe these ash-cursed bandages," he grumbled. "Of course, it may be with purpose that he keeps himself apart. Perhaps he means to wait inside his room while Refuge tears itself to pieces with doubt and joy, and then walk away over the ashes of our community."

Axane caught her breath. "Does that mean . . . have you decided he's not the Next Messenger, Father?"

"No." Habrâmna shook his head. "No. I'm no closer to understanding what he is than I was two days ago." He paused. "I think about what happened yesterday. Would a demon seek out a Communion ceremony? Would a demon accept Communion marks? But then why am I still uncertain? Why do I still fear for Refuge?"

"Remember, Father, you said he may be testing us."

"Yes. I did say that."

For a little while he was silent. She wrapped his left arm, and began on his right. The aromatic vapors of the ointment stung her eyes; her palms and fingers were numb with it.

"I have been wondering," Habrâmna said softly. "Whether it's possible to destroy a miracle. Whether doubt, or fear, or whatever it is that drives us to question the things that come to us, might so compromise the astonishment and humility we should give a miracle that we become incapable of perceiving it. I say to myself this cannot be—surely the work of the god does not depend on human understanding. Surely if there *is* a miracle, it will prove itself no matter what we do or do not do." In the yellow lamplight his face was brushed with shadow; the lines in it seemed very deep. "I pray I won't be punished for such questions when the time of cleansing comes."

Habrâmna was not a doubting man. His faith in himself was as steadfast as his faith in Refuge; he thought long and carefully before deciding, but never reconsidered once a decision had been made. Axane could not remember, ever in her life, hearing him speak as he just had. Her heart contracted with dread.

"Ârata sees your soul, Father," she said. "He knows you think only of Refuge. He knows your questions rise from that."

"Axane." He smiled, the darkness lifting for a moment, and reached out to touch her cheek. "My faithful child."

She tied the last bandage at his wrist, and cleaned her hands. "Is there anything else you need, Father?"

"Not tonight. Kiss me, Axane." She obeyed. "Now help me to bed and blow out the lamps."

She gathered up her supplies and returned to her room to put them away. With her basin, she went out again onto the floor of Labyrinth to fetch water for Narstame. Walking back from the cistern, she glanced toward the prayer groups, still defiantly present, but clustered now at the back of Labyrinth where they were less in the way. Her father was right: There were more of them than there had been that morning.

The dread that had risen in her father's apartment gripped her again. How long would they wait for answers, the faithful and the doubters both? And the Shapers, with their examination?

She had perceived the strangers' danger on the day of their arrival. It had not meant a great deal to her then; they were fascinating, extraordinary, but they were strangers, and she had no reason to care for them. But she had washed Gâbrios's limbs, fed him porridge spoon by spoon. She had secured splints around Diasarta's leg. She had felt the pressure of Teispas's dark hawk-gaze. She had sat face-to-face with Gyalo Amdo Samchen; she had given him secrets she had never shared with anyone and listened, rapt, as he spoke about his world. She knew them now. It was no longer possible to be indifferent to their fate.

Returning to Labyrinth the next morning with Parimene, Axane saw a procession emerging from the shadow of the entrance. Habrâmna led the way, with Gyalo Amdo Samchen by his side. Teispas and the ten members of the council followed.

They halted by the pulley apparatus that brought water up from the river; Habrâmna spoke and gestured, presumably explaining its operation. Then they came on, slowly, moving at Habrâmna's labored pace. Axane and Parimene pressed back against the rock to let them by. Gyalo Amdo Samchen looked haggard; in the harsh sunlight his uneven coloring— red-brown across cheeks and forehead, paler at scalp and chin where the skin had been protected by his hair and beard—was like a mask. Axane found herself hoping he would look at her, but he did not spare her so much as a glance.

Inside Labyrinth, the prayer groups had finally dispersed. Axane and Parimene tended Gâbrios, then visited some of Parimene's other patients: a woman whose monthly blood would not stop, a little boy who had knocked over a lamp and burned his leg, a carpenter who had sliced his thigh with an adze, an elderly man with a wasting sickness similar to Narstame's.

It was Habrâmna who had decided Axane should be a healer—as her mother had been, before she vanished into the House of Dreams. Typically, he had not consulted her. Still, it had been a good choice: She did not enjoy the endless herb preparation and packet sewing and bandage rolling that made up the bulk of the junior healers' duties, but the tending of patients was deeply satisfying to her. Even those who could not be saved could be helped—their suffering eased, their fear comforted. The sick did not care who she was; it was what she did for them that mattered. In healing, the pretense she lived each day of her life in Refuge drew closest to her true, hidden self.

But today her attention was not on her work. In her mind, she followed Gyalo Amdo Samchen on his journey through Refuge. Habrâmna would bring him first to the Treasury, conducting him through the workshops, the storehouses, the food-processing areas, the long hall at the back, where each year on the anniversary of Refuge's founding the ordained Shapers gathered to shape great quantities of wheat, flax, and salt—the Three Essential Elements the Plains of Blessing did not provide. They would continue on to the House of Dreams—would they go inside? Perhaps not, because of the risk of disturbing the Dreamers—then to the outdoor workshops and perhaps down to the Plains, to view the fields the community maintained along the banks of Revelation. As the morning dragged on, dread grew in her that Gyalo Amdo Samchen would say something, make some error that would solidify Habrâmna's doubts into certainty. He should never have consented to this tour. The strangers' mystery protected them; the more they exposed themselves to observation, the less that would be so.

Toward noon, from the herbary balustrade where she had gone to tear linen for bandages, Axane saw the group returning. It had acquired a crowd of followers, men and women and children who had left their work to trail along. They laughed and jostled as if it were a celebration; Axane knew her father must disapprove, but he had not tried to stop them. He walked at the procession's head, deep in conversation with Gyalo Amdo Samchen: She could see nothing to indicate that anything was amiss.

Just short of the Treasury, a knot of children came pelting

up from behind. One little girl stumbled and fell at Gyalo Amdo Samchen's feet. He stopped, bringing the entire procession to a halt, and lifted the weeping child upright. He spoke to her; she nodded, and her face broke into a smile. He smiled back. Axane felt her heart turn over. For an instant it seemed to her she glimpsed a different man, freed from the shell of injury and care.

"How strange he is to look at."

A group of workers had come to join Axane at the balustrade. It was a trainee healer who had spoken, her voice hushed as if she feared she might be overheard.

"He's the Next Messenger, girl," said a cook. "To Ârata, who made him, he isn't strange."

"Will he speak to us?" the trainee asked. "Now he's come out?"

"What do you think, Axane?"

Their faces turned toward her. She felt the pressure of their hope, their longing. "I don't know," she said quietly.

Parimene was called away that afternoon to a difficult childbirth, giving Axane at last the opportunity she needed. She had to take a trainee with her to help with Gâbrios, who still required lifting; the girl was so awed and frightened she could barely follow Axane's instructions and fled gladly when she was dismissed. Axane hurried down the passage, her heart racing. The tour had finished sometime earlier; Teispas had returned, but Gyalo Amdo Samchen's room was empty.

She stood before it a moment. Her disappointment was so acute she felt like weeping. At last she turned and walked back down the hall, and paused before Teispas's chamber. He was sitting against the headboard of his bed, his legs streched out and his arms folded across his chest, still as a man carved out of wood. His eyes rested on her, but she had the sense he did not see her.

"Excuse me," she said. "Do you know where the . . . the Next Messenger is?"

He blinked; there was a moment of blankness, as if he

were drawing his attention back from some great distance. "The Shapers took him," he said. "After we finished inspecting your facilities. Is he not returned?"

"No." Axane felt a constriction in her chest. "Did they say why they wanted him?"

He shook his head.

"I see." Belatedly, she remembered why she was supposed to be here. "Is there anything you need? Anything I can fetch for you?"

He watched her. He had not shaved his chin and scalp, as Gyalo Amdo Samchen had, but he had trimmed his beard and braided back his hair, and no longer looked so wild. His eyes were as black as her father's, but with a peculiar light-less quality that made them seem, somehow, more than merely dark. Did he know about her? Surely Gyalo Amdo Samchen would have passed on to his companions what she had told him. But she could read nothing in that hard face.

"Thank you," he said. "I am content."

Axane returned to the herbary. Her heart beat too fast; she barely saw what was before her. The Shapers were examining him—right then, that moment. What would they ask? What would they expect? Would they show him the treasures they were charged to keep—the sheets of bark, too fragile now to be unrolled, on which Cyras and Mandapâxa had set down their histories in ink made of soot from the cook fires; the eleven scrolls, one for each of the bloodlines, where the genealogies of Refuge were recorded; the reliquary that contained a lock of hair from each of the First Twenty-Three; the sheet of parchment on which, dreaming of her death, Risaryâsi had written out the story of her calling? Would they bring him to the Cavern of the Blood? She dreaded that she had not explained enough, or warned enough; she dreaded that he might, in his frustration, do as he had threatened the other day, and deny his Messenger-hood. Even if he dissembled successfully, how long could the truth be forestalled?

At the Communion ceremony, all the Shapers were present. They had finished with him, then. She could not read anything in their demeanor; they seemed as calm, as deliberate as always. She could hardly wait for the evening meal to end, so she could visit her father on some healing pretext and get him to tell her what had occurred. But he decided that night to go in to Vivanishâri, and when she came to his chamber with an infusion for him to drink, she found it empty. She stood, irresolute. Could she go to the strangers' apartment? But if she did, she would be seen, and there would be gossip, for she had no reason to be there at this hour. Better, she thought reluctantly, to wait until tomorrow.

She gave the infusion to Narstame and helped the old woman prepare for sleep. Then she went to her room, where she sat on her bed and stared unseeing at the entrance curtain. During the dry season, when Revelation sank low in its sandy course across the Plains, the ordained Shapers often mounted to the summit of the cleft to call in rain. As a child, Axane had liked to follow them to that high place and watch the storm clouds gather. There was a heavy, pregnant quality to the air at such times, a sense of great forces stirring just below the threshold of perception. She had that feeling now, and it frightened her.

Vivanishâri attended to Habrâmna after the nights they spent together, so Axane's duties the next morning included only Narstame. Returning to the apartment with her stepmother's morning meal, she saw Râvar striding purposefully toward her—alone for once, without his followers. Her heart sank. He had stayed away from her these past days—still angry, she supposed, about what had happened between them. She quickened her pace. But he was faster, and intercepted her before she reached the entrance.

"Axane." He was like a flame today, in a red tunic sashed with orange, his hair bound back with crimson cords. "I need to speak with you."

"What about?"

He shook his head. "Not here. I don't want the rest of e listening in."

"I have a lot to do, Râvar."

"It's important. It won't take long. It's nothing to do with us." This was said with some bitterness. "If that's what you're worried about."

Axane felt a burst of anger. "Do you really think I'd go anywhere alone with you, after last time?"

His lips thinned. "I won't touch you. You have my word. Just come with me." And then, when she did not reply: "Please."

She stared at him, amazed. Please? That was not like him. Perhaps it really was important. She did not trust him, not a bit; she could not look at him without thinking of the storm he had made, the storm that had destroyed the strangers' expedition. And yet . . . he and Sonhauka must have been there yesterday, when the Shapers took Gyalo Amdo Samchen. Perhaps, if she agreed to listen to him, he would tell her what had happened.

"All right," she said. "Just for a little while. Let me bring this to Narstame first."

He waited, impatient, while she did, then set a swift pace out of Labyrinth, turning toward the Temple. The sun blazed down from a sky as hard as turquoise. She averted her eyes from the glances of passersby, imagining what they must be thinking; already, she regretted her decision. They passed the Shapers' quarters, and she realized that he meant to climb to the summit. She halted.

"I won't go to the summit with you." She had to raise her voice to be heard above the roar of Revelation.

He turned. "But I told you, I want to talk privately. And it's quieter up top."

"I won't go up there."

"I said I wouldn't touch you. I gave you my word. Isn't that enough?"

"I will not go up with you," she repeated. "Talk to me down here, or don't talk to me at all."

He glared at her, struggling to master his anger. She tensed, ready to turn about and flee.

"Very well," he said. "Have it your way." He drew

breath. His beautiful face smoothed, grew solemn. "Axane. I told you this wasn't about you and me, and I meant it. I'm speaking to you now as a manifest Shaper. It's not safe for you in the strangers' apartment. You must go to your father and ask him to find another healer to tend those creatures."

She stared at him; a premonitory sense of dread drew a thread of cold along her spine, despite the simmering air. "What do you mean?"

"They are not men, Axane. They're demons, creations of Ârdaxcasa."

"Why," she said carefully, "do you think that?"

He said, with frustration: "Isn't it enough for you that I'm a manifest Shaper, giving you a warning? Is there nothing I can say to you that you will hear?"

"Râvar, I've tended these men. I've seen them close, I've talked to them. I've seen nothing to make me think they aren't as human as I am."

"They're cleverly made, I admit it. But they aren't what they seem. Axane, I swear to you it's so."

"Something happened yesterday." She could no longer keep from saying it. "Didn't it?" For the first time, his eyes slid from hers. She stepped toward him; it was difficult to keep the urgency from her voice. "Râvar, I know the Next Messenger went with the Shapers yesterday. Everyone knows it. Did he do something, say something, to make them think him false? Is that why you're telling me this?"

"I'm not supposed to tell you anything at all." He was half-turned away from her, leaning against the cleft wall. With one slim hand he traced the striations of the rock beside him, his eyes following the path of his fingers. "These are Shaper matters. They aren't meant to be shared."

"But if it's true, all of Refuge must know eventually, yes?" He did not reply. "Râvar, you can't just tell me something, something that goes against what I've seen with my own eyes, and expect me to believe you simply because you've said it! You don't have a Shaper's authority. You aren't even _ained. I don't even know how you know this!" She was ___ that her voice was rising, but could not control it.

"Convince me. Convince me, or I'll walk away right now and go back to my work!"

"All right!" He slapped his palm down hard against the rock, and turned to face her fully. "All right. I was there yesterday. I and Sonhauka. The ordained Shapers brought . . . *him* . . . into the Shaper quarters. They showed him the scrolls and the relics, the things only Shapers see. He asked questions, many questions—about our training, about our vows, about what's written in the scrolls. He was curious about how Refuge was made—he wanted to see how we work the stone. It was not . . . proper, what he asked. The Next Messenger should know our ways. He should understand, without having to be shown."

"Perhaps he was testing you."

He shook his head. "That's not how it seemed. Then it was our turn to question him. Some questions he answered, some he did not. When we asked to see the Blood he wears—or the thing that seems to be the Blood—he said he had not brought it with him, and when we asked him to fetch it he refused! I didn't talk to him, you understand—I only watched. But I could see—I could see that *he did not want to speak to us.* He did not want to give us answers. If he truly were the Next Messenger, why would he be so secretive? Why would he refuse to share with us what he knows?"

He spoke these questions as if she might actually be able to answer them. In his face she saw no anger, no Shaper arrogance, but some struggling emotion that seemed closer to horror.

"He asked us to bring him to the Cavern of the Blood. Haxmapâya and Oronish thought it was too soon, but Gâvarti persuaded them. The way he stumbled as he followed us, the way he looked around him—it was as if it were all completely unknown to him. And then, when we reached the Cavern . . ." He had shifted away from her again, his fingers moving upon the rock. "At first he just stood there. He looked"—he drew in his breath—"*stunned.* As if someone had struck him. Then he fell to his knees. He reached out to the crystals. He . . . he put his hands on them. The facets cut him. We saw the blood." He swallowed, convulsively. "Oronish cried out; I don't know what she might have done if Haxmapâya hadn't held on to her. We waited, I don't know for how long. Finally, he got up. He was staggering. Gâvarti had to help him down the stairs. When we got to the ledge he broke away. He didn't stop, didn't look back. We let him go."

He pushed himself away from the stone and met her eyes. He was sweating heavily, perspiration sliding down his smooth throat to darken the neck of his crimson tunic.

"From the first moment I saw him I suspected him, Axane. His face, that necklace, his companions—all of it felt wrong to me. How could the Next Messenger be so . . . so human? So weak? So ignorant? But in the Cavern, I knew for certain. He wasn't prepared for what he saw there. He knew only that dead semblance of the Blood he carries, which was made for him by the Enemy, who is all darkness and cannot create light. When he saw the living fire of the true Blood, he couldn't bear it. That's why he shed his own blood on the crystals, to corrupt them. Gâvarti and the others went back afterward and unmade what he left behind. The Cavern is safe now. But we are not. Refuge is not." His face, his body, were taut with urgency. "They are demons, the strangers—you must believe me. You must promise me you won't go back to tend them."

Axane felt as if iron bands had closed around her heart. The world seemed to shake to the rhythm of her pulse. "What do the other Shapers think?"

"They're divided," he said reluctantly. "Gâvarti feels as I do, and Haxmapâya and Sarax and Oronish. But Jândaste and Aryam say it's a test of faith, and Uspardit and Varas won't commit themselves either way. I don't know what will happen. But Axane, I know I'm right. I've never been so certain of anything in my life."

"Has Gâvarti spoken to my father?"

"Yesterday afternoon. Axane. I've told you everything, all I know. Will you promise as I ask?"

"Yes," she said. With her whole being she desired flight;

below her feet, the headlong rush of Revelation mocked her stillness. "I will."

"You mean it." His eyes searched her face. "You're truly promising me."

"Yes, Râvar."

"Good." The tension seemed to leave him all at once. He sighed and reached up to rub sweat from his eyes, using the heels of both hands, like a child. "That's all right then."

"I have to go, Râvar."

"Axane." He reached toward her, but then—remembering his promise perhaps—let his hand fall. "Don't tell your father I've spoken to you. I'll be punished if Gâvarti finds out."

"Yes, Râvar."

"I did this for you," he said intensely. "I disobeyed my teachers, I put my Shaperhood second—for you, to keep you safe. I didn't know . . . until yesterday, I didn't know I was capable of such a thing. Will you believe me now, when I tell you I love you?"

His river green eyes burned into hers. How many times had he asked this question? How many times had she dismissed it? His inexplicable fixation on her was not love. How could it be, with the differences between them? He only wanted her because she hid from him—because she would not, like everything else in his life, give herself easily into his hands.

Yet this time was not like the others. Perhaps it was the way he looked at her, his face utterly open and defenseless. Perhaps it was the knowledge that he was willing for her sake to betray the Shaper mysteries she knew he honored above all things. Perhaps it was the strangeness of the past days, transforming the world around her so that everything in it, even Râvar, seemed new. She did not know. But in that moment, the sun like iron on her shoulders and urgency filling her so she could scarcely breathe, she found she did believe him—fully, at last, believed he loved her.

Her heart seemed to fold in on itself. She did not want to know it. Not then; not ever.

"Good-bye, Râvar."

She saw the hurt flare in his face. Then his mouth tightened, and his brows drew down. He turned toward the cleft wall again, standing silent as she left him.

Her body urged her to run. It took all her self-control to walk sedately down the ledge and into Labyrinth, to climb quietly up the stairs. Inside the strangers' apartment she abandoned caution and raced along the passage.

Gyalo Amdo Samchen was in his room, kneeling on the floor beside his bed. He appeared to be deep in meditation; in the dimness, his face was utterly serene. She stepped a little way inside the entrance.

"I'm sorry to disturb you. I need to talk to you." He did not stir. She raised her voice. "I need—"

"He won't answer."

She gasped and jumped around. It was Teispas, coming up behind her as silent as a spirit.

"I startled you." He smiled, faintly. "A bad habit of mine."

"What . . . what do you mean, he won't answer?"

"He's been like that ever since they brought him back yesterday. I don't think he's moved at all."

"Is he meditating?"

"I don't know what he's doing." He moved past her into the chamber and took the small lamp—again, the only one alight—from the table. Shadows fled before him. He crouched and brought it close to Gyalo Amdo Samchen's face. "Look."

She went to stand beside him. She could see, now, that Gyalo Amdo Samchen's eyes were turned up inside his head; beneath his half-open lids, only the whites showed. A fine tremor ran through his body, and sweat sheened his skin—the neck of his tunic was dark with it, and there were deep wet circles under his arms. There was no sign he was aware of them, or of the flame so near his face.

"I've seen him meditate," Teispas said. "But never like this." He looked up at her, frowning. "What happened yesterday? Do you know?"

Axane dropped to her knees. She reached out and touched

Gyalo Amdo Samchen's forehead, expecting fever, but he was cool. His breathing was regular, if a little slow, and when she set her fingers against his throat his pulse beat strong. His hands rested on his thighs; she took them and turned them over. The palms and fingers were marked with lacerations, neat as knife cuts and crusted with dried blood. There were stains on his tunic where they had lain.

"Ash of the Enemy!" Startled out of his hard composure, Teispas lowered the lamp to get a better look. "What is this?"

Gently, she held the wounded hands. In her mind she saw the scene Râvar had described: Gyalo Amdo Samchen, falling to his knees before the Cavern of the Blood, reaching blindly toward the burning crystals. She heard his voice: *There's no Blood in the world of men. . . .* Râvar was right, though he did not understand the truth of it. She knew what Gyalo Amdo Samchen believed, knew what he must have expected to see inside the Cavern. Instead he had seen . . . what was there. And, like Risaryâsi, he had recognized it.

It rose in her again, the impulse that had gripped her three days ago—to reach out to this man in comfort, to blot the sweat from his face and throat, to soothe the lids down over his upturned eyes. Now, as then, she sensed it was something he would not want. And yet she might have done it if Teispas had not been beside her.

"These cuts need cleaning," she said.

"Ârata's wounds, woman!" Teispas gripped her shoulder, trying to turn her toward him. "If you know what happened to him, you must tell me!"

Once—long ago, it seemed—it might have frightened her to be handled by this stranger. Not now. She twitched herself from Teispas's grasp, and replaced Gyalo Amdo Samchen's hands softly on his thighs. She turned and met Teispas's eyes.

"Do you know about me?"

He blinked. "Know about you?"

"Did he tell you what I told him? About Refuge? About what my people believe?"

"Ah. That." He sat back on his heels and put the lamp on the floor. "He didn't say who spoke to him. But I saw you, the other day, walking past my door. I guessed it must be you." His lightless gaze moved past her. There was a complicated expression on his face. "Another man might not have told me anything. There's offense between him and me—perhaps he mentioned that?"

"No."

"Ah." That faint smile again, but bitter this time. "Will you tell me now what happened to him?"

"I can tell you what happened to his hands. The Shapers took him to the Cavern of the Blood. The crystals are sharp—he touched them, that's how he got the cuts. I'm not sure why he's like"—she glanced at his unresponsive face—"this. But you must find a way to rouse him. You must leave here, all of you, as soon as you can. Four of the Shapers have decided you are false, and it's only a matter of time before they convince my father and the council. I'll help you, I'll do anything I can, but you must go."

He frowned. "False?"

"Yes! Didn't he tell you what my people believe about the outside world? That there are no human beings in it besides us?"

"Yes," he said, cautiously.

"Now four of the Shapers have decided he is not the Next Messenger, but a creation of Ârdaxcasa, a demon, and all of you with him. I don't know what will happen to you if you stay here. You must leave. You must go." And then, when he stared at her and did not speak: "You must have known this would happen! *You* know he's not the Next Messenger! You can't be completely unprepared!"

"No. It's just that I'd hoped to have more time." He sighed. "Very well. We'll do as you say."

"I'll get as much ready as I can this afternoon. Tonight I'll come for you."

"Gâbrios. He can't walk."

"There are litters in the Treasury. I'll show you where they are. Once you get out of the cleft, you can follow Revelation. Halfway to the western ocean the stone barrens end—you can turn north there."

"Would it be possible to get us knives? Perhaps a bow and arrows?"

"Yes, of course." She drew a breath. "There's something else. There may be pursuit. The Shapers—" She faltered. "They may not want to let you go."

He nodded. "I understand."

"I don't think you do. They can open crevasses under your feet. They can make a rain of stones to crush you. They can call storms—you already know what those are like. Whatever they choose to do, you won't be able to avoid it or outrun it. I'm trying to tell you that even if you leave Refuge, you may not survive."

"I *do* understand," he said gently. "Believe me. I thank you for your concern. But we do not fear your Shapers."

For the first time, it occurred to Axane to wonder if he were entirely sane. Well, she had given warning; she could do no more.

"I must go now." She pushed herself to her feet. Teispas rose also, leaving the lamp flickering on the floor. "Parimene will be with me when I come back. I don't want her to see him like this. You must tell her he's meditating and can't be disturbed."

He nodded.

"I'll bring bandages and salve for his hands. I'll leave them under Gâbrios's bed."

"This is dangerous for you, too, isn't it? Your people wouldn't forgive it if they discovered you'd helped us."

"No one will discover it. I'll make sure."

He touched his lips with both hands and held them toward her. In his harsh face, she saw something like admiration. "We're in your debt, lady."

She glanced back as she left the room. He had pulled a

blanket from the bed and was folding it around Gyalo Amdo Samchen's shoulders. His hands were gentle; there was nothing in his manner of a man who carried, or had given, offense. *I wonder what it is between them*, she thought. And then, with an odd contraction of her heart: *Now I'll never know.*

—11—

Axane fetched Parimene and returned to Labyrinth to care for Gâbrios. Afterward she went back to the herbary, to pursue her tasks among the dwindling corps of healers. Once before the noon meal and once just after, she paid surreptitious visits to the storerooms, gathering food into bags— dried meat, dried fruit, a pelletlike grain that could be crushed and mixed with water and baked into travel bread. The knives and bows Teispas had requested would have to wait till night; Refuge's hunting equipment was carefully monitored, and she could not take anything without accounting for its use.

As the day drew on, her nerves pulled tauter than parchment stretched for curing. Despite Teispas's concern, she was not really worried for herself. If she were caught, she could claim to be acting from devotion, spurred by Râvar's warning, which she could say she had disbelieved; she would be punished, but nothing more essential than her judgment would be called in question. It was for the strangers that she was afraid. She feared her father and the council might choose to act too soon. She feared the escape might be discovered. She feared what the Shapers might send in pursuit.

Behind her fear lay the imminence of the next day, when they would be gone. For the past days she had lived beyond her normal life; even the most ordinary activities had been illuminated by the mysteries and possibilities of the strangers' presence. Her forced union with Râvar, which had eaten up all her thoughts before Gyalo Amdo Samchen came, had hardly troubled her. It seemed impossible that this should still be waiting—that in the morning she should simply continue on as always, as if there had been no interruption.

It was on the second of her storeroom visits that it came to her: When the strangers left, she could go with them.

She stood as if struck to stone, the supply bag in one hand, the other buried in a basket of dried fruit. The world seemed to turn over beneath her feet. *No*, she thought. *It's not possible.* What guarantee was there that the strangers would survive Shaper pursuit? And even if they did, there was still the Burning Land. It must be possible to travel it without a Shaper's power, or they could not have gotten here—and yet there had been many of them, with animals and supplies, and now there were just four, only two of them fully able. And supposing they did reach the outside world, and she with them—where would she go, how would she live? Was it reasonable to imagine that Gyalo Amdo Samchen might protect her? Why should he even agree to let her accompany him—a woman, a burden, another mouth to feed?

And her father. How could she think of leaving her father?

She forced herself back into motion, stuffing the fruit she held into the bag. She went on filling it, handful by handful, trying to compose her thoughts even as her imagination raced forward into a mad vision of the future. To walk the outside world . . . to look with waking eyes upon the kingdoms of Galea . . . to live in a place where Dreamers could freely choose their lives, where she would not have to keep the secret of what she was . . . With all her soul she longed for that, with all the force of her years of concealment. It was not a new longing; it had been with her since she first began to believe in the reality of the outside world. But like her adolescent yearning to be beautiful, there had been no thought it might ever be fulfilled. Now, in an instant, everything had changed. It still might not be possible to reach the outside world—but for the first time, it was possible to try. If she remained in Refuge, she would spend the rest of her life wondering what might have happened had she gone.

What would she grieve to leave behind? Not her extended family. Not her fellow healers. Not the work she did. Not Labyrinth or the Treasury—not even Revelation, whose song was woven into nearly every memory of her life. And not Râvar—never Râvar. If she remained, what was the likelihood that she would escape intent with him?

There was only her father. In the whole of Refuge, her love for him, her duty, was all there was to hold her.

No, she thought, frightened now. *How could I betray him so? How could I give up all I know for something so uncertain? It's mad. Impossible. I will not think of it.* She pulled the neck of the bag closed, knotting the drawstrings with a savage yank, and hid it with the others. Then she went back to work.

Midway through the afternoon, she was summoned to the council chamber: A meeting had been called, and she was needed to record it. She felt light-headed as she walked down the stairs, or as if she might be sick. Four councilors were already present when she got there, clustered near the table's foot. Habrâmna sat stiffly at its head, his twisted hands clasped before him; she forced herself to smile as she took her place beside him, but she could not make her eyes meet his. Writing implements had been laid out for her—an inkwell fashioned from the shell of a marrow nut, a reed pen, a folio made from squares of stiffened linen stitched together down one side.

Singly and in little groups, the rest of the councilors arrived. There were eleven in all, including Habrâmna, one for each of the bloodlines sprung from the First Twenty-Three. Each bloodline chose its own representative; the community as a whole elected Refuge's leader from among them. Representatives (and the leader) could be removed by a similar vote. But that had happened only a few times over the course of Refuge's history—in practice council members served for life, or until they voluntarily retired.

When everyone was present, Habrâmna spoke.

"My thanks to you for coming together at such short notice. An hour ago, the Next Messenger"—only Axane, perhaps, perceived his hesitation over the title—"sent word to me. It's at his request that I've called you here. He wishes to address us."

He's awake, was Axane's first thought; and then, frantically, *Why*? Had Teispas not explained the danger? Surely he did not think to reason with the council, to try and persuade them from suspicion . . . it would only make things worse.

The councilors were looking at each other.

"Does he intend to declare himself?" asked Dâryavati. She was representative to the Utani, the larger of the bloodlines sprung from Refuge's two original Dreamers, a handsome woman with amber skin and hair that had gone prematurely silver.

"He did not share his reasons," Habrâmna said.

"The ordained Shapers should be here," said Omida, a rope-thin elder past the age of manual labor, representative to one of the seven Forceless bloodlines. From her father, Axane knew that Omida was among those who had most strenuously questioned Gyalo Amdo Samchen's authenticity.

"They have been summoned."

Soon after, the Shapers arrived. They filed into the room and ranged themselves along the wall. Râvar and Sonhauka were with them; Sonhauka looked nervous, but Râvar was composed. His eyes slid to Axane's as he entered, then away.

"We're ready," Habrâmna said. "Cistâmnes. Send someone to fetch the Next Messenger."

Cistâmnes—representative to the Mandapâxan Shaper bloodline, whose yellow eyes bespoke his close kinship to Narstame—rose and left the room. The council waited. In the lamplight, the walls of the meeting room glowed like a hand held before a flame; the broad yellow band below the ceiling seemed as bright as beaten gold. The sounds of the Treasury filtered faintly through the silence, and the smell of its abundance hung in the air: grain, spice, the tang of smoke. Axane took the lid from the inkwell and laid the pen ready across it. Her hands were unsteady; she hid them in her lap.

Gyalo Amdo Samchen arrived at last, Teispas at his side. Four councilors—Dâryavati, Cistâmnes, and two of the Forceless representatives—sprang to their feet, bowing their heads in reverence. There was some uneasy stirring, then most of the others followed suit. Only three remained seated: Omida, another Forceless councilor named Kariyet, and Habrâmna. The Shapers watched, unmoving.

"Welcome." Habrâmna did not excuse his failure to rise. He gestured to the single empty chair, at the table's foot. "Please."

Axane could not take her eyes from Gyalo Amdo Samchen. It was difficult to believe this was the same man she had seen just hours before, eyes rolled up inside his head, face dewed with chilly sweat. Gone was the exhaustion, the transparent frailty of a man pushed beyond his limits. Energy sprang from him, like radiance from the sun; confident purpose spoke in every line of his body, in his firm-set mouth and the steadiness with which he met Habrâmna's hooded gaze. And it seemed to Axane that she saw something else as well, shining up through the surface of his skin, like lamplight through linen—some inner core of . . . joy? Triumph?

Horror seized her, an absolute premonition of catastrophe. *Turn around*, she wanted to cry to him; *go back, don't speak.* But even if she had had the courage to do it, it was too late. It had been too late the moment he walked into the room.

He strode forward and sat, folding his hands before him on the smooth surface of the table, echoing Habrâmna's stiff pose at the other end. His palms, Axane saw, were neatly bound with the strips of linen she had earlier slipped beneath Gâbrios's bed. Teispas took up a stance beside him, feet apart and arms clasped across his chest. His features were impassive; but his eyes moved ceaselessly, scanning the gathering.

"Thank you for receiving me," Gyalo Amdo Samchen said. "I've come before you today to tell you the truth of who I am."

Axane's heart pounded. She could hardly breathe for dread.

"I know your beliefs." His voice was clear, assured. "I know that some of what I have to say will not be easy for you to accept. I ask only that you hear me out. Hear me out, then decide.

"I am not the Next Messenger your Dreamer Risaryâsi said would come for you. I am a vowed Âratist, as your ancestors were—not a divinity, not a demon, just a man. The jewel around my neck, which you mistook for the Blood, is an image, a replica, made of glass and gold. Every vowed Âratist wears one, as a symbol of their service to the god."

The hush was so deep it was like a solid substance. The councilors sat as still as boulders; beside Axane, Habrâmna was a man made out of wood. Only his eyes seemed animate, two glittering black gems fixed on Gyalo Amdo Samchen's face.

"Risaryâsi misinterpreted much of what she dreamed. It's not surprising. She was alone, exiled from all she knew, fresh from the hardships of a terrible journey and desperate to understand what had happened to her. Her visions were powerful and full of meaning, but there was no one to help her read their symbols. She did her best. But she went astray.

"Here are her errors. An age did not end, as she believed. There are no cycles of repeating history. Ârdaxcasa did not rise. There was no new cosmic battle; humanity was not destroyed. Even now, as I sit speaking to you, the kingdoms of Galea exist exactly as they did when your forebears were forced into the Burning Land, ruled by the Way of Ârata under the guidance of the Âratist church. One of them, Chonggye, is my home, where I was born and took my vows and spent all my life till recently. Another, Haruko, is the home of Teispas"—he gestured with one bound hand toward the silent man beside him—"though in his soul he is a citizen of the seventh kingdom, Arsace, from which his ancestors, like yours, were cast out. The persecution that exiled him and you, the corrupt regime of atheism and oppression, is ended now. Its armies have been defeated, its officials and administrators deposed and punished. Arsace's rightful rulership has been restored. The Way of Ârata is once again the way of the Arsacian people.

"I tell you this from my own experience, from my own knowledge, and I give you my solemn oath that it is true. But you can confirm it for yourselves. Send your Dreamers outward—tell them to Dream across the Burning Land, beyond the Range of Clouds. They'll see the kingdoms of Galea. They'll see Arsace, newly free. They'll see I've spoken to you honestly."

He paused, gazing around at the gathered faces. Silence; no one stirred. Axane had given up the pretense of note-taking; her pen hung from her fingers, drops of ink falling from its nib to blot the folio page.

"Risaryâsi's errors were grave. But in the center of her understanding, in the core of her revelation, she was *not* mistaken. I admit . . . I admit I could not believe it, not at first. I saw the light shining above the cliffs at night, I heard the words of your faith—and I did not believe. But then . . . I *saw*. I looked upon the living fire in the crystals. I set my hands above them." He held his hands up, palms outward, their bindings faintly stained where blood and ointment had seeped through. "And I knew, I knew that it was *I* who was mistaken. It was *I* who had gone astray. Ârata has woken!" His voice did not rise, yet it was as triumphant as a shout. "And now I know the truth, the truth you have guarded in exile, while the world went on as if the god were still asleep."

At last someone spoke: Omida, his voice unsteady with anger. "First you say our beliefs are false. Then you affirm the truth of what we already know, as if we were ignorant of it! What are you telling us? What's your purpose here?"

Gyalo Amdo Samchen met the old councilor's gaze. "I want only for you to understand that *I* know the truth."

"Why should it matter to us what you know?"

"For this reason. I've said that I am not your Next Messenger. But I *have* been sent to bring you out of the Burning Land. The leaders of the church of Ârata know the injustice that was done your forebears. They wish to redress it, to restore you to your rightful place within the world. I ask you now to return with me to the kingdoms of Galea, where your brothers and sisters in Ârata wait to embrace you. I'd ask it even if there were no revelation, even if the Cavern of the Blood were not . . . what it is, for I would not leave you here in exile. But because there *is* a revelation, because the Cavern *is* what it is, I ask it even more urgently. Return with me. Help me bring the news of Ârata's rising to the church that was built in his name, so that it may begin to prepare for the time of the Next Messenger—the true Next Messenger—which is now at hand."

"You must think we're fools," Omida said furiously.

"Omida," said Habrâmna, warning in his voice.

"Someone must speak!" Omida turned on him. His creased face was taut with rage. "Someone must acknowledge the truth!"

"You have said enough."

Omida's ropy throat worked; for a moment it seemed he would not yield. But at last he sank back in his chair. Habrâmna turned his gaze upon Gyalo Amdo Samchen.

"This is what you ask of us?" His voice was as cold as the waters of Revelation. "That we follow you into the Burning Land?"

"Yes."

"Even though you tell us you are not the Next Messenger? Even though you say the understandings we have cherished for more than seven decades are false?"

Gyalo Amdo Samchen drew a breath, as if to explain or protest, then let it out again. "Yes," he said simply.

"And if we refuse?"

"I hope you will not refuse."

"But if we do?"

"Then I and my companions will return alone. It will be harder for me to bring this news, without your voices to confirm the truth of what I say. But I'll do what I must."

His eyes held Habrâmna's across the length of the table. For a moment, it was as if there were no others in the room.

"Is that all you have to say to us?" Habrâmna said at last.

"It is."

"We'll speak of it among ourselves. When we decide, we'll send to you."

Again Gyalo Amdo Samchen hesitated. But then he nodded and rose to his feet. He moved toward the chamber's entrance, Teispas close on his heels. Axane watched them go. He had sealed his fate by what he had just done. She knew it as surely as if she had already lived the hours to come.

For a moment there was silence. Then Omida turned to Habrâmna.

"You stopped me before. But I will speak now. He is false. A creation of the Enemy. He has been sent here to destroy us—if we go with him into the Burning Land, we'll die. Can you still have any doubt?"

Habrâmna said, through lips that barely seemed to move, "I would hear from the rest of you."

"He's false." Kariyet, a tiny dark woman who sat silent through most meetings, was the first to speak. "From the moment I saw that . . . necklace of his I was suspicious. I'm ashamed it took me so long to heed my doubts."

"He is false," said Ixtarser, one of the councilors who had made eager obeisance when Gyalo Amdo Samchen entered the room. He did not sound angry, as Kariyet did, but shocked. "Before this hour, I would not have thought it possible to say such a thing. But the Next Messenger could never utter such disgusting blasphemies." Revulsion shivered in his voice. "Not even to test us."

"He is false." "He is false." One by one the councilors and Shapers spoke—some decisively, some reluctantly, some with a kind of stunned disbelief. Two of the Forceless councilors abstained, declaring themselves unable to decide. Only Cistâmnes and Dâryavati, stubborn, proclaimed their unaltered faith; Aryam, youngest of the Shapers, and Jândaste, the eldest, also held fast.

"It is a test," Jândaste said. She suffered from an inflammation of the joints similar to Habrâmna's and stood with her hands braced on the head of a heavy walking stick. "He is trying the strength of our will to believe. He wants to see whether we can be tempted to reject him. He needs to know if we are strong enough to follow him."

"Absurd," Omida said. "The Next Messenger might test us, but not with such revolting blasphemy."

"How do you know?" Cistâmnes fixed the old councilor with his disconcerting yellow eyes. "And leaving that aside, who could he be *but* the Next Messenger? For more than seventy years our Dreamers have veiled us from Ârdaxcasa's sight. How could the Enemy's creature find us?"

"If you close your eyes and throw a stone often enough, you're bound to hit something," said Omida. "For all we know, he's been wandering the Burning Land since Risaryâsi first dreamed her revelation."

"And in truth, he didn't find us," Ixtarser pointed out. "It was our hunters who found him."

"No." Dâryavati shook her head, with its shining coils of silver hair. "I don't believe it. Ârata would not allow the Enemy's creature to come among us. He would have intervened to protect us."

"Ârata's attention is elsewhere," Omida said. "That is *why* the Dreamers must Dream the veil."

"Don't you suppose that if the Enemy sent a false Messenger, he'd make a better job of it?" Cistâmnes demanded. "Wouldn't he send a creature that fulfilled our expectations instead of one that contradicts them in every possible way?"

"Ârdaxcasa is darkness," said Gâvarti, entering the discussion for the first time. "Ârdaxcasa is chaos. He has no light in him, and he knows nothing of order. He could not do what you describe, Cistâmnes. It's precisely by this creature's contradictions that we recognize the Enemy's hand."

"But even if this false Next Messenger were made as

badly as you say, would he not at least claim to *be* the Next Messenger? Why would he admit that he is not?"

"Because," Gâvarti said, "he means not merely to destroy us, but to utterly corrupt our faith. To tempt us to put his blasphemies in place of Risaryâsi's revelation. To turn our minds so fully, to distort our belief so utterly, that we become willing to surrender our wills to one who is the obvious opposite of Risaryâsi's Promise—a Messenger who denies his Messengerhood, whose jewel is false, who rejects Risaryâsi's revelation and spins tales of a world that cannot exist. Would that not be a triumph for Ârdaxcasa—not just to lead us to our deaths, but to trick us into abandoning his bright brother's truth before we die?"

Beside her, all the Shapers but Aryam and Jândaste murmured assent. Râvar and Sonhauka—unordained, with no voice in such matters—were also silent; but Râvar's face was fierce with agreement.

"I say again—we are being tested." Jândaste leaned forward, supporting herself on her stick. "If we are to follow the Next Messenger through the Burning Land, if we are to rebuild the kingdoms of Galea, our faith must be stronger, purer, more powerful than it has ever been. It must be so strong that we believe even when there's nothing to confirm it, so pure that we believe even when everything gives us challenge, so powerful that we believe even when it disgusts or frightens us to do so. We must be capable of holding to the truth *even when everything contradicts it. That* is the challenge here. *That* is the test. To follow the Next Messenger even when he tells us our faith is false. To believe in him even when he denies his own nature."

"Yes." Cistâmnes was nodding. "Yes."

"If we reject this Messenger," Jândaste continued, "Ârata may one day forgive us and send another. But what if he does not? What if, in renouncing this chance, we renounce forever the destiny Risaryâsi promised us?"

"We must go to him," Dâryavati said urgently. "We must tell him we will follow him. We must show him we believe.

He'll reveal himself then. He'll reject the blasphemies he
spoke today."

"He wouldn't need to reject anything," said Omida. "For
in your blindness you would excuse him again and again.
You've swallowed his falsehood whole."

"And you," said Dâryavati, "have failed his test."

For a moment no one seemed to want to speak.

"We'll take a final vote." Heavily, Habrâmna broke the silence. "What say you all?"

Jândaste and Aryam, Cistâmnes and Dâryavati, held fast
to their declaration of belief. One of the abstaining councilors continued to abstain; the other had changed his mind
for falsity. The rest, again, voted false—as did Habrâmna,
speaking last.

"This . . . testing is not part of Risaryâsi's Promise," he
said. "I cannot believe, if we were to be tried in this way, that
she would not have warned of it."

"A test has no value," Jândaste said, "if it is expected."

Habrâmna shook his head. "The majority has spoken.
There remains the question of what to do."

"He must be destroyed," Omida said, instantly. "He and
his men."

Jândaste struck her stick against the floor. "That is unthinkable!"

"No!" Dâryavati's amber skin had gone ashen. "You can't
think to take his life!"

"I agree." Ixtarser stirred uneasily. "I'd have him gone, but
I don't want his blood on our hands. No matter what he is."

"Let him leave," Cistâmnes said. "Let those who believe
in him follow. That way, we may all answer our consciences,
and you'll be rid not just of him, but of those who have faith
in him. For mark my words, those who believe will not easily give up their belief."

"Divide Refuge?" Kariyet said, incredulous. Axane could
not recall the last time she had spoken twice in a council
session. "Allow our people to march to their deaths? Are
you mad?"

"Can you not see that Refuge is already divided?" Cistâmnes turned on her. "That if he is put to death, it will bring us to open war among ourselves?"

"We will all be cursed utterly to destruction." Jândaste trembled visibly with anger, or perhaps with horror. "Believe him false or not, can any of you say without the shadow of a doubt that you are correct? That there is no chance, no chance at all that you are wrong?"

"I can." Omida, flinty, met her gaze.

"No matter what our decision here today," Gâvarti said, "darkness will be brought on Refuge. But Omida is right. It is not enough to banish him. The Enemy made him for our destruction. He will not rest until his task has been accomplished. If we refuse this persuasion, he will try another. If we allow him to take only some of us into the Burning Land, he will come back for the rest. There is only one way to end this. We have no choice."

Back and forth the discussion went. This time the majority was not so clear. In addition to Ixtarsher, Dâryavati, Cistâmnes, and the two Shapers, three of the councilors who had voted false, as well as the one who had abstained, were unwilling to take the irrevocable step of condemning the strangers to death. Even Omida's angry exhortations, and Gâvarti's calmer interjections, could not sway them.

Axane, listening, felt strangely distanced from it all. Since Gyalo Amdo Samchen had left the room, it was as if a veil had fallen across the world; nothing before her—the councilors, their arguments, their urgency—seemed quite real. Beside her, Habrâmna sat motionless. His face, his posture, were controlled and commanding, but she saw by the way he gripped the arms of his chair that he was in pain. At last, either because he had heard enough or could bear no more, he held up both hands for silence.

"It seems to me that there is nothing to be gained from further discussion," he said. "Our positions are set, and I do not believe that either side will sway the other. Yet this is a judgment that should not be quickly made. Whatever we decide, we'll bear the burden of it for the rest of our lives. I would not have such a thing done lightly or in haste. Let us end this meeting now. Let us take the night to think, to meditate, to search our souls. Tomorrow we'll come together again and take a final vote."

He gazed around the table. Many of the councilors glanced away, but Cistâmnes met his eyes.

"What would be your vote," Cistâmnes asked, "if you were to vote now?"

Habrâmna said, without inflection: "I would vote for death."

Dâryavati put her hand to her mouth. Cistâmnes looked down at the table. For the first time, Axane saw defeat in his face.

"Gâvarti," Habrâmna said. "Take your Shapers. Go to the strangers. Confine them in their chambers. I don't care how you manage it—just make sure it's done so no one but a Shaper may free them, and so it is not apparent to those outside."

Gâvarti nodded, and began to turn. Jândaste stepped forward, placing herself in her superior's path.

"You put your hand to blasphemy if you do this thing."

"You know my mind," Gâvarti said quietly.

"I will not be part of it." Jândaste clutched her stick. "I declare myself in opposition. I refuse all further actions. May Ârata hear me, and remember, at the end of time."

"I refuse also." Aryam stepped to Jândaste's side. "May Ârata hear me, and remember, at the end of time."

Gâvarti nodded. Her seamed brown face, with its wreath of white curls, was somber. "I accept your opposition. Now I demand your oath. Swear you will not hinder us, or seek to undo our work."

"I cannot," Jândaste said.

"Nor can I," said Aryam.

"Then you must accept confinement at our hands." She gestured. "Haxmapâya, Oronish. Varas, Sarax. See to it."

The Shapers she had called came forward. Haxmapâya and Oronish took Jândaste's arms; Varas and Sarax took

Aryam's. They drew their colleagues toward the entrance. Their faces—prisoners' and captors' both—were like the faces of people going to their deaths.

"Râvar, Sonhauka," Gâvarti said. "Accompany them."

Sonhauka obeyed. But Râvar did not move.

"Let me be part of this," he said. The words shook with the force of his desire. "I know I have no vote. I know I'm not ordained. But please, let me serve Ârata in this way. Let me help to defend Refuge."

Gâvarti watched him—a long, clear, unblinking gaze. "Do you understand what you ask? What we go to do is beyond anything any of us have ever done, or will ever do again. Light or dark, it will be with us always. Do you truly wish to carry such a burden?"

"I would carry any burden. I would do anything. Risk anything. You know it's so."

Gâvarti nodded. "Yes," she said. "Very well."

Axane had to look away from the exaltation in his face.

Gâvarti moved toward the door, Râvar and the remaining Shapers behind her. The councilors rose and slowly followed.

"You did not write, daughter."

Axane looked at her father, at the blotted folio. Carefully, she set down the pen she still held.

"No, Father."

"It's just as well. I'm not certain I'd wish to have a record of this." Habrâmna pushed back his chair, its legs crying out against the stone of the floor. "Come, Axane. I need your arm."

She rose. Her body felt insubstantial, as it did when she dreamed; any moment, she thought, she would rise into the air and float away. Habrâmna took his stick and gripped her shoulder with his other hand. Step by slow step, they made their way out of the coolness of the Treasury, into the heat of late afternoon. The clamor of Revelation rose up to greet them. The way ahead was shadowed, but the summit still blazed with the pure light of the falling sun. The sky was a fathomless blue, as if a second, more peaceful river ran above their heads.

"Did you believe in him, Axane?"

Axane looked into her father's face. He seemed to have aged a decade in the past hours—she had never seen him look so old, so ill. His eyes searched hers; she seemed to see in them a question deeper than the one he had asked aloud.

"No, Father," she said, in a voice that did not sound like her own. "I never did."

"I'm glad." He sighed. For a moment they walked in silence. "I believe I've made the right decision. I believe it is what's best for us. For Refuge."

"You always do what's best for Refuge, Father."

"Ah," he said, so softly she almost did not hear him. "If only I had Ârata's gift of knowledge, so I might be sure."

— 12 —

When they reached Labyrinth, Gâvarti, Uspardit, and Râvar were already descending the stairway. Workers and others paused to watch, curious, but the Shapers' quiet progress gave nothing away, and most people soon turned back to what they had been doing. Gâvarti halted to speak with one of the cooks; the other two moved on and out of Labyrinth. Râvar passed Axane and Habrâmna without a glance; his face was no longer exalted, but dark, absorbed.

A little later, Gâvarti presented herself in Habrâmna's chamber and described how she and Râvar and Uspardit had mounted to the strangers' apartment and shaped clear crystal across the entrances of their rooms. They were thus inescapably confined, yet in a way that would not be visible to anyone glancing casually in from outside. The cooks had been told that the strangers planned to spend the coming hours in meditation and were not to be disturbed, even with food and drink. Gâvarti spoke quietly, but she moved as if her limbs were weighted, and her ancient face was like a mask.

"It has begun," Habrâmna said to Axane after Gâvarti had gone. He did not speak again.

That evening, for the first time in memory, the calling horns were late in blowing; and at the ceremony Aryam, Jândaste, Varas, and Sarax were absent. Axane heard the talk as she left the Temple, and afterward, in the eating gallery—was there sickness? A disagreement? Did it have something to do with the Next Messenger? Habrâmna, who despite his exhaustion had insisted on attending the ceremony, also insisted on sitting through the evening meal, though it was clear to anyone who looked at him that he was ill. Vivanishâri hovered over him, jumping up to fetch him things, urging him anxiously to eat and drink; when the meal was done she tried to take charge of him, but he waved her away and beckoned Axane instead. Axane saw the mingled hurt and fury on Vivanishâri's face, and knew she would not soon be forgiven for this slight.

Habrâmna kept up his pretense of strength on the way back to his chamber, but once inside he allowed himself to yield, so that Axane had to all but drag him to his bed, while he clenched his teeth against the groans of pain he could not suppress. She removed his sandals, which had left deep grooves in his swollen flesh, and untied the sash of his tunic. Then she fetched bandages and ointment and a flask of sleeping mixture from the store of household remedies in her room.

"Stay with me, Axane," he whispered after she had salved and bound his limbs and administered a dose of the sleeping mixture. They were the first words he had spoken since the ritual phrases of the Communion ceremony. "Until I sleep."

She obeyed, sitting on the edge of the bed, giving him her hand to hold when she saw he was groping for it. She watched him as he struggled for unconsciousness; between the ravages of his pain and the events of the afternoon, it was almost as if she were looking at someone she did not know.

Death, he had said. She could still hear it. *Death.*

She closed her eyes, shutting out his face. It was wrong, she knew, to blame him. It was not cruelty that drove him, or any other base emotion—he was not like Râvar, burning with the desire for retribution, eager to inflict punishment with his own hands. He truly believed he defended Refuge. Had she not been witness, these past days, to his doubt? Had she not, earlier, seen his hesitation?

Yet they were innocent, the strangers. They did not deserve to die for the terrible mischance of their arrival, for Refuge's mistaken beliefs. She imagined their fear and horror as the Shapers blocked them in. She saw Diasarta shouting, pounding futilely on the crystal, and Teispas standing with that stillness of his, regarding the barrier with his lightless eyes. And Gyalo Amdo Samchen . . . what had he done when he realized he was a prisoner?

His face rose up inside her mind—anguished, as it had been when they first met; smiling, as she had seen it the other day; transfigured, as it had seemed this afternoon. How could he have been such a fool? Surely, between what she had told him and the warnings Teispas must have passed on, he could not have imagined the council would listen to him, let alone accept what he had to say. She had seen the certainty of his belief, in the brief time they had spent together, but she would not have thought him the sort of man to follow conviction against reason. She must have judged him wrong.

A bitter rush of anger took her. She hoped he regretted it. She hoped he suffered now, knowing that he had cast aside for nothing the chance of escape she had offered. But then she thought of him as she had first seen him, lying on his bed with his back turned to the entrance of his chamber; and her anger slid away. It came to her, coldly, that if the council voted death the next day, the sentence was already all but accomplished. The crystal could simply be left in place until the strangers died.

Habrâmna stirred and muttered something inaudible, his fingers tightening on hers. She looked down into his dark, pain-lined face. She would talk to him in the morning, plead for the strangers' lives. He was Refuge's leader; he could choose, if he wished, to overrule the council. She did not think there was much chance he would. Still, she had to try.

She did not want to wonder, over the dreary years that lay ahead, whether there was anything she had left undone.

At last, when he had fallen fully asleep, she disengaged her hand and bent to kiss him softly on the forehead—for he was her father, and for all he had done, for all she could not feel it in herself just then, she knew she loved him. She left his room and tended to Narstame, and retreated at last, with relief, to the sanctuary of her own chamber.

She put on her bedgown and unpinned her hair and then, on impulse, went to her leaf-carved chest and took out her meditation square and Communion beads. She spread the square and knelt, and told off the affirmations and responses of the ceremony one by one. It had been a very long time since she had spoken her beads alone; it felt strange, and somewhat false, to do it now.

When the last bead had been told, she prayed. *Ârata*, she thought, *if you are still upon the earth, reach out your hand and save these men. They shouldn't die for Refuge's error. Don't let Refuge take their lives.*

She remained a little longer on her knees, striving for some sense her prayer had been received. But all she felt was silence, and her own growing certainty that there had been no point in praying. At last she got to her feet and blew out her lamps, and went to bed.

Sleep would not come. Images of the strangers' incarceration rose relentlessly before her inner eye. She saw them dying slowly behind their crystal walls, while the life of Labyrinth went on around them. So vividly did she imagine their fear and anguish that as the night wore on it began to seem like her own. Yet was it not, in a way? She was a prisoner, too, her fate as immutable as theirs. Perhaps she would not have found the courage to go with them, if they had managed to escape—but now she would never have the chance to choose. It seemed worse to know that, somehow, than to think she might have chosen wrongly.

At last she flung back her tangled covers, unable to bear the walls around her a moment longer. She must get out, out of Labyrinth. Quickly she tied on her sandals and pulled a day gown over her nightclothes. Wrapping herself in a stole, she left her father's apartment, emerging onto the nightbound floor of Labyrinth, where the coals of the cook fires winked red in their beds of ash, and fire pots made islands of illumination along the gallery walls. To her right, the arch of the entrance framed a slice of starry sky, the blackness of the cleft wall rising up beneath.

That was where she meant to go. But all at once a different impulse gripped her, and she found herself turning to the left, toward the stairway up to the tiers. *This is pointless*, she told herself even as she began to climb. *You can't help them—there's nothing you can do*. It made no difference; it was as if her mind and feet were not connected.

She stepped onto the third tier. Before her lay the entrance to the strangers' apartment, spilling over with soft lamplight. She halted, one hand against the wall, feeling the slickness of Shaper-wrought stone beneath her palm. Gâvarti and the others had done their work well. The crystal that blocked the rooms was faultlessly transparent, all but invisible to the casual glance. And yet . . . there was an odd distortion at the crystal's center, or at least at the center of the crystal that closed the closest chamber, the one where Gâbrios lay. The lamplight seemed to fall a little differently there—an irregularity in the material, perhaps. Or something inside, casting shadow.

Or . . . an opening?

Her heart began to pound. *No,* she thought. *Impossible.* But even as she thought it she was plunging down the passage, stumbling to a halt before the entrance. Unbelievably, it was so. There *was* a gap in the crystal, just big enough for a man to pass.

Beyond it, the room was empty.

She ran from room to room. All four crystal walls were breached. All four chambers were vacant. The blankets and linen had been removed from the beds, and two of the tables had been broken up—to make a litter for Gâbrios, no doubt.

Before the last room, the room that had been Gyalo Amdo Samchen's, she halted, panting. The floor seemed to heave beneath her feet; she felt dizzy and a little sick. This was the work of Shapers—in the water-smoothness of the openings, their rounded edges, it could be nothing else. There was no other force, in any case, capable of piercing such a thickness of stone. But who had done it? Aryam or Jândaste, escaping from custody? Another ordained Shaper, stricken by a change of heart? Yet the openings were crude, irregular, entirely unlike the expert Shaper stonework with which she was familiar. The one in front of her was the roughest of the four; it looked like a hole pushed into wet clay, or as if part of the crystal had briefly liquefied. She could not imagine the ordained Shapers, or even one of the older trainees, producing something so crude—and surely they would not have bothered with openings at all, but would have shaped away the crystal entirely. One of the younger trainees, then, creeping out after everyone had gone to sleep? But at that level of inexpertise, trainees were not capable of the sustained effort required to make an opening of any size, let alone one large enough for a man to slip through.

There was another possibility. One of the strangers was a Shaper.

It took her breath away. Why would they have hidden it? And yet, cast among strangers in a place that had so disastrously mistaken their identity, did it not make perfect sense that they would keep such a secret, against a possibility exactly like the one that had overtaken them? The more she thought of it, the more it explained: how they had gotten across the stone barrens after the storm destroyed the expedition. Why Teispas had been so unconcerned about the possibility of Shaper pursuit. Why Gyalo Amdo Samchen had risked speaking to the council: With shaping at his disposal, he did not need to fear their hostility. Even, perhaps, why the shaping was so rudimentary—for she knew shaping was practiced differently in the outside world, and perhaps this Shaper had not acquired stoneworking skills.

Most of all, it explained what was inescapably obvious as she stood before the entrance to Gyalo Amdo Samchen's chamber. The other openings appeared to have been made by someone standing outside the crystal—widest at the outer thickness, narrowing toward the inner. But the one in front of her was the opposite. As if it had been created from within.

It's he, she thought. *Gyalo Amdo Samchen is a Shaper.*

And they were gone. Escaped. Free.

She raced from the apartment, down the stairs, across Labyrinth's deserted floor. The night received her. She skimmed past the Temple, past the Shaper quarters, until she reached the stairway to the summit and, hastily knotting up her skirts, began to climb. On the summit she dashed westward, to the point where the cleft walls began to slope toward the Plains of Blessing. There she halted, gasping with the speed of her flight, and looked north.

The moon was only half-full. But it was enough to show her, after a moment or two of scanning, a small moving darkness upon the smoky dimness of the Plains. Behind spread a wake of trampled grass. They had already covered a fair distance; if they walked the night through, dawn would find them nearly at the stone barrens. A few hours more, and they would be out of sight.

She sank to her knees on the rough sandstone. It was hers again, the chance she had thought lost. But not for long. Every second took them farther from her. Soon they would be so far she could not catch them.

She must choose now, to stay or go.

Panic swept her, as it had that afternoon. All the reasons why she could not, should not go rose up before her. But if I stay, she thought . . . if I stay . . .

She seemed to see, spread before her like the shadowy expanses of the Plains, all the possible courses of her life in Refuge. Râvar. A child, marriage, the daily dread that he would pierce her lie. Perhaps he would, and denounce her, and she would be cast out. Perhaps he would not, and her secret would perish with her; but still she would have lived every day of her life in fear. Or perhaps she would prove barren after all, and become single again, caring for her father till he died and she was left alone to begin her own descent into old age. Different lives, different futures—yet each the same, each bounded by the same duty, the same deception.

She saw more, unfolding relentlessly like a Dream she could not control. If she stayed, she would go on dreaming—Dreams no different from the Dreams she dreamed now, yet not the same, for she would always know that what she saw in sleep she might have seen in waking time. She saw how her hidden knowledge, which she had hoarded like treasure, would grow hateful in its reminder of what could have been. She saw the emptiness of a wisdom that could never speak itself aloud, the burden of a falsehood she must carry always. She saw how she would grow to hate that falsehood across the monotony of the years—how she might even learn to wish she had embraced a Dreamer's fate. Once, she could not have conceived of anything more horrible. But for the first time, she grasped that what she had chosen was no better. It, too, was a kind of living death.

It was terrifying, this understanding. She had never seen so pitilessly what lay ahead for her. Yet never before had there been anything to set her life against in contrast. The strangers' coming—Gyalo Amdo Samchen's coming—had changed everything. She could never be what she had been, whether or not she remained in Refuge.

This is the only chance for me, she thought, agonized. *The only chance ever, my whole life long. How can I let it go?*

Something seemed to tear inside her. She folded herself around the pain, bowing her head onto her knees. She thought of how her father's hand had groped for hers as he fought his way toward slumber, of how he had whispered *Stay with me.* She felt as if she were a child again, tormented by her sleep, caught between a Dreamer's fate and her own desperate desire to be free. She had chosen freedom then— over faith, over duty, over love and guilt. But it had not been a reasoned choice, for she had been too young to understand the consequences. It was different now—years different. She knew exactly what it meant for her to choose.

She wept, crouched upon the summit. Even as she did, she knew the choice was made.

The tears stopped. She used the stole to dry her face and got to her feet, her mind already turning to practicalities. She must return to her room, pack blankets and clothing. Then to the Treasury, to retrieve the bags she had prepared earlier. Gyalo Amdo Samchen might be a Shaper, but food would still be welcome.

Would they accept her? The question, which had come to her that afternoon, stirred again. It was the single thing that could undo her choice. She had her healing skills to offer, her witness to Refuge. Gyalo Amdo Samchen wanted witness—he had said so this afternoon. Would it be enough?

Ahead, the golden effulgence of the Cavern shimmered above the summit. She looked at it, an idea forming in her mind. What if she brought him better witness than just her words? What if she brought him the most indisputable witness possible—a crystal of the Blood? Surely he could not refuse her then.

Something in her drew back, shocked. *Defiler,* it whispered. She pushed it away—that was what Refuge would say, what Râvar would say, and she had already turned her back on both. How could it be wrong, anyway, to give a crystal to someone who would use it to bring news of Arata's rising?

Swiftly she crossed to the stairway and descended to the ledge, and turned east, up the flow of Revelation. The walls of the cleft began to rise; the ledge, too, inclined upward, gradually at first, then more steeply. She leaned into the slope; despite the darkness she could see clearly, for the Cavern's radiance rose around her like a false dawn. The clamor of Revelation increased and, below it, something else, a deep shuddering roar.

The cleft curved sharply and straightened. Its terminus lay directly ahead. There, with all the violence of its long descent from its mountain birthplace, Revelation vaulted over the summit, plunging more than three times the height of Labyrinth to meet itself below. The force of that collision was elemental. It fractured the air and shuddered through the rock; spray shot up from it in great clouds and veils, obscur-

ing the point of impact. Just below the summit, directly behind the falls, the light of the Cavern flooded into the night,
turning the streaming cataract to gold. Refracted brilliance
leaped and dazzled along the cleft walls, as if they were fili-
greed with precious metal.

Axane had come there more times than she could count—
for the annual celebrations that marked the day of Risaryâsi's revelation, on personal pilgrimage with her father
when she was small. But those visits had been made during
the day, under the relentless blaze of the sun, which largely
eclipsed the Cavern's brilliance. She had not seen it at night
since she was a child, creeping out with playmates when she
was supposed to be abed. Awe, now, drew her to a halt—at
the unearthly beauty of it, at the blind, enormous power of
all that light and water. The percussion of the cataract pulsed
in her chest, her belly, her bones. Her very blood yielded,
her heart beating to its rhythm.

She forced herself forward again. The ledge ran well beneath the summit; to reach the Cavern it was necessary not
just to climb out over the sheer drop below but to ascend a
considerable distance. Risaryâsi, perilously, had scaled the
water-sculpted lip of the narrow flame-shaped fissure known
as Risaryâsi's Ladder, then edged along a natural ridge that
sloped up to the Cavern's mouth. For the ease and safety of
Refuge, Cyras and Mandapâxa had created a stairway.

Axane stepped past the black mouth of Risaryâsi's Ladder
and began to climb. The air was saturated with moisture;
within moments her hair and clothing were soaking wet. She
placed her feet carefully—the steps were broad, and a guide
rope was strung through loops of iron driven into the rock:
but even so the going was treacherous, and it was impossible
not to think how easy it would be to slip and tumble into the
deadly tumult of Revelation below. She reached the edge of
the cataract and passed behind it; the Cavern's splendor
spilled out above her, dancing on the inner surface of the
falls as if some great hand poured out an unending stream of
jewels.

Beyond the final stair, a passage ran back into the rock. At the passage's end the Cavern pulsed gold, as if it were alive and breathing. It was too bright to be looked upon with naked eyes; pilgrims wore eyemasks made of bark, so they would not be struck blind. Axane had no eyemask, so she cupped her hands before her face, peering through the gaps between her fingers. The din of the cataract fell away as she advanced, though she could still feel its thunder beneath her feet. It was deeply cold, a chill born both of the rock and the frigid breath of Revelation; in her wet clothes, she was already shivering.

The Cavern was not high—twice as tall as a man, perhaps. But it was vast, extending hugely back and out within the rock. Unlike the cleft, it had not been water-shaped; its ruddy sandstone surfaces were jagged and irregular, as if great slabs had been clawed or torn away. Across its floor and up its walls spread a thick encrustation of golden crystals, accreted here and there into fantastic shapes, heaped up in mounds where the fragile structures had collapsed. At the heart of every stone danced a core of fire, each throbbing to a separate rhythm, as if harried by its own private wind. These small flickerings, magnified by the crystals' facets, joined to form great waves and coils of light, sweeping across the Cavern like wind across the grasses of the Plains, or the currents of heat at the heart of a bed of red-hot coals.

At the Cavern's center, a great fissure cracked the floor. There were no crystals here, only a vaguely man-shaped scar of naked stone with a slash of blackness at its heart, stark amid all the scintillant gold. This, according to the lore of Refuge, was where Ârata's body had lain across the eons of his slumber, as his thousand wounds slowly closed and time turned the blood that flowed from them to gems, trapping within each a faint shadow of his divinity. The fissure had been made by his great weight, for gods' flesh was far heavier than mortals', and even the depth of rock below the Cavern had not easily supported it.

Axane stood at the threshold of the Cavern, a footstep from the blazing crystals. As a child, this place had awed and terrified her, for it seemed, despite the tales that bound it to

Refuge and its faith, utterly alien. How fearsome the being that had such fire in its veins! How awful the processes that turned living blood to stone! Later, she grew preoccupied with questions she knew better than to ask out loud: How had Ârata gotten inside the rock? How long, exactly, had he lain there? How had he emerged without tearing the Cavern apart? Still later, in the dwindling of her belief, the Cavern itself became the question. Was Risaryâsi right or wrong? Had this truly been Ârata's resting place, or were the crystals, amazing as they were, only gems?

She had the answer now: Gyalo Amdo Samchen had provided it. Standing before the Cavern for the last time in her life, trembling with cold and the enormity of her choice, she understood that she had come full circle, back to the fearful certainties of her childhood. Something rose in her—the sense of trespass that had gripped her on the summit, but much more powerful. She seemed to feel a pressure in the air, as of great fingers folding round her. *Thief*, a voice whispered inside her head. *Defiler.*

She gasped, and dropped to her knees. Narrowing her eyes to the merest lash-veiled slits, she took her hands from her face and pulled off her wet stole. She folded it in half and, with the cloth to protect her, reached out to the carpet of crystals, probing for any that might be loose. She could see only a fiery blur, her arms a dark blot within it. It seemed an age before she found a crystal that moved at her touch. She twisted it free, flinching at the snap as it broke off.

She bundled it in her stole and got to her feet. As she did, her eyes came a little open. The Cavern's brilliance seemed to spring at her, as if the waves of light had suddenly grown liquid. In her mind burst an image of fire, reaching out to snatch back what she had stolen. Terror seized her. She whirled and ran, the crystal clutched to her chest, her thoughts filled with flame. She stumbled at the mouth of the passage, half-falling onto the stairs; she dashed down them, heedless of the treacherous footing, and raced along the ledge.

Just before the angle of the cleft, beyond which the Cavern fell out of sight, she halted, panting. Turning, she looked back. Below the summit, the Cavern poured glory upon the darkness. The river, dropping past it, coruscated gold. Nothing had changed. Nothing had followed. In the darkness, she was alone.

She still held the bundle of her stole tight against her breast. She lowered it. The fabric pulled open a little; the glow of the crystal bled through, a tiny echo of the enormous luminance ahead. The barter for her passage, she thought. But now, for the first time, she saw a different meaning in her intent. She would give the crystal to Gyalo Amdo Samchen; he would bring it with him out of the Burning Land. But was that not Ârata's Promise, as his people understood it? Would they mistake him, as Refuge had, for the Next Messenger?

She stared down at her hands. Surely it could not be the same. The people outside were not like the people of Refuge. They did not spend every moment waiting for the Next Messenger to arrive. Anyway, they already knew who Gyalo Amdo Samchen was, or at least the people who had sent him did. A mistake like Refuge's was impossible.

Unless, something seemed to whisper from deep inside her, *it's true. Unless you* make *it true, when you give him the Blood.*

Her heart seemed to stop. For an instant the world around her grew utterly alien, not like any place she knew. Then she drew a breath, and the moment passed, and she saw how absurd it was, to imagine that so much could come of anything she did. This is exactly what I want to leave behind, she thought, with sudden anger: The constant searching for significance, the shadowing of every moment by divine intent. She wanted to live her life—she did not want to think about what it meant. She had made her choice. She would give him the crystal. He would take it to his superiors. It would mean no more than that.

She tightened the folds of her stole, extinguishing the crystal's small radiance. Turning her back on the Cavern, she began to walk. She could feel it behind her, its light reaching across the darkness; but she did not turn. She had looked on it for the last time. From that moment, she started new.

She was shuddering convulsively with cold by the time she reached her chamber. She dragged off her wet clothes and put on dry ones, then bundled gowns and chemises and stoles into a blanket and rolled the blanket up and tied it with a sash.

She went next to the Treasury, where she lit a lamp at one of the fire pots and went into the storerooms to retrieve the two food bags she had prepared. She climbed to the herbary and gathered into a carrying basket a selection of herbs, salves, bandages, needles, knives, and other healing materials. On top of them she placed the crystal of the Blood, secure in its wrapping. She laced the basket closed and pulled it onto her back, then returned downstairs for the food bags, which she slung over each shoulder. It was a heavy load. But she had borne heavy loads before.

She left the Treasury. She passed the House of Dreams, moving swiftly through the wash of light that sifted from its entrance, then the outdoor workshops and the mortuary caves, with their drifting odor of spices and decay. The moon had set long ago, casting the cleft deep into shadow; she slid her hand along the wall, guiding her way. She emerged at last onto the Plains of Blessing. Beside Revelation—broad and docile, purged of the violence of its entry into the cleft—she paused to fill the water bag she had brought with her, then began searching for the strangers' trail. She found it at last, the springy chest-high grass pushed aside where they had walked, and began to follow, setting her feet where theirs had been. The weight of what she carried slowed her, but she thought she must still be moving faster than they, hampered as they were by Gâbrios and Diasarta's splinted leg. By morning, hopefully, she would have closed much of the distance—and gone far enough from Refuge that the Shapers, mounting to the summit to spy out their escaped prisoners, would overlook her small self upon the hugeness of the Plains.

She plodded on. The stars wheeled overhead; the night seemed endless. But at last a glimmer to the east announced the imminent sunrise. The gray of dawn stole out across the Plains, then the first long light of the returning sun, restoring color to the world. She stopped, then, and looked back. Across tossing distances of silver grass, the red sandstone of the cleft reared abruptly up, resembling, in its rounded contours, a series of misshapen loaves of bread. To the west, the trees that marked Revelation's course meandered toward the horizon, their pale trunks lit orange by the lifting sun; behind and to the east, fire-colored cliffs folded upward toward the distant mountains. The dazzle of the Cavern could still be seen, fading, like the stars, with the coming of day. It was beautiful, peaceful—and in its utter stillness, somehow innocent, like something just created.

I will never stand here again, she thought. *I must remember this moment. I must remember it always.*

She turned and walked on. When the disk of the sun stood fully above the horizon she stopped to rest, sipping a little water and eating a strip of dried meat, then sitting for a time in a kind of utter, blank exhaustion. She would have liked to sleep, waiting out the heat of the day, but she was afraid to let the strangers get too far ahead. At last she untied her blanket roll and pulled out a pale-hued stole and wrapped it around her head and shoulders, to protect her from the sun and also to hide the darkness of her hair amid the Plains' silver grass. She shouldered her burdens once more and resumed her journey.

It was past noon when the first breath of wind touched her sweaty skin. She halted, her heart contracting with dread, and looked back. Where she stood the sun still blazed, and the sky arched blue and hard as stone. But above the cleft a storm was taking shape. Black and gray and purple clouds billowed angrily into being, the sky around them trembling with prismatic light, as the Shapers bent the substance of the air to their will. A huge shadow crept down the cleft, staining the red stone dark, dimming the Plains beneath. The wind, increasing, tossed the grasses and pressed Axane's gown against her body. Still the storm grew, devouring the sky. She could hear thunder now, booming like a distant rockfall, and see the bolts of lightning that lanced the boiling turmoil of the tempest's heart.

The storm reached its full and awesome strength, and the Shapers let it go. Like something out of nightmare it rolled toward her, sending darkness before it, flattening the grass. At its center, a fat black finger of cloud had taken shape, snaking slowly toward the ground. Even from a distance she could see it was following the strangers' trail. She began to run, racing through the whipping grass, away from the storm's trajectory.

The wind roared down on her. It threw her to the ground and ripped away her stole. It scoured her exposed skin, beating her with the grasses more painfully than Narstame had ever thrashed her when she was a child. Thunder shook the earth; lightning seared her eyes even through her closed lids. The rain came, with such force that it seemed each drop made a bruise upon her skin.

Then, quite suddenly, it was past. Light returned—not the crack and flare of lightning, but steady daylight. She felt the sun again, burning through her sodden garments. Painfully she sat up. Above her, the sky was clear. To the north the clouds swept on, the air beneath them gray with rain, the probing cloud-finger drawing behind it a swath of destruction.

But now there was a change. The tempest seemed to slow. The clouds' tight coherence flattened, spreading out. The cloud-finger quivered, as if uncertain; then, slowly, it tore free. It dissipated as it fell, like smoke—tatters, a transparent haze, gone. Clouds still massed across the sky, but they were only rainclouds. There was no longer even thunder.

Gyalo Amdo Samchen, Axane thought. He had met shaping with shaping. He had torn the heart out of the storm.

The Shapers tried again. This time the clouds did not even reach Axane before they were tamed. A third time the gale was called; a third time it was dispersed. And then there was nothing—no darkening of the sky, no rumbling of earth quake, no rain of stones. Only clear air, and silence.

Axane got to her feet and wrung some of the water from her hair and clothing. Her dress was ripped, and there was a swelling contusion on her calf where something had struck her, but otherwise she was uninjured. Her baggage, too, had survived, the food and water bags caught beneath her as she fell, the basket strapped to her back. She shouldered the bags again and began to walk toward the great furrow the storm had cut across the Plains, which would bring her again to the strangers' trail.

She thought of her father. He would have marked her absence when she did not bring his breakfast; he would have gone to her chamber to see if she were ill, and when he did not find her, sent someone to search her out. Had he guessed, when the strangers were found missing, where she had gone? Had he known she was on the Plains when he sent the Shapers up to make their storms?

Something stirred in her, painfully. She pressed it away. She had abandoned him, abandoned Refuge. Why should he protect her?

She walked on. The straps of the bags cut into her shoulders; sweat ran down her body, and her leg ached where it was bruised. But her mind was fixed beyond such discomforts. Refuge was behind her. Her life lay before her, a blank folio page waiting to be filled. The whole world spread out beneath her feet.

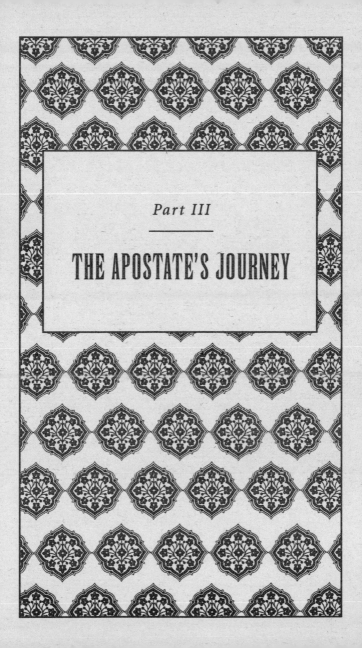

Part III

THE APOSTATE'S JOURNEY

—13—

Gyalo had wrapped himself in a blanket against the cold. But he could still feel it, for the night was very chill, and the blanket, like his clothing, was much the worse for wear. Stars massed the sky; at his back they poured like a rain of crystal to the distant curve of the horizon, but ahead, a thrusting darkness cut their flood abruptly off: the Range of Clouds. Day by day, for the past weeks, they had been rising larger. Now they seemed to divide the world in half.

Another week, or maybe a little more, and they would reach Thuxra City.

They were already among the mines. The way Gyalo walked was riddled with pits and passages, and humped with mounds of earth, the ugly detritus of opal diggings. The going was treacherous, but the half-moon and his own pearl-colored lifelight lit the way, and his Shaper pattern-sense showed him, in the grouping of the shafts and the angles of the terrain, the hidden craters and sinkholes where the ground might collapse beneath his weight. Flows and shimmerings spoke to him of the differing temperatures of the earth; if he were to glance back, he would see his own trail—the patterns of disturbance his feet had printed on the soil, the faint swirling traces left by the progress of his warm body through the cold night. Everywhere, he perceived the processes of change—accretion, transformation, decay, the same properties that lay at the heart of a Shaper's skill.

It had been too much for him at first, this way of seeing. The patterns, the colors, the auras that wreathed even the smallest living thing—they had overwhelmed his senses, an assault so unrelenting that he had had to wrap cloth across his eyes to give himself relief. He had known only a shadow of it before, in the controlled release of Âratist ceremony— he had never understood, until his shaping was untethered, how tightly manita truly bound him. He thought often of the Refugean Shapers, their ability free throughout their lives. Their strength and skill had awed him; he had not known it was possible to shape on such a scale. The stories of the Shaper War were all about destruction, but in Refuge he had seen creation, the use of shaping not to damage and to ruin but to preserve and build. Still, the risk of ruin was always there. He had met it face-to-face, in their killing storms. He had confronted it, to his peril, in his own clumsy practice.

And yet it was as natural now as breathing to live this way—to view the world through Shaper eyes, to touch it with his shaping will. It terrified him to think of returning to the fettered mode of being that, before this journey, had been all he knew.

His mind shied away from that, moving backward instead, across the months.

He had been on fire that day in Refuge, emerging from his long meditation. He had gone in to Teispas and Diasarta and told them everything. He did not care that Diasarta was angry and afraid; he did not care that Teispas had no faith. Before the exaltation of his knowledge, such things could not stand.

Diasarta protested—resistant not so much to the truth of Ârata's rising as to the idea that it had been given to heretics to find and guard his resting place. Patiently, Gyalo answered him, until the light of belief dawned in his face and he fell silent, overcome. Teispas only listened, his expression unreadable. When at last he spoke, it was not to dispute or question but instead, calmly, to address practicalities. They were in danger, he said: The healer, Axane, had told him so. In the circumstances it would be madness to address Refuge's council, half of whom already thought them demons. Better to accept the opportunity Axane had offered—better simply to slip away.

Gyalo knew Teispas was right. But though his task was no longer the one that had sent him into the Burning Land, he could not entirely abandon that original purpose—could not, in conscience, depart from Refuge without offering its people the truth and a chance to follow, though he knew it was unlikely that any would listen. His shaping, which he had kept hidden out of shame and despair, now promised protection, should the council answer with hostility. He and Teispas argued; in the end Teispas capitulated—not, Gyalo suspected, because he was convinced, but only because he recognized that Gyalo would not be swayed.

His shaping did free them—but it was dismayingly difficult to pierce the Refugean Shapers' crystal walls, and he feared afterward that his ability would not prove equal to whatever might be sent in pursuit. But as he was to discover, it was easier to perform large sweeping acts of shaping than smaller, focused ones. And he was lucky—instead of pitting himself against the entire storm, he concentrated instead upon its deadly cloud-finger, hoping only to reduce the winds so they would be survivable. That, it turned out, was the key. By destroying a portion of the tempest he managed to tear apart the whole.

He expected the Shapers to try again. For days he or Teispas or Diasarta kept constant watch. But the third storm was the last of Refuge.

Or almost the last. As they sat resting at the margin of the pebble plain, where the rich grasses of the Plains of Blessing gave way to arid, stony ground, a woman appeared, staggering with fatigue. Her head was down; her unbound hair fell across her face. Even so, Gyalo knew her, for that astonishing lifelight could not be mistaken. It was Axane, the healer.

She gasped when she saw them, and sank to her knees. Teispas sprang forward to assist her, helping her shed her bundles and drink from the waterskin she had brought with her. Reviving a little, she told them—flatly, in a way that dared contradiction—that she intended to go with them.

Gyalo was not altogether surprised. He had perceived, in the brief time she had spent in his chamber, her fascination with the outside world, and also guessed the difficulty of her life in Refuge. Even so, it was no small thing to abandon family, friends, and home to undertake a journey none of them might survive—all for no more than the promise of an uncertain future in a world for which she could not possibly be prepared.

He and Teispas questioned her. She reiterated her rejection of Refuge's beliefs; she also spoke, haltingly, of a forced marriage she was desperate to avoid. They left her where she was, with Gâbrios laid out on his litter beside her, and went off to confer. Diasarta, for whom even the blankets they had brought with them carried the taint of Refuge's heresy, wanted to send her packing. But Gyalo already knew she must come with them. She was proof in her own person of Refuge's existence, and her healing skills would be useful. More than that, by following them she had irreversibly corrupted herself in her people's eyes. To send her back was likely to condemn her to whatever fate they would have suffered at Refuge's hands. Teispas—who, Gyalo could see, admired her—agreed.

When they told her their decision, she sighed and closed her eyes, too worn-out to show much emotion. Then, turning to the basket she had carried on her back, she opened it and removed a bundle, which she offered to Gyalo. The radiance of what was in it pierced the fabric as he pulled aside the wrapping. Even before he parted the final layer he knew what he would see.

"Ârata!" Diasarta whispered, beside him. Teispas drew in his breath, like a man receiving a knife cut.

"I took it from the Cavern," Axane said, in her oddly accented Arsacian: the sound of more than seventy years of isolation. "Because you said you wanted proof." She paused. The air around her flickered emerald, sapphire, aquamarine, jade—the tangled gem colors of her lifelight. "It's a gift. For you. To do with as you will."

Gyalo stared at the pulsing jewel. He felt as if he had been emptied out and filled up again with light. Reverently, he drew the wrappings back across the crystal, hiding its heart of flame.

"Thank you," he said. And then again, though it did not seem even remotely adequate: "Thank you."

Axane nodded. Her face, with its dark proud features, was sharpened almost to ugliness by exhaustion. Softly—and not, he sensed, to him—she said; "I will be Galean now."

It took them twelve days to cross the pebble plain—a desperately hard journey, with Diasarta in his splints and crutches and Teispas and Gyalo, still weak from earlier rigors, burdened by Gâbrios's makeshift litter. At the plain's far side they rested for a time, then went in search of the oasis where the original expedition had waited for its scouts to return. They found it at last, and in it, undisturbed, the equipment the expedition had left behind, canvas and cooking pots and candles and discarded clothing. There was also, incredibly, one of the expedition's camels, sheltering in this place of abundant water. It bore signs of injury, half-healed cuts and abrasions on its flanks, but otherwise was in sound health. "Ârata's blessing," Diasarta declared, and Gyalo could not disagree. They would be able to take all the equipment with them. And Gâbrios could ride, freeing Gyalo and Teispas of the awkward litter.

They moved on into the vastness of the Burning Land. Gyalo still had his battered travel pack, and inside it his travel journal; they followed the maps he had made on the southward journey, walking in reverse the trail of footsteps he had drawn. They measured their progress by the expedition's red-and-gold markers, and the cairns and blazes that had been left where there was water or good camping. It was spring, and there were often torrential rainstorms, trapping them where they were till the flooded plains drained. Later the storms gave way to the aridity of summer, and a heat that forced them to travel only in the morning and afternoon, waiting out the blazing hours of midday beneath squares of canvas they improvised into cloaks and hoods to protect them from the sun.

Slowly, they hardened to the journey. Gyalo and Teispas regained their endurance; Axane's feet, which had blistered badly in her leather-soled sandals, healed and callused over the cotton wrappings she improvised from among their supplies. Diasarta unbound his splints and threw away his crutches; he limped a little, for the broken leg had knitted slightly shorter than the other, but otherwise was fully healed. Gyalo had never much cared for Diasarta, whom he thought narrow-minded and ignorant, but under the press of necessity the soldier revealed a better side of himself, relaxing his initial hostility toward Axane and swallowing his smoldering resentment of Teispas, submitting to something like the soldier-to-officer relationship of the journey out. As for the truth of the Cavern of the Blood, he had wholeheartedly embraced it. He even abandoned the amulet he wore—the twisted flame of Hatâspa, an Aspect popular among soldiers—for, he said, with Ârata risen there was no longer any need to beg the Aspects' intercession.

Gâbrios, too, recovered physically, though his mind was sadly impaired. His memory of the time before his injury was clear, but he had lost comprehension of the present, and could not understand for more than a few moments at a time where he was and what was happening to him. As he grew stronger he began refusing to ride the camel; but if they allowed him to go on foot, he wandered off, so Teispas fashioned a harness for him, and Axane became his keeper, walking beside him during the day, tying his leash to her wrist at night, patiently answering the questions he asked over and over and soothing him when, as often happened, he grew agitated. There were many reasons by then to be glad she was with them, for in addition to her healing skills she was a competent camp cook and a steady, uncomplaining traveler. But if she had done no more than care for Gâbrios, it would have been enough.

She also possessed a good knowledge of the plants and edibles of the Burning Land. Together with Gyalo's desert lore, acquired from Vâsparis and greatly enhanced by his freed Shaper senses, and Diasarta's accuracy with a makeshift slingshot, they were able to find and gather most of what they needed to eat and drink. But there were times when there was no water, when even Gyalo's pattern-sense could not guide him to food. Without his ability, they would not have survived.

He had not intended, after his first great act of unfettered shaping, ever to employ his gift again. In an absolute sense—the sin already accomplished, the betrayal already made—it did not matter whether he shaped or not: He was an apostate, a vow-breaker, and nothing could change that. Yet he himself, his beliefs and values, were unaltered; and the loss of his vocation did not make right what had been wrong before. He had no manita now, and could not control the way he saw the world—but he could control his actions. It seemed right and proper, therefore, as punishment and penance and also as an act of faith, to renounce the use of shaping. To choose to do right, though he himself was and always would be wrong.

The Cavern of the Blood changed everything. Over the course of the long, strange meditation into which he had fallen afterward, he came to understand not only that the god had risen, but that all that had happened had been meant. The lost Âratists had been banished into the Burning Land so that they might find the Cavern; so that the church might send a rescue expedition; so that the Cavern might be found a second time and word brought back to Baushpar. If not for the storm, the expedition would have reached Refuge without incident. But the storm—not natural, but the product of capricious human will—had destroyed the expedition, and only the release of Gyalo's shaping could save those who survived so that the Cavern might still be found. Even his apostasy, therefore, had been meant. Even as he betrayed his Shaper vow, he had done Ârata's will.

He did not make the mistake of assuming, in light of his new understanding, that he was relieved of the burden of his choice. He had not known the god's purpose when he chose; the lives he had saved could not be a weight on his conscience, but his own life was, and the truth the choice had taught him about himself—that he was not strong enough to die for the sake of his belief. Nor did he suppose he had been specially chosen. It was the purpose that was important, not the tool that accomplished it. He was simply what had been to hand.

Yet, fallen and imperfect as he was, he was still the god's servant. He had thought himself banished forever from that role; the joy of discovering otherwise was as great as the despair from which the discovery delivered him. And so he surrendered himself, with delight, into Ârata's hands. He opened himself, utterly and without question, to the god's will—which required that he and the others survive to reach Arsace, and therefore that he abandon his decision not to shape.

Late one afternoon the travelers halted beside a stand of stunted trees, where both Gyalo's desert knowledge and his Shaper senses told him there was water. Over the weeks they had fallen into a routine of making camp, so familiar through repetition that there was scarcely need for speech. Axane tied Gâbrios's leash to a tree and set about gathering brush for the cook fire. Diasarta hobbled the camel and came to help Gyalo and Teispas dig a trench in the sandy soil. When it was deep enough Gyalo waved the others back, and altered the porosity of the sand so that water welled quickly up, clear and cool.

After they had eaten he left the camp alone, as had become his habit. He had a natural instinct for shaping's use; it was this that had enabled him, new to his full ability, to un-make the rock of the pebble plain and, later, to pierce the Refugean Shapers' crystal walls and eviscerate the pursuing storms. But instinct without knowledge was not to be relied upon. So every evening he went into the desert, and strove, by trial and error and experiment, to school his aptitude into skill.

At first he had been obsessed with pattern—learning it, reproducing it. He found it easy to fix pattern in his memory; he had always owned a facility with languages, and in some ways this was similar: the secret language of the world itself. Lately, though, his interest had shifted to boundaries—of shaping in general, and also of his own ability.

Some of them he already knew. As a boy, he had been taught that Shaping shaped only that which was unliving. It was only within the inanimate world, therefore, that a Shaper could exercise the elemental comprehension of form and essence that revealed the pattern of things, and the larger patterns those things composed, and the ways in which change or removal or intrusion might shift the whole. He had wondered whether that might alter with the release of his manita tether; but it had not. His pattern-sense had become far deeper, and even in the areas that were closed to him his perception was greater than it had been. The basic truth, though, was the same. Unliving things—things never living, like stones and sand, and things severed from their living source, like a plucked leaf or a grain of rice—were like buildings, like cloth: constructions of material elements, arranged in particular ways and with varying degrees of complexity. Living things were that, and something more. It was the something more that defeated him.

Other boundaries he was still discovering. So far, he had managed to shape only single things—one grass seed, one rock, one drop of water—but he had learned to do so in quick succession, so that to an observer the manifestations would seem almost simultaneous. He could unmake any-thing, with enough time and effort, but the ability to create appeared to be confined to natural objects: He could shape a stone but not a wall, a stem of grass but not a woven mat. As for transformation, there must surely be an outer range for his capacity, but he had not yet discovered it.

He halted before a hump of gray-mottled stone. It appeared to be an excrescence of the bedrock, but his pattern-sense told him it was actually a huge boulder, more than half its bulk sunk in the fragile desert soil. It was half again as large as the last object he had transformed, and so a suitable subject for experiment.

He fixed his eyes on it, concentrating his Shaper senses on its pattern while in memory he summoned up the pattern of the rosy quartz into which he intended to transform it. When both were clear, in balance, he extended his will, probing the existing structure of the stone, urging it toward something more quartzlike. For a moment, frustratingly, it resisted. Then he felt the shift, the yielding, and knew he would succeed. Tonight would not be the night he found his limit.

That instant of distraction was his undoing. The patterns slipped out of kilter; his shaping will—which desired always to be huge, encompassing, and struggled against any limitation—escaped the tight focus he had imposed on it, like a leashed animal bursting free. He caught it back but it was too late. There was a deep percussion beneath his feet. The earth shuddered, and with a grinding roar pulled apart, a narrow black emptiness snaking swiftly north, like a line of ink scribbled by an invisible brush. The boulder, neither quartz nor its original substance, tipped from its deep home and vanished into darkness.

The tremors stopped. Gyalo crouched where they had pitched him, only a few handspans from the crevasse. His limbs were watery with shock. He had made mistakes before, but never like this. He thought of what might have happened if the crevasse had opened a little closer, or if he had been standing a few paces forward; his blood ran cold.

He climbed to his feet. His enthusiasm had soured; he did not feel like continuing. He shaped a span of stone to bridge the crevasse, then hesitated, unable to bring himself to trust it. In the end he leaped the gap, which, after all, was not so very wide.

The sun was nearly gone. All around him the desert coruscated with the small life-patterns that so stubbornly resisted his understanding. Up ahead he saw larger luminances, cobalt blue and pale green: Teispas and Diasarta, hastening toward him, alarmed by the noise and the shaking of the ground. Tersely he explained what had happened, trying not to show his annoyance at being forced to speak about his private pursuits—though in truth he could not blame them for their fear.

They headed back to camp. When the fire came in sight, Teispas spoke.

"Brother Gyalo. A word alone, if you please."

Diasarta moved on. Gyalo turned. Teispas stood still as a pole, mantled in his indigo lifelight. His arms were folded uncompromisingly across his chest.

"You must stop this experimenting," he said. "It's too dangerous."

Gyalo sighed. He no longer hated Teispas; the understandings of the Cavern of the Blood, which had changed so much, had changed that as well. But it was hard to shed the weight of so much dark emotion; he did not think he would ever again learn to feel easy with the man. It did not help that over the past weeks Teispas seemed to have appointed himself a kind of bodyguard, either at Gyalo's side with food or a waterskin or an outstretched hand, or watching for the chance to spring forward. He also seemed to feel he had the right to offer criticism and advice—which he mostly did, as now, entirely unasked.

"I know what I'm doing," he said, not bothering to keep the irritation from his voice.

"Do you? You might kill yourself the next time."

"Your confidence in my ability is inspiring."

"I have every confidence in your ability. It's your judgment I'm not sure about. At least let me come with you."

"What would be the point of that? If I pitched myself down a hole, what could you do about it?"

"It's irresponsible, this . . . this playing of yours! It serves no useful purpose. We need you to create food and water for us, not to make rocks fall out of the sky, or turn a boulder into a hill of sand!"

Gyalo felt a rush of real anger. He was aware, as his skill increased, that he devoted himself less and less to what was practical and more and more to what interested him. He recognized the truth: He experimented not just because it was needful, but because he loved it, because it thrilled him to explore the limits of his ability, because, as always in his life when he encountered something new, he desired above all else to learn. But right or wrong, it was for Ârata to judge him. Not Teispas.

"I understand your concern," he said, holding his voice quiet with an effort. "But what I do is not your business."

"It *is* my business." Teispas's hawk face was fierce. "This is my task, to guard you, to see you safe—even if it means protecting you from yourself. It's why I was sent here; it's why I survived, by Ârata's will. I have no choice."

"Ârata's . . ." Gyalo stared at the captain, his anger forgotten. "Does that mean you believe?"

For a long moment Teispas did not reply. "Yes."

"But you've said nothing, these past weeks. You've given no sign."

Teispas shrugged, the smallest movement of his shoulders. "What should I say? I spent a long time in unbelief. I hardly know how to speak of such things now."

"This is a good thing, Teispas. A wonderful thing. I'm more glad than I can say."

Silence. Teispas stood like a desert stone, his arms still clasped across his chest. Behind him, in the western sky, a line of red marked the place where the sun had vanished.

"My parents were devout." The words were soft; Gyalo had to strain to hear them. "They kept the Way of Ârata, and took Communion weekly, and prayed to the Aspects for Arsace's deliverance. That's how I was brought up. The Aspect my parents favored was Vahu, Patron of healing. But I favored Hatâspa, the soldiers' Patron. Even then I wanted to make war on the Caryaxists.

"We lived in Haruko, in the refugee quarter of Fantzon City. It was a stinking little warren down by the marshes. We called it Little Arsace, as if we were diplomats on sovereign soil, but everyone else called it Sewertown, because the city's drains emptied there. There was a lot of idleness in Little Arsace, a lot of violence. The law in Fantzon looked the other way. We made do—we had our own watch, our own justices. But it was the gang lords who really ran things."

The bitterness in his voice was like acid. The words came faster now, as if they had been bottled up too long.

"I had a friend, Naruva. We grew up together. I put my name in for the watch, and he became a runner for one of the gangs, but still we were friends—that's how strong the bond was between us. Then he insulted one of the gang lords, and the man had him strangled. I decided to get revenge. I was clever about it, or so I thought. It's known among the followers of Hatâspa that the devotee-priests can call a reflection of his spirit into a weapon and make it infallible—if you can pay the fee, of course."

"But that's a myth," Gyalo said. "A swindle. Devotee-priests found doing it are stripped of their offices and brought before a magistrate."

"Yes." Teispas laughed, without any trace of mirth. "I discovered that—though unfortunately, not soon enough. Anyway, I got the money, and I got the blessing. I took my supposedly infallible knife and went out to kill the man who had killed Naruva. I accosted him in a public place, and stabbed him—I thought—to the heart. His bodyguards ran me through with their swords and left me for dead. I was prepared for that—you don't do what I did and expect to survive it. But I did survive. I was found and taken to my parents' house. They tended me in secret, mourning as if I were dead. Because the man I struck down with my infallible knife didn't die—he survived, just as I did. If he'd known I lived, it would have been the end for all of us.

"I didn't have much to do, lying behind a false wall in my parents' cellar, but think. I knew what the devotee-priests would tell me—it wasn't the blessed knife that had failed, but my faith. But I knew that wasn't true. I did believe when I went out to kill that man—I absolutely and completely *believed* he would die, no matter where or how I struck him. If my faith was blameless, it must have been the knife that failed. And if the knife had failed, the devotee-priests had lied. And if the devotee-priests had lied, what else might be false? In the end, all I could see were lies. The ceremonies, the prayers and blessings, Hatâspa, the other Aspects—lies, all lies. I thought Ârata must have existed once—how else could this world have come to be? But not now, not for eons. It seemed to me we were alone, and all our beliefs were illusions, imaginary comforts built on a dead truth by men in mortal fear of a meaningless existence."

Remembered pain shivered in his voice. "Ah, Teispas," Gyalo said.

"My faith was never very strong—you might think I didn't lose much when it left me. But it's a terrible thing to find a void where you thought there was something solid, no matter how small and poor that thing was. As soon as I was well enough, I answered King Santaxma's call for volunteers. For fifteen years I fought for him. And then the Caryaxists fell, and I was given this assignment. I thought it would be the last—I thought that if I survived, I'd resign my commission and retire. Truth to tell, I didn't care much either way. Or so I thought, until the storm."

The flood of words had slowed. Teispas spoke now with a kind of harsh effort. "On the pebble plain I learned I wanted life. That even my empty, faithless existence was better than the nothingness that was all I believed, then, lay after death. I knew you could save me, and in my fear I threw away your manita. I didn't think to feel remorse, for I didn't believe in your vows. Yet I did feel remorse. I tried to hate you—for not throwing away the drug yourself, for . . . for . . . for *suffering* so much. Instead, it began to seem to me that by what I'd done I had bound myself to you in atonement, for as long as we both lived.

"I know now that is true, though not for the reason I first thought. I know our actions are not our own, here in the Burning Land—I know that everything we do and have done serves a larger purpose. But that's not why I took your manita. What I did was purely selfish. The truth, the bare truth, is that I wronged you. And I'm sorry for it." He drew a breath. Through the whole of this speech he had not moved, but now he shuddered, a single convulsive movement. "I've been wanting to say that for a long time. To apologize, and ask forgiveness."

For a moment Gyalo was silent. He could not imagine how much it had cost Teispas to make his confession, to draw aside so completely the normal cloak of his reserve.

"I would have had to make the choice whether you'd thrown away my manita or not," he said. "I don't know . . . I don't know, if you hadn't, whether I would have been strong enough. It was needed that you do it, just as it was needed that I break my vow. I understood that, in the Cavern of the Blood. There's no longer any offense between us. There never truly was. I forgive you fully."

For a moment Teispas did not stir. Then he nodded, as if he did not trust himself to speak.

The light at the horizon had died away as they spoke. The sky was sapphire black; the first stars showed, and the ivory crescent of the moon. A little distance on, the camp's cook fire glowed like a scrap of the vanished sun, its heat patterns thickening the air. Diasarta crouched beside it, bent over the frayed rope he was repairing, his lifelight the faded green of parched grass; Axane sat nearby, her great turmoiled aura all but eclipsing the uncertain carmine glimmer of Gâbrios, who lay curled beside her.

"I remember thinking how devout you were," Gyalo said. "While we were traveling. You took Communion every day—even some vowed Âratists aren't so conscientious."

Teispas made a sound that was not quite a laugh. "You aren't the first to tell me that."

"Why did you keep the forms of faith so diligently, if you didn't believe?"

"Hope." Teispas's voice was quiet, the bitterness drained out of him for the moment. "I thought if I behaved as a good Âratist, I might somehow become one again."

Gyalo remembered him on the balcony in Thuxra City, saying, *Isn't it what any good Âratist would do?* "So you weren't happy as an unbeliever."

Teispas shrugged. "I thought to find an earthly cause I could follow as other people followed faith. The Exile Army, the fight to liberate Arsace, seemed to be a cause like that. And I did believe in it. I still do."

"But it wasn't enough?"

"No. More and more I saw the emptiness of things. We are such petty creatures, we humans—so frail, so base. Our schemes and our crusades—they come and go, and the world is just the same. What an awful joke if there were nothing more than that."

"Was it in Refuge that you began to believe again?"

"No." Teispas was silent a moment. "When you told Diasarta and me about the Cavern of the Blood, I thought you might have dreamed it. You spent a long time in meditation after you came back; it was very strange. But when I was in Baushpar the Bearer received me, and I saw the Blood he wears around his neck. When you unwrapped the crystal Axane gave you, I knew it was the same."

"Ah."

"I saw then that everything you'd said to us might be true. It was . . ." He drew in his breath as he had then, like a man in pain. "Terrifying. For so many years I longed to believe again, and now all I wanted was to turn away. But Ârata took hold of us, on the pebble plain. Or before, perhaps . . . perhaps it was he who took my faith away, so I'd do what I did to you. I don't know. I fought it because I was afraid, but I couldn't fight for long. I have my faith back now. And more—I have purpose. The kind of purpose I was searching for all those years ago, when I joined the Exile Army."

Gyalo felt his heart sink. "Not guarding me."

"Yes. Guarding you."

"But I'm not a purpose, Teispas."

"You really don't see it, do you."

"See what?"

"That you are the Next Messenger."

"That . . ." Gyalo felt as if the captain had struck him. "What?"

"It came to me when I saw you hold the Blood. It was as if a hand had reached inside me and closed around my heart. I feared to believe it then. But now the truth of it is all I see."

"Tcispas," Gyalo said faintly. "No."

"*He will be born out of a dark time.*" Teispas quoted Ârata's Promise. "*He will come among you ravaged from the burning lands, bearing my blood with him. He will bring news of me.* All those things are true. Or will be, when you walk back into Thuxra City."

"No, Teispas. I'm just a man, a human man. The Next Messenger is Ârata's creation, made whole and entire by Ârata's hand. Not a man born of woman. Not a man at all."

"I know that's what people say. But where in the *Darxasa* is any of that written? All it says is that the Next Messenger will be born out of a dark time. And weren't you? Weren't we all? Anyway, haven't you been *re*-created? Stripped of your vow, your Shaping freed? Are you the man you were?"

"I'm still human! No human man could do what the Next Messenger must! No human man is strong enough."

"Ârata will give you strength." Teispas's regard seemed no longer fixed, but febrile. "He chose a human Messenger once before. He can do it again. Diasarta sees it too. And Axane."

"You've *talked* to them about this?"

"Diasarta came to me—he saw it for himself. And Axane . . . Axane gave you the Blood."

"Teispas. This is heresy. Do you hear me? Your faith is too

new—you've been lost too long. You've gone terribly astray. You must give up these notions. You must abandon these ideas. You must let me help you seek the proper paths of faith."

Blue light sparked in Teispas's eyes. "I already walk the proper paths of faith."

"Then you are no better than the heretics of Refuge! Do you understand what that means? Your soul will grow as dark with sin as theirs! You will burn as long, when the time of cleansing comes!"

"The people of Refuge *are* heretics. But they're not wrong in why they wait. They were not wrong about you."

"Enough! That is enough! I will hear no more!"

Teispas fell silent. For a moment they stood, eye to eye. Gyalo was the first to turn aside.

"Stay where you are," he said unsteadily. "Don't follow me."

He strode rapidly away. Glancing back after a few moments, he saw the cobalt of Teispas's lifelight stationary against the dark. He could almost feel the hot, fixed stare that emanated from it, like a barb between his shoulders.

He walked until he could see no trace of blue, then sat down on the ground, his back against a stone. His own nacreous lifelight shone out around him, an earthly echo of the drifting moon. Great sheets and plumes of heated air breathed up from the sun-stunned earth, boiling where they met the opposing currents of the sky. All the desert was ashimmer—the unmoving glow of brush and scrub, the darting glint of the insects and small animals that came out at night to hunt and feed. Their rustlings and chitterings seemed tiny in the silence, his own breathing much too loud. He was cold, and appalled, and filled with a terrible sense of familiarity, as if he had fallen back into a dream from which he thought he had woken. How could this befall him twice? Was there some awful irony at work, some cosmic pattern he did not comprehend?

He sighed, pulling his hands across his face, rubbing at his eyes, always sore from sun and dust. He should not have run away. He should have stayed, tried to reason with the captain. *I must talk to him,* he thought. *And to the others. I must put things right.* He saw again Teispas's hectic, blue-sparked gaze, and felt a sinking weariness. It would not be easy.

He stayed all night against his rock. At last, when the sky began to pale with dawn, he pushed himself stiffly to his feet. He was light-headed with fatigue. The glimmering world around him seemed subtly strange, as if it had changed during the night—or as if he had.

He had gone farther than he thought, and it was some time before he saw the camp ahead of him, the heat patterns of its fire rising toward the dimming stars. He saw the flash of blue as well, and knew that Teispas had waited for him. There was no surprise: Even as he sat solitary he had sensed that barb between his shoulders, the force of Teispas's will for his return.

He averted his gaze as he passed. He did not want to see what was in Teispas's face, or show what was in his—the telltale residue of the long, long night, during which the captain's words had taken root in him like some kind of sickness, and he had begun actually to weigh them, as if they might be true.

In the days that followed, he thought of nothing else.

What Teispas had said was so: Nowhere in the *Darxasa* was it written that the Next Messenger must be a demigod. His divinity was a theological assumption, dating from the early days of the church. Ârata had chosen a human man to be his First Messenger; why could it not be so a second time? Yet how could any human man accomplish the Next Messenger's task—to open the way, to lead the faithful out of the exile of time and death and into the new primal age? And even supposing it were possible, why should that man be he? Certainly he carried a crystal of the Blood, but it had not come to him through his own endeavor—or, as with Marduspida, as Ârata's gift. It had been simple chance that set it in his hands, chance and the choices of others.

He felt a strange sense of recognition as he asked these questions—as if they had been born not just of Teispas's words but of some understanding of his own, concealed till now in the deep bedrock of his mind. At times he was sure he must have gone insane, to give even a second's thought to something so impossible. At times the hubris of his speculation took his breath, and he shuddered to conceive such blasphemy. And now and then he saw, as stark as the vistas of the desert, the truth that lay behind the questions: That by whatever circumstance, through whatever agency, he _would_ bear both the Blood and news of Ârata out of the Burning Land. And everything in him stood still in horror, to think he might really be what Teispas named him.

Had Marduspida thought such thoughts, when he refused Ârata's summoning dream? For him, blasphemy would have been a seventh rejection. Was it a test, then—was it part of the Next Messenger's task not just to do, but to accept? To believe?

There were no answers. In the end, he resolved to renounce the questions—or rather, to take them to Baushpar along with his message and lay them at the feet of the Brethren, who, in the gathered wisdom of their centuries of consciousness, would know what must be done. Till then, he would strive simply to follow his task as he had originally conceived it, in his first apprehension of Ârata's will. He found at last a kind of peace in that decision. But it was not the peace of before. That exalted, joyous certainty was gone.

Now, alone amid the opal fields, seven days from Thuxra City, he halted and turned his face to the jeweled sky. _O Ârata_, he prayed, _be patient. Forgive my blasphemy, if that is what it is. Forgive my doubt and fear. I will come to you, if that's your will; I will give up my life for you, if that's what you require. I am your servant, always and forever—I want no more than that, and never have, my whole life long._

The prayer flew out into the indifferent vastness of the night. In the initial flush of revelation, it had seemed to him that the quality of his devotions must change. Somewhere, Ârata bestrode the world again; surely it must be possible to sense the god's great listening mind, to feel that huge awakened attention bent upon the earth. It was, of course, an irrational assumption: Ârata had been awake for longer than Gyalo had been alive, and nothing was different now but that he knew it. Still, he had had to relearn the expectation of that silence, huge as the world itself; he had had to reschool himself to acceptance of it as a mystery of faith. He knew now, as he had always known, that his devotions printed themselves upon his soul; he must trust that Ârata would read them there, when the time of cleansing came.

He turned and began to make his way back to camp. Around him all creation seethed with pattern and with life. He walked slowly, pausing often, trying to fix all he saw indelibly in memory. For memory, soon, would be all he had.

—14—

They had come in to the west of the thoroughfare cut through the mining areas, and had to spend a few days searching for it. They found it at last, and made camp nearby just before sunset, at the lip of a pit mine. Worker barracks huddled not far away; by mutual consent they avoided them, preferring the open air to such haunted shelter.

There was nothing Gyalo needed to shape tonight. Food had been gathered as they walked; the pressure well that had supplied the barracks had not been capped, and was full of sulfurous water when its cover was removed. He left the others to their preparations and went to stand above the pit. It descended into the earth like a giant's staircase, six terraces deep. The ladders the workers had used to clamber up and down were still in place, as were the hoists with which ore had been brought out, their iron pulleys scabbed with rust. Water glinted at the bottom, an artificial lake built up over the years by the desert's scarce but fierce rainstorms; its unnatural turquoise color, a product of the copper ores that had been mined there, was dimmed by the falling sun to a sullen green.

He had stood at the edges of other pits on the journey out. Then, with his ordinary senses, he had seen only their toxic ugliness, unhealed wounds in a sacred land. Now he saw much more: the stresses of the soil, the currents of the day's heat in the pit's lower reaches, the cunning way the angle of the excavation followed the strata of the earth, the small darting brightnesses that betrayed the presence of life, even in this poisoned place.

Nothing can be truly ugly to a Shaper, he thought. If it were not beautiful in itself, there was always fascination in the way it touched the world. It caught at his heart. He turned away and went back to the fire, where the lizards Diasarta had killed earlier were nearly cooked.

"There's something we need to discuss," he said, when they had finished eating.

They turned toward him, except for Gâbrios, who lay dozing with his head in Axane's lap. They shone against the night: Diasarta's watery green, Teispas's vibrant indigo, Gâbrios's hesitant carmine, Axane's glorious mesh of sea-deep hues. Nearby, the fire pulsed a dozen shades of gold and scarlet, the patterns of its heat unfurling like sheets of gauze. Beyond, in the darkness, a million tiny lifelights sparked their radiance, as if to mimic the thick-starred sky. So it had been, each night, for all the months of their journey. It would be very strange to walk between walls again, to lie in a bed, to eat food he had not gathered with his hands or created of his skill. To be in company with people who were not these four, who did not know what he knew, who had never walked the Burning Land or looked upon the Plains of Blessing.

"There will be many questions once we reach Baushpar," he began. "One of them will be how we survived this journey."

"We'll answer however you like." Teispas comprehended instantly.

"Yes." Diasarta nodded. "Only tell us, and we'll say it."

Axane glanced from one man to the other, puzzled.

"No, no. That's not what I mean. I don't intend to conceal

anything. But . . . the Brethren don't yet know what we know. I must come among them as I am—I must speak to them, as I am. And it has occurred to me that as I am—as I am now—they will fear me."

"Why?" Axane asked. "You're a Shaper."

"Yes. A free Shaper. An apostate."

"An . . . apostate?"

"One who abandons true belief to return to the false ways the belief supplanted. The Shapers of the outside world aren't like the Shapers of Refuge, Axane. We, too, swear a vow, but our vow binds us to use our shaping for Âratist ceremony only, and to tether it with a drug called manita."

"Tether it?" She looked at him. When first he met her, she had been like Teispas, very difficult to read—though it was not remoteness she conveyed, but rather a sense of complex presence, formidably controlled. This was not as true as it had been; still, it was not always easy to tell what she might be thinking. "How?"

"Manita . . . inhibits shaping ability. Binds it to latency, so it can only be used by means of special disciplines."

"I don't understand. Why would you do that?"

"A long time ago a terrible war came of the free use of shaping. Since then shaping has been strictly guarded, and all Shapers have sworn the vow I described. On the pebble plain, when the storm came, I lost my manita and my shaping was set free. I chose to use it to bring water. I became a vow-breaker, an apostate, like those unbound Shapers centuries ago. It's the greatest sin a Shaper can commit."

"But you would have died!"

"My superiors will say it was my vow I should have saved, not my life."

"How can a vow be more important than a life?" She shook her head. "That makes no sense."

"You don't know the history, Axane. You don't know about the Shaper War."

She frowned. "There's nothing in Refuge's chronicles about a Shaper War."

"No." Gyalo paused, choosing his words. "Your first

Shapers, Cyras and Mandapâxa, were vowed Âratists in Arsace. That means they took manita, and swore the same vow I did. When Risaryâsi found them, they must have been without manita for some time. Maybe they'd already broken their vows, maybe they held on until Risaryâsi persuaded them—I don't know. But by the time they reached Refuge, they'd grown to believe that the Shaper vow was wrong and that the Brethren, in decreeing it should be sworn, had wrongly interpreted the lessons of the past. They decided it wasn't fallible human will that had led to the Shaper War, but the practice of shaping outside the Way of Ârata. The Shapers who fought the Shaper War were all pagan, you see."

"Pagan?" Axane said.

"They worshiped gods other than Ârata. So Cyras and Mandapâxa decided that in the new world Refuge's descendants would one day build, shaping shouldn't be limited as it had been. All the First Twenty-Three agreed. When the story of Galea was written down, the Shaper War was left out, along with the Doctrine of Baushpar. If the Shaper vow was to be removed from history, the circumstances that produced it must be excised as well."

"Ash of the Enemy!" It was Teispas, fascinated. "How do you know this?"

"They showed me their secret scrolls, the Shapers, when they took me into their quarters. They still thought I was . . . it was before they began to think me a demon, and they wanted me to know how they'd kept faith during their exile. It's one of their duties to retain the correct memory. There's a scroll where it's recorded, the true history of Galea and the decision to alter it. No one sees it but ordained Shapers."

"Blasphemers!" Diasarta spat, and touched his eyelids in the sign of Ârata. "May the fires of cleansing roast them all to ash."

Gyalo thought of those long-dead Shapers, who in the face of death had chosen life, as he had. They, too, had labored under Ârata's will; like him, they had embraced the freedom of their shaping, for they had needed it to survive. But they had gone too far, deducing from that freedom a philosophy that twisted divine purpose into heresy. In the larger context it meant little, for the cycles in which the people of Refuge had planned to promulgate their deviant vision were illusion. Still, there could be no greater proof of the deadly arrogance of untethered shaping.

Axane was gazing into the fire, absently stroking Gâbrios's matted curls. She looked not like someone who had been informed that the very root of her own history was a lie, but as if she were fitting together the pieces of a puzzle.

"I'm sorry I interrupted," she said. "Go on."

"So." Gyalo drew a breath. "I am apostate. Now, we here tonight know that the age of human law and custom is drawing to a close, but for those to whom we go it's the only age they know. I'd be a fool and twice a fool if I thought I could simply speak and be believed, even with the evidence we carry. Even if there were no question of my vow." He paused. "So I've decided I must tether myself again, to prove my loyalty to the Way of Ârata—like Liruloro the Steadfast when she was released by her captors, or the Shapers of Ruzin, when the snows of the Bitter Winter finally melted. The Brethren still won't trust me, not at first. But at least they won't fear me so much they'll refuse to hear me."

They stared at him. For a moment no one spoke.

"No," Teispas said. He shook his head. "No. You must not humble yourself so."

Over the past weeks Teispas had continued, stubbornly, to fill his self-appointed role—following where he could, watching always; but he had been obedient, and no mention of the Next Messenger had passed his lips. This was as close as he had come to declaring his belief aloud.

"I'll be tethered again in any case. That's the sentence for apostasy."

"What? You can't submit to that!"

"I won't have a choice. And if I must do it, I'd rather do it myself, at my own pace. I don't want to be seized and drugged unconscious while my body adjusts to a massive dose of manita."

"But Brother, why should you say you broke your vow at

all?" Diasarta asked. "If you don't, and we don't, who's to know? We'll say we managed with my slingshot, and Axane's desert lore, and yours. It's the truth."

"But not all the truth. And even if it were . . . if someone told you about a group of people marooned in the Burning Land, cast on the direst circumstances, and one of them a Shaper, what would you think? The question will be asked. And I will not lie."

"I'll speak for you, then," Teispas said, intensely. "I'll tell them how you saved our lives. I'll say you were ready to die rather than break your vow, that it was only for us you did it. I'll say I forced you to it—"

"No. Absolutely not. You'd be seized as well, for suborning apostasy. I forbid you to speak of that, Teispas."

Teispas's mouth was as tight as a closed door. "You have no manita."

"There's manita at the ruined monastery on top of Thuxra Notch. I found it when we camped there." Gyalo shook his head. "It's not because I wanted counsel that I've told you this. My mind is set—I only wanted to prepare you for what I mean to do. Now, I think it's best we say as little as possible before we reach Baushpar. The Brethren should be the first to hear the news we've brought. But when the time comes to speak, you must not lie about my vow—though for Teispas's sake I ask you not to say how I came to lose my manita. You can say it was lost in the storm. That's true enough." He looked around at their faces, each in turn. "This is what I ask. Will you do it?"

Silence again. At last, with great reluctance, Teispas nodded. "If I must."

"I'll do it," Diasarta said.

"And I," said Axane.

"There's one more thing." Gyalo paused a moment, steeling himself. Though he had meant, after Teispas's revelation, to speak to his companions, he had never done so—largely because of his own uncertainty, but also because he could not bear to see them look at him as Teispas had. "I would ask you not to say anything of what you . . . of what

I . . . of the possibility . . ." He drew a breath. "Of any re-semblance between me and the Next Messenger." A cold-ness ran up his spine as he said it, a tingling sense of trespass. "I plan to lay the matter before the Brethren. But I want to do that myself, alone. So I ask you, all of you, not speak of it—to the Brethren, or to anyone."

"I don't understand these things you ask," Teispas said. "I can't see why you think you need to—" He broke off, shook his head. "But I'll do as you say. You have my oath."

"And mine," said Diasarta. Axane only nodded.

With relief he left them, and went again to the edge of the mining pit. After a little while he heard soft footfalls, and emerald light bloomed around him.

"Here." Axane offered him a blanket. "It's getting cold."

"Thank you," he said, surprised. He pulled the blanket around his shoulders. He expected her to turn and go, but in-stead she stood beside him, looking down into the pit.

"Will it be painful?" she asked. "To take the manita again?"

"I imagine it will make me sick. Manita is harsh, and I've been without it for some time."

"That's not what I meant. Will it hurt . . . to diminish your shaping?"

Gyalo had hoped it would not show, his terror at the thought of tethering himself again. He had conceived this plan after the passing of his initial transcendent certainty, when he first began to consider, in a sober way, the practical difficulties of the task ahead. It had come to him like the knowledge of a fatal sickness, unacceptable yet inescapable. In the dread he felt, he was forced to confront what he had not much wanted to think about before now: the addiction a freed shaping talent planted in the Shaper's soul, a depen-dency as absolute as manita's but far more powerful, for it could never be cured. The other symptoms of unfettered shaping—the greed, the pride, the drive to dominance—had not so far woken in him, perhaps by Ârata's grace, perhaps because he had not been free long enough. But the addic-tion—that was in him, beyond any doubt.

"It won't be so bad," he lied. "I'll soon be used to it."

She looked at him. "I wish . . ." She did not complete the sentence. Silence fell. Still she did not go.

When he first agreed she should come with them, he had not been certain she could stand the journeying. She was a daughter of Refuge and obviously accustomed to hard labor; but Refuge in its way was a place of considerable comfort, and he did not know if she had ever traveled as they traveled, walking day after day under the blazing sun, eating strange food and sleeping on the hard ground. She was a woman, too, and frail to look at. But as he was to learn, there was iron in that reed-slim body, and iron in her soul as well, for she never complained or faltered, never quailed or hesitated, and endured the embarrassments and indignities of being a lone woman among four men with matter-of-fact practicality. She did, he suspected, grieve for what she had left behind; he had woken in the night to see her sitting up, her arms around her knees, gazing south. But she never spoke of it.

They traded desert lore. She answered his questions about Refuge, for he wanted more fully to understand its ways, and he told her tales of the kingdoms of Galea, about which she had an inexhaustible curiosity. Stranger that she was, raised under the yoke of heresy, he felt easier in her company than with either of the others. Teispas behaved toward him with reverent distance, a sworn guard with a precious charge; Diasarta showed him a careful deference that he assumed stemmed from his Shaperhood, and only later realized had a different cause. But Axane treated him as a companion and, sometimes, as a teacher. It was a more human sort of fellowship, and he was grateful for it.

That had soured, with Teispas's revelation. It seemed impossible that she, who alone among her people had not seen Risaryâsi's Promise in him, could believe as Teispas did. And yet, as Teispas pointed out, she had given him the crystal of the Blood. He began to notice how her eyes followed him when she thought he was not looking, how she served him first when portioning out the food, how she offered him things—water, blankets, a bandage—before he knew he needed them. It was an attention more subtle than Teispas's, but just as constant. Was it kindness, companionship—or the reverence of a believer?

At last he could bear it no longer.

"Axane," he said to her one evening, when they had gone together to gather fruit from a stand of treasury vines, "why did you give me the crystal of the Blood?"

She glanced at him, and he sensed that she had been waiting for this question. "You said in the council meeting that it would be harder for you to bring news of Ârata without Refuge's voices to add to your own. Since you didn't have our voices, I thought I'd give you the Blood to bring with you. As proof."

"Why should you do such a thing for me?"

"It wasn't for you." She stripped a handful of fruits into the ragged stole she used for gathering. In the falling light of evening, she glimmered like an emerald. "It was for me. I thought you might not want to let me come with you. I thought that if I brought you the Blood, you wouldn't be able to refuse. But after I took it . . ." She paused. "I changed my mind. It seemed wrong to use it that way, to . . . to barter, to bargain. I thought instead it should be a gift."

"Did you think what it might mean to give me such a gift? Did you think what it might mean for me to bring a crystal of the Blood out of the Burning Land?"

He saw the comprehension in her face. "Not when I first took it. But after—yes. I did think of it. But your people aren't like my people. I didn't think it could really be the same."

"So you don't believe it, then. That I might be . . ." He could not say the words. "What Teispas thinks."

A pause. She looked away. "I don't know."

"You don't know?" It came out more harshly than he intended. But what he wanted, with an urgency he only just recognized, was for her to look at him and say, as she had said in Refuge: *I know you're not the Next Messenger.* "Why not?"

"How can anyone know a thing like that? My people

thought they knew you when you came to Refuge, but they were wrong. Now Teispas thinks he knows . . . but maybe he's wrong, too. There are a dozen ways to look at anything. A hundred ways."

"That's not an answer."

"I'm sorry." There was appeal in her face. "Gyalo—I don't want to think about things like this anymore. In Refuge, *now* is never as important as what's coming. Everything is faith, faith and waiting. I'm tired of living that way. I don't want to wait, to spend my life hoping for something that may never come. I just want to *be*. To let things happen as they happen, without always wondering what they mean."

"You may not always be so fortunate," he said stiffly.

"Who knows? Maybe I will be. Anyway, it's not as if my opinion is important. What does it matter what I think?"

"It matters . . . it matters because I want to know."

"All right, then. The truth is that I don't *want* to think about you that way. I'd rather think of you . . . I'd rather think of you as just a man."

She flushed as she said it, a long, slow flood of color rising into her cheeks. The muscles of her throat were taut, as if with effort. Her eyes were fixed to his; he saw the invitation in them, as clear as spoken words, and understood at last why she paid him so much attention.

"You mustn't . . ." He stammered, hardly knowing what he was saying. "You mustn't think of me that way either." She stared at him. "That is . . . I follow a vow—"

"A vow?"

"A vow of . . . of abstinence. To bind me to the church. I cannot . . . I must not . . . be with a woman. Do you understand?"

A moment. Then her face changed—closing, smoothing. "Yes," she said. "I understand."

She bundled up her fruit and, without another look at him, got to her feet and returned to camp.

She kept a careful distance after that. She still watched him sometimes, when she thought he did not notice; but that was all. Though he missed her companionship—missed it with surprising sharpness—he was glad of the separation. He knew the indecent marriage customs of Refuge, knew that she had lived a year in unwedded union with a man. Perhaps such casual invitations were customary among her people—if so, he told himself, he could not judge her, for she knew no better. Still, it shocked him that she had been so bold.

Now, standing beside her and wondering what had led her to seek him out after so many weeks, he felt again the embarrassment of that moment, and half wished she would turn and go.

"It's why you went off all those nights alone, isn't it." Her low clear voice broke the desert quiet. "To grow accustomed to your shaping. It's why the openings in the crystal were so . . ." She paused. "So rough. In Refuge."

"Yes." Of course she had perceived his clumsiness and inexperience. He had seen that she wondered at it. But not till tonight had he been able to bring himself to explain.

"I still don't understand it," she said. "Why you would make your shaping small. Why you would swear never to use it for anything—" She hesitated. "Anything of benefit. It seems such a waste. It seems—" Again she paused. "I'm sorry. But it seems to me you might as well not be a Shaper."

"You don't know enough to judge."

"Tell me, then. Explain. I want to understand."

Tired and uneasy as he was, Gyalo was tempted to refuse. But, he thought, she did deserve to know.

"It begins long before the Shaper War itself. For a while after Ârata lay down to sleep, men kept the memory of the primal age, when all creation existed in perfect communion with the god. Shapers honored their ability as a sacred thing, never to be used for selfish or ignoble ends. But slowly the primal age was forgotten. Shapers began to believe that shaping was no more than a tool to be used to the Shaper's will, or a skill that could be sold to whoever would pay for it. There were attempts at control—in many lands Shapers were barred from certain professions and activities, or required to submit to certain kinds of training, or bound by law to go into service. But rules aren't perfect, and there was much abuse. Where once Shapers had been revered and blessed, they came to be feared, even hated.

"This was just part of the disorder that caused Ârata to summon Marduspida into the Burning Land. In the *Darxasa,* Ârata bids Shapers to return to the precepts of the primal age, to honor the divine origin of shaping and use it only in accordance with his Way. When Marduspida brought Ârata's word to the kingdoms of Galea, many Shapers embraced it. But many others refused it."

She said, a little impatiently, "All this we learn in Refuge."

"But now we come to the part you don't learn. In the second century after Marduspida's emergence, a pagan nobleman called Nabrios decided to evict all Âratists, vowed and secular, from his domains. He wasn't a Shaper, but he had Shapers in his employ, and they helped him drive the Âratists out. Once he was done, he decided it wasn't enough—all Galea should be rid of the Way of Ârata. He recruited a great army of pagan Shapers, and began a campaign of terror. Vowed Âratists were slaughtered. Followers of the Way were forced to pagan worship. Monasteries were demolished, Âratist temples unmade to the last stone."

"It sounds like what the Caryaxists did."

"In a way it was. Except that Nabrios's weapon was shaping, and those who tried to face his army weren't just pierced by arrows or cleaved by swords, but swallowed by the earth, or consumed by storms of fire, or crushed by stones falling from the sky. It wasn't a long war, as wars go—about a year. But it was the most savage conflict Galea has ever known. Even now, there are places where you can see the scars of it. No one has ever managed to properly calculate how much was lost or how many died."

"But they didn't win, the Shapers."

"No. The King of Arsace, Vantyas, had recruited his own Shaper army, Shapers loyal to the Way of Ârata. But he felt he needed more than shaping to win victory. It was known that if dried manita leaves were mixed into a Shaper's food, his ability would be diminished—it was one of the few defenses ordinary people had. Vantyas's artificers began experimenting with manita, trying to discover how it worked, trying to find a way to make it into a weapon. They invented a method of concentrating it by cooking and distilling, and then drying it and grinding it very fine, like dust, so it could be dispersed through the air. Any Shaper who breathed it in became temporarily powerless.

"Vantyas and his Shapers went out to meet the pagan army. They used catapults to throw clay vessels of manita powder into the army's midst. The battle is named for that, the Battle of Clay. The pagans' shaping was bound—and they were physically helpless, too, for manita is incredibly harsh to breathe, completely incapacitating if you aren't used to it. Then Vantyas's Shapers opened the earth, and the pagan army was swallowed up."

"Even though they were helpless?" Axane was shocked.

"They were only helpless for a little while. The manita would have worn off—and what then? How can you imprison someone who can unmake the bars of a cell? What choice did Vantyas have?"

She was silent a moment. "What happened then?"

"After the war was over, the Brethren called a conclave in Baushpar. Vowed Âratists and kings and princes and officials came from all the kingdoms of Galea—more of them then than there are now. The Shaper War was more proof than anyone had ever wanted of the danger of free shaping. There were some who said that shaping must be cut out of the world entirely, that all Shapers still alive should be hunted down and killed, even those who had fought with Vantyas. Of course that wasn't possible—shaping is Ârata's gift, an echo of his own divine power, and we're bound by the *Darxasa* to honor it. Yet the ash of the Enemy is born into us all, and if shaping were left free, what was to prevent the Shaper War from coming again someday? In the end it was decided that shaping should be removed from the secular realm and the uses to which it was put there, and given into the keeping of the church, which was best fitted to guard it according to the Way of Ârata. How that was to be done was set down in a document called the Doctrine of Baushpar. Ever since, Shapers have sworn themselves to serve it."

"And everyone agreed to that?" She sounded disbelieving.

"Not everyone. There were other conflicts. But within a hundred years, all the shaping in Galea had been brought fully to the Way."

It was a terse description of a turbulent time. Even the Brethren had been divided on what should be done and how to do it; and many Shapers, Âratist and non-, had resisted not just the limitation of their ability, but the rule of it by men and women who were Forceless. There had been battles; there had been atrocities, not all of them committed by free Shapers. Had it not been for the fact that the Battle of Clay had swallowed up more than half of all Shapers in Galea, the effort might not have succeeded, even with the assistance of manita—a fact the official histories did not state in so many words but made clear enough.

"Do Shapers never refuse these vows?" Axane asked.

"Sometimes. If they do, they must agree to become the church's wards and take manita, just as vowed Shapers do."

"But that's no different. And how can you be sure of finding them all? Shapers must be born all the time, all over Galea."

"Not so often. Shaping isn't common. Anyway, that's one of the things our Dreamers do—search the world for signs of it."

"Refuge has had three generations of Shapers," Axane said. She had moved nearer as they spoke; they stood close enough now for the edges of their lifelights to intersect, Gyalo's steady nacre softening her restless emerald-cobalt to cloudy jade and pearlescent azure. "Never have they done the kind of harm you've just described. They revere their shaping. They revere their duty."

"Yes," he admitted. "I saw that they do, within the limits of their heresy."

"And yet they don't bind themselves to a vow like yours. They don't take a drug to make their shaping small."

"There are nineteen Shapers in Refuge—all of them free to use their shaping as they wish, unequal in strength and unrestrained by any tether but their oath. Can you say beyond doubt that none will ever misuse his or her ability? That none will ever yield to anger or greed or envy? What about that young man, the oldest trainee? I was told he's greatly gifted. But I saw the pride in him, the arrogance. Are you sure he'll be content to keep his vows?"

"Râvar would never break his vows." There was something odd in her voice.

"No, Axane." Gyalo shook his head. "These are the truths history teaches us. Your Shapers' vows are not enough. If it had really been your people's task to build the world anew, there would have been another Shaper War. It might have taken longer, but it would have happened. I think Cyras and Mandapâxa understood that, in spite of their apostasy—that's why they secretly retained the true history of the world. So there would be someone to remember, if the Shaper War came again."

She was silent, staring down into the pit. He was overwhelmingly aware, now, of the margin where their lifelights touched. A hundred times they had stood like this, before their misunderstanding, and it had never discomforted him. He edged away from her, one step, another, until her turmoiled colors were fully separate from his own.

"I should be going." Her tone was flat.

He nodded. She began to turn, then paused.

"Gyalo." She hesitated, then said, in a rush: "You can trust me. I won't say anything—not about your shaping, not about . . . the Next Messenger. I don't yet understand your world. But I don't ever want to harm you, or . . . or to discredit you, by something I might say in ignorance."

She did not wait for a response but walked rapidly away.

He stood on for some time after she had gone. The night seemed very dark with the removal of her light, and deeply empty. He thought about what he had told her, about the

Shaper War and the changes that had sprung from it. Those were the truths that had turned him from transgression years ago. The wonders he had seen in Refuge, his exploration of his own apostasy, had only deepened and enlarged his understanding of them. Yet he knew that if the men and women to whom he traveled were to see him now, they would think him no better than the pagan Shapers who had laid Galea waste, or the ones afterward who had refused the authority of the church. He himself would have seen it so, a year ago. It was not a comfortable thing to comprehend.

For a moment he allowed himself to feel it fully—the difficulty of the task before him, his dread of binding himself again. Then, as he had done many times before, he packed it all down inside himself again, and followed Axane back to camp.

They traveled on along the mining thoroughfare. Gyalo would have thought, as they drew nearer the prison, to see more signs of the reclaimers' work, but things looked much as he remembered them from a year ago. It was not until the fourth day that they began to come across dismantled mine sites.

On the fifth day, an hour or so past dawn, Thuxra City came into view, a dark blemish on the desert's upturned face. A few more hours brought them to the middens. Heat fumed off them, as thick as smoke to Gyalo's Shaper sight; ahead, the walls of Thuxra seemed to dance above the ground, dissolving in a boiling haze. Gâbrios, remembering he had passed this way and not understanding why he was there again, grew fearful, tugging at his leash until Diasarta had to grip him by the arm.

"Look." Teispas, leading the camel, pointed. "Up ahead."

Gyalo shaded his eyes. Near the prison, liquid in the heat shimmer, there was a nexus of motion—a work group of some kind, men standing in a cart shoveling something onto the midden, with two more waiting nearby. Even as he realized that, there was a babble of voices, and the motion stopped.

"They've seen us," Teispas said.

The workers stood staring as the companions approached. The guards—for by then it was plain that these were prisoners—stood with their staves angled defensively before them.

"Stop," one of them called. "Don't come any farther."

"We mean you no harm." Gyalo displayed his empty hands. "We're the remains of the expedition sent out from Thuxra last autumn."

"The . . ." The guard stared at them. "But they all perished."

"Not all, as you can see."

"Ârata's thousand bloody wounds!" The guard strode toward them, trailing the scarlet of his lifelight. He clasped Gyalo's shoulder and then Teispas's, as if to assure himself they were real. When he saw Axane—who, slight of figure to begin with and pared down even more by the journey, still could not be mistaken for anything but a woman—he checked, his eyes stretching in his sunburned face.

"Who—"

"She is a refugee," Gyalo said. "Everything will be explained. Perhaps you could escort us in now."

"Of course. Of course. Come." The guard started back toward the prisoners, shouting. "Finish up now! Hurry!"

The prisoners' task was quickly completed. They climbed down, ranging themselves in pairs at the front of the cart so the guards could harness them.

"We'd carry you," the first guard said to Gyalo, apologetic, "but I don't think you'd want to ride." And indeed what the prisoners had shoveled looked and smelled like human waste.

Their arrival produced a sensation. Grooms and soldiers crowded around, exclaiming and questioning. Someone took the camel; others tried to relieve the travelers of what they carried. Gyalo only just managed to keep hold of his battered travel pack, which some helpful soul attempted to pull out of his arms. After the quiet of the Burning Land, the long solitude with the same small company, it was too much.

The others pressed around him, as overwhelmed as he. He closed his eyes; the earth seemed to tilt, and he might have fallen had it not been for Teispas and Diasarta, flanking him. He heard Gâbrios, gabbling unintelligibly, his voice rising high and terrified, and the first guard, loudly recounting their arrival:

". . . like some kind of mirage, it was. And when I saw it was people, living people from out of the Burning Land, I swear for a minute I thought the Next Messenger had come—"

Gyalo's eyes flew open. Teispas's hands tightened on his arm.

The crowd parted. The administrator pushed through, his aides behind him. He wore a guarded expression, as if he had not yet decided whether to believe the news. That changed as he saw them: recognition, for Teispas and Diasarta and Gyalo, and then, as his eyes found Axane, shock. For an instant it held him motionless.

"Ârata be praised!" he said, recovering. "Are there no more of you?"

"The rest are dead," Teispas said.

"May they rise again in light." The administrator made the sign of Ârata. "Come. Come, let us tend you."

They entered the custodians' quarters, and the noise of the crowd fell away. Gyalo had thought he remembered this place, yet it seemed entirely unfamiliar. Perhaps it was the strangeness, after so long in the desert, of so much moist and tender green, so much flowing, falling water. Or perhaps it was his altered senses, dazzled by the dense tapestry of life around him. Only the gravel of the central thoroughfare, and the cool-hued stucco of the villas, and the tiles of the garden paths did not shine with life—and, above them, the walls of Thuxra. Seeking relief in that harsh dead symmetry, Gyalo read the patterns of enclosure that dominated all the others—holding the desert out but also confining what was within, like a jewel in a miser's strongbox.

The administrator handed them over to his household

staff. Kaluela, plump and perfect in her drifting silks, took charge of Axane, who went reluctantly, looking back at Gâbrios. Agitated, he called out for her, but then forgot her in the way of his impairment, addressing his anxious questions to the servants who took him into gentle custody.

Gyalo gave himself up to the luxury of being tended—the scented water of the bath, the deft touch of the barber, the practiced hands of the physician called to examine him and the others. It was like a dream. He could not rid himself of the sense that he must wake and find himself on the hard ground of the Burning Land, dust in his mouth and filth on his skin. Afterward, a servant escorted him to one of the second-floor bedchambers. There he found his travel pack, set by the foot of the bed. He could not remember relinquishing it. Seized by sudden fear, he knelt and dug down inside. The Blood was there, at the bottom, safely wrapped in Axane's stole.

He drew it out. Sitting back on his heels, he folded away the cloth and exposed the jewel. In the chamber's shuttered dimness, its little flame throbbed like a beating heart. It gleamed no differently, in this closed and bounded space, than in the limitless expanses of the desert.

He wrapped it up again and slipped it under his pillow. He went to pull back the window screen, for the air in the room was stuffy, then ate sparingly of the food he found waiting on a tray—simple fare, but impossibly rich to his desert-adapted palate. Stripping off the clothes he had been given, he slipped between the sheets. He felt fluid, nearly weightless. The mattress yielded unfamiliarly beneath him; the pillow was strange in its softness. But the crystal, beneath, was hard against his cheek.

We're here, he thought. And then, with something like surprise: *We survived.* He had known they must. But not until that moment had he quite believed they would.

—15—

Gyalo woke to a soft knocking. Sun fell through the window, exactly as it had when he lay down.

"Come in," he called.

A maidservant with an amethyst-colored lifelight entered with a tray of food, which she placed on the table by the bed.

"Can I fetch you anything, Brother?"

Gyalo scrubbed his hands over his face, feeling the unaccustomed absence of beard and the soft stubble of his hair, which he had chosen to have cropped close to his scalp rather than shaved. "No. Thank you. How long have I been sleeping?"

"You slept the clock round, Brother."

"Ah." He did not feel it.

"If you're well enough, Brother, the master asks if you would attend him once you've eaten."

"Yes. Yes, tell him I'll come."

She bowed and departed. Gyalo lay a moment, then got up and stiffly pulled on his borrowed clothes. He felt leaden in all his limbs, and his back ached from the unaccustomed softness of the mattress. He drank deeply from the jar of water on the tray, then, suddenly ravenous, began to eat.

When he came out onto the gallery the servant was waiting. She led him downstairs. Pattern assailed his senses: smaller patterns, wood and stone and paint and fabric, and larger ones—the arrangement of the furnishings in the rooms he passed, the rooms' relationship to the greater space inside the house, the stresses the stairway placed upon the wall against which it was built, a hall whose pristine plaster told him exactly where it meant to crack. He was used to the patterns of the Burning Land, sparser and less variable and also, because they were naturally occurring, more orderly; but here pattern piled on pattern, a furious man-made clutter in which each separate thread competed for his attention. Already he was exhausted from the effort of looking at it all.

The servant delivered him to a large chamber at the house's rear. In contrast to the opulence elsewhere, the room was plainly furnished—clearly the personal taste of the administrator himself, whose direct manner and avoidance of Arsacian pretensions seemed to fit much better here than in the rest of the dwelling. He sat behind the table that served him as a desk, the pale amber of his lifelight dancing on the shadowed air. Before him in a cushioned chair was Teispas. The Exile uniform the captain had been given hung on him as if he were made of sticks; the sun-blasted skin of his face was raw, and his cracked lips were smeared with salve. But his hair had been sheared to shoulder length and sleekly combed, and his once-shaggy beard was now trimmed close to his jaw.

"Brother Gyalo. Welcome," the administrator said in his Tapati-accented Arsacian, rising courteously to his feet. "Rani—another chair." The servant obeyed. "Thank you, that'll be all. Will you have some wine, Brother?"

Gyalo seated himself. "I don't think that would be wise. I'm still only half-awake."

"Have all your needs been met? You are comfortable?"

"Very comfortable. Thank you."

The administrator smiled, wide cheeks creasing. "Good. Good."

The room's order was soothing after the confusion of the rest of the house. Gyalo felt his senses settling. At the administrator's back a colonnade opened upon the garden. Hinged screens were set between the columns, half-closed against the heat; beyond them, the garden shimmered with sunlight and with life, the steady luminance of grass and leaf stitched through with the darting spark of insects.

"Captain dar Ispindi was just telling me about your journey," the administrator said. "As it happens, I already knew half the story. The miner, Vâsparis, returned a month ago."

"Vâsparis?" Gyalo said, astonished. "He's alive?"

"By Jo-Mea's grace. He was starved and eaten up with fever when we found him, and we didn't expect him to survive. But he's tough as leather, that one."

"I'm glad to hear it. Very glad."

"If anyone had asked me, I'd have said it could not be done. There's not a single account of anyone surviving the Burning Land so long alone."

"He knows the Land as few do. He tutored me, on the journey out. It's partly thanks to him that we survived."

"So I understand. It's a lucky thing you took an interest."

Gyalo glanced away from the administrator's shrewd gaze. "The others—the soldiers who took him—what of them? Do you know?"

"Dead, one assumes. Vâsparis says he left them as soon as he found a way to slip his bonds."

"Poor Haxar." Gyalo thought of him, of his terror and confusion on the pebble plain.

"Poor Haxar?" Teispas's tone was harsh. "Have you forgotten he betrayed us?"

"No. Still I pity him. He was not in his right mind. He must have suffered terribly before he died."

"I hope he did. And that he suffers more, when the time of cleansing comes."

"We all learned much about desperation," Gyalo said mildly, "on the pebble plain."

Teispas looked away, shaking his head.

"Well," the administrator said, "I suppose we'll never know."

"Before you came in, I was talking about how we managed to survive his treachery." Teispas was staring into his wine cup, swirling the liquid in it round and round. "About the fissure we found beyond the place where he left us, thrusting water out of the ground as the pressure wells do here. I was saying that we'd all but given up hope before we saw it, for several days had passed, and it seemed certain we would die."

As he had promised, not a lie. Not the truth either—but it would do until they reached Baushpar.

"But you lived," the administrator said. "And went on. And found them—the lost Âratists." He shook his head; there was wonder on his broad brown face. "When I saw the woman . . . truly, I thought I must be dreaming. My wife says she has the manners of a nun, and will hardly speak a word but 'please' and 'thank you.' "

"How much have you told your wife of who she is?"

"My wife knows everything, Brother." The administrator met Gyalo's eyes. "It's no longer a secret, what you and your people went into the Burning Land to do. Vâsparis said things, in his delirium. I thought truth was better than rumor, so I told it."

"That's just as well. It would have had to be told now anyway."

"What's it like, the place where you found them?"

"There's a great grass plain, with a river running through it. The Burning Land has a far more variable terrain than any of the accounts indicate, and that plain is as habitable as any place in Galea. They live above the river in a rocky cleft, in caves they've furnished and improved. They call their settlement Refuge."

"Refuge," the administrator repeated. "Are there many of them?"

"About three hundred."

"Three *hundred!* How do they survive?"

"Hunting and gathering mostly, and a little farming. They brought skills with them from the monasteries—weaving, smithing, healing, stoneworking—and monastery discipline as well. It's quite ingenious, some of the accommodations they've worked out. They've achieved a comfort that would surprise you."

"They'll be brought back now, surely. To Arsace, as was originally planned."

"I can't say what will be decided." Gyalo hesitated. "I know you're eager to hear more. But I think I've said as much as I should. These are matters that should first go to the Brethren. You understand."

The administrator nodded, unsurprised. "What shall I tell my people? I must say something. There are many questions."

"Tell them what I've told you. Ask them to be patient. Say that everything will be known in time."

"I'm afraid I shall have no peace from my wife. She's determined to solve the puzzle of how people could live so many decades without piped water and tiled ovens and not revert to a state of utter savagery." He smiled, with a ruefulness that did not disguise the fondness behind it. "You'll stay with us a little while, I hope, before starting back."

"Yes." Even as he said it, Gyalo felt his exhaustion, pulling at his limbs like a weight of water. "We do need to rest."

"I'll supply an escort for you when you go. The disputes over land reapportionment drag on—there's still considerable lawlessness where there are no lords to see the roads patrolled."

"Thank you. I'd like to send a dispatch to Baushpar, as soon as I may."

"A courier left yesterday with news of your return. I can send another today if you wish."

"Yes. Please. Could you see I'm brought writing materials?"

"Of course. If you can spare another moment, Brother—" The administrator's demeanor had stiffened. "There is one more thing I'd like to discuss. The men who brought you in yesterday. I expect you noticed they were under guard."

The prisoners, Gyalo thought. Until that moment, he had forgotten that this was something he was not supposed to know.

"Doubtless you'll hear of them when you reach Baushpar, but I thought it right to tell you now. They are prisoners." The administrator's gaze was steady, though it seemed to take effort. "There are still some few hundred of them here at Thuxra, on the King's authority—criminals we cannot set free and have no place to send. That wasn't known to the Brethren when you were here before. But it has since become general knowledge."

So Utamnos got my message, Gyalo thought. He reached for the righteous anger of a vowed Âratist just informed of terrible religious violation, but found he was too tired to dissemble.

"I see," he said.

"I'm a faithful Âratist, Brother," said the administrator, defensively. "I honor the Aspects and keep the Foundations of the Way. But I'm under orders. I must do as I'm commanded, even when I don't like it."

"Yes. I understand. I commend your honesty."

A pause; the administrator seemed to be waiting for something else. When it did not come he sat back in his chair. "Well," he said. "I'm glad you see it that way."

"I'm really very weary." Gyalo braced his hands on the arms of his chair and pushed himself to his feet. Teispas, instantly, did the same. "I think I'll return to my room now."

"Of course. I'm the one who should apologize, for keeping you." The administrator rose also. "I beg that you will consider my house and staff wholly at your disposal. Whatever you wish, simply ask. If it can be found, you shall have it."

"Thank you. We're grateful for your care."

"Good afternoon, then, Brother. Captain."

In the passage Gyalo paused, bewildered by the crowding patterns and his own weariness, unable to remember how to go. Teispas, coming up behind him, took his arm; closing his eyes against the turmoil of his senses, he allowed himself to be led. Teispas delivered him to his room and departed without a word.

A servant came with ink and paper, and Gyalo composed his dispatch. Tersely he confirmed the fate of the expedition, the names of the Âratist dead and those of the survivors, and his intent to journey with all speed to Baushpar once he and his companions were well enough to travel. Then he thought for a time, and added a final paragraph:

> We found what we were sent to find—and something very much greater. I will not write the details here, or speak them until I stand before you. I will say only that I bring news of change. I bring also a wonder, which I will give into your hands, and a woman, a descendant of the lost Âratists, who will bear witness to all I say.
> Great is Ârata. Great is his Way.

He signed the message and addressed it to the Bearer, sealed it with the church seal he had carried in his pack across the Burning Land and back, and summoned a servant to take it away. Then, as fatigued by the small task as if he had done a day's hard labor, he returned to bed.

For the next few days he did little more than sleep and eat. In the Burning Land he had not often thought of his physical condition; pain and fatigue were givens, and he went on in spite of them. But now that he no longer needed to strive, all strength seemed to abandon him. He could barely keep awake for two hours at a time. The walk from one end of his room to the other exhausted him. It seemed, sometimes, too much effort to breathe.

Three days after their arrival, Vâsparis came to see him.

"No, no," the little miner said, as Gyalo made to push himself up against his pillows. "You don't look as if you've got the strength to turn over, never mind sit up."

He dragged a chair to the bedside and sat down. He was

shockingly wasted, his face and arms scabbed and peeling with old sunburn and healing injuries. His hair had been shaved off to ease the fever of his infection; the stubble, growing in, was grayer than Gyalo remembered. His lifelight was the color of tarnished silver, almost the same hue as his eyes, roiled with smoky currents. Gyalo had never seen it before; Vâsparis had not attended the ceremonies he conducted in the Burning Land.

"It knitted wrong." Vâsparis gestured to his left arm, which was bound across his chest. "They broke it again after I got here, but it'd been too long, and the muscles had withered. They say I won't ever have much use of it again."

"I'm sorry, Vâsparis."

The little miner shrugged. "My working days were over, anyway."

"What will you do now?"

"Go back to Arsace, I suppose."

"Will you be all right? Do you need money?"

Vâsparis grinned, the expression skull-like on his ravaged features. "Oh, I'm a rich man, Brother, what with finder's bonuses over the years and never spending but a fraction of my wages. Of course it was only scrip before the Caryaxists fell, but I'd saved up a nice bit before that. And I wasn't stupid enough to bank it, either. It's buried out there"—he gestured with his good arm, toward the open desert—"safe as can be."

"That's good. I've often thought of you, Vâsparis. I never dared hope you'd survive."

"Truth to tell, Brother, nor did I." The grin was gone. "I was sick for the last part . . . I don't remember much. They said I only made it to the middens. If there hadn't been a work detail out that day, a guard who was looking in the right direction . . ." He shivered, though the room was hot. "I dream about that, Brother. I dream no one was looking."

"Well, someone was. And here you are."

"Like bad luck."

"I—we—owe you a debt. What you taught me about the

Burning Land while we were traveling—it was part of what saved our lives, on the journey back. I'm glad to have the chance to thank you."

"Things happen for a reason, eh, Brother?" Vâsparis grinned his death's-head grin and shook his head. "What wonders you've seen. A city carved into a cliff, a running river in the Burning Land! Who'd have imagined such a thing?"

"Do you know what became of Haxar and the others?"

Vâsparis turned away, toward the room's south-facing window, where sun streaming through the window screen laid a filigree of light across the tiles. "I killed them."

"You—" Gyalo stared at the little man. "How?"

Vâsparis made a motion of his shoulders, not quite a shrug. "I told everyone I'd escaped. But you—" He flicked a glance toward Gyalo. "I won't lie to you, Brother. I made them trust me. I made them think I'd've gone with them by choice, if they hadn't seized and bound me. When I said the roots of colic grass were good to eat, they believed me. There was a big stand of it—they ate it up like pigs. After they were dead I went on alone."

There was a silence. Vâsparis kept his face averted, staring at the patterns on the floor.

"When did that happen?" Gyalo asked.

"Maybe a week after we got across the pebble plain. The camels died . . . we'd no carrying water, no supplies. I tried to get them to search out a place for resting, but Haxar said Ârata would smite us if we stopped for so much as half a day. Him and Nariya . . . they couldn't agree on which eye to open first in the morning. And Cinxri, with his complaining . . . Haxar stuck a knife in his arm one night just to shut him up. I could see what was coming." He shook his head. "It wasn't so much death I feared—I just couldn't stand that I'd be killed by their stupidity." He made a sound that was not really a laugh. "I buried them. Took me a whole day to do it. They'd've rotted the same on the ground as underneath it, but I couldn't leave them there." He sighed. "I suppose now you'll have to turn me in."

"Is that what you want?"

"No. I don't know." He paused, then went on in a rush, "I've never been much of a believer, Brother, you know that. Never much thought about what comes after death. But I'm damned now, aren't I? I'll be burned to nothing at the end of time."

"Do you repent what you did?"

Vâsparis's mouth twisted. "Burn me, Brother, but I do. They're a burden on my conscience, those useless men."

"Well, then." Months ago, Gyalo might have answered differently. But he knew now about desperation, about the tyranny of the will to survive. "You've taken on a burden of darkness, that's certain. But Ârata sees everything, not just one thing. He'll judge not just what you did, but what was done to you, and how you went on afterward. If he can be merciful, he will be."

Hope struggled in the miner's face. "You really think so?"

"Yes. I do."

Vâsparis sighed again. "Thank you, Brother."

There was a pause. Scent drifted through the window, the honey perfume of the exotic blooms in the administrator's garden. Gyalo felt the pull of his fatigue; it was a struggle to keep his eyes from falling closed.

"*Will* you turn me in, Brother?"

"That's not up to me. The choice was yours; what must be done about it is also your choice."

"We all make choices, don't we?" Vâsparis's eyes were like silver coins in his sun-black face. "In the end, it's all about survival. You know that, same as I do, don't you, Brother?"

The room seemed, suddenly, to have grown much smaller. In what he saw in Vâsparis's face, Gyalo understood that the miner had deduced the truth. And why not? Vâsparis had been there. He knew there was no water on the pebble plain. He knew there was only one way Gyalo and the others could have survived.

"I won't tell anyone, Brother," Vâsparis said softly. "I'm

not exactly fit to judge what someone does to stay alive. You don't need to worry about me."

Gyalo could think of nothing to say.

"Well. I should be on my way." Vâsparis pushed back his chair. "Good-bye, Brother. It was good to see you again."

"Good-bye, Vâsparis."

Vâsparis moved stiffly toward the door. For the first time since Gyalo had known him, he looked like what he was: an aging man, worn by the rigors of a harsh life.

"Vâsparis." The miner turned. "Come see me again, will you?"

Vâsparis smiled—a real smile this time, not that stretched grin. "Be sure of it."

Toward the end of the week, the need for rest became less pressing. Gyalo felt able, now, to sit on the gallery during the day, even to walk in the administrator's garden. His Shaper senses were also adjusting, and he no longer found the complexity around him so intrusive. He had asked that he be brought a drawstring pouch and a leather wallet on a neck strap; inside these, the Blood's light was effectively hidden, and he was able to take it with him wherever he went. It was not really that he feared it might be found or stolen; it was just that he had carried it for so long and did not like to be parted from it.

He also began to take the evening meal in company on the open terrace downstairs. Teispas, with the almost inhuman resilience that was characteristic of him, had begun coming down two nights after their arrival; Diasarta followed a few days later. Gâbrios was absent: He had been sent to the infirmary, where he could be given the constant care he needed.

As for Axane, she descended for the first time the same night Gyalo did. She, too, had been bedridden, and Gyalo had not seen her since they arrived; he was startled by the change in her appearance. Kaluela had mounted an energetic campaign to undo the cosmetic ravages of the Burning Land, ordering unguents for Axane's damaged skin, special baths to remove the ingrained grime of travel, manicures to repair her cracked and broken nails, oils to smooth her roughened hair. A wardrobe of Arsacian gowns had been assembled for her—some Kaluela's own, cut down, some donated by the other women of Thuxra. She was much too thin, her face still shadowed by the fatigue of long journeying; but she looked remarkably good in her new clothes, her large eyes enhanced with kohl, her heavy hair fastened up with enameled pins. Kaluela, proud of her handiwork, invited compliments, causing the younger woman to blush—that slow painful flush of hers, like coals burning below the surface of her skin.

They were informal occasions, the meals. The administrator's aides were not invited, and only the administrator and his wife, and sometimes Vâsparis, were present. The food was simple, in deference to the travelers' recent starvation, and their hosts did not ply them with questions, making it a point to talk instead of things beyond the Burning Land. In this way Gyalo learned how the world had moved on during their absence. The restoration of the Âratist temple-monastery complex in Ninyâser, half-complete when he had passed through a year ago, was now nearly done. King Santaxma had married a daughter of one of the noble houses that had not escaped Arsace—a popular match, for the honor it gave the surviving lords-in-hiding, who had suffered so much more than the returning lords-in-exile—and the new bride was already with child. The Lords' Assembly was still at odds over the continuing difficulties of land return, as well as the apparently ineradicable plague of banditry and the question of what to do about the Caryaxist warlords hanging on in Arsace's arid southwestern quarter. Elsewhere in Galea, the young King of Aino and his consort had produced an heir. A sea monster had appeared off the coast of Kanu-Tapa and was terrorizing Tapati fishing boats. Tiny mountain-locked Isar had closed its borders against a black-fever epidemic in neighboring Yahaz, and tensions were escalating over a disputed strip of land along the border between Chonggye and Haruko.

A year ago, Gyalo had taken a vital interest in such matters—not just as they affected the church but because of his own inexhaustible curiosity about the world. But now they seemed to touch him only lightly, as if he were a traveler hearing news of a foreign land. He suspected that his physical depletion played a part; it seemed harder these days to summon up any sort of strong emotion. But it was more than that. The Age of Exile was drawing to a close. All these human doings, and their consequences, were soon to pass away. To rejoice for Santaxma's heir was also to comprehend the imminence of a time in which royal succession was irrelevant. To feel pity for the victims of Yahaz's epidemic was also to understand how soon their souls would rise into the light of the new primal age. To look upon the enclosing pattern of Thuxra's walls, to experience the luxury that had been built on blood and pain—the things that had disturbed him so, when he had been here before—was to know the gladness of a future in which no such place would ever again exist. It was not that the happenings of the world had lost meaning; joy was joy, and suffering was suffering, and humankind must embrace them for yet a little while. But they had grown transparent to their own finitude. They could not matter to him as they once had.

At Teispas's urging, he agreed to extend their stay at Thuxra by another week. It was longer than he would have wished; but they were all still weak from their ordeal, and he accepted the captain's judgment. Also, as Teispas pointed out, Axane needed time to practice the riding skills in which he had begun to instruct her.

Returning to his room from this conference, Gyalo encountered Axane sitting on the gallery, playing a game of sticks-and-circles with little Eolani, who had taken a passionate fancy to her and followed her about like a puppy when Kaluela would allow it. He paused to tell her what had been decided.

"I wish we could just walk," she said, grimacing, at mention of the riding lessons. She was clad in a spring green gown today; her sea colors boiled around her, shading toward amethyst where they intersected Eolani's yielding rose.

"Why? Is it not going well?"

She sighed. "I'm a terrible pupil. Teispas has grown very impatient with me."

Gyalo was aware that she struggled with more than just inexperience. There were no large animals on the Plains of Blessing, and though she understood the idea of beasts of burden (there were paintings of horses on the walls of Refuge's Temple, after all), the reality was something else. The camel had terrified her; it had been days before she would go near it, and even when her feet were blistered she had not consented to get on its back.

"Would you like me to speak to him?"

"No!" She shook her head. "No. I'll manage."

"Don't worry, Axane," Eolani said. "You'll be a *good* rider."

"I hope you're right, sweetheart. At least once we're traveling I won't have to wrap myself up in a dozen veils. I thought I'd faint yesterday from the heat."

"Why do you have to wear so many veils, Axane?"

"Because your mother wants me to spare my skin from the sun."

"Why?"

"Because people with dark skin are ugly."

"You're not ugly!" the little girl said indignantly. "You're beautiful!"

"Don't be silly, sweetheart."

"I'm not silly! The man said so too, the riding man. He said it to my mother. I heard him."

"That's enough, Eolani." Axane was blushing. She bent toward the game board, hiding her face. "Look. You've knocked over your pieces. We'll have to start again."

"Can Brother Gyalo play?"

"I'm sure Brother Gyalo has better things to do."

"Actually, I don't have anything to do." Gyalo dropped to his knees. "Now, I don't think I know this game, Eolani. You'll have to teach me."

He soon wished he had refused. The constraint between the two of them, which had eased on the night he told her about the Shaper War, had fully reasserted itself, and he felt the awkwardness of it more strongly with each passing moment. Luckily, Eolani chattered enough for all of them, and after only a little while grew bored and dragged Axane off by the hand. Gyalo watched them out of sight. The gallery seemed very dark once they had gone.

The day before they were due to depart, Gyalo led a Communion ceremony. In the absence of ceremonial substances, he improvised with colored rocks, salt from the kitchens, charcoal from the cooking fires, and oil he consecrated himself. He had not wanted to perform the ceremony, which in strict terms he was no longer entitled to conduct, and whose ancient phrases were mostly contradicted by the understandings he had gained in Refuge. But he had known it would be asked of him, and so he was ready. It felt very strange to step back into the ways of Âratist Shaperhood, to accomplish the tiny changes that once had been the whole sum of his capability and now were as insignificant as blinking.

Among the communicants were Teispas and Diasarta. He spoke to them and marked them, as he spoke to and marked the others. He read in their faces the knowledge they shared, the revelation they had together carried out of the Burning Land. In this crowd of strangers, he felt the ties that joined him to these men—whose companionship he had not chosen, whose belief in him he did not accept, who were not friends, and yet were bound to him as closely as anyone ever in his life.

When he returned to the administrator's house, he found Kaluela waiting.

"Brother Gyalo!" She hurried toward him, her rosy lifelight vivid in the daytime dimness of the entrance hall. "May I offer you refreshment? You must be tired after such a long ceremony."

"Thank you, no. I think I'll just go upstairs."

"Brother—I don't mean to impose. But if you could spare a moment—"

He resisted the impulse to sigh. "Of course."

"Not here." She looked around, almost furtive. "Come."

She led the way to the back of the house, where the terrace's flagstones ran up against the verdant tangle of the garden. Graveled paths snaked between the beds, opening here and there onto paved areas where fountains played, fetching up unexpectedly against the lavender-tinted stucco walls that formed the garden's boundary. The plantings rose higher than Gyalo's head, isolating him and Kaluela in a narrow green world. With his human gaze he saw the shade they cast, but to his Shaper eyes they blazed with life. The air was heavy with the scent of flowers, and, beneath it, the darker odor of vegetal decomposition.

"Which do you think is the worse darkness, Brother?" Kaluela's gaze was fixed upon the path. "To violate a trust because it's your duty to speak, or to know something terrible and keep it secret out of loyalty?"

"It depends upon the secret."

She sighed. "I'm a good Âratist, Brother. I'm also a good wife. I've been asking myself, these past days, which I can best bear to betray."

"Lady, I can't counsel you if you speak to me in riddles."

"I don't mean to. But this is very hard." She halted. Behind her, a vine scrambled up an iron trellis, throwing out yellow flowers on long curving stems. "I must speak. I know I must."

Gyalo waited. She drew a breath.

"We've discussed politics a little, these past evenings. But we haven't wanted to . . . distress you, so we've avoided certain things. One of the things we haven't spoken of is a resolution that has been brought before the Lords' Assembly. Some of the lords have proposed that the mines at Thuxra be reopened."

"Reopened? Surely not."

"It's true, Brother. A group of lords-in-exile proposed it in Assembly, just after the break between His Majesty and the Blood Bearer."

"Break? What break?"

"It happened after you left last year. It's said their friendship is at an end—no one knows why. Some say the lords took advantage of that when they brought the resolution, that they believed the King would be more receptive because of it. Publicly His Majesty will not take a position. But privately, he supports the mining."

"Supports it? How can that be?"

"His Majesty believes he has no choice. The expense of restoring Arsace is more than anyone imagined. The Caryaxists left nothing in the treasury. The other kingdoms of Galea will send money to the church, to refurbish monasteries and temples, but not to Arsace, to rebuild roads and rehabilitate the land. There's wealth in the Burning Land, all the wealth His Majesty needs and more. He believes Ârata wouldn't refuse the use of his resting place if he knew the suffering of the first of his kingdoms."

Gyalo shook his head, incredulous. "How do you know all this?"

"My husband has received orders, direct orders from the King, to halt the reclamation of the mines. To hold things as they are, in anticipation of the resolution's passage. It's a deadly secret, Brother—only His Majesty and those closest to him know of it. Even the lords who would open the mines again believe that Thuxra's reclamation continues."

Gyalo stared at her, rose-hued against the dark core of growth behind her, itself limned in light. For a moment there was silence.

"Your husband told you this?" he said at last.

"My husband tells me everything, Brother. We're alone here, and there's no one of his own rank he can speak to. It burdens him, what he does in this place." Her large brown eyes had filled with tears. "He thinks I don't really understand."

"The King truly believes that this . . . resolution will pass?"

"My husband says he does."

"But surely there's opposition. Surely the Brethren have spoken against it."

"The Brethren have declared that any lord who endorses the resolution will be declared heretic. Even so, support is growing. Twice it's been forced to the vote, and each time the number of supporters is larger. It's near a third of the Assembly now. My husband thinks that if it weren't a question of heresy, they'd already have a majority."

"They're no better than Caryaxists, then!" Gyalo drew a breath. "Your husband is following these orders." It was not a question: He understood, now, the lack of change he had seen as he and his companions walked among the mines. "For how long?"

"Six months. He has to do it, Brother. He'd be found guilty of treason if he refused." There was entreaty in Kaluela's voice. "He's a good man. Please don't judge him harshly."

"It's not my judgment you should worry about."

"Do you think I don't know that?" The tears spilled over, trailing kohl down her cheeks. "Do you think I don't?"

"I'm sorry, lady." Gyalo was struck with guilt. She did not deserve his anger, this soft, kind woman who had set her conscience above her loyalty. "My anger isn't for you. I know what it must have cost you to tell me this."

"Do you?" She turned away from him and plucked one of the yellow flowers near her hand. Its tiny light winked out at once, dead in the instant of its severance. "I've betrayed my husband, whom I love, who trusts me. How will Ârata judge *me*?"

"He'll judge you for your faith. And for your courage in following your conscience. You've done the right thing in speaking to me. I'm grateful."

Her mouth twisted. She closed her fingers on the flower, crushing it, and let it fall. "I must go back now. I'd like to go alone."

"I understand. Lady . . . thank you."

She turned without reply, and moved off down the path. The garden swallowed her; her rosy light glinted a moment longer between the leaves and stems, and vanished.

Gyalo walked on until he came to a place where benches were arrayed in a circle around a trickling fountain. There he sat, as the afternoon dwindled, his hand resting in what had become a habitual gesture upon the leather wallet that held the crystal of the Blood. He breathed deeply, trying to set aside the disgust that had claimed him. These were the end times. Ârata no longer lay within the Burning Land; it could not, therefore, be defiled. Yet the King and his nobles did not know that. What they did was blasphemy, as surely as if Ârata still slept.

It was twilight when he got to his feet and sought the house, making his way between the glowing banks of vegetation. He felt the world to which he would go out tomorrow, as close around him as the moist air of the garden. Finite or not, the world went on. And its currents were as treacherous as they had ever been.

—16—

They departed midway through the following morning. They were a party of eight—Gyalo, Axane, Teispas, Diasarta, and the four Exile soldiers the administrator had given them as escort. It had been decided that Gâbrios would remain behind, in care of Thuxra's physicians, until he could be returned to his family in Haruko. Axane had gone the day before to bid him good-bye, coming back silent and sad.

Gyalo was aware he had not yet regained his strength, and the first day of riding proved how true that was. He was grateful when Teispas decided to call an early halt—not for his sake but for Axane's, who suffered greatly from saddle soreness given her limited riding experience. She had become an adequate rider, but not an easy one; her fear was apparent in the rigidity of her seat and the way she clutched the reins. She was too stiff to dismount on her own; Teispas had to lift her down, supporting her until she pulled shakily away. As usual, she did not complain.

This was an altogether different sort of journey from the one just past. The long hours were the same, though, and the routine of making and striking camp, and in the days that followed the companions fell back into the easy interdependence of the Burning Land, where each had been so familiar with the others' roles and competences there was hardly need for speech. The Exile soldiers kept themselves apart. It was clear they found much about this expedition curious, from Gyalo's decision to travel incognito to Axane herself, who, brought impossibly out of a lifeless land, must seem as exotic to them as a dream.

Gyalo had not been certain how he would bear this time, as they approached the ruined monastery and what he must do there. Yet though that arrival was present in his thoughts, though he could feel time narrowing toward it, he found himself unable to fear or brood. A strange, exalted mood had come upon him. The world, in all its great variety, filled his Shaper senses: the glassy clarity of the light as the elevation increased, the gem-sharp hues of his companions' colors against the stark grays and duns of the cliffs, the ancient patterns of stress and change written upon the mountain landscapes, the boiling cataracts of frigid air that raced down from the peaks, the convoluted poetry of rockfalls, the heat and scatter of sunlight on stone. Everywhere his eyes fell, vision entranced him.

On the fifth day they reached the overlook where he had first glimpsed the Burning Land. He waved the others on and, dismounting, approached the edge as closely as he dared and knelt. A year ago, he had seen only desert spreading out below, red and green and hazed with distance, overwhelmingly immense. It was still too huge to grasp in its entirety, even for an unbound Shaper. But now it was not just the Land he saw, but the whole sweep of its history: the shadow patterns of what it had been—dry riverbeds, lost forests, the bowls of vanished lakes; the clear patterns of what it was, speaking even from afar of drought and dust and hidden, paradoxical abundance; the inchoate patterns of what it would become, sculpted by time and the elements. Heat skeined up from it like smoke; cold plunged from the heights, and where they met the air danced and the light fractured into colors not known in nature.

For a long time he knelt, gazing outward. As in meditation, past and future fell away, leaving only the present, a single ecstatic instant like a note struck on a perfectly tuned instrument. When at last he rose to go, he felt his heart might burst from the beauty of the world, and from gratitude he had been born a Shaper, that he might see it so.

A week later, in the middle of the afternoon, the monastery came in sight, strange in its man-made regularity amid this wild and uneven land. Gyalo's joy vanished like a pinched candle flame. Now at last dread filled him, more terrible because he had held it back so long. By the time they reached the monastery, it was as if great hands bore down upon his shoulders, and the world that had been so vivid, so full of depth, had gone pale and flat. He was aware of his companions' glances, a shared understanding he did not dare acknowledge for fear it might undo his resolve.

Teispas and Diasarta and the Exiles—who, affected either by the atmosphere of the derelict building or the mood of the others, were tense and edgy—bedded down in the ruined refectory. Axane chose to sleep alone in the room next door. It was the room the Dreamers had used; Gyalo, glancing in on his way to the third floor, saw her spreading out her blankets by candlelight, her stormy colors roiling round her, and thought of Seiki in her red-curtained bed. Axane's head began to turn; he quickened his steps and was past before she saw him.

In the third-floor chamber he had chosen, he set down what he carried. He was calm now, a brittle tranquillity that sat above his fear like a skim of ice. He busied himself with his bedding and turned to his travel pack—new, like his clothing, but containing many of the same things: the travel journal he had kept on the journey to Refuge, his meditation square, the church seal, the book of poetry that had been Utamnos's gift, the tattered remains of his last Shaper stole, his simulacrum (which he had taken off in Refuge and never put on again), and the silver box that held his manita equipment.

He removed the meditation square and the box. He spread

the square beside his blankets and arranged the contents of the box upon it. He retrieved what he had brought upstairs: his manita pouch, full of powder from the store in the monastery's cellar. He had never been certain why he had salvaged the pouch after Teispas emptied it, but he supposed he had reason now to be glad.

With the silver scoop he dipped out a single measure of the drug, placing it on the disk in two small heaps. It was just one-eighth his normal tether, but he did not know whether his body retained any tolerance at all after so much time. He vividly recalled the harrowing process of adjustment and had no wish to repeat it.

He set the scoop back in the box and removed the tube. In his mind, he saw himself performing the actions that came next: bending to the disk, lowering the tube, inhaling the powder. He could almost feel the burn of the drug as it entered his system. But he knelt before the meditation square, the tube gripped in his fingers, and did not move.

He did not know how long he hesitated. He was aware of the silence of the room, of the coldness of the night, of the press of darkness beyond the small gleam of his candle. At last, from somewhere within him, resolve emerged—not gradual, but immediate, full-blown. *Now,* he thought.

He leaned forward and took the drug in two fierce inhalations.

Fire burst behind his eyes. Fire bloomed in his throat and chest. For an awful moment he could not breathe; then he did drag in a breath, but it came out as an explosion of coughing, so violent it overbalanced him. Facedown on the floor, he clawed another breath, and coughed again, until it seemed his throat would come out through his mouth.

The world around him turned blue, then green, then blue again, a light he could see even through his clenched eyelids. He felt arms come around him, holding him against a warm body while he hacked and gasped and wept, his lungs striving helplessly to rid themselves of what he had forced them to take in. At last the paroxysms diminished. He was able to take two breaths, then four, then more. The embracing arms released him. The body they belonged to adjusted itself, so that he lay on his back with his head cradled upon the width of a thigh. There was a waft of air, and warmth enveloped him. A soft cloth blotted his forehead, and gently cleaned the spittle from his mouth and chin.

He opened his eyes. They burned, like his throat, and a haze hung across his vision. The face bent over him was blurred, its corona of light smeared and indistinct, like something reflected in a piece of greasy metal.

"Axane," he whispered, not knowing he spoke till he heard the rasping sound of it.

"Shhh." She pressed the cloth against his cheeks. "Rest now."

"Too much noise . . ." Another coughing fit took him. He had not wanted her, or anyone, to come to him; nor could the Exiles be allowed to guess what he was doing. That was why he had chosen this distant room. But he was grateful for her presence, so much he could have wept; he had not known until this moment how much he feared to go through this alone. "Didn't mean . . . to disturb you. . . ."

"Hush. You didn't disturb me. I was waiting on the stairs."

She bent closer. Her face swam into focus: the dark skin, the proud nose, the generous mouth, the great black eyes. Not a soft face, or a pretty one—but to him, in that moment, she seemed beautiful. He reached up, hardly knowing what he was doing; she caught his hand and placed it gently on his chest. He drew a breath and coughed again.

She stayed with him, steadying his head, wiping the sweat from his skin. At last he fell into an exhausted sleep. When he woke, wrung-out and groggy, the sun was slanting across the rubble-strewn floor, and she was gone. So confused were his memories of the night that he might almost have thought he had dreamed her. But she had left behind the cloth she used to blot his face: one of the stoles Kaluela had given her, torn in half.

He packed up his things. His head pounded, and his throat was raw, and the muscles of his chest ached where they had tensed and strained during the night. The world seemed a little distant, a little blurred around the edges. But he still saw as a Shaper. He had feared the change would be immediate—it had taken an act of will, when he first woke, to open his eyes.

Unsteadily he made his way downstairs, his stomach turning at the smell of the porridge the Exiles had boiled up over a fire on the hearth of the derelict refectory. He got a cup of water and sipped at it, relieved to find that he could swallow; when he had been given the drug in childhood he had not been able to eat or drink anything the day after the first dose. He was aware of Diasarta's covert scrutiny, and Teispas's more open observation. The Exiles watched also, their faces closed and suspicious.

Teispas and Diasarta went out to unhobble the horses, while the Exiles packed up supplies and utensils. Gyalo went to Axane's room, meaning to thank her. She was kneeling on the floor, her back to the doorway, rolling up her blankets. She had not yet braided up her hair; it fell forward across one shoulder, exposing the back of her long neck.

He opened his mouth to speak. But as he did, a vivid, tactile memory overwhelmed him—of her arms around him, of the warmth of her body, of the feel of her breasts against his back. Heat suffused him, from the soles of his feet to the crown of his head. He had just enough presence of mind to step aside before she turned and saw him.

He leaned against the wall, his heart pounding. The heat drained away, leaving him shamed and dizzy. *What is this?* he thought. He liked Axane, respected her; he was conscious of her as female, as he strove for honest consciousness of all who surrounded him. But even after she had offered herself to him in the desert, she had never tempted him, as a woman to a man.

He pushed away from the wall, turning toward the rear of the building. He could not speak to her now, with that memory still in the forefront of his mind. Outside in the windy morning, Diasarta and Teispas and the Exiles were saddling the horses. The cold air was welcome against Gyalo's overheated face. But the sun did not seem quite bright enough, and the distant peaks were indistinct, as though there were a film across his eyes. He blinked, blinked again. His vision did not clear.

He felt a twisting in his chest. Fear opened up in him, black and huge. The moment just past vanished from his mind. He had been wrong that morning: The change had come upon him after all.

They crossed the Notch and began to descend toward Arsace. It was a longer trip than the climb from the desert, but easier, for the Range of Clouds was not so rugged on its Arsacian side. The rocky heights gave way to dry foothills, then to a region of grassy steppes, uninhabited but for migratory tribes whose origins were lost in the mists of history. The Caryaxists' road followed the course of one of the many swift, shallow rivers that ran there; the nomads, who once had used it to water their herds, avoided it now, and in all the time it took to cross the steppes the travelers saw no human faces but their own.

Each night, Gyalo took manita. He had previously maintained a morning schedule, but it seemed better, while reacclimating, to keep to evenings, which allowed him the hours of darkness to recover. As soon as he could ingest a dose without reaction, generally about four days, he increased it—by a half measure only, for he did not want to repeat the experience of the first time. Because of the need to keep what he was doing hidden from the Exiles, he was forced to leave the campsite, under pretense of wanting solitude for meditation, returning anywhere from an hour to half the night later. He feared Axane might try again to tend him, and prepared himself to reject her if she did. But, as though sensing he would allow it only once, she did not follow.

Slowly the tether of manita drew down tight within him, a hard knot in the region of his heart, like something he could not fully swallow down. He did not track its growing grip by what he was capable of shaping—he had not shaped since the ceremony at Thuxra—but by the changes in the way he saw the world. For much of the first week, this was no more than a slight hazing of perception, as if his eyes were gummed with sleep. With the next increase, the obstruction thickened, not a haze now but a veil. By the time they reached the terminus of the steppes, four weeks past Thuxra Notch, he felt as if he were going blind. He could still see, of course; but it was a very poor vision, flat and dull and deprived of dimensionality, like a sculpted frieze worn by the elements or a piece of fabric faded by much washing. The light of life was no more than colored shadow now, his pattern-sense a vague inkling of potential meaning. He could still, with concentration, perceive how things fitted together, the qualities that made them what they were; but this effortful comprehension was a sad change from the easy mastery of before. He had forgotten what a random, ill-made place the world could be, to unaided human perception.

He thought sometimes of seeking comfort in the ways of his former Shaperhood, of working the inner disciplines that loosed the tether of the drug so his shaping might be as free within him as it could be. But even free, a fettered ability was only the ghost of a natural one. It seemed less painful simply to embrace the change.

For now, he told himself each time he took a dose. It was the only way he could bring himself to think of it—not as a thing he must do forever, but as a thing he did this day, this moment. But now and then, as he bent to the manita or sat afterward coughing or woke from uneasy sleep in the deep hours of the night, the truth of what he did opened up in him, and he felt the press of a grief he knew would swallow him alive if he let it go.

He was aware of his companions' concern. In the first village they passed through after they left the steppes, Axane searched out a healer, trading one of Kaluela's dresses for herbs that could be boiled with water and honey to soothe his throat. Diasarta, who since the Notch had taken it on himself to see to Gyalo's horse and to load and unload his baggage, was more direct.

"I still can't say I understand why you're doing this, Brother," he said in his rough way one evening. "It's tearing you up. Anyone can see."

"I know what I'm doing, Diasarta. I'll be all right."

"We've been down a long road together, haven't we?" Diasarta's homely face was a shadow in the deepening twilight. "Seen sights other people can't dream of. Known hardships they can't dream of either."

"Yes."

"What I mean to say—" Diasarta paused. "I'm not a brave man, Brother, nor a clever one. Ârata knows I haven't done much with my life, nor left much good behind me. But— what I mean to say is that I'm with you. No matter what. I'd follow you anywhere—even back into the Burning Land. Even into death."

"I wouldn't ask such a thing of you." Gyalo felt, suddenly, very weary. "I wouldn't ask it of anyone."

"Doesn't matter whether you'd ask it. What matters is I'd give it. I can't stop you from doing what you do. But it works the other way, too."

Gyalo shook his head. "Once we've spoken to the Brethren, Diasarta, our task will be done. You owe no duty beyond that. To them or to me."

"I just wanted you to know, Brother." Diasarta's steady gaze made no acknowledgment of ending. "Good night."

He turned and walked away, with the rolling gait forced on him by his shortened leg.

Teispas came to Gyalo also. With the air of a man who had lost a protracted battle to restrain himself, he demanded that Gyalo discontinue the drug. It was unworthy, he said, unnecessary, dishonorable—all the arguments he had made when Gyalo first announced his intent, but offered now with much greater vehemence and coupled with an angry assessment of Gyalo's health. To Gyalo, short-tempered with stress and fatigue, it seemed that this showed less care for him than for the prejudices of Teispas's unwelcome faith. Brusquely he cut the captain off and forbade him to speak of it again.

"It was Ârata's will that set you free!" Teispas called out furiously as Gyalo walked away. "Whose will is it that you bind yourself again? Who are you to throw away the gift Ârata gave you? What does it mean that it's a man like me who must tell you that?"

Still, if these things were difficult, Gyalo was at least prepared to face them. But that moment of heat in the hallway of the ruined monastery—he had not in any way been prepared for that. As the days drew on, he understood that it was not, as he first told himself, a stray consequence of the difficult night. Something fundamental had altered. He was now infatuated with Axane, an irresistible force of desire he could neither banish nor control.

He had battled with celibacy in his youth, just as he had struggled against the limitation of his shaping. Trainees, no less than vowed Âratists, were expected to be chaste— though this rule, like the restrictions on shaping's use, was often violated, and in Rimpang and other monastery cities there were prostitutes who catered specifically to postulants. Gyalo had sought this release just once, when he was sixteen; afterward he felt such shame that he swore never again to yield. He had kept that oath, relying furtively on self-gratification, hoping that passing time and growing knowledge would release him from the prison of desire. Instead the hope itself became a prison, a dark room beyond which the light of chastity gleamed, unattainable.

He was not honest with his preceptor, fearing he might be judged unworthy and suffer the fate of Shaper castoffs and apostates. But his preceptor was no fool. When Gyalo was eighteen, two years away from swearing the Sixfold Vow, his preceptor confronted him. Gyalo, ashamed almost to speechlessness but also strangely relieved, confessed his torments.

"You think you are the only one who suffers so." His preceptor was an elderly man, with an ugly mobile face and an inexhaustible abundance of kindness. "Believe me, you're not alone. It's one of the hardest things in this world to set aside your carnal self, for it means setting aside not just the crude fulfillment of lust, but married love, children, family.

Much, in fact, that makes life joyous. Do you know the danger of your condition?"

"That I will stray," Gyalo muttered.

"No. No, the danger is that you will come to hate your celibacy, to see it not as a gift you give Ârata so you may love him without division, but a punishment forced on you, an injustice. That you will grow angry at what's denied you, and serve Ârata not in love and duty but in bitterness and resentment. I know you know such service is not worthy. I know it's not what you want."

"What can I do then? How can I get free?"

"You will never get free." There was enormous compassion in the old man's gaze. "Your carnal nature is part of you, part of the world Ârata created out of the substance of his own bright self. If you try to pretend it doesn't exist, you'll be a liar to yourself. If you try to crush it to nothingness within you, you will twist and pervert your essential being. You must accept it, embrace it, comprehend it—and choose, even so, to be abstinent. And it must be a choice, Gyalo. That's perhaps the most important thing of all. It's something of a paradox for us Shapers, for unlike other Âratists we cannot elect our service—we must either enter the church or become its wards. But if we see it so, as something outside us to which we're forced, we will never find balance, never love Ârata as we should. Even if you're required to make it, even if there is no other, *it must be a choice.*"

"A choice," Gyalo repeated, wondering, for it seemed such a simple understanding. Not a test. Not a burden. Not a penance. A choice.

"And not a choice made once," his preceptor said. "With each temptation, you will have to choose anew. Every day. Every hour, sometimes." He smiled. "Time will make it better. And Gyalo, when desire troubles you, tend to yourself. Ârata requires our single love, but he doesn't ask us to change our natures. Our bodies were made to know pleasure. It's no shame to honor that."

It was a turning point. The struggle did not become much easier, not for some years; but it was possible to place it in context—not a solitary battle waged in the dark, but one element in the larger task of dedicating the whole of himself, mind and body, to the service he wished above all things to follow. In the end, as his preceptor promised, time and the habit of discipline delivered him from the feverish needs of adolescence. There were lapses—periods when he was distracted by an access of unfocused desire, or swept with sudden infatuation. But with the clear-eyed scrutiny he strove always to turn upon himself, he grew to recognize what seduced him, what aroused him, what tempted him to forget, and so to better know what to reject and what to avoid.

It had been a long time since he had been troubled as he was troubled now, in his thoughts and in his dreams. He thought he understood the cause: It was the void made in him by the dwindling of his shaping, struggling to fill itself with some equivalent passion. Soon they would be in Baushpar. Axane would pass from his care then; the infatuation would wither, as others had. He had only to endure until it did.

They rode into Ninyâser at the beginning of the seventh week, and took lodgings at the Âratist temple complex, where guesthouse accommodations were provided free of charge to travelers. The expedition party had been housed in the monastery itself during the Ninyâser stopover, and Gyalo and Teispas had taken meals with the monastery's administrator; concerned they might be recognized, he had given serious consideration to staying at an inn. But the funds Thuxra's administrator had advanced them were not unlimited, and two of the horses needed to be reshod. They would simply have to be discreet.

Tending to the horses forced them to remain an extra day. Gyalo spent the morning in the temple, making the offering he had promised Seiki before she died. He knew, without really allowing himself to think about it, that he would likely not have the chance in Baushpar; the Brethren, learning of his apostasy, would probably take him immediately into custody. In a somber mood, he took the midday meal in the men's guesthouse. Then he set out for the markets of Ninyâser, where he planned to purchase Âratist attire for the return to Baushpar.

In the guesthouse courtyard he encountered Axane, sitting on a bench built around the trunk of an ancient, spreading fir tree. He was close enough to his full tether now that he could perceive the light of life only in the largest and most vigorous of living entities; he could just see the fir's radiance, strongest at the base, fading along the branches. He could glimpse Axane's powerful lifelight as well—a blue-green shadow in his peripheral vision that vanished when he looked directly at her.

She got to her feet as she saw him. "May I come with you? I won't get in your way, I promise."

It was diffidently said, but she could not quite hide her eagerness. Gyalo's first thought was to refuse. But he recognized the impulse as purely selfish: A few weeks ago, it would not have occurred to him to say no.

"Very well."

They passed out of the complex and into the wide brick-paved streets of Ninyâser, where pedestrians and vendors and beggars jostled with lumbering drays and hurtling rickshaws and the occasional palanquin borne by uniformed carriers. Multistoried residences crowded on either side, with jutting balconies and screened windows and curve-eaved roofs of red and green and yellow tile. Charcoal smoke hazed the mild autumn air, adding to the varied stinks of animals, food, refuse, incense, and drains. The shouts and rumblings of the streets formed a continuous din; beneath it, the larger voice of the city could be heard—the deep, formless roar of a million souls all going simultaneously about the business of life.

Gyalo had spent some time wandering Ninyâser the year before, and had an idea of where he was heading; even so, he had taken the precaution of asking directions from one of the monks, and now was glad, for his memory was not as accurate as he had thought. His right hand rested on the wallet that held the crystal of the Blood, concealed beneath his clothes. There were pickpockets and footpads in Ninyâser, and it might perhaps have been better to hide it in his baggage, but he had not been able to bring himself to leave it behind. After he and Axane twice were separated by passersby, he held out his arm; a little hesitantly, she took it. She was careful at first to maintain a separation, but quickly forgot herself in spellbound observation of the city, and soon was pressed against his side. Since it could not be helped, he gave himself up to enjoyment of the contact. Her lifelight stirred faintly at the corners of his eyes. He thought of how it must enfold him, invisibly; he felt a deep quaking at his center and hurriedly turned his mind away.

They crossed a stairstepped bridge over a green canal, its waters as populous with boats as the streets were with foot traffic. Beyond lay the district where the religious paraphernalia-sellers had their shops. Under the Caryaxists such wares could not be sold, but on Santaxma's restoration the businesses had sprung up again at once. Offerings, incense, prayer ribbons, Communion beads, meditation squares, simulacra, fabric for Âratist clothing and tailors to sew it—all were available in an enormous variety of qualities and prices. Axane, as usual, was helpful: She turned him from the saffron silk he was considering to one whose dye was better fixed, and found a tight-woven red linen that she said would be more likely to hold its shape when washed, as well as a beautiful length of marigold-colored wool for a cloak. She looked on, fascinated, as he bargained for the items; she understood barter, but Refuge had no currency, and she found it difficult to comprehend the notion of purchase.

He took the fabrics to a tailor, who recorded his measurements and for an extra fee agreed to sew the garments overnight. Then they started back, Axane taking his arm without being asked. He glanced down at her, watching how she watched the city, with the rapt, open wonder of a child. He thought of her fear of the camel, and of the horse, the first large animals she had ever encountered; this teeming, noisy, stinking place had to be far more alien to her than that, yet she showed no timidity at all, only ardent interest in all she saw, no matter how strange or squalid.

It rebuked him, a little. He was finding it much too easy to sink into self-pity—to think, as he had been thinking that afternoon, not of what he saw but only of how he would have seen it had he not been tethered by manita. There was wonder in the world, and beauty, even to limited senses; the truth of that was clear in Axane's eager face. And even if he no longer perceived it, he nevertheless understood, of his own direct experience, the true appearance of the world—a knowledge he could not lose, any more than he could lose his Shaperhood. Bound, he still could not be other than what he was.

He felt his spirits lift. They passed a woman selling sweets; he stopped and bought one for each of them. The sticky confections were shaped like lotus buds, each with its own little cup fashioned from a leaf. Axane was delighted; she examined hers from all angles before cautiously biting off a tiny piece. Her eyes widened.

"Oh! What is it?"

He could not help smiling. "Almond paste, mixed with honey."

"Almond . . . ?"

"A kind of nut, ground up fine."

"Oh. Oh, it's wonderful! I never thought anything could taste so good!" She finished the sweet and licked her fingers, then held up the little cup. "What should I do with it?"

"Toss it aside." He gestured to the littered street. "Every night the sweepers come and clear all of this away."

She looked at it. "No. I think I'll keep it."

Carefully, she slipped it into the pocket of her stole. Then she took his arm again—there was a certain familiarity to it now—and they walked on, she gazing about, he content simply to proceed at this leisurely pace, his mind fixed on nothing more than what was in front of him. It was as close to peace as he had been these past few weeks. Even the sense of her body next to his had changed, not disturbing now but companionable.

"What's that?"

To their left, the crowded buildings drew apart. Between them was set a low milk white structure, with columns carved to resemble sheaves of grain and a domed roof like a pale fruit sliced in half.

"That's a temple of the Aspect Tane."

"Tane?" She frowned. According to the lore of Refuge, the Aspects had vanished when Ârata rose, reabsorbed into his being. When he slept again, he would dream them back into existence; but they would not necessarily be the same ones, so Cyras and Mandapâxa had not bothered to make a record of their worship. "Which one is he again?"

"She. Tane is Patron of crops and the moon. Her temples are among the most beautiful of all the Aspects. . . . That dome should be covered in silver leaf, and the columns set with copper."

"Did the Caryaxists take those things?"

"I assume so. They must have turned the temple to some secular use. I can't imagine why else it would still be standing." He glanced down at her. "Would you like to go inside?"

"Oh, yes!"

They passed through the entrance into a low-ceilinged lobby, dimly illuminated by braziers. Most of the floor was occupied by a shallow pool. A broad walkway extended across it, just under the surface of the water.

"Take off your sandals," Gyalo said. "We have to walk through the water. It's meant to purify us."

They left their sandals on the shelves provided for that purpose. Beyond the pool lay a narrow dark passage, symbolizing the falling of night. The illumination of the inner temple, moonstone-pale, showed the way through.

They emerged into a great round space entirely fashioned of milky alabaster. Sheaf-shaped columns circled its perimeter, bereft of their copper inlay like those outside. Offerings were set before them in shallow basins—a bunch of grapes, a stalk of tufted grass, a pomegranate, a scattering of flowers—all perfect, unblemished, as offerings to Tane were required to be. At the center of the space lay a large sunken area, ringed by alabaster benches. It held another pool, with an image of Tane at its bottom. Since this was an Arsacian temple, her face was an Arsacian face, but otherwise she appeared according to tradition, clad in flowing grass green robes, with grain and fruit twined into her saffron hair and a phase of the moon cupped in each of her four hands. Directly above the pool, the dome of the roof lay open to the sky. There was no other source of light. Tane's temples were illuminated only by the sun, the moon, and the stars.

Gyalo led the way to the benches. The great voice of the city was just perceptible through the dome, a formless whisper below the embracing quiet of the inner temple.

"It's so peaceful," Axane murmured.

"Yes. I always liked coming to Tane's temple, when I was a child. My mother was devoted to her."

"Tell me about your mother."

"There's not much to tell. She was a servant in a nunnery, and died when I was seven. I don't remember very much—her hands, her hair, the way she smelled . . . she used to tell me the stories painted on the gallery walls of the temple of Ârata. Tane's stories, too."

"It's confusing. How can you worship more than one god?"

"The Aspects _are_ Ârata, or rather parts of him, given reality through his dreams. When you worship them, you worship him, though in a more limited way. I was never drawn to it, but many are. People do forget, though. In the time before the First Messenger, the Aspects were mistaken for independent gods . . . and there's a famous heresy that held that the Aspects didn't spring from Ârata at all, and only become part of him when his missionaries subdued them."

There were only four other people present: an old woman in Caryaxist peasant clothing, a middle-aged man with earth-stained hands, and a wealthy matron accompanied by her maid. Among these citizens of Ninyâser, Axane looked in no way out of place, her fine turquoise-colored dress caught at the shoulders with silver pins, her heavy hair pinned up as Kaluela had taught her, one of Kaluela's silver bracelets on her narrow wrist. She might have lived there all her life—a prosperous merchant's daughter, perhaps, or the wife of an official with small children at home.

"Is it everything you thought it would be?" Gyalo asked her.

She turned her large eyes to his. "What?"

"This. Ninyâser. The outside world."

"Oh." She smiled, the wide full smile she seldom showed. She was one of those people whose faces are entirely transformed by smiling or laughing; for a moment, she radiated joy. "Oh, yes. I wasn't sure I'd seen it . . . that is, that I'd imagined it properly. But it's even more wonderful than I expected."

"I should think you'd find it very strange."

"It is strange. But that's part of what makes it wonderful."

"You don't miss Refuge, then?"

A shadow passed across her face. "I miss my father. And there are some things . . ." She paused. "But not many. I knew what I was choosing when I decided to follow you—or maybe it'd be truer to say I knew what I was choosing not to choose. Still, I was afraid . . . afraid I might have been wrong. But I wasn't wrong. I'm happy." She smiled again, with wonder this time. "I actually am."

"I'm glad," he said, feeling, somewhere within himself, an entirely unexpected twisting of envy.

"You can't begin to imagine how different it is here," she said. "In Refuge, everyone knows everyone else. From birth to death we know each other. It's hard to keep a secret, hard to do anything at least a dozen other people don't know about. And oh, it is so tedious to wake every morning knowing you'll see the same faces you saw the day before, and that those are the only faces you'll ever see, your whole life long! But here . . . even if you tried every minute of every day, you'd never know them all. A city full of strangers—a place where you can walk all day and not see one person you recognize—a place where nothing is expected of you, except that you leave others alone—"

"A place where you can be whatever you wish."

"No," she said, intensely. "A place where I can be what I *am*."

There was some significance in that he could not read. Again with that spark of envy—at her happiness? at the comfort she seemed to have found in an alien world?—he said, "I'm glad for you."

She looked away, pensive, as if reminded of something unpleasant. "There's something I should tell you."

"Yes?"

"Teispas has asked me to marry him."

For a moment Gyalo could not speak. "When?"

"Two weeks ago. He thought we could do it here, in Ninyâser, before we reached Baushpar."

"So . . . you've accepted?"

"No. I've told him I need time to think."

"To think?"

"Yes. It's . . . you know it's different among my people." She was looking down at her wrist now, twisting the silver bracelet round and round. "I am . . . I think I may be barren. To marry me, not knowing if I could bear a child . . ." She shook her head. "How could he want that? How could any man want it? But I've told him, and he says . . . he says he will take the chance."

"Then," Gyalo said, "there's no impediment."

"But there is. I don't love him."

Gyalo felt something turn over in his chest. "Many excellent marriages aren't made in love. Other needs and interests can be just as binding."

"Don't you think love is important?"

"Of course. But it's not the only reason for a marriage, or even the best one."

She dropped the bracelet and looked up at him. "Why not?"

"Because romantic love is rarely constant." He felt like a

hypocrite. What did he know of such things? "But common interests, common needs—those things are solid. Lasting."

She turned away. "So." Her voice had flattened. "You think I should do it."

"It would be a practical match for both of you. You need to think of how you'll live, now that you're in Arsace. A marriage would be a good answer. For him—for him too it would be good. I think he needs a wife. But—" It was extraordinarily difficult to continue. "It's more than that. I've seen how he watches you. It's clear he cares for you."

"I know. I wish he didn't." Her eyes were fixed on her hands again, laced tightly in her lap.

"You must have some means of support, Axane. You could claim protection from the church, if you wanted, but I think you'd hate a cloistered life."

"Why must I do either? There are other ways to live."

"What other ways?"

"I'm a healer. A healer's skills are always needed. I could be a midwife—if there's one thing a healer learns in Refuge, it's how to birth babies. I could live here, in Ninyâser. I talked about it with Kaluela, when we were in Thuxra—I've been thinking about it ever since. I even have a pouch of coins. Kaluela gave them to me. She said they'd be enough for a while, if I was careful."

"But you don't even understand how to use them!" Gyalo was horrified. "You don't know the first thing about how to live in a place like this!"

"I can learn." She looked at him, defiantly. "I'm not a fool. I know it will be difficult. I know life is hard for a woman on her own—and that's not something I had to come here to find out. I've spent hours thinking about all the reasons why I should do the practical thing and marry Teispas. But all my life I've been practical. I'm *tired* of living that sort of life. I'm *tired* of being careful. In Refuge I knew just one thing about myself: that I could keep a secret. But now I know something else: *I can do what's needed*. I'll go with you to Baushpar, because I promised, and because—because—" She broke off; she sounded, suddenly, as if she might weep. "But after that, I'll come back here and make my own way."

Gyalo looked at her. She meant it; he could see it in her face. "You'll be all alone," he said.

"That won't be anything new." She got to her feet. "I'd like to go now."

They left the temple, returning to the noise and turmoil of the streets. She did not take his arm this time, nor did he offer it. They walked in silence. She had retreated fully behind the wall of her reserve, and Gyalo could think of nothing to say.

"Thank you," she told him, formally, when they reached the courtyard. "For escorting me. And for the sweet."

"It was my pleasure," he replied, with equal artificiality.

She vanished into the women's guesthouse. He thought he saw a flash of green, trailing on the air behind her.

He sought his own chamber—more of a cell, really, with just space enough for a bed, a chest, a table with a basin and water jar, and a window facing onto the courtyard. He drew the chest over to the window and sat looking out. Afternoon passed into evening; night folded around the city, and the waxing moon drifted toward the apex of the heavens, a half disc as perfect as the image in Tane's hand. Slowly, like water sinking through sand, the agitation that had gripped him drained away, leaving behind it understanding, dry and stark.

Impossibly, absurdly, it had been jealousy that seized him today, when Axane spoke of Teispas's offer. He did not want her to choose someone else. He did not want her to pass from his life. This was no temporary infatuation, no involuntary groping after passion to fill a deeper void: He had been deceiving himself when he dismissed it so. Somehow, over the time they had spent together, he had fallen in love with this woman—with her uncomplaining strength, her quiet reserve, her quick intelligence, her beautiful blue-green lifelight. With the whole of her. And not until that moment had he realized it.

And she. What did she feel? He thought of how she had offered herself in the Burning Land—of how she had held his eyes, the blood rising in her face. He thought of how she had continued to watch him, to care for him, even after he refused her. He remembered how she had said of Teispas, *I don't love him.* He remembered the tears he had heard in her voice at the end.

He felt something move inside him—deep, like the molten rock at the earth's core. He lowered his face to the windowsill, his fingers gripping its edges, the painted wood cool against his heated skin. He was a vowed Âratist. Whatever he had been, whatever he had done, whatever he might become, he was pledged to Ârata first, fully, and without reserve. It was not simply a question of vows, of celibacy. Celibacy was only the door closed against a greater danger. Earthly love split the heart in two. It demanded; it required. Bound that way, how could he be certain of following without hesitation where the god demanded he go? And yet a part of him—a part that, over the past weeks, had been growing more insistent—said it was too late: The door was already open. A part of him cried out that a new age was dawning; did the god still require, in this time of ending, the old fidelities?

He sat on. Insects rasped in the courtyard trees, and the air smelled of spice and onions from the guesthouse kitchens. At last he closed and latched the window screen and, turning back to the room, struck a flint and kindled the lamps. Moving to his bed, he took the wallet from around his neck and lifted out the crystal of the Blood. He had rarely done so, in the Burning Land. In the desert, where there were few distractions beyond physical discomfort, it was not difficult to remember purpose. Even after Teispas shattered his first ecstatic certainty, he had not needed to look at it to know he carried it. But here in the domains of men, it was terrifyingly easy to become distracted by feeling or experience and drift away from larger truths. The world, in its teeming multiplicity, seemed profoundly permanent, possessed of its own determination to go on, regardless of what faith knew about ending; it was frighteningly possible to become lost in this, and forget the change now rising across the earth. Since Thuxra, he had more and more required the affirmation of the Blood.

The crystal winked from its pouch. He gazed at it, opening himself to the truth it told, to the whisper of divinity contained within it. Slowly his mind settled, and his heart, falling back into their proper shape. Once again he knew the clarity of purpose. Once again he comprehended sacrifice not as loss, but as necessity.

He wrapped the crystal up again and replaced the wallet around his neck. He got out his manita equipment and took his dose. In a few days he would add the final measure. His Shaper senses would be entirely gone then; not even the ghostly traces he had seen that day would remain.

He took off his clothes and blew out the lamps. Already, the peace the crystal had given him was slipping away. His thoughts returned to Axane; he closed his eyes, and jade and cobalt swirled across the darkness of his lids. His body grew restless with the familiar need. Sometimes he could turn his mind to other things, but not tonight. At last he surrendered and granted himself release, quickly, wanting to get it over so he could sleep. He fell toward unconsciousness, grateful for the dark.

—17—

A little over two weeks later they reached Baushpar.

The holy city had originally been a mountain fort, guarding the border of a much smaller Arsace against a hostile northern neighbor, long since conquered and absorbed. By the time King Fárat gifted it to the Áratist faith, it had not served a military purpose for more than a century. But its fortifications had never been taken down, and though much else within Baushpar was razed to make room for the First Temple and the Evening City, the Brethren had allowed the walls to stand as a reminder of Baushpar's history. They were built of the local blood granite, lit now to rusty garnet by the declining sun. The city, which had long ago overspilled their confinement, lay tangled at their feet, an untidy weaving of streets and squares, dwellings and shops and warehouses and, at the outskirts, the great houses of the wealthy, with their sprawling outbuildings and formal gardens.

Gyalo had sent one of the Exiles ahead, so that the Brethren might know when to expect them. Two tattooed Tapati guards were waiting by the south gate. They spurred their horses forward to meet the companions, then conducted them along the outer curve of the ancient fortifications, toward the western gate and the Avenue of Sunset. The expedition party had ridden forth this way nearly a year and a half before; it had been midsummer then and was nearly winter now, but as he passed into the echoing shadow of the Avenue's high, enclosing walls, Gyalo was seized with the sense that time had doubled back on itself, returning him to the moment of his departure. He placed his fingers on the wallet at his neck, holding to it like an anchor. Beneath the din of hooves and harness, he could hear the voice of Baushpar: a dense texture of ordinary city noise, stitched through with the music of bells from the city's hundreds of shrines and temples.

The Avenue terminated on the Sunfall Gate, the rear entrance to the Evening City. In the great stable yard beyond, grooms took charge of the travelers' horses, and servants were called to unload their baggage. The guards conducted them deep into the Evening City, leading a labyrinthine route through hall after hall, court after court—a parade of intact magnificence and dusty dereliction that showed no logic in what had been restored and what left untouched. They arrived at last in an open courtyard, with a delicately scalloped gazing pool at its center and a tile-roofed porch running around all four sides.

"You'll stay here," one of the guards told Gyalo. He gestured to the servants. "They'll fulfill your needs—you have only to ask."

Gyalo nodded.

"You'll be summoned to the Brethren tomorrow. In the meantime, I'm ordered to bid you not to go beyond this court."

"I understand." Gyalo was not surprised. It was reasonable to assume that the purpose for which he had left Baushpar was no more widely known now than it had been a year ago.

"Come, lady," the guard said to Axane.

"But—shall I not stay here?" Gyalo saw the fright in her face. Over the past days, she had grown increasingly apprehensive; since Baushpar had come in sight, she had barely uttered a word.

"More suitable accommodations have been prepared for you."

The guards escorted her away. One of the servants went with them, the chest that had been Kaluela's parting gift to her slung on his back. The other servants finished stowing the companions' baggage and followed. Diasarta went after them, to try the door.

"Locked," he said. He made as if to spit, then thought better of it. "Well. What now?"

"We wait," Gyalo said.

The chambers were lavishly appointed, the newness of their refurbishment apparent in the bright tints of the plaster and the crisp lines of the muraling. Standing by his bed, Gyalo passed his hands over his naked scalp—shaved just that morning—then took off his cloak, and, with relief, his stole. The Ninyâsan tailor had done a good job, but it felt odd to wear Âratist garb after so long. He had also resumed his simulacrum; it was heavier than he remembered, and bumped uncomfortably against his chest when he moved.

The servants returned. They set braziers around a table under the overhanging porch eaves, and laid out a meal. The companions ate in silence. There was no need for talk; they had already thoroughly discussed what was to come.

Gyalo sat on after the others went inside. The braziers glowed softly, chasing the autumn chill; lanterns hung from the eaves like little moons, drawing a few late moths to bump and blunder at their panes. Somewhere someone was playing a sithra, the plucked-string sound as mournful as a dream.

There was the scrape of a turning lock, clear on the quiet air. At the end of the courtyard, the door swung open. Two servants entered, bearing a carrying chair. The lanterns' illumination swept across the face of the occupant: Utamnos.

Gyalo leaped to his feet, his weariness forgotten. He dropped to his knees and crossed his arms before his face.

"Great is Ârata," he said. "Great is his Way."

"Go in light." Utamnos held out both hands, smiling. "How very good it is to see you, my Third Hand."

Gyalo rose and went to him. Emotion closed his throat; he could not speak.

"Won't you invite me inside? It's cold for an old man, out here in the dark."

"Of course! I'm sorry. Come, Old One."

In Gyalo's chamber, the servants set down the chair and withdrew at the old Son's signal.

"Will you sit more comfortably, Old One?" Gyalo gestured to one of the low-backed, cushioned seats with which the room was supplied.

"Better I stay where I am." Utamnos's smile was wry. "My legs don't serve me well these days."

"Old One!" In the indoor brightness, Gyalo could see that his master was not, after all, so unchanged as he had seemed under the dim lantern glow outside. Utamnos had lost flesh; his dark skin was slack, and his eyes, in their nest of wrinkles, seemed sunken.

"Don't concern yourself, Gyalo. It's just the shell that clothes me, wearing out. Soon I shall have a new one." He smiled again, with great affection. "Come here by me, so I can see you."

Gyalo obeyed, sinking to his knees beside the chair. The old Son's eyes moved across his face.

"The Burning Land has marked you," he said softly. "More deeply, I think, than just your skin."

Gyalo felt his breath catch.

"And yet—" Lightly Utamnos touched Gyalo's cheeks, his brow. "You are the same. I see that, too. In your core, in your heart—still strong. Still steadfast. Still my cherished Third Hand."

Gyalo thought of tomorrow, when he must confess his apostasy. He bowed his head. Utamnos's fingers clasped his shoulder, a slight grip, very warm. For a moment they remained that way.

"Tell me, Old One, what's happened while I've been gone. How does the work progress?"

Utamnos smiled. "The work feeds upon itself. There is always more than can be done."

For a little while they discussed the events of the past months. It felt strange to talk about these things, like memories of a different life. At last a silence fell.

"There's something I must tell you, Old One."

"No." Utamnos set his fingers briefly against Gyalo's lips. "Whatever news you bring of the Burning Land, I would not hear it before my Brothers and Sisters do."

Gyalo shook his head. "This is something else, Old One. Something I learned while I was at Thuxra City."

"Ah?"

"The wife of the administrator came to me, just before we departed. Apparently her husband has received orders directly from the King to halt the reclamation of Thuxra's mines. The King supports the resolution that's now before the Lords' Assembly, to re-open the mining operations. He's privately preparing for its passage."

Utamnos sat back, folding his knotted hands in his lap. "Ah," he said again. He did not seem surprised.

"You already knew this, Old One?"

"Yes and no. Do you trust this woman? Do you think she tells the truth?"

"I do, Old One. It seems to be her husband's habit to speak to her very frankly about matters of this kind. I think her conscience was deeply troubled."

Utamnos nodded, slowly. "How familiar are you with the current political situation, Gyalo?"

"Only generally, Old One. I know about the resolution, and the conflict it has caused. I also understand that there has been a break between the Bearer and the King."

"Sadly, that is so."

"The administrator's wife said it had come before the

mining resolution was brought. Was it the matter I wrote you of? When we came in from the Burning Land we were met by prisoners, and the administrator felt he needed to explain this. He told me that the presence of prisoners at Thuxra is now common knowledge."

"That lies at the root. But it's my spirit-brother's political ambition that's really to blame. He is still determined the Brethren must have a representative in the Assembly, and the lords still oppose it. Last year, in his frustration, he asked Santaxma to intervene. Santaxma refused—wisely, I think. But my spirit-brother was angry. Santaxma owed him a debt, and this was how he believed it should be repaid."

"A debt, Old One?"

"Some time ago, Santaxma came to my spirit-brother to beg that Thuxra's destruction be postponed. My spirit-brother agreed."

Gyalo was too shocked for a moment to speak. "You knew, Old One?"

"No, Gyalo. None of us knew. The King came in secret, and my spirit-brother agreed in secret. When I brought your letter to him, I thought he would be as appalled as I. Instead he told me the truth." Utamnos's dark face was somber. "He said he had not come to us because he did not wish to risk the chance of our refusal. I don't doubt it was for their long friendship that he did it, for the sake of the bond between the two of them. But my spirit-brother is a clever man. I believe he saw the chance to put Santaxma in his debt and could not let it pass."

"But surely they could not imagine such a secret could be kept. You and others were already impatient with the delays, even before I left for the Burning Land. Even if I'd never passed through Thuxra, it couldn't have continued hidden for much longer."

"They never intended it should continue, or at least my spirit-brother did not. Three years was what Santaxma asked—time to settle into his kingship, to address the other problems of Arsace. After that, he swore to turn to Thuxra as he had been supposed to do from the beginning. My spirit-

brother, I'm certain, believed him. But I think that even then
Santaxma did not mean to honor his oath."

"And now he seeks to go beyond even that betrayal."

Utamnos nodded. "After my spirit-brother confessed the
truth to me, I ordered him to lay it before the rest of the
Brethren. To his credit, he did not question me. It was a dark
time for us, very dark; the shadow of it is on us still. We
summoned Santaxma to defend his actions, but he refused to
come. Instead he spoke the truth himself, before the Lords'
Assembly, making it seem he had undertaken on his own to
deceive the Brethren—all the Brethren, including my spirit-
brother. Thus he took the sole responsibility for a thing that
would be far more damaging to my spirit-brother, if it were
known, than to Santaxma, who after all is a secular leader.
And in keeping my spirit-brother's secret, the King turned a
thing that had been meant to bind him into a thing that bound
his friend. Ah." Again Utamnos shook his head, reluctant admiration in his face. "He is a formidable man, Santaxma."

"Did he think the Bearer then wouldn't dare oppose it,
when the mining resolution was brought to the Assembly?"

"I think he would have preferred to influence my spirit-
brother privately. It was to my spirit-brother that he first
came with the idea—in secret, as before. He asked for my
spirit-brother's support; after all, if the Blood Bearer called
for the mining of the Burning Land, how could the lords refuse? Perhaps he only invoked the ties of friendship; perhaps he attempted to call in the debt. Whichever it was, he
went too far. My spirit-brother ordered him to abandon his
intent or be declared heretic. Santaxma capitulated—or appeared to. But within the month the resolution was brought
to the Assembly. To all appearances it's an independent ini-
tiative, and Santaxma has made a show of disavowing it. But
we've always suspected it came from him. You see, Gyalo,
why I wasn't truly surprised by your news."

"Surely the King's part in this can be revealed. I'm certain Thuxra's administrator will obey, if he's ordered to
speak under threat of heresy—he is a devout man and according to his wife these orders trouble him."

"No, no." Utamnos was shaking his head. "Santaxma cannot be weakened, with Arsace still so wounded. Deficient in faith he may be—a thing that I have always suspected, by the way, though my spirit-brother would never heed my warnings—but he's a fine ruler, and there's no one capable of taking his place. No. He cannot be discredited."

"What, then, Old One? The resolution gathers support, or so I was told, even with the threat of heresy attached. Will you allow your authority to be challenged so?"

"Calm yourself, Gyalo." Utamnos's eyes, in their web of wrinkles, were sharp. "You are very much a man of the straight path. But we who guard the Way of Ârata cannot always afford to be so direct. We must work toward a subtler end. Do not fear for our resolve. This is not our first encounter with the wiles of kings. Nor will it be the last."

And yet, Gyalo thought, *it will be the last. For Arsace will never have another king.*

Out of nowhere joy fell him, the incandescent jubilation that had shaken him so often in the early days in the Burning Land, but only rarely after that, and since Thuxra not at all. He could not help himself; he laughed aloud. He heard the sound it made in the quiet room: exalted, triumphant.

"Gyalo?" Utamnos was frowning.

Gyalo felt as if he stood upon a sunlit peak, gazing down at Utamnos in obscurity below. *Tomorrow,* he thought. *Tomorrow I will lift all of them up to stand beside me.*

"I'm sorry, Old One." He breathed deeply, reaching for composure. "I'm very weary."

Utamnos's brows were still drawn. Something Gyalo could not read had come into his face.

"I should be on my way. Will you fetch my servants?"

Gyalo obeyed. The servants came in and ranged themselves between the carrying bars. Gyalo knelt.

"Great is Ârata. Great is his Way."

"Go in light." Utamnos's face was grave. "Till tomorrow, my Third Hand."

* * *

Gyalo lay awake for a long time that night. Joy blazed in him, hot and pure as the red ground of the Burning Land, clear and clean as his first rapturous certainty. He fell at last into a deep sleep, from which the servants roused him a few hours later, setting breakfast on the porch outside. He lay a while, then rose, and washed and shaved and dressed. The exaltation of the night before had slipped away, leaving behind a deep, powerful calm. So it had been in his competitive running days, on the mornings before a race.

The guards came at noon and led another swift progress through the halls and courts of the Evening City. They came at last to a large forecourt, where two more guards stood watch before a pair of vermilion-painted gates. A third guard was waiting, with Axane. She was dressed soberly, as Gyalo had advised, in a high-necked indigo gown, her hair drawn back into a single braid; she looked strained and fearful, and the ends of her blue stole were wound around her fists. When she saw them she took a step forward, then checked, as if remembering the presence of the guard.

Gyalo moved to stand next to her. His companions ranged themselves alongside: Diasarta, breathing through his mouth as he always did when forced to walk fast on his shortened leg; Teispas, impenetrably composed.

The gatekeepers grasped the gates' thick brass bars and set their weight against them, pulling them slowly inward. Beyond lay a vast courtyard, walled in blood granite and paved with ironstone. Brass discs topped the walls, rayed to represent the sun, Ârata's symbol. Brass, not mortar, ran between the flagstones, as if a golden net had been tossed upon the ground. A raised walkway led to the court's far side, built of great blocks of honey granite; where it ended three terraces of the same material rose toward a wooden pavilion, with gilded pillars across its front and a roof of crimson tiles. At equidistant intervals along the walkway, towering honey granite images depicted Ârata in each of his four guises: the World Creator, smiling his enigmatic smile, cupping a gilded sun between his hands; the Primal Warrior, fierce of face, with his sword of golden fire; the Eon Sleeper, wounds welling gold, floating upright in slumber; the Risen Judge, terrible in righteousness, aureate flames leaping from his outstretched palms.

This was the Courtyard of the Sun, where for more than a thousand years the Brethren had gathered to receive dignitaries and visitors, and conduct ceremonies and the business of the church. The Caryaxists, running wild through the rest of the Evening City, had not touched it; the returning Brethren found it intact, even to the gilding on the images. So close to noon the entire courtyard was in sunlight, flooding hotly down from a sky of such flawless blueness, and reflected back with such intensity from all the shining metal, that had it not been for the chill Gyalo could almost have imagined himself back in the Burning Land—breathing fire, his eyes filled to dazzling with vistas of red and gold.

The guards led the way forward; the companions followed. Gyalo had entered the court only once before, for a celebration of thanksgiving just after the Brethren's reestablishment in Baushpar. Then, it had been packed with people, the air almost solid with noise and incense smoke. In emptiness it seemed far larger. The Ârata images gazed with stony serenity into nothingness; looking up, Gyalo marked the damage the centuries had done, blunting the images' features, pitting their surfaces. Time was visible here—in the wear of the brass inlay and the overlaps where it had been patched, in the waterworn surfaces of the ironstone, in the depression at the walkway's center, where countless feet had passed. And yet all these signs of change and dissolution spoke a deeper, opposing truth: the massive, millennium-defying permanence of the church of Ârata.

A long stairway mounted through the terraces. At its top the guards moved aside, leaving Gyalo and his companions to pass alone into the shadow of the pavilion. Here the Brethren waited, the scant twelve men and women who, in these post-Caryaxist times, made up the ruling council of the church. They sat in vermilion-painted chairs, arranged in a semicircle at the pavilion's center. Some had brought their spirit-wards to kneel beside them. The Bearer occupied a gilded, low-backed bench, raised above the others on a dais. His arms were folded across his broad chest; at his neck, the Blood pulsed light inside its gleaming cage. Vimâta, his ward, crouched below, one hand resting on the bench's cushioned seat.

The companions approached. The Brethren were as still as carven images; the force of their collective gaze was a thing that could be felt. Four red mats had been set out before the Bearer. Reaching them, Gyalo knelt and crossed his arms before his face. His companions followed suit.

"Great is Ârata." The words rang clear in the silent room. "Great is his Way."

"Go in light," the Bearer replied in his sonorous voice.

Gyalo lowered his arms. The room was paneled and floored in dark spicewood; the only illumination came from horn-sided lanterns suspended from the gilded ceiling and what light spilled in from the court outside. Except for the Bearer's necklace, and his golden bench, and the great sun-mural at his back, picked out in gold leaf and yellow jewels, everything was drowned in gloom.

"We rejoice at your return," the Bearer said. "We grieve for those left behind."

"May they rise again in light." Gyalo was aware of Utamnos on the Bearer's right, his ancient face as impassive as any of his spirit-siblings', his gaze as intent.

The Bearer turned his regard upon Axane. "This is the woman you wrote of in your dispatch?"

"She is, Old One."

"What's your name, child?"

"Axane, Old One." Gyalo had taken care to coach her in the proper modes of etiquette and address. Her voice was low; he was close enough to her to feel that she was trembling. "Of the Risaryâsan bloodline, of the city of Refuge."

"A city, you say." The Bearer regarded her. "Are there so many of you?"

"We number more than three hundred, Old One."

The Bearer blinked. The Brethren murmured in surprise.

"Why do you call it Refuge, child?"

"When my ancestors were driven out of Arsace, Old One, they wanted only to find a place, a good place, where they could live in peace. When they found it they named it Refuge, for that was what it was."

"You remember Arsace, then. Your origins."

"Yes, Old One. We are exiles. Exiles don't forget such things."

"Indeed." The Bearer returned his gaze to Gyalo. "Now we would hear from you, Gyalo Amdo Samchen. We would hear how you found this . . . Refuge, and of the journey that led you there. We would hear of this wonder you say you carry with you. We would hear this news of change."

Gyalo drew breath, and began.

"What I have to tell you, Old One, will not be easy for you to believe. Indeed, you may find it almost impossible. So it was for me, when I first learned of it. Not until I saw the reality with my own eyes could I accept that this . . . amazing thing was true. I've brought with me a small piece of it, so you, too, may look and understand, as I did. I beg you to hold that in mind, as you listen to me now.

"In the land the lost Âratists found, there is a river that passes through a rocky cleft on its way to the plain below. Refuge is built in that cleft, above that river. It was placed there not just for its own protection, but to guard what is at the river's end—a great cavern, in which lies a miracle." He paused, and set free the words he had come so far to speak: "The resting place of Ârata. Empty. This is the news I bring you. Ârata has risen."

Silence, profound with shock. The Brethren and their spirit-wards sat as if struck to stone. The Bearer's eyes were fixed to Gyalo's, sharp as grappling hooks.

"Explain yourself," he said.

"I will show you, Old One. May I approach?"

The Bearer nodded. Gyalo crossed to the dais and knelt again. He drew a folded cloth from the pocket of his gown and laid it on the dais. From the wallet at his neck, which today he wore outside his clothes, he took the pouch that held the crystal. Untying the drawstrings, he shook the crystal carefully onto the cloth. Its small light flashed; he heard Vimâta gasp. Gathering up cloth and crystal, he rose and offered them to the Bearer—who did not take them but sat transfixed.

"How can this be?" His voice was half a whisper.

"This crystal of the Blood was taken from the cave I spoke of, Old One." Gyalo's heart raced. Joy boiled in him—the joy that had transported him when the revelation was brand-new, that had burned in him in Refuge's council chamber as he told a different group of men and women this same truth, that had returned to him last night. "In the cavern there are a thousand thousand crystals like this one. They cover the floor, the walls—all but a space at the center, a space of empty rock shaped like a man, but wider and taller than any human man could be. I've seen this with my own eyes, Old One. I've watched the crystals blaze. I have laid my hands upon them—I have the scars of that still, on my palms. It is the god's resting place—it can be nothing else. I say to you: Ârata has risen. The Age of Exile is at an end!"

The words rolled out of him like thunder. In that moment it was not he who spoke, but the world that spoke in him— waking, like Ârata, to the dawn of a new age.

"Is it so, Brother?" A voice—Gyalo could not tell whose—cut urgently through the silence. "Is it truly the Blood?"

Slowly the Bearer leaned down and took the crystal into his hands. Feeling struggled in his broad, strong face: wonder, astonishment, reverence.

"It is the Blood." His voice was hushed. "By my immortal soul it is."

"Show us!" someone called. And someone else: "Let us see!"

"Vimâta," the Bearer said. "Bear this to your Brothers and Sisters."

Vimâta rose. His hands shook as he held them up to receive the crystal. He descended the dais, stepping as if the floor might crack beneath his feet, and slowly moved around the semicircle of the Brethren, pausing before each and offering the crystal for inspection. There were exclamations, indrawn breaths. Some leaned forward after Vimâta passed, studying Gyalo, who had returned to his place on the mat, as intently as they had studied the Blood.

Vimâta finished his circuit. The Bearer took the crystal from him and whispered something. Vimâta slipped behind the Bearer's bench, where a door gave onto a warren of meditation and preparation and tiring rooms, and returned with a small table, which he set on the floor before the dais. Receiving the crystal once more, he placed it carefully at the table's center, where its small dancing light could be seen by all.

The Bearer looked at Gyalo. His expression was controlled, his voice quiet.

"Tell us how you discovered this."

Gyalo began the tale. The Brethren interrupted, questioning him about the traveling, about the Dreamers' guiding visions, about the Burning Land itself; but the narrative went quickly, and it was not long before he reached the passage across the pebble plain.

"In my dispatch, Old One, I wrote that most of the members of our expedition were carried off or killed by a storm that came upon us as we crossed a barren plain of stone." His pulse was racing again, and his mouth was dry. "We who remained were betrayed by some of the survivors, who stole most of the water and departed on their own. We were left with water only for a few days, not enough to take us across the plain in either direction. We would certainly have died." Reaching up, he began to unwind the golden silk of his stole from around his arms and shoulders. Beside him, he felt his companions' tension. "But the storm, which took so much, took my manita also. My tether was broken, and my shaping was released. I could not withhold the help that would save my companions' lives . . . and my own." The stole was free; he dropped it in a soft heap on the floor before him. "I no longer have the right to wear the gold, for I stand before you as an apostate. But not as a heretic. I have retethered myself.

My shaping is bound again by manita, as it was before I left Baushpar."

A beat of quiet. The Bearer's face was as blank as glass. "You confess to apostasy?" he said.

"I do, Old One."

"Guards!" The Bearer's shout seemed to shake the pavilion. "Seize this man!"

The guards, who had retired to wait on the stairs, leaped forward. Gyalo found himself on his feet, with no memory of rising. Teispas and Diasarta had sprung to stand before him; behind him, Axane clutched with both hands at his gown. Gyalo dragged frantically against her grip, terrified of what Teispas and Diasarta might do, of what might be done to them—

"Halt!"

The authority in that cry stopped the guards in midstride. For a frozen instant no one moved. Gyalo pulled himself free of Axane, and turned.

It was Utamnos. He had pushed himself to his feet, using the arms of his chair for support; Gyalo could see his shoulders trembling with strain. Now he lowered himself again. His muscles betrayed him before he was quite done, so that he fell rather than sank into his seat.

"Younger Brother," he said, breathless. "I believe he speaks the truth. I believe he is tethered."

"We have no proof, Older Brother." The Bearer's face was implacable, like the Risen Judge outside. "I can count on the fingers of my two hands the number of apostates, in all the centuries of the church's existence, who of their own will have resubmitted themselves to manita."

"I know this man, Younger Brother. He has that sort of will. And he is like those few in another way—he is *involuntarily* apostate. He did not choose his corruption. It was forced on him by the elements, which no man may control."

"For that, too, we have only his word."

"If he truly had turned heretic, would he have confessed his sin before us all? Would he not have hidden his apostasy? If he had abandoned the Way of Ârata, would he have brought us . . . what he has brought us? Would he have given us such news?"

The Bearer hesitated. His eyes moved to Gyalo. "You claim tether."

"Yes, Old One." Gyalo found it difficult to control his voice. He could hear Diasarta behind him, breathing harshly through his mouth. "My dose is the same now as when I left Baushpar."

"How can that be, if your manita was lost in the Burning Land?"

"There was a cache of it, Old One, in the cellar of the monastery ruins atop Thuxra Notch. It had been well stored—it was still good. I resubmitted myself as we traveled here. My companions can confirm it."

"You may as easily have conspired with them to lie." The Bearer studied him. "Why should we believe anything you say, apostate?"

"For the very fact that I am here before you, Old One, saying it. Because I have come into this place and freely told you a thing that damns me when I could as easily have kept the secret. I'm tethered now—you may send manita masters to verify it, I'll submit to any test you wish. Had I not confessed, you never would have known. It's as my master said—if I were heretic, if I meant you harm, would I not have hidden my sin? Instead I speak the truth—because it *is* the truth, because I have sworn to tell *all* the truth, no matter how it darkens me in your eyes, so you may be certain that nothing, *nothing* I say to you is a lie."

"Be very sure you will be tested," the Bearer said. "And that, whatever follows on this day, you will endure an apostate's punishment."

"I understand, Old One." Gyalo closed his mind to that, as he had done so many times during the journey. "I am prepared. I beg only that you hear me."

The Bearer looked toward his spirit-siblings. "What say you, Brothers and Sisters?"

"I would hear him." It was the Son Baushtas. He was a

slim man of middle years, Harukoi in this incarnation, with a smooth, handsome face. Growing up, he had been Utamnos's ward and was still one of the old Son's closest associates.

"There's nothing *I* wish to hear from an apostate's mouth," said the Daughter Kudrâcari. She was Aino-born, a rawboned, awkward woman who looked older than her twenty-six body-years. "His companions can finish this tale."

"We must hear his companions," Baushtas said. "But we must hear him also. How can we properly judge this matter unless we listen to them all?"

"He is *apostate,* Brother!"

"But what a tale he has to tell us, Sister! What a wonder he has brought us! If it's true, this thing he claims, does it matter who brings us news of it?"

"I agree." This from Sundit, the Daughter who had instructed Gyalo before he left for the Burning Land. "If he's truly tethered as he claims—and like Utamnos, I'm inclined to believe it of this man as I would not of another—he is no danger to us."

"And if he lies," said Baushtas, "the guards stand ready."

Back and forth the discussion went. Gyalo listened, his heart racing; this was the moment of greatest risk, the moment in which they might choose not to hear him. At last the Bearer raised his hands for silence. His heavy-lidded gaze came to rest again upon Gyalo's face.

"My Brothers and Sisters have spoken. We will hear you."

"Brother, I protest." It was Kudrâcari.

"Your objection is noted, Sister. Guards, keep watch. And you three—" his eyes flicked to Axane, Teispas, Diasarta "—take your places now, or I'll have you removed."

They obeyed in haste, Axane stumbling as she bent to retrieve the stole she had dropped. Only Gyalo remained standing; his legs were trembling, and he feared to fall if he tried to kneel.

"So." The Bearer folded his arms once more. "Continue."

Gyalo took up the story. He was aware of the guards behind him, standing in the Tapati at-ease posture, arms folded under their stoles so that they could easily reach the throwing knives strapped to their sides. He was aware of his own stole, a soft drift of saffron at his feet. He was aware of the Blood—gleaming at the Bearer's neck, flickering on the little table below the Bearer's dais. He was aware of the Bearer's steady observation, of the stony stares of the Brethren, of the half-fearful gazes of their spirit-wards. He was aware of Utamnos's regard—gentler, he thought, than the others', though perhaps he was deceiving himself. Utamnos had spoken for him. Not until this moment had he allowed himself to acknowledge how greatly he had hoped for that. But he would be foolish to imagine that anything remained the same between them.

When he reached Refuge's heresy and its disastrous assumption of his identity, the Brethren's silence broke on a flurry of shocked questions.

"Do you subscribe to these beliefs, young woman?" the Bearer said sternly to Axane.

"No, Old One. I haven't believed as my people do since childhood."

"And why is that?"

"I grew up believing, Old One, but as I became older I could no longer accept what my people thought was true. Brother Gyalo has explained to me the Way of Ârata as it should be followed."

"And do you accept that true Way? Will you declare before us and before the Blood I bear that you reject, absolutely and without reservation, your people's heresy?"

She hesitated. Gyalo tensed. For her safety, she had to repudiate Refuge's beliefs as quickly and as strongly as she could. But when he had explained this to her, she had balked. "My people aren't guilty of Risaryâsi's mistakes," she told him. "You said so yourself, in Refuge. I don't want to condemn them." Eventually she capitulated, and memorized the words he gave her. Now he found himself, again, fearing what she might say.

"I do reject it, Old One." Her voice was clear and strong.

"I denounce my people's error, and condemn their fault, and declare that I am grateful to be delivered from their darkness. With all my heart, I embrace the true Way of Ârata."

"Fair words, child," the Bearer said, holding her in his brooding gaze. "If they are true."

Gyalo moved on, to Refuge's Shapers—whose strength and numbers produced incredulity, and in some cases flat declarations of disbelief—to the Cavern of the Blood, to the escape from Refuge, to the journey home.

Finally, he was finished. For a moment no one spoke or stirred.

"We have been long at this," the Bearer said. "You have given us much to think on. With my siblings' consent, I propose that we adjourn."

There was a murmur of assent from the Brethren. The Bearer nodded to the guards.

"Take them away. See that the apostate is held separately."

The guards stepped forward. Gyalo fell to his knees and crossed his arms before his face.

"Great is Ârata." His voice was hoarse from so much speaking. "Great is his Way."

There was a long, long pause. "Go in light," the Bearer replied at last.

The guards gripped his arms and hoisted him to his feet. They drew him away; his companions followed, the third guard bringing up the rear. The Brethren watched them go; Gyalo felt the pressure of their gaze again, freighted, this time, not with expectation but with judgment.

Most of the afternoon was gone. The shadow of the western wall lay long across the Courtyard, and Ârata's images cast huge shade upon the stones. They passed through the vermilion gates and the forecourt beyond. There Axane's guard turned, escorting her away. She looked back as she went; Gyalo saw the terror on her face.

At a diverging hallway, one of the two remaining guards pulled Gyalo aside.

"Where are you taking him?"

Tcispas's voice followed him. There was a sound of scuffling, an oath. Gyalo pulled against the guard's grip, looking back. Teispas stood in the middle of the corridor, his dark face—which had remained perfectly impassive this whole day, even when he sprang to Gyalo's defense—suffused with rage. Diasarta crowded close behind him. The remaining guard stood before them, hands held up in warning.

"It's all right," Gyalo called wearily. "Don't make trouble."

"But where are they taking you?"

"I don't know. Don't worry. Nothing will happen to me."

The guard urged him on. There were no more sounds from behind.

They came at last to an open doorway, beyond which lay a tiny court. The guard pushed him through and slammed the door. He heard the rasp of the lock.

He leaned against the wall. He felt a weariness so profound the world seemed to sway beneath his feet.

It's done, he thought. *The message is given. Now I can rest.*

—18—

The courtyard was exactly twenty-three steps across. Twelve long flagstones paved the distance; seventeen courses of yellow brick brought the walls to eye level. At the court's midpoint, the flags were worn down all the way across, as if others before Gyalo had paced to pass the time. Water pooled in this hollow when it rained, and ragged black-green moss bulged up between the stones.

It was not an uncomfortable incarceration. The court was pleasant when the sun shone into it, and the single room was adequately furnished, with blankets and lamps enough and two braziers for warmth. There were servants to bring meals and water for washing, to empty the slop basin and take linen away for laundering. Still, it was lonely, and also very dull, for he was not allowed any reading matter to pass the time. The noise of life intruded—the percussion of a hammer, a woman singing, the falling cry of a hawk circling overhead—but for the most part the only sounds he heard were those he made himself. It seemed quite possible, sometimes, when he had not seen another face for hours and the silence had grown so oppressive he had to stamp his feet or clap his hands just to remind himself he had not gone deaf, that the rest of the world had vanished while he waited, and only these four walls remained.

On the evening he had been locked in the court, a group of Forceless monks wearing the saffron badges of manita masters arrived to test his tether. He was sleeping, wrung-out with exhaustion; they had to beat on the door of his chamber to wake him. They had brought, from his travel pack in the other courtyard, his supply of manita and his silver implements; they set these out and watched as he dosed himself—proving his habituation by the lack of adverse effect. They departed, taking everything with them. The next morning a single master returned, with a new supply of drug, a set of plain brass implements, and a directive: From now on Gyalo was to take not eight measures, but fourteen. It was the apostate's punishment: a tether that would bind him so firmly that not even the learned disciplines of Âratist Shaperhood could release him.

Obediently he bent to the little heaps of powder, feeling the master's alert regard like a hand at the back of his neck. *For now,* he told himself; but as he made to inhale a sudden panic seized him, and for a vivid instant he saw his future, the whole horrifying powerless stretch of it. His head spun; he dropped the inhalation tube, which struck the edge of the table and arced spinning to the floor. The master took a sharp step forward. Gyalo fell to his knees and scrabbled for the tube, and, closing his mind, forced himself to take the drug. The increase doubled him over, choking. The master waited long enough to satisfy himself that Gyalo would not suffocate, then departed. Hours later, when a guard came to summon him to the Pavilion of the Sun, Gyalo was still hoarse from coughing.

On the day he delivered his message, he had told himself he could rest. It was not so, of course. There was still the questioning.

The summonses were unpredictable. He might be called twice in one day or not at all; he might be kept for an hour, or

an entire afternoon. Always he was brought alone—he had
not seen any of his companions since they were separated.
The Brethren wanted him to speak first about the Cavern of
the Blood. They had his travel journal, but he had not written
in it after the storm, and it contained nothing about Refuge.
He was asked to describe in detail the Cavern's features and
qualities, the landscape that surrounded it, how it was approached. He was asked to estimate its dimensions. He was
given pen and ink, and ordered to draw sketches.

"I don't like it," hatchet-faced Kudrâcari declared, early
in this process. "In the *Darxasa,* it's said that Ârata slept and
the earth rose up to cover him. Not that he climbed a cliff
and hid himself inside the rock."

"That's what I thought also, Old One, when I first learned
of it," Gyalo said. "But it has been eons since Ârata lay
down, and the earth must have changed greatly in that time.
I saw marks of earthquake in the cliffs around Refuge, and
there are fire-mountains to the south. The Cavern may have
been raised up where it is by some cataclysm."

"It would be a cataclysm indeed," said Kudrâcari scorn-
fully, "that tossed *below* as high *above* as you describe."

"What he says is sensible enough, Sister," Baunhtas said,
mild as always "We know of our own experience how much
the earth has altered since our spirit-father brought the
Darxasa out of the Burning Land."

"I do not believe, Brother, that if Ârata had lain above the
earth, he would have told our spirit-father he was beneath it."

"And yet, Sister, if this is not Ârata's resting place, how
do you explain his Blood within it?"

"I don't have to explain it." Kudrâcari fixed her narrow
eyes on Gyalo's face. "That is the apostate's task."

"I can put forward conjectures, Old One," Gyalo said.
"But nothing I can offer will answer all questions beyond a
doubt. What *is* beyond doubt is what I saw—what *you* see."
He gestured to the crystal of the Blood, which during these
sessions rested always on its little table before the Bearer's
dais. He missed carrying it, with an acuteness he had not an-

ticipated; the place on his chest where it had lain felt wrong without it, as if his flesh had been scooped away. "I would suggest, Old One, that questions of how and why are less important than such witness. That the rest may be accepted as a mystery of faith."

"Do you presume to instruct me in matters of faith, apostate?"

"Never, Old One. I suggest only what you might in your wisdom consider."

"It's this . . . Refuge that I'm uneasy with," said the Son Ariamnes. He was eldest in his body after Utamnos, immensely stout, with a smooth, moon-shaped face. "This community of heretics. It offends me to consider that Ârata might have given it to such people to discover his resting place."

"I doubt Ârata paused to think how _you_ would feel about it, Brother." It was the Son Martyas, a dwarfish, prematurely wizened man who delighted in needling his spirit-siblings. "Given what else he must have been preoccupied with at the time."

"And why should he wait so long to reveal his rising?" Ariamnes went on as if he had not heard. "If the apostate's story is to be believed, it has been seventy-five years at least since Ârata woke. Seventy-five years! Where, then, is the Next Messenger?"

"Yes," the Son Dâdar said. "And in that time there has been no shortage of flood and drought, plague and famine. If Ârata no longer dreams, why does the world still suffer these misfortunes?"

"Perhaps," said practical Sundit, "the world has changed over the millennia of his dreaming. Perhaps these disasters have become a natural part of it. Perhaps they create themselves."

"Really, Sister!" Dâdar's face, deeply pitted by skin disease, twisted in an expression of distaste. "If I heard that from any ordinary vowed Âratist I would suspect her of heresy."

"There are many mysteries here," said Baushtas. Despite his conciliatory ways he possessed a formidable will, and rarely conceded an argument. "I'll grant it would be pleasant to know how they might be resolved. Yet we must not forget that Ârata is a god, his purposes not necessarily comprehensible by humankind. A mystery of faith, as the apostate says. A truth stands before us: The Blood of Ârata has been brought out of the Burning Land and given into our hands. We must not spin around that fact such a web of inquiry and disputation that we lose sight of its significance."

"I agree," Sundit said.

"Well, that's hardly surprising," Kudrâcari said acidly, "since you always follow where Baushtas leads."

"While you, Sister, walk your own road," Sundit replied, with unruffled calm. "And no one follows you at all."

Gyalo, kneeling on his mat, thought that this was not correct: It seemed clear that pockmarked Dâdar was Kudrâcari's ally, at least in this. Still, among her spirit-siblings she did appear to stand alone—plain and graceless, smoldering always with the heat of some perennial anger.

He had been called before the assembled Brethren many times in his career, but he had not before now attended meetings like these, in which they freely spoke their minds to one another. It was their custom to confer alone, apart from their aides and secretaries and assistants, and to promulgate any directives through the scribes who sat behind screens at the back of the Pavilion. He was aware that these gatherings could be contentious: Utamnos, who spoke to him more frankly than many Sons and Daughters did to their aides, had described the complicated web of affinities and dislikes that bound and separated the spirit-siblings, based not only on their current incarnations but on the centuries of their rebirths, over which each had done every other a thousand favors and disservices. Even so, it was startling to experience it. They were, truly, like members of a family, who knew one another so well that the knowing had become a kind of ignorance.

He was not comfortable perceiving them so. Mortal the Brethren might appear to be, but those who served them closely never forgot their otherness, and the gulf of that difference yawned even in the most affectionate exchanges. But now, in their disputes and disagreements, their irritations and annoyances, their interruptions and exclamations and rolled eyes and upflung hands, they seemed deeply, in some cases almost basely, human. It was difficult to glimpse behind this veil of body-nature the greater verity of their being.

Perhaps it was the lingering discord of the Bearer's deception that put them so at odds; but if that were true, Gyalo could not separate those stresses from the rest. The Bearer sat on his golden bench, arms folded on his chest or chin supported on one broad palm, Vimâta crouching like a shadow on the dais below. He intervened now and then when discussion grew heated, but otherwise rarely spoke. His eyes turned often to Gyalo. Gyalo could not interpret that gaze, but he could always feel it.

Utamnos watched him, too. Occasionally surprise or expectation marked his face, but the old Son was schooled in impassivity, and Gyalo could not often guess what he might be thinking. Since that first day, he had uttered not a word.

From the Cavern of the Blood, the Brethren turned to Refuge's Shapers. Many found it difficult at first to believe Gyalo had not misinterpreted or exaggerated what he had seen; even those who, like Utamnos, had not expected the Shapers' abilities to dwindle in exile, were astonished by what he told them—of Refuge's making, of the weather called and the storms raised, of the storerooms filled yearly with the salt, flax, and wheat the Plains of Blessing did not provide.

"And you would truly have us believe that with all this power, all this . . . strength—" Dâdar delivered the word like a curse "—these apostate Shapers are not massively corrupt?"

"They are arrogant, Old One." It had been plain to him from the beginning that they wanted tales of greed and dominance, perversion and cruelty—all the baseness that, according to Âratist history, characterized Shapers who remained apostate for more than a little time. It was plain to him, too, that to provide such stories, with the proper expressions of outrage and disgust, might improve his own standing in their eyes. But he had not seen such things, and even for his own protection could not say he had. "And jealous of their ability, whose practice they keep largely secret. They knowingly perpetuate the lie on which Refuge is founded. And of course, in the magnitude of their works the danger of shaping is clear—the storms they sent to kill us, for instance, which they normally use to nourish the Plains of Blessing. But the individual corruption the histories describe—that I did not see. It's my impression that the vows of duty they take hold the worst excesses away."

"Pah," Dâdar said. "Without manita, what does a vow mean?"

"Precisely," fat Ariamnes said. "The woman swears that none of them have ever gone beyond their vows, but I cannot believe it is the truth."

"It is the truth as she understands it, Old One," said Gyalo. "If there have been transgressions, it would be in the Shapers' interest to conceal them. It certainly would not be the only secret they keep."

"A full nineteen of them." Blind Haminâser, who had been born a pauper's child in Aino and wore a band across his eyes to hide the marks of the accident that had taken his sight, shook his head. "In a population of just over three hundred. When not more than thirty Shapers are born yearly into all Galea."

"It's hardly surprising, Brother," said little Martyas. "They let their Shapers breed."

"Intermarriage between Shaper lines has ever been encouraged, Brother," Kudrâcari snapped.

"And those with the actual ability are gathered to the church, where they must be chaste. Don't pretend, Sister, that you don't remember our deliberations ten centuries ago, when we persuaded the secular rulers of Galea to give shaping into our hands."

"Hsst, you fool! Do you speak so before an outsider?"

"What if I do?" Martyas shrugged. "He has no use for the knowledge."

Briefly Gyalo saw his future in the small Son's words, and felt a deadly cold come over him.

The questioning moved on to Refuge's heresy. At the Brethren's request, Gyalo repeated Refuge's own tale of its founding—which, he suspected, they had already heard from Axane—and described what he believed to be the cause of Risaryâsi's errors. He recounted Cyras's and Mandapâxa's revision of Galea's history, and the plan the two Shapers had drawn up against Refuge's emergence from the Burning Land: the single state, ruled not by secular kings and princes but by the church of Ârata; the reformed church, governed by Shapers free of any tether but their vows of service.

"What of the Brethren?" the Sons and Daughters asked him, and he told them that Cyras and Mandapâxa had believed those ancient souls had been consumed when Ârdaxcasa rose, never to be reborn.

"The Dreamer's heresy," said Baushtas in his thoughtful way, "was not willful. She was weak, deluded, but her intent was not actively evil. But the two Shapers did not mistake the truth—they chose deliberately to hide it, to fabricate a lie to take its place. In this, as in their works, we see the arrogance of untethered shaping. Theirs is by far the greater transgression."

"There are more heresies here than I care to think about," Kudrâcari said, harshly. "The fault of the Dreamer, the fault of the apostate Shapers, the fault of those who accepted these abominations and passed them to their children. As far as I'm concerned, they are all equally repellent."

"Yet those who live in Refuge today did not choose the way they follow, Sister," Sundit said. "It was chosen for them, by people who now are dead. They are heretics not because they rejected the true Way of Ârata, but because they know no better. Say what you will, it's a lesser sin."

"Heresy is heresy," Dâdar growled. "All the theological thread-splitting in the world can't turn it into something else."

"With respect," Gyalo interjected, "I would say that in their most essential nature Refuge's heresies are a paradox. They are false, but the web of their falsehood is spun around a truth. They are blasphemous, but the darkness of their blasphemy is founded upon a miracle. The people of Refuge are fatally mistaken in their beliefs, in their understanding of who they are and the nature of their guardianship. But they're not mistaken in their understanding of what they guard."

"Do you defend them, then?" Kudrâcari's face was predatory. "Do you condone these blasphemies?"

"May I burn for all eternity, Old One, if I should ever condone blasphemy. I mean only to remind this council that at the heart of Refuge's error lies the truth of the Cavern of the Blood."

"You name them guardians." Martyas fixed Gyalo with a gaze as sharp as a thorn. "This first Dream of Risaryâsi, this supposed revelation that called her into the Burning Land. Tell me, do you think there's any truth in it?"

"About the Dream itself, Old One, nothing can be said, since the story is all that remains of it. Like any story, it may have grown distorted over the years—or perhaps Risaryâsi herself distorted it, to better support what happened later. But behind the story—yes, I do believe there is truth. I believe Ârata used the lost Âratists to his purpose. I believe she was meant to find his resting place."

"So you think she was really called by Ârata?"

"In some sense, Old One, I believe she was."

"And you, apostate. Were you called? Was it Ârata's will that you, sent to search for these lost Âratists, find what this Dreamer found?"

Gyalo looked into Martyas's wizened face, his bright malicious eyes. "I don't believe I was called, Old One. But I do believe I was used."

"Used?"

"I believe, Old One, that Ârata intended Risaryâsi and her descendants to survive, so the Brethren might send searchers after them, so what they found might again be discovered and word brought to Baushpar. I believe our expedition was meant to reach Refuge. But it was destroyed, and I and my companions were all that was to hand. It was left to us to complete the task."

"So you claim Ârata's blessing for your broken vow?" Dâdar cried. "You dare justify your apostasy thus?"

"Old One, I do no such thing. I'm entirely aware of the darkness of my choice. I didn't know what was to come when I broke my vow. I broke it not for Ârata, but because I could not accept death for my companions . . . because I could not accept it for myself. And yet I am certain the god required it of me, just as I am certain he requires me to stand before you now."

"Disgusting!" Kudrâcari hissed.

"I accept your condemnation, Old One. I embrace the punishment it will bring me." He turned from Kudrâcari's sallow fury and gazed around at the faces of the others. "Sons and Daughters of the Brethren, I've never denied my sin. I've confessed it freely, given myself up to your judgment. Yet I have also told you a great truth. I have brought you a great miracle. Do not allow my unworthiness to taint those things. Turn from me if you like—yes, turn from me, but if you do, look there." He flung out his arm, toward the table where the Blood lay glimmering. "The Blood of Ârata lies before you, irrefutable. It speaks louder than I ever could. Heed it, I beg you."

He felt the weariness of these words, whose basic argument, it seemed to him, he spoke at least once at every session. Look at what I say, not at me. Look at the Blood, not yourselves. It seemed dreamlike, sometimes, that he should say such things to the Brethren, these souls so ancient in experience and wisdom.

"Yes," Baushtas said, quietly. Kudrâcari turned on him.

"Do you say, then, Brother, that you *believe* this man?"

"I say this, Sister." Baushtas met her glare with his usual composure. "Once, long ago, all living things shared Ârata's mind. When he lay down to sleep that link was severed, and we were left to go our own way in the dark. Choice has been our lot since then—choice for good, choice for evil. And many of us do choose badly. But if a potter selects poor clay to make a jar, is the wine that's poured inside it poor as well? The wine is the wine, no matter what contains it. Let us keep in mind the unimportance of the vessel, Brothers and Sisters, as we debate the finer points of faith."

So it went, day by day.

Gyalo disciplined himself not to think in terms of time or progress, to go willingly to each session and welcome each question as another chance to speak. He turned his mind from Kudrâcari's contempt, Dâdar's hostility, Martyas's malice, Utamnos's silence. Nor did he dwell on Baushtas's quiet support, or the occasional rebukes Sundit offered her more zealous spirit-siblings—for just as he could not allow resistance to undermine his resolve, he could not permit himself to take sympathy for granted. *The message will be heard,* he told himself when he woke in the middle of the night with his heart pounding, or returned from the Pavilion of the Sun with the wounds of Dâdar's scorn still fresh upon him. *It needs only time.* One day he would look into Kudrâcari's hatchet face and see faith dawning there, as it had in Diasarta's face in Refuge. One day he would see them all struck speechless by belief.

He thought much of his companions, prisoned like himself, suffering no doubt under the same questioning. He prayed that Teispas would restrain himself, that Diasarta would keep calm. He prayed that Axane was not too afraid. He could not forget the terror in her face as the guards led her away that first day; it lacerated him to think of her, all alone in this world she knew so little of. At night, she came to him in dreams.

He was aware, as the Brethren extracted the knowledge

that was in him, squeezing him as dry as an orange, that there was one matter that remained unaddressed. In the Burning Land, he had determined immediately to recount Teispas's revelation and lay before them the question of the Next Messenger. But passing time had made him less certain of the wisdom of this. Moments came when he might have spoken, but always he held back. Day followed day, and still he was silent.

Very late on the fifteenth evening of his captivity, he paced his courtyard, back and forth along the path other feet had worn, too restless to sleep. It was a clear night, luminous with stars. He had wrapped himself in a blanket against the chill and left the door to his chamber open. The light from within made a yellow wedge across the stones.

Abruptly there came a chinking sound, and then a scrabbling and a sliding. A dark shape dropped over the eaves, landing with a thud. Gyalo leaped backward, letting out an involuntary cry of astonishment.

"Ash of the Enemy!" the shape hissed. Then: "Brother Gyalo?"

"... *Teispas?*"

"Yes. Burn me for a clumsy fool. My ankle's twisted."

"Teispas! What . . . how . . . what are you doing here?"

"Paying you a visit." Teispas moved and caught his breath. "Come. Let's get inside. Do you need a hand?"

Teispas shook his head. He limped toward the room. Gyalo followed, latching the door behind them. The captain seated himself in the room's single chair and bent to examine his ankle. His feet, Gyalo saw, were bare.

"No swelling, thank the Aspects. That'd be a nice thing, wouldn't it, if I found my way here and couldn't get back again."

Gyalo settled himself cross-legged on his bed. "How on earth did you discover where I was? And how did you get here without being noticed?"

"You can travel all around this section of the Evening City

by climbing over the roofs. It's tricky in spots, but not bad if you're careful. I have a map."

"A map?"

Teispas straightened. "Axane gave it to me. The three of us were called to the Brethren the other day. When they took us away she broke from her guard and came and clasped my hand as if to say farewell. She left it in my palm, folded up small."

"Where did *she* get it?"

Teispas shrugged. "Maybe she bribed a servant. It's accurate—I've already found Diasarta."

"Diasarta and you have been separated?"

"They took him away the night they took you. We're not far from each other distance-wise, though there's a perfect maze of passages in between. Here. I copied it for you." He reached into the breast of his tunic and drew out a twist of fabric. Unfolded, it revealed a confusion of lines and squares, drawn in some brownish substance that was obviously not ink. "Here. You're the *G*." Teispas pointed. "See? And I'm the *T*. And so on."

"Well. Thank you." Gyalo refolded the diagram and stowed it in the pocket of his gown. He found it incredible that Teispas had taken such a risk to bring this scrap of cloth. Yet it was a long time since he had glimpsed any faces beyond guards' and servants' and the Brethren's; he was surprised how pleased he was to see this dark, discomforting man. "How are they treating you, Teispas?"

"Oh, decently enough, if by 'decent' you mean endless stretches of idleness broken at intervals by unkind questioning."

"I'm sorry. Has it been very difficult?"

"In truth, not really. Boring, mostly."

"And Diasarta?"

"The same."

"And . . . Axane." He had to glance away as he spoke her name, for fear his face would show too much. "How did she seem, when you saw her?"

"She seemed afraid."

"Afraid?"

"Gyalo." He could not recall Teispas ever before using his name unprefaced by his title; it gave him an odd feeling to hear it now. "I haven't come just to give you the map. I need to warn you."

"Warn me?"

"There are some of the Brethren who want to discredit you. Four of them came to my courtyard the other day. I don't know for sure, but I got the feeling the others didn't know of it. They asked me about a lot of things, but mostly about you—how you used your shaping in the Burning Land, whether you'd shown any signs of madness or corruption. They seemed to think you might have coerced us into lying for you through some sort of threat or bribe, and they spent a lot of time trying to get me to admit it. They also asked about Axane. Whether . . . whether you'd lain with her."

"What?"

"They asked me whether her gift of the Blood had corrupted you and made you believe you are what Refuge named you."

Gyalo stared at him. "They asked you that?"

"Asked me, ordered me, threatened me with damnation. It was as clear as that lamp over there that they wanted me to denounce you. Of course I said nothing. When they saw I wasn't going to crack, they went away." His face was somber. "One of them, the woman, was very angry."

Something heavy had settled in Gyalo's chest. "A woman? Was she young? Hatchet-faced?"

"Yes, with a tongue to match. And there was an older man with pockmarks on his cheeks, and one even older, very fat. And a younger one, not much taller than a child, with misshapen legs. Gyalo." There was urgency in Teispas's voice. "The map shows the outer walls of the Evening City. There are places where the roofs run right up against them. It won't be easy, but we can climb out of here. We can escape."

"Escape?"

"Haven't you heard what I've been saying to you? It isn't

only me they've talked to—they've been to Diasarta, and I'm sure Axane as well, and probably the Exiles who brought us from Thuxra too. Of course Diasarta and Axane won't say anything, but the Exiles don't have any reason to hold their tongues."

"What can they say, other than that they suspected I was tethering myself? The Brethren already know that. Teispas, none of what they suspect me of is true. If they can find no one to say it is, what do they have but suspicion?"

"Come, Brother, you're an intelligent man. You know as well as I do that lies can work as well as truth to poison minds. Suppose these Brethren do manage to discredit you. What will happen—to you, to us? Personally, I'd rather not wait to find out."

"These are the leaders of the church of Ârata, reborn souls more than a thousand years old. Not some . . . some group of village elders." Gyalo shook his head. "Anyway, what you've told me is new only in the details. I already knew those four opposed me."

"I take it then you will not go."

"I came here to fulfill a task, Teispas. It hasn't been completed yet. If my courtyard door were left unlocked each night, I wouldn't go."

"Very well." Teispas sighed, with a resignation that suggested he had not expected anything else. "You can always change your mind. If you do, use the map. I'll be waiting."

"I won't change my mind."

A silence fell. The captain sat with his arms folded, his gaze fixed on the brazier at the center of the room. Gyalo watched him, thinking of the long way they had traveled together, of the way they traveled still. An image rose into his mind: Teispas, on the night he had revealed his unwelcome faith, ashimmer in his indigo lifelight, planted like a stake amid the vastness of the Burning Land.

"You believe it still, don't you," he said. "What you believed of me in the desert."

Teispas looked up. "Of course."

"I thought about it a great deal after you spoke to me."

Gyalo glanced away from those black eyes. "There was a time . . . a time when I almost thought it might be possible. But since we've left the desert it's passed out of me, like a sickness. I wish it could be the same for you."

He could feel the captain's troubled gaze. "If you think to drive me away with words like that," Teispas said, "you won't succeed."

Gyalo sighed and shook his head.

"Well. I've said what I came to say." Teispas pushed himself to his feet.

"What about your ankle?"

"It'll carry me."

Limping only slightly, he moved to the door.

"Teispas." The captain turned. "I've been dishonest with you. In the Burning Land, when I said there was no longer offense between us—it wasn't true. I hated you for what you did on the pebble plain, and I never truly let that go. And then, when you told me what you believed . . . oh, I was angry, not just for the error of it but because you wouldn't let me turn away. But that's gone now, all of it. The path we've walked, the knowledge we share, the truth we've spoken together before the Brethren . . . that's what is important. You've been brave and steadfast, and I have been selfish and unkind. I'm sorry for it."

Teispas grinned—that wolfish expression of his, full of bitter humor. "I'd say that makes us even, Brother."

"Thank you, Teispas. That isn't even remotely adequate, for all you've done . . . but thank you."

"Good night, Brother. Take care." He pointed at Gyalo's chest. "Don't forget that map."

And he was gone.

Gyalo went to sit in the chair Teispas had vacated. The room seemed much too quiet now; the lamps, flickering in the draft from the window screen, made shadows jump in the corners. What he had learned lay heavy in him, despite the resolute face he had put on. It was one thing to know he had enemies, quite another to see the substance of their enmity laid bare. His confident words seemed hollow—was he truly so sure of the Exiles' honesty? Was he really so certain Ku-drâcari and the others would not stoop to lie? And yet, he told himself, he had the advantage. For now he knew they worked against him.

He felt a surge of baffled rage. *They have the Blood of Ârata,* he thought. *Brought from the Burning Land, placed in their hands! Instead they look to me. To my apostasy.*

He closed his eyes. He should not feel this. It was the fire he should feel, the fire that had blazed so high in him the night before he faced them. How long had it been since he felt the touch of flame? He went when he was summoned; he answered what was asked; he strove unflinchingly to tell the truth. But it was only words, only will. That roaring joy, that sense of history speaking through him, had not visited him again.

It was a long time, that night, before he slept.

The next day brought no summons from the Brethren. A second day slid past without word, and then a third and a fourth and a fifth. They had never let it go so long before. Gyalo began to grow anxious, imagining accusations and denunciations made in his absence. The need to speak burned in him: It was his only tool, his only defense.

To distract himself, he had begun to perform again the drills and exercises he had followed in his competitive running days. He turned to them near noon on the sixth day after Teispas's visit. The sun beat down into the courtyard, heating the still, enclosed air to a temperature that recalled spring rather than autumn, and he stripped to his breechclout to spare his gown and trousers, which were all the clothing he had. He had been at it for some time when he heard the lock turn. He looked around. Utamnos and his carriers were entering the court.

For an instant astonishment held him frozen; then he scrambled to his knees on the sun-warmed stone.

"Great is Ârata. Great is his Way."

"Go in light." The old Son's eyes moved over him. "How thin you are, Gyalo. I did not realize."

"Old One, let me cover myself."

In his room, Gyalo toweled the sweat from his skin and put on his clothes. Astonishment had given way to unease, for he could not imagine that Utamnos had simply come to visit. He closed his eyes and breathed twenty-five deep breaths for calm, then returned to the courtyard and settled on his knees before the carrying chair. The servants had gone.

"It's been a long time since I visited this part of the Evening City." Utamnos was gazing around the court. "It was just before the Caryaxists—I must have been all of four years old. I can't remember why I was here, only that Haminâser brought me. Haminâser as he was then, I mean."

"Of course, Old One."

"It's odd how the body tricks the mind. I have more than a thousand years of memories of the Evening City. But because I've been absent from it in this incarnation, it seems strange to me now . . . and I'll have to learn it all over again, when I am reborn."

The words trailed into silence. The old Son sat sunken in his chair, wrapped to his chin in the folds of a crimson cloak. A year ago, two weeks ago, Gyalo would not have hesitated to break the pause, to ask plainly why Utamnos had come. But he was acutely conscious of the barriers the past days had raised between his former master and himself—the barrier of his apostasy, the barrier of all he had asked the Brethren to accept. He knew nothing now, not even whether Utamnos believed him.

"I've come to ask you a question." Utamnos spoke at last. "It's not an easy thing to say, so I will simply say it. Do you believe you are the Next Messenger?"

For a moment Gyalo could not speak. "No, Old One."

"Do you swear it?"

"By Ârata himself. Old One—why do you ask me this? Has someone suggested it?"

"Surely, Gyalo, you can't have failed to perceive the significance of your return from the Burning Land with a crystal of Ârata's Blood."

"No." Gyalo swallowed. "I haven't failed to perceive it."

"But you've never mentioned it. All this time, you've never once addressed it."

Gyalo glanced away from the old Son's steady gaze. "I have meant to speak of it, Old One. But each time I came to it . . . it seemed too presumptuous. To even raise the possibility—I feared it would seem I wasn't posing a question, but making a claim."

Utamnos shook his head. "There are those among my spirit-siblings who have come to see a claim in your silence. They fear you say nothing because you believe it true, encouraged by Refuge's false naming of you and the woman's gift of the Blood. They fear you conceal it because you mean to act on it in some way."

"Act on it?" Gyalo could not believe it. "How? I'm imprisoned, I face a lifetime of imprisonment! If that was my intent, why would I retether myself, return to Baushpar, surrender to an apostate's fate? Why would I give up the Blood?"

"So I have argued, and others with me." Utamnos sighed, and pulled his cloak closer around him. "But my spirit-siblings see only their own logic."

"So . . . you don't believe this of me, Old One?"

For a moment Utamnos was silent. "Before you left Baushpar, I would have wagered my life that you would never break your Shaper vow—you, of all men in the world. But here you are, apostate, condemned out of your own mouth. When my spirit-siblings brought these questions before the council, I argued for you, but really I did not know what to think. I asked myself, do I truly know this man? Can I say with any certainty what he would and would not do?" The old Son paused. The harsh sun picked out his faded tattoo, the folds and wrinkles of his face. "But then I remembered the night you returned, when I looked into your eyes and saw the alteration there—but also, more deeply, that you had not changed. And I thought to myself, this is my Third Hand. He would not lie. He would not scheme. I'll go to him and ask, and he will tell me the truth. I wasn't certain before I came here today, Gyalo. But I do wholly believe you now."

Gyalo looked down, at the smooth flagstones beneath his

knees, at his hands clasped upon his thighs. He no longer had the right, he knew, to expect his master's unquestioned loyalty. And yet it was hard to have this proved. "I'm grateful, Old One."

"Gyalo, you are in danger." Utamnos leaned forward in his chair. "It's important that you know it. As yet there are just three who speak against you, and they have suspicion only, no proof. But they are persuasive, and determined."

"Three, Old One?"

"Kudrâcari, Dâdar, and Ariamnes."

"Not Martyas?"

"In fact, Martyas speaks for you."

Gyalo digested this. "And the rest?"

"Baushtas, Artavâdhi, and Sundit believe you innocent. As do I. The others only listen and won't commit themselves. But I fear that will soon change. My Brothers and Sisters are afraid, Gyalo. So much faces us now. The task of Arsacian restoration is more massive than anyone imagined, and the costs are staggering. The people's faith is free at last, and it is like a flood, uncontrollable. Blasphemous rumors surrounding the fall of the Caryaxists spring up as fast as we can counter them. Village children see visions of Ârata. Miracles are reported in the temples of the Aspects. And then there is the discord with Santaxma, and his actions in the Assembly. We have not known turmoil like this since the Shaper War, nor have there ever been so few of us to face these challenges. My Brothers and Sisters feel themselves besieged. They are quicker to fear—and I am afraid they will also be quicker to judge."

"And the Bearer? Has he spoken?"

Utamnos shook his head. "He hears all and says nothing."

Gyalo thought of the Bearer, sitting silent through the interrogations, his heavy eyes turning again and again to Gyalo's face. It was the Bearer who cast the final vote in actions of the council; in times when the council's membership comprised an even number, as now, his vote was counted twice. He also possessed the power of veto, though it was rarely used.

Gyalo closed his eyes. Dread turned in him. *This is my fault*, he thought. *By keeping silent, I've brought this on my-self.*

"Old One—" He hesitated, and then went on in a rush. "Old One, I told you the truth. I don't believe I am the Next Messenger. But there was a time, when I was traveling the Burning Land, a time when it seemed . . . possible."

Utamnos watched him. "Go on."

"It came to me against my will, this possibility. I hardly dared hold it in my mind, for it seemed the most appalling blasphemy. And yet I thought of Marduspida, who six times rejected Ârata's dream. For him, a seventh rejection would have been the sin. It seemed . . . it seemed to me there might be as much danger in not asking the question as in asking it."

He paused. Utamnos waited.

"I was sane enough at least to realize that I was not the one who could answer. I resolved to lay it all before you, be-fore the Brethren, when I reached Baushpar. But . . . once I was in Arsace again, and began to feel the world around me, it began to seem not just blasphemous, but . . ." he paused, searching for the proper words ". . . impossible, *absurd*, the questions I'd been asking. I'm a mortal man. I received no revelation. No divine act brought me the Blood—if Axane hadn't given it to me, I would have returned empty-handed. And the destruction that is supposed to follow at the hands of the Messenger, and the generation . . . what sign is there of that? I came to my senses. It's hard for me now to imag-ine I ever considered such a thing. I wish with all my heart I'd been strong enough not to fall into such error, and it shames me that I was not. I think I must have gone mad for a time, in the Burning Land."

Utamnos was quiet a moment. At last, slowly, he nodded. "I understand better now why you never spoke," he said. "You must not say this to my Brothers and Sisters, Gyalo. You must not breathe a word. They could never understand."

Into Gyalo's mind rose an image of Kudrâcari's face. He drew a breath, pressing it away.

"But I must address them," he said. "I must speak directly to these accusations."

"Yes," Utamnos said. "That you must do."

"It's been almost a week since I was last summoned. When will they call me back?"

"Soon. I'll see to it. You have my promise."

"Old One—all mistakes have been mine. My companions are blameless. No matter what happens to me, they shouldn't suffer for anything I've done or failed to do. If I should . . . fail . . . will you intercede for them? Will you try to see they're set free?"

"If you are judged heretic, it will go ill for the two soldiers, for it's plain they are loyal to you. I doubt there will be anything I can do." Utamnos hesitated. "In any case, they must first perform a service for us. They are to be our guides into the Burning Land."

Gyalo caught his breath. "You mean to go again into the desert, Old One?"

"We've decided we must look with our own eyes upon this Cavern. There's also the question of the heretics—how can we leave them in exile? They must be returned to Galea, to the true Way of Ârata, and their settlement must be razed, the Land made clean of it. And of course the Shapers must be dealt with. We will not attempt to subdue them—you have most thoroughly convinced us of their strength, Gyalo. Instead we'll do as King Vantyas did, at the Battle of Clay."

"You will *kill* them?"

"We will execute them. They are far too dangerous to be left alive. You, who were capable of re-tethering yourself, surely understand that. It will be hard. But it must be done," Utamnos said, and then again, heavily: "This *must* be done."

Gyalo was silent. Images possessed his mind: the Cavern of the Blood, Refuge, the faces of its people. He was not certain why any of this should surprise him.

"What of Axane, Old One? Will you speak for her?"

"Ah. The woman." Utamnos shifted in his chair. "That's another matter. We are not convinced she speaks the truth when she denies the teachings of her people. It seems very

likely that what Kudrâcari and her supporters say is true—
that by giving you the Blood of Ârata she sought deliberately to corrupt you."

"What? Old One, that is not so!"

"Can you be so certain, Gyalo? I don't know the face she
has shown to you, but to us she is defiant. She resists our attempts to guide her. She does not behave as a penitent
should."

Gyalo felt a falling within himself. "Old One, she doesn't
understand our ways. But she's no heretic, I swear it on my
life. When I was in Refuge, she was the only one who understood that I was neither their Next Messenger nor a demon,
but just a man."

"You are young." Utamnos spoke gently. "You've never
before encountered true transgression. This woman was
born in heresy, raised in it—a heresy so odious that even I,
who have lived long and seen much blasphemy, am shocked
by it. It's wound deep into her soul, this ugly thing, and
though I am prepared to concede the possibility that she may
honestly believe she has cut it out, somewhere in her the
roots remain."

"Old One, let me speak to her. I know I can make her understand."

"No, Gyalo." A coldness had come into Utamnos's face.
"The matter is decided. She cannot go free, any more than
her people may, when they are returned to Arsace. In this I
am in full agreement with my spirit-siblings."

"What . . . will happen to her?"

"There's a nunnery in Kanu-Tapa, where women go who
choose to vow the Way rather than serve a magistrate's sentence. She'll be sent there. If she's as quick-witted as she
seems, she'll recognize the mercy of it. We might as easily
have chosen to imprison her. It will be a better life than she
could have made for herself, alone and without protection. A
better life than the one she had."

Into Gyalo's mind came an image of Axane, in the temple
of Tane, scandalizing him with her plans of returning to
Ninyâser. *I'm happy,* she had said. *I actually am.*

The afternoon was far advanced now, and shadows lay all the way across the court. Utamnos glanced up at the sky. "It's growing late," he said. "Come, Gyalo—I would give you my blessing."

Gyalo slid forward on his knees. Utamnos's hand came softly to rest upon his scalp.

"Go in light, child of Árata. May you find the will you need to walk your way. May you know the kindness of compassionate hearts. May you—" He paused. In the quiet, Gyalo could hear the tap of his own pulse, and, very faint, the rasp of Utamnos's breathing. "May you learn the strength that is born in solitude. Go in light."

The gentle fingers released their grip. Gyalo looked up into his former master's face, creased and seamed with age and weariness. There was no coldness in it now, only a sadness that took Gyalo's breath.

"I love you still, my Third Hand," Utamnos said. His eyes brimmed with tears. "Apostate though you are. I cannot help it. It breaks my heart that you must spend your life confined."

Gyalo felt his own eyes fill. He could not speak.

"Fetch my servants now."

Gyalo rose and crossed the courtyard. He banged on the door; it opened at once. The servants entered and ranged themselves between the shafts of Utamnos's carrying chair.

"Good-bye, my Third Hand."

"Old One." The words rose, irresistible, to Gyalo's lips. "You believed me in the Pavilion of the Sun, when I said I had retethered myself. You believed me a little while ago, when I told you I don't believe . . . as I'm suspected of believing. But the news I've brought. Do you believe that?"

There was a long, long pause. It was chilly, in the shadow; Gyalo realized he was shivering.

"You've told me a great deal of truth today," Utamnos said finally. "I owe you at least as much. But this is all I can give you. I wish with all my heart we had never thought to go into the Burning Land."

The words seemed to shock the hushed air. In Utamnos's

amber eyes, dry now, Gyalo saw something he did not want to read. He bowed his head and knelt again, crossing his arms before his face.

"Great is Ârata. Great is his Way."

"Go in light," Utamnos said. "Farewell."

—19—

The sun was gone; twilight had claimed the world. It was not just chilly, but cold. Still Gyalo paced the courtyard.

He was weary with thinking—of the errors he had made, of the peril that threatened, of what might yet go wrong. More and more, as the afternoon drew on, his mind had come to dwell on his companions—Teispas and Diasarta, tainted with his suspected heresy, forced back into the Burning Land; Axane, locked up for life in some grim nunnery for the sake of beliefs she had left behind long before she departed Refuge. It would destroy her, to be confined like that. She would pine away, like a wild thing in a cage.

They had given him their trust in the Burning Land, their loyalty, their faith. Even, perhaps, their love. He had not wanted any of these things, except perhaps the trust; yet he had assumed they would follow him, would stand and speak with him, for no better reason than that he needed them to do so. Now, for his lapses, his mistakes, they faced punishment and worse. He feared for them; but deeper than his fear was shame.

He halted where he was, at the courtyard's center. Over

the past hours the flagstones, the walls, the dimming sky seemed to have grown subtly unfamiliar. A sense of unraveling possessed him, of things tipping out of control—like standing on a sand dune and just beginning to feel the sliding beneath his feet.

He knew what must be done to put it right.

Full darkness fell. A servant brought a meal and returned to take it away again. Gyalo waited, counting off the minutes as he counted breath in meditation. At last, when it seemed late enough, he took out Teispas's map and spread it on the table. He studied it until he was certain he had committed it to memory. Then, blowing out his lamps, he slipped into the courtyard.

Beneath the roof where Teispas had come down, he paused, looking up. He thought to frame a prayer, but no words came. This was not a thing he did for Ârata, in any case, but for himself.

He breathed deeply, and leaped for the eaves. He had to try three times before his fingers got a solid purchase on the curving tile. With an effort that made all the muscles of his arms and shoulders crack, he hoisted himself up and got a leg over the edge. On hands and knees he climbed the slope of the roof, then began to make his way crabwise along the peak, clinging to its spiky ceramic decorations.

Remembering that Teispas had been barefoot, he had left his sandals behind; despite the cold he was glad he had, for the slick-glazed tiles were treacherous. Open courtyards passed below—small ones like his to the right, larger and more elaborate ones to the left, all darkened and apparently deserted. According to the map, this section of the Evening City was a honeycomb of such courts, accessed from a series of passageways like the one whose roof he now traversed. He reached a higher, crosswise passage; he pulled himself up onto it, scaled its peak, crept down the other side, and continued on.

Two more crosses and one sickening near fall later, he found himself above the court where the map had shown a *T*. It was the same one in which they had been confined together: He recognized the scalloped gazing pool at the center. He sat on the roof edge and carefully lowered himself, turning as he did so that he hung by his hands. He struck the flagstones with a jolt that knocked him over onto his back. He lay a moment, winded, and climbed to his feet.

Light showed through one of the window screens. He knocked softly on the adjoining door. A pause, and the door swung open. Teispas stood there, fully dressed.

"Ah," he said, as if this were entirely expected, and stood aside so Gyalo could enter.

"When you came to me the other night," Gyalo said, not wasting time with greeting, "you told me you thought escape was possible. Do you still think so?"

Teispas leaned against the door and folded his arms. "You've changed your mind, then?"

"Do you think it can be done?"

"I've already scouted a route." Teispas smiled. "I'd a feeling it would be needed."

"Good. I've learned something." Quickly Gyalo related the gist of what Utamnos had told him. "So if I were judged heretic, you and Diasarta would be judged along with me and probably imprisoned. Even if that doesn't happen, you'll be forced to cross the Burning Land again, and who knows what may come of that? And Axane will be shut up for the rest of her life, imprisoned among strangers." He drew a breath. "You must leave here. All of you."

Teispas regarded him. "What about you?"

"I told you before, I have to see this through."

"Even if at the end of it you're judged a heretic."

"I don't believe that will happen."

"Why? Do you think you can persuade them otherwise?"

"I *must* persuade them otherwise."

"Suppose you can't. What will they do to you?"

Gyalo looked away. "The sentence for heresy among vowed Âratists is blinding."

Teispas was jolted from his casual pose. *"What?"*

"Ârata is brightness. His symbol is the sun. Heretics forfeit the right to light."

"You can't accept that!" Teispas took a step forward; his face burned with outrage. "You can't risk it!"

"Why? Because of what you believe I am?"

"Because of what I *know* you are. A good and honest man, and no heretic. Gyalo—Brother Gyalo—I saw it in the faces of the ones who came to me. There's only one way this can end. You're throwing away your sight, your freedom, the rest of your life, for nothing. I wouldn't send an enemy to such a fate, never mind a friend. That's how I think of you—not just as the Next Messenger, who I'd follow into Ârata's own fires if I had to, but a friend, the first true friend I've had since Naruva died. I won't let you do this."

"Teispas, I can't argue this with you. There isn't time."

"I'll stay, then. I won't abandon you."

"No! I don't want you here. Ârata's Blood, if you won't do it for me, do it for Axane! She'll need protection, once she's away. I know you care for her. She told me about your offer."

"She won't have me." Teispas's face had turned to stone. "Did she tell you that?"

"At least this way you'll have the chance to persuade her."

"It may be worse for you if we go. Have you thought of that? They may blame you."

"How will they know I was involved? You said they've summoned the three of you together, but me they've only summoned alone. More likely they'll think you saw what was coming and deserted me. Teispas. Teispas, you *must* go."

They stood, eye to eye. Teispas's resistance was a physical presence upon the air. At last the captain dropped his gaze.

"Very well. Tomorrow night, we'll go."

Gyalo drew a long breath. "Thank you."

"I'll climb and tell the others."

"I will . . . I will go to Axane."

Teispas looked at him; there was uncomfortable perception in that dark gaze. But all he said was: "Tell her we'll be coming late."

Gyalo nodded.

"Brother Gyalo." Teispas's tone was formal now. "Give me your blessing before you go."

"A blessing from me is worth very little."

"I traveled far enough with you to know that isn't so. I want your blessing. Will you give it?"

"Yes. Of course."

Teispas sank to his knees and bowed his face into his hands, his sleek black hair falling forward over his fingers. Lightly Gyalo laid his palm on the captain's head.

"Go in light, child of Ârata. May the god hold you steadfast in his care. May he cherish the honor in you and treasure the strength. May he grant you the peace you have sought so long. May he raise you up at the end of time, cleansed and perfected, to dwell in bliss beside him. Go in light, child of Ârata."

He felt Teispas shudder under his hand. He stepped back. Teispas rose.

"I won't say good-bye." The captain's voice was rough.

"I'll never forget you, Teispas."

Teispas turned away. "Go."

Gyalo did.

The route to Axane's courtyard took him back the darkened way he had come and then, beyond his own court, into areas lit and populated. He was forced to pause several times as someone moved past below, and was grateful for the overcast sky, which made it hard for him to see but also difficult for anyone, looking up, to glimpse him. The tiles were cold under his bare feet; the sound of his own breathing filled his ears like the murmur of the ocean. Anticipation of her presence was a pressure beneath his heart. Perhaps he should have let Teispas go to her; but he had been unable to deny himself the chance to see her one last time.

He came to the court that, according to the map, was hers. He lowered himself over the eaves and dropped onto the flagstones. This time he did not fall.

No light showed behind the window screen. "Axane," he whispered into the fretwork, and tapped softly. "Axane!"

Silence. Then a reply, very quiet: "Who's there?"

"Gyalo."

"*Gyalo?* Wait." There was a rustling, and a small light

flared inside the room. Shadows moved. The door opened. "Gyalo?"

He crossed the threshold. She closed the door and turned to face him. She wore a white linen bedgown, and had pulled a blue stole around her shoulders. Her hair tumbled unbound about her face, and her feet were bare on the wide planks of the floor. She looked exactly as he remembered her—and nothing like at all, for in his thoughts she was always cloaked in the gem colors of her lifelight, which now he could not see. The old desire, the old yearning, swept over him with tidal force. He retreated toward the wall, putting the shadowy spaces of the room between them.

She spoke low. "How did you know where I was?"

"Your map. Teispas copied it."

"He found you?"

"Yes." The urge to move, to undo the separation he had made, was overwhelming. He put his hands behind his back, curling his fingers against the unyielding plaster of the wall. "I've come to tell you something. You should . . . perhaps you should sit down."

She went to the bed and settled herself among her blankets, and looked at him expectantly.

"There has been . . ." He cleared his throat. "You're in danger."

"Danger?"

"The Brethren have decided you're not to be set free. When these inquiries are finished they'll send you to a nunnery in Kanu-Tapa and keep you there for the rest of your life."

She drew in her breath, shocked. "They'll imprison me?"

"Yes."

"But . . . but why?"

"They can't forget you were born in heresy. They fear the ways of your people are too deeply rooted in you to be cut out."

"But over and over I've told them I don't believe as my people do. Do they think I'm lying?"

"I think perhaps you haven't been as . . . repentant as they feel you should be."

"Repentant? What do I have to be sorry for? Oh, Gyalo." She clutched the stole around her shoulders. Her voice was tight with panic. "I couldn't bear to be imprisoned. I'd die."

"I know. Before I came here, I went to Teispas. Tomorrow night, you and he and Diasarta will leave the Evening City over the roofs. Can you manage that? Can you climb?"

"Yes. I can climb. I can do anything." Her great eyes searched his face. "You aren't coming with us?"

"I have to stay. I have a task to finish."

She did not protest, but only looked down at the tumbled bedclothes. "So I'll never see you again."

It pierced him to the heart. He could not speak.

"Gyalo . . ." She paused, then went on in a rush: "The Brethren have asked me so many questions about Refuge. I think . . . I think they must mean to go there."

"Yes."

"What will happen to my people?"

"They'll be brought back to Arsace. They'll . . . probably be shut away, like you."

Her face tightened. "Even the Shapers?"

"Not the Shapers." He could not tell her less than the truth. "The Shapers will be subdued and executed."

"What?" Horror dawned upon her face. "They'll be killed?"

"Yes."

"But . . . but . . . why?" She leaned forward, her stole sliding from one bare brown shoulder. "They aren't dangerous. They're not corrupt. They aren't . . . greedy and mad for power, the way those cruel old men and women think! Oh, they tried to get me to say so, but I wouldn't, I wouldn't, I closed my mouth and stayed silent no matter how many questions they asked. Even when they told me I had to speak to prove my faith, I wouldn't say what they wanted me to!"

"Oh, Axane." Gyalo could see it all too clearly.

"Should I have lied? You're a Shaper, Gyalo." There was pleading in her voice. "You were free. You aren't those things they say. Can't they look at you and see how wrong they are?"

"I wasn't free for very long, Axane. When they look at me—" He stopped. "I prove nothing."

"But they've never even *seen* our Shapers! How can they condemn to death people they've never even seen?"

He did not answer. What was there to say?

"So they'll kill all the Shapers. And the others, the Dreamers and the Forceless, they'll drag them back to Galea and lock them up . . ." The stole had slipped from her other shoulder; she wrenched it up again, her hands fisted in the soft blue fabric. "Oh, it's too cruel! Why must they go to Refuge at all? Why can't they just leave it be?"

He shook his head. All the explanations in the world would make no difference, even had he wished to make them.

"I'm sorry." She was quiet now. "It's not your fault."

"They're your people. It's natural you should feel so."

"They *are* my people." She looked down at her cloth-wrapped hands. "It's strange. I always thought I hated Refuge."

A lamp burned on a table by her bed, its tiny flame as perfect as a jewel. For the first time, Gyalo noticed the meagerness of the furnishings: the table, a chest, a chair, the single bed with its disordered covers. The walls were unmuraled, the floor bare of carpets. It was an accommodation little better than a servant's.

She looked up at him again. "Won't they blame you, if we go?"

"They'll have no way of knowing I had anything to do with it."

"And once all this is over. You said . . . in the desert . . . that they'd confine you, for breaking your vows. Is that still true?"

"Yes."

"Even if you make them believe that Ârata has risen?"

"Yes."

She nodded. With something like panic, he felt the imminence of ending: the moment in which he would have no more to tell her, and she no more to ask him. He cast about for something to say.

"You'll be ready, then. Tomorrow night."

"Yes."

"They'll come late."

"Yes."

"You should bring only what you can carry on your back. You'll need your hands for climbing."

She nodded.

That was all. There was no more: He could not draw it out a minute longer. Still he stood, his back against the wall. Everything in him denied departure—all his body, all his mind.

From across the room she watched him. The lamplight lay on half her face; the other half was shadowed. He thought of how her lifelight would have illumined all of her, if he had still been free to see it. Heat burst across his skin; longing swept him, so huge he could scarcely breathe. He tensed his fingers against the plaster at his back, knowing it would not yield. There was nothing to hold on to.

He let his hands fall to his sides. He stepped away from the anchor of the wall. He crossed the room; the floor seemed uncertain beneath his feet, and he had that sense of slipping again, of unraveling. By the bed, he halted. She gazed up at him. Her stole had fallen from her shoulders again; he could read her body beneath the thin linen that covered it—the angle of her hips, the roundness of her breasts. Below the hem of her bedgown one bare foot showed, slim and high-arched, perfect.

She pulled her arms free of the stole and held out her hands. Her eyes were locked to his; the muscles of her throat were taut. It was like the moment in the Burning Land, when he looked into her face and first understood that she desired him. He had condemned her then—for offering herself to a celibate, for following the practice of her people, who saw no need to bind their physical liaisons with any lasting union. But who was he to judge? Except for a single lapse he had been abstinent all his life; but his abstinence had not defended him, and love, when it came, had divided his heart as cleanly as a knife.

What am I doing? he thought. He placed his hands in hers, and let her draw him down onto the bed.

"Are you sure?" she whispered.

He barely heard her through the thunder of his blood. Slowly, carefully, she leaned toward him, her eyes never leaving his. He smelled her scent—clean linen, something darker and more aromatic. She took his face gently between her hands and kissed him. The tip of her tongue parted his lips. The world seemed to swing on its axis. His hands rose to grip her—her hips, her breasts. His thumb passed across the pebble of her nipple; she breathed into his mouth, shuddering. He had lost the boundaries of his body; there was nothing but sensation now, nothing but the need to devour, to be utterly devoured. It was like tipping off the edge of the earth. He could already, rapturously, feel the fall.

But in a small cold corner of his mind, he saw what it would mean for him to fall. He saw that in this moment, he could still reach out his hand.

He gasped. With an effort of will that felt like tearing his own flesh he gripped her shoulders and set her away from him. She made a sound of protest, reaching for him; he stumbled up from the bed and backed away.

"I can't." He was panting. "I can't."

"But why?" He saw the baffled need in her face, as violent as his own.

"My vow. This is . . . this is forbidden to me."

"But what does that matter now? Why should you keep your vow now?"

"It's the promise I made to Ârata." The words were like ash in his mouth. "I've broken one vow, Axane. I can't break another. I can't."

There was a pause. Then she reached for her stole and pulled it up again around her shoulders, crossing her arms defensively before her breasts. "I'm sorry," she said. "I shouldn't—shouldn't have—"

"No. It's my fault. It was wrong of me to come here."

She looked away, at the small flame of the lamp.

"I'll go, then."

She drew in her breath. "Gyalo—" Her voice was small. "Would you stay? Just . . . just for a little while, to keep me company. I won't touch you, I won't come near you. Please. We'll never see each other again, after tonight."

He hesitated. The terrible desire had drained away, leaving a cold, flat emptiness behind. But if he let himself, he could feel her under his hands, and he knew it would not take much to stir it again. Even so, his heart denied departure. "All right. For a little while."

He went to sit in the room's single chair. She moved back against the headboard, curling her legs under her; she still held the stole tightly around her shoulders, hunching into herself, disguising the shape of her body.

"Where will they send you? For your imprisonment."

"I don't know. Somewhere remote. Isar, perhaps, or one of the mountain monasteries in Haruko."

"Will they be cruel to you?"

"Of course not." He banished the image of the heated pin with which heretics' eyes were put out. "I'll have all the comforts of a vowed Âratist, except for those of faith. Apostates aren't allowed to take Communion. And I'll never be able to leave the monastery."

"That sounds cruel enough."

"Axane. You must marry Teispas."

"What?"

"When you're away from here. You'll need protection."

"I don't want to marry Teispas."

"But you'll be a fugitive. You'll have to leave Arsace. You can't go alone into lands you don't know."

Her mouth set in a stubborn line. She turned her face away. "I shall never marry anyone."

"Axane—"

"There's something I want to tell you. Something I've never told anyone before." She paused. "I'm a Dreamer."

She said it as if she were confessing to a crime. It startled him; he had never suspected.

"My mother was a Dreamer. When she was thirty-five she

went into the House of Dreams forever. Children aren't allowed inside the House, but I went in anyway, secretly, because I missed her so much. It was—" She shuddered, a rippling tremor that shook her from head to foot. "Awful. I never forgot it. When I realized I was a Dreamer myself, I was terrified. I never wanted to go into that place. So I hid my dreaming. I've hidden it ever since."

Gyalo had seen the House of Dreams when he had been in Refuge; except for the lack of luxury, it had not seemed so very different from the descriptions he had heard of Dreamer monasteries and nunneries in Aino. But in Galea, Dreamers were free to choose whether or not to vow the Way and were not compelled unwilling to a life of sleep. Axane's voice returned to him, speaking of Ninyâser: *A place where I can be what I am.* He had sensed the significance of her words, but he had not understood them until now.

"Did no one suspect?" he asked.

"No. I made sure of that. Dreaming is a sacred duty. What I did was a terrible transgression."

"But surely there were others who felt the same. You can't have been the only one."

"I don't know. I used to look at the faces of the people I knew, people I'd known all my life, and wonder if any of them were like me, and if we might recognize each other. But it never happened." In a small voice, she said, "Do you hate me?"

"For what? For not wanting to spend your life asleep?"

"For not telling you. I could have helped—I dreamed ahead sometimes, in the Burning Land. Refuge sent people after us, after you unmade the storms—I dreamed them, too. I never told you."

"Well, they didn't catch us. And we survived."

"Yes, we did." Bitterly, she said, "For this."

"Did you dream of Galea? Is that how you recognized your people's error?"

She nodded. She had freed her hands from the confinement of her stole and was pleating the linen of her bedgown between her fingers. "Refuge's Dreamers are trained to keep their minds in Refuge. But I was never trained, so my mind went where it willed." She paused. "I dreamed you, too, as you crossed the Burning Land. Once in a camp, with all your people around you, and then on the Plains of Blessing, when only you and Teispas and Diasarta and Gâbrios were left. Before I ever met you, I knew your face."

Against his will, it stirred him. "Did you dream the Evening City? Is that how you were able to make the map?"

"Yes. It used to be that I couldn't control the Dreams. They came or they didn't, and there was nothing I could do about it. But . . . I've discovered I can always dream you, if I try." She raised her eyes suddenly, and captured his. "Every night we've been in this place, I've come over the roofs, to you."

He caught his breath. Desire quaked in him. He was afraid to move or speak.

She let her stole fall and came forward on her knees. Her bare arms and shoulders were dark against the white linen of her gown. "Gyalo, come with us tomorrow night."

He shook his head. His mouth was dry. "I've told you, I have to stay."

"I won't press you. I won't tempt you. I'll go away if you like—you'll never see me again. Only come with us. Please."

"I can't."

"Is it the drug you take? The sickness that will come when you don't have it anymore? You don't need to be afraid of that. I'm a healer. I'll take care of you."

"It isn't the drug."

"Why, then? Because of this . . . task of yours? But you'll never convince those evil men and women that Ârata has risen! They hate you as much as they hate Refuge, I could see it in their faces when they questioned me. And even if you do convince them, you'll still be imprisoned, locked away forever! How can you be loyal to people who treat you so? How can you not want something more worthy of you? How can you just allow—"

"Enough!" He surged to his feet. "Enough, Axane! No more!"

"I can't help it! I can't help it! How can I just let you go?"

She burst into a storm of weeping and flung herself face-down upon the bed. Her sobs seemed to reach inside him. He knew that if he stayed, he would not be able to resist their pull.

"Axane, it's time for me to leave."

She pushed herself upright. "No."

"It's best."

"Please stay a little longer." Grief ravaged her face; he could hardly bear to look at her. "I won't say anything else, I promise."

He shook his head. "It'll be light soon, anyway."

She bowed her face into her hands. "Go then," she said, muffled. "I don't want to watch."

"Good-bye, Axane. It'll be a comfort—" The words seemed to break inside his mouth. "A comfort to me to know you're safe."

He turned toward the door. Her voice reached after him.

"Gyalo, if it had been different. If you were ... free. Would you have chosen me?"

It was a meaningless question. If he had been free, he would not have met her—and he could never have been free, Shaper that he was. And yet, in this final moment, he yielded to the deeper truth of what she asked. "Yes."

Tears streaked down her cheeks. She whispered: "I'll dream of you."

It was as if she had touched him. He fled.

Her words pursued him across the roofs. They followed him into his courtyard, into his silent chamber. They crowded in his mind as he fell upon his empty bed, remembering how her hands had moved upon his skin. And he could not help but think that there was little value in having kept the form of his vow intact when, with his burning flesh and divided heart, he so utterly violated its spirit.

—20—

Dawn came at last. The servant arrived with Gyalo's breakfast; he picked at it, then, remembering Teispas's map, took it from his pocket and set it on the coals of the brazier, where it glowed red and burst into flame, collapsing in a few seconds into ash.

He spent the day in taut expectation of the Brethren's summons. It did not come, and by late afternoon he had given up hope. With the relaxing of that vigilance, he understood for the first time just how exhausted he was. He crawled into bed, but slept only fitfully, dreaming of his companions' escape and what might go wrong. He had wondered if he would hear them, climbing overhead; but either they were very silent or he was sleeping when they passed, for he heard nothing.

It was still dark when he was wrenched awake by a great crash. It took him several groggy seconds to comprehend that his door had been flung back. A Tapati guard stood in the opening, a lantern in his hand. The guard regarded him a moment, expressionless as an idol; then he turned on his heel and departed.

Gyalo lay staring at the dim rectangle of the open door. *They know,* he thought coldly. Why else would they need to check on him in the middle of the night? It was much too soon for his companions' absence to have been discovered by servants bringing the morning meal. Something had gone wrong.

He rose and closed the door. Knowing he would not sleep again, he dressed and sat tensely down in a chair to wait. Through the fretwork of the window screen he watched dawn arrive, then day, dull and overcast. Dread pulsed in him, keeping time with his heartbeat. The hours dragged on; no servant came, no meal was brought. At last there was a knocking. It was a guard.

"Come," he said. "The Brethren have summoned you."

Gyalo obeyed on unsteady legs. Ordinarily the guards allowed him to walk unrestrained, but this one took him firmly by the arm, hustling him along like a child. A strange stillness had come over him, distancing his fear; the passages of the Evening City seemed to pass by at a remove, as if he were watching in a mirror.

They reached the forecourt, where the gates already stood ajar, and crossed the Courtyard of the Sun. Inside the Pavilion the Brethren waited, stiff as statues in their red chairs. On the floor below the Bearer's dais, legs spread and arms folded, stood another guard. Someone knelt at his feet.

Teispas.

Gyalo's false calm deserted him. He stumbled, and might have fallen but for the grip upon his arm. The guard propelled him to the dais and pushed him roughly down at Teispas's side. The captain did not move or turn. His arms were pulled behind him, bound at elbows and wrists; his back was hunched to relieve the strain. His unbound hair fell across his face.

"Gyalo Amdo Samchen." The Bearer's rich voice rolled across the silent room. He sat with both hands braced upon his knees, his back straight as a slab of stone. "You see beside you Captain Teispas dar Ispindi, who was discovered this morning before dawn, attempting to climb over the walls of the Evening City. Following his capture, a search was conducted. The soldier, Diasarta dar Abanish, and the heretic woman were found to be missing."

So the others are safe away, Gyalo thought.

"Captain dar Ispindi has been questioned, but he will not speak." The Bearer's hooded gaze was like a hand beneath Gyalo's chin. "So we turn to you. What do you know of this?"

"He knew nothing."

It was Teispas. He had straightened, as much as he could with his bound arms, and shaken his hair back from his face. With an unpleasant shock Gyalo saw the bruises that marked it, dark against the dark skin. Blood crusted the corner of his mouth.

"So." The Bearer's gaze shifted. "You have something to say after all."

"It was their idea." Teispas's voice was hoarse. "Diasarta and the woman. They were lovers—they became so in the Burning Land. They plotted together to flee. They came to me last night and offered to let me go with them. I said yes."

Ah, Teispas, Gyalo thought.

"How did they find one another?" the Bearer asked. "How did they find you?"

"I don't know."

"Why did they wish to flee?"

"Any fool can see the way things are shaping here." Teispas coughed, painfully. "You suspect us all of heresy, or worse."

"Are you a heretic, Captain dar Ispindi?"

"No! Not I. Nor any of my companions, to my knowledge."

"Do you know where they were going?"

"Haruko, maybe." Teispas coughed again, his shoulders jerking. "Diasarta grew up there, like me."

"And your companion here." With a gesture, the Bearer indicated Gyalo. "You assert that he knew nothing?"

"That's right."

"I find that curious. There was a time, as I recall, when you three were ready to give your bodies to his defense. Why would you leave him here to face, as you believed, a charge of heresy?"

"We didn't care what happened to him."

"Indeed? And what brought about this change?"

"He deceived us. Before we came here, he told us we'd only be questioned. He never said we'd be confined. He never said his transgressions would make us suspect, too. He never said there would be talk of heresy! If I'd known, if any of us had known . . ." He bit off the words. "We did not want him with us. As far as I'm concerned, he can rot."

The Bearer regarded him. "So many words," he said softly, "after such silence."

"I've told the truth. Believe it or not, as you choose."

"Will you swear to this, Captain dar Ispindi?"

"I will."

"And you." The Bearer turned toward Gyalo. "Were you truly ignorant of your companions' plan?"

Gyalo had known he must lie. He had prepared himself, in Ârata's name, to do so. Yet to lie now was also to embrace the falsehood Teispas had just spun, and thus, indirectly, to condemn him. Beside him, Teispas's body was rigid; he could feel the familiar force of the captain's will.

"It's the truth, Old One."

"Will you swear it?" The Bearer lifted the cage of golden wire that held the Blood. "Will you come to me now and, before the assembled leaders of your faith, place your hand on the Blood of Ârata and swear you had no part in your companions' flight?"

Gyalo closed his eyes. "I will, Old One."

For a long moment there was silence. The Bearer let the necklace fall. "No need," he said.

"Brother!" It was Kudrâcari. "He must swear!"

"No, Sister." The Bearer did not shift his eyes from Gyalo's face. "Either he tells the truth, in which case there is no need for oaths, or else he is prepared to forswear himself no matter what the cost. I won't dishonor the Blood by using it so."

"Brother, he lies! He must be forced to acknowledge it!"

The Bearer drew breath to reply, but answer came in a different voice.

"I've heard enough."

For the first time Gyalo realized that a stranger stood behind the Bearer's bench, concealed till that moment by its high back and his own slight stature. He came forward—a vigorous, straight-standing man in rich gold-and-yellow clothing, his neck and wrists heavily jeweled and his black curls wound with threads of gold—and halted beside the Bearer, one ringed hand on the gilded armrest. With astonishment, Gyalo recognized Santaxma V, King of Arsace.

"Your Majesty," he said, and prostrated himself.

"Get him up."

The guard grabbed the back of Gyalo's gown and hauled him upright. Santaxma regarded him with hard black eyes, set a little too close together. He was light-skinned, as most Arsacian nobility were, with a smooth intelligent face and a jutting Arsacian nose. Gyalo had seen him often in Rimpang, though never from so short a distance; close to, he was less comely but more commanding, the focused power of his attention as tangible as a scent.

"I say you lie," Santaxma told him—easily, like a man making an observation about the weather. His eyes, though, seemed capable of looking through stone. "Do you still deny it?"

"Majesty, I do."

"Then there's no point in further discussion." He turned to the Bearer. "You'll get nothing out of him by simple questioning. You need a more direct approach."

"We've talked about this, you and I." The Bearer did not quite look at the King. "I will proceed as I see fit."

"As you saw fit to keep him and his companions in open courtyards instead of imprisoning them properly, thereby making it possible for them to search for one another over the roofs? Fit, perhaps, but not fitting."

"They were not prisoners. They were merely confined."

"A fine point, and one apparently lost on his companions.

Now they run free, fugitives certainly, heretics possibly. Who knows what filthy rumors they will spread among the people, who are already half-mad with counterfeit miracles and the cant of false holy men? You lack the stomach for this sort of thing, Taxmârata." The King used the Bearer's incarnation name, which no one had called him publicly since his election. It was a token of the intimacy they had shared, but in the circumstances it seemed shockingly disrespectful. "You'd be better advised to leave it in my hands. You may still do so, if you wish."

"We have placed enough in your hands already."

"As you will." The King struck the arm of the Bearer's chair lightly with his fingertips—the gesture of a busy man marking an end and moving on. He turned again to Gyalo. "I leave you to your superiors, who will not do with you what I would do. Consider yourself fortunate." He shifted his gaze to Teispas. "This one, though, I will take with me."

"He is to be our guide, Santaxma."

"You'll get him back when I am done. Guard."

Teispas's guard bent to grip him under the arms, hauling him ungently to his feet. He made no sound. His face was still, remote; he had taken his attention from the world and journeyed to some deep place inside himself where he could not be touched. Gyalo felt a slow, disbelieving horror.

"We are not finished here." The Bearer's voice strained a little, as if he had to struggle to modulate it.

"But *I* am finished."

It was not an order. Yet, spoken in the King's brisk, emphatic tones, it carried the force of one. The silence that followed was profound. The Bearer sat like a man of stone, his gaze locked with that of his childhood friend. The expression on his face could not be read; but Vimâta, his shadow, shrank back against the golden bench, his dark eyes huge and fearful.

"We understand each other," the King said. "I'll return within the month. We have much to plan." He bowed low, Arsacian-style, holding the pose. "Great is Ârata. Great is his Way."

There was nothing in his voice or manner to suggest in-sincerity. Yet following on what had gone before, it seemed as artificial as a stage play.

"Go in light," the Bearer said. His lips barely moved.

The King turned, and descended the dais with quick, effi-cient grace. Gyalo prostrated himself again; by the time he rose, Santaxma was halfway across the Pavilion, the guard at his heels, dragging a stumbling Teispas. They passed through the columns into the pale light of the clouded day and were gone. Gyalo stared at the place where they had vanished; its emptiness seemed to resonate, like an echo.

"For shame, Younger Brother." Utamnos broke the silence.

"The man's an Exile." The Bearer did not look at his spirit-sibling. "The King's to command."

"But we are not." Utamnos seemed very frail in the heavy chair, engulfed in his crimson cloak. "You claim too little, Younger Brother, and surrender too much."

"We agreed." The Bearer's face was regaining its anima-tion. "All of us, even you. We have a need, and only he can fill it."

"And when the need is satisfied? When the thing is done? Will he still think to command us, as he did today? Where will it end?"

"It will end when the desert is clean, Older Brother."

"Then it will never end." There was grief in Utamnos's voice. "Do you forget what we have promised?"

The Bearer looked down at Gyalo, an odd melancholy in his face. "Perhaps such things no longer matter."

Gyalo felt an unfolding coldness in his chest. "Old One," he said. "Let me address you."

"We do not wish to hear you."

"But Old One, there are things I must say—matters I've neglected to lay before you—"

"Stop." The Bearer held up his hand.

"But—"

"No more!" The words rolled through the room. "All that is needful has been said," the Bearer continued more qui-etly. "Gyalo Amdo Samchen, your questioning is ended. Tonight you will be taken from Baushpar and conveyed to the monastery of Faal in Isar, there to be confined for your apostasy."

Gyalo felt as if the world had fallen into dream. He groped for words, could not find them.

"Brother." Kudrâcari spoke again. "I renew my protest. We cannot send him away now. The King is right. He must be properly questioned."

The Bearer looked at her. "This has already been decided, Sister."

"I did not dispute your decision to terminate these proceedings, Brother, for I, too, have had enough of them. I accepted your veto of our attempt to impose a charge of heresy—for we can bring the charge again. But on this I cannot be silent. You must interrogate him, and you must do it at once. We must know where his heretic companions have gone. Even now they may have begun to spread the message he sent them out to speak. Can't you see that this has been his intent from the beginning?"

"You know well the question that brought us to this decision, Sister," said the Bearer. "We will certainly pursue his companions. But he will go to Faal, tonight, as we decided."

"Where a whole monastery of vowed Âratists will be vulnerable to his corruption! If you won't question him, at least confine him properly!"

"It will be proper, Sister. Surely you haven't forgotten the restrictions we agreed upon."

"It's not enough!" Her voice scaled upward. "He should be held in isolation, his tongue cut out so he cannot speak, his fingers broken so he cannot hold a pen! This . . . this absurd leniency is based on nothing more than superstition!" There was a scraping sound, as if she had risen roughly to her feet. "Yes, I will say it—superstition! In your fear of what *might* be, you've lost sight of the present danger! Some of us at least know what he is—"

"None of us knows what he is!" The Bearer's anger cracked like a whip. "And it's you, with your arguments and accusations, who have made that so very clear!"

"I'm not alone, Brother," Kudrâcari said. Her voice shook.

"Then challenge me, Sister. Overturn my veto. Can you do it? Do you have half the Brethren with you? No? Then sit down again, and let us be done."

There was a simmering silence. Then came a rustling: Kudrâcari, yielding, returning to her chair. The Bearer brought his attention back to Gyalo. In that stern face Gyalo saw his own ending, as clear as spoken words.

"Old One." He could not get his breath. "I know I must go—but please, not yet. Give me more time."

The Bearer flicked a gesture to the guard at Gyalo's back. "Take him."

The guard gripped his shoulders. He wrenched away, turning toward Utamnos. "Old One!" he cried. "You know what I would say! Speak for me as you did before! Tell them they must hear me!"

"I have spoken for you, Gyalo." Utamnos's dark face looked ashy, sick. "I can do no more."

"Old One—"

The guard seized him again and hauled him to his feet. Panic overcame him. He struggled against the guard's brutal hold. "No!" he shouted. "Let me speak! Let me speak! Let me—"

The guard clamped a hand across his mouth and yanked his arm up behind his back so that he arched with pain. Unable to resist, he felt himself propelled toward the Courtyard of the Sun. A confusion of images wheeled before him—the Bearer, reaching down to rest a hand on Vimâta's smooth black hair; Utamnos, sunken in his chair, one hand raised to cover his eyes; Baushtas, his head turning as Gyalo passed; Kudrâcari, fixing him with a dagger gaze.

Then he was outside. A light rain had begun to fall. He could not understand the moisture on his skin, or the hardness of the walkway under his feet, or even the pain of the guard's grip. The world had fallen into pieces, and nothing in it made sense.

They took him from Baushpar that night, as they had promised.

"If you've anything personal, you can bring it with you," said the guard who came to fetch him.

"No." The sense of dream still possessed him; he was not sure he had actually spoken. He cleared his throat and tried again. "There's nothing."

The guard pointed at his chest. "You must leave that here."

There was a moment of blankness. Then Gyalo realized the guard meant his simulacrum. "But," he said, shocked, "it's mine."

"By the Bearer's orders."

With numb fingers Gyalo lifted the necklace over his head and laid it glinting on the bed. Till then he had remained composed, but this small thing threatened to unhinge him; it took all the will he had to keep from weeping.

The guard took him by the arm and led him swiftly through the halls of the Evening City. They came at last to the stable yard where Gyalo had arrived, in hope and faith, just over three weeks ago. It was still raining; the air was raw and bitingly cold. But for a closed coach such as Dreamers used, with baggage strapped behind and a double team of horses in front, and a sleepy stableboy waiting by the gate, the yard was empty.

The guard took Gyalo's wrist and locked an iron cuff around it. Expecting to be manacled, he held out his other hand, but the guard shook his head and gestured him to the coach. There was another passenger, a Forceless monk wearing the saffron insignia of a manita master. He watched without expression as Gyalo climbed inside, then leaned his head back and shut his eyes, a dismissal as final as a closing door.

The coach shook as the guard mounted to the driver's post on the roof. A pause, a jolt, and they were on their way. Canvas coverings were laced over the windows, closing out the world, but Gyalo knew, by the change in the coach's motion, the exact moment when they passed beyond the western gate and left the cobbled streets of Baushpar behind.

Over the following days he learned the boundaries of his new imprisonment. The coach, built for Dreamers, was well furnished with cushions and blankets to soften the wooden seats, coal boxes for the passengers' feet, and a pair of small lanterns. He spent the whole of the day inside it, released only for brief exercise and to relieve himself. Each morning, the manita master supervised his tether, doling out the drug from a pouch at his waist, watching with hawklike alertness as Gyalo dosed himself, then withdrawing his attention with a completeness that suggested Gyalo ceased to exist between doses. At night they stopped at inns if they could, and by the road if they could not. If there was a bed, Gyalo was fettered to it by a chain linked to the loop on his cuff. When they camped, the guard and the manita master shared a tent, and Gyalo slept beneath the carriage, his chain locked to one of the wheels.

His companions must have been instructed not to speak to him, for they never addressed to him a word they did not have to. He could see their distaste—for him, for the task of guarding him. Still, they were not unkind. If they left the coach, his cuff was padlocked to a bolt set into its wall, but while they were present he was not restrained. The window coverings must be in place when there was traffic, but when the roads were empty he was permitted to unlace them and look out. They saw he was fed, and even, now and then, granted his request to bathe.

He had traveled farther in the past months than he had ever dreamed of traveling, seen and experienced things he could not, two years ago, have conceived. Yet none of it seemed as strange as this long, jolting progress between a past he could hardly bear to think about and a future he did not dare imagine. Sometimes, watching the world roll like a ribbon past the coach's window, or circling a frost-glazed field on his daily exercise, or waking in the night to feel the weight of the chain at his wrist, he was seized by an almost visionary sense of disbelief. He was not here. This was not happening. It was illusion: what he saw, what he felt, what he seemed to remember.

Most of the time, though, it was much too real.

In the hours immediately following his banishment it seemed to him he must have dreamed, that if he blinked or shook his head, all would be as before. That passed quickly: The coach, his silent companions, the monotony of their progress, all instructed him moment by moment in understanding. Yet even so the suddenness of his banishment was difficult to grasp. There had not even been a charge of heresy—for which, belatedly, he was grateful; he did not think he could have borne to lose his sight. Kudrâcari, whose feelings toward him obviously were unchanged, had said something about a termination, a veto; but did that mean the others had wanted to condemn him, and the Bearer had overridden it? Or had the Bearer simply decided, from anger or disgust or simple weariness, to make an end?

The why of it did not matter. He had failed. Oh, he had delivered his message; he had challenged them with questions they could not ignore, Kudrâcari and her supporters notwithstanding. But he had not made them believe. Now, instead of preparing for the coming of the Next Messenger, they gathered to go again into the Burning Land—not in faith and hope, but in mistrust. In the name of the church, they readied themselves to take a free people captive and to execute apostates, some of whom were only children. In Ârata's name, they planned the destruction of a settlement that had been built in heresy but also in testament to a great truth, and was in its own way (as he had come only after leaving it to understand) a sacred wonder.

He had not simply failed: He had made disaster.

You fool, he thought—*you stood in front of them and talked to them of heresy and unbound Shapers. What did you think they would do?* And yet it had seemed to him that, learning to believe, they must, like him, perceive the finitude of the world. They, too, must comprehend that the old verities, the old imperatives, had altered. With Ârata risen, what did it matter that Refuge remained hidden in the Burning

Land? With human history drawing toward a close, what threat could nineteen free Shapers in distant exile truly be?

He had never considered failure. Even after Utamnos came to him, he had not doubted that he could mend things—speak the truth, make them understand. He was not so proud of himself or his abilities; it was simply that Ârata had given him a task, and it was unthinkable he should not accomplish it. *Ârata sees everything, not just one thing*—he had said that to Vâsparis in Thuxra City just after his return, and he struggled, now, to accept it for himself. If his choices had been bad, had not his faith been steadfast? If he had failed, had he not also persevered? Yet he could not quite believe those things would count in his favor. He had made too many mistakes. He was a tool that had failed its use, and one did not save a broken tool: One discarded it.

He thought of Axane and Diasarta, free beyond Baushpar—the only action he had taken, in the past weeks, that had turned out as he intended. How long, though, would that be so? Could they run far enough and fast enough to elude the Brethren's pursuit? He willed himself to believe it. More often, though, he saw Diasarta chained as a deserter, saw Axane bundled off to some harsh nunnery, a captivity very much like the one that had been decreed for him.

She possessed his memory always, but especially at night. At the edge of sleep, hallucinations gripped him, so it seemed he felt her under his hands again, her lips on his, her breath in his mouth. He imagined he had surrendered, and lain with her in her little room; he imagined they had fled Baushpar together and lived as man and wife. They were carnal, these fantasies, but nothing like the feverish visions that had afflicted him as they traveled to Baushpar. The yearning he felt now was more of the heart than of the body.

Did she dream him, as she had promised? He longed for it, as he had longed for water on the pebble plain. Yet he did not want her to see him like this, abject and captive.

More painful was the thought of Teispas. It still seemed impossible he had been caught; he was so careful, so capable, so skilled. Santaxma, who obviously considered the companions' suspected heresy as grave a threat as the Brethren did, would certainly have him interrogated. Teispas would say nothing. Gyalo knew it, as certainly as he had ever known anything. Even unto death the captain would resist.

I failed him, Gyalo thought. *I failed them all.* The shame of that, in its way, was as great as the shame of his botched task.

He could not forget Santaxma, glittering and triumphant in the Pavilion of the Sun. The meaning of the King's presence was starkly clear to him. *We have a need,* the Bearer had said, *and only he can fill it.* The Brethren possessed the funds for their venture into the Burning Land, but not the personnel, for a military force would be required for what they planned. So they had swallowed their scruples and turned for help to the only man who could provide it: the man who had twice conspired to deceive them, the man they knew plotted against them in the Lords' Assembly. In a just world, Santaxma would have provided his aid for nothing— if not for faith, then for fear of nineteen unfettered Shapers. But Utamnos had said something about a promise. Had Santaxma asked a price? Consent for the mining of Thuxra, perhaps?

Gyalo, knowing Ârata risen, knew the mining mattered little. Yet the Brethren, whom he had not brought to belief, could not see it so. Like Santaxma with his machinations in the Lords' Assembly, they had made their bargain in the certainty that Ârata still slept. How urgent they must think their need, to agree to such transgression, to accept such blasphemy. *This must be done,* Utamnos had said bleakly, on the afternoon he visited Gyalo's courtyard; Gyalo had thought it was the Shapers Utamnos meant, the cruelty of their execution. But it seemed to him now that Utamnos had been speaking of Santaxma's price.

Utamnos had turned from him in those final moments. Perhaps he should not feel it as betrayal, and yet he did. Of all of them, Utamnos should have believed him—Utamnos, who had raised him up, who had taught him, who had loved him, whom he had loved. Yet he could still hear the words the old Son had spoken before leaving him that afternoon: *I wish with all my heart we had never thought to go into the Burning Land.* And he could acknowledge now, as he had not been able to acknowledge then, that what he had seen in his former master's eyes was fear.

Old souls the Brethren were—deep in wisdom, mighty in faith. But he had watched them as they argued and goaded and insulted one another in the Pavilion of the Sun; and he understood, as never before, how those souls were bound by the changing bodies that were their vessels. Brief lives strung into a larger one, like beads on an ever-lengthening necklace—a long existence, very long, but not eternal. For its price was the perfected immortality of the new primal age. The close of the Age of Exile, for the rest of humankind both an end and a beginning, was for the Brethren an ending only. Perhaps, in the news Gyalo brought, they had glimpsed their own mortality, and fought, with a wholly human dread of death, to turn away.

Perhaps it was not just upon his own mistakes that his task had foundered.

Once he would have thought it close to blasphemy to consider such things. But now his mind ranged freely forth, and he made no attempt to curb it. Prisoner that he was, it was the only liberty he possessed. And there was a weight to these speculations, a sense of truth, from which he could not turn away.

They journeyed north. The Caryaxists, whose collective agriculture experiments had been concentrated on the rich grain- and pastureland of Arsace's center, had left northern Arsace more or less alone, and the neat villages and trim farmsteads stood little changed from the time before the revolution. Three weeks brought them to the pine forests that cloaked the upper portion of Arsace; there they turned east, heading for the Tarsh mountains. The trees grew in poor soil that did not adapt well to agriculture; there was some timbering at the forest's fringes, but the forest itself was nearly empty of habitation. Progress was slow—in part to spare the horses' strength, in part because of the poor condition of the road, which had received little use during the Caryaxist years.

The fifth week brought them out of the forest and into the Tarsh. Once across the Isaran border the road improved, but the steep grades made the coach impractical, and at the first inn they encountered they exchanged it for three horses and a pair of pack mules. It was more pleasant travel than the endless hours in the stuffy coach, for though the days and nights were cold, the sun shone, and the icy air was sweet. It snowed now and then, but never more than an inch or two, and the winds scoured much of it away.

They made camp one evening in an alpine meadow, framed on all sides by rising mountains, except to the west, where the ground fell away as if some huge hand had cleaved it and it was possible to see for a great distance across a wrinkled sea of peaks. Gyalo sought this precipice after they had eaten. The guard, who once would either have followed or restrained him, had grown more lenient of late, and allowed him to go without demur. He seated himself cross-legged just above the drop, huddling into his cloak against the wind, gazing out at the clear sweep of air before him. The sun was setting, descending through masses of apricot-tinted cloud.

Since leaving the forest, the tenor of his thoughts had changed. He had failed: Very well, that was done, and no amount of regret would change it. But what exactly did his failure mean? Not for him—that seemed plain enough—but for the church of Ârata, for Galea? Ârata had risen; the Next Messenger would arrive, whether or not the church was ready, whether or not humankind was prepared. What did it mean, then, that he had not brought the Brethren to belief? What was the consequence of his failure?

His mood was low that evening; but then it nearly always was. His thoughts were dark; but so had they been at other times. He could not afterward say why, on that particular night, there should be a change in him—a sudden and unbidden shifting of perception, so that all his thoughts grew transparent to new understanding.

Had Ârata truly used him, on the pebble plain?

He had spent much time, these past weeks, tormenting himself with questions. Yet this particular question had never once occurred to him. It filled his mind now with the force of revelation—so simple, so obvious, he could not believe he had never seen it. What was any of it, he thought, but assumption—that the hand of the god had touched him, that his discovery of the Cavern had been intended, that he had been given a task . . . that there was a task at all? What was there to prove that all that had happened had not been simple chance? Beyond doubt, he had confronted a miracle in the Cavern of the Blood. But the revelatory certainty of mission that filled him afterward—was it a true understanding, or had it only risen from his desperation and need— from the shame of his apostasy, the pain of his broken vow, the nascent addiction of his liberated shaping, driving him to spin out of the miracle a tissue of illusion?

Here, at last, was the answer to his question. What was the consequence of his failure? Nothing. For there had never been a task to fail.

I am no better than Risaryâsi, he thought.

His mind emptied into a kind of white horror. He sat on above the precipice as the sun sank, and the air grew bitter. There were footsteps, crunching in the snow, and a presence at his back.

"Come," said the guard. "It's late."

Gyalo climbed to his feet. He felt brittle, as if his bones might shatter if he moved too quickly. Since they reached the mountains, he had been allowed to share his companions' tent, though it was a close fit for three men. He submitted to his nightly chaining—in the absence of the coach, the guard locked the chain around his waist—and lay down on his back. He could feel the precipice's perilous edge inside him, its great falling distances. All night he crouched at its lip and could not turn away.

They reached Faal monastery a few days later.

Over the weeks of travel, Gyalo had tried not to think

about the journey's end. So when he rounded a bend in the cliffside path and saw the monastery below, panic seized him. His hands closed spasmodically on the reins, causing his horse to check, its head tossing.

"Move on!" The guard called from behind, warning in his voice.

How irrationally Gyalo might have behaved, had the guard not been riding at his back (probably for just that reason), he did not know. But even in his fear he had sense enough to see he could not get around the guard on the narrow track, bounded as it was on the right by rising rock and on the left by a sheer drop. He forced his hands to relax, and the horse moved on.

The monastery was made of the local blue-gray stone and roofed with purple slate. Worn and weather-beaten, it rose several stories high, springing from the cliffside as if it had rooted and grown there without human agency. Beside and behind it, gardens were terraced into the slope, brown now and dusted with snow; below, the cliff fell away, and there was nothing but empty air all the way to the valley beneath. In its way, it was a striking place, but as breathtaking as the beauty of the mountains that surrounded it was the utter isolation. Isar, and its neighbor Yahaz, had never fully come to Ârata; like most of Galea in the time before the First Messenger, it worshiped as independent gods a number of deities long recognized by the church of Ârata as Aspects. There were seven Âratist monasteries in the whole of Isar, all of them as remote as Faal. Those who vowed the Way in this land bound themselves to a lonely existence.

As they descended, it became clear that the monastery was not a single structure, as it had seemed on first sight, but three separate buildings, pressed together like slabs of clay and angled to follow the line of the outcrop on which they stood. There were no gates; the track led directly into the courtyard, a great stone-flagged expanse above which the buildings brooded like smaller copies of the cliffs that supported them.

The guard waited with Gyalo while the manita master

went in search of the monastery's administrator. He came quickly, a reed-slim man wrapped in a Shaper's golden stole. Isarans and Yahazites were the result of racial mixing; they had the round eyes and large noses of Arsacians, and the light skins typical of the other kingdoms. The administrator's face was the color of undyed linen, and his eyes seemed to look past, rather than at, what they regarded.

He made a beckoning gesture. "Come."

With an effort of will, Gyalo dismounted. The administrator led him away from the central building, with its great square entrance, to a smaller door in one of the wings. They mounted several flights of stairs and turned down a long hallway. Everything was very plain—the stone of the walls unplastered, the ceiling faced with unvarnished planks, the floors tiled with dull brown-glazed clay. Cast-iron lamps hung from the ceiling's crossbeams, each shedding its own pool of yellow light.

The administrator opened one of the doors and passed into a large room, with red hangings on the walls and a low plank table set before a window. He arranged himself cross-legged behind it, and gestured for Gyalo to kneel.

"Faal monastery has never had an apostate." He folded his hands, marked with devotional tattoos, before him on the surface of the table. "Nor did it ever expect to have one."

Gyalo said nothing. He was short of breath and afflicted by a sense of constriction, as if the ceiling were too low or the walls too narrow. He fixed his eyes on the window at the administrator's back, trying to calm himself. The shutters were partly pushed aside, despite the cold; he could see the sky, the far humped shapes of mountains.

"We have no precedents, therefore, for your care." The administrator's Isaran-accented Arsacian possessed a clipped quality that suggested he found the words distasteful; it was not possible to tell whether this were his normal manner or a reaction evoked by Gyalo himself. "The Brethren, fortunately, understand this. I have been given a list of conditions and requirements. I thought it best to review them with you at once. That way, we may begin as we mean to go on."

Gyalo made himself nod.

"First, you may speak to me, but to no one else. No one at all. Do you understand?"

"Yes."

"If I find you've disobeyed, you will be confined entirely to your room. Second, some contact with the brothers is unavoidable, but it is to be minimized. Your room will be locked when you are in it. Your meals will be brought to you there. I've worked out a schedule whereby you may take exercise and visit the bathhouse when others are not present."

Again Gyalo nodded.

"Third, you will not be allowed writing materials, but you may have anything you wish from the library. Fourth, you may request permission to visit the chapel of Ârata, and any of the Aspect shrines you desire. Fifth, you are to be allowed to take Communion once a month. I shall administer it." He paused. "It has always been my understanding that the sacrament of Communion is a privilege forbidden to apostates. But the Brethren have ordered it, and I will do as they instruct."

His opinion of this was clear, even through the professional impassivity of his expression.

"Your travel companions will depart as soon as your manita master has had a chance to instruct mine. From now on, you are solely in our care. We are not wealthy here. We don't live in luxury, as they do in Rimpang and Baushpar. But you'll have every comfort we ourselves enjoy, save only freedom. It will not be said that Faal was derelict in its duty."

"I understand," Gyalo said.

"Do you have any questions for me?"

Gyalo shook his head.

"If ever you wish to speak with me, make this sign to the brother who brings your food." He extended one pale hand palm out, gripping his wrist with the other. "He was born deaf, and knows no speech. But he'll understand what you mean."

Gyalo nodded.

"Very well then." The administrator rose smoothly to his feet. "I'll take you to your room."

The room was in the central block, on the fifth and highest floor. It was furnished with a low bed, a table with a kneeling cushion, a chest, a few lamps, and a brazier. There was a layer of matting over the tiled floor, but the stone walls were bare. A single unglazed window was set into the outside wall. It was not barred or netted; Gyalo could climb through it if he wished. If he did, though, he would fall to his death, for the window overlooked the plunging drop at the monastery's rear.

The administrator left without a word. Gyalo heard the thud of the closing door, the click of the lock. He stood staring at the blue distances beyond the window, holding himself against the panic that battered in him, urging him to throw himself against the door and howl to be let out. He did not dare move, or blink, or draw too deep a breath, for fear he would lose his grip on this small spar of self-control and drown utterly in the ocean of his horror.

—21—

The first few days at Faal were like walking a skin of ice above a black river. Gyalo drew down into himself, made everything within him slow and quiet. He breathed shallowly, walked carefully, made no sudden moves. He trained his mind upon the moment; he strove to think no farther than the next step.

He was not always successful. Sometimes his thoughts escaped him and fled down the dark corridor of his future; the ice cracked then, and the freezing water roared up around him. Yet it never quite closed over his head. Always he managed to struggle back above the flood.

As time passed and his surroundings grew familiar, he did not need to exercise such rigid self-control. The more he learned to know his chamber and its contents, the more they became for him simply what they were, rather than horrifying reminders of his exile. He no longer forgot where he was during the night; if he spent too long at the window, what he saw when he turned toward the room again did not shock him. The growing knownness of the little space in which he

lived became a sort of haven, a place for his mind to rest—
still close above the flood, but better able to bear his weight.

His routine, such as it was, was invariable. Four times
every day his door was unlocked: once for Faal's manita
master, who supervised his tether just after dawn, and three
times for meals, brought by the deaf attendant, a big young
man with the white stole of a Forceless monk. Every second
day this same attendant fetched him for exercise, leading
him out of the monastery and walking behind him, like a
drover with a prize cow, as he crossed the courtyard and
paced a little way up the track. Once a week the attendant
delivered him to the bathhouse, helpfully pouring buckets of
water to rinse the soap, then standing by as Gyalo soaked
briefly in the copper tub.

It was apparent the young monk did not know who or
what Gyalo was, for he did not hold his face distastefully expressionless, like the administrator, or avert his eyes and
make the sign of Ârata, like the brothers they occasionally
encountered in the hallways or the courtyard. Sometimes he
made signs, clumsy sweeping and clutching motions of his
hands, seeming disappointed when Gyalo shook his head or
shrugged. For all that, he understood his duty well enough.
He never failed to lock the door, and when they were abroad
kept close on Gyalo's heels.

Gyalo did not really need a guard, of course, or even a
lock on the door. His tether, so large now there was every
chance he would not survive withdrawal, was an imprisonment as effective as iron bars. It was the rest of the
monastery the young monk guarded—against the taint of his
apostasy, the danger of the beliefs of which the Brethren
suspected him.

And yet his status was not quite so unambiguous. He had
guessed this even before he reached Faal, and discovered the
odd conditions of his exile—that he was to be far more prisoned than ordinary apostates were, yet allowed a privilege
apostates were prohibited: the solace of worship and Communion. This was not a thing the Brethren gave him: It was a

thing they did not dare deny him, just as they had not dared to blind him as a heretic. *None of us knows what he is*, the Bearer had said, that last day in the Pavilion of the Sun. Forced to consider the possibility of a false Next Messenger, they must also have been confronted by the chance he was not false at all.

How ironic, and how bitter, that they should have arrived at the same point of question he had left behind in the Burning Land. He could have told them this, and explained how he had passed beyond it; but they had had him dragged away before he could speak. How they must have feared what he would say! What a burden of decision they would have faced, if he had actually proclaimed himself the Next Messenger. Even in denial, the questions would remain. Easier just to silence him; easier simply to banish him to Faal—a sentence appropriate for the apostate he indisputably was, but that, should he prove to be what they could no longer say with certainty he was not, was not irrevocable—and let time prove it one way or the other.

He spent many hours at his window. He had drawn the table up beneath it and folded a quilt into a bolster so he could kneel in comfort with his elbows resting on the sill. It was a spectacular view, all the way across the valley to the far gray peaks on the other side. Most of the valley floor was neatly stitched into a patchwork of fields, showing brown through their covering of snow. At the center lay a lake shaped like a pointing finger, the color of lead in shadow but lapis blue when the sun struck it; a town sprawled along its southern shore. It was like looking down into the bottom of a bowl. Still, he was close enough to make out fishing craft on the lake, beasts in the fields, the traffic that passed along the roadway—a little pocket world, above which he hung as fixed and permanent as a star.

When he had been a month at Faal, he made the sign the administrator had showed him when his attendant brought his noonday meal. The young monk smiled and nodded, as he always did; Gyalo was not really sure he understood. But soon he heard the sound of the lock, and the administrator entered.

"You wanted to see me?" he asked, his pale face blandly composed.

"I'd like to visit the chapel of Ârata."

"I won't have the freedom to attend to you until tomorrow morning."

"I don't wish to take Communion. I want to spend time in the chapel. Half an hour, perhaps."

The administrator looked at him. "It must still be tomorrow."

"Very well."

"I'll see to it."

The young monk came for Gyalo the following afternoon. The chapel was located on the ground floor, at the back of the monastery's central block. Like everything in the place, it was austere, with plain cut-stone walls and a utilitarian tiled floor. Its ceiling was beautiful, though, a smooth arch of formed planks painted red and gold in alternating bands. A row of narrow windows ran down the outside wall, each framing a slice of the view across the valley.

At the chapel's far end reclined an image of Ârata Eon Sleeper. He was sculpted of some glossy golden stone, portrayed unusually not as a beautiful youth but as a mature man. His body bore no adornment of jewels or gilding, and there was no elaborate composition or stylization: He was just a man, grievously wounded, who might be either dead or sleeping. The artist had been very skilled; there was both pain and strength in the unconscious face, the long loose limbs, the muscled torso.

An altar stood before the image, with a little heap of ribbons and papers and amulets gathered ready for that evening's Banishing ceremony. Gyalo knelt before it. He rested his eyes on Ârata and schooled himself to quiet—not attempting meditation, simply seeking a state in which his mind could rest. There were no braziers, and the room was cold; the floor quickly numbed his knees through the linen of his trousers. He knelt on, finding a kind of equilibrium in his discomfort, until his attendant touched him on the shoulder and signaled that it was time to go.

Back in his chamber, he went to crouch before the window, gazing sightlessly down at the valley below. His faith had never needed the bolstering of temples or images. From the time he was quite young he had been able to meditate easily—to find identity, in his small human way, with Ârata's transcendent unconsciousness. He had embraced the god's silence as a mystery of faith; even after he understood Ârata awake, the silence no longer slumber but choice, it had been possible to do that. But since his banishment, he seemed to have lost touch with such things. He had not meditated at all during the journey, unable to summon up the will. Now he tried, and could not lose himself. When he attempted to pray, as he had sometimes done in the Burning Land, Ârata's silence was a roaring in his mind, and the words of his prayers flew back at him, like ashes tossed into the wind.

He had thought it might be different in the chapel. It had not been. It seemed to him this should trouble him more than it did. Lately he had been conscious of a flatness within himself, a kind of dwindling. Hunger, boredom, fatigue, the interest of the view beyond his window, the pain when he struck his shin against the low edge of the table—all such things seemed indistinct, attenuated. Even the black river did not seem so close these days. Perhaps it was aftermath—an exhaustion born of too much experience, an emotional cautery like the numbness that follows on traumatic injury. But sometimes he wondered if the ice he walked so carefully were thickening, and he was freezing with it, moving slowly toward some permanent inner winter.

Would that be so bad? he thought. *If I must spend the rest of my life in Faal, would it not be easier to do so without feeling?*

He still stood on that precipice inside his mind. There had actually been a sort of comfort, once the first shock passed, in thinking he might have been so wrong. If there had been no task, there could be no failure. If there were no divine intent behind what he had done, his mistakes held no cosmic significance, no meaning at all beyond themselves. It did not make them any less humiliating, nor did it relieve him of responsibility for his companions' fate—or for Refuge's. But oh, to think he had not failed the god, that he had not been cast from Baushpar with a task undone! Oh, to imagine himself only a deluded fool!

Yet even in the sharpness of his disillusion, he could not quite bring himself to believe it. He understood, as never in his life before, the danger of assumption, no matter the knowledge on which it was based. To fear he had been wrong in the Cavern of the Blood was to recognize the fallibility of all his understandings, even this one. He could suspect the truth, but he could not know it—not for certain, not as he had once thought he knew it in Refuge. Ârata's rising he did not doubt. But he did not think he could be so sure of anything else, ever again.

Belief had always come easily to him. He had struggled with aspects of his vocation, but never with the service he had chosen. Faith had mapped his life; the Way of Ârata had been a broad, level road along which he confidently pursued his earthly journey, its precepts clear-written markers by which all his choices might be guided. He was not a fool: He knew there would be joy and achievement, but also pain and hardship. He knew he would stumble, and fall, and fail. But there was nothing, he had believed, from which faith could not forge understanding.

In the Burning Land, he had gone beyond the map. Even so he had had the signposts of the Way to guide him. He had walked in the footsteps of the First Messenger; he had learned the hidden abundance of the Burning Land and seen in it the fecundity of Ârata himself. Breaking his vow on the pebble plain, he had still been bound by faith—for he had known what he should not do and had chosen even so to do it. Even in the question of the Next Messenger, belief had directed him, for he had thought to yield the inquiry into wiser hands. As for the Cavern of the Blood . . . the understanding had been absolute, immediate, ravishing. There had been no questions, none at all.

But he no longer trusted his own perceptions. If one could believe so deeply and still go so far astray, what certainty could there ever be? For the first time in his life, faith offered him no standard by which to choose.

And why should I choose? he thought. He was bound in Faal, and would go nowhere else ever again. Why should he not remain where he was inside himself as well, on the precipice's edge—unable to launch himself entirely into doubt, knowing too much to turn away? Why should he not allow himself to change slowly into ice?

This is a darkness, he thought, *and if I follow it, my soul will be blackened even more than it is already.* Yet just as part of him longed to be a fool and not a failure, there was temptation in the cold. Not to feel. Not to regret. To look back, and find his life as small, as distant as the world below his window.

His mind ran much upon the past these days. Not the recent past, which he had all but worn out with thinking, but his youth—his childhood, his postulancy, his early training. He thought especially of his father, and of how his father had tried to get him back after his mother died, though he could not say why his thoughts should return so often to these fragmentary memories. His father and several comrades had tried to storm the monastery and bring him out by force; there had been commotion in the hallways, pounding on the outside doors, shouting. His father had cried his name— Gyalo had heard the cries even through the walls of the storeroom where the old brother who watched him took him to hide. They made him desperate; at one point he scrambled to his feet, ready to yield, to go out to this man he barely knew, just to make it stop. But the brother had reached out to him, and he had crouched again, weeping—whether for fear or anger, he could not recall. He could still feel the brother's hand upon his back, patting him in awkward comfort.

He had been relieved, the year after, when he learned of

his father's death. Now no one could stop him from vowing the Way, from serving Ârata all his days. Had he grieved at all? He could not remember. It shamed him to think he might not have.

It was a strange thing to come to, after so many years.

The sun had dropped behind the peaks. The valley floor was in shadow, and he could see the flicker of lights in the town. He turned from the window, back to his dim room. Time to kindle the lamps. Soon his silent attendant would bring his supper and take away the dishes from his noonday meal. He would kneel at the table and eat his food, then read a while—poetry, perhaps, or one of the historical treatises he had requested. Then he would wash his face and body at the basin his attendant filled each morning, and go to bed. He would sleep. Tomorrow it would begin again.

Winter drew on, bringing storms and wind, then, reluctantly, retreated. The air grew mild. Snow melted off the monastery's roofs; all day long water fell past Gyalo's window. In the valley the fields were plowed, then planted. At Thuxra Notch also, spring would have unlocked the ice. The army the Brethren had bought from Santaxma would be assembling, gathering at Thuxra City, preparing for the march on Refuge.

One summer night he came suddenly out of a sound slumber, with the sense that something had woken him. He lay, listening, but could hear no sound. The silence of the monastery was complete, as deep as the distance between it and the valley below.

He sat up. He had left his shutters open to the balmy air. The full moon hung in his window as if some hand had pinned it there, pale as a pearl. His heart beat too fast; a strange anticipation gripped him, like light running under his skin. What had he dreamed, to wake this way? But he could not remember dreaming.

Then it came: a scraping noise outside his chamber. Faal kept dogs for vermin-hunting, but even so there were rats; he sometimes heard them scratching and scurrying in the hall and under the floor. But this was no rat: The noise of metal on metal was unmistakable. It was a tiny sound, but in the quiet it seemed loud as a thunderclap. Someone was trying to get into his room.

He had been waiting for this, he realized—for the stealthy entrance in the night, the mortal blow, the choking grip. In many ways, it would be welcome. Yet he could not lie helpless on his back and let it happen. He slid out of bed and crossed the room, pressing himself into the corner farthest from the door. The outer walls still held winter in their stones; cold ate through the wool of his bedgown. But the white moonlight flooding through the window would show him at once the face of whoever came through his door, while he would be cloaked in shadow.

The lock clicked. The door swung open. A man slipped through. He was dressed in dark clothing, and a bag hung over his shoulder. He turned. Moonlight fell across his face, and Gyalo realized he was dreaming. For it seemed to him the man was Diasarta.

Diasarta stepped toward the bed. He checked, seeing it was empty; his head came up, and he scanned the room. His eyes found Gyalo—a shadow in the shadows, but not shadowy enough to elude night-adapted eyes. He came limping swiftly across the chamber, his hands rising. Gyalo felt no surprise; the logic of dreams made it perfectly sensible that Diasarta had come to kill him.

A few paces away Diasarta stopped. His hands fell. "Brother Gyalo." His whisper was breathless. "It *is* you. For a minute I thought I had the wrong room."

Gyalo stared at him.

"It's me, Brother. Diasarta. Don't you know me?" He stepped closer. "What's wrong? Have they done something to you?"

Gyalo reached down deep within himself, and dredged up words. "You're a dream."

"No!" Diasarta whispered a laugh. He closed the distance

between them and took Gyalo's shoulders in a warm, firm grip. "See? No dream. I'm as real as you."

"No."

"Yes!" He shook Gyalo a little. "Brother, you're half-asleep. Wake up!"

"But . . . but how . . . what . . ." The world seemed to swing around; Gyalo caught at Diasarta's wrists to balance himself. "How did you . . . how could you possibly know where I am?"

Diasarta grinned. "Every man has his price. Even the Brethren's scribes."

"You . . . bribed the Brethren's scribes?"

"Just the one."

"Wait. I—I can't . . . I can't get my mind around this. I never thought—I never expected . . ."

"Come, Brother. Better sit down." Gently, Diasarta urged him over to the bed, and supported him as he half fell upon it. "Put your head down. That's right. Now breathe deep."

Eventually the room stopped spinning.

"Better, Brother?" Diasarta knelt before him. The soldier's back was to the window; silver moonlight shawled his shoulders.

"I can't remember the last time I spoke aloud," Gyalo said. "I don't think I've said a word to anyone for . . . well, weeks, at any rate."

"Now you'll be able to talk all you like."

"You were supposed to go somewhere safe, Diasarta. You were supposed to escape."

"I did. I'm here, aren't I?"

"Where's Axane?"

Diasarta looked down at his hands, braced on his knees. "I lost her. We ran, when Teispas was captured. All those bloody twisty streets—we got separated. I searched everywhere. I never found her."

"Did she—did they—"

"Catch her? I don't think so. They were still looking for both of us when I left Baushpar."

So she was free. And alone . . . but that was what she had wanted. "You saw Tcispas captured?"

"Yes." Again Diasarta looked away. "It was my fault."

"Your fault?"

"The walls were high, so he'd twisted sheets for a rope. There was a roof that ran right up against the walls—he tied one end to the ridge tiles. He held it while Axane and I went down. When I turned around, he was drawing up the rope. I saw he meant to go back. I didn't think—I just jumped and caught it. He pulled, and I . . . I pulled, too. Enemy take me, I know it was stupid, but I wasn't thinking straight. He slipped. Tiles came loose—the noise they made was like thunder. We heard shouting. I yelled at him to jump, but he untied the rope and threw it down and turned away. We ran." Painfully, he said, "What else could we do?"

"He was going back? Back inside?"

"Yes. I don't think he ever meant to come with us."

Gyalo closed his eyes. "Ah, Ârata," he said. "Stupid, stupid man. What did he think he could accomplish by staying?"

"Anyway." Diasarta shrugged, not carelessly, but as if pushing off bad memories. "I set myself to try and find out what had become of you. It took a while. And then I had to get myself here, and that took longer. Then I had to find out where they were keeping you. I was close to a month working in the kitchens here, and bloody horrible it was, too." He drew a long breath. "I'm sorry, Brother. I'm sorry I couldn't be quicker."

"Why? I never expected to see you at all."

"Well. Now I've found you. We can go."

"Go?"

"Why do you think I'm here? I've come to take you out of Faal."

Once again Gyalo's head was spinning. "That's impossible."

"Everything's prepared, Brother. We can leave right now."

"But—"

"What's wrong, Brother? Don't you want to escape?"

In fact Gyalo had never once thought of it. Now and then

he still found himself speculating about what might have happened if he had chosen to leave Baushpar; and he had not been able to prevent himself from leaning out his window and wondering how it would feel to fall. But escape—actual exit, alive, from Faal—was something it had never occurred to him to imagine.

Now he did imagine it—clumsily, fumblingly, as if he were employing a sense he had not used in some time. Escape. A life not spent between these walls—a life of open air and unfettered motion, of speaking and being spoken to, of choosing for himself, hour by hour, what to do. A secular life—for the church, his vows of service, would be left behind forever. A fugitive life—for he would have to take a different name, fabricate a different history. An apostate life. For his shaping would be unbound.

Desire burst in him—deep, painful, like tearing open an old injury. It had been a long time since he had felt anything so keenly. To be free. To be in the world. To have his shaping alive within him again; to see again with Shaper eyes. Ah, he wanted that, more than anything in the world. Did apostasy still mean what it had, at the end of the Age of Exile? Must the Doctrine of Baushpar, the rule the church had made to protect the world during the time of Ârata's slumber, still be followed now that the god had woken? Did he still owe allegiance to the Brethren, who had turned from the truth of Ârata's rising? Whether or not that turning had been his fault, he had come to understand, beyond doubt, that it was also theirs.

He caught his breath. This was the voice of his addiction, he thought, the craving of his tethered ability—the madness that could never be cured or mastered, the reason he was closed up in this little room. His apostasy on the pebble plain had been a choice, but it had been brought on him by circumstances beyond his control. If he freed himself now it would be truly corrupt, for it would be entirely deliberate, forced by no hand but his own. There was the manita withdrawal, too—how could he go through that again? Would he even survive it? And if by some miracle he did, how would he live without the church to order his hours, to dictate his employment, to overlook his actions? How would he support himself?

"Brother." It was Diasarta, patient on his knees. "Is it the manita sickness you're afraid of? I'll be there to tend you. I took manita from the store here—I thought maybe you wouldn't get so sick if you didn't have to stop taking it all at once."

"My dose is much higher than it was, Diasarta. Even gradually . . . the withdrawal might kill me." The shadow of that awful nausea clutched at him as he said it. "Anyway, they wouldn't just let me go. They'll send people after us."

"No." Diasarta nodded toward the window. "When they come to your room tomorrow and find it locked from the outside and you gone, they'll think you jumped."

"But then they'll discover that you and I disappeared at the same time. That's too much of a coincidence."

"Oh, I'm cleverer than that. I quit my post two weeks ago. Besides, when they go down the cliffs to search for you, they'll find what they're looking for."

"What—"

"Best not to ask." Diasarta's face had hardened. "You see, Brother, I've thought of everything."

It seemed he had.

"You can tell me no if you want to, Brother. I'll not force you. But I swore an oath to Teispas I'd see you safe if he couldn't, and I mean to keep it. If you refuse tonight, I'll come back. I'll come back as many times as I have to, till you say yes."

"Why would you do this?" Gyalo said wonderingly. "Why would you tie your life to mine this way?"

"You really are a fool, Brother, Ârata burn me for saying so. Don't you remember I told you once I'd follow you anywhere?"

Gyalo felt his heart contract. "You can't still believe I'm the Next Messenger, after all that's happened."

Diasarta shook his head. "Maybe if *you* believed it, Brother, you wouldn't be here."

Gyalo stared at the soldier. Something moved in him—

turning, shifting, as it had on the precipice, traveling to Faal. And he thought: *Is it not that I've believed too much, but that I have not believed enough?*

Did Ârata look at him, out of Diasarta's eyes?

It was only the edge of an idea, the shadow of an intuition. Yet he saw at once where it might take him, if he let it.

"You must decide now, Brother." Diasarta's whisper was urgent. "I can't wait much longer. We must be well away by dawn."

Gyalo closed his eyes. *Ârata, guide me,* he thought. *Is this your will, or is it only mine? Is it your call I hear, or am I spinning more illusion?*

There was no answer. So had it always been. So, perhaps, it would always be. Yet all his life he had believed, in defiance of that silence. Was that not, in the end, what faith was—a shout into the void, a choice made in the dark? It terrified him, the darkness, for this time the choice was entirely his: There was no imperative of survival, no religious miracle, no guideposts at all. Yet was it not better to choose, even wrongly, than to stand always on the edge looking down?

He opened his eyes. He drew a breath. "I'll come with you."

Diasarta's face broke into a grin. He swung the bag off his shoulder. "I've brought you clothes. Leave your gown—they have to think you died naked."

Gyalo stripped off his bedgown° and pulled on the garments Diasarta gave him. Dread and exaltation filled him. Diasarta took up the bag again. They moved to the door. Gyalo glanced back; the moon watched them through the window, a round, knowing eye. For no reason at all he thought of his father, and of the day he had decided to remain in Rimpang. That choice had bound him to Ârata's church. This one severed him from it forever.

In the corridor, Diasarta pulled the door closed and knelt, working some instrument in the lock. It clicked. He tried it to make sure, then took Gyalo's arm and set off swiftly down the vacant hall. Gyalo let himself be guided. His heart raced; he felt sick, as if the manita withdrawal were already upon him. The world had never seemed so huge, or so quiet.

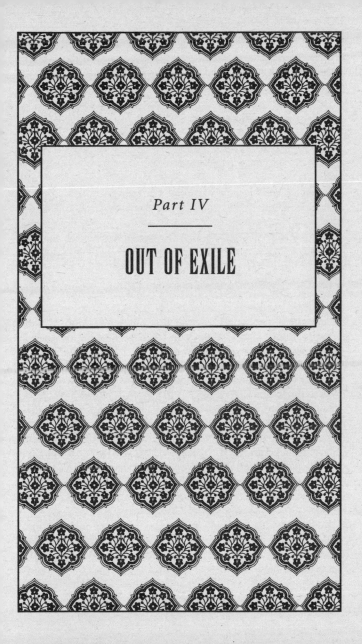

Part IV

OUT OF EXILE

— 22 —

Axane sat waiting, her knees drawn to her chest and her arms
wrapped around them. The light of late afternoon pierced
the heavy canvas of the tent, bathing the interior in a ruddy
gloom. It was so hot she could barely breathe. At her feet lay
a blanket roll, a bundle of clothing, a food bag, and two full
waterskins, bound to a frame to carry on her back. Outside
the tent, the stone barrens spread vastly out beneath the hammer of the sun. Their southern margin lay perhaps two days
distant—and beyond them, Refuge.

In a little while, when the sun fell far enough, it would be
time for her to go.

She glanced to her left, where Vâsparis lay deep asleep.
He had been astonishingly kind to her over the six months of
the journey; it troubled her that she had offered so little in return, apart from her healing skills, which he had scarcely
needed. Once, a few weeks after they left Thuxra City, he
had reached out in the night and placed his hand on her
shoulder; she had lifted it and returned it to him, and he had
not tried again.

He had come to visit her soon after she arrived at Thuxra,

in the bedroom where Kaluela had hidden her. Axane did not know how the other woman managed to arrange it, for the force—really, a small army—that had been assembled to march on Refuge was strictly segregated from Thuxra's ordinary population, living in a separate camp outside Thuxra's walls. Vâsparis arrived in the middle of the afternoon, when most of Thuxra was sleeping—a better time for secret visits, according to Kaluela, than the late hours of the night.

He was as brown and leathery as Axane remembered, but much fitter, though his left arm hung mostly useless at his side. He asked after Gyalo; she knew they had been friendly but had no idea if he were aware of Gyalo's apostasy, and anyway had little desire to talk about what had happened, so she said she had not seen him after they reached the Evening City and did not know what had become of him. She had already practiced the lie on Kaluela; it came a little easier the second time.

"A good man, Brother Gyalo," Vâsparis said. "I owe him some peace of mind. I hope he's prospering."

She had to look away.

"So. The mistress says you want to cross the Land."

"Yes." She told him the story she had prepared: that she was homesick, tired of life in a strange place and desperate to rejoin her people; that she had run away from the Evening City, where the Brethren wanted to keep her, and returned here, thinking to follow the army back to Refuge; that she had tried to attach herself to it but had been turned away. This story, too, she had given Kaluela, who, sentimental and kind, had not questioned it. But she was aware that Vâsparis, who was to be the army's guide and surely knew the real reason it marched on Refuge, might not be so accepting. Around them, the sleeping house was silent; the scent of flowers drifted through the window screens.

When she was finished, he said at once: "That's easily solved. I'll tell 'em you're my wife. I was in Ninyâser more than a month before they hired me back—I'll say we met and married then."

For a moment she was too surprised to speak. She had been thinking more along the lines of disguising herself as a boy and asking him to get her taken on as a servant or a cook. "They said no women. Though I did see women in the camp."

"Yes—wives. Or at any rate, those with a man to say they are. It's not official, but so long as they've some useful skill the officers don't make a fuss."

She shook her head. "Why should you do this for me, Vâsparis?"

He gave her a steady look. "I'm only guessing, lady, and you'll forgive me if I'm wrong. But you were in the Evening City, and I'm thinking you know more about what's in store for your people than you're letting on. I'm thinking it's not just for homesickness you want to get back across the Land."

She felt herself flush. "I—"

"No." He held up a hand. "You don't have to explain. If I was in your shoes, I'd probably do the same."

"But . . . but . . . why should you help me? I mean, if you know I want to warn them . . ."

He watched her with his strange light eyes. "That army out there isn't exactly what you think. When it marches out, twenty-five untethered Shapers will be part of it."

"Untethered Shapers?" She still did not feel confident in her comprehension of the outside world's strange proscriptions of shaping, but she had seen enough, these past months, to understand clearly the consequence of trespass. "But that's forbidden."

"Indeed it is. But no rule's a rule if you need it not to be, so long as you're the one who made the rule in the first place—if you take my meaning, lady. In times of dire danger, Shapers can be unbound by order of the Brethren—so they've told us, at any rate."

"The *Brethren*?" She felt a shock of pure outrage. "They freed their Shapers, when they mean to murder Refuge's Shapers for being free?"

"That's right." Vâsparis did not ask how she knew about the plan for Refuge's Shapers, just as he had not asked how she had known about the army. "The army couldn't get across the Burning Land without 'em, never mind back again with all your people with them—there's not enough camels in the world to carry supplies for so many, and I could never scout enough water. And once we get to Refuge . . . well. The army's carrying manita—more than King Vantyas himself had, I'll wager. But they want to be sure. They say your Shapers are very strong."

"Did they say that some of them are children who've hardly begun their training?" Axane asked bitterly.

"Oh, we've heard plenty of stories about your people, lady. Heresy, apostate Shapers, blasphemous ceremonies, all kinds of dark tales—most of 'em lies, if I'm any judge, but even if it was true, I can't say it'd mean much to me. What's the difference what your people do, so long as they keep it to themselves? To my mind, this trip's a dirty business. The way things are right now . . . well, it just seems to me the odds need a bit of evening."

She looked down at her hands, folded in her lap, trying not to weep. "I'm very grateful. Thank you."

"Now, you mustn't repeat any of this, not even to the mistress here. Thuxra knows only that we go to finish what the other expedition started, and bring the lost Âratists back—it hasn't even been said that they're heretics."

She nodded.

"Once we get there, you'll be on your own. I won't be able to help you then."

"I understand." She hesitated. "Vâsparis—if you don't like what the army is doing, why did you agree to guide it?"

"You think they told me any of this before I signed on? They hadn't planned to use me at all, you know. There was another fellow set to go, one of those who came back with you. But it didn't work out, so they turned to me." He looked at her. "If I'm honest, lady, I can't say I'd've told 'em no, even if I had known. To travel the Land again . . ." He paused, shook his head. "Ârata help me, but that month in Ninyâser was the worst of my life."

"I won't be a burden to you, Vâsparis, I promise."

"You were born to the Land. I'll wager you'll do better than most." He got to his feet. "I'll go now and beg an audience with the commander. I'll send for you as soon as I may."

"Send for me?"

"If you're to be my wife, it'll look odd if we don't live together, wouldn't you say? Don't worry—you've nothing to fear from me. You'll have your own side of the tent."

"I didn't mean—I'm sorry. I hadn't thought of it."

He grinned, his sun-black face creasing. "Till then, lady."

She sat on after he had gone, thinking of the peril that threatened Refuge, much greater even than she had known. The army's manita did not surprise her, for she remembered what Gyalo had told her about the Shaper War. But twenty-five unbound Shapers . . . They were not trained to act in concert as the Shapers of Refuge were; they were inexperienced in the free use of their ability, and perhaps would be clumsy, as Gyalo had been. But Refuge had had only eight Shapers ordained when she left it. She had been gone more than a year—Sonhauka might by now have taken his place among them, and of course there was Râvar, with his huge gift; but either Gâvarti or Jândaste or both might have died, so the total number might not have changed. As for the others, they were trainees in various stages of learning, from Axane's cousin Randarid, not long past his conversion, to the two fifteen-year-old girls—sixteen, now—who were oldest after Râvar.

She felt the outrage again, so sharp it made her shudder. *Hypocrites,* she thought. *Vile, arrogant hypocrites.* She had not thought she could learn any evil thing about the Brethren that would surprise her. But this she would never have imagined.

She had seen at once she must go back, on the night Gyalo came to her—an understanding so certain, so absolute, it was as if she had always known it must come to this. Even so, she had tried to argue herself out of it. She no longer hated Refuge—knew, in fact, that she never really had, for to feel separate from a place, to chafe at its restrictions, was not the same as hatred. Strangely, it was the Brethren who had shown her this, with their angry questions, their strange suspicions, their rich contempt. They had made a kind of mirror for her, in which she perceived, as never when she had been there, the wonder and worthiness of her birthplace.

And yet she would not by choice have turned toward Refuge again, even for the sake of her father, whom she missed with a sadness that partook as much of guilt as it did of love. She understood she could not have Gyalo, whom she wanted most of all things in the world—but she had also, deeply, wanted the life that beckoned her in Refuge, the life whose shape she had glimpsed so clearly when she passed through Ninyâser on the way to Baushpar. Until Gyalo told her of the fate decreed for her people, she had believed that life would be hers; it was like dying to know she must give it up. She sat for hours after he left her, enumerating to herself the difficulties of return, the odds against success; but even as she did, she recognized that her deeper mind, her deeper heart, was set. Once before, she had known the truth and done nothing. She could not make that choice again. This disaster, after all, was partly of her making. At last she surrendered to certainty and to grief—grief for Gyalo, grief for her own lost freedom—and wept as she had not wept since her mother vanished into the House of Dreams.

She had always intended to slip away from Teispas and Diasarta after they were free, for she knew that if they discovered her intent, one or both of them would insist on accompanying her, and she could not bear the thought of forcing them into the Burning Land again. She wasted no time, therefore, searching for Diasarta after they lost each other in the aftermath of the disastrous exit from the Evening City. From an untended wash line in an unlocked courtyard she stole boy's clothing, bound her hair up under the wrapped head covering worn by Arsacian laborers, and left Baushpar.

She was not foolish enough to imagine she could cross the Burning Land alone. From the beginning, she had planned to find a way to attach herself to whatever force the Brethren sent to Refuge. She had no idea what the force would be, or when and where it would assemble, but it must, logically, pass through Thuxra City, so that was where she headed. She recalled almost nothing of the way she and Gyalo and Teispas and Diasarta had traveled, and had to seek assistance—asking not for Thuxra Notch, which she feared might seem suspicious, but for the first town they had come to after the great steppes beyond the Range of Clouds, whose name, Fashir, she had managed to remember. When questioned, she answered with a story of her parents' death, which forced her to travel to her brother there.

Past Ninyâser, she abandoned her boy's disguise. She knew the Brethren must be seeking her, but she needed her healing skills to exchange for food and shelter, and no woman would accept a laborer boy as midwife. She had reason yet again to be grateful to Kaluela, for the gowns the administrator's wife had given her, though increasingly shabby and travel worn, were recognizably of good quality, and supported her tale of a respectable woman fallen upon hard times.

It was a miserable journey—far more miserable, in its way, than the long trek across the Burning Land. It was winter by then, and cold in a way that she had not known was possible. Many of the people she encountered were kind, offering shelter or meals or rides in the backs of carts or wagons; but most were indifferent, glad to accept her skill in exchange for food or a bed, equally ready to turn away if she had nothing they wanted. And some were cruel, taking her for a beggar and chasing her off with stones or sticks. She came to understand more clearly how difficult it would have been to make a life for herself, alone in an alien world. Still, she thought she could have done it if she had had the chance; and in each town she passed, with each healing service she performed, she could not help but think of how it might have been if she could have stayed.

She grieved for her companions—for Teispas, discovered on the roofs of the Evening City; for Diasarta, who, if he had not been caught, was a fugitive like herself. Night after night she willed herself to dream of them. But she was not tied to them as she was to Gyalo, and the old unpredictability of her dreaming betrayed her. Not once had she seen them in her sleep.

Gyalo she did see, and wished she did not.

She promised when he left her that she would dream him. But after he was gone she could not bear the thought of it, and for three nights after she left Baushpar she did not allow herself to sleep, desperate to outdistance the bond that drew her Dreams to him. At last staggering exhaustion forced her to take shelter in a barn. Even as she slid into slumber, she knew the weary distance she had walked was not enough. She could feel the tidal pull of him, like a cord around her heart.

She came upon him not in the Evening City, as she expected, but outdoors, sleeping on blankets beneath a large wheeled conveyance of some kind. Shocked at the change, transfixed by the pain of seeing him again, she did not at once notice the odd way his arm was stretched above his head. Then she did, and saw the thick cuff that locked his wrist, the chain wrapped around the carriage wheel.

Understanding wrenched her awake. She lay stiffly, staring into the soft, animal-smelling darkness of the barn, too desolate even to weep. It had come for him, then, the end he had predicted. He was a prisoner, journeying into exile.

She had not really believed him in the Burning Land, when he explained how the Brethren would view his apostasy. The rules and limitations he described made no sense to her, and even his tale of the Shaper War did not render them less absurd. How could it be a sin to save one's own life, the lives of one's companions, if one had the means to do so? Would the Brethren have expected him, slipping off a cliff, not to put out a hand to save himself? But when she stood before them at last, and looked into their faces as he told them what he had done, she saw she had been wrong. It was true—all of it, exactly as he had said.

It was her fault, too, what had happened to him—though she knew that only in hindsight. Gyalo had spoken to her of faith, on the journey from Refuge: of the real Way of Ârata, the correct belief from which Risaryâsi and her descendants had strayed. But his talk of the two Messengers, of the single flow of time, of the imminence of the world's ending now that Ârata was awake, did not settle in her with any greater weight than Risaryâsi's story, which she had long recognized as false. All her life she had known Ârata awake, but she could feel him no more closely now than she ever had. Every day she looked upon the world, which in its growing and withering and multiplying and dying created itself afresh with each passing moment, and try as she would she simply could not believe that all that multiplicity and change could simply stop, simply finish. She did her best to hide this from the Brethren—but everything she said to them was hollow, and she knew, as certainly as she knew the rhythms of her own body, that they perceived it. Nor was she able to bear their contempt for Refuge. As time went on she became more and more unwilling to condemn it as they urged her to do.

She had understood that her defiance might bring punishment for her. But she had never thought that what she did and said might reflect upon Gyalo. She had sensed their aversion to him, their skepticism of his message; but not until much too late did she realize that she must have helped to make it so.

With all her heart, she wished she had never given him the crystal of the Blood. In fearing what might come of that, she had seen what it might cause others to believe of him—a fear she had been quite correct in dismissing, for the Brethren, coldly interrogating her about the crystal and why she had taken it, clearly had not for an instant mistaken Gyalo for the Next Messenger (though they seemed to think it possible she might have done so). But it had not occurred to her to consider what it might cause him to believe about himself. He had never actually said he thought himself the Next Messenger; the one time they spoke of it he had seemed to shrink from the idea. But why else would he have gone on so stubbornly, in the face of the Brethren's adamant rejection? Why else would he have refused to leave Baushpar, when the possibility of escape was offered? Perhaps he had believed he would be saved—that Ârata would put out a hand before the end and rescue him. Did he still wait for that deliverance, in his imprisonment?

She knew well it would not come. The force of Teispas's faith had briefly shaken her, in the Burning Land, for she had not quite left behind the shadowy intimation of significance that had come to her just after she took the Blood. But she had never believed it, not really. Even if she had, she knew something now about herself that she had only partly known before: She did not care. Gyalo was a man, and she loved him; that was all that mattered. If she had it to do over again, she would not give him the crystal—no, not even if it meant setting her will against Ârata himself. He would have come with her, then, out of the Evening City. He would be with her now.

For a while Dreams of him came nightly, and she grew to dread her sleep. But soon enough, mercifully, the growing distance of their mutual journeying did its work, and her Dreams became random again, as they had been before she met him. At last there came a time when she did not dream him at all.

Just before she reached Fashir, she saw him again. She skimmed low over forests, above mountains, across a long valley, arriving at last at a harsh building on an outcrop above a plunging cliff. Windows pierced its walls; most were dark, but in one a little light gleamed. He was there, unchained, looking out at the night. There was nothing between him and the spinning drop below. As she watched, he braced his hands upon the sill and leaned forward. Farther he leaned, and farther still, as if he strove to see something on the wall beneath his window. Her heart stuttered with dread. *Don't,* she cried to him, *you'll fall*—forgetting that in her Dreams she did not have a voice.

Abruptly he straightened and stepped back. His face was

blank, utterly without expression. He turned from the window and moved toward the bed. He wore only a bedgown; the lamplight shone through the fabric, and she saw how gaunt he was, almost as gaunt as when he came to Refuge.

She woke gasping. This, then, was the shape of his exile: the bleak building on its cliff, the bare room, the drop below the window. She saw again the way he had looked down, the terrible stillness of his face. How long would it be before he allowed himself to fall?

Will I know? she thought, agonized. *Will I feel it when it happens?*

It was the last time she dreamed him.

At a farm beyond Fashir, she learned to her dismay that Thuxra Notch was locked in ice and snow and would not be passable until spring. The farmer, whose abscessed forearm she had drained and bandaged in exchange for a meal and a night's shelter, took pity on her and offered her a place for the rest of the winter if she would do the work that was growing difficult for his pregnant wife, and stay to birth the baby. She was thankful, though not even in her worst moments in Refuge had the time seemed to pass so slowly. She knew the Brethren's army could no more get across the winterbound Notch than she, but she could not help but fear she would arrive to find it gone.

The child came at last, and she set off again, equipped with blankets and supplies by the grateful farmer. As she neared the foothills of the Range of Clouds, she began to be overtaken by companies of cavalry or convoys of wagons. Halfway up the Notch, another cavalry company came up behind her; she could not hide among the grasses as she had before, so she simply stepped off the road and let them pass. They glanced at her, curious, but did not pause. A little later she heard the sound of hoofbeats, and looked up to see one of them trotting back toward her. Fear leaped up into her throat.

"You're traveling alone?" the soldier inquired, reining in. His expression was open, his manner courteous.

"I'm going to my husband in Thuxra City." It was the tale she had told the farmer.

"You'll starve to death before you reach it, if that's all you're carrying." He leaned toward her, reaching down a hand. "I'll see if I can talk the captain into carrying you with us."

She hesitated, but only for a moment; the prospect of not having to walk the rest of the way was too tempting to resist.

The captain agreed to the cavalryman's request, allowing her to ride one of the packhorses. In exchange she donated her small store of food to the general supplies, and sewed up a cut or two and wrapped a few bruised limbs. She slept in the open, next to the tent of the soldier who had rescued her; when one of the others tried to climb inside her blankets one night he woke and chased the man away, and thereafter no one bothered her. He had been stationed at the military garrison at Darna, he told her, and had left his wife and baby son behind there. When she asked him why he was riding to Thuxra, he shrugged and said he did not know. From the way his eyes avoided hers, she knew he lied.

They reached Thuxra, and he left her outside the encampment. Drawing her stole around her face, she began to wander among the tents. Within a few moments she was halted by a sentry.

"What's your business?" he inquired brusquely.

"I'm looking for work."

"There's no work for women here."

"But I can see women." She gestured toward a nearby fire pit, where several women were preparing food.

"All right, since you want it plain—no doxies. No camp followers or hangers-on either."

"I'm not a . . . a . . . camp follower—"

"Have you a husband, then?"

She looked at him.

"I didn't think so. Go home, woman. Even if you could, you wouldn't want to go where we're going."

He escorted her from the camp. She stood for a time where he left her, breathing hard with the effort of not yielding to her desperation. There was one possibility remaining: Kaluela. She had kept it for a last resort, for she did not know how much Thuxra might have been told about Refuge and its heresy and the army's purpose there, and was not certain how Kaluela would receive her.

She trudged to the prison. She feared she would be stopped, shabby and dusty as she was, but no one seemed to remark her as she passed quickly through the courtyard and slipped into the custodians' quarters. She made her way to the administrator's house and climbed over the wall at the back of the garden, where she knew Kaluela liked to walk most afternoons, and hid herself amid the vegetation to wait. Her abrupt appearance made Kaluela shriek, but after the first astonishment the older woman seemed pleased to see her. She listened, exclaiming now and then with sympathy, as Axane told her half-true, half-made-up story.

"I don't know if there's a great deal I can do," she said, doubtfully, when Axane was finished. "The expedition force keeps separate; even the commander doesn't have much to do with us."

"Oh." Axane felt something flatter than despair.

"But I can ask Vâsparis. He's to be the guide—he must know all about the arrangements. Maybe he can help."

"Oh, Kaluela! Thank you!"

Kaluela reached out and took Axane's hands in hers. "You may not think it, my dear, but I know what it's like to be separated from everything you know and love. For years I've been living here and there and anywhere, following my husband. I can hardly say how much I long for Kanu-Tapa, where I was born. My sister died in childbed last year—by the time I got the letter she was more than a month buried." Her eyes had filled with tears. "You must go home, Axane. You must see your father."

Emotion rolled over Axane, a long dark wave of exhaustion, fear, relief. She closed her eyes, holding to Kaluela's soft, painted fingers as if they were the only safe thing in the world.

It was not practical for her to remain in Kaluela's house,

where she must be kept hidden for fear the administrator or the servants would recognize her; so while she waited for word to come from Vâsparis, Kaluela arranged for her to stay in an empty apartment in one of the long barracks-style dwellings where ordinary soldiers lived. The older woman came each afternoon to visit; the hours they spent together were among the most pleasant Axane had ever known. Not since she was young had she had a female friend in whom she could confide. Kaluela was curious about Refuge, and she found herself talking about her childhood, which before her mother left her had been happy, and describing the things that were beautiful in her memory: the flaming colors of the cleft, the dancing grasses of the Plain, Revelation's joyous song. She spoke also, guardedly, of Baushpar and her flight from it—even, at last, of Gyalo and her hopeless love for him. For the first time in weeks, she allowed herself to weep for him. Kaluela took her into a scented embrace and stroked her hair, awakening in her a vivid recollection of her mother's hands. Not for years had she thought of this; she felt then she might die of grief.

It was Kaluela who wept, when Vâsparis finally sent for Axane. She was, in her way, as much a prisoner of Thuxra as Axane had been of Refuge; for her, too, the brief friendship they had forged across the gulf of their differences was like no other in her life. She had already assembled a lavish travel kit, containing not just the ordinary essentials, but things only a woman would give another woman: salves against the ravages of the sun, lengths of linen for Axane's monthly courses, a supply of hairpins. Now she gave gifts: a braided cord for Axane to wear around her neck, strung with five enameled amulets; an ivory-handled knife in a metal sheath to tie at her waist; a beautiful box, its small compartments stocked with healer's supplies—herbs, little flasks of oil, powders, needles, knives, waxed linen thread.

"It's a joy to me to do this for you," she said when Axane protested the rich presents. "Every woman needs gifts. I think you haven't had many in your life."

She kissed Axane tenderly before she left. When the army departed, she was not there to see it off.

Occasionally, restless with the need to be away, Axane had veiled herself and climbed Thuxra's battlements, to look down on the army as it assembled beyond the walls. Even from a distance, it had looked huge. Now, from within; it seemed far huger. According to Vâsparis, it numbered two hundred soldiers (horse-mounted, since the Shapers would ensure adequate water), two hundred and fifty pack camels, fifty grooms and camel-handlers, fifty or sixty assorted servants and cooks and farriers and drovers and medics and wives, a herd of swine and another of goats—and, of course, the twenty-five Shapers.

There were no horses for the wives and servants; given the choice of riding pillion behind Vâsparis or walking at the back with the other foot travelers, Axane chose to go on foot. The harsh sky above her head and the sun's savage weight upon her shoulders told her she was in the Burning Land, but apart from that she might have been anywhere, for the press of men and beasts blotted out the desert and wrapped everything in a shroud of dust. Where the army passed, the Land's shallow soil was churned to powder, its fragile scrub and grasses trampled flat. A broad trail of manure and litter stretched behind, edged by the ugly holes and fissures the Shapers made to bring up water. Vâsparis, with his love of the Burning Land, was troubled by the destruction.

"The other crossing was different," he told Axane. "Except for the markers, you can't tell now where we passed. It'll be years before the Land heals herself of this."

The swine and goats provided meat, and the camels carried quantities of flour and dried fruit paste, but the Shapers were responsible for everything else, from grain to water. At Thuxra they had had their own encampment, and they maintained that separation, traveling on the army's flank, setting up their tents some distance from the rest, allowing no one to see them in the employing of their ability. Most of the soldiers did not seem greatly concerned by the fact that the ground they walked and dug and bled and defecated upon was held sacred by their faith, but they feared the Shapers. When a dust storm held the army captive for a day, it was rumored that some careless act of shaping had called it up. When a scouting party sent to canvass a route through a region of arid dunes failed to return, it was whispered that one of them must have displeased a Shaper. In dread of the Shapers' scrutiny, many avoided oaths and the profane use of Ârata's name; they made the sign of Ârata, furtively, if any of the Shapers happened to pass.

What waited for the Shapers, Axane wondered, once they returned to Arsace? She had noticed that though they wore the loose red gowns and trousers of vowed Âratists, they did not wear their golden stoles. She asked Vâsparis, but Vâsparis did not know.

She had no difficulty passing herself off as Vâsparis's wife. There were perhaps thirty other women, most of whom had long experience following their men on campaign. They tolerated her kindly enough, though she mostly held apart from their conversation, having no true history she could share with them and not certain of how to invent one. Too, she hated the avid stories they passed among themselves about the army's destination—half- and quarter-truths and many pure inventions that transformed Refuge into a place of repulsive iniquity, with strange heretical rites and a cadre of insane Shapers. The women's tales, she knew, came from their husbands; she could not tell whether they were falsehoods the men had been deliberately given by their superiors, or tamer stories distorted in the telling. She had always feared for Refuge's destruction and her people's abduction, should her warning fail, but she began to be afraid in a different way—for if this were what the soldiers believed, how would they treat her people if they succeeded in capturing them?

They must not succeed, she told herself. *They must not.*

The women speculated also about the mysterious pair of travelers who had joined the army just before it left Thuxra City. The army had had to wait for them, in fact, delaying departure by nearly a week. No one knew who they were; even Vâsparis had no idea. They did not show their faces, wearing hooded robes whenever they went abroad and traveling during the day in the army's vanguard in closed litters slung between pairs of camels. At night, their several servants pitched their red tent well apart from the rest. It was clear they were important; the army's commander had been seen to visit them, and so, occasionally, had the leader of the Shapers. But were they nobles sent by King Santaxma to oversee the expedition? High functionaries within the Âratist church—Shapers, perhaps, or servants of the Brethren?

Axane was often in demand for her healing skills; the army's medics, whose expertise lay in stitching wounds and setting bones and dealing with flux and fever, were mostly helpless when it came to treating the endless variety of sap burns and insect bites and skin eruptions the Burning Land bestowed on those who traveled it. One night, returning from a visit to a man covered over his hands and face with weeping blisters, she passed along the margin of the camp, where the travelers' tent stood in its customary isolation. As she neared it the flaps of its entrance parted, and one of the travelers, hooded as always, ducked through. He straightened; the breeze that sprang up at dusk came skipping through the camp, belling canvas, plucking ropes, stirring spirals of dust. It lifted his hood and tossed it back over his shoulders, revealing his face.

Axane halted in her tracks, paralyzed by recognition. It was Dâdar, the hard-eyed, pockmarked Son who had been her most relentless questioner.

She was bareheaded and in plain view—there was nothing she could have done if he had turned toward her. But he did not. Casually he caught his hood up again and moved on toward the cook fire, where his servants were preparing a meal. Axane forced herself into motion, turning and stumbling toward the crowded safety of the camp. It took all her will not to run.

In the tent she shared with Vâsparis she sank down on her blankets, trembling. How many times had she gone out in the evening without her hood? Thinking about it, she felt faint. He must never see her. He would understand at once why she was there; before she knew it she would be a prisoner again, or abandoned to the desert.

Was the man with him also a Son? In hindsight, she thought perhaps she should have guessed. It made perfect sense that the Brethren would accompany the army, to command the apostate Shapers, to oversee the razing of Refuge, perhaps to look with their own eyes on the Cavern of the Blood—of which, among all the rumors, there were no stories at all, the one thing about Refuge, apparently, that had been kept secret. It made sense also that they would travel incognito; they would not wish to stir the sort of speculation that would be spun were their presence known. There was no one with the army who had any reason to recognize their faces, but the tattoos on their foreheads would identify them at once.

Their secrecy is a good thing, she told herself. *If I'm careful, they'll never know I'm here.*

It seemed to her Vâsparis should know, and so she told him. When she was finished, he shook his head.

"Now I've heard everything," he said. "Who'd have thought I'd ever get within spitting distance of the Brethren?"

It seemed to mean no more to him than that.

Often in Baushpar, looking into the Brethren's cold faces, Axane had wondered if they could truly be what Gyalo claimed they were: ancient souls, endlessly reincarnated. It was a thing that held no place in the lore of Refuge; it had seemed preposterous to her even before she came before them and thought that beings so old should surely have learned more compassion. But from the moment she recognized Dâdar, she was never again quite free of dread—as if he truly were more than human and might somehow see her not just through the veils she was always careful to wind about her face whenever she went abroad, but through the clouds of dust, the walls of canvas that lay between them.

In the months of travel, he never had. And soon she would be gone, beyond his reach.

The sun had fallen far enough now. Still she sat, in this pause before the last stage of her journey, her heart beating with something that was not exactly fear. It was a little like standing atop the cleft, as she had on the night she left Refuge—only now what she saw was not the trackless distance between herself and the kingdoms of Galea, but the circle of her passage there and back again. While she waited, the circle was not closed: She still touched, a little, the world in which she had so briefly held a place. Once she left the tent, once she passed beyond the camp, it would all be behind her. There would be only Refuge.

I must go now, she thought, *or I never will.*

She hitched herself to her knees and began to pull on her robe. There was a stirring beside her.

"It's time?" Vâsparis said.

"Yes. I want to be well away by sunset."

He assisted her with the pack, adjusting it so it lay comfortably on her back. He had devised its frame, cannibalizing wood from the collapsible skeleton that supported their tent, experimenting with the arrangement of bags and bundles to make it balance properly.

"Well." He sat back on his heels. "There's not much to say, except good luck."

She nodded. "Vâsparis . . . be careful."

"Oh, don't you worry about me. I've got my own plans." He watched her with his silvery eyes. "Maybe I'll see you again one day."

"Maybe. Good-bye, Vâsparis."

"Good bye, Axane."

She slipped through the tent flaps and got to her feet. No sentries were posted, for the only enemy was the sun. There was no one to see her as she made her way swiftly through the camp and struck off across the barrens.

— 23 —

Axane walked through the night, guiding herself by the stars, which over the past months' travel had fallen again into the patterns she knew. The barrens spread around her in perfect emptiness. The moon came up, bright enough to cast her shadow out beside her. When it set, the darkness seemed very deep.

She continued as the sun rose, until the stone began to burn her feet through the worn soles of her boots. She halted and drank from her waterskin, then lay down on her blanket, drawing her robe over her body like a shroud. She waited out the broiling day, dozing and waking and dozing again, drifting in a dream of incandescent heat. At last she roused to dimming light and cooling air. She drank again, forced herself to eat, and moved on.

She passed one more day upon the barrens, reaching the Plains of Blessing just before moonset the following night. The desire to rest was overpowering, but urgency pressed her forward; she thought she must be at least a day ahead of the expedition, which trundled along much more slowly than a single person on foot, but she could not be sure. The shapes of the distant mountains told her she had come in to the east of the cleft, and she moved west for a time before turning south. Exhaustion forced her to stop at last.

When she woke, the morning was well advanced. The air was hot, but not cruelly so, and a breeze stirred the tasseled grasses, brushing shadow across her face. She lay a moment, staring at the sky, smelling all around her the odor of the Plains, drawn upward by the heat: a melding of dry grass and rich earth, with undernotes of sun-baked rock. It was familiar in a way that went beyond mere recognition; it released in her a flood of emotion, not memory but something deeper, a visceral sense of place. She had taken with her many memories when she left, but this one was too fragile to carry. It had been lost to her until this moment.

She got to her feet, her abused body protesting motion. The tossing grasses enclosed her to the waist; she stood amid them like a swimmer, gazing across the distance at what she had never thought to see again: the rounded russet contours of the cleft, the mountains beyond it lofting skyward, Revelation in its cloak of trees winding west across the Plains. It was beautiful, more beautiful than she recalled. For an instant, dizzily, she had the feeling that she had never left—that she had only closed her eyes a moment and dreamed she had been gone.

She drank, and ate, and plodded on. She had tried, over the past months, not to dwell on the uncertainties of the task that awaited her in Refuge, to focus all her attention simply on arriving. But now she was there, and the difficulty of what she must accomplish rose before her like the cleft itself. How would Refuge receive her, who had run away with demons? What would her father say when she stood before him? How would she explain what she had done, what she knew? How would she make him believe? What if he rejected her warning?

What if he were not alive?

She reached the cleft in the last light of sunset. At its mouth, where Revelation eddied into shallows, she paused to drink and, quickly, to bathe, for she was unspeakably filthy and did not want to come that way before her father. She tossed her soiled clothing into the river, letting the water take it; she yanked the tangles from her hair with her fingers and dressed herself in a chemise and gown saved clean through all her journeying.

She shouldered her pack, ready to move on. But now, for the first time in this apparently unchanged world, she was gripped by the sense that something was not right. She paused, looking around. It was a moment before she saw it. A little distance downriver, the community grew crops, in eight irrigated fields whose use was rotated so that one was always left fallow. But three lay unplanted. And not just unplanted: It looked as if they had not been plowed, for the soil was rank with weeds and silvery stalks of Plains-grass. The grass, which spread quickly by means of long runners, was incredibly difficult to eradicate once it became established. Getting rid of invading shoots was a constant labor, never to be neglected.

Strange enough that the fields should not be planted. But that they should be allowed to go back to grass . . . it was unthinkable.

She had tried to dream of Refuge during her months in Arsace. In the random manner of her ability, she had rarely been successful. Once she entered the Burning Land again, however, the Dreams began to come of themselves, growing in frequency as the distance narrowed, and over the past few weeks her sleep had carried her to the cleft nearly every night. Perhaps her father really had given her up to the Shapers' storms—but that did not mean she ceased to love him, and that love drew her, as her love for Gyalo had drawn her. But in all these Dreams, she experienced the resistance Gyalo had once described to her—a slippage or deflection that clouded her Dream-vision and held her away from Refuge itself. Though she skimmed above the cleft and glimpsed the light of the Cavern of the Blood, though she raced like a shadow above the grasses and skipped along the river's western course, she was never able to approach the cleft itself, much less to drift inside.

That had not alarmed her, for she knew it was the Dream-veil, spun by Refuge's Dreamers to conceal it from the En-emy, concealing it from her as well. But now, looking at the derelict fields, which her sleep had never brought her quite close enough to see, she was suddenly terrified. She had been away nearly two years. What might have happened in that time?

Swiftly she moved toward the cleft. No workers were about, but that was not surprising—the calling horns would some time ago have brought Refuge to worship, and the community would be gathered in Labyrinth for the evening meal. She reached the mortuary caves, with their faint odor of decay; she saw there had been no increase in the number of screened openings and felt a loosening of relief, for she had thought of fever, of epidemic. But then she came to the outdoor workshops and dread gripped her again. Three forge fires had been burning when she left; now there was only one.

The House of Dreams was quiet, a wash of lamplight sift-ing from its round opening—but then it always was. The Treasury was deserted, darkened but for the glow of fire-pots—but that was normal, once the workday was done. Ahead gaped Labyrinth's great entrance. She paused, one hand on the rock beside her, unable for a moment to go on. She could see a slice of its interior—the galleries rising up-ward, the openings of the first apartments. All seemed as it should be. She heard no sound from within; but that meant nothing, given Revelation's clamor. She could hear her heartbeat, though, drumming in her ears.

She forced herself to step forward.

The first thing she saw was the fire pits. All six had been in use when she departed; now the three closest to the en-trance were empty, swept clean. In the eating gallery itself, the glow of lamps fell across a gathering of people. But the lamps were lit only at the gallery's front. Its rear was dark—dark, and vacant.

She had known she would see something awful. Even so, the shock halted her. More than a third of the gallery was unoccupied. Hunting and gathering bands often stayed away for several nights, but never in numbers like these. Where was the rest of Refuge? Plague, she thought again—but if so many had died, would the number of mortuary caves not have increased?

Her father's face rose up inside her mind. It broke her stasis, pressed her forward again.

They saw her then. Hands stilled; heads swung round. By the time she reached the gallery they were all turned toward her, motionless as the sculptures on the Temple's façade. She halted by one of the supporting pillars. She knew every face there, and Habrâmna was not among them.

"Where is my father?" she blurted out, her voice harsh in the silence.

There was a pause. For the first time it occurred to her that they might not recognize her, or that they might think her a spirit, a ghost. But then one of the women raised her arm, pointing toward the galleries: toward Habrâmna's apartment.

Axane did not remember how she got there. The passage, with its little lamps, was just as she remembered; the curtain hung as always across the opening to her father's chamber. Beyond it, the chamber, too, was unchanged: the hanging lamps, the color-banded walls, the round table, the six chairs. Habrâmna lay in the great bed, heaped with coverings, his head propped up on bolsters and his hands clasped upon his chest. His eyes were closed. Vivanishâri sat nearby, a swaddled infant in her arms.

Fear rang through Axane; in that second, she knew that he was dead. She plunged past the curtain. Vivanishâri bolted to her feet, clutching the baby, her face stretched into a rictus of terror.

"Begone," she gasped. "Begone, spirit!"

Axane barely heard her. Vivanishâri darted forward, planting herself in Axane's path.

"Stay away!" Her voice cracked. "Don't come any closer!"

"Let me by." Axane tried to step around her, but Vivanishâri dodged to block her. "I'm not a spirit, Vivanishâri! Let me by!"

"You look like Axane." The baby had started to cry. "But Axane is dead."

"I'm as alive as you. Now get out of my way!"

She shouldered past. Vivanishâri staggered; the baby began to howl. Axane bent over the bed. Habrâmna had not stirred. But she saw the motion of his chest, and knew, with a relief that for an instant turned the world black before her eyes, that he lived.

"Father," she said. "Father!"

"He won't hear you." Vivanishâri's voice came to her over the infant's cries.

"Why?" She rounded on the other woman. "What's wrong with him?"

"The pain in his joints has been bad. I gave him a sleeping draught." Vivanishâri jogged the baby against her shoulder. Her eyes were still wide, but her face had lost some of that stretched quality. "It's the only way he can rest."

Axane turned again to her father. He had been ill—she could see it in his sunken eyes, his hollowed cheeks—and his hair and beard were grayer than she remembered. But his jutting nose and proud mouth were the same, and his large hands with their swollen knuckles. She sat down on the edge of the bed and slipped her fingers around his palm. It was warm and a little rough, utterly familiar. Something pressed in her, larger than either grief or love. She felt wetness on her cheeks: tears. She wiped them away.

"It really is you." Vivanishâri spoke softly. She had managed to soothe the baby back to stillness. "But we thought . . . we were sure you must be dead. Where have you been all this time?"

Axane shook her head. She had no desire to explain anything to her father's partner. "Vivanishâri, what has happened here? Where is everyone?"

A shadow passed across Vivanishâri's face. For the first time, Axane noticed how thin she had grown. She wore no cosmetics or jewelry, and her rich curling hair was drawn into a simple braid. The hands that held the baby were chapped, the nails rough. Vivanishâri had been vain of her hands—it was one reason she had so disdained domestic tasks.

"I'll tell you," she said. "Just let me put the baby down."

She moved to the table. Beside it was a carrying basket. She stooped and laid the sleeping infant inside.

"Your new sister," she said, rising. "She's six months old. She's named after you." She did not need to add that this had not been her choice.

Axane swung her pack off her shoulders and sank into a chair. She felt ill with exhaustion and the aftermath of fear. Vivanishâri seated herself opposite, folding her damaged hands in her lap. Her smoke gray eyes traveled across Axane's face.

"You look terrible."

"I've been traveling." Axane pushed back her still-damp hair. "Tell me, Vivanishâri."

Vivanishâri drew a breath, let it out. "The first of it was that the false Messenger and his companions escaped. The ordained Shapers had imprisoned them—well, you know that, you were at the council meeting where it was decided. The Shapers made them secure, but somehow they got out. The Shapers sent storms, which they unmade. The Shapers wanted to do more, but Habrâmna wouldn't let them—he'd discovered you weren't in Refuge, and he feared you were on the Plains. Later on, when you never came back . . . well, he assumed you'd been caught up in the storms and killed."

He stopped the storms for me after all, Axane thought.

"He ordered all of Refuge to gather on the floor of Labyrinth. He stood with the council and the ordained Shapers, except for Aryam and Jândaste, who were in custody because they believed in the false Messenger, and Uspardit, who was watching them. He began to tell us about what the false Messenger had really been and how he had lied to us. But then Cistâmnes and Dâryavati broke from the council and challenged him. They said it wasn't a false Mes-

senger who had come but a true one, and that Refuge had
cast aside its destiny when it drove him out. They said we'd
failed Ârata's test. Oh, there was such an uproar! Habrâmna
ordered them to recant, but they wouldn't obey. So he banished them."

"Banished them?" Axane said, shocked.

"What choice did he have? They wouldn't be silent. It was
a terrible time, terrible. There was anger and grief. There
were questions, especially about how the false Messenger
had escaped. Suspicion fell on Aryam and Jândaste, but
they'd been set to sleep with the Dreamers' sleeping mixture, and Uspardit swore they never stirred. But she was lying, or else she freed the false Messenger herself, because
two days after the false Messenger fled she let Aryam and
Jândaste wake, and the three of them came into the Temple
in the middle of Communion and called on Refuge to go after him. He had gone ahead, they said, but with Shapers to
lead, Refuge could still follow. What could Habrâmna do?
He ordered them from Refuge, too. He told the other
Shapers to see them gone, and open the earth beneath them
if they tried to turn back. But then . . ." Vivanishâri dropped
her eyes, gazing at her sleeping child. "Something terrible
happened. People began to follow. All that evening they followed, and all that night. Habrâmna ordered the Shapers to
block the ledge, but it made no difference. People climbed to
the summit and lowered themselves on ropes. Some leaped
into Revelation, in hopes it would carry them down."

"Into *Revelation*?"

"Yes."

Axane was horrified. She had known Gyalo's coming had
divided her people. She had known there must be consequences. But she had never imagined that those wounds
would not heal—that in the end Refuge would not gather itself up and go on as it always had. She had been certain she
must find it, if not entirely unchanged, essentially as she remembered it: united in false faith, still watching for a Messenger who would never arrive.

"We unblocked the cleft," Vivanishâri said, "and let them

go. We thought it was over. But then Sarax made up his mind to follow. Not so many went with him as with the others. But enough."

"How many? How many went, in all?"

"More than a hundred." Vivanishâri drew a breath. Tears glinted on her lower lids. "From every bloodline. From almost every family. Even now, sometimes, people slip away. They believe Ârata will sustain them on their journey."

"Have any come back?"

"None." The tears overflowed; Vivanishâri reached up to wipe them away. "My youngest brother and his family went when Aryam and Uspardit and Jândaste did. And my sister—she went with Sarax. She left her husband and all her children. I didn't know she meant to do it, I didn't even know she was gone until her husband came to tell me. We ran after her, we took her hands and begged her to stay. But the others who were with her pushed me aside, and one of them struck her husband so he fell unconscious. I watched her walk out across the Plains, and I knew she was going to her death. And there was nothing, nothing I could do."

Axane understood now that she had dreamed this, or some of it, as she traveled away from Refuge two years before: knots of people on the Plains of Blessing, and later on the stone barrens. But she had believed they were pursuers, sent by Refuge in the wake of the Shapers' failed storms; she had assumed, when she ceased to dream them, that they had turned back. Was Vivanishâri right—had the Burning Land claimed them all? The desert was vast, and Axane's dreaming was erratic; but her ability was drawn to living things, and it did not seem possible, if the people of Refuge had survived, that her sleeping mind should not at some point have found them. Of the three Shapers who departed together, only Aryam had been young. Perhaps the rigors of the journey had been too much for Uspardit and Jândaste, and Aryam alone had not been able to provide for those who followed him. And Sarax . . . Sarax's ability had always been smaller than the others'.

She leaned forward. "Vivanishâri, how many are left?"

Vivanishâri rubbed her eyes again, a rough, angry gesture. "Two hundred and fifteen. Thirty-three of them Dreamers in the House of Dreams. Twelve of them Shapers."

"*Twelve?* But you said only four Shapers went."

"Four *ordained* Shapers went. Some of the trainees followed with their families."

Axane felt a falling inside her. "How many ordained Shapers are there now?"

"Six. Râvar and Sonhauka took their vows after the others left. But Gâvarti is very ill. Râvar is principal Shaper now."

"*Râvar?* But he's . . . surely he's too young."

"It was Gâvarti's choice. She said he was the only one whose faith in Refuge never faltered." Abruptly there was spite in the smoky gaze, the old Vivanishâri emerging briefly from this new, careworn shell. "He hasn't married, you know. He hasn't even declared intent."

Axane hardly heard her. How could Refuge defend itself, with only six—no, five, if Gâvarti were so ill—full-trained Shapers? She wanted to weep. She wanted to lay her head on the table and go to sleep forever.

"Where have you been all this time, Axane?" Vivanishâri still watched her, the malice of a moment ago transmuted into something harder. "There were some who thought it wasn't an accident—they said you spent too much time with the strangers, that maybe you followed them when they fled. Habrâmna never believed it. He thinks he killed you. He grieved so—he has never been the same."

Axane turned her face away. Guilt pierced her.

"Nisha." A hoarse voice came from the bed. "Nisha, where are you?"

Vivanishâri sprang to her feet and hurried to the bed. Axane rose also, then found she could not stir.

"Yes, my love." Vivanishâri bent over Habrâmna, taking his hands in hers. "What is it you need?"

"Get me another draught." The words were slurred.

"My love, you had the last not two hours ago."

"I need another. My back pains me."

"You take too many draughts, Habrâmna. It isn't healthy—"

"Ârata's Blood, woman!" He threw off her grip. "Do as I say!"

Vivanishâri turned to the table by the bed, where there was a flask and a cup. Habrâmna's eyes shifted, moving beyond her, to where Axane stood frozen by her chair.

"Who is that, Nisha?" He raised a hand, as if to shade his eyes. "Who's standing over by the table?"

"I'm sure she'll tell you," said Vivanishâri tightly, "if you ask her."

Axane forced herself to move. His eyes followed as she approached. She saw the instant in which he recognized her—an absolute transition, a shifting of all his features.

"Am I dreaming?" he said hoarsely.

She reached the bed. Her heart beat so she could scarcely breathe.

"Is it really you, Axane?"

Her throat had closed; she could not answer. He reached toward her, his hands shaking. She folded down onto the bed, burying her face in his chest. His arms went around her. Wrackingly, she wept.

"You've come back," he murmured. His fingers moved gently in her hair. "You've come home."

She got control of herself at last and sat up, rubbing at her eyes. When she lowered her hands he captured them, holding them in both of his. His gaze moved over her, hungry.

"You've grown so thin, daughter." In the shock of her return, he seemed to have cast off the lingering effects of the sleeping draught; his voice was stronger, his diction clear. But oh, how worn he seemed, how frail. "Are you hurt? Are you ill?"

"I've been traveling, Father. It was a hard journey."

"But where have you been? Where have you been all this time?"

"I'll tell you, Father." She drew a breath. "It's a strange story . . . I think you won't find it easy to believe. But Father, I swear to you it's true. All of it is true."

"Dearest child." His fingers tightened on hers. "You've never lied to me. Why should you make such oaths?"

There was love in his face, such love. She closed her eyes. As much as she dreaded the struggle of bringing him to believe her, she dreaded more the other truths she must tell, the truths she understood that he did not know: that it had been choice, not mischance or necessity, that had taken her from Refuge; that she had abandoned him of her own will.

Behind her, there were footsteps.

"Axane?"

She felt her heart stop at the sound of that voice, which of all voices in the world she had most wished never to hear again. She turned. Râvar stood just inside the entrance. His green eyes devoured her face.

"I don't believe it," he said softly. And again: "I don't believe it."

He was dressed in the red and gold of an ordained Shaper. Even from where she sat it looked shabby—the overrobe limp, the tunic frayed at the hem. His wrists and his long, smooth throat were bare of jewelry, his hair tied carelessly back. He looked older, older than two years should have made him, and very weary. Yet he was still heart-stoppingly beautiful.

"What are you doing here?" The words seemed to leap across the space between them. "Why have you come back?"

"Râvar," Habrâmna said, with mild rebuke. "She has come home."

"Why?"

"She was preparing just this moment to tell me. Now, daughter, you may tell us both."

"Father." Axane's heart had begun to race again. "I'd rather talk to you alone."

"No," said Râvar, with a flatness that denied any contradiction.

"What I know, Axane, Râvar knows. He speaks for me now in many things." Habrâmna smiled a little, wryly. "I'm not as I was. Some days I cannot rise from this bed. I rely on Râvar to assist me."

Râvar had advanced to stand beside the bed. He moved fluidly; his features were composed. But his green eyes were like nails, and anger rose off him like a scent. *He knows,* Axane thought with sudden certainty. *He knows why I left.* She felt a stirring of fear.

"Go on," he said, still in that flat tone. "Tell us."

Axane drew a breath. "There's a force of men out on the stone barrens." She spoke fast, wanting to get it all out before she lost her nerve. "An army. They're a day behind me, perhaps two days. There are more than two hundred of them. Twenty-five of them are Shapers. They have weapons, and a drug that kills shaping ability. They're coming to Refuge. They mean to destroy it. They mean to kill Refuge's Shapers and take the people of Refuge captive and bring them away, never to return."

Silence. They stared at her—her father, Vivanishâri, Râvar. She saw no comprehension in their faces at all.

"I know it's hard to believe," she said. "But it's true, all of it. I've seen this army with my own eyes. I . . . I traveled with it, to get here. It was the only way I could come back and warn you. These men are real, I swear it—I swear it by the Cavern of the Blood."

"What are you saying, daughter?" said Habrâmna. He seemed not merely disbelieving, but bewildered. "That there's some sort of demon army approaching Refuge? That it . . . took you captive?"

"No, Father. Not demons. *Men.* Real men, *human* men, from the outside world. From the kingdoms of Galea."

Habrâmna's brows drew down. "What madness is this?"

"Father, the false Messenger told the truth. The kingdoms of Galea never fell into ruin. The outside world is still there, all of it, beyond the Range of Clouds—still living, still thriving, just as in our histories. I've seen it. I've traveled its ground, I've breathed its air, I've eaten its food. That's where I've been all this time, Father—in the outside world."

"You have the sun sickness, Axane," Habrâmna said. "You're delirious. Nisha, go fetch a healer—"

"Father, I don't need a healer! I don't have the sun sickness! Look. I can prove it." She fumbled at her waist, un-buckling the belt Kaluela had given her, with the knife in its chased metal sheath. She pushed it into his hands. "Look at this. Have you ever seen its like? It comes from the outside world. And look at these." She untied the leather cord around her neck, with Kaluela's enameled amulets. "There's no work like this in Refuge. They come from the outside world, too. And if you look at my pack, you'll see the frame is made of wood that doesn't grow on the Plains of Blessing, and if you unroll my blanket, you'll see it's not woven the way we weave. Where could I have gotten these things, if what I've told you isn't true?"

Habrâmna held the knife as if he had forgotten how to use his hands. "I don't understand. How can this be?"

Râvar stepped forward and twitched the knife from Habrâmna's grip. He turned it over, frowning; he drew it out of its sheath and held it up to the light to examine the blade. Then he thrust it back into the sheath and tossed sheath and belt onto the bed, wiping his fingers down the front of his tunic as if to clean them.

"This proves nothing," he said. "We know well, here in Refuge, how easily demons can imitate what human beings do. But there is something I'd like to know." His gaze fixed her like a spear. "Wherever it is you really went when you left Refuge, I think you didn't go alone. Am I right?"

Axane swallowed. "Yes."

"You followed the false Messenger. Didn't you?"

"Yes." There. It was spoken. "But he wasn't a false Messenger. That was Refuge's mistake. He never said he was the Next Messenger, never. He tried to explain that he wasn't."

"He . . . compelled you, daughter?" Habrâmna's words were thick again, as they had been when he woke. "He made you go with him?"

"Yes." It was only a small lie. "He compelled me."

"Ah." He turned his head on the pillow, back and forth, his face creasing with grief. "My poor Axane. No wonder your mind is filled with these terrible fancies."

"Father—" Axane felt like weeping. "Father, please, they

aren't fancies. You must believe the army is coming. It's close behind me, very close. You must prepare, you must, or Refuge is lost!"

"Enough, daughter." He pulled his hands from hers. "I have no more strength for this. Râvar, take care of her. Get her to a healer. Nisha, my draught—"

Vivanishâri stepped forward. Râvar grasped Axane's arm and drew her off the bed.

"Father—Father, listen to me—"

But all Habrâmna's attention was on the cup Vivanishâri held to his lips. He did not look up as Râvar dragged her from the room.

"Râvar, where are you taking me?"

He did not answer. His face was like stone.

"Please tell me." She was really frightened now. "What are you going to do?"

"Be quiet." He tightened his fingers around her arm, a vicious pressure that made her gasp.

They came out onto the floor of Labyrinth. Most of Refuge had retired for the night; only a few cooks remained, banking the fires, stacking the cleaned dishes in the gallery. They paused to watch as Râvar propelled her toward the stairs; their faces were alight with the avid curiosity she remembered so well. She stumbled as he pushed her up the steps; he righted her like an unwieldy bundle. Past the second tier he guided her, and out onto the third. She realized he was making for the first apartment, the apartment where Gyalo and his companions had been housed, then imprisoned.

He halted before the chamber that had been Gâbrios's. The breached crystal was gone; the room beyond was a pit of darkness. In the dim light filtering in from outside, his eyes looked black.

"You lied," he said, soft. "You were not compelled."

She did not dare to speak.

"I went to your room that day, after your father ordered us to halt the storms. I saw what you'd taken with you. I warned you they were demons, the strangers. You swore you'd stay away from them. You lied. They'd already corrupted you. I understood that when I went to your room. Your father couldn't believe it of you. But I could. Oh, I could."

"Râvar." Her mouth was like a desert. "I don't care what you think of me. But all I've said is true. Tell the Dreamers to dream outward—they'll see—"

His face twisted. "Bitch. Liar. I wouldn't have stopped the storms. I would have let them tear you apart."

He thrust her into the chamber, powerfully, so that she staggered and fell. His face went blank. The entrance trembled like an open mouth; there was a burst of light, a sound like thunder, and the opening vanished.

Stunned by the suddenness of it, she was unable for a moment to comprehend what had happened. But then the darkness clamped down like a fist, and rage and terror wrenched her to her feet. She collided painfully with the rock that stretched where the entrance had been; she beat at it and screamed, knowing it was pointless, unable to stop herself. At last she slid to the floor and huddled there, her hands aching, her eyes wide upon the blackness.

The floor was chilly, and her gown was still damp from being pulled on over wet skin. Shivering, she crept forward on hands and knees, searching for the bed. Gyalo and his companions had disassembled the furniture in other chambers to make a litter for Gâbrios, but in this one things had been left intact, though the bed, when she found it, was bare of either sheets or blankets.

She curled up on the mattress, grateful to be off the stone. The darkness was like a solid substance; she imagined she could actually feel it, a pressure against her skin. She thought of the dilation of Râvar's eyes, his incandescent fury. Her mind fled down terrible paths of speculation—how long would he hold her like this? What would he do to her when he let her out? *Would* he let her out? *My father will ask for me,* she told herself; *he'll have to come for me.* But if the army reached Refuge first . . . if Râvar were caught and killed before he could release her . . .

She lay rigid, trembling. The dark bore in from every side.

She slept at last. She woke blind, with no idea of where she was. Panic vaulted her upright; then she remembered, and pulled her knees to her chest and laid her forehead on them, panting. Mundanities intruded: hunger, thirst, the needs of her body. She slid to the floor and felt under the bed, but there was no chamber pot. She used the corner of the room, then navigated oceans of blackness back to the sanctuary of the bed and curled up on her side.

She was still afraid, but it was quieter now. Had any part of what she said been heeded? It was what she had most feared: to speak and not be believed. But even in her worst imaginings she had thought to have the chance to argue, to persuade. Now she did not even have that.

She fell in and out of sleep, tormented by thirst. She was awake when Râvar came back for her at last; in the deep dark she was not aware that her eyes were open, and the burst of light as he shaped the entrance back into being slashed her vision like a blade. She gasped, huddling inward against it like some subterranean creature.

"Come with me," he said.

She sat up. The dim illumination of the corridor seemed almost unbearably bright. Within it, Râvar was a pillar of black.

"Don't make me force you."

She got off the bed and went to him. He stepped aside as she emerged and motioned her ahead of him out of the apartment. There he took her arm and urged her toward the stairs. Below, Labyrinth was deserted. Through the great arch of the entrance she could see the late-afternoon sky. She felt a jolt of fear; she had lost track of time in her dark hole, and had no idea how long she had been imprisoned.

"Where is everyone?" Her mouth was so dry she could hardly form the words.

"At Communion."

"Râvar, I must have water."

She thought he might refuse, but when they reached the floor he steered her over to the cistern and waited as she drank her fill. Then he pulled her out of Labyrinth, turning toward the Temple. "Up," he said, when they reached the stairs to the summit. She obeyed. At the top he took hold of her again and drew her to the summit's northern edge. He dropped her arm and pointed. "Look."

She followed his gesture. It took a moment, but then she saw it: a dark mass upon the Plains, some distance to the east.

"It's your army, isn't it?"

"Yes," she said, heavily. "I warned you. You didn't listen."

"Oh, I listened. Ârata help me, I listened. That's why I came up here."

She looked at him. The wind blew the skirts of his Shaper overrobe back like wings, and tossed his unbound hair around his face. She could sense no anger in him, only a kind of hard-held tension, as if his body were a rope winched too tight.

"Do you believe me, then?" she said.

He turned to her, shading his eyes against the falling sun. "Let's say—just for the moment—that I do." He spoke quietly. "Tell me about this army."

"There are two hundred men, soldiers, skilled with weapons and trained in fighting. There are twenty-five Shapers to defend them. The army carries a drug called manita, which cripples shaping ability if Shapers breathe it in—they mean to use it on you and the others, so you won't be able to protect Refuge with your shaping. Once they've overcome you, they'll kill you. Everyone else they'll take prisoner."

He watched her. "Why?"

"The people of the outside world . . . they believe as Risaryâsi did, before her revelation. They don't believe the Enemy rose. They think Ârata is still asleep. They don't believe in the cycle—they think there's just a single history, that Ârata will rise just once, and there will only be one Next Messenger."

"That's the same blasphemy the false Messenger spoke."

"Yes. He's of that world—he believes as they do. To them

it's Risaryâsi's revelation that's blasphemous. Heresy, they call it. It's a great sin for them, even when it's too far away ever to touch them."

"Heresy," he repeated.

"So they'll take Refuge's people captive, and take them to the outside world. And when they're there, they'll order them to renounce Risaryâsi's revelation. Then they'll imprison them. Lock them up forever."

"And eventually those from Refuge will forget they were ever Ârata's chosen people, and the truths we've guarded here will be lost. I see." He nodded, slowly, as if he really did understand. "But the Shapers will be killed?"

"Yes. Shaping . . . shaping is different in the outside world." He already knew this, historically at least, for he was ordained now and must have read Cyras's and Mandapâxa's secret scrolls; but she did not think it would be safe to reveal that she knew of them. "Shapers can only use their ability for ceremony, in Ârata's temples. And they . . . they bind it, they limit it, make it small, by taking this drug manita. So no Shaper has more strength than any other."

She could read nothing in his face. "Why do they cripple themselves like that?"

"They fear shaping, the people of the outside world. A terrible war of shaping was fought far back in their past, and since then they can't tolerate Shapers who are free."

"And the punishment for freedom is death?"

"For the Shapers of Refuge it is."

"You said they have Shapers with them. Are they crippled?"

"No. They've been released, so they can defend the army. That's how much the people of the outside world fear Refuge—they're willing to break their own laws to destroy it."

"Are they as powerful as we are, then?"

Axane hesitated. "They've been free for months now. I think they must be strong. But before that, they were locked up all their lives. . . . I think, if all our Shapers were here . . . but now I don't know. There are so few of you. And there are twenty-five of them."

He turned away, looking out again over the Plains, toward the distant mass of the encamped force. The red light of sunset tinted his skin almost to the color of the sandstone beneath his feet. She thought again how much older he seemed—in the set of his features, in the way he spoke, in the sober attention with which he had heard her out. And yet she could still feel the tension in him, the tight stretching of control; and she could still hear the ugly words he had spat at her before he thrust her into the chamber—a day ago? Two days ago? At least, she thought, if Refuge survived, and she were allowed to remain, he would not try to claim her. It was clear that he had come to despise her.

"They'll come tonight," he said, still gazing east. It was not a question.

"Yes. Ten soldiers will be sent ahead. They'll steal up the cleft while Refuge is sleeping, go to the Shapers' quarters, and use manita on them." She had learned that from Vâs-paris, who had passed on to her all he knew of the army's plan. "The main force will follow along the base of the cleft. They'll wait until first light, then come up into Labyrinth and take everyone captive."

"It really cripples shaping, this drug?"

"Yes. They have it in vessels that will break if they're dropped or thrown—it's like dust, it flies everywhere. It's very harsh. Anyone who breathes it in will cough and choke as if he were dying." Briefly she remembered Gyalo, on the floor of the abandoned monastery. "They'll use it on the people of Refuge, too, if there's much resistance."

"How will they protect themselves, then?"

"They have masks to wear across their faces."

He was silent. How much of what she had told him did he believe? And even if he did believe, was there hope that anything could be done in the small time remaining?

"They know a great deal about Refuge." The wind drew a strand of hair across his face; he brushed it back. "Do they know about the Cavern of the Blood?"

"Yes."

"Was it he who told them? The false Messenger?"

"Yes," she said reluctantly.

"Is he with this army?"

"No. He is . . . he's still in the outside world."

"But it's on his word that this army has come."

"No." She shook her head. "No. He told the Brethren about Refuge. But he only wanted them to believe in Ârata's rising. He never wanted this."

He flicked a glance at her. "You defend him."

"I'm only telling you," she said carefully, "what happened. It was the Brethren who decided to send the army. They're the ones responsible."

"Who are these . . . Brethren?"

"They are—" How could she explain to him? "They're the leaders of the men and women of the outside world who are sworn to the service of Ârata."

"To the service of Ârata!" He laughed, harshly. "I doubt that. And they sent *him*. The false Messenger."

"Yes, they did send him, but he wasn't a false Messenger—"

"They made a false Messenger." He continued as if she had not spoken. "To tempt us into the Burning Land. And those of us who didn't follow to our deaths were left divided, weakened by dissension and by grief. And now they've sent this army to finish us, and all the Dreamers' Dreams can't turn it away, for the false Messenger walked among us and learned the shape of our refuge. Ah." He drew in his breath. "This is the Enemy's work. And Refuge will be destroyed, and its people turned against their faith, and the human race will perish. And where is Ârata? Where is Ârata?"

What was it she heard in his voice? Dread? Anger? Despair?

"And you." He wheeled suddenly to look at her. "You, who went with this abomination of Ârdaxcasa into the Burning Land. You who survived, as the others who followed him did not. How do you know so much about what's to come?"

"I told you. I learned it in the outside world."

"Did you go with *him* before these masters of his?"

She did not dare admit the truth. "No."

"So you didn't betray Refuge?"

"No," she said, and it was like dust in her mouth, for she knew it was a lie.

"Why should I believe you?" The light of sunset glinted in his eyes. "When you went with him of your own free will? How can I even know you're what you seem to be? You might be some dark thing made in Axane's form, sent to deceive us."

"No, Râvar. I'm real. Look at me—I'm the same woman who left here, the same woman I've always been. Why would I give warning, if I wanted harm for Refuge? Why would I come back at all? I could have stayed in the outside world. I could have stayed, and then you'd have no idea they were even coming for you."

For a long moment he watched her. Then the tension seemed to leave him all at once, as if a cord had been cut. With a kind of sigh, he sank down upon the stone and buried his face in his hands.

"What am I to do?" he said. "What am I to do?"

She was still a moment, startled by this sudden change. Cautiously, she crouched beside him. "You must tell my father."

He shook his head, his face still hidden. "It's no good. He won't decide."

"What do you mean?"

"He no longer makes decisions. It began after Sarax left, when his health began to fail."

Axane thought of the way her father's head had turned fretfully upon the pillow, the bewilderment in his face as he held Kaluela's knife. . . . Her throat tightened with guilt and sadness. "Gâvarti, then," she said.

"She's too sick." He let his hands fall, "No. I'm principal Shaper. It's up to me. There's no one else."

He stared out over the Plains, where dusk was beginning to settle across the grasses. His shoulders sagged with utter weariness. A memory returned to her, unbidden: Râvar in the council chamber, just after Gyalo and his companions had been judged false. *I would do anything,* he had said. *I would carry any burden.*

"What have you been doing all this time, Axane?" The question was quiet. "While you've been gone?"

"Traveling. Living. It's no different from here, Râvar. They believe different things . . . but life—life is the same."

He shook his head. "It's illusion, this outside world of yours. A perfect illusion spun by the Enemy. You haven't been living, you've been dreaming, wandering among the ruins."

She said nothing. What did it matter what he thought, as long as he accepted the reality of the army?

"Did you believe he was the true Next Messenger? Is that why you followed him?"

"No. No, I didn't believe that."

"Why did you go, then?"

She sighed. "How can I explain, since you don't believe the outside world is real? But I believed it—for a long time I believed it. I was certain there was more than Refuge. And then he came . . . and I knew I had to go, to find that place, that bigger place. I knew there would never be another chance to do it."

"But you *must* have believed in him. To do such a thing."

"I believed he could take me out of Refuge. That's all."

"I never knew you were unhappy, Axane. I never knew you thought such things."

"No one knew."

"I saw you didn't want me. But I thought . . . I thought you were only afraid. . . ." He bowed his face so that his hair veiled his profile. "But I was wrong, wasn't I. That was part of it, wasn't it? It was so disgusting to you, the thought of our union, that you preferred a demon to keeping intent with me."

There was real pain in his voice. For the first time she was reminded of how young he was. "Râvar—"

"No," he said. "Don't deny it. I don't believe you, and I don't want to hear you lie."

They sat in silence. To the east, the black blot of the army merged with the growing darkness. Was it her imagination, or was it already moving? At last Râvar straightened and shook back his hair. His face was composed again, controlled.

"One thing's certain," he said. "Refuge mustn't be here when the army comes. I'll talk to the other Shapers. We'll make a plan." He braced his hands on his knees and rose to his feet in a single graceful motion. "Come. We've been up here long enough."

Axane followed him to the stairs, and down. Just before the entrance to the Shapers' quarters, he halted.

"You can't come in here."

"I'll wait in Labyrinth."

"No." He grasped her shoulders and pushed her back against the wall of the cleft. There was a burst of light, a sound like clapping hands, a sudden pressure. She looked down, uncomprehending; it seemed the stone had reached out an arm and clasped her around the waist.

"What—"

"I've listened to you only because it was necessary. I don't trust you any more than I did before."

"How dare you!" In the shock of it she forgot to be afraid. She slapped the hoop of rock. "Let me go!"

"Would you rather be walled up again?"

She saw he meant it. She bit her tongue and kept silent. He turned, rigid as a knife, and vanished into the entrance.

The restraint was not painful, but it embraced her too snugly for any hope of escape. Since there was no alternative, she yielded, folding her arms before her on the stone. She looked up at the darkening sky. The first stars had appeared. Below her feet, Revelation sang its tumultuous song, mocking her with its freedom.

Where would she be the following night, when the stars came out?

Full night had fallen by the time Râvar emerged, a lamp upraised in his hand. After him walked the other ordained Shapers: massive Haxmapâya and tiny Oronish, elderly Varas and the boy Sonhauka. Their arms were burdened with boxes; they bore bundles on their backs.

"Râvar," she called, but he did not pause or turn. He and the first three vanished through Labyrinth's great arch. Varas went on, toward the Treasury and the House of Dreams.

She clenched her fists in rage, but there was nothing to be

done. After a time a small crowd of women came out of Labyrinth and hurried toward the Treasury, followed by a knot of men; the men came back quickly, carrying litters and lances, bows slung over their shoulders and quivers on their backs. The women reappeared after a more extended pause, laden with bundles and carrying baskets. They kept close, these hasty groups, as if the shadows were hostile. The light of Labyrinth, falling on their faces as they entered it, showed their strain and dread.

Axane was beginning to grow fearful. Could Râvar mean to leave her behind when Refuge departed? The soldiers, if they found her, would not look kindly on her defection, and the Brethren . . . she caught her breath. No, she thought— her father would not allow it. But her father was much changed; and she had not seen him since she first arrived. If Râvar told him she had died of sun sickness, why should he question it?

Râvar did return, after what seemed a very long time. He paused as he reached her; a flicker, a tiny percussion, and the pressure at her waist was gone.

"Come." The lamp he held illuminated his features, but she could not read them. "Your father wants to see you before he goes."

"Am I not to go, too?"

"I want you with me. I may need your knowledge for Refuge's defense."

"Defense? Râvar, you can't think to fight them!"

"What's here must be defended." It was said without expression. "Come. We have little time."

She followed him, her heart pounding now with a different sort of fear. The people of Refuge were huddled by the fire pits. Oronish, Sonhauka, and Haxmapâya moved among them, organizing them, giving direction, checking bundles and occasionally confiscating something. There was some milling about, some low-voiced conversation, some weeping and complaining from children or uncomprehending elders; but most stood silent, subdued by shock. Their dread was as visible as a shadow.

Habrâmna lay apart from the rest, propped on a litter. Vivanishâri stood tensely at his side, her infant, Axane's namesake, in a cradle on her back, her children huddled around her. Bags and bundles lay at their feet—and, set on another litter, Habrâmna's bloodgrain cabinet, its doors bound closed with rope. It seemed incongruous, but only for a moment. It was his journals Habrâmna would want to save, in preference to all else.

"Axane," he said when he saw her, reaching out his hands. She went to him and knelt.

"I did not believe you, daughter." His voice was thick; she could see, in his heavy eyelids, the effects of the sleeping potion. "It seems I should have."

"It doesn't matter, Father."

"Râvar has asked that you remain with him. He says you know this . . . demon army that comes for our destruction, and your knowledge is required for Refuge's protection."

"Father," Axane said urgently, "Father, they are too many. They have twenty-five Shapers, *twenty-five*, and more soldiers than all of us here. We can't fight them—"

"Refuge must be defended," he said—not stonily, as Râvar had, but firmly, a command. "And that which it guards. I've given my consent. I know this is what you want, Axane, in your heart—to do your duty for Refuge, as you did your duty in bringing warning."

He was, suddenly, much more the man she remembered. She knew that nothing she could say would sway him. She bowed her head. "Yes, Father."

"Kiss me, Axane."

She leaned forward; he caught her face between his palms and pressed his lips against her forehead, holding them there a moment. "I am not prouder of my sons than I am of you," he whispered as he let her go. He looked up at Râvar; for a moment the whole of his old fierceness was there in his gaze. "I leave her in your hands. *Remember what you have promised me. Keep her safe.*"

Râvar nodded once, tightly, then turned and beckoned. Four men came forward. Two raised Habrâmna's litter; two hoisted the cabinet. Vivanishâri and her children took up their bundles.

"Move out!" called Oronish. Sonhauka and Haxmapâya took up the call. "Move out!"

The people of Refuge obeyed—igniting torches in the embers of the fire pits, shouldering baggage, lifting children, supporting elders or the sick. Slowly the crowd shaped itself into a procession, with Habrâmna and his family at its head. Axane saw another litter amid the press, and recognized the blanket-shrouded form of Gâvarti. Beside her walked four Shaper trainees, each with a box carefully cradled in his or her arms: the treasures of Refuge, taken for the first time in memory from their secret place inside the Shaper quarters.

Râvar stood beside Axane, watching as Labyrinth emptied. He was, if possible, more tight strung than before. Sonhauka, Haxmapâya, and Oronish, their duties complete, came to wait nearby. As the last stragglers vanished into the night, Râvar took Axane's arm in a hard grip and led her after them. The others followed.

At the House of Dreams Varas waited, with the drugged, sleeping Dreamers laid out on improvised litters. Their attendants lifted them and fell in at the procession's rear; Varas came to join the other Shapers. Down the cleft Refuge marched—past the outdoor workshops where the lone forge fire still burned, past the mortuary caves, past the openings and fissures Revelation had carved over the centuries into its confining bed of stone. The torches bobbed like fireflies on the blackness; the roaring of the river obscured all sound but itself. Near the mouth of the cleft, the lead torchbearer tossed his light into the water. The others did the same, making a brief rain of fire. Part of the night, the people of Refuge moved onto the Plains, following the margin of the river, among whose turns and timber they hoped to hide themselves—all but one small group, which turned aside and vanished into the grasses.

Râvar had drawn his party to a halt as the torches began to fall. They stood watching Refuge go.

"Are none of the Shapers to accompany them?" Axane whispered.

"They have Gâvarti and the trainees. The rest are needed here."

"But if something goes wrong—"

"Nothing will go wrong."

"Râvar, this is madness." She knew in her heart it would do no good, but she could not stop herself. "You can't defend this place. There aren't enough of you."

His fingers tightened painfully on her arm. She did not dare say more.

When the procession could no longer be picked from the darkness, he led them back up the ledge. At the mortuary caves he halted, the others beside him, turning to face the way they had come. He released Axane and bent to set down the lamp.

"Shut your eyes."

She heard the tension in his voice. She obeyed.

Soft as a breath, he said, "Now."

Light exploded, searing Axane's eyes even through closed lids. A huge percussion shocked the air. Heat slapped her like an open hand; the ground bucked beneath her feet, and there was a roaring that eclipsed even Revelation's, as though the cleft were collapsing above her head. She dropped to her knees, scrabbling for purchase on the stone, expecting any minute to feel the crushing impact. Her throat ached—she was screaming, though she could not hear it.

Then, abruptly, it was over. Dark returned. The world grew still. In the silence, the river's great song seemed small.

Cautiously, she opened her eyes. She was unharmed; the ledge around her was clear. But a little distance away, in the blackness of the cleft, a deeper blackness had taken shape. Râvar lifted his lamp. A massive wall of rock now blocked the way down to the Plains, extending across the entire breadth of the ledge, rising all the way to the summit. It was as rough and fissured, as jutting and irregular, as the cleft's natural walls. There was nothing to suggest it had not always been there.

Axane felt awe shiver through her, like the chime of crystal. She had seen much shaping in her life, but never like this. Even the tales of Cyras and Mandapâxa did not tell of a feat so great.

"That'll hold them," said Oronish, her voice betraying satisfaction.

"It's only the beginning." Râvar turned. Lamplight trembled on his face; the harsh shadows painted there made him seem half again his true age. "To the summit now."

Back they went, past the House of Dreams, the Treasury, Labyrinth, the Temple, the Shapers' quarters. Light fell tranquilly from the open entrances, as if everything were normal. And in some sense that was so, for the greatest part of Refuge was still present and intact—its furnishings and ornamentation and fabrics and tools and weapons and foodstuffs, all the accoutrements of its people's life. But that life itself was gone, and with it the knowledge and purpose and memory that gave significance to the rest. Refuge lay like the shed skin of a serpent, or an empty beetle casing—its shape preserved, its meaning gone.

At the stairway Râvar left his lamp behind, needing both hands for purchase, and they mounted in almost total blindness, finding their way from one step to the next by touch. As they emerged on the summit, the moonlight seemed brilliant by contrast. Râvar caught Axane's arm again and led the way over to the summit's northern edge. To the east, the radiance of the Cavern of the Blood bloomed above the cleft; below, in the same direction, the black mass of the army showed clear upon the silver sweep of the Plains. Axane caught her breath to see how close it had drawn.

"What do you think?" Râvar murmured. "Two hours?"

"Maybe a little less," replied Varas. He was the eldest of them, more than twice Râvar's age, yet he deferred to Râvar as if it were he who were the younger.

Râvar nodded. "One more time, then. We'll let the ones they've sent ahead approach unharmed. When they go into the cleft, Kiruvâna and his men will follow and kill them. If any escape, the barrier will turn them back."

The others nodded.

"Meanwhile we'll wait up here." He spoke tightly, with authority. There was no trace of the burdened boy who, earlier in this same place, had bowed his head into his hands

and asked aloud for guidance. "We'll form two groups.
Varas and I will be one, and you three will be the other. We'll
let the army draw near, so they'll believe for as long as possible that we don't know they're coming. When I make my
signal, Haxmapâya and Oronish and Sonhauka will shape a
rain of boulders. At the same moment, Varas and I will open
up the ground beneath them. Are we clear?"

"Yes," four voices said.

"If we're lucky, all we'll need is that first attack. But we
don't know what their Shapers are capable of, or how prepared they are. So Haxmapâya and Oronish and Sonhauka
will continue to bombard them, and Varas and I will call fire
across their line of advance and at their back, and open the
earth between. If we can keep them trapped, if we can force
them to use all their strength in defense, it'll only be a matter of time before we overcome them."

"I still say we should call storms," Haxmapâya said in his
rumbling baritone. "Blow them back upon the barrens."

"No," Râvar said tightly. "We've discussed this. It takes
too long to build the winds. Anyway, the false Messenger
will have told them of our storms and how he unmade them.
I don't want to do anything they may expect."

"We all agreed, Haxma," Varas said.

Haxmapâya shook his head, but held quiet.

"Now, we know they are demons," Râvar said. "But they
come to us in the form of men, and that's how we must oppose
them—as if they were as real as we. And we must stop them
here, on the Plains, for our barrier will only hold them if they
have no Shapers with them. They mustn't get to Refuge. Especially, they must not reach the Cavern of the Blood. We defend the whole of Refuge, but that more than all the rest."

"How close will you let them come before you start?"
asked Sonhauka. His voice shook a little on the words.

"We'll strike just before they pass below us. I want to be
able to see." Râvar hesitated. "How are you, Sonha?"

"I'm all right." Sonhauka drew in his breath. "It's just . . .
I've never killed anyone before."

"They are demons, Sonha." Oronish set her hand gently on Sonhauka's shoulder. "It'll be well. You'll see."

Sonhauka nodded. His eyes shone like an animal's in the moonlight.

"So. Are we clear on what must be done?" Râvar said.

"Yes," they all replied again.

"We're fewer than they. But we are strong, as strong as any Shapers in Refuge's history. And Ârata is with us. We are his chosen people. He will not abandon us. We will prevail." He turned to them, reaching out. They stepped close, joining their hands with his in a many-fingered clasp. "For Refuge," he said.

"For Ârata," said Haxmapâya.

"For Ârata's chosen people," said Oronish.

"For Risaryâsi's Promise," said Varas.

Sonhauka caught his breath. "For the Cavern of the Blood."

They broke apart. The other Shapers moved eastward along the summit. Râvar sank down where he was. Axane crouched next to him; Varas, on the other side, did the same. Râvar stared north. His profile, edged with silver moonlight, was still, almost tranced. But Axane was close enough to hear his breathing quick, a little labored, not tranquil at all.

It was cold. She drew up her knees against it, and pulled her skirts down over her feet. Earlier, watching Refuge depart, everything in her had strained across the gap, desperate to follow; but her fate was sealed now, and the compulsion to flee had left her. There was a kind of inevitability to sitting this way, bird high above the Plains in the deep hours of the night, as if she had always known her long journey must end here. She thought of the cool way Râvar had instructed the others. She thought of the barrier they had made—so perfectly created, in such seamless unity of skill and purpose. No Shapers of the outside world, she was certain, were capable of such a thing. Even so, she could not bring herself to believe that Refuge's Shapers could prevail.

— 25—

The moon sank slowly toward its setting point. The army came on. After a time Râvar ordered Axane and Varas to lie down, and extended himself full length on his belly, dangerously close to the summit's rounded edge, propped on his elbows so he could see. A little distance to the east, the others imitated him. Axane was truly afraid now, so much so she felt sick.

"Look," Varas whispered, pointing. "Down there."

It was the advance force, a black knot of moving figures, skimming fast and stealthy through the grasses.

"Soon now," Râvar murmured. He was trembling, an almost imperceptible vibration of his body that Axane could feel only because she was so close to him.

Closer the army drew, and closer still, until it was possible to make out the individual figures of mounted men, and hear, faint from so far down, the muffled thunder of their passage. They rode in a long column, ten abreast, moving along the base of the cleft at about the distance of a javelin's throw.

"It's time," Râvar whispered. He put his fingers to his lips and whistled a long falling note, a fair imitation of the call of a hawk.

For just an instant, stillness.

Then light pulsed in the sky, on the grasses. A deep double percussion cracked the air. Out of nothing a rain of boulders plummeted upon the army, and the ground before it heaved and dropped away. The first ranks of riders plunged into yawning blackness, the ranks behind struggling desperately to pull back as the Plains unmade beneath their feet. Screams rose, audible even above the thunder of shaping.

The advantage lasted only a moment. With astonishing swiftness the army's Shapers sprang to action. The falling boulders vanished in a blaze of blue-white brilliance. The earth shuddered and rumbled and held steady. Lightning spat along the ground as the chasm Râvar and Varas had opened strained to close. The riders, scattered by the attack, milled and wheeled; their numbers were visibly diminished. But many remained, and Axane could see them already drawing inward, trying to re-form.

"Fire!" Râvar shouted. "Now!"

Varas cried out. Before the army, at its back, the Plains erupted into flame, walls of solid fire that seemed to leap half the height of the cleft. Unable either to advance or retreat, the column dissolved entirely into chaos—horses panicking, men fleeing frantically from the heat. Some attempted to turn north, but another flaming barrier blasted into being there, cutting off escape.

"It worked!" Râvar panted, exultant. "They're pinned!"

They attacked with renewed fury. Sonhauka and Oronish and Haxmapâya hurled down boulders, some half as big as a man; Râvar and Varas made the ground dance beneath the soldiers' feet. Stubbornly, the army's Shapers defended, bracing the earth, unmaking rockfall after rockfall. Beyond the battleground it seemed that half the Plains was ablaze, the fire leapfrogging across the grasses, roaring like a living thing; but though the flames strained to rush inward upon the army, the Shapers threw them back, and they could take no ground. Thick dark smoke billowed up; Axane could smell it, even from so high above, and taste it at the back of her throat. The wind blew south, now drawing the smoke like a veil across the scene, now tearing it aside so she could see, in brief searing glimpses, the men and horses that had fallen, those that still stood, the rocks that had found their mark, the crevasses that writhed open and sealed again as Râvar and Varas strove to bury the army and their opponents fought to thwart them. The dazzle of shaping and the spreading conflagration lit these things almost as bright as day.

It was a stalemate—each side holding the other, neither able to gain advantage. In the light from below she could see how Râvar's face ran with sweat, how Varas, beside him, clutched at the stone and gasped for breath. How long could they continue? She glanced east, to see how the other Shapers fared; but the air was hazy with smoke, and all she could make out were the outlines of their bodies, prone upon the stone. Beyond them, smoke partially obscured the luster of the Cavern, and the sky was gray with approaching dawn. She stared at it, disoriented; how had so much time passed? It seemed to her that only moments had gone by.

She began to turn away; and then paused. Surely the eastern summit was too high for smoke to mass so thick above it. Yet smoke there was, black and curdled against the brilliance of the Cavern—almost as if a blaze had been kindled atop the cleft. *How strange,* she thought. It was coiling, swirling . . .

Moving?

Yes, moving, sweeping swiftly across the stone, toward the place where Sonhauka and Haxmapâya and Oronish lay. Understanding burst in her.

"Râvar!" she shouted. "Over there—"

He turned on her, furious; but even if he had looked in the proper direction it was too late. The smoke tore apart. Two figures darted forward, hurling something in the direction of the three Shapers, dancing back and away. A glittering cloud of dust shot up—manita, for the Shapers were writhing, rolling on the stone, clawing at their faces. With their incapacitation the clamor of battle fell away; for a moment Axane heard the awful chorus of their coughing. There was a whining sound, a thud, and another and another; and all three Shapers lay still.

It was done in the time it took Râvar to surge to his feet, shouting. Again the smoke-veil swept aside; for a moment Axane saw the knot of soldiers who had scaled the cleft, the two shaven-headed Shapers who had assisted and concealed them. The bowmen were already turning to loose another volley; she heard a whine, felt the arrow whip above her head. Then a deep concussion jarred the summit, as if a great fist had hammered down, and a fusillade of light burst from the rock. Where the soldiers stood the summit cracked, like a breaking plate. They vanished into that sudden vacancy; briefly, Axane heard their screams.

For a moment it was almost quiet. Then the sounds of shaping rose again on the Plains below—the army's Shapers, taking advantage of the respite. Râvar fell to his knees, gasping.

"Varas! We have to hold them!"

But the older man had drawn back from the edge. In the growing light Axane could see the slack exhaustion of his face. "It's no use," he said. "We're finished."

"No!" Râvar's voice cracked. "You and I are strong! We can hold them!"

"For how long? Look." Varas pointed. "They're already putting out the fires. They're too many for us. No, boy. It was a good try, but we've lost. I'll stay here and distract them as I can. You go seal the Cavern of the Blood." And then, when Râvar did not move: "Go! You know what must be done."

For a long moment Râvar stared at him. Never in her life had Axane seen a face so terrible. Then he pushed to his feet.

"Come," he said, turning that awful gaze on her. She scrambled up; he grasped her wrist and pulled her toward the stairs. She looked over her shoulder, toward the place where the soldiers had been, fractured now by a wide crevasse running all the way to the summit's edge. It had taken Haxmapâya and Oronish when it opened, but Sonhauka still lay upon the stone, his limbs thrown wide, an arrow in his chest.

Râvar went down before her, so fast and reckless she was certain he must fall. At the bottom he seized her again and began to run up the ledge, dragging her behind him. They reached the turning of the cleft, and came before the Cavern of the Blood. The rising day paled the sky, but not yet enough to eclipse the light that flooded past the torrent at the cavern's mouth.

Before the flame-shaped fissure known as Risaryâsi's Ladder, Râvar halted.

"Râvar!" Axane had to shout over the pounding of the falls. "What are you going to do?"

He dropped her wrist and turned to her. His amber skin gleamed with water; his clothes, already soaked through, clung to him. His face was no longer terrible, but utterly impassive.

"I'm going to seal the Cavern. They'll come into Refuge now. They'll see everything, but this they must not see. I'll go inside and seal it. When they're gone, I'll open it again."

"You'll seal yourself *inside*?"

"I have to stay." She saw now that the wetness of his face was not all Revelation's doing: He was weeping. "They know it's here—even if I seal it they'll search for it. I have to be here to defend it."

"No." She stepped toward him, urgent. "You have to go to our people now. You have to defend them."

"I can't." The tears welled and spilled, welled and spilled; he did not seem to be aware of them. At his back the cataract thundered down, the mists of its spray coiling toward the golden glory above. "This is a sacred place. This is where Ârata passed the ages in sleep. This is where he'll return when it's time for him to sleep again. If it's defiled, he'll have no place to rest."

"Then let him find another place! Râvar, Refuge is lost, but its people still live! When the soldiers find no one here they'll go in search of them. You can't let that happen! You have to try and stop it!"

The stone of his expression cracked, and for a second she glimpsed the agony behind it. "I can't stop it!" he shouted. "Don't you understand? I've failed! This is all I can do!"

"Râvar, listen—"

"Come with me." He seized her again, and tried to pull her toward the stairs.

"No! I'm not going to let you wall me up in there!"

"I swore an oath to your father I'd save your life."

"Let me go!"

To her surprise, he did. For a moment he watched her, his eyes moving on her face. Then he turned and set his feet upon the stairs.

"Râvar! Come back!"

But he was climbing now—backward, unmaking the steps below him as he mounted. Rage seized her, shattering and pointless.

"Râvar!" she screamed. "Don't do this! Râvar! *Râvar!*"

He reached the Cavern's opening and slipped inside. For a moment its brilliance shone on, unchanged; then there was a pulse of greater light, cold white against the Cavern's warm gold; and the gold was gone.

She ran back along the ledge, and turned. The Cavern had vanished. There was nothing to see but an unbroken cliff face with a cataract pounding past it, lit up like crystal at the summit where the sun was rising, tumbling dark all the rest of the way to black Revelation below.

She sank to her knees. A wild burst of weeping took her— fury and sorrow and terror, so tangled she could not tell which was strongest. After it passed she knelt for a time on the ledge, hoping against hope that Râvar would relent and emerge. At last she pushed herself to her feet and began to wander down toward Refuge, with no clear idea of what she meant to do. The sound of the falls diminished behind her. She began to hear again the crash and thud of shaping, muted somewhat by the depth of the cleft. Varas, she thought, still doing what he could.

Not until she was level with Labyrinth did it occur to her that the concussions had increased in volume as she moved downward, and that they were too loud anyway to be rising from the Plains. *It's the barrier,* she realized. *The barrier Râvar and the others made. They've reached it, and the army's Shapers are trying to breach it.*

She stood were she was, paralyzed. She could not let them find her. But where to hide? In one of Labyrinth's remoter apartments? In the grain bins of the Treasury? In the turning corridors of the House of Dreams? But they would certainly search those places, and eventually would find her; and the thought of huddling in darkness while their searching brought them closer and ever closer made her skin crawl in horror. Should she climb back to the summit, then? But there was nothing on that bare expanse of stone to conceal her if the soldiers climbed there, too.

Of all possibilities, she could think only to flee back to the Cavern of the Blood. Risaryâsi's Ladder was there, narrow and dark; if she went all the way inside, she would not be visible even to someone standing at its mouth. They would search Refuge's living spaces, but surely, surely they would not search the fissures.

A roar came from down the ledge. Terror shot through her. She turned and raced the way she had come. She reached the terminus of the cleft, too intent on flight to think of the strangeness of the now-dark cliff wall. Risaryâsi's Ladder opened before her. She flung herself into it. The water-sculpted walls were barely wider than her body, and her shoulders and elbows scraped against the rough stone. She came upon the fissure's end with an impact that sank her teeth into her tongue. Stunned, she turned and set her back against it, her heart trying to beat its way out of her body.

Safe, she thought. *Safe now.*

She woke with a jolt sometime later, huddled awkwardly on her side. Her body ached; her tongue throbbed where she had bitten it.

Gingerly, she pushed herself upright. The inside of the fissure was dry, its floor softened by centuries' accumulation of rock dust. The walls, in this space where the sun never reached, breathed a steady chill, and thrummed a little with the violence of the falls. Even so, the river's voice was muted; she could hear the sound of her own breathing, the rustle of her clothing. Ahead, the fissure's opening framed a slice of the outside world, like a gash in a black curtain; she could see straight down the ledge, nearly to the turning of the cleft. It had been bright with sun when she closed her eyes; but now the sun was gone, though it was not yet dark.

She sat staring at it. Into it, after a time, came people: a little group of men. Two Shapers walked in front, recognizable by their shaven heads and red garments. After them came a pair of soldiers, with crossbows at the ready. And after them . . . Axane caught her breath. Dâdar, unhooded. And another, whom she recognized as the Son Vivaniya, one of the younger Brethren.

The Shapers and soldiers came on, but the Sons paused, looking upward. Dâdar said something to Vivaniya; Vivaniya replied, and Dâdar shook his head. They began to move again, catching up to their escort, which had paused to wait for them. Wrapped in darkness at the back of Risaryâsi's Ladder, Axane felt as naked as if she stood before them unconcealed.

They halted before the fissure's mouth. Dâdar gestured; the escort fell back a little. He and Vivaniya stared up at the falls; they stepped closer to the edge, then back, then to the side, examining it from several perspectives. Vivaniya leaned toward Dâdar and spoke—or shouted rather, to be heard above the din of the water. Again Dâdar shook his head. Vivaniya shouted again; this time Dâdar pulled away, making an angry chopping motion with his hand. He gestured to the soldiers and the waiting Shapers, signaling them to remain where they were, and then took the younger man's arm and drew him into Risaryâsi's Ladder.

Axane was so horrified she nearly screamed.

The two Sons halted just inside the fissure's mouth, black silhouettes against the brightness without. They were intent upon each other; they did not glance toward the fissure's back.

"Don't speak in front of them," Dâdar said. By some trick

of acoustics, his voice came to Axane clearly. "They know nothing of what we look for here."

"They would have had to know it, Brother, if the thing had been there."

"But it is not. There's nothing, only rock and water, just as I predicted. And so they do not need to know."

"Did you never doubt, Brother?"

"Not for a moment. I always knew what I would see when we reached this place."

"Yet the apostate described it so precisely." Vivaniya shook his head. "The mouth of the cave, the stairway leading up to it. This fissure." He paused. "The light."

Dâdar shrugged. "He lied."

"But we saw the light, Brother. Above the cliff, as we approached—"

"A trick of the moon. Or of those wretched corrupted Shapers, seeking to distract us."

Vivaniya was silent a moment. "Perhaps what we see now is the trick."

Dâdar stepped closer to him. "What was in your mind, Brother, in the instant before you turned that corner? What did *you* expect to see?"

"I thought . . . I thought to see what the apostate described."

"And what did you *hope* to see?"

Silence.

"Your hope was the same as my certainty, I think. Now your hope has been fulfilled, and my certainty has been vindicated. We can return, in good faith, and say as much to our spirit-siblings."

"But what if we are wrong? What if—"

"*We are not wrong,* Brother."

More silence. At last, slowly, Vivaniya nodded. "I accept the evidence of my senses."

"Very wise. For what other evidence could there be?"

Vivaniya turned away, looking out toward the ledge. "I wish we could depart tonight. I'm eager to be gone."

"There's still work to do, Brother. And the men need rest.

This was only the beginning—a diversion, to blunt our strength. The real battle lies ahead."

"Even now I find it hard to believe there were so few Shapers atop the cliff." Vivaniya shook his head. "Such strength—I would not have thought it possible. When we find the rest of them . . ."

"Courage, Brother. We have many Shapers of our own still, and most of our manita. Our forces are diminished, but not so much we cannot do what must be done. In Ârata's name, we will prevail."

Vivaniya sighed. "In Ârata's name."

They returned to the ledge. With their escort, they departed.

Axane remained inside Risaryâsi's Ladder through the night, through the day that followed and much of the day after that. She emerged only to quench her thirst, lapping like an animal at water caught in crevices and pockets of stone. At last, near evening on the second day, terribly hungry and unable to bear confinement any longer, she crept out of her hiding place and with much caution and many pauses to listen for noises below, made her way down the ledge.

The army was gone. But before it departed, its Shapers had destroyed Refuge—pulling the cleft down around it, flattening the great spaces Cyras and Mandapâxa had created, and the House of Dreams, which human hands had not made at all. The entrances stood choked with boulders and huge slabs of rock, their exterior sculpting violently defaced. Above the Temple, the images of Ârata had sagged and run like molten metal, and there was only pitted stone where the wheel of time had been. The pulley that had brought water up from the river was snapped off at its base. Even the platforms shaped out over Revelation's eddies, where the people of Refuge had gone to bathe and wash their clothes, had been smashed.

Axane wandered past the wreckage, too stunned to take it in. How could she have failed to hear such devastation, even deep inside Risaryâsi's Ladder? How could she not have felt the cleft shudder with it, even over the pounding of the falls?

She had known they meant to turn Refuge into a place of ghosts. But she had not realized they intended to annihilate it, to rip it apart. Why punish it so, when soon there would be no one left to live in it? Why not simply leave it slowly to unmake itself?

She stood before the House of Dreams. Rubble spilled from its round pink mouth, partly blocking the ledge. There would be no more Dreams here; in time, as the people of Refuge died in their captivity, there would be no one to recall there ever had been. It was not only Refuge's spaces that had been obliterated: The whole life, the whole history of a people had been wiped away. The labor, the generations, the joy and hatred and love and sorrow and wisdom and waste—all gone, erased, as if none of it had ever been.

She sank down where she was and wept.

Dry-eyed at last, she sat as darkness fell. Belatedly, the reality of her situation was coming clear to her. Râvar might yet emerge—but for all she knew he had destroyed himself in the sealing of the Cavern, or had gone mad and would remain inside until he died. Her people were lost—not yet captured, perhaps, but soon to be. For all intents and purposes she was alone, marooned in the Burning Land.

She was afraid, but her grief and shock were still too great to allow her to feel it very much. At last, since there was nothing else to do, she curled up on her side and fell asleep.

For the first time in several days, she slept deeply enough to dream. She skimmed along Revelation's turning course, between its stands of timber. She came upon the army—not encamped, but moving forward through the night, following Refuge's trail. She circled it once, twice—counting, even in the darkness, how its numbers were reduced. Then she flew on, with a swiftness that blurred the world around her, until suddenly, at a bend of the river where a sandstone bluff overhung the bank, she glimpsed the spark of fire. It was Refuge. There was no Dream-veil to repel her: She saw the shelters her people had made and the cook pits they had dug, and knew that this was not a single night's halt but a settled camp. Here was where they had chosen to wait out the battle. Here was where the army would come upon them.

She willed herself to descend, but her Dream wrenched her up again and sent her spinning back toward Refuge, where the cleft, black and lightless, lay against the stars. Her Dream-eyes pierced the dark: She saw on the ledge below a small huddled shape—herself. She hung there for a moment, twinned. She felt the currents of her dreaming, and knew that they would obey her. She could descend, return to herself—or she could abandon her body, rise up and soar on, never turning back. Her Dream-self would vanish once her body ceased to breathe. But would that not be better than to go on living, all alone in this place?

She woke gasping, clawing for air. Revelation's clamor echoed in her ears. All around her pressed the dark of ruined Refuge, which she had never known truly dark, not once in all her life. Horror overwhelmed her. She did not want to vanish. She did not want to die.

I can follow the army's trail, she thought. They were maybe two days ahead—not so far she could not catch up. By the time she did they would have found her people and taken them captive—but surely she could contrive somehow to slip in among them. Who would notice one more prisoner among so many? Perhaps, when they reached Thuxra City, she could manage to escape. Or maybe Vâsparis would help her again, if he had survived. And if not . . . better to be captive in Arsace than to remain behind—alone.

She thought of Râvar. But if she waited, and he did not come out, she would lose her one chance. If he did appear, he would never consent to become a prisoner; he might even see it as his duty to stop her. *No,* she thought, panic rising again into her throat. *I won't wait. He chose the Cavern over Refuge—let him stay with it.*

She would have left at once, so horrible had Refuge's vacancy become to her, but she did not want to clamber over the wreckage of the Shapers' barrier in the dark. She waited for dawn, sitting with her knees drawn up and her head resting upon them, her arms clasped tight around her legs, as small as she could make herself in the vastness of the night.

She set out as soon as she could see her hand before her face. In fact there was no rubble at the barrier: The army's Shapers had pierced it with a neat passageway, and she was able to walk straight through. On the Plains she found the army's trail, easy to read in crushed grass and churned earth and horse droppings. They had buried their dead in one of Refuge's fallow fields: a double row of narrow mounds, each with a boulder at its head. She paused to count: forty-three. It startled her to see so few, until she remembered the horsemen who had been swallowed by Râvar's rifts.

She walked for three days. In the forenoon of the fourth day she reached the bend in the river her Dream had showed her, beyond which lay the sandstone bluff where her people had taken shelter.

She knew the army must already have come and gone, that the camp would be abandoned. Still she was cautious as she moved through the dappled shade along the riverbank. To her left Revelation flowed past, smooth as Shaper-worked stone, so broad and placid it was difficult to recall the violence of its passage down the cleft. The wind had fallen off as it always did in the middle of the day, and with it the singing of the insects that lived in the bitterbark trees. She could hear only the crackle of her footsteps in the leaf litter, and the sound of her own breathing.

She rounded the turn, and saw her people's campsite a little distance on. There was no smoke, no motion. Blankets and tents and bundles were thrown about—had they not been allowed to take those things with them, then?

As she drew closer, it began to seem to her that there was an oddness to these piles of debris. Surely that was an arm, flung out there—and over there, a pair of legs . . . She felt a spreading coldness, despite the breathless heat beneath the trees. *There has been a battle,* she thought. *People have died.*

And then suddenly her vision shifted, and she understood what she was really seeing. Not the litter of a hastily abandoned camp. Not a few isolated corpses. The tossed bundles, the tangled blankets—they were all bodies, dozens of them, scores of them. Under the spicy scent of bitterbark she could smell the odor of putrefaction.

For an instant she stood as if struck to stone. Then she flung herself forward.

Beneath the sandstone bluff, the people of Refuge lay dead. It had happened more than a day ago, for the blood from the sword thrusts and arrow shots that had killed them was dark and congealed, and their bodies had begun to bloat. There was no indication of struggle or resistance, no weapons to hand or signs of flight: Death had come upon them unaware. The air was murmurous with flies, and the stench of decay was like a wall. Axane pressed her hands over her nose and mouth. She was a healer, and had seen terrible wounds and injuries, but never anything like this. Her mind refused to accept the truth her senses brought her. A moment, a blink, a breath of wind, and the illusion would vanish, and she would see what ought to be before her: a disordered camp, abandoned.

To the right, something pale drew her eye. A scattering of . . . . folios? Yes, for there was her father's cabinet, tipped on its side, its doors hanging open. And beside it . . . beside it. . . .

No, she thought, horrified. *I can't.*

But she had to be sure.

She forced herself to turn. Her head seemed to float some distance above her body; she barely felt her feet upon the ground. The whole world seemed to throb and flare in time with the beating of her pulse. She tried not to look at what she passed, but there was so much death that there was nothing else to see. Dust stirred under her feet, the acrid smell of it piercing even the stink of decay, and her eyes burned. *Manita,* she thought. She understood now: The army had immobilized the people of Refuge with manita, then come into the camp and slaughtered them.

She was staggering by the time she reached the blood-grain cabinet. Her father lay beside it on a pile of blankets. He had been killed with a single sword thrust to the chest. Flies crawled about the wound, at the corners of his mouth and around his half-open eyes. His belly was swollen, his

face and hands puffed and blackened. Near him was Vivanishâri, crumpled on her side, the earth stained dark where
her blood had flowed. The infant, Axane's namesake, lay by
her mother, her throat cut.

The earth turned over beneath Axane's feet, and everything went white.

She came to herself sometime later, stumbling along beside
the river. It was nearly evening. She had no memory of the
intervening hours. The air was hot—she could feel the heat
against her skin—but she was terribly cold, and her teeth
chattered as she walked. She did not know where she was
going, nor did she care. She was empty, as empty as ruined
Refuge.

There was motion in front of her, something living: a
man. Râvar. He had survived, then. Or maybe he was illusion. Maybe she had gone mad, and only thought she saw
him. But his hands on her arms did not feel illusory, or the
way he shook her, as a parent might shake a disobedient
child.

"Did you find them?" he demanded. With a distant part of
herself, she registered the wildness of his eyes. "Axane!
Where are they?"

"Behind me," she told him. "I left them all behind me."

"Behind you? What do you mean?"

"They're sleeping." She began to laugh, shocking herself.
"Go see if you can wake them up."

"Ârata's Blood!" He shoved her aside and began to run.
Into her emptiness, suddenly, rage came leaping.

"You might have saved them," she shouted after him.
"Think of that when you look at them. You might have saved
them!"

But he had already vanished among the trees. She turned
and stumbled on.

— 26 —

By the time Axane reached the cleft, she was no longer in shock. She longed for the numbness and disorientation of those first hours; what she felt instead was almost too terrible to be borne.

Under the trees, within sight of Refuge's abandoned fields, she halted and lay down. She did not know why she had returned; on the other hand, there was no less reason to seek out this place than any other. She did not close her eyes; she did not dare to sleep, for fear her Dreams might take her back to the place where her people lay murdered. Instead, she watched the mosaic of leaves above her, and in their restless, constant shifting tried to lose the memory of her father's face. Around her the whole world was in motion—the grasses swaying, the bitterbarks creaking and whispering, Revelation slipping past like oil. Only she was still. She thought perhaps she would never stir again.

She did not want to eat or drink, but her body had its own will, driving her down to the river when her thirst became too great, and to forage along the banks when hunger pushed a spike into her belly. Even so, she could feel herself growing weak. The world seemed blurred about the edges, and her limbs felt light, attenuated, as if it were not just her flesh but her bones that were diminishing.

Sometime later—she was not sure how long—Râvar returned. She heard him before she saw him, his footsteps crackling in the fallen leaves, keeping a slow and burdened pace. He paused when he saw her, and for a moment they looked at each other—all that was left, the two of them, of Refuge. He had put off his soiled Shaper clothing for a drab brown tunic, and carried a large bundle on his back. His face was haggard, streaked with dirt and sweat, but there was none of the wildness of before. She felt nothing to see him, apart from a remote curiosity as to how he had brought himself to walk among the dead, in order to take the clothing he wore and whatever it was he carried.

He turned away, and resumed his plodding progress. By the soldiers' graves he paused. Thunder growled; the spark of shaping stuttered across the ground, and in its wake the earth spread flat again, all trace of the burials gone. He moved on, into the cleft. Later, she heard noise—great crashing and grinding sounds. After a time it stopped, and she forgot it.

Night came, and morning. There were more footsteps. He loomed above her, blotting out the leaves.

"Get up," he said.

She stared at him. He seemed as distant as the sun.

"Now." He bent and gripped her arms, pulling her to a sitting position. "We're going."

She groped for speech. "Going?"

"Across the Burning Land. I would see for myself this demon realm of yours."

Arsace. She tried to comprehend it and could not. She shook her head, and subsided back onto the leaves.

"Get . . . *up*." Again he took hold of her, this time hauling her all the way to her feet, where she stood, swaying. "I'm going, and you're coming with me, if I have to make a travois and bind you to it and drag you all the way. Here." He thrust a wad of cloth into her arms. "It's for you . . . things you'll need. Now come."

It was easier to obey than to struggle, and so she followed him as he led the way up the riverbank. In her weakened condition she was soon laboring for breath. He slowed, as if to accommodate her, but it was obvious that he was as depleted as she. By the time he called a halt his golden skin looked gray, and when he swung his bundle off his back he had to clench his teeth to keep from groaning.

They picked up the army's trail the next day, looping widely around the charred destruction of the battlefield. It led them east, past the cleft, doubling back toward the point where the force had come onto the Plains. At last they reached the remains of the encampment where the noncombatants had waited out the battle, and turned north, striking out across the barrens.

They walked and ate and slept and answered the needs of their bodies side by side, the ordinary concerns of privacy made meaningless by the extremity of their situation. They spoke to one another only when it could not be avoided. Sometimes, in the monotony of the constant plodding, Axane forgot Râvar was with her and imagined she moved through the night alone. Because it was less painful to be strong than weak, she forced herself to consume the food and water he made. Even in exhaustion, he shaped with thoughtless ease: An instant's concentration called up quantities of fruit or grain, a glance and a frown pulled water from the rock, a moment's focus drew pillars of stone from the surface of the barrens, so they could drape blankets to make a shelter.

He kept them going with a grim determination that suggested purpose, though she could not imagine what purpose he could find in seeking out a world in which he did not believe. Awake, he was as closed as a wall, sunk utterly in his own dark thoughts, but she knew he wept in his sleep. She had not dreamed since the attack, but she still feared her slumber and often lay open-eyed for hours beside him.

When his control cracked, it revealed only anger. She could feel it breathing from him then like heat from a forge. Sometimes he stared at her, his eyes intent and his face very still, and she remembered how he had looked when he walled her up inside the chamber. Perhaps she should have been afraid. She had never been so utterly at anyone's mercy, not even the Brethren's. But she could not find much reason to care. The Burning Land might kill her or he might, and she did not see that it made a great deal of difference which. Why would he have brought her with him, anyway, if he meant to harm her? He had put some planning into it: In the bundle he had given her were gowns and chemises and sandals, even a comb for her hair and a hooded cloak to wear against the sun—all, she knew, taken from the dead.

One night, several weeks beyond the stone barrens, he sat across from her and watched her with that angry, brooding gaze. Normally she tried to ignore him; but this night, suddenly, it was too much.

"Stop it," she said. "Stop staring at me like that."

He did not react, did not even blink; it was as if she had not spoken. But then he said, in a voice tight with the effort of control, "You should have known."

"Known?"

"That they meant to kill them. You should have known."

She drew in her breath. If he had driven a knife into her, it could not have been more painful.

"Well?" he demanded. "Have you nothing to say?"

"I didn't know," she said raggedly.

"How could you not know?" he cried, and the heat of his released rage seemed to sear her skin. "You traveled with them. You walked among them. *How could you not know?*"

"I *didn't* know! I never heard anything—no one ever said anything—there was no sign, nothing at all—"

"So you say now." He practically spat the words.

"Do you think . . . do you think that I . . . that I wouldn't . . ." She had to stop for breath. "I came . . . all the way from Arsace to warn you. How would I not have told you that, if I'd known?"

"You abandoned Refuge." The little fire he had shaped against the chill crackled and sparked between them; in its shadowlight, his green eyes seemed black. "You chose to go among its murderers. Who knows what you're capable of?"

"I didn't know!" she shouted. "Curse you a thousand times to ash, I didn't know!"

Against her will, she had begun to weep. For he was right. Not that she had known and not warned, of course; but that she was responsible. As she lay half-starved on the riverbank, her mind had been too clouded for coherent thought; but with increasing strength had come increasing clarity, and over the past days and nights she had questioned everything that had happened, tracing back the chain of events that had brought destruction on Refuge, searching for choices that, made differently, might have forged a different chain. If, knowing the Brethren's ruthlessness, she had guessed the army's true intentions. If, listening to the stories the wives told, it had occurred to her to fear more than just the soldiers' cruelty. If she had not trusted so much the information Vâsparis gave her; she did not suspect him of deceiving her, but it seemed to her now that she should have thought to worry more about what he might not know, about plans and schemes kept between the commanders and the Brethren. If, in Baushpar, she had behaved more humbly, spoken less defiantly, somehow made the Brethren hate Refuge less. If she had never abandoned Refuge at all—never given Gyalo the crystal of the Blood, never traveled to Baushpar as proof in her own person of Refuge's existence. Perhaps they would not have believed him then. Perhaps they would simply have locked him up and forgotten about the Burning Land.

She was aware, even as she lacerated herself with such speculations, that the web of circumstance that had brought Refuge to its end was too large and too complex to turn on any individual fault. Yet always she saw her father's face, turned sightless to the sky. Always she saw the carnage beneath the bluff. And she understood, bone deep, that it *was* her fault—was and always would be. But it was not Râvar's place to say so.

"How dare you blame me?" she cried at him through her tears. "You're the one who refused to save them."

"I didn't know they meant to kill them!" he shouted.

"But you knew they'd be taken captive. You knew they'd be dragged back to the outside world and put in prison."

"I thought they could escape. They had a head start—they had Gâvarti, and the trainees—and we killed so many of those men, you saw how many we killed. I thought they had a chance—"

"A chance!" she cried wildly. "How could they have a chance—women, children, babies, men not trained as soldiers?"

"I had to protect the Cavern. What else could I do?" The fury of it brought him up on his knees, halfway toward her across the fire. "I was all alone! There was only me! *It was the only thing I could save!*"

For a moment they were eye to eye. Then he subsided, falling back heavily where he had been. He stared at the fire.

"I know what you think," he said. "You think I shouldn't have tried to defend Refuge at all. You think I should have abandoned it and fled with the others."

She said nothing, for it was true.

"Maybe I should have . . . done things differently. But we were so strong . . . we would have beaten them, I know we would have, if they hadn't tricked us. And Ârata—I thought Ârata *must* be with us. Even though he'd turned his face away before, and allowed Refuge to . . . to dwindle, to diminish, how could he turn from us in this?" He spoke painfully, as if each word required separate effort. "Maybe . . . maybe I should have known what would happen—even if you didn't tell me, maybe I should have known. But I couldn't have saved them!" There was raw anguish in his voice. "Not with all those Shapers to oppose me, and that drug—how could I have stood against that, just me, by myself? In the end they would have overcome me, and it would all have turned out just the same, except that I'd be dead now, too, and there would be no one to—"

He bit off the words. His face was ravaged. His eyes glistened. Axane watched him, feeling something stir in her. She had heard him weeping in the night, but until that moment she had not consciously acknowledged that he, too, must grieve, that he, too, must question choice and circumstance and wound himself with guilt. She glanced away, down at her hands, laced together on her knees. It felt strange to consider another's pain. Till now she had had no room for any suffering but her own.

"I buried them." Remembered horror shivered in the words. "I opened up the riverbank and closed them all inside."

He did not speak again. After a while Axane lay down in her blankets, and tried to sleep. She roused in the night to hear him sobbing—not the ragged gasps of his dreaming, but soft covert sounds that told her he was awake and trying not to be heard. Again that thread of pity stirred in her, winding strange and hesitant through the dark preoccupation of her grief, through all the blame and anger that lay between them. She wondered if she could bear to offer him comfort, if he would accept it if she did. But before she could make up her mind he fell quiet, and she knew that the moment, if there had ever been one, was gone.

When she woke at sunrise, his blankets were empty. She sat up, then got to her feet, scanning the vistas of sand and scrub. He was nowhere to be seen.

Breathless, she thought, *He's abandoned me.*

She waited. The sun climbed the arch of the sky; beneath it the Burning Land simmered, vast and vacant. She was aware of her pulse, tapping against her throat, of the depth of the desert's silence. She moved only once, to pull on her hooded robe as the sun drifted toward its apex; other than that she did not stir, not even to quench her thirst at the little bubbling flow of water Râvar had coaxed out of the ground the night before.

At last, in the metallic, mirage-quivering distance, she saw a dark blur of motion. She started to her feet. Relief flooded through her, so powerful she sobbed aloud.

By the time he reached her she was composed. "Where did you go?" she asked.

He shrugged, and bent and began to gather up their things. His face was hard and closed, as usual; looking at him, it was difficult to remember those sobs in the dark.

It was a turning point. Axane's grief was no less; the world around her still vanished from time to time, and she was on the riverbank again, staring into her father's dead face. But somehow, over the days of journeying, she had come to care again whether she lived or died. It was possible now to think about their destination, waiting beyond the heat-blurred horizon—Arsace, not a mirage but real. She did not allow herself to hope too much, or even to assume that they would reach it. But she no longer walked only because Râvar required it.

The army was returning along its outward route. New signs of passage lay atop the old—the usual litter of human debris and animal droppings, and now and then something more substantial: the carcass of a horse, a cairn of stones to mark a burial. Axane and Râvar walked beside this path of destruction but not on it, for Râvar preferred to set his feet on unstirred ground. Always they camped some distance away. The army had been many days ahead of them initially, and with its diminished numbers must be moving more swiftly than it had on the way out; and their own progress had been very slow at first. Even so, she was never free of the fear that they might draw too close and encounter some straggler or outrider.

Râvar seemed both fascinated and repelled by the army's leavings. At night, when they stopped to eat and sleep, he asked questions about the outside world—its places, its customs, its different faith. He listened intently to all she said. She had no idea what he might be thinking.

"What would you have done," he said to her one evening, "if you'd stayed in the outside world? If you'd never come back to Refuge?"

She felt the stirring of those lost dreams. "I would have gone to the city of Ninyâser in Arsace and been a healer there."

"Ninyâser," he repeated. "Why there?"

"I suppose because it was the only city I knew."

"You'd have lived there all alone?"

"Yes." She hesitated. "Râvar, do you actually believe any of what I've told you?"

He looked at her. A fire leaped between them; beyond its small illumination the moon painted the world in shades of black and silver. "Why do you ask me that?"

"It's just . . . in Refuge, you seemed so sure the outside world was nothing but illusion. Have you changed your mind?"

He shrugged. "If I'm to walk among its deceptions, I should know them as if they were real. Shouldn't I?"

"But if you think the outside world is all illusion, why do you want to go to it? Why travel to a place you believe is nothing more than . . . than an evil dream?"

He looked down at his fingers, in which he was turning a smooth pebble. "Why not? My world is gone. Why should I not go to theirs?"

She did not press. The anger in him was never far from the surface; she did not want to stir it.

They were camped by a dry riverbed in a region of low hills, where sparse stands of trees spoke of water close below the ground. Earlier, Râvar had made a flood, causing the river briefly to run again, and they had bathed and washed their clothes. She had gone apart from him to do so, beyond a bend in the river's course that hid her from his sight. In the beginning she had scarcely been conscious of him as a living being, let alone as a man—a man who once had pursued her with single-minded intensity. But now she was aware of it all the time. She had felt him watching her as she returned, her gown clinging to her damp body, and had been careful to avoid his eyes.

He sighed. "You're right."

"What?"

"I do believe you." He was still looking at the pebble, which he was now passing from hand to hand. "That the outside world is not illusion."

"You do?"

"Because we were wrong. All of us, from Risaryâsi on. It's just as that . . . creature, the false Messenger . . . it's just as he said. She had a Dream, and drew the wrong conclusions. And for all the years since then, we've lived a lie."

She stared at him, shocked. He dropped the pebble and met her eyes. In his face was a bleakness beyond despair.

"Well, what else could it be? If we were really Ârata's chosen people, how could he have permitted what happened? Why would he not have intervened to save us? No. He didn't intervene because he cares nothing for us, because we are *not* his chosen people. We are nothing—the descendants of a group of fugitives who happened by chance upon his empty resting place and spun out of that accident a web of illusion as false as anything the Enemy could devise. Why should Ârata need a chosen people anyway, to hide in the wilderness and remember the past? He's a god. He could create humankind anew at the ending of the cycle. Or not. As he chose."

"Râvar—" What could she say to him, she who did not believe?

"I thought it was our fault." He had turned away from her, staring down at his hands, empty now upon his knees. "When the poison of the false Messenger divided us, when things began to . . . to fall apart, I thought we'd brought it on ourselves, because we weren't strong enough to reject the deceptions of the Enemy. Your father said that Ârata was testing us through suffering, but I said that Ârata would never be so cruel. It was we who made him turn his face away, when so many of us embraced the false Messenger. I thought we must work to win him back. But really his face was never turned to us at all."

"Râvar." She could hardly bear the ache of pity she felt. "I'm so sorry."

"Why?" He looked at her again. "You've always known it, haven't you? I always felt something in you, some difference. It's part of what . . ." His mouth tightened; for a moment he did not go on. "It was that, wasn't it. It's why you could go with that . . . man. Why you never thought him a demon, or the Next Messenger either. You always knew Risaryâsi was wrong."

She could see no point in lying. "Not always."

"It doesn't matter. You were right."

"I never chose it, Râvar. I didn't choose not to believe."

"Well, I choose," he said. "I'm finished with belief. I'm finished with Ârata too. I won't honor a god who allows such things to happen, even to those who are unchosen. I won't serve a cruel god."

She was silent. In truth it seemed to her that what had happened spoke not so much of cruelty as of indifference. A cruel god might permit human beings to destroy each other, driven by their own darkness—but surely only a god who was utterly indifferent to the world would accept the service of men and women like the Brethren, let alone allow them to speak in his name. Until she found her people dead on the banks of Revelation, she had thought the Brethren merely pitiless, merely hypocritical and hard—but she now knew that they were far worse. She thought of Dâdar and Vivaniya, standing inside Risaryâsi's Ladder and agreeing to turn away from the truth hidden in the cliffs above. Had they also turned their backs as Refuge was slaughtered? How could a god who cared even a little about the world allow such creatures to rule the faith that honored him?

Râvar watched her. "How can you bear it," he said, "to live without belief?"

She glanced away, toward the riverbed, where a little water still glinted in hollows and on rocks. In truth, she scarcely remembered what it had felt like to believe; but she did not want to tell him that. "It grows easier."

"It must have been hard, keeping such a secret."

She nodded.

"Are there others?"

"Others?"

"Other secrets."

She heard the change, the shift of mood. Carefully, she said, "No. No other secrets."

"Are you sure? Was he your lover, Axane? Is that why you went with him?"

"No, he was not my lover."

"Did he become your lover, then? You were many days alone with him. Many nights."

"He was never my lover. He made a vow never to be any-one's lover. They do that, the Shapers of the outside world."

"So he wasn't truly a man at all," he said with contempt. "Yet you chose him over me."

"I didn't choose *him*. I chose the outside world. He was a way to get me there. That's all. Nothing more."

"You're lying. I've given you all the truth that's in me, and still you lie to me."

He spoke low, but his eyes were hot. She understood: He had revealed too much, and sought to turn on her his anger with himself. But it was more than just anger she saw in his face. She thought of the way he had watched her when she returned from bathing. All at once she was afraid.

"I'm not lying, Râvar."

"It's always been this way between us, hasn't it? I reach toward you. You draw away."

She swallowed against the dryness of her mouth. "I'm not . . . drawing away."

"Even now—now that we're the last of Refuge, now we're all alone in the world—even now you turn from me. Do you think I don't see you judging me? What right do you have to judge me?" His voice was rising. "Do you think your grief is greater than mine? Do you think your loss is greater? Answer me!"

"No," she whispered.

"You're corrupt. I knew it after you ran away. But it made no difference. I still wanted you. I dreamed of you, all the time you were gone—I dreamed you returned and gave yourself to me, all your light, all your beautiful colors. I never looked at anyone else. No other woman even tempted me."

"Râvar—I'm sorry—".

"You're *sorry*? You threw away everything I offered you, as if it were nothing, as if *I* were nothing, as if *Refuge* were nothing, and you're *sorry*? You were mine, *mine*, bound and promised, and you let another steal you, steal you and spoil you." He had risen to a crouch. He began to move toward her, his shadow preceding him like some furtive beast. "But that doesn't matter now. Because I'm spoiled, too. As faithless, as guilty as you."

"Râvar." She backed away. "Stop. Please—"

"You have no right to turn from me," he said through his teeth. "Who can there ever be for either of us now but each other?"

He lunged. She scrambled back, but he caught her by the ankle and dragged her toward him. She tried to kick him off, but he was amazingly strong. He fell on her, pinning her with his weight; she writhed and beat at him with her fists but could not get free. He captured her wrists with one hand while with the other he tore at her clothing, ripping the rotten cloth of her gown. She felt his lips, his teeth. He drove his knee between her legs, forcing them apart, and thrust into her with all his strength and all his rage. She screamed; he clamped his palm across her mouth to silence her, so tight she could hardly breathe.

It was over quickly. He lay a moment, gasping, then pulled away. She curled onto her side, drawing her knees to her chest. There was blood in her mouth. She would have given anything not to weep, but the tears came and she could not stop them.

"Axane—" There was something like horror in his voice. "Oh, Axane, I'm sorry—"

She jerked away, folding deeper into herself. After a while she heard his footsteps, moving off into the night.

She lay awake till dawn, in pain and shame and outrage. She was shocked, but when she looked inside herself she found no surprise—as if, for the past weeks, she had been watching a storm take shape, hoping it would pass over her but always knowing it might break above her head.

After that he turned to her as if by right, though never again with the violence of the first time, of which he seemed ashamed. He even attempted, clumsily, to please her; but she could not bring herself to feign response, and after a while he stopped trying and simply took her, quick and silent. She hated what he did to her, hated him for doing it; but she did not try to resist. He had brought her with him for her knowledge of the outside world or for this, or perhaps for both; he no longer asked her any questions, and if he could not use her body, why should he keep her with him? She did not want to be abandoned. All her will was focused upon reaching Arsace.

The Range of Clouds came into view, a gray stain on the horizon. At long last she began to dream again—Dreams of Galea, mostly, like the ones she had had when she was still trapped in Refuge. Now and then, though, her sleep took her south, and she saw the cleft rising from the silver grasses and soared above the trees that marked Revelation's course. She dreaded those Dreams; always she struggled to wake from them. As yet she had not come to ground, but she knew one night she would.

As the mountains rose larger, Râvar began to neglect himself, with a deliberateness that suggested some sort of self-punishment. He created abundant food and water, but barely ate. He allowed his hair and beard to grow snarled and matted. He no longer covered himself against the sun, walking all day clad in a breechclout, putting on his tunic only at night against the cold. When the strap of one of his sandals broke, he discarded both and continued barefoot. The sight of his feet, cut and swollen, moved Axane against her will, and she did what she could to treat his injuries with the meager resources the desert offered. But he refused to bind his feet with cloth, and every day inflicted new injury upon himself.

"This is ridiculous," she told him. "Are you trying to cripple yourself?"

"What if I am? Besides," he said bitterly, "I should have thought you'd take pleasure in it."

"These cuts will fester. I have nothing to use against infection."

"Then let them get infected."

"All right—torture yourself. I won't interfere. But it won't make you hate yourself any less."

She thought he would strike her. But after a tense moment

he turned away and did not say a word for the remainder of the day.

She dreamed one night of Ninyâser, where she had once thought to make a life. She flew above its streets and markets, its darkened dwellings, its silent temples. She slipped along the wide canal that cut the city in half, following the path of stars reflected there—the Year-Canal, Gyalo had told her it was called, for as many bridges spanned it as there were days in a year. On the canal's south side the streets became meaner, poorer. There she came upon a tall house with balconies hanging from its front. The small glow of lamplight drew her, like a moth. She fluttered onto the balcony and through the open shutters beyond. Inside, a man lay on a bed, one arm thrown across his face. She could see only his bearded jaw, the shape of his body beneath the coverlet; but he reminded her powerfully of Gyalo.

It woke her, that instant of false recognition. It was almost dawn, and the sky was paling, the early-morning grayness overtaking the stars. She lay looking up, tears sliding out of the corners of her eyes. She had not remembered it was possible to feel such longing. Would she dream him again in his prison, she wondered, when she was in Arsace? Was he even still alive for her to dream him?

What would happen once she and Râvar crossed the mountains? She had tried, during the journey, not to think of it, for she did not want to beguile herself with false hope. But more and more she was unable to prevent her mind from reaching forward. One thing she knew: She would find a way to get free of Râvar. Stranger though she was, she knew the outside world as he did not, and had no doubt she could escape him once they reached more populated areas. Alone, she knew, he would destroy himself. He had no experience in dissembling and must eventually reveal himself as a free Shaper. Much as she loathed him, she did not wish his death. But she would not lift a finger to save his life, if it meant remaining with him.

She knew they were close to Thuxra City. Still it surprised her when they reached the thoroughfare that cut through the mining areas.

"What happened here?" Râvar asked, looking at the great pits opening out on either side.

"These are copper mines," she told him, as Gyalo had once told her.

He stared around him with a kind of wonder. "Is it all as ugly as this?"

The following day they passed a group of worker barracks. Nearby lay a sunken area—a burial ground, Gyalo had said. At its near end, a flutter of red caught Axane's eye. She squinted at it, puzzled, then, realizing what she saw, drew in her breath. She broke from Râvar and went to stand above the pit. After a moment he came up behind her.

"What is it?"

"The Shapers," she said. "The army's Shapers."

There were six of them, their throats cut. They had not been covered over, simply tossed into the pit. Desert creatures had been at them; the sun was already beginning to turn the exposed skin of their arms and faces and shaven heads to leather. Once she would have shrunk from such a sight; but nothing could match the images of Refuge she carried.

"So few of them," Râvar breathed. "Did we kill so many?" He crouched down on his haunches, his gaze riveted on the bodies. "They did to them what they came to do to us. Why?" He looked up at her. "Why would they do this to their own?"

"They were free too long." Traveling with the army, she had wondered what lay in store for the Shapers; now she knew. "They saw too much."

"But why would they not save themselves? Why would they serve these people, if they knew they must die for it?"

She had no answer for him.

Thuxra City came in sight a few days later, a dark blot on the Burning Land's red soil, dwarfed by distance and the mountains behind it. An odd obscurity hung before the prison, a haze of dust Axane did not remember from before. Not until they were quite close did the cause become apparent. The pit mines that lay immediately beyond the prison's middens were in use again, the area around them aswarm with men and equipment.

"This wasn't here when I passed through the first time," she said. They had climbed one of the huge piles of tailings that rose beside the road, to get a better look.

"It's a good thing," Râvar said.

"Why? We'll have to go around now. It'll take twice as long."

He did not reply. After so much time alone, it was hard to think of the little moving figures as human; it was like watching the activity of an anthill, or one of the colonies of burrow-dwelling creatures that had lived on the Plains of Blessing. There looked to be more than a hundred workers, not counting the carts that rolled slowly back and forth between the prison and the pits—drawn, as far as Axane could tell, by men. Râvar crouched motionless beside her, his body as taut as stretched wire. He had been very tense over the past days, more silent even than usual, and she had begun to wonder whether he might be having second thoughts about crossing the Range of Clouds.

They moved on again, halting just after sunset. They were too close for a fire, and they sat in the growing darkness, eating the food Râvar shaped for them. When they were finished he spread out their blankets and indicated that Axane should lie down. She obeyed, her heart sinking. He had not made her yield to him for several weeks, and she had begun to hope his desire for her had died. But all he did was stretch himself beside her. He remained there through the night, his body cupping hers. From time to time he was wracked by bouts of shivering, as if he had a fever, though his skin was cool. It discomforted her so she could not sleep. By his breathing she knew that he was wakeful also.

As dawn stole across the world he drew away from her and rose. She watched through her lashes as he stripped off his tattered tunic, leaving himself attired only in a breech-clout, and sat down cross-legged in a meditation pose. He remained there as the sun climbed above the horizon, his face lifted to the rising warmth. It had been long since she had really looked at him. Now, as if for the first time, she perccived how his self-neglect had altered him. His arms and legs were wasted; every rib was visible. His fine amber skin was burned coarse and brown. The clean lines of his jaw were hidden by his matted beard, and his hair hung in a filthy tangle past his waist. His elegant feet were splayed and scarred and callused, his beautiful hands cracked and rough. He had become, she realized, the one thing she had not thought he could ever be: ugly.

He finished his meditation, or whatever it was, and got up with that fluid grace he still possessed. She shut her eyes, feigning sleep. She felt him kneel beside her.

"Axane," he said, quietly. "Axane, wake up."

She opened her eyes.

"This is where we part. You must go on alone."

It was so unexpected that for a moment she could only stare at him. "You're letting me go?"

"Yes. I have my own path to walk." He looked at her with his river green eyes, all that remained of his great beauty. "You don't have to pretend to be sorry."

She pushed herself upright, wondering if she could trust him. "What will you do?"

"I will destroy Thuxra City."

She gaped at him.

"Do you think I can't do it?" The serenity that masked his features did not flicker. "I can, you know. I don't have to un-make it—all I have to do is move the earth, and make it fall. I'm strong enough for that. There aren't any Shapers now to stand against me. There isn't any drug to cripple me."

In all this time, she had never really understood why he sought the outside world. Now she felt a leaden comprehension. "Is that the reason you've come all this way?" she said. "To get revenge for Refuge?"

He shook his head. "Thuxra City is just the beginning. There must be an act of destruction first."

"What do you mean?"

Instead of answering, he turned and rummaged in the bundle of his blankets and clothing, bringing out a leather wallet. He untied its laces and drew back its cover. Inside was something wrapped in linen. Carefully he pulled the cloth aside. Light bloomed through the fabric. The last fold fell away, revealing a crystal of the Blood as large as his fist.

"Do you understand now?" he said.

She stared at the honey-colored jewel. Its razor facets caught the rising brightness of the day; the brilliance at its heart danced like living fire. Not once had she suspected he carried it. "No," she whispered.

"They sent a false Messenger into Refuge," he said. "Now Refuge sends one in return."

"Do you mean . . ." The world around her had grown unreal; her voice seemed to come from miles away. "Do you mean you'll use this . . . to pretend . . . to be the Next Messenger?"

"Not pretend." He shook his head. "I *will* be the Next Messenger. *Their* Next Messenger. The Next Messenger they deserve. I'll make them believe in me. I'll lead them into false faith. I'll deceive them as they deceived us. And then I'll destroy them."

"But . . ." For a moment she lost the words. "But Râvar, this isn't Refuge. It's . . . it's an entire world. There are towns, cities . . . and people, more people than you can imagine. You can't destroy a world, the way they destroyed Refuge—it's impossible!"

"Perhaps. Still I will try."

"But you will . . . they will . . . how can you think anyone will believe you?"

"I come from the Burning Land, gaunt and ravaged as the Messenger should be. I bear a crystal of the Blood. I will give them destruction—such destruction! It's more than they gave us, and we believed."

"*They* gave us nothing! They never intended us to see the Next Messenger! It was our mistake, our error. The people here aren't like us. They don't believe in destiny or revelations. They aren't . . . they aren't waiting for anything!"

"Everybody's waiting for something," he said, almost gently. "Don't you know that, you who have no faith?"

"The Brethren won't believe it. They'll see you for what you are. They'll find a way to stop you."

"I mean to destroy them before the rest."

"Râvar, this is blasphemy."

"Yes," he said, and for the first time the inhuman calm that wrapped him trembled. "I will also be the Next Messenger Ârata deserves."

He's gone mad, she thought. But she did not believe it. This was the purpose she had sensed in him as he drove them relentlessly across the Burning Land. This was why he had asked questions about the outside world; this was why he had listened to her answers. All this time it had burned in him, the secret fire of this intent, just as the Blood he carried had burned inside its linen wrappings. Into her mind sprang the faces of Kaluela, and little Eolani. She felt sick.

"There are people in Thuxra," she said unsteadily. "Hundreds of people. If you destroy it, you'll kill them all."

"They killed all of Refuge." Anger roughened his voice.

"The people of Thuxra didn't kill anyone! They're innocent! Râvar—Râvar, you'll make yourself a murderer!"

"But I already am a murderer! Isn't that what you think? That I let Refuge die?" He closed his eyes, drew in his breath. That implacable calm settled once more across his features. "No. There has to be an act of destruction, to announce the next Messenger's coming. Thuxra is an abomination against Ârata, built upon his sacred land—isn't that what you told me? I'll be revered for bringing it down."

His cruelty appalled her. "There's supposed to be an act of generation, too," she flung at him. "Have you thought of that?"

Some of the hardness seemed to leave him. "Yes. Or at least—" His hands rose toward her; she flinched back, and he let them fall. "You're pregnant."

"What?" She stared at him. "But that's—you can't know that!"

"I do know it. Your lifelight's different." He hesitated. "I can see its light. In yours."

Could it be? Her mind fled back across the weeks. She could not remember when she had last bled. But her courses had always been sparse, irregular; there had been other times she had gone months between.

"No." She shook her head. "No, I don't believe you. It's a lie. A cruel lie, after all you've done to me."

An odd look came into his face. "That's not what . . . I didn't mean . . . I never meant that, Axane. I—" He stopped. "I never did."

Liar, she thought. Rage struggled in her; she felt the pressure of all the words she had never dared set free.

"Axane, will you come with me to Thuxra? Will you watch as I reveal myself? I need . . . I want a witness. Someone who knows the truth. There's only you—in all the world, only you."

Now, finally, she understood. "That's why you brought me with you," she said. "Not for what I know. Not to . . . to use me. For this."

He said nothing. But she saw, because he could not hide it, how much it mattered to him. She felt something rise up in her, a kind of triumph. *I can deny him,* she thought. *Now, at last, I can deny him.*

"No. I will not."

His face tightened. For a moment he watched her. Then he nodded.

He leaned forward and took up the crystal. He did not shield himself with the cloth that had wrapped it; its facets sliced his skin at once, and blood began to well. With that persistent grace of his, he rose, lifting his hands so that he held the crystal before his chest. Blood overspilled his cupped palms, ran in rivulets down his forearms. He was, Axane realized, the very image of the portrait of the Next Messenger in Refuge's ruined Temple.

He looked at her across the light he held. "Take good care of my child."

He turned and walked away along the road. She thought she could see the luminance of the crystal, a faint nimbus around his body.

She thought wildly of leaping up, of running to give warning. But pit mines lay to either side; the only way forward was the road, and she knew he would not let her past; he would drop her into a crevasse, or fix her feet into the soil. At last she did get up, and began to follow him. She had refused him witness; she did not want to see Thuxra fall. Yet she had been journeying for so long, and always to this end, though she had not known it. She felt bound to watch—not for him, but for herself.

The miners, their attention turned on the ground and their vision veiled by dust, did not see him until he was among them. Axane, keeping her distance, was not quite close enough to read their faces, but she saw how they dropped their tools as he passed them, how barrows fell from their hands and baskets from their shoulders. Some collapsed upon their knees; others stood as if struck to stone. Some cried out. Overseers with heavy staves came running to beat them back to work; one strode after Râvar, shouting. Roughly he gripped Râvar by the shoulder and pulled him around—and then staggered back, raising his arms as if to defend himself, as the fire of the Blood blazed from Râvar's hands. Either the hazy air intensified the crystal's radiance or he had done something through his shaping, for he seemed to stand within a corona of light, like the summer moon come down to earth.

He turned and paced on, unhurried, as if he had all the time in the world. The miners began to follow. They moved with an odd shuffling gait—chained at the ankles, Axane realized. The overseers no longer tried to discipline them, but followed also, entranced as their charges. Râvar was invisible by then, hidden by the mass of prisoners. But she could still see his light, a rising glow before and just above the crowd.

Past the perimeter of the mines, in the littered area that divided them from the middens, the crowd came to a jostling halt. Axane halted also, almost at their backs, no longer caring if she were seen. She was breathing as hard as if she had been running; the sun bore down on her like a burden too heavy to carry, and she had to fight the impulse to sink panting to her knees. She could smell the middens' stench. Ahead, Thuxra City swam in a haze of heat, its dark walls seeming to float above the ground.

Râvar came in sight again, climbing with that same measured pace onto a pile of earth and stones. At its top he paused—a stick figure, impossibly frail against the harsh landscape before him. Slowly he raised his hands, until the Blood was held high above his head. It blazed like a star, like a little sun—not a steady brilliance but one that pulsed, as if he held his own heart between his palms.

"*In Ârata's name!*" he shouted.

It rang out like a bell, hardly a human voice at all. The corona of gold enclosing him burst outward, blinding. The crowd surged back, shouting, tangling in its chains. Before the prison, the air shattered; blue-white lightning burst from the base of Thuxra's walls. The earth shuddered, a long, slow, agonized heaving like an ancient creature struggling in its sleep. The walls of Thuxra flexed and shifted, all that hard stone grown suddenly fluid. The earth jerked again; and slowly, slowly, the prison folded in on itself, subsiding like a piece of fabric, billowing up a great plume of dust. For an instant it fell in silence, as if it had no true substance. But then came the roar of collapse, rolling on and on as if it would never end; and the earth shook once more, this time with the impact of that colossal disintegration.

Finally, there was silence. Thuxra was gone; where it had been was empty air and rubble. The cloud of dust still hung above, unmoving in the windless glare of noon.

Axane stood trembling. Almost until the moment it happened, she had not truly believed he would do it—had not truly believed he *could* do it. In memory she saw the collapse; with her eyes she beheld the ruins. Still she did not comprehend it, as if she looked on something so impossible that even the sight of it was not enough to prove it had actually occurred. In her mind Thuxra still stood whole. It was what she saw before her that seemed the lie.

Râvar lowered his arms. His gleaming golden nimbus was

gone. She could not imagine, after the effort he had just expended, how he was still standing. What did he feel as he gazed upon his work? Triumph? Joy? Was he astonished by what he had done?

He turned to face the prisoners—slowly, not quite steady on his feet. His face was deathly. The Blood glowed before his chest, its fire reaching no farther than his palms.

"Thus Ârata's Promise is fulfilled," he called, in a hoarse and cracking voice—nothing like the pealing cry of before, but in the spreading silence he could be clearly heard. "The old age is ended. A new age begins. Behold the promise of the new age!"

She saw him close his eyes, saw his body tense. Across the gathering burst little flares of light, a sequence of sounds like clapping hands. And the prisoners' chains were gone.

"You are the first witnesses to the new age." He paused to breathe. "This is your task now. . . ." Another breath. ". . . to bear witness, in Ârata's name. To spread news of Ârata's Promise through the kingdoms of Galea. To speak the coming of the Next Messenger. Go now . . . go forth, and bear witness."

For a moment longer he stood on his high perch, looking outward, beyond the prisoners, toward the open desert. Did he see her standing there, bearing witness after all? She felt the cord of knowledge that bound them, like a living thing: the truth only the two of them knew. It would be with her always, no matter what path she took, no matter what fate he met. She would never be free of him.

He began to descend, stumbling, his legs betraying him in his exhaustion. The prisoners rushed forward; eager arms reached up to catch him. He vanished among them.

Axane allowed herself at last to sink to the ground. The sun-seared earth burned her flesh through the tattered fabric of her gown. She tasted dust in her throat, the dust of Thuxra City; there was dust beneath her hands, the dust of the Burning Land. She watched as the crowd of prisoners receded, jostling north. Any moment, she thought, she must hear a different sort of thunder—the huge, world-spanning foot-steps of a god, come to punish the blasphemy done in his name. But she sat and sat, until the crowd vanished around the ruins of Thuxra, and there was only silence.

—27—

Axane stood beneath an entrance porch. It had been driz-
zling off and on all day; gusts of wind tossed the rain about,
and even under the overhang she could feel her clothing getting wet. But it was not really for shelter that she had sought
the porch—just as the stole she had wrapped around her
head and face was not really for warmth, though the autumn
afternoon was chill.

Across the little square, a narrow building stood shoulder
to shoulder with several others. Balconies ran across its
front. At ground level, a doorless entrance gave access to the
stairwell, lit by a single lamp. She had never actually seen
him go in or out. But she knew he lived here, in the apartment on the topmost floor, for she had dreamed it.

It was in the desert that she dreamed him first, though she
did not realize until much later. At Thuxra City, where she
remained to help the injured, she did not dream at all; in fact
she barely slept. There were survivors of Râvar's great destruction, many of them terribly hurt. She tended them in the
makeshift shelters the able-bodied survivors had rigged up,
doing what she could for crushed limbs and cracked skulls

and lacerations and fever. When she could be spared she went with others among the ruins, searching for anyone who might still be trapped alive. Kaluela and Eolani were not among the living, nor did she ever find them among the dead, though she looked for them constantly. The administrator lived, but both his legs were fractured and the moment she saw the injuries she knew that he would die. She nursed him until he did, of gangrene and fever. He never recognized her; at the end he thought she was his wife and died clutching her hand.

Relief arrived at last, fetched from the garrison at Darna, and she departed, setting out for Ninyâser. The plans she had once made to live there seemed trivial and irrelevant, but she could not think of anywhere else to go. Past Thuxra Notch, she began to dream again: Dreams that drew her over and over to the city, to the room of the man who, in her desert Dream, had reminded her of Gyalo—except, incredibly, it *was* Gyalo, released somehow from his imprisonment and living not as a vowed Âratist but, apparently, as an ordinary man. She dreamed him sleeping, in a bed with white sheets and pillows and a saffron-colored quilt. She dreamed him on his balcony, gazing out over the rooftops. She dreamed him once in the temple of Ârata, sitting cross-legged on a cushion before an image of Ârata Creator. His face was dark in that Dream, as if he dwelled on troubling memories.

From then on, she could think only of finding him. When she reached the city she did not stop to eat or rest, but followed her Dream-vision through its streets, her heart beating so she could scarcely breathe. But when she came to the building where she knew he lived, a paralysis fell upon her. She knew what she wanted; there had seemed at least a chance, now he was free, that he might want it, too. But how could she go to him as she was? For a long time she stood, looking up. Then she turned and walked away.

Twice she had come back since then. Each time her nerve had failed her.

This time, she knew, would be the same. Sighing, she stepped from beneath the porch and crossed the square, to the alley that gave access to the wider thoroughfare beyond. Her mind was dark; she barely felt the rain on her head and shoulders, the wetness of her clothes. She barely heard the quick footsteps behind her.

"Axane!"

The familiar voice turned her to stone.

Then he was before her—changed, as she had dreamed him, but still utterly himself. His eyes searched hers; in his face she saw both amazement and dawning, incredulous joy. It was just as she had imagined he would look at her, in her fantasies of this moment. For an instant anything seemed possible. But then, inevitably, his gaze slipped downward, and she saw his expression change.

"Axane," he said again.

Shame rolled over her in a burning tide. She bowed her face into her hands, hiding from his gaze.

She felt him take her arm, turning her, urging her to walk. She went with him, unprotesting; she did not dare look at him, but fixed her eyes instead on the brick paving before her feet, shining with rain. In the musty dimness of the stairwell he paused to take a candle stub from a box and light it at the lamp, then led her up and up, to the topmost landing. There he pushed open a door and drew her into the room beyond.

The plaster was tinted coral, the floorboards painted glossy black. The shutters across the balcony opening were drawn back to let in the light; there were hanging lamps as well, and an iron brazier, glowing red with coals. Cushions were stacked against the wall. Gyalo brought one close to the brazier.

"Sit," he said.

She obeyed. He took the wet stole from her shoulders and draped it over the screen that stood at one corner of the chamber, then vanished through the adjacent doorway, returning with a blanket that he shook out and offered to her. She took it, grateful, and pulled it around her shoulders, hiding her body in its folds. From behind the screen he fetched a clay cup.

"Water," he said, placing it beside her. He drew up another

cushion a little distance away, and sank down cross-legged upon it.

To fill the silence, she picked up the cup and drank. There were a thousand things she wanted to ask him, to say to him. But now that she was finally with him, not in Dreams but in waking time, she could not summon up a single word.

"Did you dream me?" he asked at last. "Is that how you knew I was here?"

She nodded.

"You've come before, haven't you?"

She nodded again.

"I wasn't sure—it was just a glimpse of green, yesterday at the passage arch. I went down, but you were already gone."

"Green?" she said, for the modest dresses she had been given by the nuns were made of undyed cotton.

"Your lifelight. There's no one in the world with a light like yours. I knew it at once, when I looked out my window today."

Of course. Since he was no longer living as a vowed Âratist, he was no longer taking manita, and so must have a Shaper's vision again. How foolish she had been, hiding under porches, wrapping up her face.

"Why didn't you come to my door, Axanc?"

Her throat was tight; it was difficult to speak. "I wasn't sure you'd welcome me."

"How could you think that?"

"You saw me." The blood flamed in her cheeks. "I'm five months gone with child."

A pause. His eyes moved over her, dark and very clear; on his face was an expression she could not read. Once more she thought how different he was, not just in his appearance—the neat beard that framed his mouth and chin, the sleek black hair falling a little past his jaw—but because he looked so strong, so well. She had never known him well— only gaunt and battered with journeying, or haggard with the rigors of his resubjection to manita, or grim with the strain of the Brethren's questioning. Something rose in her, pressing hugely in her chest; all at once she could not bear his gaze. She bowed her head and burrowed deeper into the blanket.

Softly, he said, "Tell me what has happened to you."

So she did. She told him of the escape from Baushpar, the long trek to Thuxra City. She told him of the army. When she spoke of the released Shapers, his eyes stretched in shock.

"I can't believe it," he said. "Never has such a thing been done, in all the history of the church."

"Perhaps it's just that it hasn't been written down. The histories may not tell of this either." She described the bodies she and Râvar had seen. His face tightened.

"To keep the secret," he said. "Even with all I know now, I would not have believed . . ." He let the words trail off and shook his head. "How afraid they must have been," he said softly. "To do such things."

"The army?"

"The Brethren."

"The Brethren? *Afraid?*"

Again he shook his head. "Go on."

She told him of Refuge, of the battle and its aftermath. Haltingly she described the massacre. Shock flared again in his face, mixed this time with anger. "Ah, Axane," he said, but that was all. She composed herself and continued, telling him of Râvar and their return, though when she came to it she found she could not speak about the rape. She recounted what Râvar had done at Thuxra, and her time there with the wounded.

At last she was finished. Gyalo sat pensive, staring at the red glow of the brazier. She waited, feeling scoured, emptied out, as if after a violent sickness. Through the open shutters she could hear the sound of the rain.

"There's been word about Thuxra," he said. "It's said there was an earthquake."

"That's what the survivors thought. They were inside the walls—they didn't see him when he came. Afterward he vanished, with the prisoners he freed. I thought he'd cross the Notch and go down into Arsace, but when the relief party came from Darna they didn't seem to know anything about him. And I didn't hear a thing as I was traveling here, though I asked. I haven't even dreamed him. I've been thinking . . . I've been thinking that something must have happened to him."

But Gyalo was shaking his head, with the expression of a man in the grip of unwelcome understanding.

"I don't think so," he said. "About a month ago three men began going around the markets and temples here, proclaiming the coming of the Next Messenger. I heard one of them—he said it was the Next Messenger who had knocked Thuxra down. He said he knew where the Next Messenger was, and offered to reveal the way to anyone of true faith who was willing to go. He had scars around his wrists and at his neck, as if he'd recently been a prisoner."

Axane drew in her breath.

"I didn't really think anything of it. There've been so many apocalyptic rumors since the Caryaxists fell. I thought it was just one more group of holy madmen, or maybe a gang of confidence tricksters using the disaster at Thuxra to cheat people out of donations."

"So what are you saying? That Râvar is . . . in hiding somewhere? Sending out these people to speak for him?"

"It makes sense if you think about it. You say he wants to lead people into false faith, but if he just storms down into Arsace he won't accomplish that—and he wouldn't last long, either, for the King wouldn't be any happier about a free Shaper claiming to be the Next Messenger than the Brethren would be. Better to send out missionaries—to spread the word in advance, to prepare the way, so that when he does emerge, people will expect his coming and rally to him. Maybe—" He paused. "Maybe even to gather some sort of army, by calling converts to his side now."

"But this is so much worse," Axane said, horrified. "This way . . . this way he really has a chance."

"I remember him, you know. From Refuge. He had a really extraordinary lifelight—gold, just a margin around his body, but incredibly bright. Like the sun in eclipse." Gyalo paused. "It's a monumental blasphemy, what he's done. What he means to do."

"Yes."

"There've been false Messengers before, but they were madmen—deluded, but true at least within their own minds." He drew a long breath. "But he can't succeed. No matter how large an army he gathers, no matter how much false faith he stirs among the people. The Brethren will never accept the possibility of a Messenger. Not even a true one." A faint, bitter smile tugged briefly at his lips. "They'll go to any lengths to destroy him."

"Do you think they can?"

"Look what they've already done."

She watched him. "You aren't loyal to them anymore. The Brethren."

He did not answer at once. "I've come to think that maybe my task in Baushpar wasn't just to bring them news, but to test them. To see whether after all these centuries their faith was still true. Dâdar and Vivaniya—what you heard them say makes me even surer of that. Perhaps . . . perhaps Râvar is also a test. Perhaps Ârata in his wisdom has already begun to judge us all."

She said nothing.

"It's ironic, really. They feared me so much that they shut me away where I couldn't speak—and now the same thing has come on them, except that this time it's their own creation. I wonder if they see it."

"Râvar, you mean."

"Yes." He sighed. "I'm truly sorry. For Refuge. I knew what must happen to its Shapers, but I never imagined . . . the rest of it."

Her father's dead face composed itself uncontrollably inside Axane's mind. She was not visited by such images so often these days, but when they came they possessed undiminished violence. She closed her eyes convulsively, willing it away.

"Axane?"

She heard the quick concern in his voice. She opened her

eyes. "I knew they'd imprisoned you. I dreamed you—you were in a stone building high up on a cliff. I saw you leaning out your window, looking down. I thought maybe you meant to fall."

"I did think of it sometimes. Falling." He glanced down at his hands. "I wondered if you'd ever seen me."

"Did they set you free, the Brethren?"

"No. I escaped. Diasarta came for me. He took me out of that place. He saw me through the manita sickness."

"So you are . . . you're not . . . you're no longer—"

"A vowed Âratist?" He shook his head. "I've left that service behind. I work as a scribe now. I have a spot in the courtyard of the temple of Inriku, and I spend all day writing letters and documents for anyone who can pay me." He smiled. "It's dull. But given that I expected to be locked up in a single room for the rest of my life, I don't complain."

"Isn't it dangerous for you? To live like this?"

He shrugged. "Diasarta arranged things so they would believe me dead. Fallen from my window, as you feared."

"I meant . . . as a free Shaper."

"Ah. Well, that's not something anyone is likely to guess, as long as I don't actually use my shaping." He paused. "It's a strange thing, being free. In the Burning Land I believed there was divine purpose to it, and that made it easy. But now . . . now it's just a choice I made. I don't even know whether it was the right choice. Maybe I'm just another apostate—a true apostate this time, not an involuntary one. And yet . . ." Again he hesitated. He had taken up the hem of his tunic and was pleating it between his fingers. "I know that shaping free to human will is a terrible danger. Look at Râvar. Yet if the Brethren had never heard of Refuge, he might have gone his whole life without ever doing wrong. Freedom is a risk—but to tether shaping, to imprison it with manita . . . I don't know if that's really any better. Shaping is a sacred gift. If we can't use it properly, is it right to diminish it, to make it small?"

"Do you think Shapers should be free, then?"

"All of us?" He glanced up at her and smiled, strangely.

"Someone once told me that my shaping was given by Ârata, but my vow was made by men. I didn't understand the difference then. But I do now, and I wonder . . . I wonder if there might be a middle way, a path between destruction and diminishment." He shook his head. "But I don't know. And I don't dare use my shaping, and not just because it would be dangerous for me. You remember my mistakes in the Burning Land. I fear my ignorance. I fear the burden of ash in me, my fallible will. I even fear my fear." Again that wry half smile. "I'm just waiting now—waiting to understand what I should do."

"Do you—" She stopped. "Do you still believe you're the Next Messenger?"

He looked down at his knees again, pulling his tunic smooth across them. "I don't know what I am."

Silence fell between them. Outside, the light was fading. The rain still fell, tapping on the roof of the balcony, sheeting from the tiles.

"Have you ever dreamed of Teispas?" he asked.

"No." How long had it been since she had thought of the captain? "I tried, but I never did."

"Diasarta and I have been looking for him. Diasarta's sure he's still alive, but I'm not so certain. And Vâsparis. Do you know what became of him?"

"He wasn't among the wounded or the dead at Thuxra. He told me before I left that he had plans . . . sometimes I imagine he slipped away and went back into the Burning Land."

"Yes." Gyalo nodded. "Yes, I can see him doing that."

Again the conversation died. He stared at the brazier, as if he could read some message in its glowing coals. With a feeling like coming to the end of a long road, Axane understood that he was not going to speak—was not going to ask her to stay with him. She had hoped for it all the while she sat there, with the same absurd, impossible hope that had brought her back four times to stand gazing up at his apartment. *You're a fool,* she told herself. *Why would he want you, pregnant by another man? It was a mistake, a terrible mistake to come here.*

She threw off the blanket and pushed herself to her feet, with the awkwardness her growing pregnancy was beginning to force on her. "I should go."

He looked up, drawn from his reverie. "Why?"

"It's getting late. I'm staying at the temple of Ârata, in the travelers' guesthouses there. I don't want to walk the streets after dark."

His face seemed to have hardened. "Do you love him, then?"

"Who?"

"Râvar, of course."

For a moment she was so dumbfounded she could not speak. "No. I don't love him. I never loved him. How could you think I loved him?"

"But it's his child, isn't it?"

"Yes, it's his child, but—but—I didn't choose it! He forced me. He—he—he—" Images assailed her; she gasped. "He would have abandoned me if I had refused him. I would have died."

By then Gyalo was on his feet, too. "Then why are you leaving?"

"I thought it was what you wanted."

"How could you think that?"

"Because I have his child in me! Because you didn't ask me to stay!" She bowed her face into her hands. "Because . . . because I am ashamed."

"What he did shames him, not you."

"No. No. I should have stopped him. I should have fought harder—done more—"

"Axane, look at me." Reluctantly, she obeyed. His eyes captured hers. "Do you know why I came to Ninyâser? Oh, it's safe enough for me here, but still it would have made more sense to lose myself in Aino or Kanu-Tapa, somewhere far from Baushpar." He stepped toward her. "But I thought of what you said to me, that afternoon we went into the city together and visited the temple of Tane. Do you remember?" Another step. "You told me how you meant to return here and make your living as a healer. I thought if I were ever to see you again it would be here—that one day, maybe, you'd come back, and find me through your Dreams. I've been watching for you this past year. Every day, I've watched for you. And now you're here." Another step. "I didn't speak because I thought your heart was with him. But I'm speaking now. Stay."

"But the child—"

"When I was a vowed Âratist, the only thing I ever regretted was that I'd never have a child of my own. Now I will."

"But it's *not* your child!"

"It's *your* child. I love you, Axane. How could I not love your child?"

She could not help herself: She burst into tears. He closed the small distance between them; his arms went around her, and he drew her against the warmth of his body. She wept into his chest. He held her lightly, as if she might break.

"Will you stay?" he murmured when she was quiet.

"If you really want me." She raised her head and looked at him. "Yes."

He bent and kissed her then, softly, tentatively—a boy's kiss, not a man's, and she remembered he had been celibate all his life. Desire flooded her. The image of Râvar flared once in memory, and died. She put her hands behind Gyalo's head, her fingers tangling in the silky fall of his hair; she lifted herself toward him and opened her mouth to his. He dragged in his breath, sharply, and pulled back. His eyes were wide, his skin flushed.

"Take me to your bed," she said.

"Can we? The child—"

She smiled. "It's all right. For some time yet."

He led her into his darkened bedchamber, and pulled back the saffron quilt, and laid her down on the white linens of his bed. And it was everything she had imagined, and more, for it was real.

Axane dreamed.

She soared above the Plains of Blessing, skimming the silvery grass. Ahead lay Revelation and the cleft, the golden light of the Cavern of the Blood pulsing up as it always had.

She reached the banks of Revelation. Her Dream steered her west, close above the river's flood. Terror grew in her, for she knew where the Dream was taking her; she struggled, willing herself to slow, to rise, but the Dream propelled her on.

In the filtered moonlight she saw it: the bluff where her people had been murdered. Râvar had told her how he had closed them beneath the ground—yet in her mind she saw her father, his face turned toward the sky, and near him Vivanishâri and the child who had borne Axane's name, and beyond them the rest of Refuge, stiff and dead—and she knew, as surely as she had ever known anything, that this was what her Dream would show her. With all the horror of her grief and guilt she pulled back. *No!* she cried out in her sleep. *I will not! I will not!*

But she was already there, above the little strand where Refuge had thought to wait safe. And here, where she had so feared to return, she saw no scene of massacre, but only smooth sand and shadowed rock and sliding water, spangled pale and dark in the uncertain illumination of the moon. Râvar had not lied. Somewhere below this quiet place more than two hundred bodies lay, bones and flesh slowly joining with the earth. But the ground above them, the ground on which they had died, was innocent, unmarred.

Something breathed out of her, passing away into the night.

Her Dream took her again, urging her back the way she had come. Into the cleft she sped, between its walls. The moonlight did not reach there; but this was a Dream, and she could still see.

Near the ruin of Refuge she slowed. Râvar had been at work there, too. The collapsed openings, the defaced carvings, the debris upon the ledge—all were gone. The cleft walls rose smooth and whole, as if they had always stood so. One thing only he had left: the image of Ârata Creator that had presided above the Treasury. The god's hands were gone, and the small sun he had held, and his left leg was broken off below the knee. But his face, perfect, still smiled ecstatically from the rock—a watcher in this place where no living soul, perhaps, would ever come again.

She winged on, to the terminus of the cleft, where the Cavern of the Blood, its opening restored, poured glory on the night. Up and up she soared, above the Burning Land, speeding north, the huge distance she had so painfully crossed three times on foot wheeling past in the space of a few breaths. The Range of Clouds loomed ahead; briefly, as if hands had reached up and closed on hers, she felt herself drawn toward one of its peaks. Snow and rock filled her vision, spinning, and she thought she saw a flash of light; then she was free, arrowing on. The mountains fell behind, and the steppes, and the rich farmland of Arsace. Ninyâser rose before her.

And she was awake.

The rain had stopped. Moonlight drifted through the balcony opening, whose shutters Gyalo had pushed back to let in the air. He slept beside her, his body warm, his breathing easy. She lay a moment, the shadows of her Dream still clinging to her, then got softly out of bed. She found the flowing tunic he had so hastily pulled off, and drew it on; it fell just past the knee on him, but on her reached nearly to the ankles. Barefoot, she padded across the room and slipped out onto the balcony.

Ninyâser lay before her. At that hour most of it was dark, but here and there a lamp or candle glinted at a window or burned upon a balcony. The clouds had torn apart; she could see stars glittering in the black sky between them, and ahead, a silver nimbus where vapor lay across the moon. The air smelled of smoke and wet. Night sounds—a barking dog, a crying child, distant shouting—touched but did not stir the greater flow of quiet.

Something rose in her, deeper than joy. She was there, where she had so longed to be. There were no tasks to be accomplished, no warnings to be given. Only life, stretching out before her, unencumbered—as she had imagined it might, on the night she escaped from Refuge.

She thought of her Dream, of the peaceful images it had granted her. The memories of death would never leave her; all her life she would see her father's face. But now she would also think of him asleep beneath smooth sand, beside a peaceful river. She would see the cleft walls rising whole and healed. Râvar had done that—Râvar had given this to her.

She felt a quickening, and set her hands on her belly. He had also given her this child. A child of rape; a child she had no means to keep. Yet there had been no hesitation in the happiness she felt, once she realized he had told the truth and she was really pregnant. The conception was a miracle, and in embracing it she could at last allow herself to understand how greatly her barrenness had grieved her. From the start she had loved the child, utterly and without question.

She thought of the harsh gray peak that had drawn her as she sped homeward in her Dream, of the light that had seemed to glint there. It was not the first time she had dreamed it; now, remembering Gyalo's speculations, it seemed to her she might know why. Perhaps that was where Râvar had hidden himself, to bide his time, to send out his missionaries and gather his converts and await the proper moment to emerge. One way or another, she would find out—for while he lived it was inevitable that she come to him in her sleep. She was bound to him by what she knew, and by his child—bonds she might resist, but never break.

Gyalo's words returned to her: *Perhaps Àrata in his wisdom has already begun to judge us all.* She had not replied. She did not want to tell him of the door of understanding that had opened in her mind, just after Râvar brought Thuxra City down—of how, sitting on the hot ground of the Burning Land, the dust of Thuxra in her mouth, she had recognized in the vast hush of the desert something more than silence. Absence. It was not that Àrata saw Râvar's blasphemy and forbore to act. It was not that, indifferent, he turned away. It was that he was no longer present on the earth to witness or to punish such things. Human actions, human choices, human evil, human joy—all unfolded unobserved.

There is no one to see us, she had thought in dread and comprehension, *but each other.*

She wrapped her arms around herself, shivering, for the air was chilly. She still was not sure. The thought of such emptiness was fearful, even though she had lived with something very much like it for most of her adult life. It was not easy to imagine that this life was all there was—a spark born from the fires of the world, rising briefly, swiftly consumed. But sometimes she could feel the wonder of the freedom unbelief might grant her, if she embraced it fully. To live with no stern judging eye to overlook her fate, to be the sole arbiter of her actions, to accept no meanings but the ones she chose. And oh, how much more vivid her life must be, burning between dark and dark!

She returned to the room, pulled off the tunic, and slid softly into bed. Gyalo still slept, his face turned toward her. A strand of black hair lay across his cheek; carefully she smoothed it back, then propped herself on her elbow and watched him—so long loved, so long yearned for, hers at last. Echoes of the pleasure he had given her stirred along her limbs. How would they fare, in the time to come? His loyalties had changed, but it was clear that he believed as deeply as he ever had, or perhaps even more. His ordeal, which might have killed another's faith, had not affected his at all. He would never understand the insight that had come to her in the desert. She could never speak of it.

For a moment she felt the heaviness of it—a secret she must keep as she once had kept the secret of her dreaming. But then he sighed and opened his eyes, and smiled to see her looking down at him. Sleepily he reached up and drew her into his arms. She felt the life in her, rising on a cresting tide of blood. Past and future, grief and secrets, gods and blasphemers fell away, and there was only the two of them, blazing in the dark.

Glossary

Dramatis Personae

Gyalo Amdo Samchen: A Shaper, vowed Âratist, and servant of the Brethren

Axane: A woman of Refuge

BAUSHPAR

Utamnos: A Son, Gyalo's master

Ivaxri: A Son, Utamnos's ward

Taxmârata (the Blood Bearer): A Son, elected leader of the Church of Ârata

Vimâta: A Son, the Bearer's ward

Sundit: A Daughter

Haminâser: A Son

Baushtas: A Son

Ariamnes: A Son

Dâdar: A Son

Artavâdhi: A Daughter

Martyas: A Son

Vivaniya: A Son

Kudrâcari: A Daughter
Santaxma: King of Arsace

THE BURNING LAND

Kaluela: Wife of Thuxra City's administrator
Eolani: Kaluela's daughter
Dorjaro: Aide to Thuxra City's administrator
Teispas dar Ispindi: Commander of the expedition to the
    Burning Land
Aspâthnes: Teispas's second-in-command
Vâsparis: A former mining prospector, the expedition's
    guide
Diasarta dar Abanish: A soldier
Gâbrios: A soldier
Haxar: A soldier
Sauras: A soldier
Bishti: A soldier
Saf: A soldier
Cinxri: A soldier
Nariya: A soldier
Kai-do Seiki: A female Dreamer
Senri-dai Tak: A male Dreamer
Rikoyu: Dream-interpreter for Seiki and Tak

THE LOST ÂRATISTS

Râvar: Axane's fiancé, a Shaper
Kiruvâna: Râvar's cousin
Habrâmna: Axane's father, leader of Refuge
Narstame: Habrâmna's wife
Randarid: Their grandson
Vivanishâri: Habrâmna's second partner
Sarispes: Vivanishâri's oldest son
Ardinixa: Axane's former lover
Biryâsi: Ardinixa's wife
Parimene: A woman of Refuge, a healer
Irdris: A woman of Refuge, a healer
Yirime: A woman of Refuge, a healer
Gâvarti: A female Shaper, principal Shaper of Refuge

Haxmapâya: A male Shaper
Oronish: A female Shaper
Aryam: A male Shaper
Jândaste: A female Shaper
Varas: A male Shaper
Uspardit: A female Shaper
Sarax: A male Shaper
Sonhauka: A male trainee Shaper
Omida: A man of Refuge, a councilor
Cistâmnes: A man of Refuge, a councilor
Kariyet: A woman of Refuge, a councilor
Ixtarser: A man of Refuge, a councilor
Dâryavati: A woman of Refuge, a councilor

Historical Characters

Marduspida: Prophet of Ârata, also known as the First Messenger
Fârat: King of Arsace, first royal convert to Âratism
Nabrios: Leader of the pagan Shaper army during the Shaper War
Vantyas: King of Arsace, leader of the Âratist army during the Shaper War
Caryax: Arsacian philosopher executed for treason
Voice of Caryax: Leader of the subsequent rebellion based on Caryax's precepts
Vandapâya IV: King of Arsace, overthrown and executed by the Caryaxists
Risaryâsi: Female Dreamer, leader of the lost Âratists
Utane: Second of Refuge's two original Dreamers
Cyras: First of Refuge's two original Shapers
Mandapâxa: Second of Refuge's two original Shapers

Gods and Aspects

Ârata: Principal god of the Âratist religion
Ârdaxcasa: Ârata's brother and foe, also known as the Enemy
Dâdarshi: Aspect of Ârata, Patron of luck
Skambys: Aspect of Ârata, Patron of war and weather

Hataspa: Aspect of Ârata, Patron of fire and weaponry
Tane: Aspect of Ârata, Patron of crops and the moon
Vahu: Aspect of Ârata, Patron of healing and childbirth
Jo-Mea: Aspect of Ârata, Patron of travel
Inriku: Aspect of Ârata, Patron of learning and the arts

Place Names

Galea: Continent that contains the Seven Kingdoms

Arsace: Largest and richest of the Seven Kingdoms, birthplace of the Âratist faith

Ninyâser: Arsace's capital city

Darna: An Arsacian city

Fashir: An Arsacian town

Baushpar: An Arsacian city, traditional headquarters of the Âratist church

First Temple of Ârata: The largest and oldest Âratist temple in Galea, located in Baushpar

Kanu-Tapa: Another kingdom of Galea, known for martial skills

Haruko: Another kingdom of Galea, home to a large population of Arsacian refugees from Caryaxist persecution

Aino: Another kingdom of Galea, home to most Dreamer monasteries and nunneries

Chonggye: Another kingdom of Galea, refuge of the Brethren during the time of Caryaxist rule in Arsace

Rimpang: Chonggye's capital city, seat of the Brethren during their exile

Isar: Another kingdom of Galea

Yahaz: Another kingdom of Galea

The Burning Land: A vast desert occupying the whole of Galea's southern portion, sacred to Ârata, who according to Âratist belief lies sleeping there

Range of Clouds: Vast mountain range that divides the kingdoms of Galea from the Burning Land

Thuxra Notch: Pass through the Range of Clouds

Thuxra City: Caryaxist prison, built at the edges of the Burning Land as a deliberate desecration of holy ground

Refuge: Rock-carved settlement of the lost Âratists

Revelation: Refuge's river

Plains of Blessing: The fertile grass steppes beyond Refuge

Labyrinth: Refuge's living quarters

Treasury: A complex housing Refuge's workshops and storehouses

House of Dreams: Abode of Refuge's Dreamers

Miscellaneous Terms

Âratism (Âratist): Dominant religion of Galea

Way of Ârata: Broad term covering the secular and religious practice of Âratism; includes ethical as well as religious precepts

The Five Foundations: The central credos of Âratism—Faith, Affirmation, Increase, Consciousness, and Compassion

Vowed Âratists: Men and women who swear themselves to Ârata's service

The Sixfold Vow: The vow they take

The Brethren: The thirty-five children of the First Messenger, perpetually reincarnated leaders of the Âratist church

The Blood Bearer: Elected leader of the Brethren

Darxasa: Âratism's holy scripture, dictated by Ârata to Marduspida

Book of the Messenger: Âratism's second scripture: the life story of the First Messenger, Marduspida

Dreaming: The power of true dreaming

Shaping: The power to form, unform, and transform inanimate matter

Manita: Plant whose leaves yield a drug that suppresses shaping ability

Doctrine of Baushpar: A creed formulated after the

Shaper War, defining shaping as the property of the church

Shaper War: Ancient conflict in which pagan Shapers brutally attempted to eradicate the Âratist faith from Galea

Caryaxism (Caryaxist): Modern atheistic political movement that came briefly to power in Arsace

Acknowledgments

Much as I'd like to think I can do everything without help, I'm smart enough (sometimes) to know it isn't true. Many people have given generously of their time, wisdom, and patience to help bring this book to final form. Heartfelt thanks are due to Bob, whose objective, insightful comments challenged me to do better than I knew I could; to Ann, my last-minute savior, who helped me focus (and caught all my horse mistakes); to Michael, for maps; to Charlie, whose thoughtful criticism made me think; to Gerald, who said the right things at the right times; to Rob, plot consultant extraordinaire and unfailing source of support (and omelettes); and most of all to Alice, my first, last, and most critical reader, without whom I would be lost.